B. CRAWFORD
6-6-2018

One Dr●p — A Slave!

Eddie Price

EDDIE PRICE

Millers Mill Publishing, LLC
175 Windsong Drive
Hawesville, KY 42348

www.eddiepricekentuckyauthor.com

Book Design: Kathy Cummings, Graphic Enterprises
Cover Design: Kathy Cummings, Graphic Enterprises
Cover Image: John L. Ward, Artist

Library of Congress Cataloging-in-Publication Data

Price, Eddie, 1954-

Widder's Landing/ by Eddie Price
        p. cm.

ISBN 978-0-9985583-3-2 (alk. paper) -- ISBN-10: 0-9985583-3-8 (alk. paper)
        1. United States -- History -- 19th Century – Fiction –Suspense --Saga
Kentucky – Slavery – New Orleans – Social life and customs

2017918627

First Printing: 2018
Printed in Canada
10 9 8 7 6 5 4 3 2 1

Contents

About the Author

    Eddie Price is a retired history teacher who now writes award-winning books. *Widder's Landing*, a historical novel set in Kentucky in 1811-1815, has won gold medals for "Best Historical Fiction" at the Readers' Favorite Awards and the National Literary Habitat Awards, and was honored by the US Daughters of 1812 with the "Spirit of 1812 Award." His children's books, *Little Miss Grubby Toes Steps on a Bee!* and *Little Miss Grubby Toes Plays With Fire!* are illustrated by Mark Wayne Adams. Eddie has won gold medals at the Readers' Favorite Awards, the Florida Authors & Publishers Association, and the Mom's Choice Awards. Eddie is a world traveler who enjoys bicycling, horseback riding, and swimming. He and his wife Mary now live in Hancock County, Kentucky. He has two daughters, Sheena and Breanne.

    Eddie Price presents a number of acclaimed educational programs all across the United States. He often visits grades K-12, colleges, and universities in the daytime; in the evenings he presents for historical and genealogical societies, libraries, museums, patriotic groups—often doing as many as nine programs in a single day. If you are interested in having the author present a program for your organization or school, please visit his website at **www.eddiepricekentuckyauthor.com.** Click on "Program Info."

and "Contact" for more information. The author invites you to pay a visit to his Facebook page at **www.facebook.com/eddieprice.1954** Books are available at Amazon.com.

To get your own inscribed, signed copy, please contact Eddie Price at **eddieprice.1954@att.net**

Books by Eddie Price:

Widder's Landing
One Drop—A Slave!

An Unlikely Trio—The Winners of the 1913 Kentucky Derby

Little Miss Grubby Toes Steps on a Bee!
Little Miss Grubby Toes Plays with Fire!

Eddie Price in front of the Cathedral-Basilica of St. Louis King of France in New Orleans.

About the Artist

Kentucky artist, **John L. Ward** is known for his artistic talent and ability to capture on canvas the movements and expressions unique to his subject matter. A self-taught artist, John paints in a variety of mediums including oil, watercolors, and graphite.

John's work is distributed through galleries, catalogs, and gift shops. His print, "Masters of the Forest," was reproduced in posters and distributed to schools and universities throughout the United States and Canada. John's work has graced the covers of sporting catalogs and magazines. He has won numerous awards including selection in the design process for the 2001 Kentucky Quarter. Commissioned to create prints for private and corporate collections,

John has also illustrated popular children's books. His steamboat drawing is on the front cover of *One Drop—A Slave!*

Professionally, John is an Associate Member of the American Academy of Equine Art and a juried member of the Kentucky Guild of Artists and Craftsmen and Oil Painters of America.

About the Designer

One Drop — A Slave! was designed by **Kathy Cummings**. This is her third book project and the second book designed for author Eddie Price. Trained as a commercial artist, Kathy has been self-employed for 30 years. In addition to screen printing and various design projects she is a web designer with hundreds of websites to her credit, the first website being Pioneer Times USA. It is a living history site for re-enactors and history buffs consisting of thousands of photos and stories from living history events. From that first site sprang websites for local museums, non profits, and history groups. The past few years, she has branched out with websites for a multitude of industries. Kathy and her husband Jim, own Graphic Enterprises/Pioneer Times. The company has won four history awards from the Kentucky Historical Society.

GRAPHIC ENTERPRISES

www.graphicenterprises.net
www.graphicenterpriseswebdesign.com

Preface

How exciting it must have been to have lived in the United States from 1815 to 1818! The American victory at New Orleans ignited a surge of nationalism that swept like wildfire across the young Republic. President James Monroe's 1817 "Goodwill Tour" engendered a sense of national purpose and a strong desire for unity. Kentucky took a prominent role on the national stage, enjoying commercial success and growing political power. Henry Clay regained Speakership of the U.S. House of Representatives and actively pushed for the "American System," an economic plan that included a protective tariff, national bank and internal improvements such as roads, bridges and canals. It was a time that some would call an "Era of Good Feelings."

But this "Era of Good Feelings" did not extend to all Americans. Tensions rose as new states were admitted into the union on a "free" or "slave" state status. Nowhere was the problem of race more confusing than in the state of Louisiana. Awash in a rising tide of African slaves, free blacks, and mixed-race individuals, the court system struggled to deal with issues of manumission, illicit unions, inheritance and intermarriage. Further muddling the situation, wealthy white males openly took advantage of *plaçage,* the system that allowed extralegal, common law marriages with mixed-race females. Elaborate social events called "quadroon balls" openly encouraged these liaisons. The *Digest of 1808,* an actual law code based on the French *Code Noir* and the Spanish *Código Negro,* sought to define slavery in Louisiana. Many of its laws dated back to Roman days. Portions of the *Digest* are quoted in this story.

During the 18th and 19th centuries, numerous physicians, philosophers, naturalists and professors postulated theories of "scientific racism," claiming that empirical evidence existed for racial superiority or inferiority. Among these were Carl Linnaeus, Christophe Meiners, and George Cuvier. Some of their theories appear in the story. Quite naturally this hothouse of pseudoscience spawned an environment that enabled unscrupulous lawyers to prey upon those they could classify as slaves.

The "Year Without a Summer" (1816) most certainly occurred. Some folks called it "Eighteen-hundred-and-froze-to-death!" Global temperatures plummeted, crops froze, and famine struck most parts of the Northern Hemisphere. Although Kentuckians could not have known about the super-volcanic eruption of Mount Tambora in the Dutch East Indies, they saw and wrote about darkened skies, a diminished sun, summertime frosts and cold winds. Thomas Jefferson kept impeccable weather records at his Virginia estate, Monticello, documenting the repeated cold fronts that swooped down upon America. These and period newspaper articles helped the writer create a fairly accurate timeline. While Kentucky suffered far less than did our northeastern states, they also endured the strange events.

Wildcat banks, land speculation, fluctuating farm prices and state politics added varying elements of drama to everyday life, as did new technology. Most of the steamboats in *One Drop—A Slave!* actually plied the Ohio and Mississippi Rivers; the *Jesse P. Emmick* and *J.D. Estes* are invented, but possess structural features of those vessels built by Henry Shreve and Daniel French.

Medical practice in 1815-1818 was still in a state of medieval barbarism. Folks relied mostly on natural resistance and home remedies, some of which came from the Native Americans. Sick people stood a better chance of survival when the doctor did not visit! Many popular "cures" actually worsened the patient's condition. Without antibiotics, anesthetics, sterilization, and diagnostic imaging, doctors worked as best they could. But there were advances. Ephraim McDowell from Danville, Kentucky performed the first ovariotomy in 1809 and became known as the "Father of Abdominal Surgery"—a good model for the doctors in *One Drop—A Slave!*

I have lived in the Ohio River Valley of Kentucky for sixty-three years. What a blessing! One should try to visit our state in all of its glorious seasons. My world travels aided immensely in depicting other geographic settings. A trip to Brazil helped me paint Bahia da Salvador in a much more realistic light. The city's historic center is named *Pelourinho*—for the whipping post where African slaves received punishment for various infractions. *Pelourinho* was declared a world cultural center by UNESCO in 1985. Sailing in the Caribbean helped me describe the story's ocean voyage and provided much insight on the island of Martinique. Walking the streets of *Vieux Carré*, the Old French Quarter of New Orleans, is like taking a step back in time. The *Place d'Armes* (now Jackson Square) the levee, historic buildings and narrow streets are not all that different from the early 1800's. Some say it is as dangerous now to venture out at night. Folks then feared the "Kaintocks," wild flatboat men from Kentucky. This old Kaintock trod those same cobblestones in 2015, gleaning information for the sequel to *Widder's Landing*.

One Drop—A Slave! is first and foremost a novel. Although I use family names common to the various settings, the characters are fictitious. They do, however, move along a historical timeline experiencing actual events, and at times they interact with historical figures who did exist. When these persons speak, they say things they really said, or might have said, in a given situation. All other places and landmarks in the book are authentic. In those instances I endeavored to use the historic names by which they were called.

Acknowledgements

Richard T. Carter, to whom *Widder's Landing* was dedicated, passed away in 2014 at the age of 93. His knowledge of old farming methods provided much of the detail for that novel. Without that beginning, *One Drop—A Slave!* would not have been possible. Richard, you are sorely missed! I am sure you know that I married your lovely daughter, Mary. Sorry I took so long.

Several special people deserve my deepest thanks for their support, especially my parents, Paul and Julia Price, who taught me to love reading at an early age. Floyd Hooks was the high school American History teacher who brought the past to life and inspired me to teach history. Mary Price listened to the story in its formative stages and believed in the project from the beginning. Her suggestions helped—and she tried again, with about the same degree of success, to have me tone down the "sizzling" scenes. Trace Kirkwood, Archivist for the Kentucky Department of Libraries and Archives, offered his vast knowledge and valuable insights into Kentucky laws, documents, practices, and customs. Donn Wimmer, Editor of the Hancock County Clarion, read this manuscript and urged me to publish it. His support has been unwavering. Thanks to illustrator, designer and author Mark Wayne Adams for walking me through the publishing process. Our venture with children's books has been a joyous escapade! Paul Madden, Attorney-at-Law, his wife Ruth, retired English teacher, Linda Tongate, retired history teacher, Kay Whitehouse, author of *The Diamond Bracelet Club;* and Stu Spindel edited *One Drop—A Slave!* and helped make it a better tale. Any remaining faults in the text are mine alone.

There are others who contributed, directly or indirectly, their vast knowledge and assistance: In Kentucky—George and Mary

Gibbs of the Hancock County Archives, the Hancock County Historical Society, Breckinridge County Archives, Library and Historical Society, and the Thomas D. Clark Center for Kentucky History; in Indiana—the organizers of events at "Mississinewa 1812," the "Vincennes Rendezvous," and "Old Fort Wayne;" in New York—"Old Fort Niagara" where I viewed Jack Mathay's outstanding 18th Century surgical instrument display and toured battle sites for the prequel; in Illinois—"Old Fort Massac" and "Fort Lamotte" where black powder enthusiasts and historical reenactors abound. Numerous folks opened doors for me in New Orleans: Ron Chapman, History Professor at Nunez Community College, the park rangers at Chalmette Battlefield National Park, the City of New Orleans, and Mark Lance, Pastor at Chalmette Church of Christ. The staff at the Cabildo and Presbytère Museums were as kind and helpful as one could find in America. This holds true for the caretakers of the historic Cathedral-Basilica of St. Louis King of France. Christina Vella, PhD, accomplished writer, historian, and adjunct professor at Tulane University in New Orleans, shared valuable insight into the lives of widows in early New Orleans society.

William K. and Nicholas P. Klingaman's *The Year Without Summer: 1816 and the Volcano That Darkened the World and Changed History* makes for fascinating reading. Louis C. Hunter's *Steamboats on the Western Rivers: An Economic and Technological History* and Ben Casseday's *The History of Louisville: From its Earliest Settlement Till the Year 1852* furnished information on early steamboats. Book I, Title VI, Chapter III in the *The Digest of 1808* affords an unpleasant glimpse into the early institution of slavery in Louisiana. Oswald Jett's *Hancock County Kentucky: When it was Frontier Country* pointed me toward hundreds of excellent primary sources.

The outstanding team at the Hancock County Public Library helped me obtain scores of research books on Kentucky wildflowers, birds, wildlife, farming practices, whiskey making, folklore, architecture, Kentucky politics, laws, statesmen, early Frankfort, the Falls of the Ohio, store prices, New Orleans, steamboats and the "Era of Good Feelings." I am indebted to them all.

**Dedicated to
Mary Susan Carter Price**

Chapter One

The French Quarter, New Orleans—September 15, 1815

A sluggish breeze wafted in from the northwest, sweetened with the aroma of sugar smoke from the brick refineries located upriver on the Mississippi floodplain. It stirred the solemn gray strands of Spanish moss that drooped from the big live oaks in the courtyard, making the night just bearable for two gentlemen dining outside on the upper gallery of an elegant townhouse. Another muggy evening was descending upon New Orleans.

Jules Marie Signet gestured for his slaves to clear the table. "Fetch those papers from my desk," he ordered his negro butler. The men adjourned to a row of chairs arranged so they could view through wrought-iron grillwork the torchlit courtyard below. The butler brought a leather satchel containing Signet's important papers.

"Cigar?" Signet offered.

"Thank you," his guest replied.

"Cognac?"

"Please. You are not having any?"

"I have grown to prefer Kentucky whiskey. This decanter was drawn from the Pierre Delacroix reserve. He purchases his stock from a relative who lives on the Ohio. It is shipped downriver, directly to his warehouses."

"Then I will have the same." He watched as the butler poured the amber-colored liquor into balloon-shaped glasses.

Signet volunteered, "Delacroix hoped to manufacture the product here in New Orleans, but he claims we lack the pure limestone water for which Kentucky is famous."

Alain Morel took a sip and rolled it in his mouth. "It is, quite simply, heaven."

"Now to business, my friend."

"The doctor is not coming? He is the critical element of our plan. Without him we stand little chance; if we fail, my reputation will be ruined. I will not proceed without him."

"Not to worry. He will arrive shortly. At this moment he is paying an important call directly related to our cause. You are my lawyer and I am paying handsomely—as you well know—so I will accept nothing but complete victory. How do things look in your estimation?"

"If the doctor can work the miracle you claim, I am cautiously optimistic," Morel asserted. "Does he truly hold such influence with the judge?"

"He does." Signet gestured to the courtyard below. "Here he comes now."

A horse cart, drawn by a single mare, rolled through the carriage entrance into the courtyard. A stable boy helped the doctor step down from the cart before taking charge of the mare. From their vantage point Signet and Morel observed how stiffly the man moved, his knee joints apparently causing much discomfort.

"Are you so sure he will do your bidding?" Morel challenged.

"He is in serious trouble—on the brink of financial ruin."

"Ah! People pay him in chickens, eggs, and vegetables rather than in cash."

"No doubt you are correct, but he is also a compulsive gambler. He cannot stay out of those disreputable establishments in the American sector. My bank now holds a substantial note to which he is deeply indebted. If the good doctor acquits himself well and wins a favorable judgment, I will dismiss his note and give him just enough money to land him back into trouble."

"Apparently you have orchestrated his downfall. By allowing him to exacerbate his financial woes, you keep him firmly under your control."

"Perhaps."

The doctor disappeared below the gallery as a slave escorted him inside. Signet removed papers from the satchel—baptismal records, marriage bonds, deeds, bank records and other official documents, including a lengthy and detailed last will and testament. It was all there, except for the single piece of evidence that would nail the case shut, the one paper that would instantaneously open doors to a financial kingdom. That was why the doctor was so important.

The butler announced, "Doctor Thomas Applegate has arrived."

Signet and Morel rose from their chairs. "Ah! The distinguished Doctor Applegate! It is so good of you to come!" Signet gestured toward a small table. "Please make yourself comfortable with a whiskey and cigar."

"Don't mind if I do," Applegate beamed. His long white mustaches were tarnished dirty yellow from constant tobacco smoking. When the cigar was glowing and the whiskey poured, the doctor settled laboriously into a chair. Morel noticed the red face of a man who drank heavily and often. This impression was immediately confirmed when Applegate gulped down the first glass and signaled the butler for a recharge.

"Well?" Signet prompted. "How went the house visit?"

"The judge has followed all my prescriptions to the letter. He has not smoked tobacco in two weeks."

"I find that hard to believe."

"He has taken long walks in the afternoons."

"Yes, I saw him on the levee yesterday evening."

"He swears he has cut out excessive drinking and has followed the diet I have prescribed."

"That pronouncement transcends all imagination." The judge's excesses were common knowledge among the elite in New Orleans. It required enormous amounts of food and drink to create and maintain that massive girth.

The doctor hesitated, glancing at Morel. Signet prodded him along, "You may speak freely. Monsieur Morel is my lawyer. We are all in this venture together. As you know, there is much at stake. Pray continue."

"For two weeks he has been drinking the concoction I have prescribed."

"Will it work?" Signet asked, genuinely interested.

"We will know this evening."

Morel held up his hand. "Forgive me, but you have me at a disadvantage. What does this have to do with our case? This concoction, what is it—some kind of drug designed to control the mind?"

Doc Applegate coughed in amusement. "You might put it that way."

Signet chortled, nudging Morel. "Come on, man! Who at our ages would not wish to become seventeen again?"

"It may not happen tonight, but the judge is ready to try," the doctor asserted.

Morel shook his head, still in a state of incomprehension.

"The judge's stance on racial intermingling is well known." Signet contended. "I have heard him curse a plantation owner in open court for fathering fourteen mulatto children through five female slaves. His exact words were, 'Even the damned birds have better sense not to breed with something outside their own kind.' And he is increasingly upset by the growing number of lawsuits in parish and district courts from 'persons of color' applying for manumission and the right to inherit property. Yet, despite his distaste, the judge has sympathized with some of those plaintiffs. I find that unsettling."

Doc Applegate countered, "You waste your time worrying on that account. All those cases were supported by legal documents. Our case is different; there is no proof of manumission. Everyone knows the burden of proof lies squarely upon the slave. And a slave cannot testify against his owner or any other white man. That is the law, laid down for all to see in the Louisiana Digest of 1808."

"Can we win the case?" Morel asked, impressed by the doctor's knowledge of Louisiana law. He was clearly a wily old fox.

"There will be no trial."

"But the judge—"

"You let me worry about him. You just do your part faithfully."

Doc helped himself to another glass of whiskey and drew heavily on his cigar. He glanced conspiratorially at Signet who knew the full details of the judge's unique insecurities and peccadilloes. The banker had paid well for the confidential information, and its divulgence was an atrocious breach of the Hippocratic Oath, one of the oldest binding documents in history. This covenant, held sacred by physicians throughout the centuries, was an oath to which all medical students had sworn since the time of the ancient Greek physician, Hippocrates. One provision read thusly:

> *"What I may see or hear in the course of the treatment or even outside of the treatment in regard to the life of men, which on no account one must spread abroad, I will keep to myself, holding such things shameful to be spoken about."*

Signet murmured, "You do, of course, require further remuneration for your medical expertise, prescription costs, and other miscellaneous expenses."

"I do."

"Then you may visit me in my office at the bank on Monday. As always, I rely on your absolute discretion."

———▶•◀———

Doc Applegate drove the horse cart through the rough streets of the French Quarter. The mare's iron-shod hooves clip-clopped on the cobblestones and resounded from the buildings lining both sides of the street. Judge John Harkness' residence lay near the juncture of St. Anne Street and North Rampart at almost the farthest point from the river, so there was little chance of encountering someone at this late hour. The slave girl beside him, was wrapped in a dark cotton shawl, unlikely to be noticed by anyone. She was a delicious creature, almost honey-colored, her African skin lightened by the admixture of white blood imposed more than once into her ancestry. Doc had examined her earlier in the week, admitting that she was one of nature's finest examples of the female sex. Her flawless skin, perfect white teeth, dark eyes, and rounded curves would surely please the judge.

Harkness' wife, Edna, was a barren, spiteful shrew who hardly spoke, and then only to spit venomous complaints. The couple had grown old and bitter; physical relations between them, infrequent and unsatisfactory from the outset, were consigned to a long-forgotten past. The judge wanted desperately to change all that, but suffered from the fear he was impotent. He had bottled this inside himself for several years. Perhaps it was an accurate realization. Doc had listened to his story, familiar words from a man of the judge's age and physical constitution. Harkness struggled mightily with the words, and Doc let him purge, not bothering to interrupt. This powerful and feared authority who meted out justice, held lives and great fortunes in his hands, settled major business disputes and passed death sentences, had wept like a small child, sobbing as if his heart would break.

After Harkness had regained his self-control, Doc conducted a complete physical examination and prescribed the regimens earlier recounted to Jules Signet. It was all common-sense advice, not written down in medical books, but based on personal observations gleaned from forty-five years of practice. Those who smoked tobacco tended to die earlier, experiencing shortness of breath and other lung troubles. Additionally, for men, there seemed to be an adverse effect upon the organ causing Harkness such concern. Active people more often reported satisfying love lives. Thinner people usually remained fit much longer in life and would, quite naturally, experience a better ability to perform. Those who gorged themselves at meals, as the judge was known to do, often lost their passionate feelings. Drunkards often complained they were "willing but unable." Cutting out these harmful habits could only help the judge.

Then there were the magical herbs and potions purported to

restore youth, sought desperately by aging men from all over the world. It seemed that every continent had its own remedies, many dating back to earliest times. Long ago Doc had assessed his older male patients and decided to take advantage of the fact they would pay big money to perform as they did in their twenties. After the war with Britain, New Orleans was once again an important center of international trade. One could find anything on the global market, now that ocean-going ships had returned to the levee. Doc purchased every known potion that found its way into the port—ginseng and opium from China, powdered rhinoceros horn from Africa, roots from South America, various shrubs and shredded bark from Asia—and he had built up a lucrative business. Judge Harkness was not the only wealthy man who paid big money for such "cures."

The judge now had hope. But fear and uncertainty could easily deflate desire and ability. Doc felt for the pipe in his coat pocket. He would allow Harkness a few puffs of opium to blunt the ragged edges of fear.

They reached the residence. Doc eased the horse cart through the back carriage entrance. The judge did not own slaves, so there was no one to tie the horse. Before stepping down, Doc once more considered the slave girl.

"What are you called?" He had heard, but forgotten the name.

"Kayla," she replied, not meeting his gaze.

"Kayla, you know I hired you from your master to perform a delicate task. He assures me you are a true wonder, and you will do what I require. Did he speak to you?"

"Yessir."

"Then you know if you succeed there will be a silver dollar for you."

"Yessir," the girl barely spoke above a whisper.

"The judge needs special help, namely a willing woman's tenderness. He might not be able to carry his part through, but you treat him kindly, you hear me?"

"I hear, Doctor Applegate."

"I'll be right there in the room, so I'll know if you don't."

"I be kind to the judge."

"Rub his neck and shoulders. Whisper into his ears. Do all, gently. If he talks to you, you answer him with a sweet voice. He's an ugly old cuss, but you keep a smile on your face at all times."

Doc studied the house cautiously, watching for movement within before stepping down and tying the mare to a hitching post. Edna slept separately from the judge, ensconcing herself in a front downstairs room in the opposite corner of the big residence. There would be hell to pay if she woke up. He beckoned for Kayla to follow. Together they crept to the back of the house. The judge's room was located upstairs in the northeast corner. It could be accessed by a flight of outdoor stairs and a door that opened onto the second-story veranda. A lamp glowed from behind heavy purple drapes.

"You wait here, Kayla, while I talk with the judge. If the mistress comes out, do not speak to her. You just hurry on up and come through the door."

"She knows I here?"

"It doesn't matter. The judge is master of this house."

Doc Applegate painfully ascended the stairs. "Damned knees are down to bone on bone," he cursed. He would ask the judge for his best liquor to dull the pain. He tapped softly on the door.

Judge Harkness let him in and clutched wildly at his arm. His beetled eyebrows, in sore need of trimming, twitched anxiously. Finally he managed to ask, "You did bring her?"

"I did."

"Lordy, Doc. I don't know if I can go through with this." Harkness was sweating, his terror clearly evident.

"Why not? Have you followed the diet I prescribed?"

"I have eaten so many oysters I can hardly choke them down."

"And fish?"

"I may sprout gills any day now."

"No salt pork, no tobacco, no drinking liquor to excess?"

"None of that."

"You're a damned liar. Pour me a glass from that decanter. And fill it to the rim. Have you drunk the concoction I gave you?"

"Brewed it like tea and drank it twice a day, just like you ordered, even though it tastes like horse piss. What is in that foul infusion?"

"A mixture of roots and herbs from different continents, guaranteed to turn you into a stallion!"

"Tell me then, why am I in such a panicked state?"

"I'd call it something akin to buck fever. You've heard of a boy's first deer hunt and him getting buck fever at the critical moment? He wants that buck so bad he can't find the trigger to shoot it." Doc fumbled for the opium pipe. He pressed a gummy ball of opium into the ceramic bowl and removed the globe from the nearest oil lamp, carefully positioning the bowl over the flame while holding the pipe by its wooden stem. The opium began to vaporize. Doc inhaled, tasting the heavy sweet smoke. "Here. Take a few drags on this."

"What is it?" Harkness asked doubtfully.

"Something to thaw the creeping frosts of old age. It will also calm those jangled nerves. You're as jumpy as a damned cat."

"I have been doing some thinking."

"About what?" Doc returned the bowl to the flame.

"You know I oppose mixed-race relationships. New Orleans is full of colored illegitimates. It has created a swamp of legal problems, moral dilemmas, and—"

"Judge, we are not dealing with legality, morality, or court cases. You asked me to cure you. I laid down precise regimens for you to follow, prescribed rare and exotic medicines, and brought you one of the prettiest girls in New Orleans. And, as you instructed, she is not a prostitute. I am your doctor; you are the patient. If I say this is a medical procedure, then it *is* that and nothing more. Trust me." He held the pipe up again.

Harkness took a long draw and inhaled the sweet smoke. "Where is she?"

"Downstairs, awaiting your summons."

"Is she willing?"

"She is."

Harkness took another draw. A peaceful feeling stole over him, settling his queasy stomach and dulling his apprehension. "Call her."

Doc took charge of the pipe and leaned outside the door to beck-on Kayla. With soft footsteps she ascended the wooden stairs and entered the room. Both men gaped in disbelief as she removed the shawl. A wild profusion of ebony curls cascaded onto her shoul-ders. Her shy smile almost lit the bedchamber. Doc had made a full appraisal of her in Farron Weeks's slave quarters, even going so far as to check her internal and external genitalia for tell-tale sores common to syphilis, but even he was unprepared for her feminine presence in this dimly lit room. He took a big swallow from the whiskey glass.

Harkness could barely speak, he was so overwhelmed. He croaked huskily, "What is your name?"

"Kayla."

"Kayla, come over here."

Doc interjected, "I'll just take this decanter and make myself scarce. In case you didn't know, this is the part where you both dis-robe."

Kayla slid the simple white shift over her head, revealing her magnificent naked body. Harkness' jaw dropped as he gawked at her, taking in her breasts, smooth limbs, and thick patch of coal-black curls in the fork of her thighs.

"How old are you, girl?"

"Fifteen years, master," Kayla answered with eyes downcast.

Doc settled into a chair in the dark shadow of a big armoire to supervise the proceedings he had so carefully staged. "Come on, Judge," he urged gruffly. "Don't be coy! Shuck down those pants," He poured himself another glassful.

The judge obeyed instantly. He shrugged out of his suspenders and the enormous fall-front trousers dropped to the floor with an audible thud. Kayla helped him remove his shirt.

Doc considered his patient in the lamplight. Harkness was above medium height, obese, and covered all over with a dense pelt of body hair. Great whorls of graying black growth sprouted from the pale skin from head to foot, front and back, down his limbs to the knuckles of his fingers and toes. An enormous paunch almost hid his flaccid manhood. Now he stood in the center of the room, as uncertain as a young boy. Kayla gently took him by the hand and led him to the bed, whispering endearments into his ear. The judge grinned sheepishly and lay down on the sheets in full compliance with her proposal. He was clearly infatuated, but still unsure of himself.

Although Doc could discern no visible indication of arousal, he could safely determine that this night would not turn out a total failure. Delighted, he took another swig of whiskey, closed his eyes for a few moments, and felt the warmth steal through his veins. The judge groaned with pleasure and Doc half opened his eyes to reassure himself.

Earlier he had experienced doubt, but it seemed his medical advice was beginning to bear real fruit—a monumental testament to decades of observation and dedicated practice. Apparently the concoction was more efficacious than he believed. Or did the strict physical regimen play a role? Perhaps all the judge needed was a willing partner. The girl was unquestionably the deciding factor. Farron Weeks had not exaggerated; she was indeed a wonder, knowing instinctively how to soothe the judge's anxiety before gently arousing submerged passion. Sweet words and tender caresses slowly melted the remaining ice of unease. Her lips and tongue worked in delicate concert with silky pink palms to bring about a miraculous resurrection of that which the judge had thought was long dead. She was the skilled potter; the judge's member her clay.

Harkness felt the miracle stir and then wither away, as elusive and ephemeral as a heat mirage on a mid-summer day. The shame was more than he could bear. He clutched for the sheets to cover himself, but Kayla whispered soothingly and continued her tender manipulations. Harkness unwound and the miracle returned with an unexpected surge. This time he would not be denied. He was seventeen again—as strong as a stallion and long as a sword! He bellowed with delight as Kayla straddled and rode him, lightly at first, toward the proverbial mountaintop of pleasure.

Doc watched with more than clinical interest as the judge clumsily took control of the action. The moans and snuffles grew louder and his movements became more and more frenzied. It ended almost as abruptly as it had begun. Harkness stiffened and groaned, then collapsed, panting hoarsely from his exertions. Once again, Kayla proved her worth. She sighed such a convincing note of pleasure that Doc, with all his worldly experience, could not detect insincerity. Kayla knew that a man was always the most vulnerable in this moment. She cradled the judge's head in her arms and cooed tenderly, whispering assurances of his skill and manly attributes. The judge was totally captivated. There would certainly be demands for more encounters in the days to come.

Judge Harkness held the highest esteem for Doc's expertise. For years he had called upon him to treat his numerous and all-too-frequent medical complaints. And from the beginning Doc determined that the judge was unduly preoccupied with his body. The man believed illness was always present or lay crouching in nearby shadows, ready to pounce. Doc had treated him for headaches, heart palpitations, nervous twitches, bouts of insomnia, pains in the testicles, ringing in the ears, stomach aches, and dozens of other ills. Most of these conditions were imagined, but over the years Doc had cured real ailments—catarrh, pneumonia, bloody flux, piles, fever, toothaches, rheumatism, and dyspepsia. He had cut corns from the judge's hairy toes, lanced carbuncles on his back, removed horny growths from his forehead, and irrigated his wax-impacted ears—no easy task considering the wiry black hair that sprang from them in thick tufts. Harkness' respect had grown with each cure. After tonight's rousing success, it would increase a hundredfold.

Doc chuckled as he lifted the glass to his lips. He had earned a tidy profit, charging Harkness far more money for the girl's services than he had paid Farron Weeks. On Monday morning he would stroll into the Louisiana Planters' Bank for Signet's payment. Of course the money would not be enough to satisfy his creditors, but it would tide him over until the court inquiry. He now knew the judge well enough to proceed with Signet's scheme. One thing was certain—Judge Harkness would regard all his future medical attestations as gospel.

Chapter One

Breckinridge County, Kentucky—September 27, 1815

A Congreve rocket shrieked into the air leaving a trail of smoke reaching upward into a gray winter sky. Long scarlet lines of British soldiers emerged from the low fog that drifted in from the Mississippi River. Blue steel glinted from India pattern muskets and snare drums rolled, turning Craig Ridgeway's knees into jelly. General John Adair gave him the personal order to fire. Craig aimed his Lancaster rifle at a well-dressed, mounted British officer and pulled the trigger. The regal figure spilled untidily from his saddle. Cannons boomed all along the American line behind the deep drainage ditch of the Macarté Plantation. Once again, Craig picked out an individual target in the British ranks and pulled the trigger. A man clutched his breast and fell into the cane stubble, but his eyes remained locked upon Craig's. Again and again Craig fired, and each time a British soldier fell. He was too good a marksman to miss. The ranks thinned out, but waves of redcoats kept advancing. Bagpipes shrilled incongruously in the damp morning air. Giant tartan-clad soldiers charged diagonally across a cane field to support the wavering charge on the American left flank.

"Shoot them giants!" a Kentuckian yelled. *"They'll fall just as dead as the others!"*

The charge ground to a confused standstill. Craig drew bead on a tall Scotsman, just fifteen yards away, and pulled the trigger, wishing at the same time he could call back the shot. The man had halted and was on the verge of fleeing. The rifle ball struck him in the sternum and he crumpled to his knees with a surprised expression. He raised a bloody, accusing forefinger and pointed directly at Craig. Then he pitched forward and began to whimper like a baby. Craig felt sick to his stomach, so great was his remorse. How many men had he killed in the brief battle? He knew the answer was eleven; that did not count those soldiers he had dispatched in the now famous "Night Battle" on that dark evening after the British had first broken through to the Levee Road.

In one part of that battle he had cut down eight soldiers with two blasts from a stubby double-barreled shotgun. Two of the men lay dying and he had crouched there in the foggy darkness, forced to listen to their last words:

"I've had it, mate! I'm dying."

"Where are you hit?"

"In the bowels—the pain is horrendous!"

"I can't move me legs! He shot me through the spine, I fear."

"What kind of gun was that?"

"A bloody big fowling piece. I think he killed us all."

"I don't want to die on this cane field! Napoleon—I could have died fighting him. At least he was a real threat. What was all this for?"

The crying grew louder—just a few feet away from where he lay. Craig could not breathe. He bolted upright in the bed, gasping for air. Mary laid a soft hand in the crook of his arm.

"Craig! You are having another nightmare."

"I'm awake now," he muttered. The horrors of the past January 8 revisited him often in his sleep. The memory was always there, haunting him even in the daytime.

Mary rose to feed the baby. Ruth was five months old now and almost sleeping through the night, but when she woke, her cries could bring down the rafters. It was her crying that coincided so perfectly with the nightmare.

The cabin had grown chilly in the pre-dawn hours. Craig swung his legs from beneath the covers. The floor was cold. Soon he would start wearing long stockings to bed. He crossed the polished puncheons to the fireplace and stoked up the coals before tossing on some split oak firewood. The fire crackled to life, lighting the room so he could see the little trundle bed. Isabel, their oldest daughter, slept soundly, undisturbed by the crying. Whenever Craig woke in the night he always checked to see if she was breathing, and to know all was well with her.

Mary brought the baby, wrapped snuggly in a soft linsey-woolsey blanket, over to the rocking chair. She first changed the soaked linen diaper. Craig turned to warm his back by the fire and he watched as Mary opened the top of her nightshirt to bare an ample breast. The crying ceased and turned into soft sucking sounds. Craig gazed sleepily at his beautiful young wife with her curly dark brown hair and turquoise-blue eyes, and he thanked God for keeping him alive and bringing him home from battle. Mary smiled at him knowingly. It was a shared, intimate moment in the near silence of the cabin.

Ten months earlier, fearing he would never again see his family, Craig had gone downriver with his brothers-in-law to fight the British at New Orleans. And, truth be told, the battle on Chalmette Plantation had been a near-run disaster. General Andrew Jackson was vastly outnumbered and hopelessly outgunned. With fewer than a thousand bluecoat regulars he had knocked together a ragtag force of volunteer militias from various states, naval and marine units, wealthy plantation owners, free blacks, slaves, pirates, Frenchmen, and Choctaw Indians—and he had beaten the mightiest power in the world. The British had charged his rudimentary defenses, a mud and log rampart hastily erected behind an agricultural drainage ditch, and were hurled back with appalling casualties. Jackson's victory had resounded across the nation. If there were ever doubts about America's survival as a nation, these were forever dispelled on the cane fields below New Orleans.

Like so many other Kentuckians, Craig came back along the Natchez Trace, a dangerous route known for the outlaws who earned their income by robbing and murdering farmers who sold livestock, lumber, crops, and other produce in New Orleans and returned overland toward their homes with money bags jingling. Most of the soldiers had been paid in Spanish silver "mill" dollars which were far more common than silver coins minted in America. The silver must have made for a tempting prize, but few outlaws were fool enough to try taking it.

Craig had returned to Widder's Landing, his farm on the Ohio River, just in time for the spring field work, throwing himself into the long hard days of plowing, harrowing, planting and hoeing. There was new ground to clear, tobacco, corn and hemp to plant, and large vegetable gardens to put out. Ruth was born in April, keeping Mary busy throughout the day and most nights.

"That's a good baby," Mary cooed when Ruth finished her feeding. She patted the baby's back until she produced a resounding burp. Before she could turn back the crib covers, Ruth was asleep.

"Are you coming back to bed?" Mary asked.

"I'm wide awake now," Craig protested with a yawn.

"You don't sound like it. Come to bed. It's a long time before daylight. You'll need your rest. Pa and my brothers are helping you cut corn today."

"You are right, of course."

Mary held the covers open for him and when he lay down she wrapped her arms around him from behind, fitting herself against his back so they fit together like spoons in a rack. She kissed the nape of his neck. "Was it another bad one?"

"They always are," Craig whispered. The recurring nightmares seemed to be intensifying, with the vivid details coming to him in waves, usually just before dawn.

"Craig, you behaved no differently than the other men there. You acted under direct orders. The British could have taken the city. Many more men could have been killed, including my brothers. Instead, you and they contributed to a great victory. We are now at peace with Great Britain. I read that our countries are even trading with each other again. America is more unified than ever—we are entering a new era of progress and good feelings. You helped bring that about!"

"I killed so many men. They were just like us—family men with folks back home, many with wives and children."

"And men on our side died as well. Father Badin heard your confession this summer and granted you total absolution."

Craig reflected upon this. The traveling priest had held Mass at St. Rumoldus, the newly-completed log church in Hardinsburg some eleven miles distant. Craig had confessed and the priest had abruptly, almost perfunctorily, absolved him of all guilt. When Craig tried to discuss the nightmares, Father Badin admonished him in his still-present French accent. "Get on with your life, young Ridgeway. What you did down there was not murder. Governments possess the lawful power to make war; this has been so since the days of the Old Testament. You acted merely as an arm of the government. Jesus Christ himself tells his followers to 'render unto Caesar the things which are Caesar's and to render unto God the things that are God's.' You were obeying his commandment." The priest then dismissed him and turned to deal with the long line of penitents waiting to confess everything from adultery to horse thievery, drunkenness to sloth. Craig was certain it was the same at every church; Father Badin must hear the same litany of sins amassed during the long periods of his absence on the circuit.

"Did you hear me?" Mary prodded him with her knees and pressed her breasts more firmly against his back.

Craig sighed, "I hear. But his absolution doesn't change the fact it happened."

"Pa says it will take time, that one day the bad dreams will stop coming."

"I sure hope he is right."

"Do you want me to say something to him?"

"It sounds like you already have. What else would you say?"

"I could tell him how your memories trouble you. He fought in two wars. Surely he has experienced some of the same feelings."

"Please, say nothing," Craig snapped defensively. "I don't want him or your brothers thinking I am a weakling."

"They would never think that!"

"Let's not talk about it anymore. I'll work through it; I always have."

The rest of the night passed slowly. Craig listened to the regular sounds of his family's breathing accompanied by the soft crackle and hiss of the fireplace. He burrowed deeper into the covers, happy to be home in familiar surroundings. The firelight revealed heavy rafters festooned with strings of dried vegetables—onions, beets, carrots, beans, peas, and herbs. Mary grew several different herbs for cooking, and the hanging bunches imparted a familiar and comforting fragrance.

A whippoorwill's haunting cry rose from the woods behind the cabin. Slowly Craig drifted off to sleep.

———●———

After milking the cows, Craig carried the fresh milk down to the springhouse. The docile brown cow gave rich milk, high in butterfat. Later, Mary would churn it into butter. The tall, spotted cow supplied sweet milk for drinking. There was always an ample supply of both. On his way back to the cabin, Craig roused the hens in the henhouse and gathered their eggs; usually these were Mary's chores, but the baby had wakened again.

The fire needed stoking and he noticed that the stack of firewood and kindling had dwindled. While he carried in more wood, Mary started a big breakfast of eggs, bacon, gravy, and hot cornbread. She bounced the baby on her hip while she worked the swinging fire irons and long-handled skillets with practiced dexterity.

Craig helped with the eggs, scrambling them and adding a splash of buttermilk and a pinch of salt. Mary finished baking the bread and joined him at the table. They said Morning Prayer together before he helped himself to a half dozen strips of sizzling meat. The bacon tasted sweet and smoky, far superior to other bacon in the area. Mary claimed the flavor came from the whiskey mash they fed their fattening shoats. The mash was a natural by-product left over from the whiskey they manufactured, a heavy fermented sludge containing cracked corn, red wheat, and barley sprouts. Three or four times a year he and Mary amassed the necessary ingredients, purchased white oak barrels and ground up bushels of shelled corn before beginning the fermentation process in giant wooden cypress vats. They charred the insides of the oak barrels and fired up the 110-gallon copper still to make a top-quality, double-distilled whiskey that attracted buyers from as far away as New Orleans.

Mary smiled at him over the heavy maple wood table. "You did a nice job cooking the eggs, Craig. I think you would make a perfect houseboy."

"No thank you. I was born for the outdoors." He poured their coffee into thick mugs, adding a touch of sweet cream to his. Mary liked hers black. They were fortunate to be able to afford real coffee; some folks drank only brew steeped from chicory root or burnt corn.

"You are so sweet to help with breakfast." She pursed her lips and made a kissing noise.

"Well, you'll have your hands full enough when Isabel wakes. I can't believe you want another baby so soon." Mary had been giving off subtle indications that, after five months, she was ready to resume lovemaking. Although he felt it was too soon for yet another child, he knew he would not resist her when the time came; in fact he had caught himself thinking more and more often about those delights that would put her in the family way once again.

"Look at Ma! She had babies every eighteen months or so."

He grabbed a hunk of cornbread and grinned at her. "You will get no argument from me." Looking at her he knew the time would be sooner than later. Nothing would be nicer than to jump back under the covers and act upon the wave of passion he was feeling, but the children were wide awake. Isabel left the trundle bed and scampered across the floor to climb onto his lap, snuggling against him, still half asleep. Life was changing on his little farm, just like it was for the growing American nation.

———➤•◄———

It was still dark outside, but Craig could see the day would dawn bright and the sky would be clear. His breath fogged in the early morning moonlight. Although the crisp autumn air suggested frost, it was a heavy dew that bejeweled the grass. Old friends waited for him in the barn. The big plow horses and heavy oxen jostled each other for their morning measure of grain. They had been grazing on summer grass, but Craig had started feeding them again in preparation for the plowing that always followed corn cutting. His saddle horse, Blue, a magnificent seventeen hand-high blue roan, nosed in for his share. Craig moved among the animals, greeting each one with familiar words and pats.

This year's tobacco was already cut and hanging in the barn's north shed, curing nicely and taking on a rich reddish-brown color. The leaves were dry and brittle now, but the morning river fogs of October would soon bring it into "case," a condition where the leaves became soft and pliable. Hopefully the crews could finish cutting corn in time for the stripping season. When that time arrived, farmers would climb into the barn rafters and hand down wooden sticks, each stick holding five to six split tobacco stalks. They would slide the stalks off the sticks and then strip every leaf from every stalk. Finally, the leaves would be pressed into wooden hogsheads, giant barrels weighing up to eleven hundred pounds. These were usually rolled on board flatboats or keelboats for shipment downriver to New Orleans.

But there were new vessels on the river. Some folks speculated that steamboats would soon play a dominant role in commerce, hauling passengers and freight upstream as well as downstream. Craig was inclined to agree. He recalled the first steamboat on the Ohio, the *New Orleans*. On his way to Kentucky he saw the engineering marvel under construction in a little creek known as Suke's Run, just off the Monongahela River in Pittsburgh. The steam-powered vessel, first of its kind on western waters, had passed by his farm four years ago, decked out in her new white and sky-blue paint, black smoke belching from a tall stack, water thrashing and foaming behind side-mounted paddlewheels. Craig saw her again at the New Orleans Levee on his first trip to the city. Since that initial voyage, there had been other boats to steam down the Ohio and Mississippi Rivers: the *Comet, Vesuvius, Dispatch, Aetna,* and *Enterprise. Enterprise* made a spectacular, history-making return journey upstream, reaching Louisville just twenty-five days after leaving New Orleans. She waited there until high water before continuing on above the falls, pounding against the Ohio's strong current to Pittsburgh, and then to her origin at Brownsville, Pennsylvania on the Monongahela. This voyage, a distance of 2,200 miles from New Orleans, proved to most doubters that steamboat commerce was the new future. The feat had made all the newspapers. Craig's father-in-law, Martin McDonnell, read about the journey in a copy of the *Western Courier* in Rosenbotham's store. Most papers were several weeks old, but when Rosenbotham got one he usually posted it on a signboard near the front of his store in nearby Cottonwood Bend so everyone could read it.

More changes loomed on the horizon. As he finished putting an edge on the corn knives, his hired hand, Romulus, appeared at the tool room door. Craig never ceased to be amazed at the man's size. While his brothers-in-law stood at least six feet tall, as did their father, Romulus towered over them, a good half-foot taller; and, where they were lean, he was a thick mass of bulging muscle. Romulus had been a slave on a nearby plantation, sold at an auction to a Tennessee planter and separated from his family. Craig, at Mary's insistence, purchased the wife and child. A few months later, she persuaded him to take a short detour on his return from New Orleans to buy the slave. Craig found Romulus on a farm north of Nashville. The giant had made several previous attempts to escape, and each time the owners had captured and severely punished him—cutting his hamstrings, blinding him in one eye and grossly disfiguring him. Craig purchased him with hard-earned money and reunited him with his family.

Mary had originally intended to set them free, but they had soon discovered this was all but impossible. Craig had offered all his slaves their bills of sale, but harsh reality negated Mary's well-intentioned idealism. Any slave traveling on the road, even in the free territory of Indiana, could be apprehended by "paddy rollers"—slave-catchers—who would seize them, rob their papers, and sell them to southern slave owners. Some freed slaves were even seized in Canada. Of course this was illegal, but the potential for lucrative and easy profit drew all sorts of unscrupulous opportunists. A prime field hand was worth several hundred dollars in the South, and the price was rising with the rapid postwar expansion of cotton acreage.

Romulus and his wife Vergina yearned for their freedom, but they stayed on with Craig, hoping to find a viable way out, waiting for the right time to head north. Craig treated all his slaves as free persons and had even entered into a lucrative partnership with Diogenes, the ancient leather tanner, but legally everyone in his community were still slaves, for the Breckinridge County Sheriff counted them all in the annual property tax Craig paid each year. Still, Craig regarded them as free field hands and paid fair wages, encouraging them to raise crops and livestock. He had also offered to ferry them across the Ohio River. Perhaps, if they were cautious, they could make it to Upper Canada, but it would be a dangerous undertaking for a black man with a wife and two young children. Romulus decided to stay put, save his money, and bide his time. For the past three years they had all struggled to find a solution. Even Martin McDonnell with all his age and wisdom could not come up with a satisfactory plan.

Romulus cleared his throat and spoke in his deep bass voice, "Mornin', Craig."

"Good morning to you Romulus. Are you ready for a hard work day?"

"Ready as I ever be."

"We've got the McDonnells coming over to help us."

"Then it should go fast." The cheerful tone sounded forced and Craig could tell that something weighed heavily with him. The big man was about to say something important. Craig waited patiently, putting an extra edge on the last corn knife. It had taken months for Romulus to lose his smoldering bitterness toward all white men and to open up to him. Mary and Vergina were good friends from the start, but it had taken Romulus much longer. Now they shared meals at outdoor gatherings—sometimes it was a venison roast at Craig's cabin or a catfish fry at Romulus' house. Their children played and laughed together at these events. The other slaves were always welcome—old Diogenes and his wife Maggie, and the three older women, Penelope, Adah, and Eliza. Craig was indebted to them for staying with Mary while he was in New Orleans. The women had worked together spinning flax fibers into thread and weaving the thread into fine linen cloth that brought fair prices at Rosenbotham's store and in Hardinsburg.

Craig looked the giant in the eye. "What is it, Romulus?"

"Me and Vergina decided we's goin' north to Canada."

A little shock slid up Craig's spine. He had known this day would come. He and Romulus had talked it over on several occasions, but the man always decided against taking the road. This time was different; Craig could hear it in his tone and see it in his dead-set expression.

"When?" There was really nothing else to say.

"At the end of corn cuttin' season."

It was final then, and close at hand. "The least I can do is ferry you across the river. Perhaps I can ride escort with you the first night to get you farther along."

"You already done so much for me, Craig. You saved me from that hell in Tennessee, brought our family together, gave me good wages, and made me see that all white men ain't bad."

"Several men feel the same way I do about slavery. My father-in-law has always opposed it, while I was once content not to think about it."

"Mister McDonnell is a good man too," he conceded.

"It will be awfully cold out there on the road north, and much colder in Upper Canada. Why don't you at least wait until summer? The weather will be warmer and the leaves will provide better cover when you decide to hole up."

"Because then it'll be plantin' time all over again. Won't have the heart to leave you then."

"Romulus, you know I will miss you—and not because you are the strongest and best worker I will ever have. You have taught me much about life. Few people could have survived what you did and put it behind them without bitterness."

"You and Mary helped."

"Just tell me when you are ready. My boat is big enough to hold you and your family in a single trip." He could see the gratitude in the man's eye as he handed him a corn knife and a thick spool of hemp-fiber baling twine. "Right now, we need to head for the cornfield. The McDonnells may already be down there."

The old man seemed ageless, timeless, moving across the bottomland with the straight-backed posture and limber stride of a man much younger than his seventy-five years. His grey-white hair was full and soft, pulled back and tied into a long queue that reached down to his shoulder blades. Martin McDonnell had fought in two previous colonial wars, the French War and the War for Independence from Great Britain. The legends of his exploits were famous. One of Breckinridge County's most prosperous and respected farmers, he was descended from a long lineage of devout Irish Catholics who migrated to Maryland in the late 1600's. Martin had moved on after the Revolution—passing through Virginia, crossing the Cumberland Gap, and settling in lands forbidden by the British Empire. One branch of the family planted roots in what was now Bardstown, Kentucky. But Martin came down the Ohio River to Cottonwood Bend and bought a 680-acre farm, transforming wilderness into a gem of civilization, planting his fields in corn, hay, and tobacco. Fine beef and dairy cattle grazed upon his pastures. He built Welcome Hall with bricks fired from the clay on his land. Lawyers and judges, priests and nuns, senators and representatives—all had stayed there and enjoyed its comforts.

Martin was Craig's father-in-law; he had been since 1811, the year Craig married Mary in a big celebration on the lawn of Welcome Hall. He had done much to help Craig make the transition from gunsmith to farmer. When Craig and his brothers-in-law decided to join the fight against the British in New Orleans, it was Martin who advised them to go ahead of the poorly-armed and outfitted Kentuckians, to seek an old acquaintance in the French Quarter who would see they were assigned choice positions in the fighting.

Martin never ceased to amaze Craig with his depth of knowledge and expertise. Craig figured he was an authority on just about everything. The library at Welcome Hall was one of the finest in this part of Kentucky. Martin received agricultural pamphlets and political treatises from Europe, old newspapers from Philadelphia and Pittsburgh, and Rosenbotham's copies of the *Kentucky Gazette* and the *Western Courier* that arrived on flatboats at the Cottonwood Bend riverfront. He was knowledgeable on matters of history and politics, science and agriculture, business and new inventions. Craig regarded him as America's equivalent to the English gentleman farmer—an enlightened man who possessed the wealth and audacity to experiment with new agricultural innovations. Indeed, Martin practiced the system of crop rotation first employed by Flemish farmers and introduced to England by such pioneers as Jethro Tull and Viscount Charles Townshend. He also embraced the practice of Pennsylvania farmers, planting red clover on acreage where the soil showed signs of depletion. Very few farmers in this part of Kentucky bothered with such foreign and unfamiliar methods; many wore out their soil and moved farther west. Fortunately for Martin, most of his acreage was prime bottomland, enriched almost annually by spring floods. On the higher, less-productive ground he pastured his beef cattle herd. And as George Washington had on Mount Vernon, he planted wheat where he had grown tobacco the year before. He constantly made improvements, and through careful management and continued hard work, his profits increased. Recently, he had switched some of his acreage to hemp production, after first studying the crop and analyzing the market potential. Martin owned the farms on both sides of Craig's land and, as the various seasons demanded, everyone helped each other.

Craig and Romulus quickened their pace as they descended the steep track to the narrow strip of bottomland where Craig grew his corn. Beyond the cornfield the Ohio was turning bright silver-blue in the early morning light.

Martin was flanked by two of his four sons, Owen and Stephen. Craig had gone with his brothers-in-law to New Orleans. Together they had fought the British and survived, forging a bond stronger than that of many blood brothers. Both McDonnell brothers were tall and lean like their father; both were handsome, industrious, and intelligent. Owen had married a wealthy Louisiana girl and now lived on a large, neighboring plantation Martin had acquired. Stephen, the youngest, was just shy of seventeen.

The oldest brother, Patrick, now lived in Nelson County where his McDonnell kinfolk resided. In addition to growing grain, he raised some of the finest horses in Kentucky. The other brother, Daniel, had tragically fallen at Fort Meigs in 1813. There was a daughter, Brigid, who practiced dentistry in Bardstown. The family was strongly steeped in the Catholic faith; one would have to search long and hard to find better folks. Craig counted himself lucky to be a part of the family.

"Good morning, Craig, Romulus," Martin greeted them in his resonant baritone. "I think we picked a good day for corn cutting." He set down an armload of corn knives. "The hired help will be here directly. Figured we'd get an early start."

"I appreciate it, Martin," Craig said, lowering with relief the heavy spool of hemp twine. Romulus laid out two bigger spools.

The old man squatted to examine the thick, twisted fiber, twirling it with his fingers and testing it with a few practiced pulls. "I have to hand it to Mary and her helpers. This is strong stuff. No wonder she gets such a good price. No doubt she makes more money on her twine than we do selling raw fiber to the keelboat men."

"She is quite a girl," Craig agreed with pride. Rosenbotham from Cottonwood Bend and the storekeepers in Hardinsburg kept her busy with orders, as did some of the local farmers. During the war, when there was no real market for agricultural products, most folks in the Ohio River Valley struggled to make ends meet. But Mary and her slave women industriously manufactured liquored chewing tobacco and cigars, selling both to storekeepers and wealthy customers. They wove flax fibers into fair linen cloth, and spun hemp fibers into twine. They wove coarse hemp thread to make feed bags which attracted the attention of the local miller, Levi Matthews.

"Let's get to it," Martin suggested. He rolled up his sleeves to expose long, sun-browned forearms corded with lean muscle.

Long ago, the old farmer taught Craig how to cut corn in square blocks of sixteen-stalks and then how to bind the stalks into great shocks. The center four stalks would remain uncut, and their tops were twisted together to form a support for the shock. The remaining stalks in the square were chopped off with a corn knife and leaned around the support. When the shock was full, it was tied with twine, or sometimes with twisted vines or cornstalks. It was an art that took some time to master, but now Craig could do it without thinking, cutting and building shocks that he secured with Mary's twine. He wielded his corn knife with skill, chopping through the stalks and keeping the blade out of the dirt to prevent dulling. The field resounded with varied rhythms of chopping corn knives. Soon, long rows of brown shocks emerged behind them, transforming the bottomland into a magnificent scene of beauty.

Shortly after sunup, the twelve field hands arrived. After the New Madrid earthquakes in 1811-1812, Martin had taken in three destitute families, providing each with a house and employment. He then hired them on as permanent workers after purchasing two large farms that had suddenly become available. The farmhands had proven invaluable during plowing, planting, and harvest seasons. This year his hay and tobacco crops were already in the barns; the hemp was cut and shocked in the fields. Martin's crew would help finish this field long before suppertime.

Craig loved this twenty-acre strip of bottomland that lay between the Ohio River and the wooded limestone slopes. In the slanting rays of sunrise it was more picturesque than usual. It was past mid-morning before the sun could temper the previous evening's chill. With each passing day it banked farther in the south, and each day's warmth noticeably diminished. Already the sumacs and sassafras were changing, splashing reds, golds and oranges against the pale yellow-greens of late September. Yellow goldenrod and purple ironweed blooms adorned the fringes of the field. In a few days the first frosts would fall. On Sundays Craig and Mary would gather walnuts, hickory nuts, pecans, and persimmons that grew on the hillsides below the cabin.

Winter was Craig's least favorite season, but it had its good qualities. The never-ending work slowed somewhat and there was more time to enjoy the land's bounty for which they worked all year. It was hog-killing season when families worked together cutting up meat, salt curing, smoking hams and shoulders, and enjoying big dinners with roast tenderloin. It was being together beside warm fires, long evenings of talking and laughing and storytelling, forging familial bonds and strengthening friendships. But there was always firewood to cut and haul. Blocks of ice must be chopped or sawed on the coldest days and stored in deep underground ice houses and packed in straw and sawdust. When the flatboat men pulled to shore there were usually buyers aboard, looking to purchase the year's produce. In late January sap rose in the sugar maples, and families would tap the trunks to make maple syrup. February was the time to think about plowing and harrowing, putting out an early garden, and getting ready for spring, the time of hope and renewal.

But for many British soldiers there would be no more spring seasons. Craig had seen to that with his long rifle. Perhaps two dozen soldiers had fallen to his aim. At least one was a high-ranking officer; perhaps it was General Pakenham himself. It seemed almost incongruous that a beautiful instrument as the Lancaster rifle could deal such death and destruction. After the battle, Craig and his brothers-in-law could have collected the paltry payment offered by the United States Government, but they had not signed their names on any official roster and had chosen to return home ahead of Jackson's official command allowing the army to disband. Craig would not have accepted payment for killing British soldiers.

Martin called a halt just before noon. Some of the workers had brought loaves of bread, cheese, and apples, and they sought shade at field's edge to eat their midday meal. Others drifted off to their homes. Martin and sons joined Craig at the cabin where Mary had laid on a big dinner of beef stew and pan-fried cornbread. Romulus declined Craig's invitation to eat with them, but he stopped in briefly to say hello to the children.

"Best get home to the missus. She join us after we eat."

"She does plan to help," Mary informed them. "I spoke with Vergina this morning."

"Then we should have our corn cut and shocked today, with time to spare," Craig speculated. Vergina stood taller than him and could work as hard as any field hand. Romulus grinned knowingly. He set off for his cabin across the Hardinsburg Road.

As Martin sat down at the table, he rubbed his right shoulder, the one injured long ago by rifle ball and tomahawk. "We are in for rain, if I do not miss my guess. You would not think that wounds from nearly threescore years past would still ache every time rain threatens."

Mary ladled steaming stew into wooden bowls and the family joined hands to say grace. Craig liked the way she made stew with thick chunks of beef, stock thickened with flour, plenty of potatoes, onions, carrots and peas. She always knew how much salt and pepper to add. The cornbread was hot enough to melt the sweet butter. It was the perfect meal for hardworking farmers.

"Will you finish today?" Mary asked.

"I am almost sure of it," Craig answered.

"We will," Martin confirmed. He winked at Isabel. "How have these grandchildren been behaving?"

"Miss Isabel and I had a little disagreement about her climbing the loft ladder," Mary replied. "Someone got their bottom whacked—again." She rose to pour coffee and dish out servings of blackberry cobbler.

Isabel appeared contrite and Craig rolled his eyes. "I'm glad I wasn't here to see that. We don't want you to break your head! You'd best listen to your mother, young lady. "

"I will, Father," Isabel replied. Apparently the incident had occurred just before they arrived for dinner. Craig's heart ached for her, but he knew Mary had her fingers firmly on the pulse of things. If it was left to him, Isabel would probably be swinging from the tall oaks that surrounded the cabin. He wished he could stay longer, but dinner ended all too soon. Vergina and Romulus waited in the dogtrot.

Stephen sighed in contentment as they returned to the cornfield. "That Mary sure is a good cook! She can come down to the house any day."

"Who do you think taught her?" Owen asked. "You'd best not say anything like that around Ma!"

"I won't."

Martin added. "When you marry, you must always brag on your wife's cooking. There is no better food in the world; that is the golden rule. Never say your mother cooked better, or that she kept house neater. That is looking for real trouble."

Craig figured he was lucky in every way a man could be. Mary was an excellent cook, always inventing new recipes, making even plain meals enjoyable. When it came to sewing new clothes, there were few women who could compare. She was industrious and inventive, and earned income to afford a few luxuries. If perhaps the cabin was cluttered at times, he knew to keep silent.

The river sparkled in the sunlight, achingly blue beyond the riverbank, contrasting with the trees along the Indiana Territory shoreline. These were still pale green, but their color would soon change. The afternoon remained bright, but a slight breeze blew out of the north, chilling the sweat on Craig's neck. It was dusty work, but the buff-colored shocks soon grew in number, changing the field's scenery. Vergina kept pace with Martin; both of them outworked most of the hired help. Craig, Owen, Stephen and Romulus moved out ahead of the others, but dropped back periodically to catch them up.

Chapter One

Very little daylight remained when they bound the last shock. Martin surveyed the field with pride. He chuckled and whispered to Craig and Romulus. "I need Vergina in the fields more often. Those hands hate to have a woman outwork them. They've never worked so hard."

"For a while I thought she might pass me!" Craig exclaimed.

Romulus flashed a wide grin showing wide gaps where the previous slave owner had knocked out several teeth. Craig felt a pang when he remembered that he would soon be leaving.

"We'll meet over at the Arbuckle farm tomorrow," Martin informed everyone. "Sharpen those corn knives tonight. You'll need a good edge in that field. We'll see what we can cut before the rain sets in."

The Arbuckle farm lay to the east of Widder's Landing. Stephen had tried living there shortly after Martin purchased it, but the young man soon missed the comforts of home and his mother's cooking. That short-lived experiment lasted less than one week. Craig guessed Stephen would try again when he was married. In the meantime Martin allowed his best field hand to house his family there. The workers set off for their respective homes.

"Thank you for the help, Martin. I will see you tomorrow," Craig said.

As he, Romulus, and Vergina climbed the track to the high ground, Craig studied the sky. To the west the sun sat like a giant red orb on the wooded hillsides, partially obscured by flaming scarlet clouds. Golden rays fanned upward, painting the western clouds from yellows and oranges, to various whites and pinks. The entire sky was rippled with patterns of tiny clouds, millions of white puffs that dappled the light blue background with swirling patterns fading from brighter colors in the west to purples and steel grays in the east. Martin was right—it would rain, probably tomorrow. The three of them walked abreast when they reached the top of the hill, not speaking until they reached the barn. After they put up the twine, Craig decided to broach the subject of their leaving, still hoping to persuade them to stay.

"You've been great friends," Craig told them. "Mary and I will miss you."

"Still got a few days left," Vergina argued. "We make the most of them."

Craig saw a shadow of regret pass across Romulus' face. "I guess Romulus told you, I will be glad to ferry you across the river."

"He did."

"I have decided to give you a little bonus to help send you on your way. But if you could see fit to stay on with us, I could negotiate a bigger bonus after the crops sell."

"We got enough saved. What good is all that money if you can't have a place of your own?"

"Well, you do have one, practically. I could legally deed some land to you, but you have refused. I have always encouraged you to grow the crops you want and to raise stock. And whenever you wanted to sell anything, I have always helped."

Vergina's determination showed in her expression, and her voice was firm. "We knows you care. There ain't no finer people than you and Miss Mary. But it ain't the same as bein' free and you knows it. We got bigger plans."

"I understand," Craig nodded. "And I wish you all good things in life."

"See you tomorrow mornin', Craig," Romulus spoke softly, his voice tinged with remorse.

"Good night then," Craig replied. He watched the couple walk away in the gathering twilight. A rising moon reflected off the clouds, lighting the dirt road in places where trees did not block the light. Craig fed the farm animals and headed for the cabin. At the dogtrot he kicked off his boots and shook out of his dusty clothes. He would tell Mary about Romulus' plans at the supper table.

Chapter Two

New Orleans—October 6, 1815

Blue tobacco smoke mingled with sharp fumes of cheap rum, raw whiskey and human sweat, creating a haze as solid as a brick wall. One could hardly see the drinkers across the room. Oil lamps glowed like dull yellow smudges in the darkness, barely casting enough light to make out any real features. It was week's end and the bar was full of river rats and keelboat men from Kentucky, dark brooding Spaniards from the Caribbean islands, crews from ocean-going vessels, and local planters from the smaller farms in surrounding parishes. Like moths drawn to a flame, they all came to Emmett Barnett's Tavern for a rowdy good time. It was noisy beyond belief. Shouts and laughter clapped and pealed off the stone walls. Women of all shapes and sizes worked the crowd, ranging in color from pale white to darkest ebony. Some were skilled pickpockets; others had male accomplices waiting outside in the shadows for unsuspecting victims. And still others contracted their services with relative honesty and delivered on their promises.

Barnett's Tavern was the perfect retreat for Doc Applegate. In his present condition, it would not do for him to appear in the finer establishments of the French Quarter. Many of his patients came from the highest echelon of society and they still afforded him a measure of respect. He preferred to mingle with the affluent and other professionals, enjoying expensive liqueurs and sophisticated conversation, but not on this night. Instead, he had crossed Canal Street and negotiated his way through the warren of muddy streets and cesspools until he found Barnett's. He had been here several times, on medical calls. The last time, two men had mixed it up in a knife fight and soon, others joined into the fracas. Emmett Barnett had drawn a sawed-off shotgun from beneath the bar and unloaded a blast of bird shot into the crowd. Incredibly, only one man died, one of the knife fighters who suffered a deep gash in the lower abdomen. His guts had spilled out, perforated in several places. The blood loss was horrendous. To ease the man's agony, Doc had administered a strong dose of laudanum, perhaps powerful enough to be lethal in itself. The struggle had not lasted long. He spent the rest of that night extracting birdshot from a dozen victims, including Emmett Barnett who lost an eye from a ricocheted pellet.

Barnett had invited Doc to come back, offering him a free jug of his choice and guaranteeing full protection while on the premises. No one would dare cross the squatty little tavern owner with the hair-trigger temper, so Doc was there to collect on his offer. Barnett clubbed aside an unwilling patron in order to open up a corner table. The whiskey was raw, cheap and full of sediments, a fiery, single-run batch made somewhere in Kentucky or Tennessee.

Doc was in a sorry state and he knew it. He looked like a roughed-up old game rooster that had fought in one too many fights. His dingy white hair was unkempt; long, greasy tendrils snaked out in all directions. White stubble frosted his face. His cream-colored linen suit was rumpled and soiled with dark yellow stains in the armpits and other unidentifiable splotches down the front. Long handlebar mustaches drooped sadly into the chipped porcelain mug, dribbling little streams of whiskey onto the table whenever he took his mouth from the rim.

Last night's madness at the gaming tables had turned into catastrophe. He was ruined forever. He had struggled against the temptation, but that damned Lanouette let it slip that some businessmen from Philadelphia were getting up a game. Supposedly these outsiders were wealthy beyond normal standards of wealth, sloppy drinkers, and inexperienced gamblers, therefore easy pickings. Doc declined at first, but in the end he could not resist. Over the past several years he had lost a fortune at the faro tables and in playing other popular games of skill and chance brought to New Orleans by early French settlers. These games had caught on quickly in America. Gambling and the frontier lifestyle shared similar characteristics—a spirit of adventure, opportunity, and risk taking. New Orleans, with all its wealth and allure, quickly became America's principal gaming town. This was bad news for someone like Doc, for vice was always close at hand.

Doc lost his last money at *poque*, a card game descended from the German game *pochen*. The literal meaning of the word meant "brag" or "bluff," and this game required substantial measures of both skills. It was played with a pack of thirty six cards. Players purchased an equal amount of chips and plunked down an agreed-upon number into six pools on a game board. The *poque* pot could swell to an enormous size, and at game's end, all would be won in a showdown by the player holding the best hand.

That was the thrill which kept luring Doc back to the table, time after miserable time. He knew full well he could not survive another loss. But it had all seemed so easy. At first he did win—as he always seemed to do—not a great amount, but a respectable sum for a man of his means. He could have left the game at any time. But, as losers dropped out, the stakes rose dramatically and Doc had stayed in. For once the cards seemed to fall his way. Then, one of the big losers, a fat, jowly entrepreneur who appeared the most gullible and unsure of the lot, bet everything on the entire pot. Doc matched his bid and lost everything in a single play.

The madness compelled him to sign yet another note to buy an additional round of chips, which he promptly lost. He knew he would never raise the money to redeem those notes. Creditors would seize his house in New Orleans, all the furniture, horse and carriage, and everything else of value, perhaps even his medical instruments, medicines and supplies.

He had exhausted all his options. True, the banker Jules Signet had advanced money on several occasions. The last time he had consolidated all the promissory notes into one loan for easier payments, but these new losses far exceeded even that brilliant stratagem. Doc knew he could not present him with another note.

In truth this was a sickness. For years he had diagnosed it in others, a compulsion as powerful as drinking or womanizing. Only recently had he recognized it in himself. He put the jug between his lips and took several gulps. The effect was almost immediate. He closed his eyes and buried his face into his hands. Emmett Barnett moved in to confiscate the jug and protect him from the women who were hovering around like vultures, waiting for the opportunity to strike and pick the pathetic creature clean.

The opulent Hôtel d'Orleans took up a half city block in the French Quarter, constituting almost an entire city within itself, complete with restaurants, bars, courtyard and shops. The establishment could sleep and feed several hundred guests. A new chef had arrived from Paris and his creations were the latest rage among the city's elite. Jules Signet dined in private at his usual table, served by two waiters. The claret was delightful and he ordered another glass. As this was poured, the maître d'hôtel crossed the room in an inconspicuous manner in order to approach the banker from behind the right shoulder. It was proper, formal etiquette for this dining room.

"I am sorry to impose, monsieur. But the man you mentioned earlier has arrived. He wishes to see you."

"You may send him to me."

The maître blanched momentarily and then murmured, "But of course."

When the informer arrived from behind, Signet realized that the maître had discreetly bundled him through a back entrance. Otherwise, the restaurant's reputation might suffer. The banker risked a glance over his shoulder and scrutinized the informer.

"How bad is he?"

"Bad enough that Barnett took charge of the bottle. Emmett usually don't give a shit for nobody but hisself. But not long ago Doc dug a shotgun pellet out of his eye and won his respect. Guess ol' Emmett was worried about him. Doc looks like he's been to hell and back."

"You say your man is still there, watching over him?"

"He is, but I wouldn't worry if'n I was you. Emmett won't let nothin' happen to him. One of the girls tried to fleece him and Emmett nigh split her skull. He's got a fist like a sledge hammer. The other girls carried her upstairs. She's done for the night."

Signet took a piece of Spanish silver from his purse. "Very well. Bring him to my house on Royal Street. Do you know it?"

"I do. What do I tell Emmett? He's meaner'n a cottonmouth snake. He might think we are trying to harm the Doc."

"I will compose a letter for him." Signet asked for a pen, inkwell, and piece of paper. When these arrived, he wrote out a brief explanation and handed it to the man who tucked it away without glancing at it.

"Hate to be the one to tell you this; Emmett can't read."

"Then read it for him."

"Can't read neither."

"I am through bandying words with you. If you want the rest of your payment, find a way to get the doctor to my house. That is all." He waved his hand in a gesture of dismissal. The maître d'hôtel stepped in to escort the man out through the back entrance. Signet returned to his meal, reflecting upon the different world that lay beyond Canal Street.

———●———

Doc Applegate lay on the bed, studying the strange ceiling upon which the plaster patterns were swirling. He wondered vaguely where he was, but his scalp itched, distracting him. For a moment he thought of scratching it, but he decided against such folly, fearful that the top of his skull might just come off. Swallowing was difficult; his tongue felt dry and swollen to more than twice its size. His stomach rumbled and a foul taste rose in the back of his throat. The bed pitched and heaved like a raft adrift on an open sea. Never in his sixty-four years had he experienced such nausea. And worse, he feared his head would crack open, so intense was the pain.

The sun's rays filtered through the drapes, tinted with the pale orange-red glow of late afternoon. That meant he had lain unconscious for the whole night and most of the day. He tried to lift his head, but abandoned the effort. Something stirred softly in the corner. Doc rolled his gritty-feeling eyeballs toward the sound, just in time to see a well-dressed slave leave the room. Presently the slave returned with the banker, Jules Signet. Now he knew where he was. Fortunately, Signet sympathized with his condition, for he spoke softly.

"Well, my friend, you gave us quite a scare. Welcome back to the world of the living."

Doc smacked his lips and muttered hoarsely, "Coffee."

"It is coming, Doctor. Can you try to sit up?"

"Not yet," Doc sighed.

"That was a foolish thing to do. You could have killed yourself. Then how would I win my judgment?"

"I'm sure with your means you would find another way."

"There you are wrong. Your testimony is the heart of our plan."

A female slave brought in a silver serving tray and set it on the nightstand next to the bed. She poured steaming black coffee into a delicate china cup. The aroma piqued Doc's senses and he struggled to rise. Both slaves helped him into a sitting position, propping pillows behind his back for comfort. Doc groaned with every movement, but he reached out for the cup with shaking hands, clinging to it as if it were his salvation. His teeth chattered against the rim as he drank it down.

"Water!" he gasped.

The female slave poured a glassful and he guzzled greedily, feeling his body tissues soaking it up. Doc knew he was dehydrated, and he held out his glass for a refill. Again, he drank, making pathetic whimpering noises as he swallowed. Exhausted by the effort, he sank back onto the pillows and closed his eyes.

Signet dismissed the slaves and considered the man upon which so much expectation rode. In this condition the doctor could not possibly deliver the performance so critical to winning the case. The presentation must be flawless, and the individual arguments executed with perfect timing. Right now the doctor could not manage even a simple line of argument. For this reason he must be kept under strict watch—no more gaming, and certainly no more drinking binges. The man was a physical wreck. Doc had been brought here last night, head rolling, suit coat streaked with vomit, piss soaking the front of his trousers. He still reeked with filth. Tomorrow morning the slaves would burn his old clothes and clean him up. In the meantime Signet would send for the tailor and order new clothes, perhaps a couple of suits. It would take work to get the man into shape for the courtroom.

"I'm ruined, you know," Doc croaked.

"What do you mean?" Signet asked, surprised he was still conscious.

"I lost eight hundred dollars last night."

"That was two nights ago, Doctor. I warned you to stay away from those tables. You did not heed my advice." Signet felt only a slight twinge of guilt. It was he who had arranged the poque game and hired Lanouette to "leak" the information about the businessmen. He had bought all the players, paid for their chips, and even determined the game's outcome—for the gaming house owner was also in his employ.

Doc spoke again, like a man teetering on the verge of death. His hand crawled laboriously toward his heart and then, as if it could creep no farther, flopped limply onto the bed sheet. "Well it's all over now. I see no need for me to continue with this undertaking. I'm an old man, gravely ill and tired of living. I want nothing more than to be free of this world."

Signet was dismayed. The whole plan was unraveling right in front of him. Perhaps he had pushed the man too far. Applegate resembled a dying man—ashen complexion, slack mouth, and bloodshot eyes underhung with purple bags.

"Wait and see. You will feel differently tomorrow morning."

"No, I won't."

"Please! You are still suffering from the whiskey." Signet tried to mask his rising alarm. There was so much at stake.

"It's not that." Doc protested.

"What then?"

"I can never repay that note. I have lost everything."

Signet breathed a sigh of relief. So that was it. "Then rest easy, my friend. I will simply consolidate your note into a new loan."

"You can do that?"

"I am bank president. I can do anything I want."

"But I will still have a mountain of debt when all is finished."

"Our original arrangement was this—you win a favorable judgment and your loan will be cancelled. It applies in equal force to the new loan, for I never specified an exact amount. On my word of honor you will stand free and clear. And I will still pay you the promised three hundred dollars. Does that ease your pain, Doctor?"

"It does," Doc sighed.

"Very well, but now I must add these stipulations—no more heavy drinking and no more gambling. You must live here as my guest until after the hearing. That way I can keep a close watch on you. I will furnish you with new clothes, but you must rehabilitate yourself physically and mentally. I do wish for you to maintain your close relationship with Judge Harkness. Do we have a deal?"

"We do."

"Then rest well, Doctor. I will have one of my slaves watch over you while you sleep. And I will see you again tomorrow morning."

"Good night," Doc answered. "And thank you."

When the door closed, Doc grinned, immensely proud of his acting ability. Once again he had dug himself out of a bad scrape. He really should have been on stage. The thought made him chuckle and that set his head to hurting. He asked the slave to send for his medical bag. It contained medicinal powders that would work wonders on a headache and upset stomach.

The Ohio River—October 18, 1815

A hunter's moon rose over the wooded hills to the east, transforming the Ohio River into a path of sparkling quicksilver. The big canoe surged ahead with every stroke of the paddle. They made little noise, only the gurgle of displaced water and an occasional thump of wood on wood. Romulus sat in the back, using his powerful muscles to propel them on a slightly upstream angle. Vergina sat in the middle with her children among the heap of supplies. She too, wielded a paddle, contributing her considerable efforts to their escape. Craig paddled in the bow, watching for snags. He could sense the couple's excitement. For years they had dreamed of this moment. They were setting out on the ultimate adventure, tinged with the thrill of escape. Craig was truly glad to be helping them. They were not leaving because of maltreatment or impoverishment; in many ways they lived higher than Martin's field hands. They were escaping the cruel institution of slavery. In Kentucky freed slaves might own land, but they would not stand as equals with white men. They would find it difficult to invest money and advance financially beyond what little Craig could arrange for them. Perhaps in northern Indiana or Canada life would be different.

What they were undertaking was perfectly legal. Long ago Craig and Mary had given them their bills of sale. Last night they had penned glowing character references and attestations that the slaves were truly emancipated. Martin and Agnes, Mary's mother, had signed the letters as co-witnesses. The old man had advised Craig to free the slaves as close as possible to Romulus' planned date of departure. News like that would travel fast in Breckinridge County, alerting those human predators who would profit by capturing and selling them to some southern slaveholder.

Very recently Craig had appeared in open court to acknowledge the Deeds of Emancipation. The entry was recorded in the Breckinridge County Court Order Book G, page 105. It read:

> *Know all men by these presents that I, Craig Ridgeway, of Breckinridge County do think proper and do by these presents forever manumit, liberate and set free from henceforward, my certain negro man named Romulus, about forty years of age, and his wife Vergina, both of black color, and their children Leta and Gabriel, also of black color, to have their full and perfect freedom from me, my heirs, executors or administrators and all and every person or persons besides.*

As the former slave owner Craig was required to post a bond, with security, guaranteeing that the former slaves would not become charges upon Breckinridge County. This expense came as an unwelcome shock; Craig should have known that any court transaction would cost him money. His only financial consolation came from knowing that in future years he would not have to pay the property tax the county imposed upon slave owners.

The wooded shore of Indiana Territory drew closer. Lights from a farmhouse glowed through the trees about a mile downstream. No one spoke as they crossed the river. Craig did not know exactly what lay due north of the riverbank. Despite his excitement, he felt a twinge of unease. The family would not be free just because they set foot in Indiana. Even if they managed to avoid the paddy rollers, they might encounter other troubles. Romulus, with his imposing height and muscle, looked menacing to the average person. Vergina's usually stern expression would win no sympathy in a conflict. If a crime was committed in a town they were passing through, they would surely be blamed. And both were fighters. If threatened, they would react with violence, rather than with words. A confrontation would end badly for them. He tried to put the vision out of his mind. Mary often accused him of imagining things that might never happen. She was probably right. He resolved not to spoil the family's happy occasion.

The canoe crunched onto a sandbar just off the bank. Craig hopped out and pulled the craft to shore. Vergina passed the children to him and began unloading their belongings. Romulus hopped out and shoved the canoe further onto the bank. Vergina took the infant from Craig while Romulus hefted the remaining sacks and scooped up Leta.

"I reckon that's it, Craig," Romulus sighed.

Craig clasped his forearm and said, "I guess so, Romulus. You have the extra money I gave you?"

"Vergina's got it now. She keep charge of it."

"Then take good care of yourselves. If I were you, I would travel all night and lay up in some thicket before daybreak. Stay hidden until dark before setting out again. The nights are growing longer, so you will have more time to travel in darkness. You have food enough to last you for several days, perhaps all the way into Canada."

"Miss Mary done seen to that," Vergina assured him. "We was all packed and she brung us bread, yams, and half a smoked ham."

"We are sorry to see you go," Craig replied. "But we are truly happy for you. When you are settled, have someone write a letter to let us know you are safe. Have it sent to Rosenbotham's Store in Cottonwood Bend."

"We will," she promised.

Without further words, the family disappeared over the riverbank and headed north on their new adventure in life. Craig waited a few moments, listening for them. He offered up a silent prayer for their safety and success. If anyone deserved happiness it was this family.

The return trip across the Ohio was easier, for what little current there was helped him on his way. He studied the stars, recognizing the arrival of new autumn constellations twinkling in the dark vastness above. It would frost again; the days had grown cooler, somewhat earlier than usual. Martin sensed that something strange was afoot in nature, but he could not put a finger on it. Things had been unsettled since 1811 and 1812. Those years marked a number of strange occurrences—squirrels and snakes moving in great migrations, passenger pigeon flights that blackened the daytime sky, eclipses, the Great Comet of 1811 and cataclysmic earthquakes that shook most of the eastern United States, even Canada. Recently, the sunsets were explosive riots of color, almost eerie red—on some nights the whole sky appeared as if on fire. Martin felt as many of the older folks in the area did; nature held yet another nasty surprise in store for them.

Most young people did not fret about such things. Instead, they looked forward to the upcoming autumn gatherings on the farms surrounding the little settlement of Cottonwood Bend. Tomorrow evening Owen would host a great corn shucking party at his plantation. It promised to be the social event of the season. Owen's wife, Lucinde, had asked Mary to help her prepare some of the refreshments. A side of beef was already slow-roasting on the spit, and Martin planned to contribute several jugs of apple cider. Craig offered to bring a keg of whiskey to liven things up. Other families would contribute various foods and beverages to provide for the workers that would come from miles around. There were other shucking parties scheduled in the area, but none would be as entertaining as this one promised to be.

———————◆———————

Mary baked three pies—apple, peach, and blackberry. She also cooked a pot of green beans flavored with salt-cured ham hocks. Twice that day she drove the wagon down to help Lucinde prepare for the evening. Now she held Ruth in her lap and kept watch over the food as Craig negotiated the wagon down the steep track below the cabin. Isabel sat between them, enjoying the ride. It promised to be an exciting evening.

Corn shucking was an old tradition brought to Kentucky from Virginia, a thoughtfully planned social event designed to draw neighbors together for work, fellowship and fun. Most farmers usually lived a monotonous "hog and hominy" existence, not often leaving their farms due to the enormous amount of work required just for survival. But an occasion such as this offered escape from the doldrums of everyday labor. The food was always good, and usually the host provided some kind of music for dancing and merriment. A time for neighbor helping neighbor, gatherings such as this brought about a sense of community spirit and belongingness.

Folks began arriving at Owen's plantation toward late afternoon. The corn shucking commenced before sunset. Over one hundred and twenty people showed up for the fun—and this type of work truly was fun. It gave people a chance to interact with others and catch up on all the latest news. While they worked, men discussed politics and farm prices. Women whispered about prospective romances, confided marital issues, and gossiped about infidelities. Young children played hide-and-seek among the corn shocks; even older children constantly sought opportunities to play. Sweethearts might be allowed to work on a shock together under the watchful eyes of their elders. More than one marriage proposal had been made at a corn shucking.

There was an enjoyable tradition that sometimes happened at a corn shucking—the boy or man who happened to find a red ear would be given the privilege of kissing the prettiest girl present or dancing with her when the work was done. So far, no one had found a red ear.

Stephen, Craig, Owen and three other field hands drove their teams slowly through the field while the workers tore ears from the stalks, shucked husks, and tossed ears into the wagon. Some of the women who chose to work in the fields were gossiping in hushed tones about a married citizen of Cottonwood Bend who was paying regular court to a woman recently widowed. Although they tried to be secretive, Craig could hear them talking in the stillness of the cornfield.

"That Wilfred has been playin' with fire again!" said one woman. "Heard he is a-seein' Cecilia Dowell."

"I heered it too," another woman chimed in, shaking her head. "This ain't the first time ol' 'Mister Walk-on-Water' has been caught with his hand—or his whatever—in the honey jar."

A couple of the younger women giggled in mock embarrassment.

"Heered the poor woman was in need of 'legal and financial council' and he's been a-helpin' her. Sometimes it takes the Judge two or three nights to get her affairs all straightened out!"

"Does Violet know?"

"She suspects somethin's amiss. Told Sarah Wheatley he bought new underdrawers at Rosenbotham's store."

"That's always the first of many signs," clucked one woman, shaking her head in a world-weary manner.

"Poor Violet. She has put up with a lot."

Craig drove his wagon through the field, pretending not to listen. They were talking about Cottonwood Bend's most prominent citizen, commander of the local militia, Judge Wilfred J. Bozarth. The man truly was an enigma. An educated lawyer and judge, he was also the consummate politician, constantly running for various offices. Rumor had it he would try again for the State House of Representatives, perhaps one day even run for Governor. One could not help but like him, for he possessed an easy, cosmopolitan manner, a face that some might call handsome, a brilliant, big-toothed grin, and an enormous mane of salt-and-pepper-colored hair.

Although he dressed like royalty and spoke like an actor on stage, Judge Bozarth knew how to ingratiate himself with the common folk. As Craig's lawyer, he had accompanied him to the log courthouse in Hardinsburg and assisted in securing the deed to Widder's Landing. He had advised Craig on paying taxes, helped him to collect the Governor's rewards after dispatching three violent outlaws, and fought alongside him at the Battle of New Orleans. Like most people, the Judge was not totally good or bad; there were many shades of gray where he was concerned.

Most folks in Cottonwood Bend, and many in Breckinridge County, viewed him as a great personage, a true champion of the poor and downtrodden. Indeed he had helped Craig when he was just a newcomer to the area—and in the process helped himself to big legal fees. Yes, he had assisted with the outlaw rewards, but sent those papers in with his own, describing in a flamboyant account how he, Wilfred J. Bozarth, Attorney-at-Law, Judge, militia commander, and future candidate for the Kentucky House of Representatives, had brought the outlaw leader to justice.

Yet he possessed a common touch which no one could deny. Years ago, one of his clients, a proper church-going lady, came to see him on legal business; when he offered her a chair, she refused to sit down. Clearly something was physically wrong. For weeks she had been in pain and would not disclose her symptoms to anyone, not even her closest family members. Somehow the Judge broke down her defenses and got her to confess that she suffered from bleeding hemorrhoids. Using his considerable powers of persuasion, he escorted her over to Doc Emmick's house, which doubled as an office and surgical room.

The country doctor examined her and discovered a massive tumor in her lower abdomen. He first administered a strong purgative and washed out her intestines with an enema, then performed surgery on his kitchen table. The Judge stayed in the room and watched everything, assisting with the surgery and holding a big washtub to collect the twenty-six pound mass and a segment of the woman's large intestine. That was eight years ago and the lady was at Owen's corn shucking this evening, helping with the dinner table. The Judge truly had helped save her life—and he let everyone in the county know it time and time again.

A similar situation had occurred with an elderly gentleman in Cottonwood Bend. The man's wife appeared at the Judge's door, begging him to come quickly to her house. Judge Bozarth followed without question, sure that something was seriously wrong. The little shack smelled like an outhouse, but the Judge bravely entered to find her husband lying in diarrhea-covered sheets, looking like a corpse. Somehow the man summoned up enough energy to curse his wife for exposing his shame. Judge Bozarth ordered him, in the name of the law, to shut the hell up and ready himself for a short wagon trip. He ran back to the shed behind his house, hitched the horse to the buggy, and returned to drive the man over to Doc Emmick's place. Emmick diagnosed the condition as "bloody flux." Pinching a handful of skin on the back of the man's forearm, he noted how it stood up, not immediately snapping back to its original position—a sign of severe dehydration. The doctor brewed some herbs for a medicinal tea and ordered the man to drink it along with lots of cold water. Somehow the man survived. Once again the Judge had performed a great humanitarian deed. In the following weeks, he made it known to all in Cottonwood Bend that he was looking in on the "infirm one" to ensure there was no relapse.

Sometime later, the recovered man walked the aisle of his church and publically thanked the Judge for saving his life. Every word of the ordeal was gospel, now permanently engraved into community legend. Of course the Judge did not fail to make as much political hay as possible from it all.

Aside from his pompous nature and long-winded speechmaking, the Judge was a true fighter. No one could refute that. At Tippecanoe he had charged into a mass of howling Indians, dealing death and destruction with rifle, pistols, and saber. He had ended the depredations of several outlaws in his role as peace officer, and he was a decorated hero of the Battle of New Orleans. Wherever he traveled, he liked to recount his experiences and extol his virtues. Of course he was always the hero of these long, convoluted epics. To hear his account you would think he had slain half the British Army at New Orleans and rescued scores of American soldiers from certain death. Still, Craig admitted he would not mind having the Judge at his side in battle. Like everyone else who knew Judge Bozarth, one could only laugh and shake their head—as these women in the field were doing. No doubt he would win his upcoming election, despite numerous hints of scandal.

Craig had already heard the news. People were talking about it at Levi Matthew's grain mill. The Judge was traveling to Hardinsburg more frequently and paying calls on Adrian Dowell's widow. By all accounts Cecilia was gorgeous, pleasingly plump, rounded in all the right places, dark-haired, with fair complexion and blessed with what some people called "bedroom eyes." Some menfolk remarked that they could not blame the Judge, that throughout history men far greater than he had been lured to stray.

The miller, Levi Matthews, had overheard the rumors and weighed in with one of his characteristically vulgar opinions. "They should castrate that old bastard to keep him home and out of trouble!" This remark had drawn a round of ribald laughter and comments from his customers.

But Craig recalled how worried Judge's Bozarth's wife, Violet, had been during his forays into battle. On those occasions she almost made herself ill, taking to drink during the Indian campaign that culminated in the Battle of Tippecanoe, and again when the Judge rode off to fight the British in Ohio, the Michigan Territory and Upper Canada. As his legal secretary, assistant, and wife, Violet had stood with him through thick and thin, traveling with him on his many political campaigns, even to Frankfort to meet with Governors Scott and Shelby. It sure didn't seem fair to her.

Darkness closed over the cornfield like a dark blue cloak as the sun dipped below the horizon. Faint shouts and halloos rose from the far end of the field, announcing it was suppertime. Craig tied his team to a sapling and headed hastily for the flatbed wagons. Martin had built up a big bonfire and planted torches to light the area around the serving wagons. People lined up to get their share of some of the best foods in the county.

The women had spread a wide variety of cooked dishes on farm wagons and long tables at the field's western edge. They spooned generous helpings onto open plates. Martin and a few of the older gentlemen kept busy cutting slices of beef and serving them to the guests. Agnes' shredded pork, swimming in a savory sauce, disappeared quickly as did her hot potatoes cooked with apple cider vinegar, butter, and fiery green peppers. On one table Craig could choose from various cuts of beef, venison, pork, fried chicken, rabbit and savory meat pies; on the next table he could load up on corn, green beans, peas, and carrots; and he could sample all different kinds of sweet potatoes—fried, baked, roasted, and mashed. Fresh-baked breads, rolls, and gravies were also available.

At the next wagon he took stock of a wide assortment of liquors—peach brandy, blackberry, elderberry, and grape wine, hard apple cider, rum, and whiskey. He passed these by. Later he would return for a noggin of cold water.

Mary and Lucinde served desserts at the last table. Next to the beverage wagon this was arguably the most popular station, for there were all kinds of pies, cobblers, cakes, puddings, and other delicacies on display. Fortunately Mary had saved him a slice of her blackberry pie.

"Where have you been?" she greeted him with a smile. "You almost missed out."

"I was at the farthest end of the field when they called," Craig replied as she found room on his plate for the thin slice. Mary looked stunning in the gathering darkness, her soft features highlighted in the flickering torchlight. In his eyes she was far and away the most beautiful woman present. He hoped the finder of a red ear would not choose her to dance with, or worse, kiss her. He would punch the daylights out of anyone who tried.

His sister-in-law, Lucinde, was also a beauty; her smoldering good looks attracted the stares of a good many young men. Her hair was raven black and her skin a lovely olive color, even though she stayed indoors more often than not. Only the immediate family knew she was one-sixteenth negro, something her father, Pierre Delacroix, had divulged when Owen had gone to New Orleans to investigate the offer of a semi-arranged marriage. Delacroix was among the richest men in New Orleans, and after the death of his son, Jean, Lucinde was his only child. Owen would stand to benefit greatly from the marriage. Lucinde had wanted to leave the city, its abominable heat and humidity, rampant immorality, and glaring injustice of slavery. Fortunately, the two young people fell instantly in love, and a marriage ceremony was quietly arranged.

Lucinde had settled easily into running the household of a large plantation—without slaves. She loved the changing seasons and the wildness of Kentucky, the abandonment of old world customs and freedom from the pretenses of city life. Although Kentucky was a slave state, the institution was not glaringly prevalent, especially here in the west; at least she was not surrounded with it on a daily basis as she was in New Orleans. Owen, like his father, hired local families to work on the land, moving them into the old slave quarters and paying fair wages. Everyone liked Lucinde, even if she seemed a bit mysterious. She kept mostly to herself, but at family gatherings and social occasions such as this, she mingled well and never spoke an unkind word.

"Lucinde, you and Owen have certainly outdone yourselves," Craig congratulated her. "I think everyone in the county showed up."

"Thank you, dear brother," Lucinde replied. "We appreciate you and Mary being here. The musicians have arrived from Hardinsburg. I think you will enjoy the entertainment later this evening."

"I am sure we shall."

Soon Mary joined him by the fire. She brought him a noggin of fresh apple cider to wash down the meal. As the sky deepened to darkest indigo and the first stars of the evening began twinkling into life, the temperature dropped. Craig moved a little closer to the warmth of the flames.

"There'll be frost on the pumpkins tonight!" Martin exclaimed. "You'll have to break out extra blankets!"

"Don't remind me," Craig grumbled.

"Poor Craig never has liked cold weather," Mary commiserated.

"It has turned cold earlier than usual," Martin said. "Tonight will be clear, so the heat will go quickly. But we will have a full moon to work by." He turned to serve up another plate of beef.

"Will you come out to the fields tonight?" Craig asked Mary.

"Perhaps later," Mary offered. "First, I will help Lucinde clear the wagons. Owen wants to put on the sideboards so we can move them into the field."

"That's good thinking on his part. The six wagons we have now can't keep up with so many workers throwing corn."

"I may also want to have a word with Violet."

Craig nodded. "I heard the women talking. It is a shame the Judge is stepping out on her. Do you think she knows?"

"I believe she suspects—and in some cases that is worse than knowing."

"What will you say to her?"

"Nothing concerning the Judge, for I do not know myself. I only want her to know she has a friend and that I am here for her."

"You are far and away the finest person in the world," Craig said. "I am so fortunate to have you as my wife. You would never gossip like the women I heard tonight. They almost seemed to revel in the hearsay."

"Perhaps they do it because they realize it could one day happen to them," Mary surmised. "Maybe they are amazed that wealthy and influential folks are people like them and can suffer the same calamities. We will never know. But remember that Violet, for all her arrogance, is a human being and she is hurting terribly."

Craig had never liked Violet Bozarth. She girded herself in the trappings of the Judge's wealth and station, treating most people as if they were beneath her. If anyone deserved a bit of come-uppance it was her. But this did seem excessive. She had based her whole life on the marriage and she undoubtedly loved the Judge. Mary's words gave him some real food for thought.

———————•———————

A fat harvest moon rose over the river bottoms, illuminating the cornfield. Workers poured back into the fields, attacking the shocks with real vigor. Wagons began to fill rapidly with golden ears of corn. People talked and laughed, full of good food and anticipating the musical entertainment. The musicians climbed up on a flatbed wagon and began tuning their instruments—a banjo and four fiddles. One man had filled three jugs with different levels of water to produce different musical notes. The playful twang of a jew's harp cut through the other sounds. A set of spoons clacked in assorted rhythms.

"Found a red ear!" someone shouted.

"Who is that?"

"Why, it's Martin McDonnell!"

"Are you sure he didn't have one already hidden in his coat pocket?"

"Someone better fetch Agnes!"

"I'm right here!" she called. "I'll have that kiss, Mister McDonnell!"

Folks watched as the gallant old Indian fighter stooped to embrace and kiss his bride of forty-five years. Cheers and laughter carried across the field as workers searched for another red ear. There would be no trouble discerning color, for the moon was so bright it created the illusion of daytime. Soon Craig's wagon was filled and he drove it down the field to unload in Owen's big double corncrib. This building was constructed on a hillside with wooden slats to allow air to circulate and thus dry the corn. Craig used a shovel to scoop and pitch the corn through small doors near the crib roof. On his return trip, Mary flagged him down for a ride. She needed no help as she climbed onto the box to sit beside him.

"Lucinde has offered to watch the children. May I come along?"

"Of course. It seems strange, not having them with us."

"She has also volunteered to take them this Sunday afternoon." The way she said this was charged with meaning. She snuggled close and buried her cold hands inside his open coat.

"That sounds intriguing." He could not suppress a grin. They rode on in contented silence.

"Craig, I spoke with Violet."

"Does she know about the Judge?"

"Yes, she has known for some time. I offered to visit with her. She did not accept, but I can see she wants so desperately to open up to someone."

"Craig nodded. "You should let her make the first move."

"I believe you are right. Let's not spoil the night talking about it."

"Agreed. Guess who found the first red ear?"

"Who?"

"Your Pa."

"Really? Did he kiss Ma in front of everyone?"

"He sure did. Would you like one, Mrs. Ridgeway?"

"Very much, Mister Ridgeway."

She put her arms around him and planted a big kiss that went on for a long time. The draft horses plodded resolutely toward the cornfield as if they knew exactly where to go. Soon they arrived at a spot where folks waited with heaps of corn. Mary hopped off and helped toss ears into the wagon. When that pile was loaded, Craig drove on to the next piles. The wagon filled almost to the tops of the sideboards.

The moon was hanging high overhead when the musicians struck up a lively jig. Harvesters quit their work and streamed in through the shocks to gather round the flatbed wagon. Ed Mattingly and Bill Tindle sawed on their fiddles, swaying and dipping theatrically with the music. James Earl Flood and Dan Skaggs strutted around the wagon, plucking the strings of their fiddles, all the while making eyes at the ladies. Big Tom Wheatley had brought his slave down from Hardinsburg to play the banjo. Old Eleazar sat immobile on a tall wooden stool, gripped in a trance of pure delight as he plucked joyously on the instrument, fingers rippling lightly over the strings, producing rolling notes and drones to make it sound like a whole wagonload of instruments.

The banjo came from Africa, derived from an instrument called the *mbanza* or *banjar*, which was made by stretching animal skin over a gourd and adding a long neck with strings to produce notes. Captured African slaves, brought to the new world in bondage and not allowed to play drums, started making their *banjars* to provide entertainment at outdoor weddings and gatherings. Virginia planters happily allowed this, even paying top players to perform at some of their finest outdoor events. The music had flourished, spilling across the Appalachians and into Kentucky. Some people, mostly the Baptists, saw this queer instrument as a musical outcast, lowlier even than the fiddle, which many "righteous people" swore came straight from the devil.

Eleazar had crafted this banjo himself, using fine cherry wood for the long neck and round pot instead of a round stick and traditional African gourd. He covered the pot's open face with a treated cat-skin lifted from a marauding bobcat that Wheatley trapped near his henhouse. This skin was stretched taut and secured with small brass tacks that Wheatley had provided. For the strings Eleazar chose gut over horsehair, and these he twisted and waxed so they could be stretched in different tensions to produce the bright, sassy notes for which the banjo was known. By trial and error the old slave discovered that a separate wooden plate, attached at the back of the pot, would increase the banjo's resonance and project the sound forward to give it more volume.

The musicians increased the tempo, switching from three and four-handed reels, to square sets, and then to jigs. Tim McCoy twanged the jew's harp; Lester Hinton puffed on jugs to produce alternate bass tones; Bob and Alton Coomes thwacked sets of spoons to set up a counter-rhythm. Couples danced over the ground, trampling on scattered husks and corn stalks. They whooped and hollered and sang. Some couples disappeared over the riverbank and into the brush, not to return for a time.

Eventually, the revelers resumed their corn-shucking, but the music went on through the night. It was well past midnight when Owen called a halt. The guests and other workers had shucked almost the entire field, and the corn cribs were crammed full of ears. Craig promised to help Owen and his farm hands finish the job the next morning, but he had to stifle a yawn in mid-sentence. He half dozed on the drive home. At the cabin he stoked up the fire while Mary tucked the children into their covers; then he unhitched the horses and fed each a measure of grain. There wasn't much night left when he finally fell into bed.

———————•———————

When Agnes invited them over for Sunday dinner, Mary packed extra blankets, cloth diapers, and children's clothes—and Craig remembered her mentioning that Lucinde would take the children for the afternoon. The recollection struck him like a charge of buckshot. On the drive over and all throughout the meal he felt charged with the irresistible thrill of sexual desire. Mary had not mentioned it since the corn shucking, but Craig could see it in her eyes, feel it in her touch, the way she brushed against him as she set various dishes on the table, the way each casual contact turned into a lingering caress. He hoped the family would not notice.

Lucinde was as good as her word. When the meal was finished she volunteered, "Mother Agnes, I will help with the dishes. Mary and Craig have some business they must attend to this afternoon. I have offered to watch the children."

"Why, that's awfully sweet of you, Lucinde," Agnes replied, unsuccessfully feigning innocence. Her syrupy tone and expression revealed that she knew exactly what was happening, and Craig blushed bright red. Fortunately Martin and his sons gave no indication of knowing.

"I'll just get the horse and wagon ready," Craig said, heading for the back door. "Thanks ever so much for dinner."

Mary joined him on the stoop where he struggled to pull on his knee high moccasins. "Why, Craig Ridgeway!" she laughed merrily. "You shouldn't be embarrassed. After all, we are married, and we have done the same favor for Owen and Lucinde."

"I know, but let's not hang our laundry out for the whole world to see!"

He lifted Mary into the wagon and clucked to the big tan horse, executing a smooth turn in the circular drive and heading out onto the Hardinsburg Road.

———●———

The fire cast just enough light to reveal soft, tender mounds and dark, intriguing hollows. Two childbirths had not spoiled Mary's figure; perhaps she had gained a little weight, but Craig found this even more alluring, for she had filled out in all the right places. He gently traced her outline in the near darkness—her lovely face and soft neck, smooth shoulders, outward flaring hips and the flowing lines of her legs—enraptured by her shape, symmetry and beauty. Farm life had not damaged her creamy complexion, for she always took care to cover up when working outside. His hard, sun-browned hands looked almost black against her inner thighs.

"You are so beautiful," he sighed, almost breathless with desire. "And I am so fortunate you are my wife." He enfolded her in his arms and drew her to him, feeling her ample breasts against his chest, her thighs against his thighs, and the maddening sensation of her most intimate anatomy pressed against his. "I love you, Mary."

"I love you, Craig," she murmured, gazing deeply into his eyes. It was as if she could read his mind, his very soul.

In the next instant, they clutched at each other in a wild, almost violent urgency, consumed with desire. They came together in a slippery, spine-tingling collision that engulfed them wholly, blotting out all else except each other. Craig wanted to draw out the experience, to make it last the whole afternoon, but he was hopelessly lost in the overwhelming maelstrom of passion that followed. It was a thunderstorm roaring in his ears, coursing through every fiber of his being, sweeping him along in its turbulence. Conscious of every movement—Mary's embrace, her silken heat gripping him as he moved within her, her heavy breathing, and cries of rapture—Craig fought to hold on, but to no avail. The storm surge burst with a force that left them both breathless, clinging to each other in sheer ecstasy.

Suddenly, Mary was on top. Craig felt the delicious squeeze as her muscles contracted, and she cried out once more.

"Oh, Craig!" she exclaimed. "That was wonderful!" She kissed him softly, repeatedly on the lips. This intimate moment soon passed as the next storm crashed upon them.

It was nearly dark when Craig rose to stoke the fire. The sunsets came noticeably earlier with each passing day. He dressed by the fireplace, still light-headed in the afterglow of love, wondering what the McDonnells were thinking. Then he thought on what Mary had said. They were fully married in the eyes of the church, and the family was more than used to babies. He went out to hitch the wagon. When he returned, Mary was dressed and waiting on the dirt track beside the cookhouse.

New Orleans—October 30, 1815

Jules Signet regarded Doc Applegate's transformation with a great deal of pride and, even more, relief. Doc had responded beautifully to all the pampering. Good food, plenty of rest, and hot baths had done wonders for his appearance. The scoundrel had cleaned up much better than expected. Signet's barber had wrought a minor miracle, washing and clipping off most of his discolored, dead hair, trimming and styling it into short silver-white curls and leaving long, yet closely-cropped sideburns in the current fashion. Steaming hot towels and hot soapy water softened Doc's raspy stubble for the straight razor. The barber cleaned this up with several crisp strokes. He did not stop with the beard, shaving off his wispy, tobacco-stained moustaches.

Signet's slaves worked with Doc Applegate daily, seeing that he bathed and shaved, applying cold oatmeal and coffee poultices to his face and gently pressing tea leaves under his eyes to draw out the swelling. They served his breakfast out on the gallery where he could dine in fresh air and read the *Louisiana Gazette* in the autumn sunlight. Most importantly they kept the liquor cabinets locked, making sure his beverages remained limited to fruit juices, coffee, tea, milk and water. Doc looked positively rakish in his tailored navy linen suit and gold silk cravat which contrasted beautifully against a snowy white shirt. His new boots gleamed with fresh polish. He enjoyed using, and showing off, the new ebony cane topped with an ivory head the size of a large duck egg. Even on close inspection one would think him wealthy, for Doc knew how to put on airs.

He certainly fit in with the clientele at *Café des Améliorations*. In fact, he was almost a celebrity. More than one patron approached him with some outpouring of gratitude, or merely to shake his hand. One gentleman pressed a ten dollar American gold piece into his hand, apologizing for not paying him for previous medical treatments. Doc took all in stride, thoroughly enjoying the attention.

The coffeehouse, located at the corner of Rampart and Toulouse, catered to wealthy, older Creoles who still struggled with the American purchase of Louisiana. French was about the only language spoken in this establishment. In the mid-afternoon few customers were present, so it was easy to find a private table. Signet ordered a *café au lait*; Doc ordered his coffee black with brown sugar and a dash of nutmeg. The waiter soon brought the hot beverages with a plate of assorted pastries.

"Are you enjoying yourself, Doctor?" Signet asked.

"I am indeed. It is nice to be back in society."

"Is the coffee to your liking?"

"It is."

"Tell me—are we ready to proceed with our plan? You are physically and mentally ready?"

"I am."

Signet glanced around to make sure no one was listening. He lowered his voice. "And will you be able to sway Judge Harkness?"

"There are no absolute guarantees, but I am confident."

"How is our man progressing?"

"He has surprised the hell out of me. He sends for the girl several times a week. What is most important, he wholly trusts my judgment in matters of the flesh."

"And your man, Farron Weeks, has he approved of your free 'scientific' examination of his slaves? He has no objections to the judge observing this?"

"You are correct. In fact, he wishes me to certify the blood mixture of his stock and attest in writing each slave's ancestry."

Signet could not help but admire the Doc's plan. A charade of this sort would almost certainly smooth the upcoming path. "When will the experiment take place?"

"Tomorrow morning."

"Then you must allow me to provide my carriage and driver. We want to impress the judge, do we not?"

"You're getting jumpy," Doc observed. "You shouldn't be concerned. I really think we have this game in the bag."

The banker smiled, but his trepidation remained. The stakes were extremely high. If tomorrow's events went well, he could begin setting the plan into motion. Alain Morel had submitted the brief to him for final consideration. Signet was impressed by the line of reasoning and sequence in which the legal arguments would unfold. Signet had devised the original plan; Morel had refined it, supporting everything with evidence, except for a critical piece of documentation they lacked. But Doctor Thomas Applegate, as he had from the beginning, held the key to a successful outcome.

———————◆———————

After one of the coldest winters on record, New Orleans was again experiencing an unusually cool autumn. Outside the city limits the breeze was refreshing. Signet's liveried slave drove the carriage smartly up Levee Road, past sprawling plantations and into the countryside. Most of the sugarcane was already cut, but brick smokestacks at the nearby mills spouted brown, sweet-smelling smoke, a sign that the outlying plantations were still harvesting. A line of wagons waited at the nearest mill. Doc knew that harvested cane must be rapidly processed, for once cut it began losing its sugar content. He pointed this out to his fellow carriage rider.

After enjoying a night of carnal delights, Judge Harkness was in a chipper mood. He had cleared his calendar and was looking forward to attending Doc's examination. He hoped the outing would prove instructive. The number of lawsuits involving persons of color was growing with each passing year. Some of these cases possessed real merit, especially the ones arguing for child maintenance and inheritances. In some instances these "coloreds" had been legally manumitted, but in most cases they had not. And the Louisiana Digest of 1808 had drawn rather strict guidelines concerning slaves and "persons of color."

"Persons of color" could mean almost anything, for human flesh in New Orleans and the surrounding parishes ran from darkest purple-black to palest white, and every shade in between. There were actual terms used to designate people of mixed-race, especially where ancestry could be proven. Words such as *mulatto, quadroon, and octoroon* were the most commonly used, borrowed either from Spanish, Portuguese or French colonists, the ones who had brought slavery to the new world. A *griffe* was usually a slave with three-fourths negro blood. The term *mulatto* indicated a person who had one white and one black parent. Harkness shuddered to think that the sire would ever be a negro. Beyond that point classification grew increasingly murky, unless there was clear documentation, usually found in bills of sale. The word *quadroon* was borrowed from the Spanish *cuarterón* which had its roots in the Latin *quartus*, meaning "fourth." A quadroon was the product of one black and three white grandparents. The lines blurred even further when one considered the *octoroon*. This word, rooted in the Latin *octo*, meaning "eight," referred to a person with one-eighth negro origin, a descendent of one black and seven white great grand-parents. *Terceron* and *mustee* were terms synonymous with octoroon. The labels *mustefino* and *quintroon* went a generation farther, designating a person of one-sixteenth negro blood, while some lawyers even bandied the word *hexadecaroon* to describe the next rung on the ancestral chart.

How far could this concept be taken without records to serve as some form of provenance? Skin color was not always a reliable method of assessment. True, there were certain physical features that characterized the different races, but with all the mixed ancestry in New Orleans, it was becoming almost impossible to classify a person.

This mixed-race breeding could be traced to earliest times. In those days Louisiana was dominated by explorers and male colonists. Conditions in the New World were harsh, making it difficult to persuade women to leave France. Due to a shortage of white females, colonists often took negro slave women as consorts. The French *Code Noir*, or "Black Code" attempted to prevent what authorities saw as wrongs. First, it expressly forbade marriage between the races and precluded the clergy from sanctioning such unions. The French government imposed severe fines upon white men for having sexual relations with black females. Additionally, if any issue resulted from the intercourse, the slave and the children would be removed from the man's ownership. Despite these measures, mingling of the races continued. A white man might take a slave girl as young as twelve as his concubine and, quite naturally, children were born from these unions. In some cases the mistress was later emancipated, along with her children, and sometimes they took the surnames of the white man.

After his experiences with Kayla, Harkness could now sympathize with a plantation owner taking physical comfort from a beautiful black girl. He had almost convinced himself that it was the natural order of the universe, the strong having dominion over the lesser creatures. White blood certainly raised the price of female slaves, qualifying the fairest complexioned ones to enter into long-term relationships with wealthy men who would take responsibility for their welfare.

A strange social system called *plaçage* had evolved during the colonial years, despite the *Code Noir*. A sizeable class known as "free people of color" soon proliferated in New Orleans. From this class wealthy white men would often choose mistresses. Many of the fairest, light-skinned girls were showcased at a now-famous event called the Quadroon Ball. These dances were elegant affairs, designed to appeal to wealthy white men. The girl attending these balls hoped to become a white man's mistress, whether he was married or not. A quadroon's mother usually negotiated formal terms with the admirer, demanding generous compensation for having the girl as his mistress. Usually this included a financial payment to the mother, housing arrangements, financial security for the daughter, and a promise to recognize any children the union might produce. A man would build, purchase, or rent a house for his mistress and he often took part in and arranged for the upbringing and education of their children. Some white men even succeeded in making their mixed-race children primary heirs over other white descendants or relatives, something that increasingly disturbed Judge Harkness.

The "free people of color" were growing in number and at an alarming rate. After the revolt in Saint-Domingue, in the late 1700's and early 1800's, a tide of nine-thousand refugees washed ashore in New Orleans, adding a new wave of French-speaking coloreds to the city. Open unions were rampant, now that the Americans ruled. Plantation owners continued to breed with their slaves, producing children of mixed race.

At one time Judge Harkness believed that the admixture of white blood could only improve the race. But in recent years he had begun to consider the flip side of the coin. Could not the mongrelization of the white race result in its downfall? He had discussed this at great length with his friend, Doc Applegate. Doc sympathized with his views, but could not provide a solution. The judge pressed him for an answer.

"What do you think about this surge in the colored population?"

"I think it will ultimately lead to societal disintegration. You do not see this happening in the advanced European countries." Doc did not know if this was true, but it sounded plausible. "And look at the Chinese. When they import black males, they demand up front that their knackers be clipped. Then there is no chance of slaves breeding with Chinese females."

Harkness had read an article on the Indian Ocean trade. The castrated slaves were dubbed "China Birds." Castrated in the barracoons on the east African coast, only one quarter of them survived the ordeal. It was a harsh policy, but one must hand it to the Chinese—they allowed no mixed-race breeding.

"Racial features here have become so indistinct, it becomes difficult to make informed judgments in court cases."

"I can imagine," Doc sympathized. "Can you grasp the future implications this will have for marriages?"

"What do you mean?"

"Well, imagine a young white man engaged to marry a white girl. He comes from a fine family—strong European heritage, wealth and position, all the good attributes in life. Do you have that image?"

"I do. Please proceed."

"He marries the white girl who is fair of skin, with blue or green eyes, possibly with fair hair. She too comes from a family of equally high standing."

"Very well. Let us hope it is a love match."

"Why not? They marry and produce offspring. A few years into the marriage the couple discovers that the wife's mother was a quadroon, the product of a mulatta and a white slave master. What is her legal position?"

"We have the 1810 territorial court case of *Adéle vs. Beauregard* as a partial guideline. But new cases are sure to challenge. Was quadroon a free woman?"

"Perhaps, perhaps not. But where did *she* come from? Let's say for the sake of argument the quadroon's mother was a documented mulatta slave—and no manumission papers were ever granted."

"Hmm," Harkness mused as he studied the supposition. "I would have to know all the circumstances related to your case, but I must commend you, Doctor, this is a good exercise of the mind. I can share that I once ruled in favor of a young woman in similar circumstances. But she possessed manumission papers in addition to a signed, notarized will. I awarded her one tenth of her father's property."

"I wonder…" Doc trailed off in midsentence.

"What do you wonder?"

"What if the case was reversed? What if the husband carried negro blood in his veins? What if *he* were one-fourth negro, but a paler version than most quadroons? What would be his legal position in the event of no manumission papers? Is he free or slave?"

Judge Harkness' mouth snapped shut and a menacing scowl darkened his countenance. His bushy eyebrows narrowed into a single furry row. He was disgusted. Doc took this as an encouraging sign to press home the image.

"Worse, what damage could this do to the wife? What about their children? Can you possibly imagine the shame this would bring upon her family?"

"I prefer not to consider that scenario as even a remote possibility."

"But surely, you are aware that these people often successfully pass themselves off as white? What is the French term for this—*passe blanc*? As the free, colored population increases and becomes more intertwined with our white population, more than one white woman will be deceived into a so-called legitimate marriage." He paused for effect, for it was his intention to paint as ugly a scene as possible. "And surely as the sun rises, that mongrel's seed will strike and take hold. The child she bears could be a black throwback, so everyone would know her shame. I have seen it happen all too often in the colored world, but now I am talking of her world—her universe. How would that world treat her and her child then?"

"You trouble me, Doctor."

"Then, let us forget it. This conjecturing has my mind racing beyond limits of extreme possibilities." He dropped the subject for the time being, for he had engraved the images firmly in the judge's mind.

Around mid-morning, they arrived at Farron Weeks' plantation. Their driver turned up a red dirt road leading to a cluster of buildings. This farm lacked the cultivated grandeur of the great river estates. While the barns appeared in good condition, the main house looked in need of a coat of whitewash. There were no flower gardens, no manicured lawns, just a few live oaks, a scraggly orange grove, and some assorted sheds and slave cabins scattered on the property. Despite the roughness, it was evident that this was a working plantation. In the distance, slaves hacked away on a great block of sugarcane, cutting the stalks near ground level, knocking off their leaves and tops, and loading them into waiting wagons. Oxcart drivers continuously moved the cane out of the fields to the nearest sugar mill.

Farron Weeks trotted up on a fat, dun-colored horse. He swung easily out of the saddle and handed the reins to a waiting groom that appeared from almost nowhere.

"Doctor Applegate, Judge Harkness, it is good to see you both. Won't you join me for some refreshment on the front veranda?"

"Thank, you," Harkness replied. He noticed that Weeks carried a machete in his waistband, two double-barreled pistols and a short, double-barreled fowling piece. The German Coast Slave Rebellion was just four years in the past and most planters had since taken to carrying arms.

While they settled into cane chairs, Weeks signaled for his slave woman to bring refreshments.

"How goes the harvest?" Doc inquired.

"We will finish cutting in a few days."

"How are prices this year?"

"Not as high as we expected," Weeks sighed. "Our British friends are selling West Indies sugar at unbelievably low prices to the eastern seaboard merchants. This has driven the price of American sugar downward."

"That's one argument for a protective tariff," Judge Harkness observed.

Doc winced, for the tariff was a thorny issue with southern planters, as it was all over the United States. Various people in different sections of the country had their reasons for wanting or opposing it. Weeks seemed to take it all in stride, not coming down on either side.

"Even in Louisiana folks have mixed feelings about the tariff. No one wants American industry to suffer, but neither should southern states be forced to buy goods only from northern manufacturers. Additionally, a tariff would ruin newly-revived business arrangements with Great Britain. Hopefully our legislators can arrange something that will benefit everyone."

Doc and Judge Harkness were acutely aware of the situation. Shortly after the Treaty of Ghent, British merchants began flooding the recovering American markets with inexpensive goods, hoping to crush competition from new, fledgling industries. Manufacturers in northern and western states clamored for protection to save these industries. A high tariff was needed, but it would have negative consequences for other groups in the republic. When Britain retaliated with high tariffs of its own, it would force Southerners into purchasing American manufactured goods at higher prices instead of buying cheaper goods on the overseas market. A tariff could hurt the South in other ways, by damaging recently-renewed export ties with Britain, and ruining the burgeoning cotton market rapidly spreading across the South. Southerners enjoyed strong support from New Englander shippers who hoped to restore trade relations with European markets.

But almost everyone admitted that something must be done to give American industry a fair chance. It was one of the many problems facing the new nation. The tariff issue would certainly dominate politics in the upcoming Election of 1816.

The slave appeared, carrying a large serving tray laden with coffee, fresh-baked bread, and fruit. She poured the steaming brew into porcelain mugs and sliced the bread. It was a welcome delight, sure to sustain the visitors until dinnertime. A cool breeze blew in from the river, rustling through the live oak leaves and fanning the men on the shaded veranda.

Weeks noticed Doc's black medical bag. "Do you have everything you need for your examination, Doctor?"

"I do. Do you have the bills of sale, ink, quill, and paper?"

"Of course." The plantation owner turned to his slave. "Delphine, go and fetch those papers from my desk."

Doc informed him, "I have asked the Judge to countersign my statements and affix his seal to the documents. He has agreed. Where do you wish me to examine the slaves?"

"Why not here, on the veranda?"

"Very well."

"The first ones will arrive momentarily. I asked them to report here before dinner. The females will be first."

Doc noticed that Judge Harkness stirred restlessly in anticipation. No doubt the old goat hoped to catch a few glimpses of nakedness. He would not be disappointed.

Presently the slaves appeared from the back yard. They had been working in the cane fields and looked tired and soaked through with sweat. Apparently they knew what to expect, for apprehension showed in their faces.

"Step lively, girls," Weeks commanded. "Sooner Doc looks you over, sooner you can head to the kitchen." Delphine returned with a thick sheaf of papers. Weeks began rifling through them and found what he was looking for. "Kayla, step up here so Doc can get a good look at you."

The slave girl gave no indication that she knew Judge Harkness, or that she visited his bed two or three times each week; she merely stepped forward with firm resolution, not glancing once in his direction. She waited patiently while the doctor put on his spectacles and laid out his instruments.

"Kayla, come over here." Doc beckoned. He perused her papers and nodded in agreement. "This bill of sale is correct. It establishes that the girl is a quadroon. As you can see, her skin color is darker than that of a white person, but she is lighter than most mulattos. This is the general yardstick most plantation owners use when they purchase their slaves. In most cases they buy what they see. But there are other indicators that may be valuable for use in future court cases or in other instances we discussed earlier.

"Let's start with the top of her head. Note the black hair color and its predisposition to kink. That frizzled texture is one of the first signs of negro blood. Now consider the cranium. He unrolled a tape measure and wrapped it around her head, making a big show of examining her skull and tapping on it with his index finger. "Hmm, the head may seem bigger than a white person's; that is because the bone is thicker."

Judge Harkness watched as Doc used a pair of calipers to measure three different sections of Kayla's nose. "I have often wondered how people can accurately determine racial classification, especially when there are no papers."

Doc grunted as he traced the girl's jawbone with his fingers, examined her lips, and checked her teeth. "It is a relatively new science. There are books on the subject. Carl Linnaeus, a Swedish physician, zoologist and botanist, has labeled five varieties of the human species in his book *Systema Naturae*. The French naturalist, Georges Cuvier, believes there are three distinct races in the world and he assigns ranks based on their skulls and the quality of their civilizations. The German professor Christoph Meiners describes two race divisions, calling them—and I quote—the 'beautiful white race' and the 'ugly black race.' Other researchers have written treatises on the subject. You will find that, in addition to studying physiognomy, scientists also delve into the social and moral characters of the races."

"What do they say about the black race?" Harkness asked.

"None of it is kind. Their labels include the words 'inferior, immoral, animal-like, crafty, sly, and careless.'" All of the researchers point to a 'sad lack of virtue' and 'terrible vices.' Cuvier approximates them to the monkey tribe and explains that is why they have always remained in the most complete state of barbarism."

Harkness said nothing, but listened as Doc continued his discourse.

"Meiners has studied the sex habits of the races and he concludes that African negroids have unduly strong and perverted sex drives."

"How about us?"

"He claims that the White Europeans have it just about right."

"And this is science?"

"It is still in the pioneer stages." Doc looked over at Weeks. "Can you call for Delphine?"

Weeks nodded, "I can." He did not have to call; the slave woman was waiting at the door. She reluctantly stepped out onto the veranda.

"Have her stand over here beside Kayla. We are going to do a comparison. Would you agree she is one-hundred percent negro?"

"Her papers say she is," Weeks nodded.

Doc knew that physical differences existed in negro females as they did in white females. Some were beautiful and otherwise well-favored; others were not. This was also the case with black and white males. Judge Harkness was proof of that, for he most certainly was absent when the good looks were handed out. The same could be said for Delphine. The slave was a large, corpulent woman, not the prettiest female example of her race. She was coal black, the perfect specimen for a contrast.

"How old are you, Delphine?" he asked.

"I reckon about forty."

Doc adjusted the caliper to measure the bridge of her nose and then transferred the instrument back to Kayla's nose. There was a noticeable gap between the nose and one tip of the caliper. "Uh-huh. Can you see the difference, Judge?"

Harkness was noncommittal. He could see, but he remained silent.

Doc continued. "Delphine's lips are tumid, her teeth bigger, and her jawbone much more pronounced. Meiners attributes these characteristics to the carnivorous negroid that rose up in the darkest jungles of Africa. And note the skull." He looped the cloth tape around her head. Delphine was a large individual and her skull measurement naturally reflected this difference—almost four inches more in circumference. The judge remained stone-faced. Doc could not tell if he was convinced or not.

"Delphine, show us those big udders. Kayla you do the same."

Both women glanced uncomfortably at each other making no

move to disrobe.

Farron Weeks stepped forward and spoke in a low but menacing tone. "Does the doctor have to ask again?"

Both women obeyed instantly. Judge Harkness' eyes bulged and took on a glassy stare. Doc pointed out the differences. Again, he had seen all sizes on white women patients, but he was quick to point out certain features.

"Just observe the size of those mammaries! Linnaeus has studied nursing negro women and has even measured their milk output. To phrase it in his exact words, their 'mammary glands give milk abundantly.' Did you ever wonder why, when a white woman's milk dries up, doctors always send for a Negress who has recently had a baby? They know she gives enough milk to feed a whole litter of suckers. This common knowledge that we all possess has now been documented in scientific observation."

He turned to Kayla. "Now this creature is blessed with lovely, pear-shaped little breasts. They are small, but firm. Remember, we have established that she has three quarters white blood in her."

If the judge had any objectivity, it was lost in this display of human nakedness. His eyes devoured Kayla's young body and shifted only occasionally to Delphine's pendulous mounds of flesh. Doc allowed them to cover themselves and he bade them to sit down in the empty chairs.

"Kayla, kindly put your foot up on this table." Cautiously she obeyed. "Observe this young woman's ankle and heel bone." The slender foot was dirty from the fields, but this did not deter Doc, for he was now in full swing. "One thing that always gives a *passe blanc* away is the heel bone. It is usually much longer in black folks. And the muscles in the backs of their legs are similar to those found in the black bullfrogs of the 'Dark Continent.' That is why blacks can jump so high and so far. These characteristics are not so pronounced in this youngster because they have been almost bred out of her. I'll prove it to you. Let's check out her toes."

Doc began to twist on them, bending them at odd angles and with such force that Kayla whimpered in obvious pain. "There, did you see that? I assure you her pain was genuine. Now watch what happens with this one." He took hold of Delphine's massive foot and began the same experiment. It did have a pronounced heel bone, and fortunately, for the sake of his next argument, her toes were abnormally long. He would not mention that Harkness' toes were as long as any he had seen. Drawing upon his medical knowledge and considerable acting skills, he manipulated the toes, making it appear he was applying tremendous pressure. Delphine looked amused, but showed no pain. Doc renewed his efforts, but could produce no outcry.

"What are you trying to prove?" Judge Harkness asked.

"Some of the top European physicians and zoologists have confirmed that negroids have stronger and more freely movable toes than any other race. The toes are generally prehensile; they are skilled at grasping objects by wrapping around them. Scientists posit that negroids are more closely related to the apes, because when apes climb in trees, they hold onto branches with their toes. You noticed that when I moved Delphine's toes she did not feel pain? Meiners states that the negroid feels less pain than any other race because they have such thick nerves."

Harkness could not tell where Doc Applegate was going with this discourse, but he certainly enjoyed the examinations, especially when invited to classify some of the slaves. On one occasion he classified one female as a *griffe* when her papers stated she was a full black. Doc made a few measurements and congratulated him on his discovery, although it really made no difference. Later, Doc ordered more women to disrobe, calling attention to various textures and patterns of their body hair. The judge was an enthusiastic student in this instruction.

His enjoyment diminished when the males arrived. When Doc ordered the first slave to drop his pants, Harkness almost left the veranda, but what he saw rooted him in his tracks. The first slave was as black as tar, just over five feet tall and by far the smallest male of the lot, but he was abnormally hung all out of proportion to his size. Even Doc, who had seen all, was impressed. He noted the judge's expression, one of fascination and sheer horror. "Can you believe it?" he asked. "And this is the littlest negroid in the bunch!" The selection was no accident; Weeks had informed him beforehand of the anomaly and now it created the desired impression.

Harkness mopped at his face with his handkerchief, more to hide his eyes than any other reason. He was obviously rattled. "Is it truly that way with them all?"

"I am afraid so." Doc knew this was not the case; black males differed in size just like the whites.

"I really do not wish to see more of this."

"The rest of this examination should go quickly. Most of these slaves are full blacks, maybe a *griffe* and few mulattos among them. You should know that all other racial characteristics observed in the females apply equally to males. We are conducting one more demonstration that will interest you. Mr. Weeks, could you assemble your male slaves into two rows?"

"You heard the gentleman!" Weeks snapped. "Form a double line!" The slaves seemed to understand this and formed themselves into two rows stretching about half the veranda's length.

"Spread out!" Doc added. "Get yourselves about this far apart." He held both arms outstretched and they obeyed. "Now I want you to stand in place and jump as high as you can. Ready? Jump!"

The slaves hopped undecidedly.

"Higher! As high as you possibly can! And keep in place!"

Weeks slapped his riding crop on the veranda railing. "Do it! Jump! Get those feet up!" He began walking up and down the lines, cracking his whip near the bare feet of the less energetic.

The slaves began jumping in earnest; some attained amazing heights. Doc leaned close to Judge Harkness and said, "Watch the muscles at the backs of their legs." Then he shouted to the slaves, "Turn and face that barn. Higher! Up! Up!"

The slaves obeyed and Harkness watched the display of agility with interest. He had never in his life seen anything like this. Most of the trousers were three-quarter length or less, so he was afforded full view of their calf muscles. The slaves were lean and most were in good physical condition.

"That's enough!" shouted Doc. "Now line up here while we get these papers sorted. And kindly move downwind. You've worked up a powerful sweat."

Harkness busied himself with bills of sale while Doc finished the examination. Most documents consisted of plain, beige-colored paper with handwriting executed in elegant cursive. These bore signatures of New Orleans or surrounding parish court officials, depending upon where the slaves were purchased. Very few were stamped with seals. Some were written in Spanish, dating before the United States took possession of the Louisiana Territory. There was one French document dated 1803; most were dated between 1803 and 1812. Doc wrote a few lines on some papers, but it was mostly for show, as this whole exercise had been. He hurried through the last of it, for he had more than achieved his purpose. Farron Weeks was grateful for Doc's scientific attestations, and for the judge's seal on his documents. Both would add extra provenance in a sale or auction.

———————•———————

On the drive back to New Orleans Judge Harkness remained mostly silent, absorbed deeply in thought. Much had transpired that day—Doc had overwhelmed him with scientific information and educational demonstrations. The naked bodies would plague his sleep until Weeks brought the young slave girl to his house. Before leaving the plantation, the judge had paid Weeks handsomely for another month of visits.

When they reached the city gates, Doc felt emboldened enough to speak. "I hope today's experience was an educational one."

"Oh! There is no doubt about that."

"I made every effort to apply the latest science to the examination. I believe you were able to make some informed classifications yourself."

"Possibly. I intend to order those books and pamphlets you mentioned."

"I will gladly lend you what books I have."

"It has always been obvious to me that the races possess different physical and, perhaps, social characteristics. And I have long believed that when the races mingle, it creates an imbalance in nature. The unintended mélange of humanity can only result in an increasingly messy tangle for our courts. I also believe it could destroy our whole society as it did in Ancient Rome."

"You are right to speak of an imbalance in nature. All modern scientists, physicians, and zoologists agree upon one universal principle—the races should remain separate. I believe the Louisiana Digest of 1808 attempts to redress this imbalance. But it will be up to our courts to interpret the laws. A few court decisions could reverse the damage already done."

Chapter Three

Breckinridge County, Kentucky—November 4, 1815

Craig hated stripping tobacco. For him, the work was more monotonous than any on the farm, even worse than pulling young tobacco plants from the plant bed. At least then he was outdoors in fresh air and sunshine. The dark confines of the stripping room swirled with pungent tobacco dust that burned his nose and throat. Although he enjoyed the conversation and proximity of family and friends, he preferred climbing up into the barns, handing down sticks of tobacco, sliding plants off the sticks and hauling stripped stalks away on flatbed wagons to scatter in the fields. Stripping seasons came and went without much notice, depending entirely on humidity, so there were some days he could not escape. To combat the dust's effects, Mary made him a long linen handkerchief which he tied around his face. This earned several jibes from Martin's field hands and brothers-in-law who likened him to a highwayman, but it provided some protection as he stripped the pliable leaves from the stalks.

Agnes, Craig's mother-in-law, came to his rescue. "Don't listen to them, Craig. If it helps you feel better, you just go ahead and wear it." She talked as she deftly stripped the reddish brown leaves, tying them into tight, neat hands.

"Thanks, Mother Agnes."

"I am sorry we couldn't have you over for your birthday dinner."

"Jesse Greathouse held a corn shucking at his farm that night."

"Yes, but there is nothing going on tonight. When I left Welcome Hall, Mary and Lucinde were cutting up chickens for frying. They'll be soaking the pieces in cold salt water, so we have some time yet. I have baked a pumpkin pie."

"I can't resist that!" Craig laughed. He knew that whatever meal Agnes chose to cook would be a good one. There would be all kinds of bounty from the farm, and more than likely a glass of warm peach brandy afterwards in the parlor where Martin was sure to have a fire roaring. In the McDonnell household food and drink did not last long.

"Just think—you are twenty-six years old! Why you were just a babe-in-the- woods when you first arrived. I can scarcely believe how much you have changed."

Craig nodded thoughtfully. It had taken time to learn the basics of farming and to gain acceptance from the folks in Cottonwood Bend. His association with the Widder Fuqua, the old outlaw woman who previously owned his farm, had not made that acceptance any easier. Mary and her family had wrought the biggest change. Martin had transformed him into a farmer; the family had accepted him as one of their own; Mary had made him into a man.

"Twenty-six?" Martin chuckled. "He's still just a pup."

"Pa, when can we quit?" Stephen asked.

"Soon enough," Martin replied. "We need to press that hogshead once more."

"Well, I am going to the house," Agnes announced. "Mary and Lucinde will need help with supper. Don't work much longer." She left the barn with a field hand's wife. Each woman took a lamp to light their path.

Everyone lapsed into silence. The only sound was the snip-snipping of leaves as they were stripped from the stalks. Craig tried his best to do his share, even though he despised doing it. Every now and then he encountered some stubborn tips—the top tobacco leaves. When these tips clung tightly, it threw him off his rhythm.

In no time the piles of bare stalks grew into small mountains. Fortunately, Martin asked him to help Stephen load them onto the flatbed wagon parked just outside the door. It was pitch black, for the sky was overhung with a thick blanket of heavy gray clouds, as it had been since yesterday. Craig lowered his handkerchief and guzzled clean moist air like it was a cold, clear drink of spring water.

While he and Stephen cleared the stripping room of stalks, Martin, Owen, and a field hand packed hands of tobacco into two hogsheads, giant barrels that could weigh up to eleven hundred pounds when fully packed. Long ago Martin had constructed a heavy tobacco press from a flat, circular millstone suspended horizontally from a thick oak beam. This was partially counterbalanced by a heavy square stone, hewn from the limestone cliffs and grooved with channels to help prevent the ropes from slipping. The beam could be maneuvered so that the millstone, just slightly smaller than hogshead's diameter, could be positioned directly over the newly-loaded tobacco leaves. By carefully lowering and fractionally maneuvering the stone so that it just cleared the iron rim, it could be sunk into the hogshead. The men operating the press then eased off the beam, allowing the disc's full weight to compact the leaves. While the stone did its job, workers could begin filling another hogshead. It saved money when the pressing was done right. For his own tobacco Craig used a thick circular wooden board and piled on pumpkin-sized rocks. Most farmers in the county employed this method. It was much more difficult and time-consuming than operating a mechanical press, but it got the job done.

Finally, Martin called a halt. He and his sons took the lard lamps and candles with them; workers went their separate ways, while Craig walked back to his farm with the slaves.

These old folks did not burn with the fire for freedom that Romulus and his wife did; perhaps this was because they were freer than they had ever been. While they were free to go anywhere, there was simply no place for them to go. Instead, they had become Craig's and Mary's responsibility. Diogenes and Maggie still enjoyed relatively good health, but the three older women were declining. They had always been steady and dependable tobacco strippers. Craig paid them all fair wages, gave them a hog at butchering time, helped them tend their gardens, and shared extra milk or eggs when needed. Penelope was growing visibly more fragile. Craig held her arm and steered her over the rough ground, aiding her on the climb uphill.

At the cabin he paid them their wages, and as they left for their cabins, he banked the fire in the hearth. Then he milked the cows, toting the wooden buckets to the springhouse. It was a long walk back down the hill and across the bottomland to Welcome Hall. A cold drizzle began to fall as he vaulted the wooden fence separating the McDonnell's lawn from pastureland. Instead of skirting the orchard, he wound his way through the trees and grape arbors, taking a more direct path. He could smell food cooking on the damp breeze. Smoke curled from the chimneys and warm candlelight streamed from the windows of the red-brick Federal-style house.

On the stoop, Craig kicked off his boots before washing his hands and face in the wash basin. The women finished setting the big maple wood table and everyone joined hands for the blessing. It was a glorious spread. Agnes had brought out her fine dishes and beeswax candles. The chicken, dredged in egg, flour, salt, pepper, and herbs, was fried golden brown and heaped onto two platters. Mary had quarter sliced potatoes in their skins, rubbed them in bacon grease, coarse salt and pepper, and baked them in the brick oven in the cookhouse. She and Lucinde had prepared dishes of corn, green beans, and carrots along with other delights like white gravy, onion soup, breads and desserts. They also took turns with the youngsters, feeding them and tending to their needs.

"Well, Craig," Martin said. "This is your fifth birthday with us."

"I can scarcely believe it." Craig replied. "I would not be where I am today if it were not for you all. I appreciate everything you have done for me."

"We are happy for you and Mary. You have been good for each other. And you have both done a wonderful job with your farms."

Craig now owned three farms—his home place Widder's Landing, the Jennings place across the Hardinsburg Road where his slaves resided, and most recently, the Smithhart farm, six hundred acres consisting of mostly virgin timber, some rolling pastureland and about eighty acres of arable land. This farm lay beyond the Jennings place and adjoined that farm. The small house, stone silo, and mid-sized barn formed the basis of a sound investment. He had yet to harvest the timber from this land.

"I am the lucky one," he said. "Mary is too good for me."

Mary squeezed his hand and smiled warmly at him.

"We sure miss Romulus and Vergina. They were great field hands. It shows even more glaringly now they are gone."

"I wonder where they are tonight," Stephen mused.

"If they haven't run into trouble they could be halfway to Canada by now," Craig hazarded.

"What will you do for workers?" Martin asked. "Aren't you planning to log the Smithhart farm this spring?"

"Yes. I imagine Levi Matthews will have to hire an extra man or two for his logging crew."

"It will take four men to do Romulus' work," Owen observed.

"How *is* Levi doing?" Martin asked. "I have not seen him around."

"He's as bad-tempered as ever," Craig said. "The grain mill and the lumber business take almost all of his time."

"Not all of his time," Mary pointed out laughingly. "Elizabeth is with child again."

This was news, judging from everyone's expressions. Levi was one of Cottonwood Bend's wealthiest citizens. A Mennonite outcast from the Indiana Territory, Levi had crossed the Ohio River and put his considerable carpentry skills to good use. During the day, he had worked in the sawmill at Spigot Run; at night he crafted expensive furniture for some of the finest homes in the settlement. Then, he purchased the sawmill and, farther upstream, the grain mill. Craig had met him when they were both on their way up the financial ladder. Despite Levi's foul mouth and nasty temper, Craig had made friends with the little carpenter. Levi had engineered and supervised the building of Craig's cabin, cookhouse, smokehouse, and large barn that housed whiskey barrels, tobacco, hay and livestock. He had also built a smaller tobacco barn and other sheds and outbuildings, most recently a heated stone still house.

Talking was free and easy at the supper table. Craig enjoyed being part of such a nice family. After dessert, everyone adjourned to the parlor to enjoy brandy in front of a crackling fire. Agnes served this in balloon glasses while Martin poured himself something a bit more medicinal, a tumbler of heated whiskey. Craig usually gave him a barrel at Christmas and this lasted him throughout most of the year. The conversation turned back to farming.

"How about hired hands?" Martin pressed. "You will need at least one more, unless you decide to pull in your reins next summer. It won't hurt to farm a little less and concentrate on improvements. There have been times where I allowed poorer land go to pasture, to let it recover."

Craig nodded thoughtfully. "I may do that. I could tell a difference in my hill corn this year. The plants and ears were smaller. But Mary and I plan to make more whiskey. Even Rosenbotham is offering better prices for it."

"If he is offering more, then you know the riverboat men are getting good prices in New Orleans," Owen commented. He rarely spoke, but when he did, his words carried weight.

Hiram Rosenbotham, the Jewish storeowner, was known throughout Breckinridge County for his close business dealings. He had hailed from New York City more than two decades ago when Cottonwood Bend was nothing more than a collection of cabins. He had purchased a sizeable tract of land, bought a license for a ferry, and situated a crude log trading post at the midpoint of River Street, enabling him to command most business coming in from the river and from both ends of town. The trading post soon became a major store, drawing customers from miles around, even from across the river in Indiana Territory. Because of it, Cottonwood Bend had grown into a thriving little town. Today, the big brick store was the undeniable centerpiece of Cottonwood Bend. Like most stores, it served as the lifeblood of the settlement, functioning as a post office, a polling place, and as a sort of bank where one could obtain credit. You could catch up on more gossip there than you could ever hope for.

"I understand your sentiments for wanting to grow more corn,"

Martin sympathized. "It is a tough decision not to plant more, with prices as high as they are. Just remember that corn exhausts soil faster than some crops. Sometimes the only alternative is to let your acres rest for a time. Even in medieval times Europeans argued for letting land lie fallow for one year and serve as pasture for another year, before trying to grow crops again. Today, the more enlightened minds argue for various patterns of crop rotation. You might be better off buying ground corn meal from your good friend Levi."

Craig knew he would have to give that advice some serious thought. It might indeed be a good time to cut back on his corn acreage. If he grew just enough for livestock feed and whiskey-making, he could spend more time clearing his new farms. In that time his whiskey would age, mellowing in charred white oak barrels, acquiring the taste and smoothness that had taken Europe and America by storm.

One hundred and twenty eight barrels of whiskey were aging in the barn's long south shed, but there was room for many more. Levi Matthews had devised an ingenious ramp, hoists, and a series of sturdy wooden racks for storage on several levels. Craig left enough space on each level to rotate the barrels a half turn.

"We should soon be thinking about killing hogs. The weather sure has been cold enough," Owen volunteered.

"I expect we will do that during the next cold dry spell," Martin said.

Craig knew they would be eating well in the near future. He already had a big store of hickory logs stacked beside the smokehouse. During his first year at Widder's Landing, Martin had taught him the intricate process of hog butchering—how best to kill, hang, bleed and eviscerate a hog, how to scald and scrape the hair off the skin, and how to make various cuts. Craig soon became an expert with knife and cleaver. Agnes taught him about sausage and lard-making. Then he had learned the art of slow-smoking the larger cuts—hams, shoulders, and sides of bacon. As in other farm tasks, the whole family worked together. It was an integral part of their survival.

After another spell of talking, the McDonnell brothers began yawning. Work always began before dawn, except in mid-summer. Craig glanced at Mary and she nodded that it was time to leave.

"Mother Agnes, thank you for supper. I certainly do not deserve it. Lucinde and Mary, I appreciate the trouble you took. Everything was delicious."

"Well, we're just glad we could finally enjoy a meal together," Agnes laughed. "We have all been so busy!"

"Happy to oblige, dear Brother," Lucinde smiled from across the room. She and Owen each held a sleeping child. Craig thought they made a nice-looking family.

Martin saw them to the back door and handed Craig a lard lamp. Outside, the rain still drizzled. They set off on the long walk back to the cabin. Craig toted Isabel wrapped snugly in a deerskin cloak; Mary carried Ruth bundled in layers of soft blankets. An icy blast swooped in from the northwest, slapping their backs and setting the treetops to howling in the bottomlands. A gust of wind blew out the lamp flame. Craig set it down next to the fence, opened and closed the gate with his free hand, picked it up, and caught up with Mary who kept on a straight path toward home.

"Is it cold out here, or is it just me?" he complained.

"It is terribly cold," Mary answered. "I would not be surprised if it snows tonight! I am glad you stoked up the fire before you came over."

"I might just need some extra warming when we get home."

"Me too," Mary smiled.

Craig could just make out her features in the darkness.

New Orleans—November 5, 1815

Jules Signet's butler entered the upstairs dining room bearing a sealed envelope on a silver tray. He crossed the floor to where Doc Applegate enjoyed his midday meal. Life at Signet's townhouse had settled into a pleasant, orderly succession of fine meals, long uninterrupted periods of reading, discussion, and occasional enter-tainment. Doc took the unexpected envelope, surprised at the mild annoyance he felt—that he would consider a mere letter an intrusion upon his daily routine. He opened the envelope and mumbled in irritation.

"What is it, Doctor?" Jules inquired, looking up from his news-paper.

"Yves Guillot's daughter has gone into labor."

"That would explain their absence at Mass," the banker nodded thoughtfully.

"There are no doctors available in the entire city and the mid-wives are concerned the baby is turned wrong. Apparently the girl's water broke sometime this morning."

"Will you go?"

"I must. It is what I do." Doc rose and folded his linen napkin on the table. "I'll collect my bag."

Guillot's liveryman waited anxiously in the entrance hallway. "Massah Yves says we should hurry. His daughter is very weak."

Doc grunted noncommittally. He had delivered hundreds of ba-bies in his long career. He had observed that people panicked more over an impending birth than impending death. Women had been having babies since the dawn of creation and they would continue doing so. He wondered where his colleagues Roundanez, Chevalier, and Arceneaux were. Surely they would have been among Guillot's first choices. It was possible they were out on other house calls, but there were a half dozen other good doctors in New Orleans includ-ing two new American surgeons. Whatever the reasons, Guillot had sent for him. For the first time in weeks a sense of purpose stirred within Doc's veins. After all, this was his chosen profession and he had practiced it all his adult life. Some folks, even the younger doc-tors in New Orleans, called him "gifted."

Dark blue-gray clouds hung heavy and low over the city. The chill mid-afternoon air hinted at rain. Doc was glad for his cloak and he wrapped himself in its voluminous folds before stepping into the open carriage. The liveryman drove at a fast clip down North Rampart, for Guillot's townhouse lay on the eastern edge of the French Quarter. They turned off onto Esplanade, heading toward the river. Guillot's residence was an imposing two story house, situated on a large plot among live oaks and palmettos. The liveryman swung across Esplanade and onto a circular front drive paved in cobblestones. Guillot heard them drive up and he appeared in the front door, waving frantically.

"Hurry, Doctor!" he called.

Doc Applegate eased out of the carriage, favoring his bad knee as he ascended the low steps. Guillot ushered him into the foyer and a scene of near hysteria. Two young women, apparently his daughters, were weeping in the front parlor. A female slave brought in clean sheets from a back entrance. The expectant mother's shrieks rose above the other commotion. "My baby! My baby!"

"This way, Doctor," Guillot gestured.

Madame Guillot stormed from a back bedroom, blocking their passage. "Yves, I warned you—that broken down whiskey barrel will not touch Annette!"

"But Madame, he is all we could find!" Guillot apologized. "We have sent for the other doctors. At least let him assess her condition before they arrive. It could be some time."

"He is a disgrace to medical science and a danger to others!"

"Now, Louise—"

"I mean it, Yves!"

"Allow me," Doc edged past Guillot. "Madame, if you don't stand aside I will bash you with this cane." He raised it threateningly and stared straight into her eyes. "It may be too late already. You must at least allow me to see what can be done. Then I will let you decide whether or not to proceed."

Louise Guillot relented and bowed her head. Doc entered the room. Two midwives hovered over Annette, their faces set in grim masks of defeat. The expectant mother was drenched in sweat, her complexion ashen, eyes red-rimmed and swollen. Her belly was grossly distended, rock hard from internal pressure. She arched in the throes of another contraction.

Doc set down his bag, removed his cloak and rolled up his sleeves.

"When did her water break?" he asked the midwives, pressing gently upon the young woman's distended abdomen, feeling for the baby inside.

"Madame Guillot called us at four this morning."

"And what was her condition?" he asked. He already knew the answer, for it was evident the baby was trapped in the breech position.

The older of the two midwives answered, "She was in labor even then. Her contractions were more frequent and much stronger than they are now."

"Yes, the young lady is worn out. The baby is in the breech position. Did you attempt to turn it?"

Both women shook their heads. "We did not."

"Get me some clean water." He uncovered Annette and performed a brief examination. "We must hurry."

Louise subsided into a chair. Yves embraced her, blocking her view.

As he washed his hands, Doc announced, "This baby must be turned. I would prefer that to cutting and risking mortification of the incision. Do I have your permission to proceed?"

Yves glanced over his shoulder and nodded in grim affirmation.

"Then let's begin," Doc sighed. He gestured to the younger midwife. "I want you to hold her shoulders, but in a way you can lift her on a moment's notice. I may order you to turn her to one side or the other. Be prepared to do so."

"Yes, doctor."

"And you," he addressed the other midwife. "You must push upon Annette's abdomen where I indicate. Follow my instructions to the letter and do not hesitate. The coordination of our efforts will be of utmost importance." He unfolded a cloth and laid out a glittering array of instruments. "If we cannot turn the baby, then we will undoubtedly have to cut."

Louise let out a muffled wail, but did not rise to protest. The whole family had arrived at something akin to resignation, and they clung together in desperate hope as Doc bent forward to do his work. With experienced hands he felt for the baby's position. He took the midwife's hands and placed them on the right side of the abdomen. Annette grunted at the pressure.

"Do you feel that?" he asked.

"Yes, Doctor."

"When I tell you to push, you push like hell in that direction. We are going to turn this baby around, and when we do, we must be quick. The cord could wrap around its neck and strangle it. Are you ready?"

"Yes," the midwife whispered.

"Hold her shoulders!" Doc commanded. Without further ado he guided his hand inside Annette's passage, manipulating the baby back from the vaginal canal. He used his other hand to push from the outside. He felt the baby ease backwards, and its hindquarters shifted to the left. Annette screamed in agony, trying to writhe free.

"Get ready!" he barked at the older midwife. "Now! Push like hell!" The nurse firmly pressed laterally from right to left—she could see and feel what needed to be done—and the baby miraculously turned. "You!" Doc ordered the young midwife. "Raise that right shoulder. Roll her partially to the side."

Louise fainted and hit the parquet floor with a dull thud. Doc paid her no mind as Yves stooped to look after her. Annette ceased screaming, her head lolling in semi-consciousness. Doc guided the infant until he lost contact with the bottom—the midwife had positioned it properly. It was providence that had brought her here. He must remember to take her name for future assistance. With his free hand he pressed on Annette's opposite side, guiding the baby's upper body around until the head touched his embedded hand. Gently he withdrew and issued a rapid-fire string of commands.

"Lift both shoulders!" The young midwife obeyed instantly.

"Push downward! Help her push the baby out!" With both hands the older midwife worked determinedly, pressing at an angle.

"Annette! Wake up! I need you to bear down! Now!

Through mists of pain and weakness Annette heard and struggled to obey. She groaned with the pain of another contraction. The top of the baby's head appeared.

"That's a good girl! Again! The baby needs your help, Annette! Everyone, push!"

The older midwife pushed from the top of Annette's abdomen with a firm pressing motion. This time the baby's head and neck emerged, covered in white mucus membrane. Doc eased his fingers in and found the shoulders, then guided the baby into the world. He observed with relief that the umbilical cord was not entangled around the neck; he also noticed that the infant was a girl. Taking her by the feet, he held her upside down, allowing blood to rush to her head. She resembled a little pink bat with scrunched facial features and pug nose, still connected to her mother by the fleshy tube. Three sharp whacks brought the mass of inert tissue to life. Doc felt the familiar, but always miraculous, impulse course through the legs. The infant gasped and let out a high-pitched shriek, followed by repeated cries of outrage. Doc liked the sound; in most cases that meant the baby was strong. He reckoned it must be a shock to be expelled from such warm, protective darkness into a bright and harsh alien environment.

Annette, exhausted after a half day of struggle, smiled wanly. Doc laid the infant on her mother's abdomen. The older midwife handed him a pair of clamps. With his left hand he clamped down on the cord.

"Scissors?" He needn't have asked; the midwife was ready with the surgical scissors. Doc cut above the clamp. "I'll just keep the pressure on for a bit. Then we'll tie off the baby's cord."

He considered Annette. There was a small outer tear, but no abnormal bleeding and, judging from the cord's length, separation had already occurred. As he tied off the baby's cord, the younger midwife began working on Annette. Doc watched as she kneaded gently, below the womb, ready to caution if she pushed too high or too hard.

"This room is cold," he announced to Yves. "I suggest you have someone build up the fire right away." He wrapped the baby in a soft blanket.

The older midwife eased Annette into a sitting position, propping pillows behind her. She then helped her hold the infant. Doc observed as Annette instinctively cleaned the baby's lips and nostrils with her tongue, just like a mother animal would do. Then she put the baby to her breast.

"That's right," Doc chuckled. "Let that baby suck. You will feel some strong contractions down there. It is perfectly normal, nature's way of getting you to expel the rest of that cord and afterbirth."

A cold rain pattered softly against the window panes. Guillot's house slaves began lighting candles and lamps, for dusk came early this time of year. Doc stayed on well past nightfall, making sure the afterbirth was expelled and Annette was out of danger. Louise and Yves hovered near, relieved it was all over, overjoyed at the birth of their granddaughter. Annette's sisters sat on either side of the bed and chatted gaily. Doc and the midwives stood back, forgotten for a time.

Yves was first to remember them. "Doctor, I am grateful for the miracle you wrought today. It is an absolute certainty that you saved Annette and my granddaughter—you and these wonderful angels of mercy. I thank you all from the bottom of my heart."

"We just helped nature do its job," Doc demurred.

"You are too modest, Doctor," the older midwife admonished. "Before you arrived, we had about lost hope. It was impressive, the way you came in and took charge. Your healing gifts far transcend what I have observed in the medical profession."

"Speaking of healing gifts, you, most assuredly, are not lacking them. Your instincts were accurate and the execution of my commands flawless. We worked well together. Perhaps, in the future, we may join our medical experience in other deliveries. May I know your name so I may call on you for assistance?"

"It is Solange Tourigny," she replied. "I would be happy to work with you again, Doctor."

Doc leaned over to listen once more to Annette's heartbeat and breathing. He also placed his ear to her abdomen. Another brief examination revealed no abnormal bleeding. He listened to the infant's heartbeat and breathing. It appeared the crisis had passed. Both mother and daughter were sleeping. This was the most rewarding part of his profession—to save life, to bring it into the world, and to enjoy the gratitude of the family and loved ones. Tonight that gratitude shone in all their faces, although Louise could not meet his eyes.

He drew back the drapes and cocked an ear to the glass windowpane. "I do believe it has stopped raining. I shall take my leave. You know where to find me if there is trouble in the night. I presume the midwives will stay?"

"Just Marie," Guillot announced, indicating the younger woman. "My driver will drive you back to Signet's. You do not mind if he first drops Madame Tourigny off at the convent?"

"I do not."

Doc instructed the young midwife, "You may allow the mother plenty of liquids, but withhold rich foods. Start her on small amounts of bland fare that will form consistency but will not be hard to pass. We do not wish to aggravate the tear as it begins to heal. Keep her clean and dry down there and let nature work its own healing magic. I will look in on her tomorrow morning."

Guillot ordered his butler to summon the carriage driver. He escorted Doc and Solange into the parlor. "Please wait here while I fetch your payment." He stepped into another room, presumably his office, and returned shortly with two cloth purses. The first he handed to Solange. "Thank you again, Madame Tourigny. Your assistance tonight proved more than I hoped for."

"Thank you, monsieur," Solange ducked her head and curtsied.

"And you, Doctor Applegate, will be in my prayers every day until I die. I trust this sum is sufficient to reflect my deepest appreciation for saving Annette and my granddaughter. Also, I apologize once again for my wife's cruel, personal attacks. She was overwrought and acted stupidly from fear."

"Well, if stupidity was a sin, Hell would have filled up long ago from overcrowding," Doc chuckled easily. "It is already forgotten." He considered with satisfaction the weightiness of the purse, hoping the coins were gold and not mere silver. It took a great deal of restraint not to open the drawstring to take a peek. He tucked it deep inside his bag and covered it with a white cloth, placing a razor sharp scalpel on top.

The covered carriage rolled up to the doorsteps, lanterns glowing from all four corners. "Thank you again Doctor, Madame Tourigny," Guillot bade them goodnight. The driver stepped down from his seat to assist both Solange and Doc into the seats.

A chilly fog drifted through the narrow streets as the driver negotiated his way toward the Ursuline Convent. A pale quarter moon appeared from behind the clouds, but it provided scant light. Doc wished he had primed the little double-barreled pistol concealed beneath the false bottom of his bag. Fortunately the French Quarter was much safer and better patrolled than the American sector. It was a short trip to the convent, just a few streets down Esplanade before turning right onto Decatur and into the heart of the city.

"So you actually live in the convent?" Doc cleared his throat. For some reason he felt a bit nervous. "I distinctly heard Guillot call you Madame."

"My husband, Léon, died of the fever just last year."

"I am sorry to hear it. What did he do to earn his living?"

"He was a merchant. He owned a small warehouse on the levee. We were not rich, but lived respectably. Then he was cheated by his banker. I do not wish to recount all the details, but he was sued for breach of contract. We took the case to court, but our lawyer was hopelessly outclassed. We lost the warehouse and the goods inside, then our home and all of our savings. Shortly after that, Léon's health broke and the fever took him."

"You have no children?"

"I have a son who returned to France to fight with Napoleon. I am not sure he is alive. I have written him many times, but he has not replied."

Doc felt his heart go out to her. "What did you do then?"

"There were several offers of marriage; there always are, but I was not ready. Still, I had to live somewhere. The sisters graciously took me in and now I do what charitable work I can. When I earn money, I turn it over to them. They will be pleased tonight. I am not usually paid so generously."

"Nor am I." Doc assured her. "It is absolutely remarkable that you give all your earnings to the convent. I have never met anyone quite like you." He tried to make out her features in the dark carriage, wishing he had taken more notice while they were at Guillot's house. She was slender with high cheekbones, perhaps fifty years of age, with gray strands in her short, otherwise dark hair. At one time she might have been ravishing, for she still possessed a beauty and a quiet assurance he found intriguing.

The carriage wheeled one block up *Avenue des Ursulines* before turning right onto Chartres Street. The driver pulled to a halt at the front gate.

"May I escort you inside?" Doc offered.

"I know my way. Thank you, Doctor."

Before he could stop himself, he blurted, "May I call on you at some future date? Perhaps we could enjoy a meal together."

"Perhaps," Solange replied. In the near-darkness he could just detect the hint of a smile. "Good night, Doctor." The driver opened the carriage door and she stepped lightly down, slipping lithely through the stone portals of the convent wall.

"We will just wait here until she is inside," Doc ordered the driver.

"Yes, Doctor."

They watched as she neared the front door, looking small and delicate against the convent's imposing height and severity. The building appeared more austere than usual in dim moonlight. Doc had been inside it several times, once after the Battle of New Orleans. On that memorable eighth of January, 1815, the convent portals were thrown open to admit a long train of wounded soldiers—British and American. Day-school classrooms were converted into hospital wards, and the Ursulines, ever true to their founding principles, became nurses, displaying the utmost tenderness and generosity in their caregiving. Doc remembered working with them and he could easily believe the stories of recovered British veterans weeping when they were obliged to leave.

For years the sisters had used the ground floor as an orphanage and the second floor as their residence. The convent had survived the massive fires of 1788 and 1794 and was rumored to be the oldest building in New Orleans. Because the Spanish were in control at the time of rebuilding, the "French Quarter" was actually more Spanish in style, but the convent stood as a classic example of French architecture and design.

Solange rang a bell and the clanging reverberated across the wet grounds. The door swung open to reveal an Ursuline sister fully dressed in habit, coif and veil, holding a lit candle. Solange stepped inside and the door closed.

"Drive on," Doc commanded. His heart raced at every check in speed; each time he was certain a would-be robber had caused the slowdown. It was not until Jules Signet's butler locked the front door behind him that he sighed with relief. He was equally glad to learn that Signet had gone out, for he really did not wish to engage in conversation.

Doc ascended the staircase to his bedroom and locked the door. He opened his bag, retrieved the purse, and slowly spilled a small cascade of gold coins onto the counterpane. American eagles and half eagles, British guineas and Spanish doubloons clinked with a satisfactory sound. Doc counted it with relish—over two hundred and twenty dollars! He wished that all his patients paid like this. Then he could settle his debt and disentangle himself from Signet's diabolical web of conspiracy.

For the first time he reflected upon the magnitude and malignancy of the scheme. And for the first time it troubled him. They were about to commit an evil that would trample all bounds of human decency. It was almost unthinkable that he, the doctor who saved life, would have an active hand in destroying one.

Today he had resurrected his gifts and performed a medical miracle, winning the lifetime gratitude of an entire family. It validated his whole existence and made him feel worthwhile and alive. He thought about Solange, her goodness and selflessness, even in the face of adversity—she would never engage in the duplicity in which he was involved. He wished there was a way out, but he was in too deep to quit. And the inquest was now close at hand.

Breckinridge County, Kentucky—November 8, 1815

Mary asked Isabel to help her make cornbread for dinner. It was so pleasurable having the children always near her and to experience their unconditional love. Isabel enjoyed the special attention. After all, this was an important, grown-up task, and it made her feel like a big girl. Ruth was now sitting up alone and she watched all with interest from the corn tick mattress that Mary had placed just back from the stone hearth. Isabel glanced over at her younger sister from time to time, proud of her newly acquired skill.

"That's right, dear," Mary encouraged her. "Mix the salt into the cornmeal." While Isabel stirred the dry ingredients with a wooden spoon, Mary greased the spider, a long-handled three-legged skillet, with an ample amount of bacon drippings and set it over the fire to heat. From a stone crock she spooned a dollop of butter into a tin cup and placed it near the coals to melt. "Now let's mix the rest in the other bowl. Can you pour the buttermilk in without spilling it?" Mary had already filled the wooden noggin from the springhouse bucket. "Careful," she clucked. Isabel poured with such a look of intense concentration that Mary was forced to stifle a laugh. "Good! Now I will add the egg." She cracked it on the bowl's edge and separated the halves, spilling the contents into the milk. "You must blend it all, so we cannot see the yellow egg yolk." After a time, Isabel changed hands.

"I will take over for a while," Mary offered. "It makes your hands and arms tired, doesn't it?"

"Yes, Mother," Isabel agreed.

"When I get tired, I will ask you to mix again. Aren't you glad we are here to help each other?" She took a metal whisk and finished mixing before combining everything into the big stoneware bowl that Ma gave her on her wedding day four years ago. After stirring in the melted butter, she let Isabel use the whisk for a while. "Very good, darling! You have made your first cornbread! Won't your Father be surprised?"

Isabel beamed proudly.

"Now, let's cook this before he comes in for dinner." Wrapping a thick cloth around the handle, she eased the skillet back from the coals. She carefully poured the batter onto the sizzling grease, making sure it was evenly distributed. While the children played with the little dolls she had sewn for them, she watched the cornbread until the edges began to turn golden brown. A short time later she inserted a small wooden stick into the center. It came out clean, with no batter clinging to it.

"The cornbread is done!" she announced.

As she lifted the skillet off the coals, a horse and wagon pulled up outside. Someone rapped lightly on the door. "Isabel, don't let your sister get near the fire," Mary cautioned. She raised the latch and opened the door.

Violet Bozarth stood before her looking forlorn and uncharacteristically disheveled. In fact, she was almost unrecognizable. Instead of her usual immaculate dress, she wore one of her husband's heavy coats, wrongly buttoned so that it gave her a lopsided appearance, and a hastily-tied scarf over limp hair in sore need of fixing. The town gossips would give their eye teeth to see her like this. Most women pretended to admire her and even did her bidding, mainly to stay in her good graces and to avoid being on the wrong side of her wrath. Unbeknownst to her, they despised her high and mighty *I'm-better-than-you* attitude. Now she was a victim of the hierarchy she had created, having no close friends in whom she could confide.

Mary took one look at her grief-stricken face and felt her heart go out to her. "Violet! Won't you come in, dear?"

"Thank you," Violet replied, stifling a sob, her eyes red and swollen from crying. She noticed the children and glanced around the cabin. "Your husband is not in?"

"He soon will be. It is almost dinnertime. Come and sit at the table. I'll make us some coffee."

Violet staggered in on unsteady feet and slurred, "I need something much stronger than coffee."

Mary caught the whiff of whiskey on her breath and the smell of over-worn clothes and unwashed skin. Gently, Mary steered her toward the table and helped her sit down. "Oh Violet, what is wrong?"

Violet hesitated for an instant. Then she blurted, "You already know. It's that damned Wilfred. He's been spending nights with Cecilia Dowell. And, what is worse, everyone in town knows it. I will confess he has always been predisposed to wander, but this time I fear he will leave me."

"I am so sorry, Violet."

"May I rely upon your complete discretion? You won't repeat what I say to others—especially your mother?"

"I promise."

Just then, Craig opened the door. "The Judge's horse got loose. I brought it back and tied it to the post by the smokehouse. That wagon was not hitched up right. The traces were twisted and—"

"Craig, Violet has paid us a visit," Mary's tone bore a soft undercurrent of admonition.

"Oh, I'm sorry. How are you Violet?" Craig removed his hat and scarf. "I didn't realize. Anyway, I've sorted everything out." He strode over to the hearth and embraced the children. "Something smells good!"

"I made cornbread for you, Father!" Isabel boasted.

"You did?" he kissed her cheek. "Well, then we will just have to try some!"

"Violet, will you join us for dinner?" Mary asked.

"I am not hungry, thank you." Violet managed to gather some of her reserve. She was clearly irritated at Craig's presence and, although her hostility was not open, her subtle glances and body language conveyed that he had interrupted her and she wanted him gone.

"Well, I am starved!" Craig rubbed his hands together, rolling his eyes at Isabel as Mary set the cornbread on the table. He would not allow Violet to make him feel like an intruder in his own home. It was incredible she would do this, especially when it was she who had arrived, unannounced, at dinnertime. As they said Grace and made the sign of the cross, Craig noticed her, a 'hard shell Baptist,' wincing in obvious displeasure.

Mary forked a smoked pork chop onto his plate followed by a half panful of her best fried potatoes, a generous ladle of beans, and a wedge of Isabel's cornbread.

"Let me put butter on it!" Isabel pleaded.

"Fine!" Craig agreed. After she daubed the cornbread with a few clumsy smears, he took a bite, making a big show of how much he enjoyed it. "Mmm! This is good! It is the best cornbread I have ever eaten!"

Mary winked knowingly at Isabel. Although they enjoyed the meal and each other's company, Violet's presence put a slight damper on the occasion. It was especially awkward when Mary retreated to the bed to nurse Ruth and put her to sleep, for Craig was left alone with their guest.

Seeking to make conversation, he asked, "How is the Judge doing? Is he keeping well?" Violet slumped forward, her head thumping down upon the table. Craig noticed a lot of gray mixed in with the dark brown. She burst into tears.

Isabel looked as if she might cry also. Craig suggested, "Let's climb up into the loft and see what is up there. I'll tell you a story." He found the little coat Mary had made and put it on her. Next, he took a heavy blanket from the cedar chest and they climbed the hickory-pegged ladder to the loft. He shouldered aside the wooden door that trapped heat in the main cabin. It was hard to see in the near darkness, but they found a place among rolls of hemp twine and other stores where they could sit.

"It's cold up here, isn't it?"

Isabel nodded.

"Would you like a story before your afternoon nap?"

"Yes, Father," she snuggled up against him. "Tell me the one about the three little bears."

"Hmm. Let me see if I can remember." Craig usually made up his stories on the fly; as a result he could not always recall the minor details. But Isabel remembered them all, and she corrected him whenever he strayed from the original story. She dropped off to sleep before he reached the ending. Craig focused his attention on the conversation below. From his angle in the loft he could just make out the tops of their heads.

"This is the literal end!" Violet declared. "That man has humiliated me for the last time! Playing in the muck with Cecilia Dowell, of all people! And everyone in Cottonwood Bend knows it. Oh, I hear them whispering behind my back. Do you have any idea what that feels like?"

Craig heard Mary softly reply, "Yes, I do. I know exactly how it feels."

"But how could you? You have a man who loves you and would never play you false."

"You are forgetting I was once married to Jedediah Carpenter."

"But I am a woman of high station!" Violet protested. "A respected leader in the community. So is Wilfred. We should be immune to those animalistic passions that afflict the poor."

Craig almost lost his control at this pronouncement. He wanted to shout down to her, to tell her to get the hell out and peddle her domestic problems elsewhere.

Mary inquired gently, "Do you honestly believe that other people suffer less because they are poor or uneducated or without political power?"

Violet did not answer.

"How do you think I felt when I heard about Jedediah's cheating? In addition, Jedediah was a mean drunk. I will admit he was a fair worker and he made good money, but he was broke all the time. He spent it all on coarse women in Yellow Banks, and on Joe Phillips' daughters. You remember what they were like, servicing half the river rats that came down the Ohio. Jedediah dallied with them all the time; he even came home smelling like them. One of the girls actually confronted me, boasting she would steal him away. "

"Yes, yes," Violet sought to dismiss her. Clearly she was not interested in Mary's past. "I am truly sorry for you."

Craig knew that Mary was going somewhere with this and would not be deterred. He recalled meeting her four years ago, saving her from a savage beating, and claiming her as his own, even though she was still married, when the possibility of annulment within the Catholic Church was almost naught. Jedediah had solved the problem for them, riding up to Craig's shack with a band of outlaws, intent on murder. In a blazing nighttime gunfight Craig killed two of the outlaws and Mary had wounded Jedediah, driving him away. Judge Bozarth, the subject under current scrutiny, had then led a Party of Regulators down to 'Cottonwood-Under-the-Bluff' and dispatched of the remaining outlaws. It was an epic shootout, resulting in a deadly conflagration that destroyed the shantytown and most of the riff-raff in it. Jedediah's charred corpse was identified among the dead which included Joe Phillips and his four prostitute daughters. Since then, Mary never spoke of Jedediah, and Craig never asked.

"I know you are hurting," Mary sympathized. "It makes you feel cheap and humiliated. You secretly wonder what it is that *you* lack that would cause him to wander. This is especially true when you do all in your power to be his helpmate, sharing in his successes and consoling him in his failures, cooking his meals and washing his clothes, sharing your body and mind with him. And when you have done all of that, it is a bitter pill to swallow—to find out he is embracing another woman, sharing physical intimacy and perhaps innermost secrets that should be reserved only for you."

Violet dropped her pretentiousness and listened attentively.

"I left a wonderful home and family. I was so innocent and full of hope, not knowing what I was about to marry into. Jedediah acted so properly, right up until our wedding day, and then he changed. He even declared that he owned me. We moved into a miserable little shack. Many nights he was away, working in Yellow Banks. I was all alone, often times wondering where my next meal would come from. Pa and Ma looked in on me. When Jedediah came back to Cottonwood Bend, he spent most of his nights with Tawny Phillips. He would finally stagger home and tell me all the things they did together. The whiskey made him mean and he beat me. The last time he blacked my eyes, bloodied my mouth, and kicked me in the stomach."

"I knew there was some trouble. I did not realize it was that bad."

"Has the Judge ever come home drunk to you?"

"No." Violet replied. "I can honestly say he has not."

"Has he ever boasted about his affairs in order to hurt you?"

"No."

"Has he ever denied you a good living?"

"We live extremely well. Better than anyone else in town."

"Has he ever beaten you?"

"Absolutely not."

"I will hazard he has probably tried to conceal the affairs from you in order to spare you any grief. It is possible he experiences feelings of guilt."

"You may be right," Violet conceded.

"Have you ever discussed your feelings with him?"

"Only once, when we were younger. He promised then never to cheat again. I have since suspected he has, and I have heard much gossip, but have borne my suspicions in silence. I am too afraid he will leave."

"I do not think he wishes to leave you, Violet. I believe he loves you very much. He has a weakness, but in many other ways he is a fine man with many wonderful qualities."

"But I do not want him loving another woman!"

"Then you must have it out with him. Let him know how you feel."

"Would you be with me when I do?" Violet pleaded.

Mary was taken aback. "Oh, I do not know, Violet. Perhaps that is best handled in the privacy of your own home. You could consider having Brother Kreisle present."

"That old windbag! He would surely tell his wife and she would have it all over the county before next Sunday's services!" Violet swayed and disappeared from Craig's view. He heard a resounding thwack as her head hit the oaken floor puncheons.

"Craig!" Mary called. "Violet has fallen! Can you help me?"

Carrying the still-sleeping Isabel with one arm, Craig used his free hand to climb down the ladder. He put her into bed and covered her before crossing the room to help Mary. Violet was sitting up unsteadily, holding her head in her hands. Craig took one arm and Mary the other.

"I should leave," Violet protested.

"You are in no condition to drive home," Mary argued, shaking her head. "Why don't you lie down for a while?

Violet crashed down upon the bed and began snoring. Craig lowered the loft door and stoked up the fire. Mary joined him at the hearth and laid a hand on his forearm.

"Craig, I think you should go and fetch Judge Bozarth."

"You are not serous! He is all the way over in Hardinsburg. It would be better to just let her sleep it off. I'll drive her home this evening when we finish work."

"But the Judge may be on his way back now. What would he do if he comes home and finds Violet missing?"

"It hasn't seemed to bother him before now. You heard her— he's been staying out nights."

"Please do this for me, Craig."

"We are stripping your father's tobacco. The season doesn't last forever, you know. Besides, I don't know where this Cecilia Dowell lives."

"Pa does. You can ask him for directions when you explain why you must be gone for the afternoon."

"You promised Violet you would tell no one."

"Pa is different—he will keep it to himself. Just make sure Ma is not around when you tell him. This is the kind of gossip she would love to spread."

Craig sighed in defeat. Mary asked for so little, yet she always gave so much of herself. There was no way he could refuse her. "Very well; you win. I'm not sure the Judge will come, even when I tell him why."

"Trust me—he will come."

"What makes you so sure?"

"He loves her, Craig. He just can't help himself when it comes to other women." She turned his face and kissed him on his lips.

Craig checked the shotgun loads to ensure the weapon was ready in the unlikely event that Mary should need to use it. He shrugged on his warm coat, possibles bag and powder horn, lifted his rifle from the mantle and stomped out to the barn, annoyed at Violet's intrusion, angry at the waste of valuable time it would consume searching for the wayward Judge. He did not look forward to explaining why he had come. It would undoubtedly create an awkward situation for the long ride home.

As they always did when he approached them, the animals came running, expecting a feed. His saddle horse, Blue, reached him first. Craig caught hold of his halter and coaxed him over to the harness room, tied on a lead rope and looped it to the hitching rail. It took some time to hunt out his saddle, blanket, and bridle stored in back of the room behind oxen yokes, plow horse collars and harnesses. He had not ridden for several weeks, and now, Blue behaved a bit skittishly. Craig spoke reassuringly and poured a double handful of oats into the trough. While the roan munched on grain, Craig took a comb and groomed him, checking for burrs and sores. Satisfied that there were none, he positioned the blanket and lifted the saddle onto his back, making sure it seated snugly. He then drew the girth strap tight, fastened the buckle, and slipped on the bridle. At first Blue resisted the bit, but Craig managed to get him to accept it, giving him a pat on the neck. After tightening the girth strap another notch, he led Blue out into the cold gray afternoon, swung into the saddle and headed downhill to cut across his back field to Welcome Hall.

Martin was carrying an armload of tobacco stalks from the strip-ping room when Craig rode up. He heaved the bundle onto a flatbed wagon and met him outside the open door. "What is it, Craig?"

Craig motioned for him to join him a little distance from the barn, knowing that Agnes was probably inside stripping leaves. In hushed tones he explained the situation, not concealing his disgust.

Martin nodded thoughtfully. "Mary is right. You should go. The Judge has a serious problem on his hands."

"One of his own making," Craig qualified.

"Yes, but he is a man worth having on your side. Remember, he is not without influence and if you ever find yourself in a pinch, he may one day prove valuable. None of us is perfect—this just hap-pens to be his weakness. We cannot condemn. If you do him this kindness now and keep it forever in confidence, he will repay you. Of that I am sure."

Martin had advised Craig several times over the past four years and his counsel had never failed.

"Tell me how I can find him."

"Old man Dowell settled on this side of Hardinsburg just off the Hardinsburg Road. His son, Cecilia's husband, bought part of the home place and some land adjacent to it. From your farm keep to the main road, ride east down into the next valley and then climb about four miles through some limestone outcroppings. When you reach the ridgetop, the ground opens up into farmland and pasture. Do you know the big gray barn with a double corncrib on the right hand side?"

"Yes, I do." Once every few months, when Father Badin passed through on one of his vast circuits, he and Mary accompanied the family to Mass at St. Rumoldus Church in Hardinsburg. He remem-bered that landmark.

"You will find the Dowell place on the right hand side about two miles beyond that barn—a white house with double chimneys and green shutters, tucked among a fruit orchard. If you are not sure, ask some of the folks around there. They'll set you straight."

"Thanks, Martin. I appreciate this."

"Don't worry about our tobacco. It will still be here tomorrow morning."

Craig wheeled Blue around and headed him onto the Hardinsburg Road. At first the roan worried his head around the bit, but he soon fell into a long springy gait, climbing smoothly uphill around the sweeping curve. Craig slowed when he reached his three farms. On the left he observed his home place, enjoying it from a traveler's perspective. He admired the stone entrance, and carved wooden sign his friend Levi Matthews had fashioned. The carpenter had thoughtfully renamed the farm "Mary's Landing." His cabin, with distinctive dogtrot and cookhouse, sat on a low knoll just two hundred yards back, and Craig could clearly see blue smoke curling from its stone chimney. Behind the cabin, past the orchard of young fruit trees and grape arbor, stood his barn, perhaps the county's biggest. The other buildings harmonized beautifully with pasture and large oak trees. It took all his resolve not to turn in.

A number of small cabins, barns, and sheds occupied the Jennings place, his second farm. Smoke curled from all the cabins, except the one recently vacated by Romulus and Vergina. Craig remembered that he would soon need to cut and haul more firewood for the older folks. When he passed his final holdings, the Smithhart farm, he encountered less familiar ground. He had first traveled this road in 1811 on his way to the county seat of Hardinsburg. Judge Bozarth, acting as his lawyer, had accompanied him on Court Day to help him register the deed to his farm and to pay back taxes owed by the previous owner, the Widder Fuqua.

The track plunged downward into a wild valley known by locals as Hite's Run, so-named for the early Virginia land surveyor, Isaac Hite. From his vantage point Craig estimated the valley at about three or four miles across. He studied the forested hills beyond. Most of the summer leaves had fallen, but among bare branches generous splotches of color survived. Along the water courses, maples were still clothed in soft gold. Sweet gums and sassafras flamed yellow, orange, scarlet and purple. Only the stubborn oaks retained their semblance of green, but even they were beginning to turn brown. Halfway across the bottomland a small creek cut across the road. Water rippled and purled around big rocks littering the creek bottom. Someone, perhaps a local farmer responsible for this portion of the road, had constructed a simple bridge of giant beech logs and rough wooden planks. Blue shied a little as he clattered across the planks, but thankfully he did not balk or pitch.

Despite his anger at having to fetch Judge Bozarth, Craig found himself enjoying the ride through the valley. He urged Blue into a comfortable lope, drinking in cold air as they crossed relatively open flats. The road was little more than a wide trail, deeply rutted and covered with stumps. Craig slowed to a walk and let Blue pick his way when they reached the opposite hills. They wound upward through whippy scrub brush, dark green cedars, and tall hardwoods. Limestone outcroppings jutted on either side of the steepest grades.

It was mid-afternoon when he reached the summit. Craig looked back at the road behind him. He knew that darkness would fall early, especially on this cloudy day, and he hoped to find the Judge before then. The summit appeared more settled, running mostly to rolling pastureland with cattle grazing in cleared fields. From his rare, previous trips to Hardinsburg, Craig recognized several landmarks, mostly small farmhouses and barns, including the one with the double corncrib Martin had described. He met a farmer walking west, the first person he had encountered on his journey. The man waved and spoke a greeting.

"Gonna be a cold one tonight!"

"I think you are right," Craig replied. "Am I on the right road to the Cecilia Dowell farm?"

The farmer chuckled knowingly. "And what business do you have with her?"

"I am looking for someone."

"Then you may just find him there."

Craig recoiled with shock. Violet was right. It seemed that everyone in the county did know. "How far?"

"Another mile and a half on your right."

"Thank you, sir."

"Just watch yourself in the clinches, lad. That woman is more trouble than you could ever hope to handle."

Craig rode on, wondering just how he would break the news to the Judge. Presently he arrived at the farm. It looked just as Martin described it—white wooden house, freshly painted with green shutters and orange-brick chimneys on both ends, tucked neatly behind a well-pruned orchard. At the orchard's edge Craig stopped to dismount and hurriedly scoop up a few shriveled apples as a treat for Blue. He also plucked a brownish-yellow pear. The horse had behaved beautifully, conveying them to this destination without incident. Craig resolved to spend more time in the saddle during winter.

He led Blue past the house to the barn and tied him to a rail alongside the nearest animal stall. A horse nickered from within its depths. One look was all Craig needed. He recognized the broad-rumped chestnut mare belonging to Judge Wilfred J. Bozarth, Attorney-at-Law, commander of the Cottonwood Bend Militia. He shook his head and set about taking care of Blue. He did not unsaddle, for he intended to stay no longer than it took to deliver the message.

After forking some hay into a feedbox, he found an oaken bucket and filled it with water. He watched Blue drink almost half before feeding him the tidbits of fruit. Then he strode resolvedly toward the house.

Chapter Four

New Orleans—November 8, 1815

"Madame Tourigny, once again you have proven yourself an able midwife," Doc Applegate praised. "I am glad you consented to assist."

Solange nodded, accepting his compliment without reply. Between them they had accomplished another successful breech birth, although in surroundings far less elegant. Farron Weeks had summoned Doc to the humble plantation shack to deliver a slave infant. It was the slave's third child and, coincidentally, her third breech birth. The first infant had died before a doctor could intervene. The second one had been born breech, but left crippled in its right leg and, in Weeks' words, 'rendered a complete idiot, barely able to understand and complete simple tasks.' This time Doc and Solange brought a healthy baby boy into the world. It was glaringly apparent that this baby was half white, more than likely the unmarried master's offspring. The nun who had accompanied them from the convent expressed her disgust at this realization.

Farron Weeks appeared at the door, obviously pleased with the outcome. "I tell you, Doc, you got a way of working with the human body. The last doctor sure botched things up."

"Well, I am blessed to have a good assistant."

Solange blushed as she busied herself with cleaning up the baby and mother.

Weeks drawled, "If'n you don't mind, I need you to look in on another slave. She's been feeling right poorly. You've examined her before." The nun's fierce expression drove him outdoors.

"Can you manage here?" Doc asked Solange.

"Indeed, Doctor." she replied. "I will build up the fire and keep watch while you are gone."

"Then I shall return for you shortly."

Weeks directed him across the dirt track to another slave cabin. When Doc opened the door he recognized Kayla, lying on a straw mattress, wrapped in blankets, appearing listless and ill.

"Kayla, what is wrong with you?" Doc inquired.

"I don't rightly know, Doctor."

Doc could take an educated guess. "You been sick to your stomach, mornings mostly?"

"Yes, Doctor."

"You been tired? Pissing more than usual?"

"Yessir," Kayla nodded.

"I'll hazard you've missed your last moon."

Kayla began weeping. She covered her face with a blanket. Doc raised the blanket and felt of her lower abdomen. Then he placed both hands on her breasts. He could feel the nipples, hard as pebbles and popped out firmly from the dark tips.

"Your titties hurt?" He squeezed them and she winced in pain. "Well, I can tell you now, Kayla—you are plumb knocked." He liked using the new expression that had turned up in New Orleans as recently as two years ago. Some folks claimed it came from the phrase *"knocked down by the auctioneer, knocked up by the purchaser."*

The girl certainly knew what it meant, for she wailed in despair. Doc rose from the pallet and let her cry it out.

"Has there been anyone other than Judge Harkness?" He glanced at Weeks who had watched the examination with interest.

Weeks' face registered shock. "I've left her alone, just as you ordered. There's plenty of other wenches on this plantation."

"It the judge's sucker," Kayla confirmed. "There ain't been no other man."

"Why are you crying?" Doc asked. "Most women are happy to have a baby."

"My baby—it be an ugly, hairy monster like the judge?"

Doc suppressed his mirth. "It will be part you, Kayla. My professional guess is that it will turn out just fine."

"What do we do with her?" Weeks' asked.

"Let her rest a few days. Don't let any of those young bucks get to her and for God's sake don't work or beat her."

"What about Judge Harkness?"

"You let me worry about him. And take care not to tell a soul. The judge is a nasty-tempered, powerful man. If the news gets out, he could make us all go away—permanently."

———•———

For the past two days rain had fallen, almost incessantly, turning the river road into a muddy mess. Signet's carriage slewed back and forth, bogging down at times in deep ruts. Doc cracked the whip, urging the horses through another quagmire, noting how the mud sucked at their hooves. His passengers rode in the back seat, wrapped in their winter coats to ward off the damp chill of late afternoon. Doc took every opportunity to talk to Solange.

"Nasty business, breech birth," he commented. "It has killed many a young mother. But you will agree today's case was not as difficult as last time."

"How is Annette?" Solange asked.

"I saw her this morning. Both mother and baby are doing well. I met her young husband yesterday."

"That is right. I recall he was not present at the birth."

"Away on business at the time. He seems a nice young man."

The road cut through bare cane fields with their brown stubble and silent brick sugar mills pointing smokestacks at a sullen sky. This time it was Solange who spoke.

"That negro baby was Farron Weeks' child, am I right?"

"Presumably," Doc replied. "It is not my business to inquire."

"It is a horrible crime, punishable by God!" the nun growled.

"Well, he owns her."

"Slavery is a worse crime, for it propagates other crimes like the one we witnessed today," Solange stated freely.

"Unwanted children," muttered the nun.

"Oh, make no mistake; he is proud to have that male child," Doc replied. "Farron will turn him into a fine field hand."

"Surely you cannot accept that? Slavery is a horrible, abominable system. By its own nature it promotes laziness, physical violence, lust, and cruelty. One day our nation will rise up and abolish this offense against God."

"I wouldn't proclaim that too loudly around some of these plantation owners, especially Weeks—and he isn't the worst."

"Those slaves are human beings, Doctor. They have souls and they deserve the same rights we enjoy under our Constitution. Even our former enemy, Great Britain, has outlawed the slave trade. There is a growing movement within the empire to end slavery altogether."

Doc was impressed with her knowledge of world affairs. In 1807 the British Empire had indeed abolished the slave trade; in particular it focused upon the Atlantic slave trade, which had direct consequences in America. He decided to turn the conversation to his advantage.

"Then you know our country has also outlawed the slave trade."

"But not slavery itself."

"No. But let us applaud the British for making inroads. In a series of brilliant diplomatic treaties they have worked hard to stop the trade. They brought the Swedes to the table in 1813, and the Dutch in 1814. Both countries have now outlawed the trade. Your beloved French, under force of yet another Anglo-engineered treaty, will abolish it in four more years. They have declared publically that the slave trade is, and I quote, 'repugnant to the principles of natural justice.' Even recalcitrant Spain has promised to suppress its trade by 1820."

Solange was impressed, but not distracted. "You avoided answering my question, Doctor."

"And what was that?"

"Do you accept slavery?"

"I was not aware you had asked."

"I am asking now."

Doc knew he must choose his words carefully. Solange obviously held different views on the institution and he suspected she was even more passionate than she revealed. The argument came to him like an epiphany.

"Forgive me for bringing attention to my own actions, but you must certainly agree that actions speak louder than words. In the past three days we have worked together, side by side, on two almost-identical medical cases. Did I at any time demonstrate partiality toward one mother? Did I use different instruments or practice dissimilar procedures? Could you claim that I provided shoddier care for the slave infant?"

"You are a man after my own heart, Doctor Applegate."

"Then, will you dine with me at some time in the near future?" he asked.

"I would be delighted," Solange replied.

Breckinridge County, Kentucky—November 8, 1815

Craig rapped on Cecilia Dowell's front door. He could make out hushed voices, male and female. After a few moments, he rapped again. The talking ceased and presently the door opened a crack. It was dark within and he could barely make out the woman's face.

"Yes? Who is it?" Cecilia asked cautiously.

"My name is Craig Ridgeway, Mrs. Dowell. I have come from Cottonwood Bend."

"What is your business here, young man?"

"I am here to see Judge Bozarth."

"And what makes you think he is here?" She opened the door a bit wider and shot him a cold glance. His first impression was of a head crowned with masses upon masses of wild, curly black hair. He could smell the fumes of whiskey on her breath.

"Uh—" Craig hesitated, wrong-footed by her stare and abundant womanhood. "That is his chestnut mare in the stable."

Now it was Cecilia's turn to be uncomfortable. "I see. Wait outside, please." She disappeared from sight.

Craig stepped back to wait, watching the gray clouds and hoping it would not rain. Cecilia had carelessly left the door ajar, so he could overhear most of the conversation that came from a back room. Although they attempted to speak in hushed tones, it sounded like they were shouting.

"Who is he?" the Judge grumbled as if awakened from slumber.

"Ridge-something-or-other," Cecilia slurred. "He's a right handsome young man."

"Anybody can claim they are someone else. What does he look like?"

"About my height, perhaps a little taller with broad shoulders, dark brown hair, brown eyes. Says he hails from Cottonwood Bend."

"Umm, it sounds like young Ridgeway. He is a fine lad. We have nothing to fear. What does he want?"

"He just said he wanted to see you."

"Well, tell him I am engaged in important paperwork."

"And admit you are here—alone with me?"

"Make up a story. Tell him your aged aunt is taking her afternoon nap and cannot be disturbed."

"You are so brilliant. That is why I love you."

Craig heard kissing and slurping noises in the silence that followed. "Quit it!" the Judge growled. "Just give him an excuse and send him on his way."

"Then may we—?"

"Yes! Yes!"

Cecilia appeared at the doorway again and opened it wider. The Judge's words had dispelled her earlier reserve and now she regarded Craig with an amused expression. Her face was flushed and she was breathing as if she had run up a long hill. She tossed back the wild cascade of her thick, lustrous curls. For the first time Craig noticed her big violet-blue eyes, heavy lids, long lashes, and full lips parted from recent excitement. He saw instantly why the Judge was drawn to her.

She began her recitation. "I am sorry, but the Judge is busy with paperwork and cannot be disturbed. Also, my aged aunt is taking her afternoon nap."

"I have come a long way—and it is important."

"Then give me the message. You may rest assured I will relay it to him."

Craig struggled to find the right words without divulging specific details to her. "There is a family issue that requires his attention."

Her eyes widened with shock and perhaps guilt. "What issue?"

"I am not at liberty to say. Please tell him his presence is urgently needed." He turned to leave.

"Wait!" she commanded. "I will ask if the Judge can spare a few moments. You must understand—he is a busy man."

This time she left the door open wider. Craig heard the conversation resume.

"Wilfred, he insists that a family matter requires your immediate presence."

"Oh hell!" the Judge roared. "Give me some time to put on my clothes. Where are those contracts?"

"In the dining room chest, top drawer."

"Please, lay them out for me. And find my reading glasses. Keep him occupied until I am dressed and ready."

"How do I do that?" she whispered.

"You are not without assets. Use them as you see fit."

Cecilia giggled naughtily. A few instants later Craig heard her rustling papers in the room nearest the door. He stepped back from the porch. Sometime later she appeared with a man's greatcoat loosely thrown over her shoulders. "The Judge will see you shortly. My, but it is cold for this time of year!"

"Yes ma'am."

"I have never seen you before. What did you say your name

was?"

"Craig Ridgeway, ma'am."

"And what do you do for a living, Craig Ridgeway?" She advanced a step toward him and he judiciously gave ground. Her eyes glinted with amusement. She obviously enjoyed exercising her female dominance.

"I am a farmer, ma'am."

"Are you married?"

"Yes ma'am."

"Any children?"

"Two."

"You are a handsome man, Craig. Your wife is fortunate."

As if by accident Cecilia allowed her coat to drop, revealing an almost-sheer ivory-colored linen gown. Casually, she rewrapped the coat around her shoulders, but not before Craig caught a glimpse of her generous bosom and deep cleavage. He averted his eyes and stepped back another pace.

"I believe the Judge is ready to receive you," she announced, almost laughing. "Come inside."

Craig glanced toward the Hardinsburg Road, hoping that no one would see him enter. If that happened, he might find himself caught up the same web of gossip that surrounded the Judge. For Mary's sake he stepped inside. The house was clean and well-furnished. A pair of candles burned at the dining room table where the great personage himself was ensconced, busying himself among various sheaves of papers scattered haphazardly across the surface. He looked up, peering over a set of wire-framed reading glasses.

"Why, Craig Ridgeway!" Judge Bozarth boomed, slapping his palm on the table as if taken by complete surprise. He took off his glasses. "It is good to see you, lad! You look exceedingly well!" He did not bother to rise, but extended his hand. His normally slicked-back mane was tousled and his speech slurred from recent sleep, whiskey, or both. He sat at the table barefooted, his shirttails dangling and one suspender hanging off his left shoulder.

"Thank you, Judge," Craig pretended not to notice.

"Mrs. Dowell, would you please brew some coffee for young Ridgeway?"

"Yes, Wilfred," she addressed him in the familiar and set about brewing the coffee.

Craig noticed a slight flare of annoyance flicker across his face, but in an instant the Judge resurrected his broad, big-toothed grin, lighting the room like a sunrise.

"Please, please take a seat. As you can see, I have been busy with Mrs. Dowell's legal papers. Rather complicated legal stuff, lad, I won't bore you with the particulars. Now, why are you looking for me?"

"There is an illness in the family. I have been sent to fetch you." Craig sneaked a glance at Cecilia who busied herself at the hearth, listening to his every word. He hoped the Judge would not press for details.

"Yes, lad. We'll just have our coffee. I will finish up here and join you on the ride back." The old rogue knew exactly what the problem was; he also knew better than to ask further potentially embarrassing questions.

"We should get a start before darkness sets in," Craig pointed out. "There will be no moon tonight. I do not know the road that well."

"Quite right, lad. Not to worry yourself. I have traveled the route so often it is like finding my way to the outhouse. Mrs. Dowell, will you please hurry with the coffee?"

Cecilia brought two stone mugs to the table and then retrieved the coffee pot. She wore nothing but the sheer linen gown. Her breasts protruded like round melons, standing out firmly, with dark rose-colored circles straining against the sheer fabric. Her voluptuous hips curved outward, flattening the front of the gown so that the wide furry wedge of her sex showed through, every bit as thick, black and curly as the hair on her head. Craig glanced away and concentrated on the drapes across the room.

Cecilia stood over him and asked, "Would you like sugar and cream in your coffee, Craig Ridgeway?"

"Just cream, ma'am," he croaked hoarsely, praying that the Judge would not notice his discomfiture.

As she reached across the table to retrieve the creamer, one of her breasts brushed the side of his head. Craig recoiled, certain the act was deliberate. Glancing up, he spied the thick bush of curls in her armpit, dewed with sweat from the fireplace heat. He caught a full whiff of her musky scent and squirmed uncomfortably, fearing that, when the time came, he would not be able to rise from the table. Judging from her expression, he realized that she knew exactly the effect she had engendered.

The Judge made small talk and pretended to rifle through the papers. "It seems that everything is in order here. He downed his cup with theatrical flourish. "Drink up, my boy!" The coffee was warming and Craig was grateful for it.

"Craig, if I could impose upon Mrs. Dowell to provide you with a lamp, would you mind saddling my mare? That way I can finish up here and we can be off the sooner."

"Sure, Judge," Craig replied.

"You will find my saddlery in the same stall as the mare."

Cecilia lifted a small brass-framed, boxlike contraption from the mantle and with a pine taper lit the candlewick within. Craig noticed how the polished glass panes reflected and magnified the light. She handed the lamp to him and he retreated eagerly toward the front door.

By the time Craig saddled the mare, the Judge had donned his boots, black traveling coat, and broad-brimmed hat. He stood on the porch talking quietly with Cecilia as Craig led both horses toward them.

"Until next week, my dear?" Craig heard the Judge murmur.

"I suppose, Wilfred," Cecilia replied sulkily, eyes cast downward. She had wrapped herself in the oversized coat and looked considerably deflated, no doubt frustrated that their afternoon tryst had been interrupted and that the Judge would not be spending another night.

Judge Bozarth straightened up when Craig reached the porch.

"Yes, yes! We must be away. Mustn't keep the dear, infirm relation waiting!" Majestically he mounted his horse and swept his hat in a gesture of farewell. He clucked once and the big chestnut mare cantered smoothly toward the Hardinsburg Road. The Judge always cut a fine figure in the saddle.

Craig swung aboard his horse. "Thank you for the hot coffee, ma'am."

"My pleasure," Cecilia replied with a half-smile.

He clamped his heels and Blue galloped off in eager pursuit of the other horse. They caught up just as the Judge turned onto the road. As gray daylight waned around them they rode side-by-side, not talking. Hoof falls and squeaking saddle leather were the only sounds for a long time. Craig knew from the outset that the ride home would be awkward. What was there to say? The Judge had gone through all those silly pretenses, knowing full well he was fooling no one. He was sobering up fast and reality was beginning to crash in upon him. No longer the swaggering peacock, his regal bearing diminished sadly into a pitiable slouch. His head hung low. He had been caught out and now he was figuring all the angles, how to put the best face upon it all. Finally, he asked the question he was unable to ask at Cecilia's house.

"How bad is she?"

Craig hesitated and then decided to give it to him straight. "She showed up drunk at our house. She had done a terrible job hitching the wagon. I took care of it and the horse."

"What else can you tell me?"

"She was so drunk she passed out twice—once at the table and once on the floor. Mary put her to bed. I imagine she is still sleeping."

"Oh, dammit to hell! Does she know about—?" His voice trailed off as he leaned in for the answer.

"She knows," Craig confirmed, thankful for the near darkness. He did not want to look at the Judge.

A low, rumbling sound emanated deep from the depths of Judge Bozarth's emotions, an almost animalistic growl that grew louder with each step of his horse. It took some time for Craig to realize that the great man was weeping. This was an emotion he did not expect.

"I know what you and Mary must think of me!" he burst out.

"Well, we care—that is why I have fetched you. This is a family problem, something for you and Violet to work out."

"Oh, Lord! I do love her—with all my heart! You must believe that! I never intended for any of this to happen!" The Judge was in full swing, bawling out loud, letting all of his emotions flow. Then, almost instantly, he ceased his lamentations and pressed, "What else can you tell me?"

"I am not sure what I should tell you," Craig replied honestly. "Violet was extremely upset. She said an awful lot. You had best sit down and talk it out with her."

"You mustn't think ill of me, lad."

"I do not think ill of you, Judge." Craig almost meant it. After experiencing firsthand Cecilia's overpowering womanhood, he understood at least part of what the Judge was saying.

"You may not credit this, but it is an unsafe world for those chosen few who are blessed with good looks, power, wealth, and magnetism. Women are drawn to us, especially those women of a predatory nature. They instinctively realize that our loins are the most vulnerable of our considerable attributes, and they know precisely how to exploit them. *We* are the victims who suffer, for it is we who have the most to lose! Think of Samson, the Kings of Israel, and of all those great men undone by the so-called 'fairer sex.' You will find it recorded throughout all of history, written time and again in literature. And look you to the animal kingdom—the female of the species is invariably the deadliest!"

"You may be correct."

"Are you and Mary the only ones who know?"

"I had to ask Martin for directions to Cecilia's house."

The Judge roared, throwing his head back in real anguish. "Oh, my dear Lord! Undeniably the finest man in the countryside. My shame is complete. What a world! What a world!"

"I think he understands. He doesn't condemn, and he would never discuss it with anyone."

"I am confident I may also rely upon your discretion."

"You may."

"Does anyone else know?"

Craig remained silent. He figured that Violet should be the one to tell him the whole countryside knew. But his silence was as damning as if he had replied.

Reaching into his deep well of indignation, the Judge wailed, "It is always the same! I am forever hounded by those lesser men who question my honor, my intelligence, my honesty, my character, even my love of this fair country!"

Darkness closed upon them on the descent into Hite's Run. Craig allowed Judge Bozarth to lead the way, leaving him to sort out his thoughts. Every now and then he could hear him muttering, no doubt rehearsing for his encounter with Violet. Blue used his keen animal senses of sight, hearing, and smell to follow. Craig held back a couple of lengths to avoid getting whipped by bent-back scrub branches. The flats presented no real navigational challenge. Although it was pitch black in the valley, the Judge took his bearings on distant cabin lights, leading them unerringly to the wooden bridge. This time Blue crossed without incident. He had settled into a dependable mount, content to follow where the chestnut mare trod.

It was long past suppertime when they reached the cabin. Mary had a fire blazing, and the windows glowed from candlelight. Judge Bozarth dismounted, hesitating an instant before entering the cabin. Craig led the horses to the barn to unsaddle, water, and feed them. He also forked hay for the other stock, including Violet's cart horse. When he felt the cows' udders it appeared that Mary, or perhaps Martin, had taken care of milking. He busied himself with chores a while longer, sorely tempted to avoid the conflict within. But it did not seem fair to leave Mary and the children alone with the angry couple. He steeled himself to walk toward the cabin.

Inside, Judge Bozarth was putting on a grand show of remorse, worthy of any stage in London. He knelt before the dining table, arms outstretched in desperate appeal. His face was contorted in agony and he wept openly, great tears streaming in rivulets and glistening in the firelight. Violet sat in a chair, regarding him stonily, content to let him humiliate himself.

"Oh, Violet! You must forgive me! I would be forever lost without your love—without you!"

"Did you think of *that* while you were entangled in her arms? You were gone four nights, Wilfred. And do not presume to tell me this is the first time. That would insult us both!"

"It was; I swear it!"

"For months the whole county has been talking about it—gossiping and sniggering behind our backs! How can I ever again face the women of this community?"

"Violet! You are not to blame! I am the one at fault! I alone brought this disgrace upon our house. It is my transgression, not yours!"

"And how would you feel if I took up with another man? What would that do to your precious political career?"

"Oh, damn my weakness, my physical frailties, my surrender to that vixen's wicked snares! Pray, tell me what I might do to atone for my sins, and, even more, to make amends to you?"

"There is nothing you can do, Wilfred. It is over. I plan to take the next steamboat to New Orleans and thence travel by sea to my family's home on the Chesapeake. You may take lodging in the boarding house until such time as I can make my arrangements. I will then secure a lawyer and sue for divorce."

"Please, please reconsider! I love only you, Violet! You are my heart, my very soul!" He groaned aloud in obviously severe mental anguish.

Craig skirted cautiously around the Judge who now prostrated himself fully upon the floor, thrashing about in total mortification. It seemed there was no limit to the extent he was willing to debase himself. Mary and the girls huddled by the fireplace at the far end of the room. Craig embraced them, putting on a cheerful face for Isabel.

Tossing a few sticks of wood onto the fire he asked Mary, "Do you think we should retreat into the cookhouse?"

Mary whispered, "No, this will end shortly. She plans to forgive him, Craig."

He glanced at Violet in disbelief. "You are not serious."

"We talked again after she woke up. She is livid, understandably hurt. But before she forgives, she wants to make him suffer."

"He is doing an exceptionally good job of it. But must *we* suffer listening to this?"

"Hush and watch!"

Judge Bozarth pleaded again in earnest. "Oh please, Violet, give me another chance. Tell me what I must do to win your love as I did in those halcyon days of our youth. All I have is yours. All that I have achieved was made possible with you at my side. You are my rock, my very bastion, and I have failed you—I freely admit my guilt! Now, I must confess the real reason—I fear growing old, Violet. The affair seemed somehow a way to recapture my youth. The woman means nothing to me—I swear it by all that is sacred."

Mary took up a pothook and swung one of the fire irons over, lifting the lid from the stewpot. She ladled a generous helping of stew into the bowl. "Are you hungry, Craig?"

"Famished! Thank you!"

"There is a little coffee left. Violet nearly drank the whole pot."

The family drama played on for some time longer. If Craig were not so tired, it would have been great entertainment. The Judge's wailing intensified and his financial promises waxed ever more grandiloquently. He finally won out by promising to never see Cecilia again, by offering to host a number of expensive banquets in their home, and by appearing with her on his arm in more public events.

"That is right!" he boomed. "We will brazen it out—hold our heads high and proclaim to the world our love for each other, knowing all along that it is I who wronged you! You are the righteous one and everyone in Cottonwood Bend knows that. They will admire you all the more for taking me back."

Finally Violet agreed to allow him to return home, but she insisted on sleeping in separate rooms for the first week. The Judge agreed with alacrity. He rose from the floor and they embraced. They broke into tears and held on to each other for a long time. Despite himself, Craig was touched by the scene; for him it seemed the most sincere part of the evening.

Mary whispered, "Believe it or not, Craig, you are witnessing reconciliation and true love. Not every marriage could survive such a storm."

Craig realized with a shock that she was right. They were, despite all the theatrical pretenses, human beings with human frailties. Martin was also right—it was not his place to condemn others.

Judge Bozarth followed him out to the barn and together they hitched up Violet's wagon, saddled the chestnut mare and tied it behind the wagon. Together they walked back to the cabin.

"I want to thank you for fetching me, Craig," the Judge spoke in earnest, still shaken from his ordeal. He certainly was a different person in private, not at all the pompous public character everyone knew.

"There is nothing to thank me for, Judge. I am just glad everything turned out well for you and Violet."

"You are a young man of strong moral fiber, one of our community's finest. I sincerely regret that you and your family were forced to bear witness to such a spectacle. I am an old fool who nearly lost it all. Do not ever stray as I have done. Promise me that."

"I promise, Judge."

Mary escorted Violet outside and the Judge tenderly helped her into the wagon. The couple drove off into the darkness with Violet leaning her head against his shoulder. Craig guessed that her condition of sleeping in separate rooms would be broken that evening. He just hoped that, after his previous four-day ordeal, the Judge was up to the task.

Later, after the children were put to bed, he reached for Mary under the covers. He explored her body hungrily and pulled her to him with an urgency that surprised them both.

"My, my, Mister Ridgeway! What has gotten into you?" Mary asked, chuckling with mixed bemusement and delight.

He knew better than to mention the sheer force of Cecilia's feminine power, the enticing sights and scents that inflamed him even now. It was as if the temptress had unleashed a raw animalistic passion, goading him several times in the night to awaken with desire. When he finally slept, the nightmares of Chalmette Plantation did not return to plague him.

The French Quarter, New Orleans—December 12, 1815

Dinner at the Hotel d'Orleans was a delightful affair. Doc Applegate and Solange Tourigny laughed over the wine, sautéed shrimp appetizers, salads, and main courses rivaling those of the best restaurants in Paris. They were dining with the American merchant, James Vogel and his wife, Nadine.

Earlier that month, Doc had treated Vogel for a severe bronchial condition, and his remedies had brought about a miraculous recovery. Instead of accepting payment in coin, Doc suggested that the Vogels take him and Solange Tourigny out for a meal. The couple agreed to act as chaperones, although their presence was truly not required. Widows, especially older ones, occupied a special place in New Orleans society; they were far more independent than spinsters or married women. So long as they behaved discreetly, they could do pretty much what they pleased without arousing a great deal of criticism. Still, Doc congratulated himself on his decision. The Vogels proved great company, and they knew instinctively when to make themselves scarce. After dinner they took coffee and dessert in the spacious lounge where many of Doc's former and current patients paid respects.

"You are a popular man, Doctor," Solange acknowledged. She had obviously taken extra care with her appearance as he had with his.

"I see many people in my profession," Doc waved his hand airily. This dinner reminded him of his first courtship, but without the awkwardness of youth. He liked the current direction his life was taking; he was experiencing a complete renaissance of his career, self-respect, and place in society, as if his previous failures were forever buried.

Life at Jules Signet's townhouse was extravagant, but that arrangement would soon end. Last night Alain Morel had visited to pore over the final details of the inquest, working hard into the late hours, all under the watchful, anxious eye of his host. They planned the event for mid-January, although their victim was still completely unaware. Doc felt twinges of guilt gnawing at his conscience, but brushed them aside. To maintain a semblance of this life, he must follow through. Perhaps, after the inquest, he could begin anew in another city, perhaps become a country doctor up north, away from the humid vapors and evil temptations of New Orleans. It was a thought worth nurturing.

Solange sipped her coffee and asked, "Have you many patients?"

"Yes, I do. I treat who I can, when I can, without keeping a regular office schedule."

"And you offer your expertise to all?"

"That is included in the Hippocratic Oath. I have never refused a patient in need. Many of them cannot pay."

"Including slaves?"

"Their masters pay well enough. And I often practice in the American sector."

"Isn't it dangerous? One reads such horrible stories in the papers."

"It can be. Usually, I am called in after a disturbance and the majority of those cases are gunshot and knife wounds. Oh yes, there are often a lot of broken bones and cracked skulls."

"It sounds terribly unsafe."

"Not if you know the right people."

"From what I have seen, you move freely among all social classes. May I ask, do you now live with Jules Signet? Do not answer if you consider the question impolite."

Doc realized that Solange knew more about him than he figured. "He has employed me at the present. I own a small house in the new American sector, but it is nothing to brag about."

"Are you friends with him?"

Doc answered, "I wouldn't say that. We are more like business partners."

"Then I am concerned for your safety, doctor."

"I don't think you have reason to worry."

"The nuns claim he rescued you from the gutter. If Jules Signet is doing you a kindness, you may be certain he has an ulterior motive."

The Doc's expression fell. He had tried so hard to make the right impression, conceal his weaknesses, and put his past behind him. Did she know about the gambling as well? Silence was his only defense and it encouraged her to continue.

"It may appear he has your best interests at heart, but I must warn you. He is a dangerous man—a greedy one—who will stop at nothing to get what he wants."

"What makes you say that?" Doc had long ago come to the same conclusion.

"Remember when I told you about my husband?"

"Yes."

"Because of Signet we lost everything. *He* is the banker who brought suit against us after enticing Léon into a number of shady business deals. As a rich banker, Signet could afford the most expensive lawyers. And he is good friends with all the other lawyers, bankers, merchants, and city elite. He ruined us completely, and I am convinced he killed my husband."

"Killed him?" Doc felt a shiver run up his spine.

"Not physically. Léon's spirit was completely broken. When illness besieged, he lost his will to fight. One could not prove it in court, but I know, as sure as I am sitting here, that Signet killed him."

"Who was the lawyer?" Doc asked, but he already knew the answer.

"Alain Morel," Solange replied without hesitation. "He is the top lawyer in the city."

Doc sipped his coffee and considered this new revelation. He had not known Léon Tourigny, or heard of the lawsuit, but he could see clear comparisons in the upcoming case in which he played a major role. The guilt returned; this time he could not so easily brush it aside.

Solange continued, "That is why I now live in the convent."

His heart went out to her. "You once told me that you give all your earnings to the sisters. You will never be able leave if you do not save your money."

"What makes you think I wish to leave?"

"You are too young, too vital to remain locked up in a convent."

Solange laughed. "I am not a prisoner. Why do people view convents and monasteries as prisons?"

"I don't know, but I am quite certain of this—you appreciate life in the outside world. Credit me, a physician, for understanding human nature. I have observed you at work. You derive true satisfaction from what you do. You have a gift for healing; I know you possess a fine mind. There are many other aspects of the medical field that you could learn."

"That I do not doubt."

"The human race is an interesting one. It produces all imaginable sorts of individuals—male and female, rich and poor, intelligent and dumb, tall and short, fat and thin, moral and immoral—and every gradation in between. I have treated them all from the finest to the meanest creatures on earth. In the end, they are all flesh, blood, and bone with the same finiteness, same fears, and same ultimate destiny. They need folks like us."

"Perhaps I will one day decide to leave the convent. I am not ready yet. I confess I still grieve for Léon."

"Understandable. I lost my wife ten years ago and never remarried."

"Have you never considered remarriage?"

"Now, who would want a rotten scoundrel like me?" Doc re-

called the wild times during his first years as a widower. He had
gone on a spree, enjoying the initial thrill of freedom, dallying in a
wide selection of whores, slave girls, and loose women. Wisely, he
had abandoned that perilous course of debauchery. He would keep
that chapter forever buried.

Solange laughed, "I know several widows who long to have a
kind, like-minded companion for a husband."

Doc experienced a sense of boyish hope. Despite what the nuns
had told her, she obviously held him in some esteem. He had new
reasons to regret his involvement in Signet's upcoming scheme.

He wished the evening could go on forever, but it was growing
late. Solange shared the back seat of Vogel's carriage and they talked quietly on the drive home. Doc shared his plans to leave New
Orleans and start a new practice in a quiet northern state. Solange
listened respectfully and asked a few pertinent questions. This time,
when they reached the convent, she allowed him to walk her to the
door. She took his hand and squeezed it in farewell.

"Thank you, Doctor Applegate, for a wonderful evening."

"The pleasure was mine, Madame Tourigny."

On the drive back to Signet's house, Doc considered all Solange
had disclosed. There was no reason to doubt her. The banker had
likely concocted a number of "lucrative" business ventures to attract
eager investors. Her husband had obviously fallen into his snare. No
doubt Alain Morel had engineered the wording of the contracts and
venture strategies, as he was doing now with the upcoming case.
What she said about Signet was undoubtedly true.

*"It may appear he has your best interests at heart, but I must
warn you. He is a dangerous man—a greedy one—who will stop at
nothing to get what he wants."*

Doc decided then to move back into his own house.

Chapter Five

Breckinridge County, Kentucky—December 15, 1815

"Craig Ridgeway!" a man shouted from outside Martin McDonnell's tobacco barn. "Is Craig Ridgeway inside the barn?" The voice was strident with urgency. The horse was blowing with exhaustion; clearly something was amiss.

"Wait here," Martin counseled softly, his senses alerted to possible danger. He picked up a shotgun near the stripping room door. "It sounds like trouble."

Craig regretted he had not brought his rifle. Ever since the war he had been content to leave it on the mantle when going out to work. Now, he and the McDonnell brothers scrabbled around for farm implements with which to arm themselves. Owen slid along the inside wall and picked up a long-tined pitchfork. Stephen grabbed a long-handled hoe. Craig found a hand axe and a broad-bladed corn knife.

Then Martin called in reassuringly. "Come on out, boys. It is Calvin Ward."

Calvin was one of Judge Bozarth's right hand militiamen and recognized as one of the best game trackers in Breckinridge County. He also tracked men, on those rare occasions when the Regulators were called out. Craig and his brothers-in-law joined Martin outside the barn just as Calvin reined in his mount.

"What can we do for you Calvin?" Martin asked.

"Judge Bozarth has sent me to fetch Craig."

"Why?" Craig asked.

"Seven men come through Hardinsburg this morning leadin' your nigger and his family southward. Actually, they swung west of town to avoid folks, but Billy Rose's wife and several others seen 'em crossin' their cow pasture."

"When exactly was this?"

"I'd say shortly before mid-mornin'."

"How do you know it was my man?"

"The Judge knows. Says he was a one-eyed giant, all beat up and bloody, with a woman and two small children."

Craig felt sick to his stomach. The description certainly fit Romulus and family. He wondered what trouble had befallen them.

"What does Judge Bozarth want Craig to do?" Martin asked.

Calvin replied, "Judge wants to ride after 'em. He's certain-sure the men are no-good trash. Says they're lookin' to make some fast money with Craig's niggers and he wants Craig to meet him at Mattingly's Rock just south of the Hardinsburg Road. Judge says they're takin' the trail to Hartford. We can catch 'em tonight, if we move now. He's raisin' a force as we speak."

Although inflamed and eager to take immediate action, Craig glanced at Martin for advice. The old man nodded. "You must go, Craig. Even though you freed him, he is still your responsibility."

"I am ready now."

"Good," Calvin said. "Go fetch your weapons, powder, and shot. Saddle your horse and meet me on the road in front of your cabin. I will ride into Cottonwood Bend to pick up some of the boys and get myself a fresh mount." He spurred his horse toward the settlement.

"I'll go with you," Owen volunteered.

"Me too!" Stephen added.

Both brothers headed off toward Welcome Hall. Fear flickered across Martin's face, but only for an instant. Then it was replaced by grim resolve. "The men Bozarth seeks are undoubtedly patrollers who make their careers by capturing runaways, snatching freedmen, or even stealing slaves to resell them in the south."

"But Romulus was in free territory!" Craig seethed. "It is criminal!"

"Unfortunately these acts often occur, despite the law. Slave prices have shot so high that many lawbreakers are willing to take the chance."

Craig's anger surged anew. Romulus and Vergina had suffered unspeakable tribulations. They had overcome much of their anger and distrust, working hard and saving money for their chance at freedom. Martin was right—he must help them. They truly were his responsibility.

"Do you remember, Craig, when I told you the Judge would one day repay you? He could have easily let those patrollers pass through. This is undoubtedly his way of showing gratitude."

"You were right, Martin." Craig dashed back to his cabin where he explained the situation to Mary. She did not waste time with questions; she immediately began packing what he needed. After forking some hay for the animals, he caught and saddled Blue. The horse behaved much less skittishly this time around. Since his journey to fetch the Judge, Craig had ridden him on three Sunday outings. The familiarity between them was growing stronger. Craig led him to the cabin and tied his reins to the hitching rail behind the stone cookhouse.

Mary had laid out his .40 caliber Lancaster rifle, the stubby, double-barreled shotgun, and his brace of .69 caliber North & Cheney pistols. Craig checked the loads and primed all weapons, then packed an ample supply of paper cartridges and shot into his leather possibles bag. Knowing he might not return that evening, Mary had filled a small cloth bag with a quarter loaf of bread, some dried apple slices, a wedge of cheese, and some cooked bacon. This might have to serve as both supper and breakfast. She filled the leather water bag with cold spring water and stoppered it with an oaken plug. Craig donned his wide leather belt and slid his tomahawk and knife into the strong leather loops Mary had sewn.

Outside, Mary helped him hang and cinch the short leather saddle scabbards that would carry his pistols. Another longer scabbard held the shotgun. The last time he had lugged this much armament was right before the Battle of New Orleans.

"You have done a nice job, Mary." He kissed her tenderly.

"You will take care of yourself?"

"I intend to."

"I pray they have not been badly abused!" Mary sighed. "Please bring them back, Craig."

"I'll do my best," he promised. "The Judge is heading up a Party of Regulators from Cottonwood Bend, and he may have help from the sheriff in Hardinsburg. We should outnumber and outgun the slave catchers."

Owen and Stephen waited for him on the road. Presently Calvin Ward arrived, accompanied by two riders from Cottonwood Bend, not quite the delegation Craig expected.

"Is this it?" Owen asked when the three men rode up.

"They're all I could find. We don't have much time. Judge would like to catch 'em before dark. He should have some men from Hardinsburg with him."

Craig noticed that the men were at least well-mounted and well-armed. They all set out at a brisk trot. Blue's long springy gait kept taking him out in front as they ascended the ridge overlooking a large part of Breckinridge County. It was another gray, overcast day, but fortunately the clouds did not threaten rain. From this elevation Craig spotted the steely gray sweep of the Ohio where it curved northward at Cottonwood Bend. Calvin edged his mount alongside.

"That's a fine blue roan!" he commented. "He may be the tallest horse I've ever seen. You interested in sellin'?"

"No thank you."

"Well, I am glad I have got you alone. Before I left Hardinsburg, the Judge gave me an order. After we climb out of Hite's Run he wants you to speed up and ride ahead of us."

"What on earth for?"

"He claims you know from previous experience where to find him. When you do that, he will lead you to Mattingly's Rock, where we will be waiting."

Craig tried unsuccessfully to hide his disgust. After all the weeping and apparent repentance, Judge Bozarth had fallen back into his cheating ways. It was hard to believe, for his guilt and remorse had seemed so genuine. The Judge had behaved hysterically, so frightened was he of losing all. He had ardently and publically professed his love for Violet and, true to his word, appeared all over town with her—calling on friends, shopping at Rosenbotham's store, and hosting elaborate socials in their home. The Judge had even taken it a notch higher, singing a duet with her at the Baptist church. Her performance, underscored by the exquisite resonance of his deep baritone, had by all accounts moved the congregation, especially Brother Kreisle and his wife, to tears.

The Judge had sincerely cautioned Craig to never fall prey to the weakness that afflicted him. Had it all been theatrics? Craig did not think so. Perhaps Cecilia Dowell's considerable bedroom charms had overwhelmed his resolve. Craig decided to put it out of his mind. The Judge had offered to help, and for that he was truly grateful.

They emerged onto the high ground beyond Hite's Run where a damp southerly breeze soughed through the cedars. Patches of pale blue sky appeared intermittently among the more abundant gray clouds. Craig viewed the surrounding farms with their pastures seared golden brown by repeated frosts. He wondered where the slavecatchers had crossed the road.

Presently, Calvin signaled for him to ride ahead. Craig urged Blue into a smooth, long-reaching lope that soon carried him far ahead of the others. It did not take long to reach Cecilia Dowell's house. This time he cantered straight up to the porch, dismounted and knocked on the door. Cecilia opened it and invited him in. Judge Bozarth was seated in a big cloth-covered armchair, pulling on his boots. He was otherwise fully dressed in black trousers, white frock, black greatcoat and hat.

"Good afternoon Craig! I can see you received my message. It is helpful you have arrived so soon."

"Thank you for summoning me, Judge."

"You brought plenty of arms?"

"Yes."

Judge Bozarth rose and patted the polished wood handle of a double barreled pistol stuck into his belt. Cecilia helped him buckle on his military saber. He noticed Craig's expression. "Good. I stopped here, only briefly, to conduct business. My mare is saddled and ready to ride. Will you please fetch her?"

Craig knew exactly where to find the mare and was truly glad she was saddled. He examined the fine long rifle and brace of long-barreled pistols hanging in their leather scabbards. Bozarth and Cecilia waited for him on the porch. Obviously the Judge had convinced her he could be trusted to keep silence. She unreservedly clung to him and kissed him fully upon his lips, displaying no shame. "Take care, Wilfred. The men may be dangerous."

"Bah!" the Judge tossed his head back and scoffed, adding a reckless little laugh. "I do not fear them, Cecilia. They represent the lowest refuse of humanity. We shall soon bring them to hand." Without further ado he swung into the saddle, swept his hat in his characteristic gesture of farewell and set off for the Hardinsburg Road.

This time Craig rode out alongside him, hoping his braggadocio would not bring misfortune down upon them. Instead of turning east, the Judge reined his horse westward along the route Craig had just traveled. This was not what he had expected.

"Are we headed to Mattingly's Rock?"

"We are indeed," the Judge affirmed. "There is a game trail that cuts diagonally southwest and intersects with the Hardinsburg-Hartford-Greenville Road. It is a shortcut. I estimate we will overtake our unsavory quarry this very night."

"I really do appreciate this, Judge," Craig said.

"Think nothing of it, lad. You have done me a good turn. We shall soon retrieve your slaves."

"I think I should let you know that I freed them. They were carrying their manumission papers when they left."

"Not to worry. You may reassume responsibility for them and employ them on your farm, as long as the county is not liable for their welfare."

"I understand that. But how can they ever gain true freedom?"

"Let us take one step at a time and concentrate on delivering them from their abductors."

Judge Bozarth turned off the road onto a fairly well-defined animal trail. Dark cedars closed in around them, obscuring the bends ahead. This was wild country broken occasionally by great limestone cliffs. Tall beech trees stretched their bare, gnarled branches toward the darkening December sky as if in supplication, begging for the warm sunlight of summer. Craig clutched his rifle and searched the undergrowth for a possible ambush. The Judge unerringly picked his way through the cedar forest and into the tall timber where the brush thinned out. Up ahead, Craig spied the horses of their party. They waited at the base of a massive egg-shaped boulder locals called 'Mattingly's Rock.' This strange monolith marked where the game trail crossed the road.

Calvin waited until they drew near before speaking in hushed tones. "Howdy, Judge. I've already cut their sign and it's just as you claimed—four horses headin' south. Three of the men and Craig's slaves are on foot." He pointed to a string of green horse turds in the road. "They're not that far ahead of us."

"Good, good!" the Judge rubbed his palms together and his eyes gleamed with anticipation. It was evident that he looked forward to the impending encounter. His countenance fell slightly as he studied the Mc Donnell brothers and two Cottonwood Bend militiamen. "Is this all you could muster?"

"I figured you would also bring some men from Hardinsburg," Calvin replied.

The Judge cleared his throat in embarrassment. "Well, unfortunately I was forced to attend to some legal business and was unable to lodge a formal request with the sheriff."

Craig could have clubbed him over the head. The incorrigible reprobate had decided to rely solely on Calvin's recruiting efforts so he could spend an afternoon enmeshed in the passionate clutches of Cecilia Dowell.

"I hoped to bring more." Calvin rubbed his chin whiskers ashamedly.

"Well, like us they are seven men. We are sufficient to dispatch the likes of them," the Judge announced. His confidence did not make Craig feel any easier. They ventured out onto the road, an old buffalo trail that cut south-southwest between high banks. It was covered with a deep carpet of brown and gold leaves fallen from a dense forest of oak, maple, sweet gum, beech, hickory, elm, and sycamore. These trees towered ominously overhead. The breeze stopped altogether and the forest lay silent.

"Men, gather round," the Judge commanded. When everyone had nudged their horses into a tight circle, he laid out his plan. "First of all, you may assure yourselves that I have engaged in this sort of action a hundred times or more. I expect you to follow my instructions to the letter. It is all very straightforward. Silence is of paramount importance. Once we set off, there will be no talking above a whisper. Calvin Ward is our scout. We have worked together many times, and I trust him completely. He will ride ahead, locate the outlaws, and make a full appraisal of their camp. After he has evaluated their disposition he will ride back and provide me with full details. I will then give you a specific task and expect you to perform it without fail. We work together, not independently. That way we will succeed. Remember, we are here to rescue Craig's slaves. It is a family with young children, so I do not have to caution you to take care."

Craig felt a shiver run up his spine. The Judge was not acting now; he was giving it to them straight. Out here in the wilds of Breckinridge County there was no one to impress. Craig could literally feel the strength of purpose emanating from him. He was clearly in command and no one would question him.

"Everyone check their loads. I want all hammers in half-cock position."

Craig did as the Judge ordered and heard multiple clicks as hammers were thumbed back to half cock. Stephen looked uncertain, but resolute. Owen, a fine marksman and veteran scout at the Battle of New Orleans, was calm and confident. The other men had obviously done this before.

"Ready?" Judge Bozarth whispered. "Calvin, let us commence this operation."

The tracker moved off, melting silently into the growing darkness of the forest. After some time had elapsed, the Judge inquired, "Who among you has the best night vision?" Craig and Stephen both pointed at Owen.

"Very well. Owen, you should follow Calvin at one hundred paces. Listen sharply and keep your eyes peeled. You are there to back him up. He knows I always send out a second man, so do not worry about him shooting you. The rest of us will lag behind. When he finds the outlaws, Calvin may wish to stay put to keep them in sight. In that event he will send you back with instructions."

Owen nodded in understanding and nudged his horse into a slow walk. After a few steps, he too seemed to vanish. Craig realized that night had fallen. The Judge held them up for what seemed a much longer time, then he whispered, "Let us move out—quietly."

Craig felt the icy hand of fear grip him. It seemed foolhardy to undertake such a dangerous venture in complete darkness. The two Cottonwood Bend militiamen started off, side by side. Judge Bozarth followed and ordered Craig and Stephen to bring up the rear. The carpet of leaves lay damp and compressed from recent rains, so the horses made little noise. Craig realized that this condition favored them. There would be no rustling of brittle leaves to give them away. His senses sharpened as they advanced down the wide road. He was conscious of every twig snap, the whiff of damp oak leaves, and the pungent fragrance of an occasional cedar or pine. At one point the horses trampled over some fallen persimmons, and the sweet tang of the overripe fruit rose on the moist air. Craig could see nothing, for there was still no moon. He strained his ears to hear any noise that might presage an ambush, but the surrounding woods remained ghostly silent.

On they rode, climbing and descending wooded limestone hills, crossing icy streams and negotiating through brushy valleys. At one creek, Judge Bozarth ordered a halt. While they watered the horses and performed their necessaries, the clouds parted briefly to reveal a full moon. It reflected off the surrounding clouds, illuminating the bottomland and transforming the little watercourse into a million diamond-like sparkles before disappearing once again. Craig glanced upward and noticed the weather was clearing. He wondered how this would affect the Judge's plan.

"Good news," Judge Bozarth whispered. "We now have light—and just when we need it."

"Got the wind in our faces too," one of the Regulators observed.

Craig could not comprehend this for there was no wind at all, especially down here, in the valley's depths.

"Yes," the Judge nodded in agreement. "Let us move out again. Keep these horses quiet. We are getting close."

Craig wondered how he could tell.

They began climbing, single file, following the tortuous buffalo trail as it wound around and over a massive hill. The limestone slopes were covered thickly in cedar, pine, and moss. Consequently, the horses slid and stumbled on the steepest grades. Bright moonlight shone intermittently, sometimes aiding in their ascent, but when it vanished, they were plunged into a double-darkness that forced them to dismount and grope their way up the trail.

Finally they emerged onto an elevated, open pasture enclosed on all sides by forest. The road continued onward, a dark gash cutting starkly across the pale dead grass. A campfire flickered at the pasture's far end. The aroma of roasting beef and wood smoke piqued Craig's senses even though the fire was perhaps a half mile distant. He realized that he had not eaten since noon, and hunger pains assailed him. Now he understood what the regulator meant about having the wind in their faces.

Judge Bozarth growled softly, "Those damned outlaws have gone and killed a beef. That alone is a hanging offense."

A twig snapped to their right and Craig noticed with a little shock that Owen had rejoined them. Apparently, he had worked his way quietly around the meadow, keeping just inside the tree line until he reached the road where they were. How he managed to do this without them hearing was beyond belief.

"What news do you bring?" the Judge inquired.

"Calvin says they have already eaten and are bedding down for the night. They have posted no guards."

"I did not suppose they would. What of the slaves?"

"They've chained Romulus and Vergina to a sycamore near the horses. The children are with them. One man has made his bedroll in that vicinity." He pointed out the position. The rest of them have spread their blankets near the fire."

"Then they are damned fools, for they have forsaken the primary rule of the road: 'never sleep by your cooking fire.' Any traveler knows to proceed onward after supper and then find some secluded grove off the road. This job should be easy in comparison to others. Still, we do not wish to be overconfident." He glanced across the pasture, visualizing the upcoming confrontation. "We shall steal within a few hundred yards, dismount, and tether the horses at a suitable location. Stephen will stay behind to hold them."

"But—!" Stephen protested.

"Silence!" the Judge snapped, fixing a terrible glare upon the young man. "Are you disobeying a direct order?"

"No, sir," Stephen's short-lived defiance instantly collapsed.

"Every man will do as I say. You will stand ready to bring up those horses on my command."

"Yessir," Stephen shuffled his feet in embarrassment.

"Good, then. Craig, you will take the man nearest your slaves. The slaves are your responsibility, so I know you won't miss. The rest of you will swing out in a semi-circle and pick your targets left to right. Our left flank man shoots their man on the left and so on down the line."

"What if any of them want to be taken alive?" Craig asked.

"Trust me, they will not. When we have sprung the trap, I will shout to wake them up. Then things will unfold quickly. Bear in mind, they outnumber us. We must not let them reach their guns. If we do, one or more of us could be shot. Do I make myself clear?"

Craig swallowed in revulsion. Once again he would be forced to kill a man, maybe more, depending on how the skirmish unfolded. The nightmares of New Orleans had receded somewhat and he feared what this shootout might do to revive them. But he knew he must follow the Judge's orders for the sake of the other men and for

Romulus and his family.

"Now then, Owen, lead us around this pasture," the Judge ordered. The moon disappeared behind a cloud and they rode single file in the shadows of the tall timber. A deep fold in the meadow obscured them for a few hundred yards. When the campfire was again visible, they swung the horses back inside the tree line where the going proved more difficult. They stole quietly along the forest's edge until they drew almost level with the campfire. The Judge held up his hand. Calvin Ward was there, waiting for them in the shadow of a giant beech tree. Craig's heart leapt in his chest. Everyone reined to a halt.

"This here is a good place to tie the horses," Calvin whispered.

"Any changes?" Owen asked.

"Nope. They're pretty much down for the night, full bellies and all."

"Should we try to work in behind them, cut them off from the forest?" Judge Bozarth asked.

Calvin shook his head. "I think not. We can spread out in the pasture. See that little gulley? It snakes around that low rise and will bring us to within fifty yards of the campfire. From there we can belly crawl. They won't see us until we are right on top of them."

"Sounds like a plan. Will you take the left flank?"

"Yessir. Who's covering their horses?"

"Craig Ridgeway."

"Good. I was going to suggest that. He's packing more arms than any of us. We need him and that shotgun between the horses and those outlaws."

"Do you understand, Craig?" Judge Bozarth asked. "Do not let any of them reach their horses. No one gets away."

"I understand, Judge." He unslung the shotgun, feeling sick at heart. Somehow he figured that the Judge, as peace officer, would apprehend the outlaws and bring them back to Hardinsburg for trial. Obviously this was not his plan. It was murder rather than justice.

Calvin rigged a long rope to which he secured the horses. He tied one end to a post oak, fashioning a simple slip knot there before looping the other end around Stephen's saddle horn. "Now, when the Judge calls for you, all you have to do is pull the tree end of that slip knot. It will unravel and then you can tow all the horses at once." Stephen nodded in comprehension.

"Do not waste time, lad." the Judge instructed. "When I call, bring them up immediately."

"Yessir," Stephen replied, still burning from the Judge's reproach.

"Very well." The Judge pivoted away and began removing his firearms from their scabbards.

Craig and the other men did the same.

Calvin whispered, "Don't sulk, young McDonnell. We all started out this way. The Judge always gives his newcomers the most basic jobs. If they mess up, they're finished. So don't mess up."

"I won't," Stephen promised.

Judge Bozarth motioned for Craig to advance, while he and the Regulators ducked low and began traversing the grassy gulley to half encircle the sleeping outlaws. Craig crept silently in the dark shadows at the timber's edge, shifting his vision from the ground to the tall sycamore where Romulus and family were chained. He carefully avoided stepping on sticks that might snap and give him away. A slight rise hid the sycamore's base so he could not see Romulus or any of his family. Worse, he could not locate the outlaw guarding them. The moon receded behind a cloud and he stalked closer, searching for a glimpse of his quarry. He thought how wise the Judge was to assign him the man guarding his freed slaves. And Stephen's posting was a stroke of pure genius, ensuring he stayed clear of the fight. Everything seemed to be going to the Judge's plan.

Suddenly, a wolf howled from across the pasture, its high wail unnerving in the darkness. Another wolf howled and then another. Soon, a whole pack joined in shrill chorus. Obviously the roasting meat had attracted the carnivores. They were close, just inside the woods.

A horse nickered nervously just an arm's length ahead and to his right—it was much closer than he had reckoned. Craig recoiled in horror. The Judge's plan was fast unravelling. He thumbed back both hammers of his shotgun.

The men at the campfire stirred.

"What in hell was that?"

"Wolves!"

"Throw another log on that fire," an outlaw snarled. "They won't come near the flames."

"Yeah? You just say so."

An outlaw rose to pitch more wood on the fire. Craig saw a musket slung over his right shoulder. Contrary to the Judge's wishes, at least one of them had reached his gun. The wolves howled again. Another outlaw sat up with a rifle across his lap.

"Damn them wolves to hell!" he complained, shaking his head. "We might as well forget sleep."

Out of the darkness Judge Bozarth's voice roared, shattering the stillness with a volume far louder, far more terrifying than a pack of howling wolves. It boomed louder than the cannons at Chalmette Plantation and made Craig's blood run cold.

"Throw down, you lousy bastards! I'm Judge Bozarth of the Cottonwood Bend Militia. We've got fifteen guns on you! Throw down!"

A gunshot flashed from the outlaw camp and all hell broke loose. The Regulators opened up in one volley and their muzzle blasts thundered across the pasture. At that instant, the moon emerged, flooding the meadow with its brilliance. Craig flicked his attention back to the horses and spied a shadowy figure darting in among them. He crouched low and waited for the outlaw to emerge. The man unlimbered a long rifle, hoping to use the horses as cover while shooting at his attackers in the pasture. He did not notice Craig standing in the shadows just two feet away. Craig pointed the stubby shotgun at his head and pulled the right trigger. The blast lit the forest's edge like lightning and a full load of buckshot hammered the outlaw backward, splitting his skull and scattering his brains against the trunk of an oak tree. The horses reared and strained against their ropes, adding to the pandemonium.

Two outlaws bolted from the campfire heading straight for the horses, unaware in all the gunfire that Craig waited for them. One was wounded and limping, doubled over and clutching his abdomen. Craig held his shotgun at hip level and let the faster, uninjured outlaw get in close. He fired the second barrel at a range of about eight steps. The recoil kicked high, coupled with an earsplitting boom. The blast stopped the outlaw dead in his tracks, picked him up, and hurled him backwards in the opposite direction. He collapsed in a shredded heap.

"Mercy! For the love of God, have pity!" The other wounded outlaw crumpled to his knees, hands in the air. Craig set the shotgun aside and unslung his Lancaster rifle. He decided not to shoot this man, but a rifle ball, fired from the pasture, struck the outlaw in the temple and knocked him sideways.

Judge Bozarth bellowed, "Someone shoot that man! He is getting away!"

A single outlaw had escaped the ambuscade and was some two hundred yards distant, fleeing for the trees at the far end of the pasture. It seemed impossible he could have slipped past Calvin Ward, so bright was the moonlight. Two gunshots cracked, but produced no effect; perhaps the others were reloading. The outlaw neared the pasture's edge. Craig raised the Lancaster rifle to his shoulder and pulled back the hammer. His hand curled naturally around the sleek wrist and he nestled his check against the curly maple stock, sighting down the blued steel barrel and lining up the rear notch with the front sight. One deep breath, half released, a smooth curl of the finger, and 'bang!'—the outlaw tumbled untidily into the grass at the forest's edge.

Judge Bozarth thundered. "That was one damned fine shot! Fan out and make sure they are all dead." He whistled loudly and called for Stephen. The young man emerged from the woods, leading the string of horses. Craig was proud of him; he had proven himself worthy of service. The Judge ordered him to secure the horses at the edge of the trees near the camp.

The Regulators called out again and again—"Dead! Dead! This

one's had it." One commented, "Damn, that shotgun makes a bloody mess!"

Craig did not want to survey his handiwork. He knew with certainty his men had not survived. Instead, he dashed over to the big sycamore where Romulus and his family huddled. "Romulus! It's Craig! Are you unharmed?"

Romulus stared wildly at him in dazed disbelief. "Craig?"

"Yes, it is me! Judge Bozarth and the McDonnell brothers are here. We'll get you unchained and take you back home."

Vergina stared at him in a state of shock and said nothing, her face a mask of bitterness. She clutched the wailing children to her. The two adults were shackled in leg irons and chained tightly to the sycamore.

"Where is the key?"

Romulus indicated the dead outlaw lying near the horses. Craig strode unwaveringly over to the headless body and began searching it. It was a ghoulish act, rummaging through sticky, bloodstained clothes, but he forced himself to do it. Something jingled inside a heavy leather pouch. He worked it free and held it up to the moonlight, recognizing Romulus' family money pouch. Mary had fashioned it for Vergina, a soft doeskin purse complete with leather drawstring. That fired his anger enough to goad him into continuing the search. The money was his originally, and he had paid it out to Romulus and Vergina in good faith. They had worked hard for it, saving every penny for their journey north. It made Craig so mad he could have kicked the corpse. Instead he searched the remaining pockets. His fingertips touched a buckskin string, slimy with blood. Gingerly he withdrew the string and found a brass key tied to the end. He returned to the stunned family.

The moon now shone with the near-brightness of day, enabling him to see the slot on Romulus' leg cuff. He inserted the key and unlatched the iron band. It fell off with a clanking noise. Then he freed Vergina. Romulus rose painfully and hauled her up. Like sleepwalkers they began walking north, clearly in some state of shock. The giant hobbled like an old man, favoring one side as if his ribs were broken. Craig realized that he had been severely beaten.

"Where are you going, Romulus?"

"Back north."

"But they may catch you again."

"They all dead."

"Yes, *they* are. But there will be others. Come home with me and we'll figure something out."

"It ain't home," Vergina muttered.

"I know that, but take a long hard look at Romulus. He needs care. Come back to the house and let him mend. I promise to help get you north."

The couple relented, stopping in their tracks, shoulders slumped. Craig shepherded them over to the campfire, seating them near its warmth. He gathered up the outlaws' blankets and gave them to Vergina. She first bundled the children and then draped a blanket over Romulus' broad shoulders. While she did this, Craig wrapped one around her shoulders. The temperature was dropping and frost was forming on the grass. The Regulators dragged the dead outlaws to the gulley and rolled them in.

Judge Bozarth came to sit by the fire. He was almost giddy as he gloated over their one-sided victory. "What a triumph!" he roared. "Those low-lives didn't stand a chance! Did I or did I not tell you we could handle them?"

"You did," Calvin agreed. "But who would have figured those damned wolves would start howling? They nearly ruined the game for us."

"Bah! No other outcome was possible. True, the outlaws got off some shots, but it was over with before it began."

Craig agreed—the engagement was precariously akin to murder. But the Judge had legally covered himself by ordering the outlaws to throw down their arms. He was, after all, an officer of the law and they had fired on him. And they were outlaws, guilty of stealing slaves and killing a man's beef.

"Steaks, anyone?" the Judge chuckled. "Let us not leave it all to the wolves."

Calvin rose with a grin and drew his big knife. He strode over to the supine carcass of a spring calf. The outlaws had recently killed it and cut chunks of meat from its hindquarters. He called out to them, "Those idiots didn't even know the good part of a beef. This little feller still has his tenderloin intact. At least we will eat like kings."

"Yes, to the victors the spoils," the Judge laughed heartily. "Let us see if they have any coffee." He glanced up as Stephen approached the fire.

"Horses are all secure, Judge." The young man pointed to where he had tied the mounts. The animals grazed in the moonlight.

"You performed brilliantly, lad," the Judge praised. "Every man must do his duty—and you did yours."

Stephen fairly glowed at the praise and, perhaps more, at the knowledge he was forgiven. When the Judge suggested he help the others rustle up some food, he hopped quickly to the task. The slave-catchers had traveled rough, but Stephen found some potatoes, salt, and onions. One of the militiamen dragged an iron skillet from the packs; another cut some green sticks on which to spear the meat. Calvin succeeded in removing the long strip loin and a chunk of fat. He brought it over to the fire and began slicing off hunks for the men to roast over the coals. Stephen found a cloth bag of coffee, a ladle, and an iron boiling pot. He began brewing coffee while Vergina sliced the potatoes. She seemed to have regained some of her composure. She placed the hunk of fat in the skillet and melted it down to begin frying potatoes, sprinkling them with salt. Craig shared his bread, cheese, bacon, and apples.

At first, it seemed callous, barbaric—eating such a meal after slaughtering the enemy—like some ancient rite from pre-historic times. But there was something about it that reached out and joined them into an almost clan-like union. They had fought together and survived death; now they would dine together with wolves howling from across the pasture. Eating without utensils posed no problem. Each man roasted his own beef and dipped his fingers into the communal bag of salt for seasoning. No one protested when someone plucked potato slices from the skillet. There were no mugs, so the ladle of coffee was passed from man to man. Romulus and his family ate as if they had not been fed in weeks.

After the meal the Judge ordered the men to draw lots for the outlaws' animals and possessions. The four horses were poor mounts, but they, their saddles and bridles were divided among the Judge, Calvin, and the Cottonwood Bend militiamen. The assortment of weapons was equally pitiable, but again the spoils were parceled out by lot. This time Owen received a rifle, Stephen the sole musket. There were a few coins shared equally. Everyone agreed that Vergina should have the cooking utensils. Craig, the beneficiary of this whole affair, was naturally excluded from receiving any of the spoils. He did not feel slighted. These men had risked their lives for him. One day he must do the same for them.

Calvin handed the Judge a folded sheaf of documents. Bozarth slipped on his glasses and studied them in the firelight. "Yes, yes," he muttered before refolding them. Young Ridgeway, I believe you should take charge of these."

Craig recognized the manumission papers and agreed. He shoved them deep into his pocket with the doeskin money purse.

Judge Bozarth allowed the men to rest a while before rousting them out. "Let us depart this place," he announced. "The full moon will make our return much easier. We will be home before morning."

Craig groaned at the thought, but knew he would probably feel worse after sleeping a short fitful spell on frost-covered ground. At least now his belly was full and the coffee had warmed him. He helped Romulus and Vergina onto the outlaws' horses, securing them with lead ropes so they could concentrate on keeping their children in the saddle and protecting them from branches.

The Judge was right—the moon illuminated their path and made the going much easier. It sure beat groping their way in total darkness, but it was well past midnight when they reached the Hardinsburg Road. Craig, Owen, Stephen, the two militiamen and slaves turned west; Calvin and the Judge turned east. Craig had a good idea where the Judge was headed. It was as everyone said—Judge

Bozarth was a great personage, but cursed with human weaknesses. On this evening his infidelity seemed almost trivial in comparison to his strengths. The man had just commanded a brilliant operation with deadly efficiency. The sheer force of his personality had bonded seven men into a cohesive unit with a singular purpose, and they had all survived.

Dawn was breaking when they reached the cabin. The morning star was rising, and behind them the sky grew brighter. Romulus and Vergina dismounted and plodded wearily toward their cabin. Little Leta was half asleep, holding Vergina's hand; Romulus carried the sleeping Gabriel. Craig thanked the militiamen and his brothers-in-law before they continued westward down the big hill toward Cottonwood Bend. At that moment he wanted nothing more than to topple into his own warm bed, but he followed the family across the road, knowing that their cabin was cold. Together, Craig and Romulus built a roaring fire while Vergina dragged the bare tick mattresses to the hearth. The little room warmed quickly.

"Thank ye, Craig," Romulus said.

"I'm just glad you all are safe." He stifled a yawn as he regarded the shabby outlaw blankets. "Shall I bring you some more blankets?"

"These be fine for tonight. Fire's good and hot."

"Then get some rest. I will fetch you some clean blankets later this morning. Mary will cook breakfast; then we'll see about setting you up here until you decide what to do."

"Looks like we back where we started," Vergina sighed. "Exceptin' we lost all we had, includin' our money."

Craig remembered the papers and money pouch. "On the contrary, Vergina, I found these on the outlaw I shot." He withdrew the valuables and placed them in her hands. "I don't know how much is left in there, but it is all yours."

Vergina's harsh countenance softened. "Craig, you a wonderful man." She turned her face toward the fire and wept.

"You folks have suffered a terrible ordeal. Next time we will get it right."

Chapter Six

New Orleans—January 22, 1816

The bells of St. Louis Cathedral rang for early mass, their plaintive toll reverberating throughout the French Quarter. Horses clip-clopped through the streets as vendors and deliverymen began spreading out through the city. Down at the levee a steamboat whistle blew, a long, deep-throated blast that pierced the cold fog and signaled the beginning of a new business day.

Philippe Bouchard drew the blankets around his shoulders and pulled Chantelle to him, not yet prepared to leave the warm cocoon they shared. She snuggled against him as he embraced her, and he thrilled to the contact of her soft, naked body. He buried his nose in her tousled mane of blonde hair and inhaled her scent, quite certain he was the luckiest man on earth. He ran his hands over her sleek lines, treasuring the fact she was his. Chantelle was an exquisite beauty, the only daughter of Gustave d'Alembert, one of the richest men in New Orleans. Their marriage in December had been the talk of New Orleans.

Although just twenty-seven years of age, Phillippe had achieved heights few men would ever attain. Envious men grumbled that he had inherited his wealth, and this was in fact true. Six years ago his mother caught fever and died; a month later his father unexpectedly dropped dead of unknown causes, leaving the entire estate to his only son. This included The Bouchard Exchange, a sawmill, a small bank, five warehouses advantageously situated on the levee, three large sugar plantations, and two dozen businesses scattered throughout the French Quarter and extending across Canal Street into the newer bustling American sector.

Philippe could have easily squandered his newfound wealth, as some young men might do, but instead he had sought out Pierre Delacroix, one of his father's closest associates, to ask him for paternal and financial guidance. The kindly old merchant had taken him under his wing and instructed him in the complicated art of business. Early on, Philippe demonstrated a gift for mathematics and he quickly grasped even the most challenging business concepts. During the British blockade prior to the War of 1812 he interviewed ship captains and wrote British businessmen influential in Parliament to assess popular opinion regarding America. From these correspondences he discovered that several of the calmer heads were actively petitioning for a renewal of commerce and were working fervently to avoid an American conflict—since Britain was already engaged with fighting Napoleon. American shippers from New England also weighed in heavily against conflict. Philippe reasoned that the power of money would prevail, as it usually did. It was he who inspired Delacroix to invest in American farm products on the assumption war would be averted. Over time their warehouses slowly and steadily filled with tobacco, lumber, cotton, hemp, molasses, refined sugar, and whiskey, all purchased at rock bottom prices.

Despite his painstaking research and youthful optimism, War Hawks in the U.S. Twelfth Congress got their war. The frontier agitators had crowed long enough for it. It seemed his business speculation would lead to ruin. But as the war progressed, it became evident that Britain could not possibly win, and that peace might prevail after all. In 1814, with American peace delegations meeting in Europe, Philippe and Delacroix began quietly buying more high-quality American products at absurdly low prices. Then the unthinkable occurred. A massive British invasion force appeared on the plantations below New Orleans. If they broke through, all would be lost, for the British would seize everything.

But Andrew Jackson and his motley army miraculously repelled the invaders. Delacroix soon learned, through his vast intelligence network, that sailors on the British fleet carried news of the Treaty of Ghent. Overnight, the trading houses of New Orleans exploded into action. Speculators reasoned that the value of exportable goods could double or even treble. Manchester's looms were long-starved for American cotton. Bids on cotton, sugar, rice, whiskey, tobacco, hemp, and other inland products soared on the news of peace. In just a few weeks flatboats appeared at the levee, bringing hogs, cattle, grain, pelts, and lumber. Exotic goods such as coffee, cocoa, tea, rum, bananas, citrus fruits, spices, and luxury items from Europe arrived on ocean-going vessels. New Orleans became a booming business center once again. Enterprising Americans flooded into a cosmopolitan city that was neither French nor American. All of them looked to make money.

Philippe soon sensed that the high prices might not hold. He suggested selling while the bids still climbed. This appeal flew straight to Delacroix's heart. Ever the pragmatist, he too realized it was time to sell. Again the two investors took a cautious approach, not raising alarm among other businessmen. By the time prices began levelling off, Philippe and Delacroix had divested themselves of their inventory. They had each earned a fortune. Neither of them suffered in the ensuing plummet brought on by British merchants who began 'dumping' vast quantities of manufactured goods to thwart nascent American industry. During this present slump the two investors began quietly buying. Philippe was now recognized as one of the most brilliant financiers in New Orleans. As a result, the Bouchard Exchange ranked in the top echelon of businesses. It was one of the older exchanges, solid and dependable, but headed by a young, progressive president willing to take calculated risks.

Chantelle represented the crown jewel in his life. At twenty-two she turned the heads of everyone in town, old and young. Her striking features—fair complexion, blonde hair, blue eyes and perfect porcelain-white teeth—captivated him fully. She enjoyed dressing in new clothes, and, when she appeared in public wearing the latest fashions from Paris, she always caused a sensation. Philippe caressed the soft blonde silkiness between her thighs and she sighed contentedly, pushing her buttocks against him. The night had passed in a dreamlike blur of melding flesh and sensual delights; they were both exhausted, physically and spiritually. It seemed they could not get enough of each other.

But he realized that precious business time was slipping away. The ship captains, merchants, bankers and speculators would soon converge at the levee. He must open the Exchange doors, meet with his associates and prepare for a strategic conference later in the morning. Reluctantly, he swung his legs from under the covers and plunged himself into a new workday.

———•———

Davy Sims tapped on the door to his spacious office overlooking the great muddy crescent of the Mississippi River where the flatboats moored, hundreds of them, in many places two and three deep. Philippe glanced up from his correspondences. "Yes, Davy. What is it?"

"Two officers acting as bailiffs of the court sir," the weedy little clerk replied, hardly able to trust his squeaky voice. "They are waiting for you downstairs."

"Did they state their business?"

"Just that they need to see you, sir."

"Very well. Thank you, Davy. Please convey that I will join them shortly."

"Yes sir."

Philippe took another sip of his coffee and finished reading the letter. He placed a paperweight on the growing stack of buy and sell orders, and rose shakily from his desk, still utterly spent and feeling a bit light-headed. As he descended the wooden staircase of the Exchange, he wondered what the officers wanted. Perhaps there had been a robbery or other criminal action in the vicinity. Peace with Great Britain had brought huge financial growth to New

Orleans, but it also encouraged a vast influx of river men, foreign sailors, thieves, ruffians, vagabonds, and prostitutes to pour into the city. Quite naturally this resulted in a corresponding rise in crime and violence. The most coarse and vulgar of all the new immigrants were the *Kaintocks,* or Kentuckians. From the time of American occupation, and long before, these rowdy, unkempt and dangerous river men caused more trouble than any other element of the population. A whole underworld had sprung up, catering to the vices of the *Kaintocks* who, after three or four months on the river, came ashore volubly demanding liquor and women. If a knife or gun fight erupted over in the American sector, one could be sure a Kentuckian was involved. *Kaintocks* even became the "boogie men" in stories used to frighten misbehaving children. Creoles harbored a basic dislike and distrust of these barbarians, but tolerated them because of their money. Ordinarily the violence was contained to the western side of Canal Street, but occasionally it spilled over into the French Quarter, often on the levee near the warehouses.

Perhaps these officers wished to share some intelligence concerning possible violence or an impending robbery. The two men waited just inside the main doors. Both were in their late twenties or early thirties and stood well over six feet in height, exactly the physical type capable of dealing with brawling river men. Between them they packed a considerable amount of muscle. As did most of the elite in society, Philippe considered them with no small amount of suspicion.

Law enforcement in New Orleans was at best an ill-defined force, still evolving and fraught with many imperfections. At New Orleans' founding in 1718, law was vested in the military, alternating between French, Spanish and again French rule. The first real police department was formed in 1796, under the administration of the Spanish Colonial Governor, Francisco Luis Hector, Baron de Carondelet, who complained in writing: *"Crime has reached such proportions that a full-time city police force is required."* On November 8, 1803, Mayor Etienne De Bore appointed a committee to inspect prisons, formulate rules and write police regulations. Pierre

Achille Rivery was named Commissioner General of Police, and placed in command of twenty-five men. After numerous complaints, these men were dismissed. The council then authorized hiring mulattoes, but only under command of white officers. This move had proven unpopular. With the Louisiana Purchase on December 20, 1803, New Orleans became a part of the United States. A militia patrol was organized in 1804 under James Pitot, then Mayor of New Orleans. The *Guard de Ville* followed in 1806 but was abolished in 1808. Militia patrols were reestablished and that was where the situation stood to date.

"Greetings, Gentlemen. What can I do for you?" The two officers wore no uniforms, but Philippe strode right up to them, unafraid.

"You must come with us now," answered the nearest officer. He looked and sounded German, big and beefy with reddish-blond hair cropped short, scalp disfigured with a dozen scars, ruddy complexion and ice-blue eyes. The other man, bearded and long haired, stood even taller, also marked with visible scars on his forehead, jaw, and knuckles. He rocked forward on his feet, arms folded, looking as if he would welcome any chance at violence. Both men had obviously dealt and absorbed much punishment in their careers.

"I do not understand," Philippe protested. "What is the meaning of this?"

"We are here to escort you to Judge John Harkness' chambers."

"It is not Court Day. Am I under arrest?" he asked incredulously.

"All I know is what the judge told us. He ordered us to bring you to him— immediately."

"Do you carry a subpoena?"

"Just this," the bailiff handed him a single sheet of writing paper.

It was not a formal document; it was a letter, ostensibly written in the judge's hand and addressed to him. On the surface the letter appeared genuine. Philippe took it and read the brief message. Judge Harkness was asking him in polite terms to visit his chambers to clear up some 'legal ambiguities.' He felt instantly relieved, but still held reservations about going off with the unknown strongmen. At first he contemplated refusing, but considering their advantage in height and weight, he decided this course would be unwise.

He nodded and managed a bleak smile. "I will be happy to oblige His Honor. Will you be so good as to leave your names with my clerk?"

With trembling hands, Davy directed the officers to sign their names in the visitor's book and, for good measure, he read them out loud for everyone on the floor to hear, "Matt Irby and Brent Gibson."

"Well done, Davy," Philippe congratulated him. "I should return soon. But would you kindly send a message to Pierre Delacroix? Please inform him that Judge Harkness has summoned me to his office."

"I will sir."

Phillipe lifted his coat from the wooden rack and slipped it on. "If you gentlemen will kindly lead the way, I will join you."

"You lead," Irby countered. "We will follow you."

Philippe exited the Exchange and turned west, then north into the French Quarter toward Royal Street. Irby took up a position on his right elbow; Gibson on his left. It seemed odd that these two behemoths would wish to keep such close station on him during the short walk. After all, he was cooperating fully, and he had broken no laws. Perhaps there was more to the judge's request than met the eye.

*   *   *

A clerk directed them into the high-ceilinged courtroom rather than to Judge Harkness' chambers. The bailiffs stayed close at hand, taking up guard positions just inside the door. Philippe recognized familiar faces in the room and his anxiety lessened. But still, he could tell something was wrong. His father-in-law sat in a jury box chair in his black linen overcoat, shoulders hunched forward and expression grim. Beside him sat the banker Jules Signet with a gloved hand on his shoulder, head down. Philippe recognized others—the lawyer Alain Morel and Doctor Thomas Applegate. Judge Harkness had installed himself at his bench, but he donned a black overcoat rather than his robe of office. All the other men wore their overcoats, for there was no fire in the cast iron stove.

"Come in, young Bouchard," Judge Harkness invited. He motioned for Philippe to stand before the bench. "We appreciate your consideration in coming so promptly."

"I didn't have a choice, Your Honor," Philippe replied. "Could someone please tell me why I am here?"

Harkness nodded uncomfortably at Alain Morel and directed, "You may proceed."

The elegant lawyer strode forward, his heels reverberating on the wooden floor. He wore a black overcoat, unbuttoned enough to allow his lace collar to show. In one hand he carried a sheaf of legal documents and a thick leather-bound book that looked strangely familiar.

"Excuse me," Philippe interjected. "Is this a trial?"

"Hardly a trial," Morel replied in his smooth, oily voice. "Consider it—ah!—an investigation, a mere inquiry. We have certain questions to ask of you, certain ambiguities that must be cleared."

"What ambiguities?"

"Are you, Philippe Bouchard, the sole heir of your father's estate? Are there other claimants who should have been included in his last will and testament?"

"No, I am his only son. What is this all about?"

"Just answer the questions," Judge Harkness directed.

"Yes sir, Your Honor."

Morel continued, "You maintain you are his only son?"

"Yes."

"There are no daughters?"

"No."

"Please tell us what happened to your mother."

"She died in 1810 of the fever."

"And your father?"

"Everyone in this room knows he died the same year. Why are you asking these questions?"

"I will not remind you again, young man," Judge Harkness cautioned, scowling horrifically from his perch. "Answer the questions put before you and make no remark upon them."

"I apologize, Your Honor."

Judge Harkness subsided. Phillipe had heard stories about the judge's legendary crossness; now he was experiencing it firsthand. Harkness brooked no disrespect or deviations in his courtroom.

Morel asked, "Are you completely familiar with your lineage?"

Philippe thought for an instant before answering. "My knowledge is limited to what my father and mother told me. I confess I cannot recall every name, but they are all written down in the family Bible passed on to me."

"Is this the Bible?"

"It is. May I respectfully ask how it came into your possession?" Philippe winced, expecting Judge Harkness to reprimand him again, or perhaps levy a fine for speaking out of order. Apparently the judge was as curious as he was, as he looked to Morel for the answer.

Morel gestured to D'Alembert, inviting him to speak.

"I stopped by your house this morning, Philippe. Chantelle gave it to me. Don't worry. It will be returned."

Philippe was truly perplexed. He watched Morel approach the bench with the Bible in hand. The lawyer opened it to the front pages. "Apparently, Your Honor, the father's lineage can be traced back into the early 1400's. We have documented proof that Marcel Bouchard descended from minor nobility originating in southern France. It was obviously a respected family of some note." He turned the page slowly forward for theatrical effect. "Now we must consider Philippe's mother, Claudine Pomet. You will note there are only two ancestral entries inscribed on the family tree, going back only to her grandmother—and there the tree abruptly ends." He waved his hand dramatically and flipped back to the father's page. "Here we have an extensive lineage, fully documented and extending back for centuries; in stark contrast we have the mother's lineage with only two previous generations. Does this not seem strange?" He paused to let that sink in.

Everyone present knew that few people could recite their ancestry beyond their great-grandparents. And in many cases a woman's ancestry in New Orleans tended to be even less defined. There were sound explanations for this. To remedy the shortage of white women in colonial Louisiana, France had recruited willing farm-girls and city-dwelling women as wives. These women were commonly known as *casquette* girls, because they brought all their possessions to the colonies in a single small trunk, or casket. In 1719 the French government deported over two hundred women felons deemed suitable for the colony of Louisiana. It also relocated young female orphans known as *filles du roi*, "King's Daughters" to Louisiana. Very few of these women brought a long written lineage with them.

"Now let us consider the 'place of birth.'" Morel strutted back to Philippe with open Bible displayed. "Will you kindly read the birthplace of your great grandmother Philomène?"

"I know it already. She was born on the island of Martinique."

"Ah, Martinique!" beamed Morel, feigning a slow comprehension of the fact. "That is correct. Now the ancestral trail becomes even murkier, don't you agree?"

Over in the jury box, D'Alembert hung his head in apparent misery. Philippe noticed tears sliding down his cheek. Jules Signet sat quietly watching the proceedings with the slightest hint of self-satisfaction. Something was dangerously wrong here, but Philippe could not yet identify it.

"Martinique—the isle of sugarcane, tropical breezes, romance, temptations, and—how shall I put it—concubinage? How many plantation owners living so far from home found their comfort in a comely negro wench? Who knows? Perhaps it *was* love—manifested in its basest, most animalistic form. Your great grandfather Edouard Bouchard married twice. His first wife, Jeanne, bore him a son, Ignace. She died and he remarried Philomène—birthplace unknown—who bore him a daughter, Eugenie."

"What is it you are saying?" Judge Harkness cut short his performance, clearly annoyed. "If you are making a point, I suggest you make it and be damned quick about it."

"Yes, Your Honor," Morel bowed. "I have here a letter from the island claiming that Philomène Bouchard was an African slave, perhaps a *griffe*, if not totally black." He held the paper at arm's length and shook it with disgust as if it contained a communicable disease. "Not only that, but we have a degree of inbreeding involved. It appears that Philippe's father Marcel married his half cousin Claudine."

Philippe understood at least part of what was happening. The lawyer was making an accusation that he carried negro blood in his veins. He did not view this as a problem; he was what God made him. Many people in New Orleans were the products of mixed races. But this lawyer was also casting vile contempt upon his mother and her family. It wounded Philippe deeply to hear her presented in such a disparaging manner. And, as intended, it would undoubtedly cause social repercussions. He wanted to scream out—perhaps challenge the lawyer to a duel—but the judge had ordered him to answer only those questions put before him. Wisely he held his tongue, bridling his anger, vowing inwardly that there would be a reckoning. He would spare no expense in making this vain peacock pay. As soon as he returned home, he would begin correspondences to engage a first-class lawyer from Baltimore, Philadelphia, Boston, or New York.

"Let me see the letter," Harkness commanded. He pored over it, grunting skeptically. It was a correspondence dated November 8, 1755 written from Sainte-Pierre on the Caribbean island of Martinique, authored by a plantation owner named Rene Villemont. It was addressed to Edouard Bouchard, Philippe's great grandfather. Villemont spoke of sugar prices, shipping rates, the Lisbon Earthquake and subsequent giant ocean waves that rolled cross the Atlantic to strike the island. One paragraph dealt with slave prices and offered to purchase a comely slave girl named Philomène. The letter looked authentic, for it was yellowed and brittle with age, but Judge Harkness was not convinced. "This does not prove anything. There is no notary seal, no secondary signature or affidavit."

"No, Your Honor, but it has raised an ominous cloud of doubt among several of our top citizens, including Philippe's own father-in-law, Gustave d'Alembert. You may recall, he gave his daughter's hand in marriage less than one month ago. The marriage contract was signed under the presumption that this young man was pure white. There is now reason to suppose his blood contains at least a sixteenth, perhaps one eighth part of negro blood. You will agree this is a sensitive matter for the families involved."

"No doubt, but no proof exists that this letter is genuine, or that Philomène the slave is the same as Philippe's great grandmother."

"There are also financial repercussions to consider. Many of our merchants and investors have direct dealings with Bouchard. They would like to see this matter cleared."

"Who are these people? Who is funding you?"

"I am funding, Your Honor," Jules Signet raised his hand. Judge Harkness bade him rise and the banker stood with a comforting hand still resting on D'Alembert's shoulder. "On behalf of my clientele and their business interests I am examining specific Louisiana statutes. For this purpose I have retained Monsieur Morel to help me understand how our slave and inheritance laws should be applied—especially in the business world. I represent a large contingent of New Orleans merchants, shippers, plantation owners, and investors who are demanding clarification of those laws regarding the inheritance of slaves."

"What is their problem?"

"They believe that the Louisiana Digest is explicit regarding property, business activities, and contractual agreements. Many complain that laws have not been consistently applied. Certain inheritances have been granted illegally, perhaps deliberately, spawning unfair advantages for an undeserving class. This has created hard feelings and a growing distrust of our judicial system. I am speaking of our best citizens."

Harkness coughed in irritation. "Then I suggest they educate themselves by first reading our laws."

"They have, Your Honor," Morel rejoined the discussion. "And they construe that the Digest of 1808 expressly denies the right of slaves to inherit property."

"What does the Digest have to do with this young man? He is not a slave."

"Ah! That is why we have requested this hearing—to seek your guidance, Your Honor."

"Bear that in mind—this is a hearing, not a trial."

"We understand that. But you must understand, responsible citizens truly fear the rising surge of coloreds in New Orleans—those unfortunate mongrels resulting from illicit sexual unions—and they perceive them as a clear threat to the business and social establishment. Those citizens will ultimately present demands for our leaders to protect their families, rights, and businesses. New legislation will be proposed. Courts will be compelled to interpret those laws, as they should. Hopefully we can reverse the wrongs already committed. Morality can and should be legislated. Ideally we may one day resurrect a version of the French *Code Noir* that once punished those men who planted their hot seed in the bellies of young black females." Morel fixed a penetrating gaze upon Judge Harkness. His knowing look spoke volumes in the ensuing silence. Doc had informed him about Kayla and the fact she now carried the judge's child.

As intended, Harkness was clearly wrong-footed. He glanced guiltily at Doc Applegate who had actually witnessed him naked and engaging in the very act Morel railed against, and the knowledge made him feel exposed. But Doc's face gave nothing away as he appeared to study some detail on the far wall.

Morel continued, "We hope from this exercise you may formulate a precedent so the law may be fairly and consistently enforced. If you will indulge us for the sake of argument, we may consider today's hearing a trial gallop."

"You may proceed."

"I turn the examination over to Doctor Thomas Applegate."

"Very well, Doctor. You may state your case."

Doc strode up to the bench. "Thank you, Your Honor." He turned and scrutinized Philippe as if he were one of his medical subjects, walking around him and looking him up and down. "We all agree this is a fine physical specimen— tall, well formed in every feature, fair of face, a young man in the prime of his life. We also know that he is intelligent; at the very least he has demonstrated an uncanny aptitude for business. Perhaps this is due to his association with Pierre Delacroix, one of our leading citizens, but let us give him full credit. He descended from a father whose bloodline is thoroughly documented and unimpeachable. Throughout many years great traits of nobility have been passed down to him. No doubt this has enabled him to assume a leadership position in our society."

Philippe regarded the doctor warily, hoping that Delacroix would soon arrive. Then they would sort things out. The merchant held considerable influence in this city; even the judge respected him. Fortunately Morel had termed this affair an exercise. Harkness himself had insisted this was not a trial. For those reasons Philippe did not feel endangered. He knew they could not charge him for any offense, as long as he maintained his composure.

Doc cleared his throat and pointed to the open Bible now residing on the bench. "However, the mother's lineage presents a true dilemma. What do we know about Claudine? We have only the three generations. Her mother Eugenie was born on a plantation above New Orleans. We have her baptism and marriage record. Claudine's grandmother was born on the distant island of Martinique. We know nothing more about her—just her name. And her name matches that of a female slave owned by Edouard Bouchard, young Philippe's great-grandfather. Rene Villemont's letter supports that fact. True, the letter is not an official document. But who was this great grandmother Philomène? How can we be sure she was, or was not, a negro slave?"

"How indeed?" asked the Judge.

"Through science. We have discussed this before. Scientists from all over Europe are conducting new investigations and are following the latest methodology. They begin with a hypothesis, an educated guess, derived from what is generally perceived. In their laboratories they make detailed, independent observations, recording and analyzing vast amounts of information. This is then shared and discussed among the top minds at university symposia—at Uppsala, Paris, Göttingen, and Vienna. New classifications of the races, with their appending characteristics have been postulated."

"Yes, but how can that science be applied here in this court-room?"

"With your permission, Your Honor, I propose a physical examination in this very room. Nothing will be hidden. All questions will be answered."

"Out of the question!"

"What if all parties agree? Would it not be wise to answer this question and let everyone go their own way?"

"What say you?" Judge Harkness polled the small assemblage. Signet nodded his agreement. Morel assented. Gustave d'Alembert wept openly, his face buried in his hands, but he nodded in the affirmative. That left Philippe.

"And what about you, young man?"

"I respectfully refuse, Your Honor."

"Wouldn't you like to dispel the doubts and be forever free of suspicion?"

"I refuse to be a part of this travesty. I demand a lawyer."

"But this is not a trial!" argued Morel.

"Ha!" Doc roared. "This young buck obviously has something to hide! What is it, I wonder? Is he afraid of what we might discover?" Could it be he is in fact a *passe blanc*? I am sure we are all aware these people masquerade as whites. It happens all too often. How many of our fairest young roses have been deceived into contracting supposed legitimate marriages?" He paused to allow D'Alembert to regain control of his emotions. At present Signet held him upright to prevent him from collapsing. The man wept aloud, gripped in violent throes of humiliation. To exacerbate the man's disgrace, Doc painted the same ugly picture he had shared with Harkness on their drive back from Weeks' plantation.

"Surely as the sun rises, that mongrel's seed will strike and take hold. That tender young rose could bear a black throwback so that everyone in New Orleans would know her shame. It happens all too often in the colored world, but now I am speaking of the white rose's world—her universe. How would that world treat her and her child then?" A heart rending cry rose from the jury box. This was tearing D'Alembert apart.

The judge could stand no more. "Very well, conduct the examination."

Philippe bolted for the door and all mayhem broke loose. He threw a hard punch at Irby who blocked it with a long-practiced, meaty forearm. Ducking sideways Philippe kicked Gibson's shin. Gibson launched a hard blow to his skull starring his vision and buckling his knees.

"Order! Order!" roared Judge Harkness.

Philippe kicked, gouged, and scratched as the two men wrestled him back to the bench. Miraculously he twisted free and tried again to escape. Doc casually tripped him with his cane and sent him sprawling. The two bailiffs pounced, flailing with their stout cudgels. This time they worked him over and extinguished all resistance. Philippe's head lolled, his face streaming with blood.

"A chair for the young man!" Doc ordered. "Do we need restraints?"

Philippe shook his head.

"Very well. I am sure you won't mind these men holding you while I clean your wounds. Get a hold of yourself. This examination will not be painful. And it may well work out to your benefit."

This calmed Philippe, and he sat still, allowing Doc to staunch the bleeding with a white compress. One of the cudgels had opened his scalp and it bled profusely. One eye was blackened and swelled shut and his skull was as lumpy as a newly-picked artichoke. Doc examined his head, intentionally mussing up the thick black hair. A careless blow to Philippe's face had broken his nose and puffed up both lips. The thugs certainly knew how to do their jobs.

"Would you please remove your shoes?" Doc asked. "And your stockings." Philippe obeyed, and Doc held up one of his bare feet. "Look—this is one of the first characteristics. This young man has a definitely pronounced heel bone. Note the long, prehensile toes—just as I expected. Doc then made a considerable show of measuring the skull, now increased in diameter from the external lumps. With the calipers, he measured the bridge of Philippe's broken nose and noted the sweep of his jawline. "Almost bred out of him, but not quite." No one understood any of this, but the medical show appeared to convince.

Out of the corner of his eye, Doc observed Judge Harkness. He knew his man well enough to see he was interested. Just a few months ago the judge had participated in the race classification exercise and had since read all of Doc's tracts on the progressive science of "racism."

"Remove your shirt," Doc commanded.

"What?" Philippe snapped. The bailiffs stepped forward menacingly.

"Would you prefer them to tear it off?"

Philippe obeyed, slipping the shirt over his head. His sleek young body glowed with a healthy tone, except where angry bruises and red welts marred it. Otherwise he was lean, long-waisted, and symmetrically formed.

"I did not expect this," Doc marveled. "Even his coloring bears the subtle hues of an *octoroon*. Now look closely at that nose, those lips. Who can deny the negroid appearance?"

Even Judge Harkness admitted silently that there were now resemblances. It was as if the young man had transformed completely into what the doctor suggested.

"Now shuck down those pants!" Doc ordered.

Philippe bolted again, this time fighting like a madman. When Irby enveloped him in a neck hold, he jerked his head sideways and bit down hard, his teeth slicing through flesh. His mouth filled with the salty, metallic tang of fresh blood. Irby roared and hammered at him, but Philippe held on like a bulldog. Finally Gibson drove two hard punches into his lower back, knocking the wind out of him. Philippe involuntarily let go and Irby unleashed a massive blow to the head, knocking him unconscious. When he came to, Philippe found himself seated in the wooden chair, stripped of his pants, barely conscious of the cold boards on his bare buttocks. He could just make out what Doc Applegate was saying.

"You have observed the wounds on the bailiff's arms and I have measured them; they are consistent with the bite marks of the carnivorous, cannibalistic negroid that rose up in the jungles of darkest Africa. You also have on your desk a hair plucked from this negro's groin, bearing all the characteristic kinks of the race."

Judge Harkness recoiled violently, staring at the hair in revulsion as if it was a poisonous insect.

Doc walked over and used the end of his cane to lift Phillipe's considerable member for all to see. "And here, gentlemen, is the final, incontrovertible proof. Note the darkness of the secret-most flesh. Who would now deny he is part negro?"

"I want him killed!" D'Alembert railed. The sight of Philippe's naked body was more than he could bear. "My daughter is forever ruined!"

"Control yourself!" Judge Harkness ordered. "If you do not, I will have you escorted from my courtroom. Doctor Applegate, I will see you in my chambers." Ponderously the judge rose and left the room.

Doc followed, unconcerned, for now he would deliver the *coup de grâce.*

When he closed the door to the judge's chambers, Harkness turned on him murderously, "If this was a trial I would have you charged with contempt of court. Just what in the hell are you trying to do out there?"

"Trying to save your hide—your reputation," Doc replied.

"What do you mean by that?"

"Jules Signet has offered a way out for everyone concerned. It really is quite brilliant. Actually his solution will save several reputations. I suppose they have unofficially elected me as their emissary."

"This had better be good," Harkness growled. "Let's hear it."

"First, I truly don't care if Bouchard is part negro. But Signet and his investors *do* care. If the citizenry suspects that Bouchard has circumvented our slave laws to enrich himself and marry one of our finest white flowers, we could have a minor rebellion on our hands. Some form of violence would almost certainly ensue. People resent the secret class of coloreds who take advantage of our laws, business, and society—especially our young women. We have the power to snuff out the violence before it occurs."

"You may be wrong. Many coloreds own inherited property in New Orleans. Some even own slaves. It is not unusual."

"Then we must consider D'Alembert and his daughter. They clearly did not know the facts before the marriage. You agree that they rank among our finest families. If news broke that she married a negro, the scandal would be more than they could bear. New Orleans would most certainly lose them and their money."

"The couple is legally married."

"Their marriage will be quietly annulled."

"What if the wife is with child?"

"Then D'Alembert will quietly ship her off to his sister's house in Paris. She will have the child there, leave it at a convent or monastery, and most likely marry a wealthy Frenchman."

"And what of Philippe Bouchard?"

"Morel has the legal answer to that."

"I am certain he does."

"You should at least hear him out."

"I intend to. Earlier you mentioned saving *my* hide, but you never answered my question. What do you mean by that?"

"The slave girl, Kayla, is carrying your child." Doc watched as the realization struck an almost physical blow, draining him of color.

"What!" Harkness exploded.

"I examined her myself a few weeks ago."

"Why did you not inform me then?"

"You know how these things are. Sometimes young girls miscarry. I thought it wise not to alarm you unnecessarily—to give things time to make sure. It appears now she will deliver full term."

Judge Harkness dropped down in his desk chair and buried his face in his hands. The realization left him even more vulnerable to manipulation and Doc pressed his case.

"May I fetch Morel?"

"You had better."

The lawyer entered respectfully. "I presume Doctor Applegate has informed you of—ah—recent developments at Farron Weeks' plantation."

"He has," Judge Harkness responded weakly.

"Jules Signet is offering a way out of hell."

"For some of us maybe, but not for that young man. What of him?"

"I am glad you asked. Doctor Applegate has proven to my satisfaction that young Phillipe carries some negro blood in him."

"And what of it? His father willed him the entire estate—it was legally transferred years ago."

"Yes, but that contract is no more valid than the marriage to Chantelle d'Alembert."

"How do you argue that?"

"The governing rule, laid out in our own Louisiana Digest of 1808, is *partus sequitur ventrem,* a Latin phrase meaning '*that which is brought forth follows the womb.*' It is derived from Roman civil law, which bases the social status of a child on that of the mother, rather than the father. If the mother was a slave, her offspring, even with a miniscule amount of negro ancestry, can be legally termed a slave."

"Is there a precedent?" Harkness inquired.

"Yes. The principle was first adopted by the British Royal Colony of Virginia in 1662. You will find it in our own Digest of 1808 under Chapter Three which is entitled 'OF SLAVES.' Article Twenty-Four states, and I quote: '*Children born of a mother then in a state of slavery, whether married or not, follow the condition of said mother; they are consequently slaves and belong to the master of their mother.*'"

"Are you so sure that young Bouchard is descended from an African slave woman? And if so, could he not produce manumission papers?"

"You may well ask, but I am certain he does not have them. There are no manumission records on him in New Orleans courts. We have investigated thoroughly. We have even been to Martinique. And we could find no manumission papers for his mother or grandmother. In principle, they also were slaves. After coming here from Martinique, the Bouchards managed to conceal the female ancestry."

"And you, Doctor. Are you so certain the young man has negro blood?"

"I conducted a full medical investigation and examined all the distinguishing traits. You witnessed it yourself. Bouchard tested positive in every characteristic."

"Even if what you claim is true, he cannot be much more than one-sixteenth negroid. In Virginia a person with seven-eighths white blood is considered white."

Doc mustered as much conviction as possible to make his declaration. "According to our law, he is a slave. His mother, her mother and grandmother owned no manumission papers. He cannot produce legal proof he was ever freed. According to our laws regarding coloreds, you must agree—'*One Drop—A Slave!*'"

Harkness turned to ask Morel, "In your best legal opinion, what will become of Bouchard's property?"

The lawyer answered, "By law it must all be forfeited. Without manumission papers he is, justifiably, a slave. Chapter Three, Article Seventeen of the Digest states: '*the slave is incapable of contracting any kind of engagement. He possesses nothing in his own right and can transmit nothing by succession, legacy or otherwise; for whatever he possesses is his master's property.*'"

"What if he decides to fight the ruling in court?"

"Article Eighteen decrees that the slave is '*incapable of exercising any public offices or private trusts. He cannot be tutor, curator, executor, nor attorney, he cannot be a witness in either civil or criminal matters. He cannot be a party in any civil action either as plaintiff or defendant, except when he has to claim or prove his freedom.*' This protects us all from a retaliatory lawsuit. "

"If we reveal he is a slave, who then is his owner?"

"Here is the arrangement. If Bouchard is judged to be a negro, then he must also by reason of his mother's status be declared a slave. My client Jules Signet represents an alliance at the Louisiana Planters' Bank. He is willing to create a holding company and serve as trustee for the D'Alemberts while the situation is resolved."

"You need a witnessed signature for the transfer of property."

"We have already procured the signature—from D'Alembert's daughter. If Philippe Bouchard is a declared a slave, he has no legal right to possess or transmit property. As his legal wife, she does have that right."

"But you argue their marriage is null and void."

"Not until she makes it so. We will act in the interim, before the annulment. In that time Philippe could be declared her property."

Harkness scratched his head as he wrestled with the legalities. He could appreciate their line of legal reasoning and conceded that, on the surface, it was brilliant. And, admittedly, he believed in the medical findings of Doc Applegate, his friend and confidant. Philippe was in all likelihood part negroid. But there was nothing right about this case. It reeked of business piracy. Signet was engineering a takeover.

As if making a closing argument in a courtroom trial, Morel summed up the circumstances. "Once Phillipe is declared a slave, Your Honor's ruling on inheritance and property will conform faithfully to the articles of the Digest of 1808. We realize we are breaking new legal ground with the declaration, and are doing so in the knowledge that one day this ground must rightly be broken. Your ruling could remedy the colored crisis in Louisiana. And it will result in several immediate, positive outcomes. First, we right a racial and legal wrong, avert violence and prevent a financial crisis—noble undertakings in themselves. Next, we protect the good name of D'Alembert and his daughter. Lastly, we uphold the solid reputation of Your Honor. Signet has already offered to purchase the slave girl Kayla from Farron Weeks. The papers are being drawn up this morning. One of Signet's cargo ships, the *Lisette*, is bound for the Brazilian port of Salvador da Bahia. We intend for Philippe and Kayla to be interned aboard it. There they will be held incommunicado until the vessel departs."

"When will that be?"

"In four weeks, perhaps six."

"What will happen to them?" Harkness asked.

"They will be sold and never heard from again. Life here will resume as usual for everyone. All will be forgotten. No one need mention this day again."

Harkness knew all about Salvador da Bahia. The port served as a processing center for untold numbers of African slaves brought into Brazil by Portuguese slave traders. Nearly one third of all slaves captured in Africa were shipped there and then sold to work on vast inland sugarcane plantations. The overseers in that province were noted for their cruelty. Bahia had a reputation of being hell-on-earth for slaves.

"Leave me now—all of you. Rightly or wrongly, you have provided the information I need. I will write my decision and read it aloud for all to hear." He began writing his verdict in rough longhand.

Alain Morel glanced nervously at Doc Applegate. He had not expected the judge to deliberate on the matter. Doc shrugged unconcernedly and ambled comfortably out of the chamber. Out in the hallway Morel pulled him aside and whispered.

"You claimed this would be an open-and-shut case."

"And so it is."

"It had better be."

"Not to worry. Harkness will never allow the public to know about his bastard child or the fact that the mother is young and colored. Signet will get the judgment he seeks."

They reentered the courtroom and took seats at the counsel table. The atmosphere within was charged with bitterness. Philippe had dressed and the two bailiffs loomed over him; the young man looked even more disheveled, and Doc wondered if additional violence had occurred. From the jury box D'Alembert glowered menacingly at

Philippe. The tension was unbearable. Fortunately, they did not have long to wait, for Judge Harkness entered the room, clutching a sheet of paper. Everyone rose in deference to his position, even though this was not an official trial.

"Be seated," Judge Harkness directed. "I have reached a decision in this matter and it will not be challenged by anyone in this room." He scowled ferociously at Morel and then fixed his stare on the elegant Signet. "Do I make myself clear?"

Everyone nodded in the affirmative.

"I have one final question for young Bouchard. Can you produce papers proving your manumission from slavery?"

Philippe felt the sharp talons of terror grip him. He glanced wildly around the room, looking into the faces of cold-hearted men who wanted him to disappear.

"Answer the question," Harkness ordered.

"You know I cannot! But you all know I am not a slave!" Philippe shouted in anguish. "This is a travesty!" He subsided in shock and disbelief.

"Very well. It is obvious young Philippe is at least one-eighth negroid. The scientific examination has proven it to my satisfaction. We have viewed a written document indicating that his great-grandmother Philomène was a slave. There are no existing birth records for her or his grandmother Eugenie. The law concerning slaves is clear—offspring follows the mother's condition. This is the long-established principle governing slaves and animals."

From the jury box, Signet shot a triumphant glance at Morel. Doc sighed with relief. He would soon have his money and be acquitted of all his debts.

"Philippe's owner is declared to be Chantelle d'Alembert. Her dowry, provided by her father Gustave d'Alembert, has been merged in a null-and-void marriage contract with that of the slave Bouchard. It will take some time to realize a legal resolution. I understand that the affected party's property will be held in escrow by the banking firm of Jules Signet." Harkness raised his head and stared directly at Signet. "In exchange for my signature on any document, certain conditions must be met."

Signet looked unmoved, but Morel sucked in a quick, nervous breath. It wasn't all to be open-and-shut. Harkness ordered the two bailiffs to remove Philippe and take him down the hallway out of earshot. He waited until they were gone.

"You obviously want this boy out of the way so you can take control of his extensive holdings. No doubt his wife has entered into an agreement to transfer said holdings for a certain agreed-upon sum, and she has entrusted her father to handle the transaction. The family is distressed and willing to unburden the holdings at a ridiculously low price, an action they may later regret. You have obviously found a legal pathway to achieve all these ends and have spun an extremely clever and complex web to ensure that everyone in this courtroom has something to gain or lose by my decision. I resent bitterly any attempt at the manipulation of my person and, even more, that of justice."

The ensuing silence affected even the imperturbable Signet who saw the dream slipping from his grasp. Doc Applegate was the only person present who seemed unconcerned.

"Your legal case was well-constructed and it does you great credit, but as things stand, I cannot allow immediate transfer of property. We must all take a step back from this precipice and reflect upon the consequences of our actions. In a year's time, if no maternal birth records or manumission papers can be produced, we will then finalize the transfer."

Morel and Signet sighed in dismay but made no comment. Judge Harkness had not finished.

"I am therefore granting Jules Signet trusteeship, to hold the property in escrow with the legal right to manage Philippe Bouchard's portion of the estate owned by Chantelle d'Alembert and to see that all immovable property—estate in land, real estate and real property—remains within said estate. All other forms of property— goods and chattels, movable or personal property, and legal tender—may be managed to increase the wealth of the estate in escrow. No money withdrawals will be made other than for managerial purposes of said estate, or for those business fees currently established by the bank. Any monies gained from speculation, profits, or from the normal sale of products will be deposited directly into the estate, and all bills of sale will be retained for this court to review."

Harkness then provided an illustration packed with unmistakable meaning. "For example, if the bank wishes to sell slaves to a Brazilian plantation owner, those monies will be deposited directly into the estate with corroborating bills of sale."

Doc noticed the relieved expressions on Signet's and Morel's faces. Judge Harkness had granted Signet temporary control of the estate, albeit on a limited basis. Phillippe Bouchard could be legally sold to a Brazilian plantation owner—and would never be heard from again. Within a year Signet could finalize the takeover. It seemed fair enough.

"Additionally I will require evidence that all property has been handled in a proper, legal manner. No losses at sea, no accidental mishaps will be tolerated. I will include a provision demanding proof that any slaves sold abroad have not been mistreated and are alive at the end of the year. Do I make myself clear?"

"Yes, Your Honor," Morel agreed.

Harkness ignored him and glared down at Signet. "I want to hear it from your mouth *and* I will require your agreement in writing."

"Yes, Your Honor."

"Then, this hearing is adjourned." Harkness rose and exited the room.

Doc found himself actually admiring Harkness. The judge recognized the rottenness of the deal, had instantly seen to the heart of it. Although acting to protect himself, he served notice that the smug Signet could not have everything to his liking. And he ensured Philippe's safety—for at least a year.

Morel strode over and took Signet's hand. "Congratulations, Jules."

Signet seethed with quiet anger, his Creole dignity insulted, the long-standing animosity toward unwelcome American officials inflamed. "The effrontery of that old bastard!" he whispered. "I have never been so humiliated."

"But you have achieved all your goals. As you hoped, Bouchard was declared a slave. His property has been transferred for you to manage. Within a year it will all be yours."

———➤•◄———

On Signet's orders, the two bailiffs muscled Philippe into a waiting carriage and drove him down to the levee. Turning east, they wheeled past warehouses, multi-colored droves of humanity, piles of cargoes, and innumerable flatboats tied up at the docks. Farther downstream the masts and spars of oceangoing vessels resembled a dense forest, etching the gray sky with their stark silhouettes. Here the channel accommodated ships of the deepest drafts.

The *Lisette*, a broad-beamed three-masted schooner, lay anchored almost a mile below the French Quarter near the end of the deep water moorings. A ship's officer waited on deck, ready to oversee the transfer. Under his watch two sailors hustled Philippe into the depths of the cavernous hold. *Lisette* was not a slave ship, but, if smell was any indicator, she had carried slaves on previous journeys. The foulness struck with a ferocity that almost buckled Philippe's knees, growing worse as they neared the stern. The below-deck planks were slick with bilge water and human waste.

One sailor carried a small tallow lamp. Although the sputtering flame gave off poor light, it enabled Philippe to see the rough shelving of the slave planks. Another sailor shoved him onto a shelf and fastened heavy iron cuffs around his ankles. The cold metal struck a chill that wracked his whole body. Philippe realized that slaves endured this sort of treatment all the time. Most certainly his own slaves had been shackled in this manner during importation to his sugar and cotton plantations from the West Indies. It put things in a whole new perspective.

The sailor said, "Behave yourself and we'll bring you a plate of food toward evening. You're luckier than the others; you will eat what we eat. Captain's orders."

"Never heard of that happenin' before," grunted the first sailor.

Philippe remained silent. Delacroix would sort this out. Then only God could help those who had brought this upon him.

———————▶ • ◀———————

For days Pierre Delacroix tried, unsuccessfully, to see Judge Harkness. He left his calling card, put a watch on the courthouse, and even paid multiple visits to the judge's home. Edna Harkness claimed the judge was indisposed and unable to receive visitors. He stopped in to interview Chantelle Bouchard and was turned away at the door. No one at the Bouchard Exchange had seen Philippe. Delacroix then lodged inquiries with the militia commander, but that officer seemed unconcerned. However, he did launch a half-hearted investigation. A few days later, Chantelle informed Delacroix that Philippe had departed for Martinique on urgent business. He found this news perplexing; the young man would certainly have informed him beforehand of such a venture. Nothing about her story sounded right.

Jules Signet met him for coffee at the *Café des Améliorations*. From the beginning Delacroix discerned that something was wrong. The banker's attempts to answer questions and spread oil on troubled waters unsettled him even more. His explanations were too plausible, too elaborate to be genuine.

Delacroix had dealt with treachery many times in his long life; here he sensed evil of the worst kind. As one of New Orleans' elite citizens, he was not without contacts. Intelligence was a natural part of the business world, not confined to the levee or the French Quarter. Many of his informants came from the American sector, that wild, booming western portion of the city that lay across Canal Street. Word was circulating that Signet had employed the two court "bailiffs" sent to escort Philippe to the courthouse. On the evening of Philippe's disappearance, the bailiffs had gone drinking in one of the less reputable taverns. A quarrel broke out and both men were killed in a blazing gun battle. No one knew the men with whom they had fought. It was all too neat to be mere coincidence. Delacroix thought it wise to keep that knowledge to himself.

"Why did Judge Harkness summon Philippe?" he asked straightforwardly.

"Ah! That I do not know," Signet replied. "Bouchard spoke to me shortly after the meeting and asked if one of my ships was bound for a Caribbean port. He wished to travel immediately to the port of Sainte-Pierre, Martinique."

"Did he say why?"

"He did not."

"What did you tell him?"

"One of my ships would depart for Le Havre on Wednesday. He offered to pay for the brief diversion to Sainte-Pierre, and I agreed."

Delacroix mulled over the reasons why Philippe might go to Martinique. His relations came from there. They had owned some profitable plantations before moving to Louisiana, but sold out just before the French Revolution. As Philippe's financial advisor, Delacroix had studied all of his assets. There were now no holdings in Martinique.

"And ship's name?"

"The *Marigny*."

Delacroix nodded. The *Marigny* had indeed set sail on Wednesday. "Is there nothing else you can tell me? He is like a son to me. I feel I am responsible."

"Alas, it is all I know."

Delacroix sipped his coffee, resolving to see Judge Harkness as soon as possible. He knew he would learn nothing more here.

———◆———

Later that afternoon, Doc Applegate caught up with Jules Signet.

The banker was in an irritable mood, not wanting to speak. But Doc was on a mission. He wanted that debt cancelled and his money in hand. For the past five days Signet had avoided him and it was time to force the issue. Doc strode past the protesting clerks and into Signet's spacious office. The banker sat at his ornate Louis XIV desk reading through a sheaf of papers.

"Not now, Doctor. I am busy."

"I am afraid *my* business can wait no longer. We made a bargain, and I have delivered my end. Just hand me that note absolving me of all debt and the three hundred dollars upon which we agreed."

"As you well know, I do not yet own the Bouchard estate. I am merely a humble manager."

"That is not my concern. You contracted me to prove young Philippe a negro so Morel could have him declared a slave. All that happened—exactly as you requested."

"Still, I did not get what I wanted."

"You will have it all in one year. Philippe cannot contest the decision and no manumission papers will ever be produced. His wife will legally transfer the property and Judge Harkness will approve the sale."

"All that has not yet been realized."

"My part was critical in the decision."

"Here is *my* decision. I will hold your note until the day I receive full ownership of the estate. You will not be paid your three hundred dollars until that day."

"Are you reneging on me?" Doc's anger eclipsed Signet's.

"I prefer to call it a 'delay due to circumstances.' You will have everything when I do."

Doc knew it was folly to challenge a man like Jules Signet; the banker brushed aside enemies as casually as a man would kill flies. But Doc would not allow this man to string him along for another year.

"This is really unjust—and unwise. If you do not give me all upon which we honorably agreed, you will surely regret it."

"You are threatening me?" Signet looked almost amused.

"When I leave this office I will head straight to Judge Harkness and tell him the whole sordid story. Then I will visit Delacroix and have him mobilize the other merchants to unite and put an end to your depredations. Can you imagine the D'Alembert's rage when I tell them the truth?"

Signet no longer wore the smile. "You have overreached yourself, Doctor." He rose from his desk and crossed the wooden floor, opening the top drawer of a tall wooden cabinet. It took some searching, but he found the note, scrawled his signature on it, and handed it over.

Doc examined the heavy beige paper, then folded and slid it into his breast pocket. "I only wanted you to fulfill your part of our contract—as I did."

"Of course, you are right," Signet replied icily. Returning to his desk he opened a large leather-bound book, dipped his quill into an inkwell and began writing a chèque.

"If it is all the same to you, I prefer gold coin."

Signet slammed his quill upon the desk. He left the room and whispered instructions to one of his clerks. He returned, his expression livid. "You anger me, Doctor."

"I do not see why. We *did* make a deal."

"It is our last deal. Remember this upon pain of death—you will never discuss any of this to a living soul. "

"That was always understood. I do not wish to implicate myself. But let me warn you, I will not suffer the same fate of your so-called bailiffs. In the event of my untimely death, I have written letters which will be delivered to those persons directly involved. The letters detail everything that has happened. They are not at my house or on my person. They serve as my insurance and I pray they will never be used."

"Then good day, Doctor Applegate. We shall not see each other again—a great pleasure for us both."

Doc left with three hundred American dollars in his coat pockets, all in eagles—shiny ten-dollar gold pieces. He felt secure, knowing he was at last debt free. But the moment fell far short of his expectations. During the past four nights he had awakened from fitful sleep, disturbed by nightmares of Philippe—beaten, humiliated, stripped of his estates, ruined, and enslaved. The image of the young man's physical and mental agony tormented him, even during the daytime. Doc never counted on his emotions entering into the equation. In the beginning it had seemed like a game, an abstract test of his skill—an answer to his financial crisis. Jules Signet had picked him out of the gutter, exploited his weakness, and led him to the mountaintop, tempting him with glittering possibilities of a new life. And Doc had fallen willingly, playing the key role in a malicious crime upon an innocent man. Worse than that, he had violated all the principles of the Hippocratic Oath to which he had sworn. Instead of saving life, he had destroyed it.

A month before the hearing he had moved back into his humble home in the American sector. One could handle only so much coddling. The opulence at Signet's townhouse had grown stifling, almost cloying, lightened all too briefly by medical calls and rare visits with Solange. In fact, it was her willingness to embrace the Ursuline virtues of simplicity and hard work that inspired him to leave his comfortable surroundings and return to his house. Signet had only reluctantly allowed this, but kept a close watch to ensure there was no backsliding. At first the move had been a shock—having to buy firewood from river rats who peddled it in small carts, building his own fires, shopping for goods, and cooking his own meals, but even in the meanness he felt cleaner. At least he could temporarily escape the duplicity in which he was engaged. But now that the evil was done, guilt clung like an obscene shadow.

Darkness fell as he crossed Canal Street and entered the American sector. His home lay several blocks west and north. An average person could easily lose himself in the haphazard squalor. Sidewalks, where there were any, were simply planks or sometimes a single split log pegged into the ground. In some streets wooden drains functioned as gutters, while in others open ditches served the same purpose. Into them was thrown refuse of every description. For this reason the city stank outrageously, especially in the hot, humid months of summer. During rainy seasons the unpaved streets became impassable by vehicles, and sometimes it was necessary to make long detours to reach a destination on foot. Official street names were not posted; streets were often known locally by the names of notable residents. They also lacked the oil torchlights of the French Quarter. Prudent residents carried lanterns when they went out at night.

Doc carried no lantern this evening, but he did pack a loaded and primed double-barreled pistol. Three hundred dollars was a great deal of money. Added to the amount Guillot and other patients had paid, it made a considerable sum, enough to pay for a ship passage north and to start a new medical practice—a new life. But there were human predators out there, ever-skulking in the darkness, looking for opportunity and easy wealth. Many of them would kill for far less money than Doc possessed. Robbery and murder was their vocation. Fortunately, he was known as a man of little or no means, and his reputation as physician provided him a certain degree of immunity. More importantly, he belonged to Emmett Barnett's inner circle—and this entitled him to certain unspoken benefits, including protection. No one would dare attack the vicious little tavern owner's physician. In the New Orleans underworld few men wielded more clout.

Doc reflected upon his dealings with Jules Signet. The more he thought on his words, the more he regretted them. The banker utterly abhorred humiliation. It was common knowledge that he exacted retribution upon those who wronged him. Doc knew firsthand how cold and devious the man could be. Rumors were circulating that Signet had ordered the two bailiffs killed; usually there was some shred of truth attached to those tales. Was it done to keep their silence? A shiver of fear snaked up his spine. After all, he had threatened to tell the whole story to New Orleans' most prominent citizens. Might that make him expendable? He quickened his pace and the exertion hurt his left knee. Sharp pains stabbed with every step, but he could not afford to slow down. He glanced behind to make certain no one followed. It was impossible to tell anything in the river fog that obscured the streets.

It was time to leave New Orleans. He had a plan, but with Signet's spies stationed everywhere it would not be easy. When he reached home, he did not light a candle or build a fire. Instead, he groped his way across the room until he located the fireplace. At the base on the left-hand side, he dislodged a loose stone and withdrew the cloth money bag Guillot had given him. Counting carefully, he deposited the thirty gold eagles from his pockets.

"Thirty pieces of gold," he muttered. "Judas got only silver for his treachery."

In the darkness he found his medical case and secreted the bag of coins in the false bottom. Then he packed a small travel valise with extra clothing, shaving supplies, and other personal belongings. Quietly, he crossed to the front door and opened it a crack. A twig snapped outside and his blood ran cold. He heard approaching footsteps and spied the orange glow from a lit cigar. He drew his pistol and cocked both hammers.

"Who goes there?" he challenged.

"Louis Reynard. I come from the tavern. Emmett is sick. He sent me to fetch you."

Doc did not know anyone named Louis Reynard. His hand trembled with fear as he opened the door wider.

"What is wrong with him?"

"Who knows?"

"Is anyone else with you?"

"Just me."

Reluctantly Doc picked up his bags and followed, tucking the long-barreled pistol securely under his arm where he could draw it on an instant's notice. Luck appeared to favor, for Louis led him toward the river, turning west in the tavern's direction.

Oddly enough, it was Doc's intended destination. He had decided that Emmett Barnett's Tavern would serve as an ideal hideout. Travelers, ship captains, and boatmen sometimes rented rooms during the unloading and loading of cargoes. Of course the women in Emmett's employ made their stays much more enjoyable. These women often robbed unsuspecting newcomers, but regular patrons were protected, and this guaranteed their return business. Doc enjoyed an even more special status. Hopefully he could count on additional protection.

They soon reached the yellow stone tavern. Lanterns glowed dully in the fog, and oil torches flickered along the front porch, casting it in a golden glow. A red lantern hung near the main door, the universal sign that prostitutes worked there. Doc could smell liquor, tobacco smoke and human sweat through the green-shuttered windows. His mouth watered for a drink, but he resolved to keep his wits about him this night. Louis opened the door and cleared a path through the raucous Friday night crowd.

Emmett Barnett's Tavern was an imposing two-story building constructed of stone blocks and timber beams with a high sloping roof. Built on a simple rectangular floorplan shortly after the American annexation in 1803, it had increased in length as Barnett purchased adjacent buildings, connecting them by knocking doorways in the outer walls. The tavern owner then acquired buildings behind him and incorporated them into his holdings.

Doc followed Louis up the wooden stairs, taking note of the women coming down and going up. Louis escorted him down a long smoky hallway with rooms on either side. Behind one closed door, Doc could hear shrieks of laughter; behind another came heavy panting and moaning. At yet another door a woman protested, "Oh, you dirty, dirty devil—not *that!*"

At the end of the hallway they turned left, passing through the heavy wall of the main building and into another. Mercifully, it was quieter.

'In here," Louis directed. He rapped lightly on the door.

"Enter!" bade a deep voice.

Louis opened the door and gestured for Doc to enter. A single lamp burned at the bedside. Doc was impressed with the furnishings—floor-to-ceiling drapes, wall sconces, a fireplace, polished wooden table, and matching chairs, an elaborate armoire, French landscape paintings, and a washstand with mirror and wash basin.

Emmett Barnett lay on a brass-framed bed, shivering under the covers. As Doc neared he caught the sickening-sour whiff of fever and stomach trouble.

Emmett wore a black leather patch over the blind eye, but his good eye glittered feverishly, revealing agony and fear.

"What ails you, good friend?" Doc inquired softly.

"Guts," groaned Emmett. He was definitely not a man of words.

"Is it in the lower guts?"

"Here," Emmett raised the sheets and showed him.

"How long have you had the cramps?" Doc asked.

"This morning."

"Let me see." Doc set down his bag and knelt at the bedside. He placed his hands on Emmett's distended belly, working his fingers gently downward and over to the left side. He felt and heard the gurgle of angry gas and internal fluids. The little man flinched and groaned in abject misery. Doc felt his forehead. Emmett burned with fever. He looked horrible.

"I die."

"Maybe not. Have you suffered badly from the squirts?"

"All day."

Doc peered cautiously into the chamber pot. "There is nothing here to examine."

Emmett indicated an enormous mulatto woman sitting behind the bed curtain. "She take out and clean each time." Doc had been so focused on his patient he had not noticed her.

"Was there blood and mucus in it?"

Emmett spoke to her in a strange language, a mixture of French, African dialects, Indian, and English. She nodded. Doc hazarded that Emmett suffered from the bloody flux. Actually it could be any in a whole host of diseases common to this city, but the flux was a common malady in New Orleans, killer of many of its inhabitants.

Doc gave his first order. "Have the woman fetch someone who can take simple directions in English."

Emmett translated and sent her downstairs. The little tavern owner rolled onto his side and groaned as another cramp gripped him.

Doc knew he would have to work fast. When the woman brought Louis back, he gave a string of other instructions.

"Louis, tell her to boil several pots of clean water and carry them up here. I wish to brew some infusions. Find me the best quality black tea, and see if you can't find some lemons or limes. I also want a clean mug, a spoon and a knife."

"No knife!" Emmett roared.

"I need it to cut up the lemons. Let me be the doctor." He turned back to address Louis. "Tell no one why you want these things. No one need know Emmett is ill. Remember, you have not seen me. Now go."

In his gruff manner, Emmett ordered the woman to give Louis some money for the items. She fetched his change purse and watched as the tavern owner fished with trembling hands for a few silver bits and copper coins. With money in hand, Louis left respectfully.

Doc rummaged through his black bag. "I need more light in here," he complained. "Have the woman light some candles first; then send her to boil that water." Using the best medical knowledge available, he intended to attack the flux head on. The prevailing theory suggested that Emmett had ingested something unclean, and whatever it was, now grew in the bowels. It must be purged. Doc withdrew a blue glass bottle containing white crystalline chunks of calomel. The woman soon returned with a pot of boiled water, still steaming. She placed it on the nightstand and handed Doc a battered tin mug. He wiped it out and shook in a few calomel crystals before filling it with hot water; then he ground the crystals and stirred the mixture, allowing it to cool somewhat before passing it to the patient. "Drink this—all of it."

The woman helped the little man sit upright. Doc watched him struggle to drink down it down.

"Taste like hell! Emmett roared.

"Emmett, this is a purgative called calomel. It will flush that bloody flux and excess bile out of your guts. No matter how bad you feel, you keep on drinking—as much as I tell you to. Do you understand?"

The little tavern owner nodded pathetically, totally dependent upon Doc's knowledge. Sometime later, Louis returned with a brick of black tea, another mug, and the required silverware. He apologized that he could find no lemons.

"No matter—you can fetch those tomorrow morning."

When more steaming pots of water arrived, Doc ordered the woman to brew some tea. He then crushed up another lump of calomel and stirred it into the tea. Although Doc only used it in the most drastic cases, the remedy had been prescribed throughout the 18th Century and especially during the Revolution to treat various ailments. Doctor Benjamin Rush, the great American physician and Professor of Chemistry at the College of Philadelphia, was one particular advocate of calomel and had used it to treat sufferers of yellow fever during the Philadelphia outbreak of 1793. Rush had even concocted a proprietary purgative with calomel as one of the main ingredients. Called *Doctor Rush's Thunderbolts*, it was used by Meriwether Lewis and William Clark on their expedition to the Pacific Coast. As with many medicines, there existed almost as much poison as cure, so Doc took care to administer only small dosages.

It always amazed him how fast calomel went to work. Doc was grateful for the mulatto woman's presence; he could retreat to the far corner of the room and let her deal with the unpleasantness. Emmett made a pathetic figure, sitting on his chamber pot, doubled over in pain and groaning at every violent explosion. He struggled throughout most of the night, alternatively drinking tea and visiting the chamber pot.

Emmett Barnett was a strange human figure, unlike anyone he had ever met. The man stood just four feet-ten inches tall and his shoulders were about that broad across. He had bandy little legs and a wide, dark-complexioned face concealed partially by eyepatch, sideburns and large drooping moustaches. One might find him comical to look at, but woe be unto the person who laughed, and God help the man who crossed him. Emmett was as hard as iron and renowned for his meanness. Over two dozen patrons had died in his tavern—all at his hands. He usually kept two double-barreled shotguns under the counter, but he also packed a pair of pistols and could usually lay hands on various other weapons. Emmett was an expert knife fighter and had sliced and stabbed more men than people could count. He could also be sadistic, adding calculated atrocity to his violence. Some of his enemies had died slow, torturous deaths, like the man disemboweled and hung from the yardarms of an oceangoing sloop, or the traveler who lost both legs after making fun of Emmett's short stature. Dozens of similar legends recounted his cruelty. Doc wondered briefly if he should work so hard to save such a monster, but he shoved the thought aside. He was combatting a deadly disease responsible for innumerable deaths—one that frustrated most physicians.

European doctors reported limited success by making the patient drink large volumes of liquids to replace what bodily fluids were lost. There existed few known remedies, but Choctaw Indians in backcountry Louisiana favored a tea brewed from the blackberry root and ginseng drops. Doc had prescribed it and found it to have some efficacy. The flux was so common that he kept a good stock of the ground root on hand. Another remedy was black China tea. He had observed that those people who drank hot tea and coffee suffered fewer incidents and milder symptoms of the disease. Ship captains swore they had cured ill sailors with lemon or lime juice. Doc soon located the packet of blackberry root powder, enough to brew several large cups of tea. He mixed a generous measure of blackberry root powder into a cup of black tea, adding a splash of laudanum to ease the pain. Over time, Emmett drank three more cups, then fell back exhausted. "Oh no, dear friend," Doc clucked. "You have much more to drink."

Doc ordered Louis and the woman to boil more water and to bring up some clean towels. While they were gone, he brewed another cup of strong tea and ordered Emmett to drink it down. The tea seemed to calm his churning guts. The laudanum had definitely eased the pain. Doc kept the liquids coming throughout the night. The little tavern owner drank down each cup faithfully. Toward morning the crisis seemed to pass and everyone managed a little sleep.

———•———

A shaft of weak winter sunlight found its way through a gap in the drapery and spilled onto the wooden floorboards. Doc woke, his back and neck stiff from his slumped position. He had slept in his chair, and now his entire body ached. The tavern owner was sitting up in bed, watching him with his single black eye. A look of gratitude took some of the edge off his harsh features. Perhaps his illness softened them.

"How are you this morning, Emmett?"

"You saved my life."

Those four words spoke volumes. Doc rose painfully and crossed the floor to lay his hand on Emmett's forehead. The fever had broken. "Well, I may have played a small part. Then I stepped back, as I usually do, and let nature take its course. Your physical constitution counted heavily in the matter. In truth I have lost several patients to this disease."

"How much I owe?"

Doc spoke directly, making no attempt to hide the truth. "I need a place to hide. I fear someone is after me. I need your protection—at least until I can find passage out of here."

Emmett nodded solemnly. "You stay here. I have room."

Chapter Seven

Breckinridge County, Kentucky—February 9, 1816

Craig Ridgeway enjoyed reading the latest newspapers at Rosenbotham's Store. With increased traffic on the river, news traveled faster than ever before. Papers from Philadelphia and Pittsburgh were less of a rarity, brought down by the growing number of flatboats and keelboats on their way to New Orleans. As more steamboats pounded up the Mississippi and Ohio Rivers, even the occasional New Orleans paper turned up at the store. Copies of Lexington's *Kentucky Gazette* and Louisville's *Western Courier* arrived with more frequency. Mostly these contained reprinted national news stories from east coast newspapers and some foreign news in addition to sometimes-colorful local announcements. Above all else, the papers shared opinions on state politics and national issues regarding the American frontier. Rosenbotham regularly posted his old newspapers on the front walls for people to read.

Much was happening on the local, state, and national level. A new county— Daviess—now lay on Breckinridge County's western border, carved from Ohio County. A gubernatorial election held new prospects for Kentucky. National Elections for the U.S. House of Representatives, and U.S. Senate approached. And Americans would soon choose a new President. Due to Henry Clay's unflagging efforts, it appeared that the country's first protective tariff would become reality. Most farmers in Breckinridge County supported it. Legislators also argued for a Second Bank of the United States to provide a stable, uniform currency and a source of available credit for new business ventures.

National news stories gushed with unbounded pride and optimism. Stories of the Battle of New Orleans still ran, extolling American bravery in the face of superior, almost unbeatable odds. Overnight the war had transformed the New Republic. The United States had proven itself a real power, capable of dealing on equal terms with long-established nations of the world. Its indomitable spirit was perhaps best illustrated by the U.S. President, James Madison, and his wife, Dolley. After the British burned the President's House in 1814, the First Couple had cheerfully moved into "Octagon House" on the corner of New York Avenue and 18th Street. Now they occupied one of a series of magnificent townhouses known as the "Seven Buildings." This temporary presidential home had acquired the nickname "House of a Thousand Candles" after the Madisons hosted a reception for General Andrew Jackson and his wife Rachael in late 1815. Business continued in grand style while workmen repaired and repainted the executive mansion with white, rather than gray paint.

The year 1816 seemed full of new prospects. Craig read articles about American progress—new roads, canals, businesses, and industries. A thriving steam industry had firmly taken root; writers described new steamboats and their capabilities. One story even told of a British steam engine that could run across the ground on a set of rails. It all seemed too incredible.

Hiram Rosenbotham watched him from the counter. "You sure do like reading the papers, don't you Craig?"

"Yes I do. They keep me informed on the prices merchants pay for whiskey and for crops like corn and tobacco." Craig liked Rosenbotham, but he agreed with the local farmers—the storeowner was Cottonwood Bend's most notable skinflint. Rosenbotham oversaw the tobacco inspection warehouse and he owned several other subsidiary businesses. With his connections he kept his fingers firmly on the pulse of Cottonwood Bend and from the boatmen he usually knew the latest prices.

"I wouldn't put my trust in those newspapers," he said. "The prices are long out of date when they reach here."

"You may be correct," Craig agreed, not wanting to rile him.

"Your shipment of yeast and sugar came in last week," Rosenbotham said. "Shall I have Isaac get it for you?"

Hiram's son, Isaac, resembled his father. Both were bald and portly; during the day they both ate great amounts of high-smelling pickled beef sausage, cabbage and raw turnips. Isaac got up to fetch the order.

"Thank you," Craig nodded. It had taken some time for the storeowner to treat him with any measure of respect. In all fairness, the entire community had first regarded him with suspicion due to his association with the vile Widder Fuqua. Things had changed when Father Theodore Badin, Judge Bozarth and Martin McDonnell stepped in. His marriage to Mary, financial success, and service in the war counted heavily toward changing attitudes. These days most people greeted him warmly.

After paying for the bricks of yeast and sacks of sugar, Craig drove his wagon down River Street along the high rock bluff toward the western edge of town. A pale sun glinted weakly on the muddy Ohio, adding little warmth to the cold February morning. It had been a strange winter so far, below average in temperature, but drier than usual. For a month the sky had appeared mostly overcast, as if clouded continuously by a dry fog, making the days seem shorter than they really were. Craig yearned for the warmer weather of spring. He planned to grow more garden vegetables, to plant wheat where he had grown tobacco and sow red clover in last year's upland cornfields. This year, he would grow just enough corn to feed his stock and distill whiskey. He would also clear timber from another part of the Smithhart farm. For that endeavor he would engage Levi Matthews, the local sawyer and miller.

Levi's grain mill was his next destination. But first he would pass Levi's original enterprise—the sawmill. This industry occupied a site at the mouth of Spigot Run, a small creek that rose a few miles back from the river. The little indenture could accommodate just one log raft at a time, and the landing served only for loading and unloading. Through an ingenious scheme of swinging booms, ropes, pulleys and levers, logs were snaked up the banks and stacked in great piles on high ground. Spigot Run ran alongside the lumber yard to the sawmill. There, a small stone dam impounded water for running the saw. Most of the time there was not sufficient water to power the big muley blade. For that reason the lumber yard had two sawpits where men could employ great crosscut saws from above and below. Levi Matthews did a thriving business, cutting and selling sawn lumber for barns and houses. He also sold to flatboat men on their way downriver.

A few years back Levi purchased Cottonwood Bend's only grain mill. Located farther up Spigot Run, the mill lay tucked in a fold of ground just below the mass of steep rock hills a half mile behind the town. Water from various gullies and small creeks collected in the shallow depression that formed the final leg of Spigot Run. The previous owner had dug a small millpond and dammed it to collect the sluggish flow. At various times of the year Levi could enjoy the advantage of waterpower. He had made improvements, digging a bigger pond and partially diverting a small stream into Spigot Run. He had widened and raised the dam, improved the millrace and sluice gate, and built a more efficient waterwheel and wooden cog system. These measures had proven somewhat successful, but long dry spells forced him to fall back on his horse-powered mills. To keep things running in all weather, Levi brought up lumber from his sawmill, built a spacious open barn and added an indoor grist mill. Craig wondered how anyone could turn a profit on this measly stream, but somehow the little man had succeeded. People came from near and far, for the next nearest mill lay twenty miles east, past Hardinsburg. Levi ground grain on tenths, supplied Rosenbotham's store, and sold flour and cornmeal to the flatboat men.

When making whiskey, Craig bought almost all his red wheat and barley from Levi. He tied his team of tan draft horses to the mill's hitching post. Levi was supervising two employees loading a wagon with full sacks of corn. The little red-haired miller was an oddity, standing about five feet tall and shaped like an egg with stick-like arms and legs. He had grown thicker in the middle and the hair at his temples showed signs of gray as did his little spade-like beard. He turned and regarded Craig cynically.

"Well, there he is—the long-lost stranger! Thought you had moved west."

"Not hardly."

"Where have you been keeping yourself?"

"Working hard on the farm, Your Holiness. It keeps me out of trouble."

"Hmm, that's not what I hear," he chuckled.

"What do you hear?"

"All sorts of things. Folks tell me you've been a 'white knight,' trying to keep Judge Bozarth on the straight-and-narrow. Good luck, there! It's not happening—not until somebody castrates that philandering bastard."

"You are a crude man," Craig said, wondering how that news had escaped. "And here I thought you had gotten religion. Didn't they make you a deacon in the Baptist Church?"

"A deacon trumps your pope any day of the week."

"I hope I don't run into Brother Kreisle while I am in town. I might disclose that his deacon is disparaging the most respected member of his congregation. The Judge probably gives more money than everyone put together."

"Trust me—he's not that rich. Kreisle knows him."

"I imagine he does."

"Hey, has the Judge approached you for any money?"

"Why would he do that?" Craig was puzzled by this change in direction.

"It's what he does. He's been doing it for years. Some well-dressed fop strolls off a flatboat, spinning fairytales of a new sure-fire scheme to 'get rich quick.' Usually the fop poses as a banker or financier and packs a mile-long pedigree—all false of course. The Judge falls for it every time and starts scrambling for investors to go in with him. Our Cottonwood Bend folks know to run when they see him coming, but he's pulled in several investors from Hardinsburg. They've all lost their shirts. And the Judge has borrowed money from quite a few of them."

"I didn't know this."

"You wouldn't. All you ever do is work on that farm. Oh, I forgot—you do on occasion chase after lost slaves."

"They weren't lost—they were abducted by slave-catchers."

"People all over town are gabbing about that long rifle shot you made. Heard you killed two more of those outlaws with a shotgun. I may be crude, but you are downright dangerous."

Craig knew he was needling, but Levi had struck a raw nerve. The nightmares of New Orleans had recently returned, mingling with the new, more recent horrors, tormenting his sleep and darkening his days. He wanted nothing more than to forget it, work his land, love his family, and live in peace. But it seemed that violence continued to find him, even on his quiet little farm. And in every instance it drew him into killing someone. Craig felt as if the stench of death would forever contaminate him. He looked off toward the river and said nothing.

Levi realized his blunder and sought to make amends. "So the high-and-mighty Judge Bozarth has not approached you?"

"Not yet. What is his game?"

"Banks, land speculation, cheap paper money. Lots of folks are investing in state banks that print up bushel baskets of money."

"Who would accept paper in the place of hard currency like gold and silver?"

"You're a man after my own heart. I would take grain, chickens or hogs, anything tangible, over worthless paper, but the Judge sees printed money as the salvation of all his financial problems. If you were a debtor, wouldn't you be in favor of paper money?"

"If someone was fool enough to take it as payment, maybe I would. I fear the Judge could one day find himself in worse trouble—especially if he tries to pay his debts with it."

"A Hardinsburg farmer told me that more than two dozen people have petitioned the court to make him pay them back what he has borrowed—first come, first serve."

Craig hated to hear this news. The Judge was so likable—the

man truly did care about people and was always willing to help others in need. It was hard to imagine the great personage in such difficulty. After all, he was a pillar of Cottonwood Bend society, a justice of the peace, and a war hero who had served on Governor Shelby's military council. He was an able lawyer, official assessor for the Breckinridge County Commissioner of Tax, and local militia commander in charge of the Cottonwood Bend Party of Regulators.

"I thought he was wealthy."

"He would be if he let Violet manage their finances," Levi grunted.

"Does she know about his plight?"

"It's hard to say. She may still be sitting on a big pile of money because of her thrift. But if he has borrowed outside of her knowledge, then he's in for more trouble than mere adultery." He stepped back, away from his workers, lowered his voice and asked, "In your opinion was Cecilia Dowell worth all the trouble he got himself into?"

"How would I know?" he asked, giving nothing away.

"Word is, you saw her up close—is she the voluptuous wonder people claim she is?"

"Why don't you ride up there and see for yourself?"

Levi chuckled delightedly. He had dished out his characteristic sarcasm and shared his local gossip; now he was ready to talk business.

"So you and Mary are making another batch of whiskey?"

"We are. I need a half ton of coarse-ground corn, three hundred pounds of red wheat and three hundred of rye. I will fetch it tomorrow."

"What will you do about the barley? The weather is too cold, isn't it?

"Mary has spread it all over the cabin floor and covered it with wet sacking."

"And it has sprouted?"

"It has."

"Never heard of anyone doing that before."

"The cabin is a real mess right now. And it is a real hothouse. We have just begun drying the barley for grinding."

"That new shed will double your income."

"It better had. We paid you enough for it."

At Mary's suggestion Levi had built a stone still house, large enough to hold their cypress wood mash tubs and big copper still and located a safe distance from the barn. She then directed him to construct a stone-and-clay fire pit which he vented with an underground stone duct and chimney. Above this pit they positioned the 110-gallon still. Finally she ordered small fireplaces built at each end of the shed, making it possible to produce whiskey at any time during the year. By feeding fires round the clock Craig and Mary could keep the room warm enough in winter to allow proper fermentation temperatures. It would mean much intense work over a couple of weeks, but it would pay off in the long run, allowing them to work in late fall and winter when they could most effectively use their time.

It cost money to set up for a whiskey distilling run. Much of the initial outlay went into purchasing various grains, yeast and sugar. Levi's milling charges did not come cheap, even though Mary and the women made tough hemp sacks for Craig to trade with him. Then there were expensive oak barrels to buy. These leak-proof barrels, built for long-term storage and transportation of liquids, proved much more costly than those made by a 'dry' or 'slack' cooper.

If time could be measured in money, the preparation involved in a distilling run outstripped all other expenses. First, the copper still and wooden mash tubs required thorough washing. Then Craig must cut, haul and stack large stores of firewood. Mary worked hard to spread and cover barley grains, keeping the sacking wet and watching until the grains sprouted. It took time to drive into town, order and transport all the ingredients, wait at the mill for ground grain, and then inspect and haul the charred barrels. Usually this necessitated several round trips. The malted barley was ground at home. Then Craig must draw and tote buckets of fresh limestone water from the spring well. Watching the distilling process from start to finish took valuable time. Rolling the barrels, hoisting them by ropes and windlass, and positioning them on the racks required heavy labor, and every so often the barrels must be rotated. When one factored in all the other intermediate steps, time was by far the biggest investment.

But the profit could be tremendous. With the British no longer blockading American seaports, demands for inland products swelled. The merchants of New Orleans were paying top prices. Lucinde's father, Pierre Delacroix, had written Martin McDonnell promising to buy all the whiskey Craig could send. The demand for top quality whiskey had resurrected in France. Mary had decided they should venture more into the distilling business and Craig was inclined to agree.

"You are going to need a new barn before long," Levi mused aloud.

"We'll have room. We plan to sell some of the oldest whiskey."

"Still pretty raw, isn't it?"

"We ran our first batch in July, 1812. It is almost four years old."

"My ass it is!"

"Mary keeps sound records. I didn't believe it myself until she showed me. Time passes all too quickly."

"I thought good whiskey needs to age seven years."

"Not necessarily. Martin says that 'maturity' is the real standard, not the number of years."

"Since when did *he* become an expert on whiskey?"

"He gets all kinds of pamphlets and newspapers delivered at Rosenbotham's store. I believe he is the most knowledgeable man I know."

"I won't argue with you there. I know some folks who sell their whiskey after three weeks. They don't go to all the trouble you and Mary do."

"Well, I am willing to bet their whiskey is not as good."

"It's not. It's real rotgut."

"Our whiskey always goes into newly-charred white oak barrels for aging. Martin says the wood has caramelized sugars in it. As it matures, the whiskey draws color and flavor from the charred wood. Maturity, not a particular age, is the goal. Whiskey can age too long and become woody and unbalanced."

"How do *you* measure maturity?"

"Mary draws a sample and evaluates it."

"How?"

"She smells it, tastes it, and analyzes color and clarity by holding it up to the light in a clear glass."

"If you ask me, it's a lot of trouble."

"Rosenbotham says a Methodist preacher sold some of his whiskey for two dollars a gallon. Mary claims we can get that much for ours."

"That's sixty-six dollars a barrel! You had better hang on to that girl. She is a gold mine!"

"She is indeed," Craig agreed. "But she would be first to tell you we don't make that much. The barrels, ingredients, and milling cost dearly. And we will have to sell quite a few barrels to pay for the outlay."

"Go peddle that sob story to someone who might believe you."

"Just have my grain ready by tomorrow."

"Have I ever let you down?"

━━━━━◆━━━━━

Cottonwood Bend Cooperage stood just a hundred paces east of Levi's sawmill on River Street, and it lay adjacent to the blacksmith shop. In fact the two buildings were connected by an interior door. The master cooper, Nathaniel Jolly, had prudently located next to his iron supplier and entered into a loose partnership with the smith, George Claycombe. Jolly manufactured casks, buckets, tubs, butter churns, hogsheads and barrels of all descriptions. After Levi and Rosenbotham, Craig was one of his biggest customers.

Craig watched the cooper bend and shape a boiled barrel stave while another worker rounded off the end of a nearly-finished barrel.

It always amazed him how these barrels could be constructed from loose staves and fitted together to form a leak-proof bond. Claycombe forged iron hoops for the barrels. Under his tutelage Jolly had become a first-rate blacksmith. He also knew how to char barrel interiors for whiskey making.

Judge Bozarth waylaid Craig while they were loading the new barrels. Craig saw him approach and knew instantly his purpose, although the Judge put on a big show of first talking to the other men.

"Why, Craig, my boy! It is good to see you! How are those slaves doing?"

"Greetings, Judge. They are doing fine. Remember, they are not slaves."

"Quite so." He nudged Craig with his elbow. That rescue operation was certainly an exciting event, hey?"

"It was." Craig shifted uncomfortably, not wanting Jolly to hear.

"I might add that you acquitted yourself brilliantly. You slew three of the seven outlaws. Gentlemen, Craig made one of the longest shots I have ever witnessed! He's made a splendid militiaman."

"Your planning and leadership was the key to our success," Craig interjected.

"Yes, yes. It is second nature to me," he beamed.

"Did the sheriff send out men to bury the dead?"

"He did. As a matter of fact there was a rather large reward offered for their capture or death. I naturally appropriated it to cover the expedition's cost."

"I didn't know that."

"Yes, but I could die of old age before I see any of it."

Craig realized that the wily opportunist intended to keep all for himself.

"All loaded, Craig," Jolly announced. "Nine thirty-three gallon whiskey barrels, made of the finest charred white oak wood. That'll be twenty-seven dollars."

"Thanks, Nathaniel." Craig counted out the money and Judge Bozarth watched the exchange with interest.

"Craig, could I interest you in a drink?" the Judge asked.

"I don't drink," Craig replied. "But thank you very much."

"A whiskey distiller like yourself, and you do not imbibe?"

"I'm sorry."

"No matter," he chuckled. "I keep forgetting you are a man of principle." He put an arm around Craig's shoulders and muttered quietly, steering him out of earshot. "That is why I want to bring you further into my confidence and make you this offer."

"What offer?"

Judge Bozarth glanced over his shoulder to make sure no one was listening. He held up his thumb and forefinger to illustrate a miniscule gap. "I am *this* close to making a million dollars."

"A million?"

"Well, perhaps that is a slight exaggeration, but it is more money than you could ever imagine."

"I can imagine a lot."

"Precisely. I am onto a deal that could make us all as rich as kings!" He swept his arm in an expansive gesture. "Try to visualize a carpet of gold coins spilled across your cabin floor, and being able to afford all the modern farm implements and home conveniences— why, you could buy even more land, if that is your desire."

"I can hardly work the land I own."

"If you come in with me, lad, you could hire an entire army to work it."

"Gold coins, you say?"

"Well, as you just demonstrated by purchasing those barrels, it takes an initial investment to realize any sort of profit. You, above all people, must understand that. The tax records show that you and Mary have turned a tidy profit in the past four years."

"And those profits are eaten up in taxes and other outlays. One bad farm year could ruin me." This was not true and the Judge probably knew it. He shook his head in a show of disappointment. Craig felt sorry for him and somewhat beholden for him helping recover Romulus. He did not want to leave things on a bad note. "What is the deal?" As soon as he asked the question, he knew he had made a mistake.

Judge Bozarth's face lit up with hope, revealing the extent of his desperation. "This fellow—his name is immaterial—has lately arrived in Cottonwood Bend, after traveling downriver from Louisville. He is currently staying at the Maple Manor Boardinghouse. He represents several important Kentuckians renowned for their business skill and financial judgment. These men are combining resources to open a number of new state banks. As you know, planters and farmers are expanding their production to exploit the revived European demand. Our southern plantations have never enjoyed such high cotton prices, and their demand for Kentucky hemp bagging has mushroomed. Prices for whiskey, tobacco, and grain are soaring. *This* is the time to invest!"

"Where are these investors from?"

"From Louisville, Lexington and elsewhere. Most of them come from the ranks of Kentucky's elite. There are only a few spots left open for investors. You are an honest young man; that is why I am offering you this rare opportunity."

"Aren't most of these banks risky?"

"Nonsense, lad! Kentucky's business is booming and our population is exploding. People want land—and they need money. And they will borrow and pay it back with interest. Investors in state banks are prospering beyond belief. Land speculators are taking advantage of the loose lending guidelines. It is a 'win-win' situation for all! Have you not made money from investing in your farms? Land speculation is growing ever more profitable. Mark my words—paper money will one day be the new currency."

Even Craig could see that the two professions—land speculation and banking—could eventually work against each other. If borrowers failed, investors must surely suffer. Perhaps the Judge was playing on both sides of the financial fence. Craig resolved it would not be with his and Mary's money. He asked a pointed question.

"What if the banks overextend themselves?"

"Land will stand as collateral."

"Farm prices could collapse. Land values could drop. At some point the original investors will demand gold or silver in payment."

"Copper is also accepted as a form of currency. And why is that? Because our government says it is so. If the United States Treasury decrees that paper is legal tender and it establishes proper values of that tender, then people must accept it as such."

"Do you really think this will happen?"

"By God Almighty I say it shall!"

All of this was more than Craig could wrap his head around, but he was far too conservative to be drawn into such a scheme. He would consult with Martin, just to learn more about the new banks and paper money. Certainly that sagely old gentleman would not invest in such foolishness.

"Judge, I just don't have the money," he lied. "Maybe, when I have sold a large consignment of whiskey, we can talk again. But even then, I am not the sort of big investor you seek." He hoped he would not regret leaving the door open for another proposition.

"Well, well, lad. You must realize that this offer will not stand forever. The man leaves in a few days. If you change your mind, you know where to find me."

"Thanks, Judge. Give Violet my regards."

"I will. Take care, young Ridgeway."

The Judge strode off toward his home. Jolly emerged from his factory and shook his head.

"You didn't fall for it, did you Craig?"

"I don't have the money."

"Then count yourself lucky. That is one desperate man. Do not let him draw you in."

———◆———

February continued to remain cold and mostly dry. Even on "clear" days the sky appeared hazy, as if a gray, semitransparent shroud of smoke dulled the usual pale blue of the winter sky.

Craig saw little of the outdoors while distilling the latest batch of whiskey. After procuring the grain and other ingredients, he and

Mary plunged into the non-stop work of whiskey making. Romulus and Vergina helped tote water and grind the dried barley sprouts. Craig checked Mary's list and measured the different ground grains—three quarters corn, ten percent red wheat and the rest in rye and barley malt—pouring all into the big iron kettle partially filled with limestone spring water. He heated each batch of mash almost to boiling point, stirring it at intervals before allowing the mixture to cool. After a time, he transferred the mash into the first of three cypress wood tubs. Mary added the proper amounts of yeast and sugar and Craig mixed it thoroughly before covering the tubs with wooden lids. Now they worked round the clock to keep the two fireplaces going. The aim was keeping the room warm enough for fermentation to occur, but not too hot to spoil the mash. As the process got underway, it generated certain amount of additional heat and they backed down the size of their fires. Each step required much work and close, constant attention.

Two days after the first vat began "working"–making audible gurgling and bubbling noises—they began cooking a new batch of mash, following the same recipe, filling the second and third vats in the same way. By the fourth day, the first vat quietened down and the working grains settled to the bottom. Mary insisted on dipping and pouring the clear liquid through a clean linen cloth strainer before transferring it into the still. She also filtered the first-run alcohol before double distilling it. No sediments or foreign matter would cheapen the quality of their whiskey.

Martin visited them on the day they fired up the big copper contraption. He watched as Craig chucked split firewood into the fire pit beneath the still for the second distilling run. He squatted low to examine Levi's masonry.

"That pit draws and vents well," he commented. "Not a trace of smoke in this shed. Your friend Levi knows how to build."

"He sure does," Craig admitted as he partially closed the draft.

"Folks in town claim you and Mary plan to sell off your first batch."

"We are if the price is right."

"Old Rosenbotham mentioned he might be interested in taking the whole load off of you."

"I am sure he is. But I doubt he would pay the price we want. He would just turn around and sell it for a profit to the boatmen. I would rather sell directly to them."

"Do they stop at your landing?"

"Rarely," Craig admitted. "We are also waiting to hear from Delacroix in New Orleans. He claims he has strong demand in New Orleans and France."

"Then you should wait. But dangle that prospect in front of Rosenbotham. He knows you have a good product and he wants to buy. You might sell some of it to him by not appearing too eager."

"If he meets our price, we will consider it. I'll share the news with Mary. If she says to sell, we will."

"It has taken a lot of work, but you two have built one of the finest distilleries in this part of Kentucky. Remember that thoughtful planning, hard work, and perseverance always prevails over 'get-rich-quick' schemes."

Craig realized that Martin knew about Judge Bozarth's investment offer. News traveled fast in Breckinridge County. "Don't worry, Martin. I was never tempted. I was just trying to be respectful and hear him out."

"That is what I thought. The Judge may find himself in real financial trouble one day."

"Levi says he is in trouble now. It's hard to understand how anyone could borrow money and give it to a virtual stranger to invest."

"In this business upturn, many are attracted to new state banks and western real estate. Profits can be enormous, and this lures those folks hoping to get rich quick. You could almost forgive the Judge for believing he is investing in a no-lose situation."

"Almost?"

"Some banks *have* prospered under loose-lending guidelines, but they have also loaned out far more than their assets. Land speculators take advantage of easily available money. They buy and sell, pocket their profits and move west to purchase more open lands, cre-

ating whole towns and even developing them. Right now farm prices are high. Europe is buying. New England and Quebec suffered
early frosts last year; their crops failed, so they are buying. But that
will not last forever. Farm prices will fall; land prices will inevitably
tumble. Speculators will be unable to sell their lands. They will de-
fault on their payments and the state banks will go under."

"The Judge believes that paper money will solve any crisis."

"Would you accept printed paper over gold and silver? Would
Bozarth accept it from you?"

"Of course not."

"Neither will the original investors. The banks will fail, but you
can bet the elite will get *their* gold and silver back. It is always the
little investors who are left with nothing."

"What if someone invested and sold before the crash?"

"Then they could conceivably make some money. But most folks
get caught up in the excitement and never see the crash coming."

Craig instinctively knew the Judge was one of those people.

"Almost always, the elite are in better possession of the facts;
many sit on boards of those banks and know exactly when to jump
off."

"I pretty much figured that," Craig laughed. "We will do our
own buying and selling."

Martin said, "You and Mary are wise to consider selling a large
portion of your whiskey now. Prices are much higher than they were
a year ago, but they may not stay that way—especially if the Tariff
is passed."

Craig knew that American farmers might suffer in the likely
event of Britain's retaliation against the Tariff. Martin confirmed his
own instincts—prices were high and it was time to sell. He would
not be like Judge Bozarth and other investors who failed to recognize when to cash in.

"Will you be free to help us with the sugar making?" Martin
asked. "We have already tapped the red maples and hung buckets in
the bottomlands."

"It will take us a few days to finish the distilling."

"The weather is still too cold, but after the first warm day, sap will start running. Those buckets fill up fast."

"We will be ready." After eight days of whiskey making Craig itched to be outdoors and he looked forward to working with the family. "I have a half dozen water buckets you can take. We just finished with them."

"Much obliged, Craig."

"We have some sugar maples on the slope behind the barn. You can tap those if you like."

"There are more in the bottomlands than we could ever use," Martin said.

"I'll bring my wagon so we can keep ahead of those buckets."

The still hissed softly as steam rose into the inverted cone-shaped top, heat forcing alcohol vapors into coiled copper tubing which ran into a cold-water keg. There the vapors cooled into liquid. A tiny stream of clear whiskey dribbled from the end of the copper tubing and into a pan which they would pour into a charred oak barrel. Martin caught some on his finger and tasted it. He smiled approvingly. "You and Mary have found the right recipe. Don't change it."

Breckinridge County, Kentucky—February 19, 1816

Toward mid-February the weather warmed slightly and Martin judged that conditions were right for making maple sugar. Craig enjoyed this annual occurrence, mainly because it was one of those outdoor family affairs in which everyone shared. Like everything else on the farm, sugar making involved an inordinate amount of work, but when everyone pitched together, like they did in corn shucking, hog butchering, or gardening, work seemed more like a social gathering. It also marked the end of winter, one of the last events before taking up snow-retted hemp and beginning the spring plowing and planting. Craig had rolled his last whiskey barrel into the barn; he and the McDonnells had already cut ice from frozen ponds and stored the blocks into their underground icehouses, insulating them with packed straw and sawdust.

Beginning in late January, Martin closely watched the weather in anticipation of maple syrup season. If he tapped too early or too late, it would result in reduced production. He relied upon years of experience and some inner instinct to choose the optimum time to tap the maple trees. Warmer daily temperatures caused sap to rise, but those days must be followed by below-freezing nights. These freeze-thaw cycles were needed to maintain strong sap flow. If it stayed warm, the flow would diminish. And if the trees budded, sap would turn bitter, marking the sugar season's end. For New England farmers, the season usually lasted six weeks, but Martin always tried to finish gathering and cooking in about three.

Craig drove his wagon over to Welcome Hall in the cold pre-dawn darkness. Although it was still dark, a light covering of damp snow blanketed the pastures, making it easy to see the way. Tree-covered hillsides stood out starkly against the snow. The team of tan plow horses seemed to enjoy this outing, judging by the way they picked up their hooves, pranced and snorted, their breath fogging in the cold air. Mary had cooked Craig a full breakfast—smoked ham, hot cornbread, stewed apples, porridge, and hot coffee—but if he did not miss his guess, Agnes would have a cup of coffee for him. Lights already burned inside Welcome Hall as Craig knew they would be. Animals were fed early, eggs gathered, and cows milked. Only then would the McDonnell brothers enjoy breakfast.

Martin had just led his team up from the barn and was tying them to the rail behind the house. He admired Craig's team as he secured them.

"Those horses are in their prime, Craig. They are about the finest pair in these parts. You sure keep them well-fed."

'They are a little heavy," Craig admitted. "But I'll work off some of that weight during plowing season." He was proud of these bright tan giants with their cream-colored manes and tails, and white stockings. They handled beautifully in the field and on the road.

"Come in for a hot cup," Martin invited. "We'll have one before we leave."

They kicked off their boots on the enclosed stoop and entered the farmhouse. His brothers-in-law had finished their breakfast, but Agnes poured him a hot cup of coffee.

"Are you ready to make sugar, Craig?" Stephen asked.

"I am."

"Ma's got a big dinner planned for us. Lucinde will come and help her."

"So will Mary."

"Yes," Agnes put a hand on Craig's shoulder. "We will have to lay on a special dinner!"

Stephen beamed and rubbed his hands together in anticipation. When the three women got together under one roof, the menfolk could always count on an extraordinary meal. Craig enjoyed this feeling of togetherness and belonging. It helped to dispel the ill effects of last night's horrors.

The nightmares had visited again—dead redcoats littering Chalmette Plantation in Louisiana, outlaws bleeding out on the ground below the cabin, river pirates rotting on the banks of the Mississippi River, slave catchers splattered on a frost-covered pasture in Breckinridge County. He had awakened Mary with his trembling and sobs, unaware he was doing it. Despite all rationalizing, he just could not come to grips with the fact that the killings were all warranted. Afterwards, he had lain in bed, wondering how many people in Breckinridge County had killed another human being. Certainly not many. He imagined he had killed more men than Judge Bozarth had—and the Judge was a professional lawman and soldier. It would take great effort to suppress the thought and not let it spoil his day.

Soon, Owen and Lucinde arrived, shaking Craig from his gloom. They made a striking couple—he tall, dark and lean with dark blue eyes, she with black hair and dark brown eyes. Owen looked much darker than his beautiful wife. Craig rarely gave thought that she was the daughter of an octoroon. He just did not think of her as such—she was simply Lucinde, his sister-in-law.

"Uncle Craig!" his nephew, Owen Pierre, galloped across the

floor and embraced him. "Where is Isabel?"

"She will come down later this morning. You two can play together all day long!"

"Hurrah!" shouted the lad.

"Well, we should start collecting that sap," Martin announced. He tugged on his boots.

Craig slid on his boots. "Thank you for the coffee, Mother Agnes."

"Why, you are welcome! We will have a pot ready when you get back."

It was exciting, driving three wagons single file into the dark, silent bottomlands. The trees dripped water, and occasionally a load of melted snow fell from the branches. There was no sun, but Martin hazarded that the day would warm enough to melt the snow. Years ago he had cleared a wide path in the forest; surprisingly it was smoother than the Hardinsburg Road. On either side of the path Craig noticed trees with hanging gourds and buckets covered with planks and, in some instances, stiff cloth. Martin led the procession to an open area before reining his team to a halt.

In previous decades he had selected and marked promising maple trees, those with trunks more than twelve inches in diameter. He came back to the same place year after year. His choice tree, and the favorite of farmers in the New England states, was the sugar maple, also known as hard maple, easily distinguished in autumn by its golden leaves. Martin had learned, through trial and error, that the species yielded about one gallon of syrup or two pounds of sugar for each forty gallons of sap collected. Black and red maples yielded about a gallon of syrup for every sixty gallons of sap. The old man had already begun tapping the smaller trees and red maples.

"You have already done a lot of work," Craig observed.

"Red maples turn to bud earlier, so I wanted to tap them first. Sugar maple sap will stay sweet longer," he explained.

Over the years, Martin had purchased a number of iron spiles, or taps, from Rosenbotham's store. He had also ordered the local blacksmith to make up a big order to his specifications. These added to his goodly supply of hollow wooden taps. As a consequence, he had amassed a large store. Craig learned from him that the word "spile" originated from the Dutch word *spijl*, meaning "stake." Before tapping these in, Martin used a carpenter's hand brace to drill a small hole at a slight upward incline about two inches deep into the tree. Some bigger trees might justify two or three spiles.

Earlier in the week Martin had drilled holes, tapped in spiles, and hung buckets—perhaps half his supply. Now the buckets were filling; that is why he mustered his family to collect the sap. Everyone would chip in and haul it back to Welcome Hall for cooking, and they must stay with the job until done. Sap not boiled immediately could ferment and produce sour, 'off taste' syrup. Usually Martin kept a hot fire burning late into the night and, in some cases, around the clock to boil the sap until it turned to syrup.

The task of collecting sap required much lifting and lugging. The buckets must be taken down and carried, then handed up to Stephen who stood in the McDonnell wagon and poured the sap into white oak barrels. Craig recalled from last year that Martin owned over sixty wooden buckets and several more casks, kegs, firkins, piggins, tin pots, and other odd containers including wax-coated gourds. He had also borrowed every available bucket from Owen and Craig.

While they toted buckets, Martin tapped more trees. At one point, Craig brought over some empty buckets and paused to watch him drill. Martin fished a spile from his coat pocket. "When you do this, Craig, remember not to drive too hard. You gently tap it in so you won't split the bark or shock the tree." He demonstrated with a hammer that he hung on his belt, and Craig stored the image in his mind. He watched a clear drop of sap form at the end of the tap and drop to the ground. Then the tap began a slow, steady drip. Martin hung a bucket on the tap.

They worked all morning, emptying gourds and smaller containers into buckets and then lugging these through the mushy bottom land where the snow melted and turned the ground to mud. Craig tied his wagon a hundred yards past Owen's and began carrying full buckets back to Martin's wagon. Martin drove all his taps and hung every available container from them. Then he helped carry the remaining sap buckets to the wagons. Stephen filled the four wooden barrels first, then the kegs. Owen brought his wagon into play while Craig and Martin rehung empty buckets.

"Is it dinnertime yet, Pa?" Stephen asked. Craig wondered the same thing.

"Close enough," Martin grinned. "Let's head to the house."

They took it slow through the timbered bottomlands, retracing their route and keeping close watch on the barrels of precious sap. Stephen rode in back of Martin's wagon to make sure these would not overturn. Owen secured his kegs with ropes and Craig brought up the rear with his wagon.

Fires blazed in the cookhouse at Welcome Hall and the aroma of roast pork greeted them. Agnes, Mary, and Lucinde laid on a fine meal of chops breaded in flour and spices, baked potatoes with butter, salt and sour cream, pickled cabbage, roasted turnips, beans, and three different kinds of pies—pecan, apple, and blackberry. To drink there was cold buttermilk, spring water, apple cider, and hot coffee. The laughter and conversation was as warming as the fire. Right after dinner the children began playing and laughing.

Mary leaned over and whispered something to Martin. That gentleman smiled and his eyes twinkled with amusement as he rose and tapped the flat of a spoon on his porcelain mug, making a series of clanking noises.

"Your attention, please!" he called out in his compelling baritone voice. "I do believe Mary has an announcement."

Craig noticed Agnes' face as she exchanged knowing glances with Lucinde. Mary rose, slightly blushing.

"Dear husband," she began. "It is my joy to announce that you will be a father once again."

Everyone at the table clapped and cheered. Stephen slapped Craig on the back and shouted, "Good for you!"

This pronouncement came like a thunderbolt from a blue sky—it was the last thing Craig expected. Everyone seemed happy; he was perhaps the only one who was not. All the old worries about childbearing sprang up to confront him. Women died in childbirth all the time; anything could go wrong. He did not know what he would do without Mary. Yet he forced a grin and hugged her, despite his misgivings.

"When?" he asked.

"In August," she smiled warmly, with one arm around his shoulders. "I thought I was with child a full month before Christmas, but waited another month and then some to be sure."

"That's just six months away. You have known since November?"

"You should be happy, for I have spared you three months of worry." She nudged him in the ribcage.

While the womenfolk cleared the table and washed dishes, the men ventured outside to make maple sugar. The first order of business involved building fires under two giant kettles set up beyond the grape arbor near the corncrib. Martin and Stephen had brought up a supply of firewood, but Craig imagined he would soon be using his wagon to help them haul more. It would take much time and close watching to boil the sap into syrup and then reduce it to a sticky brown sugar that could be formed into bricks, stored in crocks, and used throughout the year in all sorts of ways. Martin brought out two of his best oaken buckets and instructed Owen to dip sap from the barrels into them. Craig transferred these to the wagon's edge and Martin slowly poured the sap through a thin linen strainer into the kettle. Stephen held the strainer, an iron hoop wrapped tightly several times with linen cloth. This filtered out any impurities.

Craig remembered his first drink of sap four years ago. He had expected it to be sweet and sticky, but it tasted like cold clear spring water, filtered clean through the tree's interior wood. Martin claimed that only a tiny portion of the sap contained sugar and that most of the water content must be boiled away. This was almost always done outside. The old Indian fighter had seen operations in Upper Canada where settlers made sugar in outdoor lean-tos and stone buildings called "sugar shacks." He liked to relate the story of young Agnes trying to make her first batch of maple syrup inside the cookhouse.

The steam had left a sticky residue on every surface of the room. He was telling this story when Agnes came outside, bundled up in her winter coat and shawl.

"You a-tellin' on me again, Mister McDonnell?" She shook a wooden spoon in mock anger.

"Oh, no! I'm in trouble now!" he laughed. He stoked up a hot fire under the two kettles, but only after Owen partially filled them.

Agnes carried a stone crock of butter under her arm. She set it down, spooned out a hunk and rubbed it around the rims of both kettles. Craig knew the reason for this. Four years ago Agnes taught him that whenever maple sap boiled, it tended to foam up and spill over kettle's sides. The process of rubbing a little butter around the rim, or dripping in a few drops of milk or cream, would help prevent the sap from boiling over.

Every year Martin iterated a wise proverb, and he did so this year: "Never turn your back on boiling sap!"

Craig knew this would not happen. Someone always watched over it, adding careful measures of new sap as it boiled down, scooping off and flicking away brown foam with a long-handled flat scoop. Sometimes Agnes chose to finish off her syrup in much smaller vessels she called "finishing pans." Usually Mary or Lucinde helped at this stage. Craig watched the process unfold, marveling at how much sap must be evaporated to turn into syrup. It was critical to keep the level deep enough so it would not scorch. As it reduced, Agnes called for them to carefully add more sap. She knew that the faster it boiled, the greater the potential for producing a higher quality product. The sap would boil until it "aproned," or ran off a flat wooden paddle in a sheet.

When Agnes determined that the syrup had attained proper thickness, she transferred it into smaller pans and set these on a bed of hot coals which Martin raked from the main fires. With her paddle she stirred briskly to prevent the syrup from scorching and from sticking to the bottoms and sides of the pans. As she stirred, the syrup became so thick it turned into a sticky paste, and then to lumps of brown, flour-like sugar. She then removed the pans and continued stirring until the sugar turned cold. In the end she produced pure, granulated maple sugar ready for molding into bricks, storing in crocks, and better yet—for eating.

At this point Mary and Lucinde brought out the children, all bundled in their winter coats and wrapped in scarves. Martin gathered a panful of clean wet snow from the drift piled behind the corncrib. From the second kettle where the syrup had begun to sheet, he scooped up a ladleful and drizzled it over the snow. The older children, with their mothers' help, twirled the treat onto small wooden spoons for eating. Ruth loved the taste and cried out for more. Even Stephen got into the act, leaving his post in the wagon.

But Martin and Agnes kept watchful eyes on the kettle. This time Mary and Lucinde helped to finish off the batch, pouring it into smaller pans and stirring vigorously until they made brown maple sugar.

Craig and Owen began refilling the first cooled kettle with cold sap, starting the process all over again. Lucinde took the children indoors, but Mary remained to help with the sugar making. Craig enjoyed having her work by his side. He watched with interest as she and Agnes made "maple cream," reducing the syrup to a soft, thick stage and then whipping it into a smooth, creamy consistency. He knew Mary would bring some home to be spread on toasted bread, pancakes, and dried fruit. She even made a delicious type of candy by rolling the cream into little balls and pressing in chopped hickory nutmeats. This event always made dreary winters much more pleasant.

At sunset Craig drove his family home. He intended to come back and help the McDonnells during the night, but it was past milking and feeding time. He first lugged in several armloads of firewood and stoked up the cabin fire while Mary started supper in the Dutch oven. Then he milked the cows, forked hay from the loft, and drew several buckets of spring water to fill the watering trough. The night had turned cold, ideal weather for sap production.

When he returned, Mary was cooking a pie made from potatoes roasted that day at Welcome Hall, crumbled bacon cooked that morning, and dried garden vegetables, chopped onions, herbs, butter and salt. He talked with the children and cleaned his rifles to pass the time, famished when she finally knocked the coals from the crenellated top and removed the lid, revealing a beautifully-browned crust. The pie was delicious and he enjoyed a second helping. Isabel talked again about how good the maple snow treat tasted. Ruth grinned and cooed; Craig was convinced she understood every word. Soon she would be talking in full sentences.

The children went to bed early, tired from their full day. Craig kissed them both goodnight, and Mary tucked them in while he added another log to the fire. Mary joined him and heated water in a small iron pot. When it reached a boil, she removed the pot from the fire and scraped black tea leaves from a pressed block into it. While the leaves steeped she took Craig's hand and held it to her breast.

"I know you are concerned about the new baby, Craig. But you can't worry about such things. There are so many good things in life; you can't spoil them all by worrying about what might happen. Having another child is a joyous occasion, something we should look forward to together."

"You are right," Craig agreed. "I am sorry. You remember I felt this way the other times. I just don't know how I could live without you."

"And I have said before—worrying will not change anything. Nothing is sure in this world; let us enjoy life while we have it."

Craig felt guilty. Mary was such a happy soul, accepting life with a calm happiness that amazed the average person. When they first met, Craig worried about her living in his little shack. Levi Matthews, who orchestrated the communal raising of their new cabin, once remarked, "That girl would be happy in a pigsty!" And he was right.

"I promise I will try hard not to worry. The last thing I want to do is spoil your happiness."

"Hopefully you will feel better when springtime comes. I want you to seriously consider talking to Father about the nightmares. You wake me up in the night."

"I am sorry. I thought I had stopped all that."

"You try so hard to keep it hidden during the day, but I see it on your face when you think I am not watching. At night you shiver and shake, cry and shout. Last night you thrashed about and struck the headboard."

"Mary, I truly did not know! I will try to stop, I promise." He was mortified to know he behaved that way.

"You cannot control it, Craig. That is why I want you talk to Father. He has suffered the same remorse, the same night terrors."

"Talking with him won't help."

"Then please, talk with Father Badin when he comes in.

"I did talk with him, and it did little good. He 'absolved' me and told me to get on with living. I *have* tried. But the nightmares steal in when I am asleep and powerless to stop them."

"It grieves me so to see you suffering."

"Just don't say anything to Martin. Not yet. I think the warmer weather will help me shake it."

"Just don't let bad past events overshadow the good present."

Mary warmed his hooded deerskin coat at the fire and when he put it on, she wrapped a woolen scarf around his neck and kissed him. They held each other for a long while. He stepped outside, not leaving until he heard her lower the heavy wooden latch.

A north breeze swirled across the bottom pasture, chilled and dampened by its recent passage over the Ohio. Although Craig could not see the snowflakes, he could feel them falling on his face. He thought hard on Mary's words, appreciating her wisdom and gentle reasoning. Life was such a fragile commodity that it really was pointless to allow worry and bad feelings to spoil the good. He feared his depressed state might drag her down. He wondered if other soldiers suffered from the oppressive millstone of guilt that he did. Obviously Martin had. During the French War, folks claimed he had killed more Indians than Indians killed whites. A few years later he began killing British soldiers in the Revolutionary War. His actions had made him a hero, but according to Mary, he had struggled for a long time after the war to find inner peace. Craig hoped that time would heal his own wounds.

The McDonnells were still tending the fire when he arrived. Craig took over for Owen who went inside to catch some sleep. He took his turn adding sap, making sure it did not boil over. The torchlight flickered in the breeze but Craig could see the foam and was able to scoop it off, stirring the syrup occasionally. Around midnight Agnes came out to reduce the final batch into sugar. Martin emerged soon afterwards. He checked the barrels and found them all empty.

"You might as well go home and get some rest, Craig. This is the last of it."

"Will you need me tomorrow morning?"

"Yes. The temperature should climb above freezing."

"Do you want me to bring my horses? We didn't use them much today."

"We will tomorrow. I expect we will harvest about three times as much sap as we did today. And I will need you to help bring up some firewood."

Craig showed up again before dawn. The wind died down, but snow covered the ground once more. Again they drove their teams into the foggy bottomlands, aware of every sound in the stillness—a woodpecker hammering, a crow cawing in the distance, and, shortly past sunrise, a flock of geese honking overhead as they winged their way northward. It amazed Craig how closely Martin was attuned with nature. Somehow his prediction for warmer weather proved uncannily accurate, for a gentle breeze rose out of the south and began melting the snow.

The gourds on the red maples had completely filled with sap. Craig admired the twine netting that supported them. Agnes had made these loose-knit baskets and Martin had hung them, tying an ingenious knot that tightened down as the gourds filled and weight increased. Some of the smaller buckets and containers had run over. The bigger sugar maple buckets were heavy with sap. Today, Martin helped carry gourds and lighter containers to the wagons. Everyone stepped lively, knowing the work load had greatly increased.

They worked long past dinnertime. Craig was grateful when they could sit down to eat. He felt guilty that Mary had walked from their cabin over wet, snow-covered ground, but he was glad to see her and his daughters. The reunion was short-lived, for after dinner he and Stephen took the big tans and drove up to the cabin. There they loaded a full cord of firewood and brought it down to Welcome Hall. Craig was glad to do this, since he and Mary would receive a generous share of the sugar. Mary would take part of her share in syrup and use it to glaze her whiskey and brandy-flavored cigars and to sweeten her chewing tobacco. She sold these products to Rosenbotham and to the storekeepers in Hardinsburg, also to private individuals. This made almost as much money as they earned selling hogsheads of tobacco.

———————◆———————

Over the next several days the family worked together at various interlocking tasks—gathering and hauling sap, staying up late to boil it down into syrup, and reducing it further to granulated sugar. Some nights Craig and his family slept over. He grew accustomed to working in shifts, bedding down on blankets in front of the fireplace, eating hot breakfasts and starting all over again. Each morning and evening he trudged home to feed his livestock, milk the cows, gather eggs, and build up a fire in the fireplace. Excepting Mary's sugar-flavored tobacco, none of the sugar making was done for income. The maple sugar would last all year to be used in many ways, making frontier meals more enjoyable.

After three weeks, Martin announced they would shut down the operation and shift to other farm work. He removed each tap with care, assuring Craig that the trees would heal themselves within a year or eighteen months. Next year, as he did every February, he would drill new holes in the same trees and they would suffer no ill effects.

On March 5, Craig and the McDonnells began taking up the snow-retted hemp that had lain in the fields during the winter months. This work must be done before the weather turned warm, for heat would reduce the fibers' strength and salability. Craig now knew how to break random stalks over his knee to check for residual stickiness, to make sure the inner fiber separated easily from the woody stem. They began working long days at Owen's plantation, raking hemp stalks into large piles, loading great armloads into open wagons and hauling them to the barn. There the stalks were placed on a "hemp brake," a crude wooden device resembling a pair of gigantic jaws. The lower "jaw" consisted of a horizontal grid of three boards set edgewise and rounded at their tops. The upper jaw had two similar boards that, when lowered, passed midway between the lower boards. One worker lifted the top jaw while another placed a small bundle of stalks across the bottom boards. Then the operator pressed sharply downward, lifting and repeating the stroke while a worker fed stalks across the brake. A few chomping motions broke up the woody stems and the outer chaff was then shaken free by whipping the fractured bundles against the brake. Only the tough fibers for making rope or cloth remained.

Martin and Owen employed all their field hands for this endeavor. Romulus and Vergina joined Craig in the fields. With eighteen people engaged, the work progressed quickly, enabling them to move within a few days to Martin's farm, then to Craig's, and finally to the Arbuckle farm, Martin's easternmost property, still named for its previous owner. Owen owned two hemp brakes; Martin had built two in 1813 from seasoned burr oak lumber. Last spring Craig hired Levi to construct a hemp brake from the same tough wood. With five operating brakes and a large crew to feed and operate them, the hemp soon piled up.

Each evening the men assisted each other in tying piles of fiber into massive bundles, each weighing as much as 150 pounds. These bundles were weighed and stored in different barns. Before leaving the fields, the workers set fire to the piles of broken stalks, turning the deepening dusk into scenes of picturesque beauty, lighting the sky with bright orange glows.

Craig had read that hemp prices were soaring in the postwar boom. Enterprising buyers purchased raw hemp and shipped it on board keelboats and steamboats to sell to the Lexington ropewalks. But flatboat men were paying top dollar to ship the hemp south for cotton bagging. Craig and Mary estimated they would keep about a third of their crop to manufacture twine and hemp bagging to sell or trade at Levi's grain mill.

During hemp breaking season, the womenfolk got outside to work the spring gardens, hoping that winter's worst weather was over. At the end of February, Rosenbotham had sold them all sorts of seeds—spinach, lettuce, mustard greens, English peas, cabbage, beets, carrots, and onion bulbs. Mary planted her seeds in indoor pots and set them on a table by the south window to take advantage of the rare days of sunshine. When the weather warmed, she would transplant them outdoors. Craig would then cover these young plants with straw to protect them from any late frosts. The lightweight linen covers were reserved for his tobacco bed.

Craig had plowed and harrowed his garden plots in late November, extending their dimensions beyond those of past years. He had also helped Martin and Owen prepare their gardens. He regretted he was so busy working with hemp that he could not help Mary plant the peas and onions. Fortunately, she enjoyed help from the old folks across the road. Diogenes and his wife Maggie were experienced gardeners. Adah and Eliza worked most days, but Penelope was hardly able to venture outside, laid up with rheumatism and a lung ailment. The weather remained unusually cold but dry, and continued frosts stopped them from planting.

One afternoon Martin rubbed his old gunshot and tomahawk wounds and announced, "I think we should rein in our planting season until we see what direction this weather takes. Something tells me winter is a long way from over."

Chapter Eight

New Orleans—March 18, 1816

Much later than originally scheduled, *Lisette* cast anchor and headed downriver, bound for the Gulf of Mexico and thence to Salvador da Bahia in Portuguese Brazil. Philippe Bouchard had spent almost two agonizing months chained in the schooner's hold. Two days before departure, Farron Weeks brought aboard a slave girl named Kayla. The sailors chained her to a shelf on the opposite side of the hull. There was no privacy. Each captive was provided with just enough chain length to stand and use the slop jar. Fortunately it was almost pitch black in the hold. Philippe tried several times to engage the girl in conversation, but she lay listless, void of all hope. In contrast he harbored a rage so intense that it fueled his will to live. One day he would make them all pay.

When they cleared the mouth of the muddy Mississippi, the sailors slapped a pair of leg irons on Philippe and Kayla and marched them up on deck. Bright sunlight seared their vision. Philippe suffered the worst, having not seen the sun in two months. Now he cringed from its overwhelming brilliance. Gradually, his eyes adjusted and he observed his surroundings. The captain put the helm down and ordered full sails on all three masts. Philippe watched as *Lisette's* crew sprang to action, climbing the ratlines, swarming out across the yards and shaking out the heavy canvasses. Each new sail filled as it took on the stiff northwesterly breeze. Astern, the low-lying delta receded into the background. The gulf was still stained chocolate brown from the vast Mississippi silt plume. Some miles farther out, the water turned bright green and then began to reflect the blue sky.

In contrast to the warm spring sun, the wind blew cold, striking through Philippe's thin linen shirt. He could tell he had lost weight, despite eating the same meals as the crew. With his stride considerably restricted by short chains, he began walking up and down the deck.

"Don't get the fool idea of throwing yourself overboard," one sailor cautioned. "Those leg irons will take you down in a flash—and sharks are already circling the ship. I doubt you'd last long either way."

Philippe ignored him and hobbled over to where Kayla crouched. She had found a place near the mainmast sheltered from the wind. "You should try to walk," he counseled. "They confined me in that cursed hold for two months. If I can walk, so can you. We must keep up our strength."

Kayla stared out to sea with a dull, unchanging expression. Her big brown doe eyes registered defeat. Philippe noticed her distended abdomen; she was obviously with child. She was victimized as he was, although in a much different way. He felt sorry for her. In that instant he thought about the slaves he owned. Perhaps they were captured in Africa, uprooted from their way of life, chained, beaten, brought to an alien land, and forced into slavery, to live at the total mercy of their overseers. If not, their ancestors most certainly were. As owner he had never dealt with the institution on a face-to-face basis, never considered its impact beyond the asset and profit sheets. Slavery truly was an abominable practice. Perhaps those northerners who spoke for abolition were not the rabid anarchists other plantation owners made them out to be.

Out there on the open sea with the wooden deck canting and rolling beneath him, Philippe made a solemn pledge to escape his predicament, regain control of his property and manumit his slaves. Perhaps he could buy this girl and free her. He looked down at her and tried again.

"You do want your baby to live, don't you?"

"It put there by a man who paid to have me."

"Well, you can't blame that on the baby, can you?" Philippe held out his hand.

Timidly Kayla took it, allowing him to draw her onto her feet. He steadied her as they walked up and down the length of the deck. The crew left them alone, knowing there was no possibility of escape. Philippe drank in the clean salt air and watched the horizon dip and swell around them as *Lisette* lumbered southward toward her destination.

Doc Applegate remained holed up at Emmett Barnett's Tavern. Despite Emmett's promise of protection, he kept his door locked with loaded pistols at hand. Occasionally he ventured outside to treat injured or sick patrons at the tavern. One morning, Emmett's mulatto woman summoned him to draw an abscessed molar from a prostitute's foul-smelling mouth. Twice he was called down to the bar to stitch up knife wounds. Other than those few incidents, he kept mostly to himself. The food was deplorable and he began drinking again.

He knew that his relapse stemmed from a crushing sense of shame. Two months of seclusion had forced him to reflect wholly upon his criminal actions—and that miserable courtroom scene kept playing over and over in his head. He had used his professional knowledge in the worst way to take advantage of his friend and patient, Judge Harkness. The slave girl, Kayla, was powerless to resist when he 'prescribed' her services for the judge. Now the delightful child was bound for a Brazilian sugar plantation carrying an unwanted baby in her belly. He had totally ruined poor Philippe— breaking up his marriage, causing undue agony for his wife and in-laws, using that spurious classification scheme to declare him a negro, and giving his enemies the weapons with which to steal his inheritance and life's work. It was almost as if someone else had committed those atrocities. Waves of horror washed over him as he remembered Philippe's anguished cries. The escalating guilt was driving him mad.

Doc wondered how he had allowed Signet to buy him. Like the wretched prostitutes at Emmett's tavern, he had sold himself for a price. Perhaps he was sicker than those he treated. Often he had wondered about the human brain. As an organ of the body, could it possibly be subject to disease? As a young doctor he had been called to the prisons to provide official declarations of death. He interviewed several condemned criminals prior to their executions, and in some cases wondered if they did not suffer from some sickness of the brain. Some of the condemned had stolen money or possessions out of need, or killed someone in a rash moment; Doc had done worse, scheming and planning deliberately over weeks to commit his evil. He wondered if he could ever expunge the guilt from his mind.

In making plans to leave New Orleans, Doc clung to something that resembled sanity. Emmett purchased his house for one hundred dollars and still refused to take money for rent. The tavern owner was wholly convinced Doc could work miracles. He ordered Louis to make discreet inquiries at the levee; twice the cohort brought encouraging prospects of ocean-going ships that could provide passage around Spanish Florida to a New England port.

But Doc held back for a number of reasons. There was so much unfinished business. He yearned to see Solange again. Something wonderful had passed between them and he could not walk away from that. His friend, Judge Harkness, was sick and not receiving visitors. And those two young souls, Philippe and Kayla were bound for a living hell in Portuguese Brazil. He wished he could undo it all. Like Judas Iscariot, he had betrayed innocent blood and was now seized with remorse. Judas had gone out and hanged himself. Doc considered the loaded pistol on his nightstand.

St. Louis Cathedral, New Orleans—March 20, 1816

St. Louis Cathedral dominated the *Place d'Armes,* New Orleans' famous public square. It stood as the centerpiece of *Vieux Carré,* the old French Quarter, flanked by the matching buildings, *Presbyteré* and *Cabildo.* Arguably the finest construction in Louisiana, the massive brick church was Spanish in concept, featuring twin hexagonal towers capped with bell-shaped roofs. A balustrade artistically disguised the low-pitched terrace roof. The building was plastered and painted in front to give the impression of marble. Three Roman Catholic churches had stood on the site since 1718. The second church burned, as did most of the city, in the 'Great New Orleans Fire' of 1788. At that time Spain ruled Louisiana. A new church was built, grander than those before, and it barely escaped the fire of 1794. Dedicated as a cathedral on Christmas Eve of that year, its bishop administered the newly created Diocese of Louisiana and the Floridas.

Doc ordered the driver to wait while he went inside. He was not a Catholic; to him the trappings and rituals of the Roman Catholic Church had always seemed a bit pagan and pathetically ineffectual. As an educated man of science, he had always viewed Catholics as a malleable, superstitious lot who followed their priests like dumb sheep. He did not recognize the supremacy of the pope, or the complex hierarchy of church administration. No doubt this stemmed from his strict Protestant upbringing. But long ago he had abandoned his own faith—he could not remember when he last attended a church service, let alone with an intent to worship.

The vast interior consisted of a central space divided into three aisles by brick pillars. Built on the same premise as cathedrals in Europe, the designers created St. Louis Cathedral to inspire awe and reverence, gracing it with a magnificent altar, religious paintings and sculptures. Candles flickered on each side of the altar, near where he hoped to find the confessional booths.

Doc crept hesitantly down the center aisle, admiring what artwork he could see on the vast, high-vaulted ceiling, but dreading what he was about to do. Like many Protestants, he considered the "sacrament of confession" unnecessary, especially putting one's sins out there for a mortal man to hear. The prospect was so frightening, he could understand why Catholics avoided partaking in the sacrament, sometimes for years at a time. But he was suffering more than he could stand. He must tell someone and unburden his soul. Hopefully the Catholic priest would show mercy, at least hear him out, and help him find peace. Doc knew Abbé Dubourg, and had actually dined with him, but the administrator was currently in Europe. No one knew when he would return. Dubourg was appointed Bishop by Pope Pius VII and consecrated at the "Church of Saint Louis of the French" in Rome on 24 September 1815. This news had circulated all over New Orleans at Christmas time.

"May I help you?" a voice emanated from the shadows.

Doc's heart leaped into his throat. "Who is there?"

"I am Father Valentin Poitier." The priest emerged from behind a pillar. He was a middle-aged man, perhaps too young to hear what Doc was about to tell him.

"I realize it is late, Father," Doc apologized. "But I must talk to someone or I will go mad with guilt."

Father Poitier sighed. "That is why I am here. And it is, of course, the Lenten Season. Come closer so I may see you."

Doc edged into the weak candlelight.

The priest gasped. "I am honored! You are the famous Doctor Applegate. One often hears of your great gift for healing. I hope you thank God daily for that gift."

"I suppose I should," Doc muttered. "Is there somewhere private we can talk?"

"You are not a Catholic, are you?"

"How did you guess?"

"No matter. What would you like to discuss?"

Doc glanced over his shoulder into the dark, cavernous cathedral. "It is a subject so horrific, so unspeakable I can disclose it only where there is no chance of anyone overhearing."

"Follow me," the priest beckoned.

Doc fell in behind him and they exited the cathedral, his cane tapping loudly on the hard cobblestones.

"Are you truly penitent?" Father Poitier asked. "Have you asked God to forgive you? Do you truly wish to turn away from your sin, and will you do penance?"

Like most men of the recent Enlightenment Period, Doc believed in a sort of nebulous Creator who pretty much operated under a hands-off policy as far as the world was concerned. But at this point he was ready to concede anything.

"Yes, I wish to turn away from it. I wish to hell I had never done such a thing. Be warned, it is a crime so horrible, so inhuman that no penance could ever banish it. And I haven't bothered asking God for mercy. Even if He *is* sitting up there on high, He would never forgive me."

"You are such an educated man, but you have much to learn and so much more to accept. First, you must believe in your heart that God is very much 'up there.' And He is with us 'down here'—right now, at this moment—waiting to hear your confession."

"But if He is all knowing, then does He not know what I am about to confess?"

"He does."

"Then why bother? I have wrestled with Him for months."

"And like Jacob, you will continue to struggle, until you surrender to Him completely. That is what the sacrament of confession is all about. In the profound sense, confession is surrender, the true acknowledgment and praise of God's power and of His mercy toward sinful man. When you accept that, you will know His forgiveness."

They crossed the dark street and entered the rectory. Doc noticed the austere furnishings—there was almost nothing in the house—but it possessed a wholesomeness that Emmett's tavern did not. Father Poitier lit a candle and bade him sit at a stark wooden table. He leaned back, out of the light, so Doc could not see his face, but Doc observed him make the sign of the cross and heard him whisper, "In the name of the Father, and of the Son, and of the Holy Spirit, Amen." In that instant, something happened—the whole atmosphere took on a charge of some sort. Doc was not a mystic; he believed that most religion was nonsense. But a presence stirred in that room, something he could not identify.

"I think you should know, I almost killed myself this evening," he began. "I came *this* close to putting a pistol to my head and ending it all. I still may do it."

Father Poitier gasped. "A gifted man like yourself? But you have so much to offer your fellow man."

"Oh, no. I deserve to die. What I have done overshadows any good I have ever done. My sins are unforgiveable."

"You may not deny the power of the Almighty God, who has dominion over all sin."

"When I tell you the crime, you will agree with me. There is no way that God, in His infinite power, could fix the evil—heal the damage—I have caused. And I fear He can never heal my rotten soul." Doc broke down in anguish.

"You are a gifted physician, and, from all accounts, the best in New Orleans. You work to heal bodies; I work to help heal souls. As human beings we do the best we can in this imperfect world. But there is a healer, far greater than you and me. It is the Lord Jesus Christ, physician of our bodies and souls. He forgave the cripple's sins and restored him to bodily health. He has willed that His Church continue in the power of the Holy Spirit. Three times He built His Church here in New Orleans, and twice it was destroyed. But after each disaster it grew stronger and more beautiful. We are all members of the Church, Christ's body. He intends that we also experience His healing and salvation. Confession is a sacrament of healing. If you are sincere, God will grant you pardon and peace. You must have confidence in Him."

Doc unloaded the whole story. It burst out like foul corruption from a lanced boil—evil, infectious, and malignant. He held nothing back, telling all in vivid detail, so there could be no doubt how ghastly the crime was. Father Poitier listened in stony silence until it was over. Afterwards, Doc felt eviscerated, numb, and strangely open to whatever might follow. He could not think of anything beyond that room.

Father Poitier spoke first. "You have fought a terrible battle, and yes, you committed a grievous sin. Like Elijah in the First Book of Kings, you have holed up in a wilderness cave—that tavern where you are now staying—hiding from your wrongdoings, avoiding your friends, afraid of those enemies who seek your life. Like Elijah, you now say, 'Enough!' and you wish to die."

"*That* is in the Bible?" Doc asked in wonderment. He saw a clear parallel in the passage. "I must have missed that one. What happened to him?"

"God told him to take care of his body, to sleep, rest, take nourishment, and to listen to His instructions."

Doc sighed. Although this was well-intentioned advice, it offered no solution to his problem. Would the priest order him to recite verses as penance? An obligatory ritual of words would not provide the peace he sought.

"Have you *listened*?" Father Poitier leaned forward into the candlelight and spoke compellingly. "God is with us in this room—at this instant. You must listen to Him."

Doc felt that presence again, but this time it was stronger, much more palpable. A shiver ran up his spine. He struggled to understand.

"Long ago the Lord's word came to Elijah on the mountain of Horeb. The Lord instructed Elijah to go out and stand upon the mount before Him. A great wind rent the mountains and broke the rocks into pieces, but the Lord was not in the wind. The wind was followed by an earthquake and a fire, but the Lord was in neither. After that, came a still, small voice. And in that voice God commanded Elijah to go forth and serve Him. He informed Elijah he was not alone—there were other survivors like him, seven thousand souls in Israel. They too lived in danger, but they did not bow unto Baal."

"What are you saying?" Doc knew that something powerful lay just beyond his grasp.

"You are so highly educated, but are you listening?

"I am trying!"

"You came here hoping that with a few words, I could absolve you."

"Yes, I suppose I did."

"Do you think I can dispense forgiveness as simply as you prescribe your medicines?"

"I don't know what I think."

"Listen! There *are* others like you. I believe you know at least one man in this city who is living under the same cloud of guilt—he has spoken often with me. Why are you avoiding him?"

Doc's eyes widened with realization, but he said nothing.

"Sin and guilt are Satan's tools. Their purpose is to cause chaos and grief, to separate us from God, from those we love, and from peace. Sin and guilt often work to keep us from asking for forgiveness. You must turn away from that sin and turn toward the true light, Jesus Christ. Only He can forgive; only He can heal."

"Father, I want that with all my heart. But I do not know where to begin."

"You came here tonight, hoping to do penance?"

"Oh, yes! I'll do anything to rid myself of this guilt. I will give all of Signet's blood money to the church."

"Shame, Doctor! Do you honestly believe your filthy lucre will make everything right?"

"No, I didn't quite mean that."

"Then let me share with you the words of our Lord Jesus Christ—for His advice never fails. In Matthew, Chapter Five, He cautions that *'whosoever is angry with his brother without a cause shall be in danger of judgment.'* Later He teaches that one cannot bring gifts to the altar and there remember that his brother has something against him. His command was: *'Go, and first be reconciled to your brother'*. That, my son, is your penance."

Doc remembered the story of Jesus healing the blind man. He had first read it as a young man. That particular passage in the Gospel of John had inspired him to become a doctor. Jesus spat on the ground, made clay of the spittle, anointed the man's eyes with the clay and told him to wash his eyes in the Pool of Siloam. When the man, blind from birth, followed Jesus' instructions completely, he came away seeing for the first time in his life.

Father Poitier's words opened Doc's eyes. The quiet, gentle voice of Jesus, the Great Physician, flashed like lightning and clapped like thunder. Like the man blind from birth, Doc was seeing the path of forgiveness God intended. He had confronted squarely his sins, accepted full responsibility, and thereby opened himself to God's forgiveness. He knew instantly what he must do. Although he still ached from wrongs committed, he must now take the even more painful steps of making things right. Like Elijah, God had freed him from his chains of depression, quelled his fear, and told him to go forth. And Jesus' words were better than any prescription he could write. *'Go, and first be reconciled to your brother.'*

"Father, I don't know how to thank you. I *see*! I understand what I must do!" Weeping unashamedly, he grasped the priest's hands in gratitude.

"Then go to him, my son. And listen to that still, small voice within you."

———◆———

Judge Harkness' house stood solemn and silent, cloaked in the dark shadows of surrounding live oaks. Doc paid and dismissed his driver, waiting until the hoof beats faded in the distance before entering the courtyard. No light glowed from the judge's room, but Doc did not hesitate as he climbed the outer stairway.

He dreaded this confrontation. Harkness had been fiercely angry during Philippe's inquisition. From that day Doc had steered clear of him. The judge had perceived Signet's ultimate goal and had probably deduced the role Doc played in setting him up.

The veranda door opened slightly. "Who goes there?" barked the judge. He obviously heard the footsteps on the wooden planks.

"It's me—Doc Applegate. I need to see you."

"What for?"

"I think you know."

The door opened wider. "Come inside," the voice lost its edge and sounded tired, resigned.

Doc entered the dark room. Harkness did not bother lighting a lamp and for some time they stood in silence. Perhaps that was for the best. Doc wondered what to say.

"You must think me a damned fool," the judge grumbled.

"I do not," Doc assured him.

"They took advantage of us both; you realize that."

This observation surprised him. Doc had expected a haranguing and was fully prepared to take it on the chin. "How do you mean?"

"They exploited your weakened condition and used you as a pawn to set me up. And I allowed it all to happen. I abused my power and defiled all I hold sacred in my profession. We ruined a young man's life. Your reasons were yours; mine was to cover up my sin."

"I was not an innocent in the affair. In fact, I concocted much of the plan and I am damned sorry for it."

"What a weak and pathetic creature I am—a federal judge behaving in such a manner. I understand why you hold me in such disregard. "

"No! You have been my friend, John. I abused that friendship and violated the doctor-patient relationship. Can you forgive *me*?"

"It is I who need forgiving. I will burn in Hell for what I have done."

"Perhaps not," Doc mused. "Let's put our heads together, you and I, and see if we can make this right."

"Are you serious?"

"I am indeed."

"Do you realize I have been unwell since the hearing?"

"Guilt often does that to a person. We must put it firmly behind us so we may reason clearly. First, let us forgive each other. Can we agree we each made a horrible mistake and that we will work together to make restitution?"

"Yes! I am more than willing." Harkness clasped his hand in the darkness.

"So am I." Doc found a chair and sat down in it.

Judge Harkness sat on the edge of his bed. He then asked the critical question, "How *do* we make this right? The boy is probably dead by now, or working his life away on some sugar plantation in Brazil."

"Maybe not. I believe Philippe is still on that ship. Farron Weeks strolled into Emmett's tavern four days ago and claimed he had just loaded Kayla on board Signet's ship, the *Lisette*. The vessel was delayed, waiting to take on a full cargo."

"How do you know this?"

"Some of *Lisette's* sailors frequent the tavern. One of them mentioned they would depart on the eighteenth."

"That was two days ago. The ship is running on the high seas by now, or soon will be."

"Then we haven't any time to lose."

"What can we do?" Harkness asked.

"We need another ally."

"I have talked often with Father Poitier."

"Yes, I already know how he can help. But for this situation we need someone even more powerful to back us."

"Who?"

"Pierre Delacroix."

This took the judge aback. "You cannot ask me to disgrace myself before that honorable man. I must confess—I have been avoiding him for weeks. He is asking questions about town. Edna has turned him away from our door three times now. I have feigned illness and stayed away from the courthouse."

"Father Poitier says we must first reconcile with our brother. We have wronged Delacroix as well. Philippe is like a son to him."

"You are right, of course."

They sat silent in the darkness, each absorbed in his own thoughts, each making plans for the upcoming endeavor. When the first gray light of morning stole into the room, Harkness spoke on the other subject plaguing his conscience.

"Thomas, is there a chance of redeeming Kayla?"

"I don't know," Doc answered.

"I have ruined her life as well. Perhaps that was the greatest injustice of all."

"Again, I confess I am responsible for that part of the scheme. I conceived the idea of procuring a slave girl and then using her as leverage. I made all the arrangements and made sure you had ample opportunity to give her a child."

"Then we must reconcile with her."

Doc was amazed Harkness was not furious with him. Admittedly the judge was a much better person than he ever could be. How right he was to consider Kayla's welfare. This scheme had harmed more people in more ways than he realized.

"Well, by all accounts she is on the same ship. If we can redeem Philippe, we might be able to arrange something for her."

Harkness' voice broke with emotion. "I love her, you know."

"I fear the feeling is not mutual."

"Of course it is not. I took advantage of her because I could. It was thrilling, for she gave me back my manhood. I guess I knew all along she was powerless to resist, but I just put that part out of my mind. Because of me, the poor girl is with child and on her way to the worst hell on earth. I must make things right."

"What do you propose?"

"I wish to buy her back and then manumit her—set her up in a small house and provide for her and the child—my child."

"And you would impose no other 'conditions'?"

"No conditions."

"We will need money to buy her and Philippe back."

"I have a little put aside. The salary of a federal judge is not high."

"You can count on me to throw in."

"That's the spirit!"

"As federal judge can you issue a summons to have Philippe and Kayla brought back to New Orleans?"

Harkness shook his head. "I am not sure how much influence

that will have. They will be on international waters or in Portuguese Brazil by the time you reach them—if you can find them. But I will go ahead and write one up. It might tip the scales in our favor."

"It couldn't hurt, but in my world-weary opinion, money is the most powerful persuader. Delacroix can help with that."

"What if I arrange a meeting with him and Father Poitier? Could we set it up for this evening?"

"The sooner the better," Doc agreed. "Hopefully Delacroix can help us obtain a ship."

"I dread talking to him," Harkness' chin sagged in mortal shame.

"So do I. But, remember, we are in this together. Delacroix is a good man. I believe he will help us."

"Thomas, do you believe slavery is truly justified? Do you believe the negro race is an inferior one?"

"When they have illnesses, I treat them the same. They bleed like us, suffer the same ailments."

"What about all that science you quoted? Is it real?"

"Some people honestly believe so. It truly is studied and taught in the highest circles of European academia. But at this point, the theories are mere assumptions—not truths. Theories must be proven to become scientific facts."

"You may not credit this, but I have always believed that slavery is inherently wrong, a conviction reflected in many of my previous court rulings, yet I deliberately committed that boy into slavery. I have always opposed intermingling of the races, but I willingly fornicated and begat a mixed-race child."

"We've been through all that. I am headed back to the tavern for some needed sleep. Please send me a message with the time and place of our meeting. Advise Delacroix that we must keep this to ourselves. Jules Signet is a dangerous man playing for high stakes."

Late that afternoon Emmett Barnett rapped on Doc's bedroom door. Doc rolled over and groaned. The sleepless night had taken a heavy toll. He had drawn the heavy drapes and slept most of the day. His head ached and it took a few moments to focus and adjust to his surroundings.

"What is it?"

"Man here to see you."

"What man?"

"Signet. He bring two men."

Doc was wide awake now, his headache fading into the inconsequential. "What kind of men?"

"Kind you'd expect."

"I do not wish to receive them up here. I will meet them in the tavern. Will you and your men cover me?"

"Give me head start. We have plenty guns!"

Doc delayed leaving his room. Why would Signet be here, in Emmett Barnett's Tavern? Had one of his spies seen him talking with the priest or leaving Judge Harkness' home? If so, there could only be one reason for the visit. Strangely, Doc did not experience the previous terror that afflicted him. After the confession, something had changed within. Perhaps a higher power now strengthened him. Of course he was on edge and would take all measures to defend himself, but he felt remarkably calm, ready to face danger. He lathered and shaved his face, combed back his hair, and donned his vest and coat. For good measure he tucked two loaded pistols into his belt, one on either side.

When he was halfway down the stairs, he paused to assess the situation. Jules Signet sat at a table directly in front of the bar. The banker wore an expensive suit, appearing conspicuously out of place. Judging from their physical build and obvious awareness, the two men accompanying him were his protectors. They studied their surroundings, scrutinizing customers who might pose potential danger. Emmett occupied his usual station behind the bar, serving drinks and watching Signet's table. From his elevation Doc spied two double-barreled shotguns propped against the shelving, both within Emmett's easy grasp. Across the room Louis and two companions sat against the wall in cane-bottomed chairs, drinking whiskey from tin cups, their free hands resting on an assortment of weapons. At another table Doc recognized two more of Emmett's men. He descended the stairs and crossed the floor.

"Doc Applegate!" Signet greeted him. "Won't you join us?"

"I thought you said we would not see each other again." Doc sat down warily.

"May I buy you a drink?"

"A coffee perhaps." The tavern brewed a fair coffee.

"I sincerely regret how we last parted. Shortly after our exchange, I realized you were in the right. You fulfilled your part of the bargain in every way. It was a brilliant concept from first to last, and you performed a spectacular piece of acting. You earned every cent of the money."

"Glad you see it that way."

"I was terribly upset with Judge Harkness' decision—I still am. But I was wrong to take it out on you. I have come to offer my apology."

Doc knew this was a ploy. Jules Signet was not here to apologize.

"Accepted."

"You sold your house, Doctor? I heard you are living here, in this tavern. Rather low conditions for a man of your standing."

"Times are hard," Doc lamented. He knew he must move out soon.

"Yes, money goes so quickly. My bank would be glad to provide you with another loan."

"Thanks—I have been in debt before. I don't like it."

"Actually, I came here to employ your professional services in another case. This time I will pay you a thousand dollars if you succeed."

"A thousand?" Doc leaned forward in a show of interest. "What do you and Morel have in mind?"

"Ah, he will not factor into this particular case, at least not in the early stages. This information is for your ears only." He waved a hand to dismiss his gunmen.

They rose in obedience and the whole tension-filled room exploded into reflexive action. With blinding speed, Emmett whipped out both shotguns and brought them down hard upon the bar. He had previously cocked back the double hammers and it was a sheer miracle that none of the four barrels discharged. In the same instant, Louis and his friends drew their weapons. Emmett's men, seated behind Doc, leaped to their feet, pointing cocked pistols at the two gunmen. Signet recoiled and his guards raised their hands.

"Out!" Emmett barked.

"We were just leaving!" The guards retreated slowly, backing out and closing the door behind them.

"Nice friends," Signet muttered, glancing nervously around the room.

"I would not advise crossing any of them." Doc signaled Emmett to put away his shotguns. The stubby double barrels threw a wide pattern and were still pointed directly at the table. Everyone sat down and talking resumed. Soon, it became near impossible to speak above the hubbub.

"Is there someplace else we can go?" Signet asked. "What I have to say cannot be heard by others."

"If it is all the same to you, we will stay here. The crisis has passed. No one is listening."

Signet glanced over both shoulders and leaned forward so only Doc could hear. "I speak freely with you because of your role in our last venture. You cannot report me to the authorities, for you will condemn yourself. If you try, I will take you down with me."

"Of that I am certain. Speak your mind."

"When I gain control, Philippe's enterprises will make me filthy rich. Shipping, merchant banks, cotton plantations, speculation—it all adds up to quite a fortune."

"I imagine it does."

"But there is a much, much bigger fish to fry."

"I do not understand."

"Philippe's case was a trial gallop, a smaller, preliminary part of a much grander strategy. And it worked, brilliantly. We corrupted the judge and coerced him into issuing a decision that has established a desirable precedent for future, similar cases."

"You have mentioned this before. What do you mean by, 'a bigger fish to fry?'"

"Delacroix."

"Delacroix!" Doc recoiled in shock. He suspected that Signet had other schemes up his sleeve, but nothing of this magnitude. The kindly old businessman had come down from Quebec after the French War and built a sprawling enterprise. Deeply religious, devoted to his family and to the city's betterment, he had helped steer the French-speaking population through several major political transitions—namely Spanish rule, French control, the Louisiana Purchase, and, finally, American statehood. He had helped finance and organize defenses during the recent British attack upon the city. Delacroix was a pillar of society. He *was* New Orleans!

"The man must be past eighty years old. He has enjoyed a good long run."

"How does this involve me?"

"You are his physician. No doubt you carry a variety of potions in your black bag. Some of the painkillers can be lethal if administered in large enough doses, inducing deep sleep and shutting down breathing and heartbeat. Suppose Delacroix went to sleep and never woke up? At his advanced age who would suspect an overdose? And, as a licensed medical doctor, don't you possess official power to certify cause of death?"

The floor lurched beneath him; his vision swam, and the tavern's loud din became inaudible. For an instant Doc thought he was suffering a stroke. He inhaled deeply, steadied himself and looked into Signet's eyes.

"You look unwell, Doctor." Signet exclaimed. "Why don't you let me convey you back to my house?"

"Thank you, no. It takes a moment for one to absorb."

"Think about it. You might even spare him a terrible illness later in life. This way he just goes to sleep—no pain, no suffering. Don't you have drugs to achieve that end?"

"I do. When would you want this to happen?"

"Not for a few months. There are some legalities to which I must first attend."

"Wait. Delacroix has a daughter, doesn't he?"

"Yes. After the death of his son, she became his sole heir."

"Didn't she marry and move with her husband to Kentucky?"

"She did indeed."

"Won't Delacroix's estate pass to her?"

"In theory, yes."

Doc understood then. Philippe's trial case had lain the groundwork for future cases. In protecting himself, Judge Harkness had set a dangerous precedent. Alain Morel would invoke the Louisiana Digest of 1808 in the daughter's circumstance.

"In her case we can actually prove she is a quintroon. We have the official documents in our possession. The negro blood came in on her mother's side. Delacroix was embarrassed and kept the details hidden. Because he was part of the city's elite, he would not risk a scandal by manumitting her."

"This was your plan all along," Doc said, exhaling in wonderment.

"Are you with me once more?" Signet asked.

"It is a tempting offer. I will think about your proposition and talk with you again."

"Can you make his death look like a natural occurrence?"

"Not a problem. It would be even easier if I am asked to examine the body."

"That can be arranged. You really should consider returning to my house until the task is completed. This tavern is not the safest of environments."

"Let me think on it," Doc insisted. "I will let you know my answer soon."

Signet rose slowly, so as not to provoke another reaction. Doc stood and shook his hand. "Good day, Jules."

Chapter Eight

Although both events promised to be uncomfortable, Doc dreaded meeting Solange far more than he did Delacroix. Just before sunset, Emmett brought Judge Harkness' sealed letter directing him to meet at the rectory at eight o'clock that evening. This gave Doc time to seek an audience with Solange, tell her what information he could, and let her know he would be leaving New Orleans for a few weeks, perhaps months. She would undoubtedly terminate their friendship, but he would not continue with the dissembling and dishonesty.

Emmett arranged for a covered carriage and assigned one of his men to serve as driver and bodyguard. Doc paid the tavern owner for his trouble and they were off, slip-sliding through muddy tracks until they crossed Canal Street and entered the French Quarter. There the horse clip-clopped along the cobblestone levee. The sinking sun burnished the Mississippi to the color of old copper, lighting the clouds' undersides in a hundred shades from lemon to apricot, cardinal red to deepest violet.

His presence at the Ursuline Convent created the usual stir, but the nuns gladly summoned Solange. She strode softly into the foyer and smiled in greeting.

"I have missed you, Doctor."

"May we talk?" Doc asked.

Solange noticed his expression and offered, "Why don't we go for a walk on the grounds?" She slid her hand into his and led him outside, instinctively knowing that he brought bad news. They walked down a crushed-shell path flanked with various shrubs and flowers.

Doc was grateful for the near-darkness. First, he apologized for not contacting her—and then he told her why. He had intended to share only basic details, but walking with her now, he could not help himself. It was important she knew everything. He described his previous human condition—before the hearing—and confessed to planning and implementing the scheme's most sordid details. At one point she stopped and withdrew her hand, but she continued walking with him.

"Oh, Thomas! You didn't!"

"I am afraid I did."

"Why, it is the most horrible thing I have ever heard! I can't believe that you, of all people, could be mixed up in such a plot—let alone conceive it."

"I regret every part I played and I am thoroughly ashamed. Signet raised me up from the gutter, and his financial offer seemed to set so many things right. He restored me to decent society and enabled me to practice medicine, which I dearly love. Over the past few months I grew fond of you. My life seemed headed down the right path and I even entertained plans of asking for your hand in marriage. I know now I am unworthy of that honor."

"Why didn't you just refuse him?"

"He held that huge debt over my head and I was convinced he would kill me if I failed him. Chalk it up to weakness and cowardice. There is no other excuse—except perhaps an innate meanness. I am a wretch."

They reached the far end of the walled grounds.

"We should go back now," Solange suggested. Doc detected a note of sadness, rather than anger.

"Yes, I understand. I just wanted you to know—because I really do care about you, Solange. We became friends, but under false pretenses. It was wrong of me to think of taking things further. You deserve so much more."

"What will you do now?" she asked.

"I spoke with Father Poitier—actually I embraced a rough form of what you Catholics call Confession. He sent me to Judge Harkness and we talked. We have both resolved to make things right—as much as that is possible."

"How?"

"We meet tonight with Delacroix to formulate a plan."

"What can he do?"

"He is as influential as Signet, perhaps more so. He will come up with something, or at least refine my poor ideas."

"And what are they, pray tell?"

"First, I am journeying to Brazil to fetch those young people back, and then work to undo the hardship I helped put them through."

"Brazil? Oh, Thomas! It is so far away, and I fear for your safety."

"I thank you for that. But I am undeserving."

They reached the convent door. Solange took his hand once more. "What will you do after you bring them back?"

"If we can restore them and bring Signet to justice, I plan to pull up stakes and practice medicine somewhere else, perhaps in one of the northern states."

"I do pray you succeed, Thomas. And I hope you realize your dream. Perhaps you will contact me when this business is finished? I would like that very much."

"You overwhelm me, Solange," Doc suppressed a sob of gratitude. He had expected a much different reaction.

"Just take care of yourself." She leaned forward and kissed him on the cheek. "Until then, Thomas."

———————•———————

Father Poitier presided over the painful, face-to-face conference. His firm hand would be needed to keep tempers from getting out of hand. Pierre Delacroix listened in angry silence as Doc laid out the entire story from beginning to end. Doc held nothing back, recounting everything in vivid detail. From time to time Judge Harkness added his commentary. The old merchant said nothing, but his rage clearly mounted. They could see it in his expression, the way his eyes glittered and jaw clenched.

"Both of you!" Delacroix exploded. His snowy white moustaches twitched in outrage. "In my wildest imaginations I could never conceive of such duplicity, such wickedness. This may well rank as one of the most contemptible acts in human history! A respected federal judge and physician—both abusing their stations and God-given gifts to ruin such a wonderful young man—I have lived eighty-one years and never known anything like it."

"We beg your forgiveness," Judge Harkness wept, mopping at his eyes with a handkerchief. "I have been unwell since the inquest and have made plans to step down from the bench."

"Much good that will do Philippe!"

"Before I resign, I promise to use the full force of my office to restore him to his rightful place, but we must proceed with caution. Signet is a dangerous man."

Doc interjected, "That is why we are here—to help Philippe. We need your help to make this right."

"Philippe's wife Chantelle is with child. Last week she quit New Orleans, in her words, forever. She is sailing to France to live with her aunt. Now I know why—it is to divorce Philippe and bear the child in secret, a child which she believes to be part negro. She will abandon her baby to a religious order and remarry a wealthy French man. You have ruined an entire family with your education and your posturing of so-called scientific beliefs. How do you fix that?"

At that point, Father Poitier intervened. "Both men have confessed their sins before me and God. They truly wish to make amends, Pierre. God has seen their remorse and He will forgive them. As a Christian you can do no less. Jesus commands it. If God wills it, He will restore Philippe as He did Job. He controls the outcome of all things."

Delacroix heaved an agonized sigh and hung his head, pressing his hands to his eyes as waves of emotion coursed through him. Doc watched him struggle to shed the grip of intense anger. In his practice he observed people overwhelmed by tragedy and then fighting to regain control. After a time, Delacroix raised his head. His outrage and hatred had abated, somewhat.

"Now then, gentlemen, what do you suggest we do?"

"May God bless you, Pierre." Father Poitier crossed himself.

"I want to fetch Philippe back—buy him if I have to," Doc answered.

"How can you hope to find him?" Delacroix asked, tears streaming down his face. "He has been gone for two months."

"We think not," Doc said. "In fact Signet's ship, *Lisette*, departed just three days ago for Brazil."

"That is correct." As a leading merchant, Delacroix knew the arrivals and departures of all ships in the port of New Orleans.

"Certain intelligences indicate that Philippe is on board *Lisette*."

"You mean to say he was there all the time, just a few yards away from my trading house?"

Doc hung his head; the question already had an answer.

"Well?" Delacroix prompted.

"We need a ship—preferably a fast one," Doc said.

"I have a fast two-masted sloop that arrived from Philadelphia two days ago. The *Arabelle* can outsail anything on the high seas. I can order her cargo offloaded and have her ready for sea in two days."

"You must expressly order the captain to convey me wherever I wish to go, and to wait for as long as I require in whatever harbors we enter. I have two destinations in mind—Salvador da Bahia and Sainte-Pierre, Martinique."

"Martinique?" Delacroix asked.

"I plan to do some investigating."

Father Poitier offered, "I will pen letters of introduction to the priests in both ports. They will help deal with local officials and provide quarters if needed."

"Very well," Doc agreed.

"Now I must divulge some information relative to this case. It is not confidential. I know Father Gérard Gaston in Sainte-Pierre. Together, we attended the *Séminaire de Sainte-Sulpice* in Montreal. Some time ago he wrote a letter, telling me that a New Orleans lawyer visited him, asking for the birth and marriage records of a

Philomène Bouchard. Nothing turned up for the lawyer in City Hall. The man wished to examine church records, but some inner voice warned Gaston not to comply. He obfuscated, requested to see the lawyer's own birth record, and generally stalled until the man left. He wrote me, asking what I knew about the lawyer. I wish I had known then what I know now."

"I'll hazard it was Morel," Doc muttered. Poitier remained silent, but his face confirmed Doc's suspicions.

"Is there a birth record lodged in the church?" Delacroix asked.

"Presumably so," Father Poitier nodded.

"Do you know what information it might contain?" Doc pressed.

"Alas, I do not. But I will write Father Gaston and ask him to let you see it and to make an official copy to bring back to New Orleans. But you must understand that it could prove Signet's contention."

"We will deal with that when the time comes," Delacroix asserted. "Now, gentlemen, you must allow Father Poitier and me some time to write the letters. Is there anything else?"

"I am afraid so," Doc replied. "This afternoon Signet offered me a thousand dollars to put you down."

Everyone gasped, stunned by this admission.

"He came to Emmett Barnett's tavern and suggested I use a medical draught to make it appear like a natural death. He even claimed he could arrange for me to affirm the cause of your death."

"Why, Signet is even more diabolical than I imagined!" Judge Harkness gasped.

"And what did you reply?" asked Delacroix.

"In order to buy time, I told him I would think about it. Hopefully I can depart New Orleans without him knowing. But Pierre, you must take pains to protect yourself. In my absence Signet would not stoop to approach another physician."

"Do not worry about me, Doctor. I have survived three terrible wars. The man is nothing compared to those. Let us all meet here tomorrow night at six o'clock. I will have your letters of introduction, travel expense money, and ample gold coin to purchase Philippe. We may be able to smuggle you aboard *Arabelle* then, so pack your necessities."

"Thank you, Pierre," Judge Harkness shook his hand.

"As little as it must mean, I am truly sorry for all of this," Doc sighed.

Delacroix took his hand. "Just bring Philippe back to me. He is the son I never had."

"I promise I will try."

Chapter Nine

Faubourg Sainte-Marie —The American Sector

An orange glow lit the entire western horizon, emanating from the American sector across Canal Street. The air lay heavy with foul-smelling smoke, the underside of which reflected an eerie light. Something big was burning. Perhaps the whole of New Orleans would suffer another great fire like it had in 1788 and again in 1794. The blaze flickered wildly as it grew in intensity. Great tongues of flame rose above rooftops, lighting up a large portion of the city. Doc could see it clearly from the open flap of his carriage. The few raindrops that entered the interior did not bother him.

"What is it?" he shouted at the driver.

"Big fire near the river!"

Curious onlookers crowded the streets and the throng increased as they drew nearer to the conflagration. Doc experienced a snake of suspicion; then he began to suspect the worst. Within two blocks he was certain—Emmett Barnett's Tavern was engulfed in a raging inferno. The driver slowed his team to a walk, halting in the open square nearest the tavern. A massive fire roared from one end of the building to the other, flames rushing from every window with the force of a blast furnace. Bottles of liquor exploded in bright flashes. Charges of gunpowder detonated. Without notice, the front balcony collapsed into the street, crashing in a shower of brilliant orange sparks. The midpoint of the roof sagged dangerously, the main beam crackling as it broke and gave way. Suddenly, the entire structure seemed to implode upon itself and a massive fireball roiled upwards into the night reflected by the angry smoke clouds above. A woman shrieked and the whole crowd fell back, erupting into an unnerving roar.

Townsmen had formed a bucket brigade, drawing water from the nearby Mississippi to wet down structures around the blazing tavern. Doc watched as they struggled to keep the fire contained. Fortunately the rain increased, and it began to appear as if the fire might play itself out. Several of Emmett's whores stood weeping in the muddy street, many wearing filmy wet nightclothes that clung to their bodies, leaving little to the bystanders' imaginations. One man wallowed in a nearby gutter, drinking liquor from a jug. Others gave way to lamentations and despair, those who moments before had been indulging in drunkenness and other fleshly pleasures. These wretched animals epitomized the uncertainty of life; now they howled angrily, cursing at the flames. The scene reminded Doc of a passage from Dante's *Inferno*, perhaps the bottom half of Michelangelo's *Last Judgment* or Bosch's *Descent into Hell.*

Doc regretted that his fine clothes, second pair of boots, and travelling valise were gone, but he patted the black medical bag at his feet. He always kept it with him and now he congratulated himself for that decision. The bag contained his medicines and instruments—his entire practice. It also held two loaded pistols and all his money. If he lost it, he would be in serious trouble.

What caused the fire? Any number of things could have started it—a broken lamp, upturned candle, misplaced cigar, or fireplace spark. But again, it might have originated from a more sinister source. Jules Signet could order powerful forces into this part of the city where justice, or revenge, was most often promulgated from the muzzle of a gun. Here, the number of weapons decided the outcome of right or wrong. Doc wondered about Emmett Barnett. Was the little tavern owner inside? At that instant a figure emerged from the darkness and entered his carriage from the opposite side. Doc clutched for his pistol.

Louis Reynard forestalled him. "It is me, Doctor!"

"What the hell has happened?"

"Signet's men came, perhaps twenty of them. They carried kegs of gunpowder and crocks of lamp oil. They shot their way inside the tavern and there was a horrible gunfight. Emmett cut down six of them with his shotguns."

"Where is he now?"

"I suspect he is dead—burned alive! They wounded him in the leg, shot several of his customers, and even killed some of his best whores!"

The collateral damage did not surprise Doc. Anything could happen in a gunfight. "How did you escape?"

"I dove out of a back window and fled down the street to the river. Then I circled back around and shot one of the men as they fled back to the French Quarter."

"How do you know they were Signet's men?"

"Two of them were the same men who came this afternoon. They directed the attack—and both escaped."

Doc mulled over this new intelligence. Had Signet found another physician willing to commit the murder? If so, he had decided to eliminate anyone with knowledge of the upcoming plot. Any scenario was plausible. Perhaps Signet hoped to burn the tavern, deprive Doc of his sanctuary and thus force him to live at the townhouse. To achieve control, the banker would not hesitate to take such a drastic measure. This seemed the most likely explanation, but Doc could not take any chances. He must get out of the square and disappear into the dark back streets.

"Is there a possibility Emmett escaped?" he asked.

"There is one chance," Louis nodded. "But I must divulge a great secret. In these circumstances I am hopeful he will forgive me." He pointed forward and ordered the driver, "Turn left at that next street and follow it down to the river."

———◆●◆———

Louis hauled a large iron keyring from his jacket pocket and fumbled in the darkness for the right key. He used his fingertips and sense of touch to discern the one he needed. It was obvious he had done this many times.

"What are you doing?" Doc asked with interest as they disembarked on the waterfront. He kept his black bag with him, despite its weight.

"I am taking you to Emmett's underground passageway. Often, pirates come up from the river, usually in the dead of night, and they bring kegs of rum and brandy. That way everyone can bypass the *collectionneurs,* the tariff collectors. And we all make more money."

They paused outside a small square house, constructed of heavy square stones and twelve-by-twelve oak timbers. The solid iron door was rusted over and secured by a massive lock. Even in the bad light, Doc could see the lock was shiny from continued use. Louis turned the key and the latch responded with a click. He hauled open the heavy door, its hinges squeaking in protest. Once they were inside, he closed it behind them, securing it with a heavy iron bar that stood in the corner. Doc could distinguish nothing in the pitch blackness, but Louis knew where everything was. He rattled around on a shelf and found what he wanted. A few brisk scraping noises produced bright sparks that caught in a wad of tinder. Louis blew gently and it burst into flame. With the flame he lit a lamp. The wick spluttered and produced welcome light. Barrels, kegs, and wooden cases were stacked ceiling high on all four sides.

"Hold this, Doctor."

"What are you doing now?"

"Just follow me, please. And hold that lamp high."

They wound through the inventory and into another building. There Louis slid back a fake wooden panel, descended a short flight of steps, and came to another door. Deftly he unlocked it. Beyond the frame Doc spied a long tunnel leading away from the river. The air was dank and the floor wet with seepage, as most underground cellars in the city were. That was why the people of New Orleans buried their dead in above-ground crypts. Louis splashed steadfastly through the wet passageway with Doc close on his heels.

"Where does this lead?"

"Directly below the tavern. There is a trap door set into the floor just behind the bar. You may not have noticed—no one goes behind it but Emmett. He has often slept there, especially to guard large shipments of liquor, guns and gold."

"But *you* know about this passageway. Why do you have his keys? Does he trust you that much?"

"I am Emmett's half-brother. And I have saved his life on three occasions, once when he was just twelve years old. Then, he fought with my mother's lover. The man had beaten her to unconsciousness and was strangling her. When he tried to cut Emmett's throat, I shot and killed him."

"How old were you then?"

"Five."

"Incredible!" Doc grimaced at this knowledge.

"On two other occasions men tried to kill him here in the tavern. I stopped them. We tossed their bodies in the river."

"Do you think Emmett is dead now?"

"We will soon find out."

Up ahead in the darkness a low, menacing growl reverberated off the stone ceiling. It sounded like a wild animal and it set Doc's nerves on edge. He reached for his pistol.

"Emmett? Is that you?" Louis hissed. "Emmett! It is me, Louis!"

The reply came back as a whimpering moan. "I am killed! They shot off my leg!"

"Emmett!"

Doc's physician's instincts kicked in. He shouldered his way past Louis and held his lamp high.

"Oh, my God!" he gasped. He stooped and ripped the torn pants.

Emmett's leg was doubled up at an unnatural angle. It appeared to be hanging on by a few tendons, twisted muscle, and torn flesh. His entire knee was shattered and his lower leg was charred black. Perhaps the flames had seared the femoral artery, at least temporarily, and the surrounding tissue was a horrid mess. Veins and smaller vessels had bled out dangerously. Copious amounts of blood soaked the cobblestone floor. In some places puddles had congealed and turned black. Fortunately, Emmett lay up on higher ground, above the dark water that carried infection.

"Here! Hold this lamp." Doc commanded Louis. "Keep it steady." He opened his bag and found a section of clean white cotton rope. It measured about a half-inch in diameter and about three feet in length—perfect for what he had in mind. He found a wooden dowel rod and fashioned a tourniquet. He wound it tight and tied it off. Emmett was just conscious. He did not react to the pressure. Doc held little hope for him.

"I die?"

"You might," Doc answered.

"I lose leg?"

"You might. I have put a tourniquet on it to stop the bleeding." He turned to the half-brother. "Louis, can you carry him?"

"I not leave money—or shotguns!" Emmett protested.

"We will have to come back for them," Louis said.

"I kill you both if you do not."

"He means it!" Louis assured Doc.

"I believe you," Doc patted Emmett's shoulder. "Let's go."

"Where are we taking him?"

"To a ship called *Arabelle*. I will operate on him there."

It took some maneuvering to lift Emmett onto Louis' back and transport him down the tunnel's full length. Doc carried both of Emmett's short-barreled shotguns and his own black bag. They emerged into the smoky night air, still fifty yards from the carriage.

A man waited for them in the darkness. "Who in the hell is that?" Doc asked. He curled his finger defensively around the trigger of one shotgun, then realized that both weapons were discharged. He had no way of reloading them.

"Not to worry! It is Raoul!"

"And who is he?"

"Another half-brother. We help each other when we can."

Raoul rushed forward to take Emmett from Louis' shoulders.

Emmett mumbled something in his ear and Louis ran back to the passageway. Doc directed Raoul to the carriage. Emmett's driver sat on the strongbox, unaware he was transporting his injured, bleeding employer.

"On the floorboards—gently!" Doc cautioned.

Louis returned, lugging a small wooden chest. Judging from the way he panted, Doc could tell it was heavy. Raoul helped him raise it into the carriage, and place it with a weighty thump on the floor beside Emmett's head.

"Is this it, brother?"

Emmett opened his eye and began cursing. He coughed painfully—a dry, hacking rasp that seemed to wrack his whole body.

"We will both go. Come, Raoul!"

Doc groused, "Don't take all night! He doesn't have that long to live."

"They bring or I kill!" Emmett mumbled.

"You'll die if I don't get you aboard that ship where I can work on you. Just lie there and be still. If I can patch you up, I will."

The two brothers returned with another, larger chest, three muskets, four pistols, a bag of gunpowder, and another of lead shot. When they had loaded everything, Doc pounded on the carriage roof.

"Drive!"

"Where to?"

"The *Place d'Armes*. And don't waste any time."

———————●———————

The carriage wheeled in darkness up Chartres Street before turning left on St. Peter and then jinking right behind the towering mass of the *Cabildo*. Doc was heading to the rectory. On the last corner, Raoul managed to hop off and disappear into the darkness. Before they reached the residence, he reappeared dragging a door, obviously kicked from its hinges. Carefully they eased Emmett onto it to carry him inside. Father Poitier answered their knock. He was bleary-eyed from sleep, but sprang into action when Doc explained what they needed. He ordered the carriage driver how to find Delacroix's townhouse and ordered him to return with all haste. He lit a candle as they lowered Emmett onto the floor.

"I must get Emmett on board *Arabelle!*" Doc cried, "I don't know where the damned ship is, or what it looks like. We need to move our departure ahead—as soon as possible." He hovered over his patient, checking him for bleeding. The tourniquet held, but the lower leg had turned black. Emmett's knee was shattered, mangled beyond all hope of repair with bone splinters sticking out at all angles. Torn ligaments hung visibly and shredded muscle lay open to expose bone, blood vessels, and the pulsing snake of the femoral artery. When Doc ascertained that Emmett remained stabilized, he asked the priest to fetch a sheet of paper and a quill. As Doc worked, Father Poitier took dictation, dipping his quill into an inkwell and dashing out a list of medicines and supplies for Delacroix to find. Emmett groaned and regained consciousness.

"Damn it to hell, Emmett! What did they shoot you with?"

"Goddamned big shotgun," he croaked through dry, cracked lips. "Need water!"

Doc knew that Emmett suffered from raging thirst. It was always that way when patients lost a lot of blood. Father Poitier fetched a pitcher of water and Doc let Emmett drink as much as he wanted. He added a few drops of laudanum to dull his pain. In a short time the opiate took effect. It showed in the constricted pupil of Emmett's single glittering eye.

Delacroix arrived in his carriage and without question he paid and dismissed the hired carriage driver, then personally drove them down to the levee. *Arabelle* lay at anchor, a dark, graceful shadow in the gloom of night, her bare masts pointing upward into the blackness. The deck watch answered their hail and Delacroix ordered him to let them come aboard. The captain provided a clean cabin for Doc and his patient, another for the two half-brothers.

"I presume they will travel with you?" Delacroix inquired, regarding them doubtfully, recognizing them by their dress and demeanor.

"We may need protection on land," Doc replied. "And they *are* Emmett's half-brothers."

"My men have been expressly ordered to protect you, Doctor. Remember, the objective is to bring Philippe back alive and well. The captain is committed to that goal—and so are his crew."

"Very well. But this crew must stay aboard. I do not wish for Signet to know I have left New Orleans."

"I understand that."

"I need those medicines as soon as possible."

"They will be delivered by my hand."

"All my clothes were burned in the tavern fire. I need new clothing, boots, shaving razor, comb, and soap. Perhaps all packed in a travel valise?"

"You shall have it. Anything else?"

"Plenty of cotton padding, several bales of clean cotton cloth, three iron pots of different sizes, clean drinking water, food."

"My men eat and drink well. You and your men will not lack for anything. I will order one of my other ship's provisioners to procure fresh water and galley supplies. At dawn an entire crew will arrive to help offload *Arabelle's* cargo so you may get underway by evening. Can you think of anything else?"

Doc considered his patient's condition. In order to save Emmett, he must amputate the leg. Gangrene may have already set in.

"Yes. Please fetch Madame Solange Tourigny at the Ursuline Convent. Tell her she is needed for emergency surgery and her assistance is critical to the patient's survival. Do not let anyone know who she will be aiding."

Without further delay, Delacroix left *Arabelle*. Doc made preparations for surgery. Twice he had amputated legs above the knee; both times his patients died. In this instance Emmett had already lost much blood, suffering broken bones and charred flesh. The ship's captain appeared in the cabin doorway, face aghast.

"Is there a ship's surgeon aboard?" Doc asked.

"Just Willoughby. He is not a doctor, but he can set bones and stitch up cuts."

"Wake him and send him here. Tell him to bring his surgical supplies."

"Anything else?"

"I want an unopened jug of wine, several of your best lanterns, and some pots of clean, boiled water. And I need clean bed linens— Delacroix is bringing more."

The captain set off to order this done. Doc began cutting away Emmett's tattered pants with a pair of shears.

"It bad?" Emmett croaked.

Doc could not believe the little man was still conscious. "You've really done it this time."

"You cut off my leg?"

"If you want to live."

"I do. I kill that sombeech Signet."

"You just hold onto that thought."

He began laying out his surgical tools—razor sharp scalpels, knives, a small surgical saw, and a larger bone saw. Then he placed clamps, threads, cotton cloth, and sponges for easy access. Just as the sailors carried in the first steaming pots of boiled water and a jug of French wine, Willoughby arrived with his medical bag. He was a large man whose manner and speech did not impress.

Doc considered the instruments in Willoughby's medical bag. "Wash these in one of those pots," he ordered as he poured a measure of wine into each pot.

"They are clean! I always wipe them off after I use them," the sailor muttered.

"Tonight you will wash everything in hot water and wine." Long ago, just before performing a rare abdominal surgery, Doc had scrubbed his dirty surgical instruments in boiling water. Hot water worked much better than cold to remove congealed blood, pus, and other matter. He had also read that French military surgeons washed their instruments in wine, and their patients enjoyed a higher survival rate. He had followed this protocol and his patient suffered no mortification at the incision site. From that day on he practiced the ritual, almost religiously, and noted that his patients.enjoyed better post-surgical results than those of his contemporaries. Doc placed his own saws and knives in a second pot and let them steep.

Presently Solange arrived in Delacroix's carriage. The merchant escorted her up the ship's ramp and into the cabin. Doc wondered how she could look so fresh and young and alert, even in early morning.

"Thank you for coming, Solange. I hated to rouse you, but I desperately need your assistance. Will you help me try to save this man?"

"Of course Doctor," she replied, her dark eyes wide with concern. "What would you have me do?"

Doc outlined the procedure to her as he added a generous portion of laudanum to Emmett's cup of water. She flinched at each description, but nodded determinedly her understanding.

"Can you do this?" he asked.

"I think so," she nodded.

"We must clamp and tie off that big artery before it bursts."

Sailors hung more lamps from the ship's rafters, brightening the cabin enough for him to begin. Doc ordered them to stay. He needed them to hold Emmett down. Delacroix left to begin filling the extensive list of medical and other requirements. Doc decided to go ahead with the instruments on hand. He spread a clean sheet on the floor next to where Emmett lay and instructed Solange.

"Use the forceps to grasp those instruments and lay them out on the sheet. Careful—that water will scald you. "

Then he turned to Emmett. "You still awake?"

"I am."

"You don't want to be. Start quaffing down this medicine—as much as you can."

"Rum!"

"You can't have any. Mixed with this medicine it could kill you."

Solange raised his head and held the tin cup to his lips. Emmett gulped it down. After two more laudanum-laced cups, his head began to roll.

Doc planned to use the flap method for this surgery. It was crude, but Army surgeons who performed it on the battlefield claimed it gave them the best results. With this method he would dissect the bone and use flaps of deep muscle and skin to close the operation. While his primary consideration was to save as much of the leg as possible, it was imperative to cut the bone a few inches above where he would join the flaps together. To ensure closure, the skin and soft tissues must be left substantially longer than the bone.

"Are we ready?" Doc asked. "Willoughby, you sit on his feet. Put your weight on his good leg and don't let him move it. You men hold his arms. Louis and Raoul, you help them." Both half-brothers were visibly shaken, but did as they were bid. They recognized Doc's certainty and seemed to draw comfort from it.

Doc cut off Emmett's pants and flung the remnants aside. As he bathed the leg with wine, he assessed the damage. The little tavern owner was correct—he had taken a full blast of buckshot in the knee. Apparently the shooter had fired from close range, for the joint was completely shattered. Perhaps Emmett had tried to escape through the floor hatch and trapped his lower leg. A burning beam might have fallen on it before he could slither to safety. Perhaps he had been in shock and could not feel the flames. Whatever the scenario, Doc knew he must amputate—well above the knee.

Solange took a position where she could hand him instruments, hold clamps, and tie sutures. Doc tightened down the tourniquet and made his first incision in a circular fashion. As the skin retracted, he began dividing the deep fascia, then the muscles in continuous circular sweeps. The cut muscle naturally retracted and he made the next division at a slightly higher level, guiding his scalpel around the blood vessels, taking care not to cut them.

"Clamp here," he instructed. When Solange did this, Doc tied a double ligature to seal off the vessel. He did this with every individual vein and artery. "Now we come to the femoral artery. Clamp here, and for pity's sake do not release your grip. If you do, Emmett is a dead man." Doc worked carefully on the high-pressure artery and made two tight ligatures. He heated his scalpel tip over the nearest candle flame and seared the end below the ligatures.

"What about the nerves?" Solange asked quietly. Doc was impressed with her knowledge of anatomy.

"We simply leave them alone. We do not crush or tie them off. You can see I have severed them at the same level as the muscles."

Now Doc used leather retractors to pull back muscle and flesh so he could cut in a circular manner through the periosteum, the bone's outer covering. Throughout the whole procedure, Emmett remained unconscious. He lay motionless, his breathing shallow, but regular. That could change in an instant. Doc had seen patients wake up when the surgeon began sawing the bone.

"Saw," he demanded. Solange placed it into his hand. "You men make sure he does not move." Without hesitating, he sawed cleanly through the bone and the leg came free. Emmett groaned once, and that was all. Doc used a small file to smooth the femur's edges and inspected the field for remaining bleeders. Then he began closing up the flaps of internal and external muscle, satisfied that no stray shot remained in the stump.

Here, Solange proved her worth as a surgical assistant, laying down neat, tight sutures while Doc pulled and held different flaps in positions to form a viable union. With each successive closure he grew increasingly confident that the bone would not later project at the anterior end as it was sometime prone to do, necessitating another risky amputation. He had left generous flaps for the stump. Earlier, Solange had boiled two setons, cloth wicks to drain the pus that would surely form. These Doc wound in a spiral fashion and placed about thumb deep in the leg. Over the next several days he would fractionally withdraw the setons until he removed them completely.

Willoughby wrapped the severed leg in a cloth and ordered a sailor to remove it. Doc heard it splash when it hit the river. The sun was up when they finished bandaging the stump with light cotton strips. Solange changed the bloody bedding and spread a canvas and clean sheets for the little tavern owner. Emmett lay flat and motionless, his normal swarthy complexion an ashen gray. His breathing remained frightfully shallow.

"Will he live?" Solange asked.

"I doubt it. But we did a near-perfect job. I am glad you came."

"So am I, Thomas." She kept vigil with him long after sunrise. Neither of them spoke; they simply watched as their patient clung to life. Presently, Delacroix arrived with medical supplies and other provisions. These would prove beneficial in the event Emmett lived. The merchant peered inside the room and blanched in revulsion. "Ghastly business, amputation," he muttered, looking away. "I have brought your medical supplies. Your personal requests will be filled by this afternoon."

"Thank you, Pierre."

"This should be sufficient money to redeem Philippe. And here are your letters of introduction." Delacroix handed him a leather purse, weighty with coin, and a leather folder containing the letters. "You will have Judge Harkness' letters before you depart."

"Please tell him I need them sooner than expected."

"Very well."

"Will you please return Madame Tourigny to the convent?"

"My pleasure," Delacroix nodded. "You two have had quite a night."

"We have indeed," Doc agreed.

"Will he live?"

"I would not bet on it. But we did the best we could."

Delacroix's second crew arrived to complete *Arabelle's* unloading. Doc could hear thumping of heavy cargo on deck, creaking of ropes and hoists, shouted commands, and foul-mouthed cursing. From the sound of it, they would soon finish their business.

"Good bye, Doctor," Solange embraced him briefly. "I will pray daily for your safe return." She withdrew gracefully. Doc turned his attention to the man on the pallet, wondering why he felt so emotionally compelled to save this monster. Certainly he owed Emmett something. But he also knew that the Hippocratic Oath, to which he had surrendered many years ago, had reached out to embrace him.

Maybe he could redeem himself further if Emmett survived. He then did something he had not done in ages—he bowed his head to pray.

———•——

Late that afternoon, the sailors cast off moorings and allowed *Arabelle* to slide gracefully, bow first, downriver. When the ship reached midstream, they hoisted foresails to take advantage of the fluky spring breezes that so rarely played upon the crescent. Pierre Delacroix and Judge Harkness watched until the sloop disappeared behind the distant bend.

"Pierre, do you think they will succeed?" Harkness asked, his eyes red-rimmed from crying.

"I doubt it very much," Delacroix replied. "If you ask me, it is a fool's mission. I thank God for the ship's captain, Nathan West. He bears duplicate letters and special instructions to intervene if the doctor fails. Some of his men are excellent soldiers, skilled in fighting on sea and land. It is all in God's hands now."

Chapter Ten

Breckinridge County, Kentucky—March 27, 1816

The winter weather clung fast to the Ohio River Valley, stubbornly refusing to relinquish its grip. There were haphazard signs of spring. Geese would pass overhead flying north, but they veered south again ahead of approaching waves of cold air. Grass tried to turn green, but withered and browned under repeated searings of heavy white frosts. Crocuses and daffodils poked their green spears above the snow, but they did not bloom. Although the sun rose at a higher angle on each passing day, it was a pale caricature of its former self, and brought no real warmth to the land. Its usual brilliance appeared muted, diffused by a gray, smoky haze that seemed to occlude the entire sky. At mid-morning the day resembled a foggy dawn, except that it lacked the usual dampness.

Craig and Romulus were improving a new section of the old Smithhart farm. Craig handled his big tan horses while Romulus plowed with the oxen. It was a monumental task, removing tree stumps, roots, and rocks, breaking up the turf, and working the soil into a fine consistency. Whenever either of them struck the roots of an old tree stump, they would call out and signal the other to help clear it. Romulus now waved his arms to catch Craig's attention. Craig halted the horses and helped him unhitch the ox plow. They secured stout ropes to the stump's base and encouraged the huge oxen to begin pulling. The animals moved with ponderous dignity, but when they leaned into the yokes, few stumps could withstand their steady irresistible force. The stump came out like a black, rotten tooth, its roots slimy with half-frozen mud.

Unexpectedly, Martin McDonnell appeared at the field's edge. Like them he was bundled in a heavy overcoat, gloves and scarf. Martin had trudged a mile over rugged ground to be there, so he obviously had something on his mind.

"Morning, Craig. Do you plan to plant this farm in corn?"

"Yes. I will cut back on corn acreage as you suggested, but this ground has never been planted." Last year Craig and Romulus had cleared part of the farm and he intended to put out about thirty acres. "Is there something wrong?"

"Oh, no. You should be fine with your yields, but I would hold off planting seed. Something about the weather concerns me. This spring is unlike any I have known. We should have seen a few indications by now. Usually the weeping willows have turned yellow, and I have seen green foliage appear as early as late February. That is not the case now. Even the red maples have not budded and here it is almost the end of March."

"Surely the cold weather will soon break," Craig offered. "I have had just about enough of it."

"I'm not telling you what to do; I'm just suggesting. Of course I could be wrong, but Owen and I talked it over and we plan to hold off. We wanted to share our decision with you."

"I appreciate that. Right now we are just improving and preparing this ground. As you can see, it is still pretty rough. I wouldn't plant corn until the last of April or early May."

"That is when we usually plant, but I am suggesting we wait even longer—and longer still for our tobacco." Martin was dead serious—some inner voice was warning him. Craig trusted him completely; he possessed wisdom and experience gleaned from decades of farming, and his uncanny premonitions were usually right.

"I promise not to move until you do. Maybe Levi Matthews and I could start logging this farm. We planned to do this."

"Sounds like a good idea."

"Think of all the firewood we can cut from felled treetops—and if it stays as cold as you claim, we will need it!"

Chapter Ten

"Come over here and look at the sun. Tell me what you see."

Craig and Romulus followed him to a gap in the trees where they could observe the sun suspended just above two timbered hills to the southwest. For the first time, Craig realized how much its power had diminished. An ashen haze scattered its direct light, allowing them to look directly at it. A dark, irregular blotch tarnished the orb's surface, blocking a sizeable portion of its radiance. The image resembled a large spider with legs extending grotesquely outward from the main body.

"What is it?" Craig asked.

"I hoped you might tell me," Martin replied, shaking his head. "I have never seen anything like it. Scientists claim there are dark spots on the sun, but this appears different. Perhaps the sun is dying. In the past five years we have seen eclipses, the Great Comet, earthquakes, war—and now this. Perhaps the preachers are right. The world could be ending."

Five years ago, when the Great Comet of 1811 blazed across the heavens, the whole countryside panicked. No one had ever seen a comet. Brush arbor preachers claimed it preceded natural disasters and war. Shortly after its passing, America experienced the strongest earthquakes in recorded history and the country plunged into war with Great Britain. Then, Martin had remained calm, mostly because he knew about comets and earthquakes—and he had fought in and survived two major wars. But this phenomenon was something unknown and he was uneasy.

Naturally, this had a chilling effect on Craig. He knew that if Martin worried, he should also worry. He shivered involuntarily, and it was not just from the cold.

"Sorry to give you a fright," Martin apologized. "Last autumn I felt it was time to draw in our reins and not plant as much. Now I am sure."

"I am glad you have shared this with me."

"Allow me to change the subject. Yesterday, one of the keelboat men pulled in at Rosenbotham's store for supplies. He claims that hog prices in New Orleans have reached new heights. I plan to sell about three fourths of my hogs."

"Three fourths?"

"Why not? We only need a boar and a few young sows to begin anew. We slaughter just three hogs a year for our own use."

"Do you advise me to sell?"

"Prices have never been higher. I counted over seventy hogs in your bunch. That's too many by far. Some of mine are running with them."

"Where did you see the hogs?"

"Over on the Arbuckle farm."

Craig glanced over at Romulus for confirmation. The giant nodded. "They was on this farm two days ago rootin' around for mast. Must have crossed the road since then. Mine was running with 'em too."

In addition to wages, Craig paid Romulus in hogs and chickens. He now owned ten hogs. A sow could throw two litters in a year and from two to six, even eight piglets in a litter. Hogs, like tobacco and whiskey, were a sound form of currency in Kentucky. Both Craig and Romulus sold hogs each year, but just a few at a time for extra cash money.

"You want to sell any of yours, Romulus?" Craig asked.

"I reckon I might sell half."

"Then we will have our work cut out for us."

Martin glanced once more at the sky. "I suppose I should leave you to your work. I will stop in to see Mary and the grandchildren." Craig watched him walk away. Where most men of his age were feeble, fading, or dead, Martin still walked upright and straight-backed. He watched the ground and chose his footsteps with care, still acutely aware of his surroundings.

"You reckon it's the end of time, Craig?" Romulus asked. Fear registered in his eyes, something Craig had never seen.

"I don't know, Romulus. We might as well ignore it and keep on working." He tried to sound calm, but without success. He risked one more glance at the sun. The spider-like specter occupied its place just above the orb's center and its "legs" extended malignantly across its surface. Hopefully the sun was not dying out as Martin suggested. It was a welcome relief to return to work, to concentrate on draft horses and furrows, cold air and crows cawing in the nearby woods. More than ever, fear and uncertainty made Craig appreciate the ordinary things in life.

———•———

The next morning Martin, Owen, Stephen and the McDonnell hired hands showed up on Craig's bottomland cornfield to build a hog enclosure. This involved rearranging Craig's fence, opening up the end adjacent to the Arbuckle farm, and creating a funnel in which to drive the hogs. At the field's opposite end, they constructed a narrow loading chute to Craig's rock landing, still known by riverboat pilots as "Widder's Landing." It was easy to affect this change, for Craig's fence was the "worm" variety—split wood rails laid with ends resting on each other in a zigzag fashion. Each section was five rails high and angled slightly from the previous section, creating an appearance of a worm or snake. No vertical posts were used to build it, so workers could lift the rails and load them onto wagons, then haul them to a desired location. Romulus came down around mid-morning and added his efforts to the project.

Martin watched the proceedings with amusement. He enjoyed overseeing and pitching in, on occasion. The plan was simple— build a half-acre pen, then drive or entice the hogs into the fenced lot, and feed them until Craig or Martin could hail a passing riverboat. By mid-afternoon they finished building the pen and loading chute. Craig listened carefully to his advice.

"You should bring down about a half wagonload of corn and scatter a few ears at your field's eastern edge, then drop them at intervals, making a trail to draw those hogs in. Pile the remaining corn along this end of the fence. The hogs' sense of smell is phenomenal. Move them in this direction and they'll soon figure where the corn is. When they are inside and eating, stack the loose rails where they came in and close off their escape. You will then have to feed and water until we can find buyers."

"Those hogs can bust out of a worm fence."

"They won't try if you keep them fed."

"Will the corn baiting work?" Craig asked.

"We may need to get behind them on foot, or on horseback, and first nudge them in the right direction. Once they find the corn, watch them run headlong into the pen. We will do the same with my hogs—but work them in from this side."

Martin owned a large number of hogs that ranged all the way over to Owen's farm and beyond. Many times, bands of hogs became intermingled; that was why every farmer had a mark to distinguish his animals. These marks were scored with a knife into the hogs' ears when they were little and easy to catch. Craig's mark was called "overbit left, two overslopes right." To achieve an overbit, Craig folded the left ear and cut out a three-cornered gap on top. The overslopes involved scoring two long strips forward on top of the right ear. This identification method was registered in the "minute book" at the Breckinridge County Clerk's office. Usually, hog owners knew the marks of other owners and respected them, often supplying reports on their location. It seemed a strange practice, letting hogs run wild all over the countryside, but the animals could fend for themselves, foraging for "mast"— acorns, beechnuts, chestnuts, persimmons, berries, grubs, bulbs, mushrooms, and roots—and they were able to defend themselves against most predators. Usually families would pen hogs they wished to eat, fatten them on ear corn and whiskey mash, and then slaughter them in late autumn, salt-curing, hanging, and smoking the meat in smokehouses. The remaining hogs were sold to riverboat men who would take them downriver, usually to New Orleans.

That afternoon while Craig loaded the wagon with corn, Romulus trekked over to the Arbuckle farm in search of the hogs. Around sunset he returned and found Craig in the barn milking the spotted cow.

"Found 'em, Craig," he announced.

"Where?"

"They done run past the Arbuckle farm into the wet ground below the hills."

Craig knew the place, for he hunted squirrels there. A jumble of oak-covered limestone hills ran parallel to the Ohio and there, runoff water created a marshy area. The oaks shed their acorns in abundance and hogs loved rooting for them.

Early next morning, Craig hitched a rope to the hollowed-out beech log and dragged it down to his makeshift hog pen. He filled this homemade trough with buckets of water drawn from the Ohio River. Then he drove his wagon down to the bottomland, halting just short of the Arbuckle farm. At that point he began scattering ear corn, throwing out more and more ears as he moved in. Romulus arrived when Craig reached the halfway mark. The giant carried a long hickory stave with him.

"You baitin' that trap real good, Craig."

"I want those hogs to know it keeps getting better the farther in they go."

"That should do it. I'm headin' over now to find them hogs."

"You want me to saddle you a mount?"

"If it all the same to you, I just walk."

"See you soon, then."

The fence narrowed as Craig neared the pen. Just inside the opening he dropped a dozen ears, then a few feet farther, another dozen. And, as Martin instructed, he piled the remaining bulk near the back fence. Craig knew this golden mound of grain would tempt any hog, especially now, at the end of winter. He drove the empty wagon back to the barn. Part way up the track, he looked down on the enclosure. It did resemble a funnel-shaped trap. Silently he thanked God for bringing him here and for giving him a father-in-law like Martin McDonnell. It seemed there was always something new to learn from him. After unhitching the draft horses, Craig helped Mary milk the cows. Stephen and Owen rode their horses over, arriving while he carried the buckets to the springhouse.

"Did you bait the field?" Stephen asked.

"I did. I can't imagine those hogs refusing to go in. Where is Martin?"

"Pa drove the wagon into town to shop at Rosenbotham's store," Owen answered. "Two keelboats docked at the store landing yesterday. The boatmen said they planned to stay a few days. Might be some buyers on board."

"Martin is working fast."

"He also plans to deal with Rosenbotham. Somehow he manages to do that without riling him. They've got a longstanding working relationship that goes way back."

"I know," Craig replied. He understood that Rosenbotham must make money like everyone else, but it irked him to watch the old skinflint hem and haw and claim how he could not afford to pay. He would pay a ridiculously low price, then turn around and sell at an enormous profit. More than once he had taken advantage of Craig, especially in those early days when he first arrived in Cottonwood Bend.

Craig saddled Blue and called for his hunting hound, Brindle. The dog came running, an unimpressive, medium-sized mongrel named for its coloring—a motley mélange of brown and black swirls. Although he ranked as the ugliest dog Craig had ever seen, he was a good hunter. Deer, coon, possum, squirrel, rabbit, and quail—Brindle could track them all.

Off they rode, down the bottomland field, turning east toward the Arbuckle farm. Brindle bounded excitedly ahead, fully expecting to hunt game. His excitement was infectious. The forest towered high above them on their right, climbing the steep slope which rose a hundred feet or more above them. Craig could make out unfamiliar limestone outcroppings and overhangs usually obscured by foliage. He and Levi Matthews had logged sections of this forest, but unlike other loggers, Levi harvested only the biggest trees, doing minimal damage to the surrounding growth. At Craig's request he left the walnuts and hickories which served as valuable food sources. Levi's German ancestors had practiced good forest husbandry for centuries and some of it had obviously rubbed off.

Blue stepped springily across the narrow ditch marking the boundary between Craig's farm and the Arbuckle farm, Martin's easternmost farm. They hunted those acres for some time, riding into the timbered hills above the farm and scouring the riverbank scrub, before concluding that the hogs had moved on. Leaving the good ground behind, they ventured into some brushy marsh country, fringed with tall, dense canebrakes. It took some serious searching to locate Romulus. Then Brindle smelled the hogs and began barking.

"Get back, Brindle!" Craig growled. The hound dropped back and fell in beside Blue, his floppy ears cocked in attention.

"Over here, Craig!" Romulus called from beyond a canebrake. "Swing out toward the river and ride round them slow-like."

The thick, buff-colored cane still obscured the hogs, so Craig and the McDonnells circled cautiously around behind them. Emerging from the canebrake, they rode abruptly upon the hogs. Craig reckoned there were a hundred rather than seventy. The animals milled around in the shallow marshlands, rooting in the mud and chomping on some unknown food source. Craig spied the enormous black boar with long, wickedly curved tusks. Some older sows stood almost as tall as it did. The hogs ranged in size and color. One red sow had thrown a recent litter of six reddish-brown piglets. These Craig intended to mark and keep. There were half-grown shoats and a mixed assortment of full grown hogs, some weighing up to three hundred pounds. Some were spotted, others solid, and still others wide-striped. Colors ran from black to white, tan to pink, red to dark brown. Most had long snouts, which they used to dig up bugs, roots, and plant bulbs found in the forest undergrowth. If they ever broke into a farmer's field, hogs could cause serious damage. Most of the time they were content to forage. Not content with plant food, hogs were known meat-eaters, especially the older hogs. They could smell out a snake, root it from under a log, trample it with their sharp feet, and eat it for its nutritional value. Young birds and rabbits often fell prey to a scavenging hog. The hogs would also consume earthworms, spiders, insects, eggs and fish trapped in the lowlands after a flood. Martin claimed that hogs would even kill and eat a newborn fawn that the mother had left lying in the grass.

"What are they eating?" Stephen asked.

"I think they's eatin' them little frogs buried in the mud," Romulus hazarded.

"Let's spread out and move in a little closer," Owen suggested. "Just enough to make them uncomfortable. We don't want to run or scatter them, just move them a little."

The horses drew near and the nearest hogs grunted their displeasure and alarm. The big boar regarded them warily, especially Brindle, but he continued munching.

"I hope he doesn't charge!" Stephen exclaimed.

"If he does, I'll shoot him dead," Craig assured him.

Some of the younger hogs began trotting toward Mary's Landing. A few of the more nervous sows followed them. Owen, nearest the trees, held up his hand for everyone to pause. Craig reined in and took stock of their deployment. He was positioned about fifteen yards from Owen's right. Romulus stood to his right at about the same distance. Stephen stationed himself out on the far right.

"Let's move again," Owen counseled. "A few steps at a time and then stop."

It took two more advances to dislodge the boar and a few other recalcitrant hogs. The boar snorted and tore out for the thick canebrake and tall timber beyond. Owen swung his mount up the slope to head him off, but he wasn't fast enough.

"Sic him, Brindle!" Craig urged.

The brindle-colored hound streaked through the brush, overtook the boar, and nipped him on his right hind leg, forcing him to wheel about. Brindle dodged the tusks, barking and snaring, forcing the boar to yield and turn back down the slope.

Craig skirted the marsh and closed in toward the trees, edging the hogs back into open ground. At one point the drove almost panicked; several frontrunners broke into a mad, squealing stampede, but halted when they realized the main bunch had not followed. After a time, the hogs settled down and coalesced into a single bunch.

Owen signaled for them to slowly press forward. In this manner they moved the hogs across the Arbuckle farm and onto Craig's bottomland. The lead hogs crossed the ditch, found the first ear corn, and began eating. In one collective instant the herd sensed what was happening and rushed to where those hogs fed. Owen, Craig, Romulus and Stephen closed casually in behind them, not pushing, but effectively sealing off their escape.

Martin's scheme worked better than expected. The hogs fought over the corn, working themselves into a frenzy. Younger shoats ran ahead, finding new ears, their excited squeals drawing the herd deeper into the narrowing funnel. The bigger hogs drove smaller ones deeper into the enclosure. When they discovered the huge pile at the far end, the entire herd surged into the pen. While they snarled and snapped, competing for a share, Craig, Romulus, and the McDonnell brothers closed off the opening, stacking loose rails to close the sturdy worm fence.

Martin returned from Cottonwood Bend and watched them from the far side. He approached now, grinning with admiration. "I'd say that was a good job of hog droving—about the best I have seen." It was high praise coming from such an experienced farmer.

Next came the job of identification. It was hard to distinguish marks with the hogs milling about. After several counts, Craig and Martin agreed that thirteen McDonnell hogs had joined with this bunch. Romulus' ten hogs were easy to identify—all were black-and-white-spotted. That left Craig with fifty-six hogs, unless some of his animals had formed up with other herds.

"Good news," Martin announced. "Tomorrow the two captains are poling their keelboats upriver to look at our hogs. There are buyers on board, but there is no guarantee they'll purchase—and if they do, they are certain to be close traders. But Rosenbotham knows they are coming and he is also interested. He may send his sons out here. That is where we stand to make our bread-and-butter money."

"What about our tobacco?"

"The law says we must take it down to the inspection station."

"And Rosenbotham gets the inspection fee?" Craig asked.

"Don't be too hard on him. He's fair enough. Most of your fee goes to the government. Once the tobacco is inspected and graded, we are free to sell. Kentucky does this to ensure a high quality product. There are unscrupulous farmers who manure their fields heavily and produce foul-smelling, unusable tobacco. Buyers need to know they are getting good quality. When they see the stamp, they will pay best prices."

Craig knew that Kentucky, upon statehood, had adopted the "Virginia System" of warehouses, quality control stations, and issuance of certificates on stored tobacco. Lots of folks used the certificates as currency and to pay fees, fines, and debts. Craig saw the whole process as a government ploy to lay hands on more of his hard-earned money. He resented that the inspectors opened the hogsheads, then extracted and carefully examined at least two samplings. Up until 1809 all trash and "unsound" tobacco was burned in the warehouse kiln in the owner's presence. After that year, it was simply returned for disposal. If the owner refused, the entire hogshead was destroyed. Good tobacco was repacked in the hogshead. The planter's distinguishing mark, hogshead weight, net weight, and name of inspection warehouse were stamped on the hogshead.

At that point they could sell their crop to Rosenbotham or allow him to sell it and pay him a commission, which amounted pretty much to the same thing. Or they could wait around in Cottonwood Bend and sell to the riverboat men, but pay the fee Rosenbotham charged for using his landing. The other option was bringing the inspected tobacco back home and trying to attract the attention of flatboat and keelboat captains at Mary's Landing. Martin counseled selling a portion to Rosenbotham for the sake of future transactions.

"Should I feed the hogs again this evening to keep them from breaking out?" Craig asked.

"You might," Martin advised. "But don't use too much of your corn. You will need it for making more whiskey."

That evening Craig hauled another half wagonload down to the enclosure and tossed in ears to the hogs. They massed greedily, fighting each other for the corn. It seemed they could eat ten wagon loads and not be filled. Craig realized he could not successfully feed them for any extended time. With cattle and horses to feed, and more whiskey to distill, he prayed the buyers would take the majority of his hogs.

At the supper table Mary suggested he should tap one of the two-year-old whiskey barrels and fill a jug to take to the landing. Craig could treat the keelboat captains to a free sample and offer it for sale.

"What about Delacroix?" he asked.

"We must save the oldest and best for him. Let them have the two-year-old stock. It is superior to anything they will find elsewhere. You can let Rosenbotham have some of the three-year-old stock."

This sounded like an excellent strategy. Craig realized again how lucky he was to have her as his wife.

———•———

Two keelboats nosed into the landing and tied up shortly after dawn. Both were long, narrow, cigar-shaped riverboats, each with a crude cabin built in the middle. The first keelboat measured about fifty feet in length; the other was much larger, about eighty feet long. Unlike the big, cumbersome flatboats, these craft were designed to return upriver. Outfitted with a keel to provide stability, these boats could be propelled upstream through a variety of methods. Some boatmen pushed with "shoulder poles," walking from bow to stern and muscling the boat against the current. Others attached hawsers to a tree or stump on the riverbank and then drew the keelboat along, hand-over-hand. Some keelboat captains mounted a windlass on deck and reeled the rope in—a method called "cordelling." Overhanging branches were also grasped by deckhands who drew the keelboat along in a tactic called "bushwhacking." Finally, there was almost always a mast and sail to take advantage of any prevailing winds. As the river changed direction, the sail could be hoisted or reefed.

Keelboats ranked as one of the more popular boats on the Ohio River, used almost extensively for transporting bulky or heavy cargo in a timely manner. These particular boats were headed downstream to New Orleans. The captains disembarked to have a look at the hogs. Each captain was accompanied by an apparent buyer, dressed in somewhat finer attire. Craig noticed that these men affected disinterested or displeased expressions, similar to the ones Rosenbotham assumed when he purchased goods. And like the store-owner, they made non-committal grunts, both claiming to possess limited spending cash. Craig let them run, waiting for them to make an offer. For the past few years he had sold to Rosenbotham, accepting his prices—which were certainly lower than what the investors paid him. Craig didn't know the going price for live hogs, but he knew the market was up. The buyers would offer a low price and he feared getting taken; at the same time he feared alienating the buyers with a refusal. Most of all, he did not want to be stuck with those hogs.

Fortunately, Martin arrived with a quarter wagonload of corn. He greeted the buyers and began tossing corn into the pen, not speaking with them further. Craig joined him to help out, noticing that the captains were impressed with the loading chute.

"Have they made any offers?" Martin asked in a low voice.

"Not yet."

"Hold your fire if they do. Act interested, but Isaac and Reuben Rosenbotham are on their way out to make an offer."

"I just hope these buyers won't pull up stakes and leave us."

"Watch what happens."

"Will you do the bargaining?" Craig asked.

"I think you can manage. Stick to your price and let them make an offer."

"What *is* a fair price?"

"Right now, salted pork is selling for fourteen dollars a barrel. In the stores it sells at seven cents a pound. Lard sells for eleven cents."

"But these are live hogs on the hoof."

"You can figure a three hundred pound hog will yield at least two hundred ten pounds of pork. The average yield per carcass is about seventy percent of the hog's weight."

Craig did some mental arithmetic, multiplying seven cents times two hundred and ten pounds. "That comes to almost fifteen dollars per hog!" he exclaimed, almost unable to contain himself.

"Not so fast," Martin said. "You can't price live hogs on par with salted pork in the barrel. You must figure the time and labor involved in butchering, smoking, and curing. Factor in the cost of salt and barrels. All of that goes into the production."

"Still, we should get at least half."

Martin tried to suppress a chuckle. "Very few of these hogs will go three hundred pounds. Most of them come in at about two hundred. The buyers must also feed them and pay shipping costs."

Craig felt totally deflated. He had estimated on fifteen dollars a hog; the figure plummeted sadly below his expectations. But Martin wasn't finished.

"Imagine yourself as a buyer. You take on a load of hogs, realizing that some may never make it to market. With live animals there is always considerable risk. As a farmer you can appreciate that."

The buyer from the large keelboat approached them. "Who owns these hogs?"

Craig replied, "I own most of them. Martin McDonnell owns thirteen and my field hand owns the ten black-and-white-spotted hogs. He is not here yet, but wants to sell five."

The man turned to Martin. "How many are you selling?"

"I don't have to sell any today. These happened to form up with Craig's bunch."

"And what about you?"

Craig replied, "I can sell most of them. I am keeping the boar, the red sow and her six shoats, and eight of this year's hogs." That meant he could sell forty hogs.

The man pulled aside to speak with his captain. In his absence, the buyer from the smaller keelboat approached. "I might take a half dozen of your best, but I must have my choice of hogs." Craig grunted noncommittally and the buyer retreated to confer with his captain.

"Look there!" Martin pointed toward the river. A large flatboat, still about a mile upstream, appeared to be headed toward them. "If they pull in, we might just sell them all!"

At that moment, Owen and Stephen arrived from Welcome Hall with Isaac and Reuben Rosenbotham in tow. The young storekeepers stepped hurriedly over the frost-covered ground, apparently not wanting to miss out on the sale. Rosenbotham had certainly instructed them on what to offer, and Craig imagined they would be more miserly than the buyers. But their arrival engendered a miraculous change in the atmosphere.

The first buyer came back, much more interested. "I'll take a dozen hogs at one dollar a head."

Craig maintained his composure. Years ago he sold a stinking old boar to Rosenbotham for a dollar. The store keeper had turned around and sold it for more—and that was in 1811, the year prices had hit rock bottom, due to impending war and the British blockade. These were fine sows and gilts, guaranteed to make good hams, shoulders, bacon, and lard.

"You are too low," Craig replied.

"I cannot do better," the buyer shook his head remorsefully. "Money is scarce everywhere."

Craig bit back his anger and dug hard for a suitable counter-offer. Fortunately the other buyer saved him from a potential gaff.

"I can. Let me have my choice of eight hogs at one-fifty a head."

Craig glanced at Martin for approval. The old man remained stone-faced, not registering whether he agreed or not. The Rosenbotham brothers whispered agitatedly among themselves. This exchange did not go unnoticed by the river men.

"I'll match that," the first buyer proposed.

"First, I wish you would sample my whiskey," Craig offered. He walked over to the fence and produced the stone jug. "It is still aging, but I need an expert opinion on how well it will sell in New Orleans—and at what price."

He uncorked the jug and offered it to the keelboat captain. The man tilted it back and guzzled, his Adam's apple bobbing with each swallow. "Damn, boy! That's good stuff!"

Craig took it from him and addressed the buyer. "He didn't even begin to appreciate it. This is top-quality whiskey. You need to smell it first, then take a sip and roll it around in your mouth, front to back and side to side. Let it ripple across your tongue before you swallow. You'll see what I am talking about."

The buyer took the jug and did as Craig instructed. Then he took another slow sip. "This is the best whiskey I have ever tasted. It surpasses anything Evan Williams ever made. I have enjoyed some aged 'Elijah Craig', but this is better. Will you sell?"

"I have promised most of it to Pierre Delacroix, a merchant in New Orleans."

"I know Pierre Delacroix."

"He is my brother-in-law's father-in-law."

The Rosenbotham brothers began whispering and arguing among themselves again as the captain and buyer from the smaller keelboat tried samples.

"One dollar fifty a gallon!" the buyer offered.

"I read where Daniel Trabue sold his for three," Craig replied. "And I know his wasn't half as good."

"He sold his by the gallon to returning soldiers at retail prices. Hell, your county tavern laws have set the top rate at twelve-and-a-half cents per half pint. I am offering the best wholesale price you can hope to get."

"I think I will wait until Delacroix orders. Now, how about those hogs?"

Isaac Rosenbotham broke in, "Father heard you were selling a batch of your best whiskey. He wants to buy some."

"I appreciate that," Craig replied. "But I want to sell these hogs first."

"He'll take twenty hogs at two dollars per head. But he wants to buy six barrels of your whiskey. That is the deal, or there is no deal."

"It is three-year old whiskey. Mary insists on two dollars a gallon, but I must be reimbursed for the cost of each barrel. Also, I want another ten cents a head on those hogs. You can put the two dollars on account at your store."

The brothers consulted hurriedly and agreed. "You will deliver both the hogs and whiskey?"

"I will," Craig nodded.

"Done!" The brothers grinned and strode off, having achieved their purpose. Craig wondered if he had sold too low. Martin's face told otherwise.

"I have created a monster," he laughed.

The big flatboat hove to and edged toward them. Obviously some enterpriser on board was interested in buying. The boatmen worked their sweeps to bring it in close. Two men threw out ropes and snagged stumps and driftwood to hold them just above the landing.

The buyer from the large keelboat glanced over his shoulder and relented. "Fair enough—I'll match those storekeepers. A dozen of your hogs, but I get to choose first. And two barrels of your whiskey."

Craig felt his spirits soar. The second buyer purchased eight hogs and one barrel of whiskey at the same prices. Stephen raced with him up the hill and helped load the wagon with three barrels of two-year old whiskey. By the time they returned, the first dozen hogs were on board the larger keelboat. Martin and Owen had helped the crew members cut out those the buyer wanted.

Craig and Stephen lifted out a chute section and unloaded the barrels, rolling them down the rock landing and onto the keelboat. The investor paid in Spanish mill dollars and British pounds, shillings and pence. Sixty-nine dollars per barrel and two dollars and ten cents for each hog. It felt good to have money in hand. The second buyer shelled out a total of eighty-seven dollars and eighty cents.

Craig ran the money up for Mary to hold. He crossed the Hardinsburg Road and found Romulus cutting firewood behind his barn. "You'd better come down to the landing with me, Romulus. There are buyers pulled in down there. I have already sold forty hogs!"

Romulus joined him at the river's edge. The first keelboat was shoving off and Martin was negotiating with the flatboat captain. "Craig, this man wants to buy my thirteen hogs, Romulus' ten hogs, and six more of yours. He is paying two dollars a head."

"I gots to keep some hogs for my family to eat on," Romulus said. "I reckon I can sell him six, but I'm keepin' four young sows."

"I can understand that," Martin nodded.

"That is fine with me," Craig agreed. "I am also holding back some young sows."

"He wants to buy two barrels of your whiskey."

"I won't have any left at this rate," Craig protested.

"It really is remarkable whiskey," the captain declared.

In the end Craig fetched two barrels and helped him load six hogs, keeping back the black boar, the red sow and her six red shoats, and just two other young sows. They watched the flatboat cast off and drift slowly westward with the current.

"I would call that a good day's work!" The old man was pleased. "You won't see many days like this in your lifetime!"

Romulus was proud of his twelve dollars and sixty cents. Craig, flush from his big pay day, figured on giving him another bonus for all his hard work. He asked Martin, "When do we bring your hogs over?"

"Let's drive your hogs and whiskey barrels into Cottonwood Bend this afternoon and worry about mine on Monday. We'll work Rosenbotham the same way—let him know we are selling more hogs at the landing."

"Maybe he will want to purchase more whiskey. I'll gladly make it a contingent that he buy some of your hogs before I sell him any."

Martin laughed, "You didn't need me to help with negotiating. You did just fine!"

That afternoon, after turning out those hogs he intended to keep, Stephen and Owen joined Craig to drive Rosenbotham's twenty hogs the six miles into Cottonwood Bend. Brindle helped work them along, nipping at their hamstrings and keeping them from straying off the road. After the first mile, the bunch settled in to a manageable entity. It was slow going, but they crossed the bridge over Cottonwood Creek and reached the storekeeper's pens before dark. Martin followed them, driving Craig's wagon loaded with three-year old whiskey.

Rosenbotham accepted the hogs and whiskey and drew up a bill of sale. Six barrels at $69 per barrel came to $414. Twenty hogs at $2.10 a head came to $42. Craig could not believe it when the storeowner counted out the money by lamplight—$454 total with two dollars on store account. Very few people had that much money in Cottonwood Bend. This probably applied to most folks in western Kentucky. The storeowner was one of the wealthy few.

"We will sell this whiskey at a dollar a quart," Rosenbotham grinned. "I have customers asking for it all the time. I shall call it 'Widder's Reserve'."

Craig wondered again if he had sold too cheaply. The river pilots had all bought barrels of his whiskey, paying the same price as Rosenbotham had. Perhaps they all knew they could resell it at higher prices. In the end, he admitted he was satisfied. As Martin advised, they were selling while prices were high. Who knew when the market would crash? Who knew what the weakened sun and cold weather might bring?

They spent the first two days of April scouring the bottomland woods, using Brindle to help track down the McDonnell hogs and drive them over to Mary's Landing. It was an enormous drove, about a hundred hogs in all. In the next eight days a flatboat, a barge, two keelboats, and a little steamboat pulled in to make purchases. Martin sold the bulk of his hogs to the river men, but at the end of those eight days Rosenbotham sent out his sons to purchase the remainder. During that time, Craig sold three more barrels of whiskey.

The weather turned fractionally warmer and signs of spring

slowly emerged. The willows greened ever so slightly and some of Agnes' flowers bloomed half-heartedly. Mary deemed it was time to plant their spring garden, provided they covered the new plants with branches, straw, or thin cloth to ward off heavy frosts. She and Craig covered their plots every night and uncovered them during the daylight, hoping the weather would turn. Martin was not wholly convinced, but he too began laying out a family garden. Throughout this time, the sun remained veiled behind an ashen fog while the dark, spider-like image continued to blemish its pale yellow face.

<hr />

Everyone agreed that the winter of 1815-1816 had lasted longer than normal. The first twelve days of April were cold and hazy, marked by an uncharacteristic drought. Martin figured that the past winter was the driest ever. Without the usual warm springtime rains, everyone's garden produce was delayed. At this time of the year, folks hankered for fresh vegetables; this season the need was becoming critical. Mary found the answer to this, venturing outdoors with the girls to pick the first green poke shoots on the slopes behind the cabin. She cooked the greens with slabs of bacon and drizzled them with apple cider vinegar. Craig could not get enough of them. His body seemed to soak up the nourishment.

He and Romulus finished working on the Smithhart farm, clearing brush and plowing. They spent several days cutting firewood and splitting fence rails. Levi Matthews drove out with a crew to select giant yellow poplar and white oak trees for logging. Craig showed him the farm section he wanted to clear next. Together they stepped off the area. The little man was in a quarrelsome mood, made worse by slipping and going down on all fours in a wet gully. He rose and plodded on, directing his men to mark the desired trees.

"I am only taking the big timber. The rest of this scrub you'll clear in your own damned time. And I don't dig out stumps. That's your problem."

"Understood."

He shook water from his wet sleeves. "Damn this cold weather!"
"When will spring arrive?"

"I am not responsible for the seasons," Craig responded. "If I
could bring on warmer weather, I would have done so long ago."

"Folks all over the countryside are complaining."

"Let's hope it breaks soon. On a happier note, let me congratu-
late you on your new arrival."

"Yep, it's another boy."

"We are all happy for you."

Levi's first wife, Tabby, had been barren and had died of an unknown ailment some years ago. Levi then married Elizabeth, the
young widow of Irvin Greathouse, a local farmer who had fallen in
Upper Canada during the War with Britain. With the marriage Levi
inherited a young stepson. Since then, Elizabeth had given him two
sons.

"Mary is due soon, I hear."

"She says early in August."

"Reckon she'll give you another girl?"

"She claims she is having twins, but there is no way she could
know that!"

"Trust me—women know things we don't. It scares the literal
hell out of me. Twins, you say?" Craig noticed the smirk that usually
presaged a ribbing. "Now Mary can have four girls helping her in
the kitchen. Have you thought of that?"

"Actually I have."

"Just as well. Any sons of yours would have to work on the farm
like damned slaves."

Craig laughed and let him have his fun. He watched as Levi
scratched out numerical figures on brown paper in his spidery scrawl.

"You'll drag the logs down to your landing and ride the rafts to
Spigot Run?" Levi asked. "We'll run it the same way we have in
the past. I'll pay market value. There has been increased demand
for lumber in New Orleans and in the Caribbean Islands. You won't

make a fortune, but it will be a good, solid income."

"Let's hope so. We are not farming as much this year."

"Why not? Prices are higher than ever."

"Martin is concerned about the weather. He thinks the growing season will be a poor one."

"He may be right."

"We have plenty of surplus tobacco and hemp to sell. And I still have a barn full of whiskey."

"Heard you made a fortune selling hogs and whiskey to the boatmen. Folks are buying 'Widder's Reserve' by the quart at Rosenbotham's Store. Sounds like you have converted that grain into real profit."

"I am trying."

"Seems like this would be the time to keep producing."

"Some of the land is wearing out. Martin feels it is time to let tired acres rest. We will plant red clover in some of those fields and pasture our farm animals on them for a time."

"So you are not planting corn?"

"Just enough to feed my animals and—of course—make whiskey."

"I hate to tell you this, but grain prices are soaring, and speculators expect them to go much higher. Last year, New England and Lower Canada suffered a late spring and early autumn frosts, and they are on track for worse this spring. Papers claim that European harvests have been devastated by years of war and cold temperatures."

"Martin reads the papers too."

"Just don't come bitching to me when you have to pay me double prices for your corn, oats, and wheat. I'll be happy to lift some of those profits you have made this spring."

"Sounds like you have been talking to Judge Bozarth."

"Well, I am forced to listen to him every Sunday morning after church. The men gather outside to smoke and jaw; that's when he tries to lure some of them into investing with him. He claims the new banks are making a killing on land speculation and loans. From what I have read in the *Gazette*, he may be right."

"Don't tell me you plan to throw in with him!" Craig exclaimed.

"Not a chance. Heard he tried to enlist you."

"He didn't get far."

"As close as you are with money, I can believe that! You did know he recently appeared in court as defendant? Several Hardinsburg men won judgments against him and he has been ordered to begin paying them back."

"I hate to hear it."

"You wouldn't feel that way if it was your hard-earned coin. When it comes to money he may be the least trustworthy person I know. And that old bastard is still seeing Cecilia Dowell on the sly. But even that has gotten complicated for him. Some widower, a big-time cattle farmer east of Hardinsburg, is sweet on her too. Hope it doesn't end in a gunfight."

Craig felt a stab of concern. He knew the Judge's predicament, perhaps more intimately than anyone. And he had kept all to himself. If Levi knew what he claimed, then the whole county knew.

"Perhaps the Judge will steer clear, now someone else is involved."

"They say she won't let him go. She keeps using that old honey trap to draw him back."

"I hope for his sake he will withdraw."

"Right—when Hell freezes over!"

The Atlantic Ocean—April 13, 1816

Arabelle skimmed the surface of an indigo ocean, her sails full and rigging taut from the trade winds standing fair off the port side. Her sharp bow knifed through dancing white horses as a constant wind drove her hard on a southeasterly heading. As he did several times each day, Doc Applegate ventured outside his cabin to walk the deck and partake of sunlight and fresh air. There was much to observe, even on an open sea with deep blue swells rising around them like mountains, then collapsing dramatically to form constantly moving valleys. It was entertaining and instructive to watch the crew bustle about the deck and climb the rigging, attending to the slightest changes in the wind. Even on the open sea, currents and cross-currents necessitated close and constant vigilance.

No stranger to sea travel, Doc fully appreciated the difference between the sheltered Caribbean and the wide-open Atlantic. In the early days, *Arabelle* ambled quietly along over a turquoise sea adorned with green, palm-fringed islands, volcanic mountains, and white sand beaches. Tropical reefs and vast shallows painted delightful swirls of color that almost took one's breath, such was their beauty. But out here, on the open main, conditions were markedly different. Steady winds blew unbroken across the vast expanse of ocean, forming long heavy swells called rollers. These waves forced the sloop to alternately climb steep inclines and then plunge downward in gut-swooping drops into vast troughs surrounded by more unending mountains of water. The ship's crew seemed to relish every bit of it. Doc decided he had seen enough. It was time to look in on his patient.

By some strange miracle Emmett Barnett had managed to survive, although his hold on life was still tenuous. The setons still drew fair amounts of benign pus from the compression bandages, but whenever Doc changed the cotton padding, he sniffed the cloths, detecting no whiff of malignant gangrene. The stump itself showed no visible signs of mortification. The little tavern owner clung grimly on, obeying faithfully every one of Doc's instructions. Mostly he rested, and this gave the stump time to stabilize and the flesh to heal. Although the Caribbean's relative tranquility had slowed *Arabelle's* progress, and they had even lain three days becalmed, this provided the ideal setting that Emmett needed. The going was rougher now, but the danger of a femoral hemorrhage was less likely. Doc examined the stump and felt immense pride in his work. The amputation was far and away his most profound medical accomplishment. Of course he had been aided by the gifted Solange. She certainly had helped bring about a successful outcome. He wondered what she was doing now.

"Closing up nicely, Emmett!" he announced.

"Scratch foot!" Emmett barked. He was dangerously bad-tempered this morning, snapping and cursing as Doc changed his bandages and exercised the stump in a series of motions designed to prevent his muscles from drawing and his hip joint from seizing up, a condition known to medical science as "contracture." The maneuvering caused intense discomfort, but the positive end benefit would be immeasurable.

"I can't scratch it!" Doc chuckled.

"Damned foot itch like hell!"

"It's those catfish nibbling on it in New Orleans! You don't have a foot anymore, Emmett." He knew it was common for amputees to complain of itching, burning sensations, cramps, or phantom pain in a limb or appendage that no longer existed. Emmett still required laudanum, but days ago Doc had begun tapering off the dosage.

"What you say?" Emmett demanded.

"One of the crew tossed your leg into the Mississippi—after I sawed it off."

"Should have buried."

"We'll toss flowers into the river when we return."

"I kill that sombitch Signet!"

"I don't doubt it."

"But first, I torture slow." Emmett's single black eye glittered like a drop of fresh coal tar. The look on his face proved that he meant it. Doc shuddered and wondered what lay in store for the banker.

Just then, Willoughby appeared in the doorway. Captain West had placed him at Doc's disposal. After Louis and Raoul had refused to help clean Emmett, Willoughby pitched in and proved himself an able assistant. The half-brothers were rough gunmen, but both balked when it came to changing bandages or soiled clothing. The big sailor balanced a thick rectangular block of wood, about two feet in length, on his right shoulder. In his left hand he toted a leather bag of carpenter's tools. He sat down near the head of Emmett's bed, crossed his legs, and placed the wood block securely in front of him. Then he spread a canvas cloth and produced a small hammer, hand chisel, and spoon gouge from the bag. He began tapping on the block.

"What have you got there, Willoughby?" Doc asked.

"He make new leg," Emmett interjected.

"I have fitted peg legs on more sailors than you can count," Willoughby announced jovially. "Emmett here is paying well, so he's getting himself a stout cypress stump. This is a nice piece of wood. I can fashion a cup for the stump and leave a wide base at the foot so he can fit a buckle shoe on it."

Doc shook his head in amusement. "You plan to do some dancing, Emmett?"

"I run Signet down and cut him into strings—while he still lives."

Willoughby considered Emmett's stump and the bandages surrounding it, measuring the thigh's length and diameter before turning his attention to the wood block. He then began tapping on the chisel. In a short time he scooped out the beginnings of a bowl.

"I will make this cup plenty big to accommodate the stump. If it is too large we can always line it with leather and pad it with extra-soft cloth."

"Better to be bigger than smaller. That stump will change in size over time." Doc doubted it would work well. He had seen wooden legs before, but most users complained of discomfort and walked as little as possible on them, usually with the aid of a crutch. Still, some amputees claimed to walk ten or more miles in one day.

"Hungry!" Emmett grunted.

"I'll have the ship's cook bring you some broth," Doc said.

"Meat!"

"Whatever the patient desires!"

"Rum—buckets of it!"

"Let's wean you off that laudanum and then we'll see."

"Don't need medicine! Can take pain!"

Doc left the cabin and made his way to the ship's galley, pleased at Emmett's obvious physical recovery, relieved his appetite had returned. There were other good signs. Where most amputees suffered depression and emotional anguish, at least in the initial stages, Emmett had come to terms with his loss and was taking significant steps to regain control of his life. His hatred for Jules Signet and the unholy desire for revenge superseded mere pain and despair. It truly was a remarkable feat for him to have survived a shotgun blast, massive burns, amputation, and the impact of severe trauma, blood loss, and infection. The iron-hard little monster seemed almost indestructible.

Plunging swiftly along on its southeasterly course, *Arabelle* still faced a long run before it rounded Cape São Roque on the Brazilian coast, the point closest to the continent of Africa. Then they would swing southward on the last leg to Salvador da Bahia, still many leagues distant. Doc shaded his eyes and scanned the southeastern horizon, hoping the lookout would raise *Lisette's* topsails, praying they could catch the schooner before her cargo was delivered.

Breckinridge County, Kentucky—April 16, 1816

Almost everyone in Kentucky thought that winter was over. Signs of spring emerged everywhere. Redbud, wild plum, and dogwood blossoms all burst forth at once. Grass turned green. Wildflowers stippled the wooded hills and roadsides. Birds sang from every leafing tree and bush. The land exploded into an outright riot of color and noise. But after a few blessed days of warmth, the entire bottom fell out of springtime. Overnight the weather took a nasty turn as a massive wave of cold air descended upon the Ohio River Valley. Craig could not believe his eyes—the ground was covered in several inches of new snow.

"What the hell!" he exclaimed, peering out at the bleak, snow-blasted pasture. "I am telling you—I have had it with winter! This is worse than January!"

"It has snowed on everyone else, Craig," Mary pointed out with an air of rectitude. "We'll just have to make the best of things."

"You are right of course," Craig apologized. He stoked up the fire and piled on logs, watching while Mary sliced bacon and mixed pancake batter to pour into a flat iron skillet. Her belly protruded outward, much farther than before. Perhaps her intuition was right—she might bear twins after all. "I don't see how you can stand upright, let alone work, carrying that much in front of you."

"It's not hard, really," she replied. "It does take a bit of practice, but remember this has all happened gradually, over time."

"And you still have four months to go!"

"Not quite. I believe I will deliver in early August."

"Let me milk the cows this morning—and gather eggs. You do not need to slip on that snow."

Craig trudged outside into a resurgent winter world, angry at the stinging cold air and swirling flurries. He forked hay down for the animals. The two cows crowded into their stall for milking. Afterwards, he carried the filled buckets to the springhouse and toted the previous day's milk to the cabin. On the way back, he stopped off to gather eggs. The henhouse bulged with multi-colored fowl; his family would soon be dining on fried chicken. His workers would also appreciate some new hens. Craig scattered a measure of shelled corn onto the floor and gathered eggs. As he closed the door, a heavy snow shower struck, completely obliterating his view of the front pasture. It was a relief to get indoors and stand next to the fireplace. He held his hands near the fire and watched falling snowflakes through the big south window. Fortunately, he and Mary had maintained their routine and covered the gardens the previous evening. Onions, spinach, and English peas might survive, for they were cold weather crops, but the other seedling vegetables might not make it, especially in a hard freeze. He wondered what would happen if this lasted forever. Perhaps Martin's speculation was correct—perhaps the sun *was* burning out.

Snow fell intermittently for three more days, but fortunately it did not accumulate. During this time, the sky remained a dreary slate-gray. Craig began to fear that his vegetable garden had frozen. He figured he must buy more seed at Rosenbotham's Store. When Martin stopped in for a brief visit, Craig voiced his concern. The old man insisted he had seen snow fall this late, although it was a rare occurrence. He assured Craig that his early spring vegetables would survive. Folks in town complained incessantly about the weather, but they all agreed that this cold snap was the last.

A welcome heat wave arrived at month's end, eradicating all vestiges of winter and transforming the backward vegetation of the Ohio River Valley into a bright explosion of green. Leaves seemed to pop out on every tree; new grass sprang up almost overnight. Many Breckinridge County farmers, sweltering in uncharacteristic heat, began planting their crops, mostly corn and tobacco. Martin still counseled against planting those crops and Craig heeded his advice, although it chafed him to see the farmers working in their fields. The aroma of fresh-plowed earth was almost maddening. He tended his tobacco plant beds, covering them with straw and cedar boughs in the evenings and uncovering them each morning after breakfast. When Rosenbotham received a large shipment of red clover seed from Pennsylvania, Craig, Owen, and Martin bought the entire stock. Craig sowed his little twenty-acre bottomland strip with it and planned to pasture livestock there later in the summer. In doing this he was following Martin's ambitious plan for land renewal. Few farmers in western Kentucky bothered with such "European foolishness," but Craig knew that Martin's land was some of county's best.

Fortunately for Craig, Levi's crew showed up at the Smithhart farm and this provided an opportunity for him to divert his pent-up energy into hard labor. For days he and the six men felled great trees, cut them into logs, and dragged them down to the landing. Much of this was virgin timber, gargantuan in size. The yellow poplars and white oaks were truly amazing. Romulus showed up and threw his considerable bulk into the work. Craig liked having him help with the ox team for he knew the animals well and handled them with special care. This time, Levi sent a team of his own oxen, a pair of gray giants as big as Craig's team. Down at the landing, the piles of logs grew to enormous heights. At week's end the riverbank was crowded with timber.

Levi showed up one morning to supervise the assembling of the great rafts which would be stacked and cross-stacked three or four logs deep. The quarrelsome little miller drove a small cart behind a chunky grey pony that picked its way cautiously down the steep track to the landing. Craig watched him approach, hop down from the cart and tie the pony to a willow branch. He was glad Levi had come. It took a great deal of rolling, positioning and lashing with strong rope, but none of his rafts ever fell apart. These masses of lumber were then floated fourteen miles downriver to the little inlet on Spigot Run. In the past five years Craig had poled numerous rafts for Levi.

"Hot enough for you?" Levi grumbled, mopping at his brow with a soiled kerchief. His ginger moustache dripped glistening beads of sweat.

"You will never hear me complain about heat," Craig assured him. "It seems with you it is always too hot or too cold."

"Looks like we will make about five good-sized lumber rafts over the next few days. We'll take them downriver to Spigot Run, one raft at a time. My crew will pilot the rafts from your landing to mine. When we clear the inlet of the first raft, I will send a crew back for the next one. You won't have to worry about getting your delicate feet wet."

"That is a relief." Craig was pleased at the unexpected offer.

"Not planting yet?" Levi challenged.

"Just some red clover and the vegetable garden. We are still keeping the gardens and tobacco bed covered at night. We don't want another frost nipping our food stores."

"I can't believe you are not out plowing and planting. You are usually way ahead of everyone else."

"Martin is convinced this winter isn't over."

"Well, it is almost May. If you wait too much longer, you'll be worrying about frost at the other end of summer."

Craig had been thinking the same thing, but 'held his fire' as far as planting was concerned. He intended to follow Martin in all things. The old farmer had prospered through unerring instinct and decades of experience, careful planning and hard work.

By noon Levi pronounced the first raft ready for the voyage. The crew cast off, using long poles to push their way into the current. They rode eight feet above the waterline, bound for the sawmill at Spigot Run. Levi then joined Craig at the cabin where Mary had dinner waiting. Never one to miss a free meal, the miller readily accepted her invitation to sit down at the table. He was a staunch admirer of Mary's cooking. Ruth and Isabel were thoroughly entertained, watching Levi eat. He never stopped talking and he never missed a bite. Enhancing his stories with wild gesticulations, he continually stoked vast quantities of food into his cavernous maw, snuffling over his plate like a boar hog rooting in a trough. Most of the meal disappeared miraculously into the pit between his red-gray beard and moustache, but some stray morsels clung stubbornly to the surrounding bristles.

He had heard the latest news on Judge Bozarth and was quite willing to tell all, but Mary tactfully sidetracked him.

"How is business, Levi?" she asked.

"Grain prices are soaring!" he accepted the decoy. "And milled flour is bringing record prices." He turned to Craig. "Got any grain you want to sell?"

"I need all I have for the stock. Remember, I bought milled grains from you to distill whiskey."

"Wait a few months and see how high those prices climb!"

"So *that* is why you want to buy it now," Craig laughed. "We'll talk about it again this autumn. Hopefully this summer will be kind to us."

Chapter Eleven

Salvador da Bahia—April 29, 1816

After five weeks of sailing, *Arabelle* slid gracefully into the haven of *Baía de Todos os Santos*—the 'Bay of All Saints.' The constant assault of wind and endless blue rollers broke hard upon the rugged triangular peninsula that afforded smooth sailing inside the sheltered bay, the largest in Portuguese Brazil. While on his second voyage for Portugal, the Florentine explorer Amerigo Vespucci sighted the bay on All Saints Day, November 1, 1502. He had promptly named it 'The Bay of the Holy Savior of All the Saints' in honor of the date and his home parish church. A massive stone fortress was soon built on the cliff overlooking the bay, and around it had grown Salvador da Bahia, the western hemisphere's biggest slave trading port and main shipping point for Brazilian sugar planters. Once the magnificent capital of Portugal's great new world colony, Bahia lost its crown to Rio de Janeiro in 1763.

Arabelle glided along the glass-smooth surface of the bay, and Doc observed the city from the starboard deck. Bahia was massive, larger than most American cities. A sharp escarpment divided the Lower Town, *Cidade Baixa*, from its Upper Town, *Cidade Alta*. The city sprawled away from the fort and enveloped the land around the bay. A haphazard jumble of houses, shops, and warehouses occupied the lower town. High up on the cliff perched the old city center, its multi-colored municipal buildings, convents, and gold-laden baroque churches bathed in the rich glow of sunset.

"Now *this* is a city!" Doc exclaimed, leaning over to nudge his deck companion. It would be a welcome relief to step foot on dry land.

Emmett Barnett sat next to him in a rope chair, smoking a foul-smelling cigar and regarding with interest the waterfront with its many taverns and inns. "Tonight I get drunk! You not stop me, or you be in one hell trouble!"

"I reckon you have earned it." Emmett had been off the laudanum for days.

"I get myself a fine, fat whore!"

"Your eye is bigger than your—" Doc suppressed a laugh. "But, if you feel up to it, you have the doctor's permission. No hard pressure on that leg. You should take things easy."

It seemed improbable that Emmett could manage such a feat, but he had improved dramatically. With his voracious appetite he had steadily put on weight, and he continued to obey all of Doc's instructions, submitting to the painful manipulations and using the ropes above his bed to hoist himself up and down, over and over, to keep his upper body hard. It was almost as if he relished the excessive pain and hardship. Doc knew he was readying himself for ultimate revenge.

Willoughby, who had rigged up the deck chair, volunteered, "I know a good tavern ashore. And I know enough languages to help him get what he wants."

"No doubt you two have planned this for some time," Doc raised a world-weary eyebrow. Emmett was clean-shaven, except for his long-handled moustaches, and wearing crisp, freshly-ironed clothes, provided from the captain's wardrobe and tailored by Willoughby.

"I have been here often," the sailor boasted. "There are plenty of women available. And the ship has a good store of mercury on hand."

Doc knew that the Portuguese officials turned a blind eye to the world's second-oldest profession. Every port had its designated areas to cater to sailors who had been at sea for extended periods of time. As a physician he knew that mercury was the preferred treatment for banishing the 'sailors' affliction,' 'the French pox,' 'the

Italian plague'—syphilis. But he doubted the overall efficacy of the treatment which he regarded as poison, and he suspected that more people died from it than were cured.

A sailor stood in the bows with a lead line, chanting depths as he read markings on the line. He would whirl the weight and cast it out ahead of the ship, let it sink and read the mark again as the ship passed over it. Captain West conned his ship by those chants and by land features with which he was familiar, also by the color shadings of the water. It was almost dark when *Arabelle* tied up at her mooring. Doc silently complimented West. The captain had performed brilliantly—he was a true professional seaman in every sense of the word. While he dealt with the harbormaster and customs officials, his first mate lectured the crew about the hazards of going ashore. Apparently the sailors had drawn lots for this honor. Some would enjoy shore leave that evening; others must wait their turns. It appeared that the sailors had heard this lecture before; most listened respectfully, but all cast burning glances at the waterfront, anxious to start the night's activities.

Doc, Emmett, and Willoughby descended the gangplank with the first lucky revelers. Despite the muggy evening, made worse by the wind's cessation, Bahia possessed an irrepressible energy few cities could hope to match. The heady blend of old European, Indian, and African cultures engendered an explosion of sights, sounds and smells that assaulted their senses. In torchlit squares and open spaces singers and dancers performed with wild abandon as if some festival were taking place. Drums pounded out powerful rhythms that reverberated against the backdrop of the steep escarpment. Urban slaves hawked their many services and wares. Bricklayers, carpenters, potters, chicken vendors, barbers, cobblers, seamstresses, and lace makers all added to the cacophony, while porters carried chests, barrels, and large hemp bags of sugar, coffee, or cacao beans; firewood, furniture—and sedans bearing white people. The aroma of cooking food wafted out onto the waterfront streets. Women beckoned from the open doors of taverns. If their language made no sense, their intentions surely did.

Willoughby carried Emmett like a child, taking care not to knock the stump against a passerby or building corner. Emmett looked as small as a child, but his expression was far from innocent. The sailor conducted them to a tavern that served good food and strong liquor. On Willoughby's suggestion, Doc ordered a platter of *acarajé*, a traditional dish often encountered in Salvador da Bahia. Made from black-eyed pea flour formed into balls or fritters, this was deep-fried in palm oil and served steaming hot, split in half and stuffed with a savory paste made from mashed shrimp, ground cashews, palm oil, hot peppers, green tomatoes, onions and garlic. Doc enjoyed the accompanying drink made from *cachaça*, a fermented sugar-cane juice, crushed limes, and cane sugar. He limited himself to one glass, nursing it slowly.

Emmett ordered a jug of dark rum and guzzled great swigs to wash down his meal. He glared about the room, his single eye searching for a suitable woman. Apparently he found his target, for he leaned over and muttered something to Willoughby. The sailor rose to negotiate with the bartender. The man grinned knowingly and walked over to speak with a group of mulatto and negro women sitting at a round table nearest the back door. Doc noticed the exchange and amused glances cast surreptitiously from the table.

"Emmett, I warn you—nothing too intense. Take care with that leg. There is still a lot of healing going on inside."

Emmett slapped some coins on the table and grinned wolfishly. "I pay for meal and drinks. You not worry 'bout me."

"I'm your doctor. It is my business to worry."

Willoughby returned. "Come on, Emmett! Your honey pot is waiting!" He scooped him easily out of the chair and Emmett flung one arm around his neck for support. In his free hand he clutched the rum bottle.

Through tobacco smoke and dim candlelight, Doc spied the intended companion holding open the back door to a hallway of rooms. The negress was tall and enormously corpulent with a full head of wild, kinky hair that accentuated her imposing height. She made three or four of Emmett—exactly what the little man desired.

When Willoughby carried him through and the door closed behind them, Doc experienced a shudder of trepidation. He thought it strange he should worry. There were medical considerations, but his concern extended beyond that. Perhaps it was the doctor-patient bond. Maybe it was because Emmett had protected him in his darker days, and Doc had desperately needed his protection, but that was not the case now. The underworld figure had lost his clout, most of his wealth, and his byzantine network of informants and gunmen. His establishment had burned, much of his liquor stock destroyed, and his ancillary enterprises scattered to the winds.

Doc drew on his cigar and tried to sort it all out. He felt no real loyalty toward the little monster. Why should he? And why should Willoughby? That was a strange relationship in itself. Perhaps Emmett was paying him well. Money often forged strange bonds. But there was more to it than money, something that ran much deeper. And suddenly he knew what it was—at least in his case. Emmett had lost almost everything, including his leg, but he had chosen to get on with life. The man was a true inspiration.

It was not like that for Doc. He recalled the most tragic event in his own checkered past—losing his beloved wife, Jeanne. It still hurt to recall, even though a decade had passed. Despite his best efforts, Jeanne had died from an ailment he could not cure. It began as a huskiness in the throat and worsened into a dry, hacking cough. For more than a year she declined, losing her ability to speak, unable to swallow, and in the end, struggling for every breath. Up to that point, Doc tried every medical treatment known to man, but despite his best efforts he could not cure her. His colleagues concurred with his diagnosis—an inoperable tumor. In the latter stages he could feel the irregular cauliflower-like mass distorting her neck, pressing upon her vocal chords, esophagus, and trachea. One morning he woke to the sounds of choking. Her face had turned gray and her eyeballs bulged from her head. In desperation he performed an emergency tracheotomy to provide some instant, if only transient, shred of relief. Jeanne expired during the procedure—a horrible death with mouth agape, tongue expelled, and eyes open, blood covering her once-lovely neck and shoulders. Doc had never fully recovered from the incident. He blamed himself for killing her and reviled himself as a failure—like the preachers who were always out saving others while they let their own families go to hell. To avoid the pain and emptiness, he had turned to drink and gambling. Rationally, he knew there was nothing he could have done to cure her—his colleagues had assured him of this, time and again. But deep inside he felt he had failed her.

Willoughby returned to the table chuckling. "That damned Emmett is insane! He will rupture something if he is not careful."

"That is exactly what I am afraid of."

"I'm not talking about his leg. Stop worrying, Doctor."

"Are you quite sure?"

"That big woman knows how to handle him."

"And where did she get her medical degree? What room is he in?"

"Come on—I'll show you," Willoughby offered with a conspiratorial grin. He led Doc through the back door and into the hallway. He stopped and gestured at a door which was slightly ajar. "In there."

Opening the door noiselessly, Doc risked a glance inside. Emmett lay enmeshed in a mountain of soft black flesh, his hairy, skinny backside clenching and unclenching in between massive thighs, each larger than his torso. With giant hands the woman clasped his buttocks to move him, so he would not have to apply leg pressure in his enthusiastic thrusting. She laughed loudly and encouraged him with deep-throated exhortations. The little man buried his head between her colossal mammaries, both bigger than his head. Submerged in all of this bounty, he moaned and growled like a wild animal. The leg stump extended beyond the raised thighs and appeared in no immediate danger. Doc choked back a laugh, closed the door, and returned to his table.

"You feel better now?" Willoughby asked.

"I hope he doesn't suffocate." Doc realized he must let his patient go. Perhaps he clung to Emmett because the man needed and respected him—in fact, revered him. If so, it was a poor substitute for his own self-forgiveness. He realized that like Emmett, he too, must get on with life. Lighting another cigar and sipping on the dregs of his liquor, Doc turned his focus to the primary objective—freeing Phillippe Bouchard.

Captain West had offered to introduce him to Joshua Adams, an American merchant with various properties on the waterfront. Adams's warehouse lay adjacent to the barracoons, and he enjoyed close connections with the officials. He might agree to serve as agent to effect an unobtrusive purchase. Doc reviewed his plans with care. Although he had not spotted *Lisette*, she was certainly moored somewhere in the harbor. He wondered if anyone from that vessel would recognize him. The crewmen were not necessarily New Orleans citizens, but it would be wise to steer clear of them and keep a low profile.

Emmett Barnett slept like the living dead, exhausted from his previous night's exploits and heavy drinking. There was no rum left in the jug when Willoughby extracted him from the woman's embrace to carry him back to the ship. Doc conducted his routine morning examination and performed the stretching exercises without the usual growling and snapping. Fortunately, the stump showed no signs of bruising or swelling.

Willoughby arrived in the cabin with his cypress block, leather strips, cotton cloth and tools. "Captain wants you to breakfast with him."

"I'm almost finished here."

"Little fellow looks plum tuckered out," the sailor observed.

"He's lucky he didn't kill himself," Doc growled. "You keep him on board tonight."

"Easier said than done, Doctor."

"He's not healed yet."

"In his mind he is."

"How is that peg leg coming along?"

Willoughby showed him his handiwork. The bowl extended deep into the block and it looked large enough to accept Emmett's stump. From the side it still resembled a rectangular block, but most of the outside wood would be shaved off as Willoughby rounded out the top and tapered down the limb, making the whole much lighter.

"I still have two more inches of this bowl to gouge out. Then I will slide it on and make adjustments."

"Do not do that unless I am present."

"Understood."

"You realize his leg will change shape and size over several months?"

"I have dealt with this many times before. The hollow must be roomy enough to accommodate those changes—and it must be shaped to fit his thigh. The leather and cloth lining can be adjusted periodically for snugness and comfort. We will fit a soft wool and linen padding in the bottom. A brace and strap will hold his leg in place. And I will make him a solid crutch to lean on until the stump hardens. Of course you will determine when he can wear it."

"Good. We do not want a setback."

After breakfast, Captain West conducted him along the waterfront, past numerous vessels flying foreign flags, to the warehouse of Joshua Adams. The merchant, a stout, florid man dressed in stylish suit clothing, recognized West from previous visits.

"Captain! What brings you to Bahia? Have you a cargo for me to examine?"

"Not this time," West replied. "I wish you to meet Benjamin Baxter, a business associate from Charleston." Doc admired West's skill in dissembling—they had previously agreed upon the alias and cover story over breakfast.

"Mr. Baxter, I am Joshua Adams."

"Pleased to meet you, sir," Doc bowed.

"How may I help you gentlemen?" He directed his question at Doc.

"I am here to purchase a certain male slave. He looks completely European, stands about six feet tall, and is in his late twenties. They call him Philippe Bouchard."

"Have you been to the barracoons?"

"We thought we would call upon you first," West interjected. "Baxter here wishes to engage your services to effect the purchase and transfer of said slave. We will pay ten percent commission on a fair purchase."

"I understand. Discretion is the key. You want me to act as your agent, purchase the property in my name, and transfer it to you immediately afterwards."

"Correct. We will, of course, pay the usual deposit of earnest money and draw up an agreement. After the price is established we will provide the money required for purchase."

Doc added, "We wish to buy a particular young female as well—a lovely quadroon named Kayla. She is with child."

"This should present no problem. We may visit the barracoons this morning and you may identify the two slaves—if they are there. If I cannot buy them outright, we may have to bid for them at the next auction."

"When will that be?" Doc inquired.

"Thursday morning, May second. The sugar planters or their factors will arrive from the far corners of Bahia."

Doc digested this information. Thursday was just three days away. Ideally they would make the purchase this morning and depart as soon as West could get *Arabelle* underway, but waiting three days seemed acceptable. Then he thought of another possibility.

"Has *Lisette* arrived from New Orleans?"

Adams looked puzzled. "The American schooner *Lisette*?"

"That is the ship," Doc confirmed.

"You are the first substantial vessel in four days. I would know if she arrived—especially if she carried slaves."

"Then we have beaten her," West affirmed. Doc could appreciate the captain's pride in himself and his ship. The sloop had performed brilliantly, sailing close-hauled to windward, but she had proven worthy on all points of sail. Delacroix was right when he claimed *Arabelle* could outsail anything on the high seas. Apparently *Lisette* had stood farther out to sea; perhaps she had chosen to trade in one of the Indies before sailing onward to Bahia.

"Thank you for your time, Mister Adams," West nodded. "You will inform me when the schooner arrives?"

"Indeed, Captain," Adams assured him.

"Then we bid you good day, sir."

Doc touched his hat brim as he and West left the building. They strode back along the waterfront toward *Arabelle*.

The captain sighed audibly. "I hated to lie to him. But Delacroix insisted that I help you."

"Trust me, you did the right thing. What we do here in Bahia will save lives. If our purpose is discovered, it could mean Delacroix's death."

"So we wait at anchor until the ship arrives?"

"Precisely. *Lisette* sailed several days prior to our departure. No one on that ship could possibly know our intentions. We have lined up our buyer in advance. I believe we have done everything we can."

"Of course the best laid plans can go awry."

"In my profession I have often encountered that bitter truth. I believe the maxim applies to all of life."

◆

Doc spent the next three days exploring the city of Salvador da Bahia. The lower town was a variegated jumble of markets, warehouses, shops, and taverns. One morning Emmett Barnett and his two half-brothers accompanied him on his tour. Willoughby carried the little man and stopped in at a tailor's shop. There Emmett was fitted for shirts and trousers. At a leather shop he purchased a broadbrimmed hat, a pair of expensive boots, a wide, ornately-tooled belt with a silver buckle, and a vest fashioned from the finest Iberian calfskin.

Emmett paid generously for their meals and each course was a culinary adventure. Bahian cuisine combined the best influences of its three predominant cultures, enhancing basic foodstuffs with local, exotic spices and other ingredients. Characterized by the generous use of *pimenta malagueta*—chili peppers—and *dende*—palm oil, most Bahian dishes contained seafood, coconut milk, banana and okra. Emmett favored *moqueca de peixe*, a traditional stew consisting of fish, onion, garlic, tomatoes, chili peppers, coriander, and other ingredients. This was usually accompanied by boiled rice or farina. Doc particularly enjoyed *bobo de camarão*, a popular dish made with cooked shrimp served in a purée of cassava meal, palm oil, and coconut milk, and ladled onto a bed of white rice.

On Thursday morning Doc found a slave lad offering burro rides to the upper town center. Gladly he took advantage of the inexpensive transportation. It proved a long and uncomfortable ride along a rough switchback path, but the alternative climb on foot would have wrought havoc on his left knee. The cliff rose steeply to almost three hundred feet above the harbor. He dismounted in the *Praça Municipal*, once the political seat of colonial Brazil.

Here stood much finer buildings, reminiscent of Portugal's past colonial glory. Doc admired the pastel stucco façades and baroque architecture of the old town. The impressive *Palácio Rio Branco*, the Governor's Palace, occupied a position of honor only slightly less impressive than the massive stone fort. Originally chosen for its strategic position, the fort had guarded against numerous attacks by foreign powers. From this vantage point Doc could view the massive bay and discern the demarcation between its lime-green shallows and the infinite sweep of the blue, wind-ruffled Atlantic. A refreshing sea breeze swept through the heights, providing welcome relief from the tropical sun that baked the cobblestones.

He strolled past public buildings and well-appointed townhouses, shops and cathedrals until he came upon the small triangular plaza called *Pelourinho*, in the city center of Bahia. Here the full impact of slavery confronted him. Doc knew that the first slave market in the Americas began in Bahia in the 1530's. The port had become the principal processing center for African slaves entering the plantation labor force. He observed the original *pelourinho*, or 'pillory,' a plain whipping post where slave owners publicly punished their slaves for various infractions. He thought it odd that the center derived its name from that device of cruelty. It was like naming your town 'Hell.' The whole city appeared to center its livelihood on slavery and the products produced by their labor—sugar, cocoa, and coffee. Popular stores sold slave accoutrements such as iron collars, wrist and ankle cuffs, chains, branding irons and wooden yokes.

A hand clapped him on the shoulder, jarring him from his thoughts.

"Baxter, my dear fellow!" It was Joshua Adams, the American merchant. "Have you come for the auction?"

Doc recovered his wits. "I might find it instructive. *Lisette* has not yet arrived?"

"Not as of this morning. Will you take coffee with me?"

"Delighted," Doc agreed. It was mid-morning, the perfect time to enjoy a brief respite.

Adams led him into a coffeehouse and ordered coffee and sweet biscuits for them. A waiter ushered them through a back door that opened onto a small jacaranda-shaded garden with tables and chairs overlooking the Atlantic. Doc settled gratefully into a cushioned wrought iron chair, removed his hat, loosened his cravat, and allowed the breeze to cool him.

The coffee was superb, brewed from the finest beans brought down from the central highlands, roasted and hand-ground with care. Doc added a splash of milk and dipped his biscuit into the hot beverage. The coffee had a rich, nutty flavor, with no hint of acidity.

"Thank you, Mister Adams. This is delightful."

"The house serves delicious meals as well—as fine as any hotel in the world."

"I must try them before we leave," Doc nodded, sipping on his coffee. They made small talk, mostly about the city and America's recent victory over Great Britain. Adams was keenly interested in the Tariff and the upcoming Presidential election; Doc wanted to know more about the slave trade. Adams was a treasure trove of information and Doc enjoyed drawing it from him.

"When will the auction begin?"

"Precisely at noon," Adams replied. "It will continue until sunset, unless all the slaves are sold before then."

"Have you any slaves for sale?"

"Indeed. We have been preparing them for over a month."

"What all does that entail?"

"Well," Adams shifted forward in his chair. "Any commodity for sale, including livestock, must appear at its absolute best. This principle holds doubly true for slaves. In fact, the Portuguese refer to them as *peças*. The singular form of the word means 'piece' or 'part.' That is what slaves literally are—individual components of a vast labor and exchange system. Unfortunately ship captains often focus on delivering quantity, not quality. When slaves arrive from Africa, they have almost always suffered deplorable conditions, usually for several weeks. Many do not survive the voyage across the 'Middle Passage.' The dead are cast overboard; survivors are weakened by poor diet, filth, and inactivity, and are often exposed to diseases. When the ship captains reach Bahia, slaves are unloaded and herded into the barracoons where we examine them for plague and festering wounds.

Doc could appreciate the toll the Atlantic voyage took upon the human body. The slave's diet was poor, and usually the drinking water became spoiled, inducing dysentery and other plague-like diseases. While some captains allowed for limited activity above deck, most voyages involved the slaves lying closely packed below decks, forced to relieve themselves where they lay. The smell became appalling—when the wind was right, the stink of slave ships often fouled parts of New Orleans. Fortunately these incidents were becoming less frequent, now that Britain endeavored to enforce the Atlantic slave trade treaties.

Adams continued, "Some slaves acquire dangerous abrasions on wrists and ankles where iron cuffs rub their flesh raw. Many open sores become infected and must be treated before auction. We fatten the slaves on a rich diet, stuffing them with boiled farina and dosing them with a concoction of molasses and lime juice to combat the effects of scurvy. As they heal and round out, we shave off lice-infested hair, polish their teeth, and rub oils into their skin to make it shine. Dishonest traders will sometimes apply boot black to hide gray hairs on the older slaves."

"How long do the slaves survive on the sugar plantations?"

"Considerably longer than the Indians do. In some instances they last three times longer. If we can get eight or ten good years' work out of them, we call the purchase a success."

"I see." Doc recalled that enslaved native Indians died within a year or two working under such harsh conditions. That is why the sugar planters imported African slaves. He had been appalled to learn that most slaves died before the age of thirty-five.

Two wealthy sugar planters took a table near them. They slurped their coffee and chuckled loudly, conversing in their native Portuguese. Adams listened for a moment and translated.

"Those bastards are two of the meanest sugar barons in Brazil. They take great pride in turning punishment into a form of celebration. Of course, they don't personally engage in the physical cruelty. They simply hire the meanest overseers and support them in all disciplinary actions. The fat one has just invited the other to visit his plantation to witness an execution. Usually this entails a festival, a beef roast, music, entertainment, hunting, and horse riding. The execution is performed in front of the plantation's slave population to serve as a visible reminder of what will happen if they break the rules."

"Why are they executing the slave?"

"Apparently he struck an overseer who forced himself on his woman."

Doc thought of little Kayla and felt his heart turn over as he envisaged her as the victim. Although he had not caused her slavery, he had taken full advantage of it. Because of him she was consigned to this nightmare of a place. He simply must intercept her—and

Philippe—before they were sold.

"You do realize the entire slave industry is in decline?" Adams asked.

"No doubt Britain is the driving force behind that."

"Yes, now that they are undisputed masters of the sea, it becomes more difficult to smuggle slaves across the Atlantic. Back in 1810 Britain and Brazilian officials signed a bilateral agreement aimed at abolishing the trade. Of course the British use humanitarian reasons to justify their pressure, but Brazilian planters recognize the agreement for what it is—an attack upon their sugar cane."

"They are probably correct."

"They most certainly are. Sugar produced in Brazil is much less expensive than sugar produced in the British West Indies. By preventing Brazil from importing an inexpensive slave workforce, the British hope to destroy the industry."

"They are doing the same thing to us on a number of fronts. That is why some of our folks argue for the Tariff."

The planters rose and left the garden.

"Well, I believe it is that time," Adams suggested. "The auction is about to commence."

They returned to the central square with its raised platform of rough-sawn planks. This was the auction block where the first slaves, a parcel of three men and two women, stood stark naked in broad daylight. Doc could see them easily over the crowd thronging the plaza. Prospective buyers ascended the platform and appraised the slaves' overall health, inspecting them as if they were cattle or horses. They felt muscles, slapped abdomens, pinched skin, and examined eyes, ears, teeth and gums. They ordered the slaves to walk, squat, and stoop; balance on one leg and then the other, and hop up and down in one place. The slaves submitted to the poking and prodding, even bending over as some buyers checked for hemorrhoids and hernias. Buyers reached in and manipulated testicles to see if they were ruptured or deficient in any way. The women's external genitalia were also examined. One buyer, an overseer from an inland sugar plantation, recoiled in apparent repulsion and roared in outrage.

"What did he say?" Doc asked. He and Adams moved to where they stood just below the platform.

"That wench is poxed!" Adams translated, shaking his head. "The auctioneer is asking for the seller to come forward. He wants a physician to verify the condition."

Out of pure clinical interest, Doc almost volunteered, but he held back to preserve his secret identity. One of the visiting ship surgeons ascended the steps and ordered the woman to bend over. She resisted violently, struggling until two male slaves were ordered to force her into the humiliating position. The Portuguese doctor knelt to examine her and he also recoiled, bellowing his shock and revulsion.

"Yes, it is definitely the pox," Adams said.

Doc caught a glimpse of the unsightly cluster of papules and concurred immediately with the diagnosis. The owner bound the slave by her wrists and dragged her roughly down the steps, through the crowd, to the whipping post. Doc shouldered his way closer to see what happened.

"By God, you have humiliated me for the last time!" the owner bellowed. He uncoiled a horse whip from his belt and laid in to the unfortunate woman, flailing at her with all his might. The leather cracked like a battery of closely-spaced rifle shots, echoing off the surrounding walls throughout the plaza. In a short time he shredded the flesh so that the white crests of her spine showed through bloody tatters of her once-smooth back. Somewhere in the midst of this horrific beating she fainted—a small mercy. Doc knew that the body sometimes had a way of insulating itself against overwhelming pain. Her head lolled and blood ran down her back, dripping onto the cobblestones, mingling with the dried blood that had past stained the stones from mulberry to dark brown. Doc was appalled. He turned away, revolted—ashamed for the role he had played in Philippe's enslavement. No one else in the crowd seemed upset. Instead, they turned their attention back to the auction block. No one offered to help the beaten woman. She hung by her cords without moving. Doc wondered if she would survive.

Adams led him away from the spectacle and warned him against helping her. "You must understand; these people have a much different perspective on humanity. Come back to the block. My slaves are up next, and when they are sold we will leave this place. Like you, I have seen enough."

New Orleans—May 10, 1816

Pierre Delacroix now acknowledged the danger threatening him. Earlier he had felt no concern. He had, after all, survived three major wars, capture by the Iroquois, who came close to scalping him, and the many floods, hurricanes, fires, plagues, and fevers that had over time beset New Orleans. At eighty-one years of age, nothing much scared him. All this changed one night during a city council meeting. Jules Signet attended with his lawyer Alain Morel at his side. As chairman he proposed a new law decreeing: *"all persons inheriting estates shall be investigated by a lawyer, and an approved and learned physician, to determine if they have a negro slave in their ancestry."* If so, notarized manumission papers must be produced—or the estate, which could not legally be passed to a slave, would be forfeited to an entity appointed by the council. This proposal received mixed reception. Some folks, especially the younger ones, applauded the concept; others questioned the intrusion it would most certainly bring. At Signet's request, Morel quoted from the Louisiana Digest of 1808 including Chapter Three, Article XVII stating: *"the slave is incapable of contracting any kind of engagement. He possesses nothing in his own right and can transmit nothing by succession, legacy or otherwise; for whatever he possesses is his master's property."*

This sparked a lively debate, but in the end, cooler heads prevailed and the motion was tabled. Signet did not appear concerned with the decision. He reminded Delacroix of a skilled swordsman. The initial thrust had been parried, but Signet had learned from it; it was almost as if he was testing his opponents' strength and skill. Certainly, he would try again, perhaps in the state legislature. It was apparent he was growing more powerful, able to wield more influence in each meeting.

As Delacroix prepared to leave, the banker made a special point of inquiring about his health. He raised his voice and added a note of concern, making sure everyone heard him. This struck Delacroix as strange. Perplexed, he wondered why Signet would ask such a question. Later that evening, at the coffeehouse, Henri de Ste. Gême also expressed concern.

Ste. Gême was a fellow merchant and longtime friend, so Delacroix felt no reservations when he asked, "Why? What have you heard?"

The little merchant, who ranked among the wealthiest men in New Orleans, perhaps in America, had replied straightforwardly. "Signet has informed us you are suffering from an incurable, terminal disease."

"I can assure you I am quite well!" Delacroix snapped. "I will write Signet a letter requesting him to refrain from making such comments. And I would appreciate it if you would circulate the news that I enjoy robust health and intend to remain in that state for as long as God wills!"

Later, Delacroix reflected upon what Doc Applegate had told him weeks ago in the rectory. At the time, Delacroix was so angry he had discounted it, but now he recalled Doc's warning—Jules Signet intended to kill him. And the banker expected to steal his hard-earned fortune by invoking the Digest of 1808 and declaring Lucinde a slave. Signet had destroyed Philippe and was now making the first maneuvers against her. There was no doubt in Delacroix's mind—he knew what he must do.

On Wednesday he strode into Judge Harkness' office. The judge had recently returned to his courthouse and appeared in much better health. Delacroix learned that Signet had approached him only once, and then only to inquire about the legalities of New Orleans' nebulous police force over which he held much influence.

"Have you heard any news from our friend, the doctor?" Harkness asked.

"Nothing yet," Delacroix replied. "I am here on other business. Can you spare me this afternoon? It is quite important."

"Gladly. What is on your mind?"

It was almost dusk when Delacroix finished talking. Judge Harkness paused, trying to absorb the information and consider all the angles.

"How long will you be gone?"

"Perhaps three months, probably more. It all depends on the transportation. There are no stage roads. At my age I do not intend to ride a horse over the Natchez Trace."

"You will let me know when you depart?"

"Of course. While I am gone, I want you to handle the legalities. I will provide you with all the instructions. You may deal with any bank not owned by Signet. I believe it is time for us to consult with Ste. Gême and a few of my other old friends. We cannot allow this to happen."

"You are right. Are you sure you want to do this?"

"I am eighty-one years old and will not live forever. Lucinde is entitled to all I have. Signet must not get any part of it."

"And you do not think that manumission papers will be enough?"

"Signet has grown too powerful. He and his lawyer could easily make a document disappear. The man has woven himself into the social fabric and is gaining more political influence—especially in the Louisiana State Legislature. He has risen to prominence in law, merchant shipping, banking, and now, the militia patrol. With his secret army of bureaucrats, lawyers, and ruffians, a mere sheet of paper can be stolen, and its duplicate record easily expunged. But please, have the document drawn it up as soon as possible. I may have to leave quickly."

"I will endeavor faithfully to do my part."

"For that I am grateful. If we work together, we can beat Signet. He is just one man. But, John, the tide is clearly changing. I fear our beloved Louisiana is heading in the wrong direction, toward a destination that could one day destroy us all."

Chapter Twelve

Breckinridge County, Kentucky—May 11, 1816

Craig felt unbound, like a wild animal released from a snare, for Martin announced that they could begin planting hemp. The tall, grass-like plant tended to resist frost better than most other crops and would stand a fair chance should a late freeze occur. Craig and Romulus hitched up their plows and began the intricate rounds of plowing and cross-plowing, and then smoothing the previous year's hemp fields with heavy wooden harrows. The days were growing longer, even if the sun did not shine with its usual brilliance. Craig did not care; he was outside, working the land he loved, reasonably confident of the ground he prepared.

Because of the autumn and winter snow-retting process, much of the hemp plants' substance was leached and returned to the soil, and this seemed to keep the fields from wearing out. Hemp could be grown in the same field year after year with only slight diminutions in yield. This was not the case with corn and tobacco. These crops sapped strength from the soil and should not be grown more than twice in succession. Even after the first year, the next yield showed drastic declines. Years ago Martin concluded that by scattering his old tobacco stalks over a depleted field and plowing them under in the spring, he could produce measurable improvements in the soil. This proved what European scientists had discovered—that soil contained essential chemical elements and these must be replenished to maintain sound production. Martin continued searching for ways to improve the soil. For now he must use what strategies available to him—manuring, spreading wood ashes, rotating crops, planting wheat and clover in his worn tobacco fields and scattering tobacco stalks over those fields.

Three days after the first planting, Craig feared he had made a serious mistake. A massive line of clouds dragged winter-like winds down from Canada, laden with cold rain flecked at times with sleet and an occasional snow flake. The winds roared for two solid days while rolls of thick gray clouds scudded southward across a sullen sky. Mary asked him to build a roaring fire and bring in the entire supply of kindling he had cut for the cookhouse. She would do all her cooking at the fireplace until the cold weather passed.

Outside it felt like a winter day. Craig's breath fogged in the somber light of a miserable dawn as he donned his hooded coat for the trip to the barn. He regretted leaving his gloves behind and was glad when he returned to the house.

"What is happening?" he groused as he toted in the milk and eggs.

"I do not know Craig," Mary replied. "This is frightening." It was still dark in the cabin and the outside cold fogged the south window. They listened to the rain dripping from the cedar-shake eaves and the rush of wind howling through the oak trees.

"Your father truly does possess an extra sense. Twice I almost started planting corn, but out of respect I held back. I will never doubt him again."

"Many farmers have already planted," Mary pointed out.

"Yes, and their corn has just sprouted. Those shoots look so promising, but they are at their most vulnerable stage. If it frosts tonight, people will find themselves in bad trouble."

"Let us pray it does not."

Next morning a light frost covered the ground, sparkling in the weak rose-colored sunlight. It lay heavier in the low-lying areas, especially along the river over which a cold fog frothed and roiled. Craig did not fear for his red clover, for it was hardy; and his hemp seeds, just planted, would not germinate for a few days. But he wondered how much longer this could continue.

Later that morning, Martin came up for a short visit, obviously concerned. He wore a greatcoat over heavy woolen wear. "You covered your gardens last night?" he inquired.

"We did," Craig replied. "And the tobacco beds too."

"Fortunately the frost was light and it disappeared quickly. If you covered, then you should be fine."

"What do you make of this?"

"I have never seen anything like it. I hoped the wind would keep blowing—at least it would have prevented the frost. A lot of folks will be hurt by this. Especially those who live north of us."

"I am truly thankful for your advice," Craig reached out and clasped his hand. He had viewed others' cornfields with envy, complaining to Mary about how far they were ahead of him; now he realized how much people in his community would suffer.

"At least you won't have to plow up your corn and start over."

"I owe that good fortune to you, Martin."

"Those winds blew hard out of the north for two straight days. I'll wager that cold wave dropped all the way into southern Tennessee. I imagine folks down there are surprised."

Seasonably warm temperatures returned on May 19th and continued for the next several days. Many farmers plowed under their frost-damaged corn and began planting again. Still, Martin counseled his family to hold off on planting. This time, Craig poured his energy back into clearing acres on the Smithhart farm. He and Romulus worked together, cutting down smaller trees and saplings, sawing up the tops left by Levi's lumber crew, piling and burning branches too small to use. Between them they cut and split hundreds of fence rails, stacking them in crisscross patterns twelve rails high. They cut many cords of firewood, hauled them to the old folks' quarters, and stacked them there, also at Craig's cabin, his cookhouse and distillery. By May's end, Craig realized that the window for planting corn and tobacco was fast closing. Martin agreed that the season had grown late, but suggested that if the warm weather held steady a few more days, they might begin planting.

"You might go ahead and plant corn on the Smithhart farm," he suggested. "It is new ground and higher up, less likely to suffer a frost than in the low areas."

"Do you think so?"

"It is a gamble, as is all of farming. If I were your age, with a recently cleared farm of new ground, I would risk it. But you must decide."

"Thanks, Martin. I will think hard on it."

Craig's feeble hopes turned to despair on May 28th when yet another cold blast howled down from the north, bringing with it a pelting rain and near-freezing temperatures. He wore his winter coat and gloves to work, unaware that life held more hardship in store for him—and it would be infinitely worse than cold weather.

It began in the old folks' quarters, but Craig had heard several days ago that folks in town were suffering from a virulent form of the grippe. Doc Emmick called it 'influenza'. People complained first of a splitting headache, raging fever, bone-rattling chills, and muscular aches. This drove the sufferer straight into bed. The symptoms were soon accompanied by nausea, a painful sore throat, and then a dry, hacking cough which soon became wet. For many, the illness worsened, turning into a form of pneumonia. Several elderly folks and a few infants had already died from it.

Early one morning Romulus knocked on the cabin door. Craig invited him in, took one look at his face, and knew something was terribly wrong.

"What is it, Romulus?"

"Penelope and Adah done died."

"Died!" Craig gasped. The shock was so great, his knees almost buckled. The two elderly women had been with them since 1811. They had belonged to Colonel Franklin Stoner, the previous owner of Owen's plantation. When he had died unexpectedly, Stoner's wife Edna sold the farm to Martin. This estate included a spacious house, a number of barns and sheds, and unsold crops of flax, tobacco, and hemp. She sold everything else in a big auction—including a number of slaves. Many of those were prime field hands, but Penelope and Adah, along with Eliza, the other old slave woman, received no bids. Even the auctioneer refused to take them, they were so ancient and in such poor condition. In the end, Edna had let Craig and Mary have them and they had become Craig's wards. Mary appreciated their skill in gardening, stripping tobacco, spinning, and weaving. For their labors Craig paid fair wages, also providing smoked meat, chickens, firewood, and a share in his gardens. He had from the first offered to free them, but they had refused, saying they were content to live out their lives on his farm. It was hard to accept they had finally reached that end point.

Romulus added softly, "They got down with the coughin' sickness. It real bad. Eliza got it too."

"How bad is she?"

"I think she dyin'."

"Oh, Romulus!"

"And my missus and the childrens done took to their beds."

"I am not sure what I can do. I will give you a jug of whiskey and some wild cherry bark. You should boil the two ingredients together and have them sip several spoonsful. And make them drink as much water as they can. I will ride into town and fetch Doc Emmick."

He fetched the jug of whiskey and rummaged in the cupboard for a packet of wild cherry bark Agnes had ground. Mary retrieved her housecoat and wrapped it around her. She rose and crossed the floor to the cupboard. From the bottom shelf she retrieved a small crock of honey.

"Here, Romulus," she offered. "Put a little of this into the whiskey for the children. It will sweeten it."

"Thank you, Miss Mary." Romulus nodded. He left quickly.

Craig dressed hurriedly, horrorstruck at this development. "Mary, please do not go over to help them—not in your condition. I will fetch Doc Emmick."

"Alright, Craig," she agreed.

"And I will tend to the milking and egg gathering." Craig flung on his coat, ran to the barn, pitched hay down for the animals, then caught and saddled Blue. The cattle wanted milking, but they would have to wait. The ride into town was miserable, for the road took him mostly on a north-westerly route, right into the wind. The sky dawned a malevolent gray and a steady gale stripped tender green leaves from the trees. Craig could barely see the road in the poor light, but he let Blue have his head, allowing him to lope most of the six miles. The folks of Cottonwood Bend had not yet begun their day. The streets appeared strangely deserted, with only one or two people scurrying from one place to another. Doc Emmick was not at home. His wife met Craig at the front door, but she did not admit him.

"The doctor is out visiting folks stricken with the grippe," she explained. "This epidemic has been a bad one—perhaps the worst we have seen in Cottonwood Bend. It has killed several folks here and in Hardinsburg."

"Will you please tell him I need his services at my place? Craig asked. "Two of my slave women have died and others are sick."

"The doctor has regular folks to care for first," she replied icily.

"I understand. Please tell him I will pay in coin." Craig hoped the promise of payment would induce the doctor to turn a blind eye to skin color.

Next, he rode to Judge Bozarth's home. Violet met him at the door, looking quite unwell. Her hair was mussed, her nose red and swollen. Craig thought that she and the Judge might have been drinking again, or worse, fighting. Then she spoke with a forced croak, her voice feeble and watery. He knew instantly that she too suffered from the disease. Somewhere in the house's depths he heard the Judge coughing, a thunderous, rasping hack that seemed to shake the building's foundations.

"What may I do for you, Craig?" Violet asked.

"Please tell the Judge that two of my slaves have died of the grippe. Another is extremely ill and may not last the afternoon. I felt I should report it."

"Have you seen the doctor?"

"He is out on several medical calls."

"It is as one would expect. This pestilence has affected many. The doctor has already visited Wilfred, who is, as you have just heard, very much under the weather. The Judge has suffered far worse than I have."

"What is the treatment?"

"Bed rest, lots of liquids, and a concoction of whiskey, honey, and lemon."

Craig realized sadly that this epidemic must be treated like all the others. No miracle medicines existed to effect a cure. The sufferers must rely upon their own physical strength and natural resistance. Some would survive; others would not.

"Thank you for your time, Mrs. Bozarth."

"I will deliver your message to him," she promised.

Craig stopped off at Rosenbotham's store and purchased the last of his stock of lemons. These looked shriveled and rather brown from age, but Craig counted himself lucky to have them. He rode back to the cabin, unsaddled his horse, milked the cows, and gathered the eggs.

"Thank God you are home, Craig!" Mary exclaimed.

"What is wrong, Mary?"

"Both girls have taken ill."

Craig experienced a violent wave of dread. This plague should be affecting others—not *his* family! "What are their symptoms?" he dared to ask.

"Both have headaches and fevers," Mary explained shakily. "I fear I am coming down with the same thing. I ache all over and my throat feels scratchy."

"Then get under the covers with the girls. I will fix up something that Doc Emmick has prescribed for Judge Bozarth."

Mary did not argue. She returned to bed and drew the covers around her. All at once, Craig realized how bad things were—in five years he had never seen Mary this ill. Hanging a small pot onto the hook of a swinging fire iron, he half-filled it with whiskey, pouring from a stone jug they kept for visitors. He added several dollops of honey and squeezed the juice of one whole lemon into it, scraping the rind into zest, tossing it in, stirring the concoction and covering the pot with a lid. He allowed it to simmer and stirred again before ladling some into a cup and bringing it to the bedside.

"Have a little of this," he offered.

Mary sat up, took a few sips, and sank back onto the bed. Craig gently woke Isabel and Ruth and persuaded them to take a few spoonsful each. Ruth fought it. Craig tried to explain, but she abhorred the taste and at her age could not comprehend that it might provide some relief. She began to cry, and this spurred a painful fit of coughing. Her throat obviously hurt. He fetched a cold cup of spring water which she drank. Then he felt of their foreheads. All of them burned with fever.

"Just let us rest Craig," Mary sighed, drawing Ruth against her. "You should look in on Romulus' family and the others."

Craig hesitated, but obeyed. After wrapping a half brick of pressed tea and three lemons into a clean cloth, he shrugged on his coat. Crossing the road, he steeled himself against what he would find. He knocked on Romulus' door and opened it quietly. Romulus sat at the fireplace stirring the honey and whiskey mixture. He seemed unaffected, but Vergina and the children shivered violently underneath their blankets.

"Here Romulus," Craig handled him the small bundle. Cut up one of these lemons and squeeze it into the whiskey. I am not sure how medicinal it is, but Doc Emmick has prescribed it for Judge Bozarth."

"Thank ye, Craig," Romulus replied glumly. "'Spect you oughta know—Eliza done died too!"

"I feared as much," Craig hung his head. "How about Diogenes and Maggie?"

"They come down with the sickness before anyone, but they's some better."

"I will see them shortly."

"Nothin' much more to do here."

"Do you want me to help you bury the women?" Craig asked.

"Cold as it is, that can wait. I ain't leavin' my family."

"I understand. I must get back to mine. They have taken ill as well."

"Maybe we try buryin' tomorrow."

"Then I will take this jug and a lemon over to Diogenes' cabin." He took his knife, sawed off a portion of the tea brick, then made for the door. "Doc Emmick should be paying a visit—I am not sure when. If he does, please let him know that Mary, Isabel and Ruth are sick too."

"I will, Craig. Hope Mary and the childrens gets well."

"Me too. Call if you need me.

Diogenes and Maggie lay in their bed under a pile of blankets and quilts. Their fire had burned down, but Craig stirred the white ashes and found coals underneath. He built up a hot fire and put on a pot of water for tea. In another pot he prepared the whiskey concoction. This he poured into a battered tin mug. Maggie struggled into a sitting position and she sipped the mixture gratefully. Craig noticed that she did not suffer from the shakes. Perhaps her fever had already abated.

"You oughtn't to done this, Mister Craig," she protested.

"Why not? Doc Emmick claims it will help. He also says to drink lots of liquids. I have brought you some tea. You should brew some, but drink plenty of water as well."

"God bless you, Mister Craig."

Old Diogenes managed a weak smile from under the covers. "We be fine, Mister Craig."

Maggie ordered, "You just sit yourself up and have a drink of this, old man!"

Never in his life had Craig felt so helpless, so afraid. His family lay in the clutches of a sinister force, something over which he had no control. This was no ordinary illness; it was a life-and-death struggle, far more terrifying than what he had faced on Chalmette Battlefield. It was heart-wrenching to hear his daughters whimpering in their half-sleep and him having no way to alleviate their pain. Mary slept fitfully, barely able to speak. All Craig could do was bring them cold water or hot tea, help them sit up to drink, feed them spoonsful of the whiskey concoction and lay cool compresses upon their foreheads. He prayed aloud, begging God to heal them, offering to exchange places with them, trying with little success to hold back his tears.

The next morning, while his family slept, he ran down to inform Martin and Agnes, hoping they might know what to do. When he arrived, it was obvious the old couple suffered from the disease, but they appeared able to get around. Martin sat at the table wrapped in a warm wool blanket and sipping hot tea, coughing violently at intervals. Agnes gave Craig a packet of willow bark powder.

"This should help their headaches and pain," she offered.

"Doc Emmick says to drink plenty of liquids, and he ordered the Judge to mix honey and lemon into hot whiskey."

"That's the old tried-and true remedy. Lord knows we have done enough of that over the years," Agnes replied, her chuckle breaking into a wet cough. "You just keep those grandchildren warm and in bed. I would not feed them until their fever has broken."

"I am so frightened for them."

"I know, Craig. Many nights I stood watch by my children's bedsides, praying for them to get well. Only the good Lord knows why these things happen. It is important you put your trust in Him, whatever the outcome. It is a frightening time when we are confronted by illness. But here is one comfort I can share—little ones can seem awfully sick and then they just turn around, sudden-like, and get well. It is almost a miracle."

"Thanks, Mother Agnes," Craig said, hugging her.

Agnes' words instilled in him a small shred of hope. He pondered them as he trudged back up the hill, praying that his past killings had not brought the pestilence. Perhaps his sins had caught up with him. Outlaws and river pirates, redcoats and slave-catchers—in the end they were all human beings created by God. God could not be pleased he had killed them. When he reached the top pasture, he spied Doc Emmick's buggy tied up near the cabin. He quickened his pace. Romulus emerged from the dogtrot and headed him off. His face appeared glum and he spread his arms wide as if trying to keep a horse from escaping through an open gate.

"Doctor says you ain't supposed to go in jest yet."

Craig stopped dead in his tracks. "Why not?"

"I don't know. He come over to our house, sayin' Miss Mary done gone into labor. Told me to bring Vergina to help, then find you. Then he say not to let you in. That all he said."

Craig fought the urge to dash around him and burst into the cabin. Somehow he managed to restrain himself, aware of how utterly ineffective his presence would be. Doc Emmick would surely call him if needed. He retreated to the refuge of the barn. Romulus followed guardedly, unable to meet his eyes, as if he knew more than he could say. Craig began to understand—the disease had harmed the unborn babies, forcing Mary to go into early labor. He wondered if they were already dead, but dared not ask. The thought of losing Mary terrified him. Blood drained from his head and he swayed on his feet, feeling tired and wholly defeated. His head throbbed, and he realized vaguely that the grippe had sunk its talons into him. It was almost as if it chose the precise moment to strike. He busied himself, milking the cows, feeding and fussing over the animals, straightening harnesses and setting tools into order, feeling worse with each passing moment.

"Romulus, come up here!" Vergina called from the cabin door. Her voice sounded deep and watery, but she seemed much better than she had yesterday.

Both Craig and Romulus came at a dead run.

"Let me go ahead, Craig," Romulus advised.

Craig stopped, certain the news was terrible, overwhelmed at how so much could go wrong, and in such a short time. Doc Emmick must have arrived just after he left for the McDonnell's house. It was terrible to imagine what might have happened had he not called. Vergina caught Romulus by the arm and spoke to him in urgent whispers. Twice she glanced at Craig, unable to conceal her expression.

Presently, Romulus returned.

"Miss Mary be fine, but she done lost the twins."

"She *what!*"

"Doctor and Vergina is takin' care of her, cleanin' up and such. He done ordered me to dig a grave. You best stay with me 'til he say it alright to go in."

Craig felt a heavy numbness sweep over him. Shakily he led Romulus back to the barn and they located the mattock and shovel. They crossed the pasture, heading northeast toward the Hardinsburg Road. Twice he wrestled with the urge to be with Mary, but he obeyed Doc Emmick's instructions. A small grove of birch and red maple trees stood at the northeast corner just off the dirt thoroughfare. This grove was broken by a small semi-circular indentation of flat open ground. Mary had once remarked that the little glade possessed a sacred air. Craig felt certain she would prefer their children to rest here, rather than on Cemetery Knob, just outside Cottonwood Bend.

With his mattock he tore angrily into the earth while Romulus shoveled the broken dirt into a pile. Craig admitted that from the time he arrived in the Ohio River Valley he had lived a charmed life—perhaps too charmed. It seemed that all he touched turned into gold. He had inherited a farm, found and married the loveliest girl in the county, become part of a wonderful family, established good friendships in the community, and prospered beyond his own expectations, even acquiring two more farms. It seemed unfair that such an insidious, unseen force could strike so quickly and snatch it all from him. As he dug, Craig suspected that God was punishing him for the deaths he had inflicted. He had read passages from the Bible, especially the New Testament, and long ago figured that Jesus Christ would not have gone down to New Orleans to fight the British.

When they finished digging, Craig surveyed the dark hole. With its blank, accusing stare, the little grave reminded him of those lives he had dispatched—of the debt he owed the earth for the dead bodies he had consigned to it. They began walking back to the cabin. Vergina waited uncertainly in the dogtrot. Doc Emmick had provided her with a blanket and a cloth bag in which to wrap the stillborn infants. She cradled the bundle tenderly as if the contents still lived.

Craig asked anxiously, "Can I go in now?"

"Doc say not yet," she replied apologetically.

"How is Mary?"

"She restin' now." Vergina coughed. "She really sad,"

Craig beckoned for her to follow. When they had covered the grave and laid large stones on top to discourage predators, they began walking back to the cabin. Craig swayed with dizziness; his legs ached to the marrow and he slogged along as if plodding through molasses.

"How about my daughters?" he asked her.

"They sleepin'. Doc still takin' care."

"What about your own children?"

"They's better. Maggie watchin' them."

Craig appreciated that the couple had left their children to take care of his family. "Shall I help you bury the three older women?"

"I already done it Craig," Romulus replied. "You best take to your bed. You don't look so good."

"Thank you for everything," Craig tried to hide his tears. Romulus touched his shoulder in sympathy. The couple turned and headed for their cabin. Craig plodded wearily to his own.

Doc Emmick met him at the door, his face grave but considerate. "Mary and the children are resting," he said. "The youngest one's fever has broken."

"Thank God," Craig wept.

"I feel confident they will survive. But you get yourself into bed."

"Thank you," Craig replied weakly, struggling to kick off his doeskin boots.

"Someone must look after you. I will stop in at Martin McDonnell's and apprise him of the situation."

"Thank you. Have you seen to the folks across the road?"

"I have. The survivors have all turned the corner. They'll live."

"What do I owe you?"

"We will settle that later. Get into bed and drink plenty of water."

"I will," Craig promised. He crawled into bed next to Mary. She turned painfully toward him, crying softly.

"Shh!" Craig attempted to comfort her. "I am here. Can I get you anything?"

"No."

"Are you in pain?"

"Yes."

"I should never have left you. I went to ask your mother and father how to better take care of you."

"You couldn't have done anything. Doc was with me when the first pains came." Her voice was afflicted that watery characteristic so common in other sufferers. "You would have so enjoyed your twin sons. I am so sorry!"

A paroxysm of shock and pain coursed through him. In the confusion and awfulness he had not thought to ask the sex of the still-born children. He began crying again, unable to hold it back. "It is I who am sorry. I killed all those men and now God's judgment has fallen upon us!"

"You cannot believe that!" Mary whispered. "God has forgiven you."

"I fear he is punishing me—and you and the children have suffered for it."

"He doesn't work that way, Craig. He loves you. He loves our two sons. They are with him now in Heaven."

Craig nodded and put his arm gently around her, thankful for her faith; it seemed to give her such comfort. At the same time he experienced an intense anger, wondering why a loving God would inflict such awfulness, especially upon someone so gentle and trusting as Mary. The fever seized him once again and he shivered violently. It felt like someone had taken a club and beaten his lower back and legs. His head throbbed with each heartbeat and he rode the undulating waves of pain that crashed down upon him.

New Orleans—May 30, 1816

Pierre Delacroix began quietly liquidating some of his principal assets. First, he sold off his two plantations that lay upriver. These were among his finest holdings, the rich alluvial silt producing sugarcane, cotton, rice, and oranges in great abundance. Both properties came with large brick sugar refineries, barns, sheds, and other outbuildings. Delacroix included slaves and livestock in the final price of each plantation. The buyer, a wealthy state senator, lived in Baton Rouge and was looking to acquire properties closer to the capital, New Orleans. Delacroix then sold another plantation several miles below the city near English Turn. Quite naturally these transactions caught the watchful eye of Jules Signet. He waited just a few days before confronting the merchant. He possessed the oily grace to make it appear like a chance encounter, but Delacroix was on to him. He had played this game before.

The meeting occurred on the floor of the Bouchard Exchange. Delacroix had just sold a huge consignment of whiskey and was remarking upon the astronomical prices to one of his associates. Signet strolled up in his expensive suit, ruffled-neck shirt, black cravat, top hat and black boots. He wore a jeweled ring on each finger and flourished a rosewood cane with its ivory head filigreed in gold. It took great restraint for Delacroix to hide his disgust.

"My dear Delacroix!" Signet began. "You look frightfully well."

"Yes, and this despite the rumors you have circulated."

"I do apologize. My source was in error."

"Apparently so."

"You have been extremely active. One cannot use the chamber pot without hearing of your brilliant business transactions. I regret I did not know earlier that your plantations upriver were for sale. Perhaps I could have offered you more."

"Perhaps," Delacroix touched the brim of his hat. "But those sales were in the works a long time."

"I understand you have sold off much of your present inventory, that your warehouses are quite empty."

"Prices are high—especially grain prices."

"It would seem wise to capitalize on such an opportunity."

"Great Britain is in serious trouble. Last year Parliament passed the Corn Law to keep foreign grain out and to maintain high grain prices, all this to satisfy the rich landowners. But prices have risen so high that poor and middle class Englishmen must spend most of their incomes on grain. They are rioting in the streets."

"Yes, I have heard," Signet waved his hand impatiently. "I also deal with the ship captains and investors."

Delacroix needled him further. "I understand conditions are much worse in France. The political situation is grave; high food prices have led to many crimes. Bad harvests are expected once again. Storms, rain and flooding have added misery to an already cold and hungry people."

"Yes, yes. Please shed some light on why you are selling all your assets."

"Why, if you will just listen, I am telling you."

"Pray continue."

"European governments have passed protective tariffs to defend their landholders from foreign competition. This has prompted America to follow suit with its own tariff. New England farmers have suffered two ruinous growing seasons, and this year may prove worse. I predict grain prices will spike even higher."

"Then why sell now?"

"The European tariffs will inevitably affect us. One cannot tell when prices will drop. When that happens I will be well-positioned to buy."

"Fair enough. But please, let me know if you decide to sell other properties."

"Of course." Delacroix touched his hat again. "Now, if you will excuse me, I must return to my work."

"Then I bid you good day, Monsieur Delacroix."

Chapter Thirteen

Breckinridge County, Kentucky—June 6, 1816

The epidemic took much longer to run its course than it did coming on, leaving its victims temporarily incapacitated and in excruciating pain. Eyelids felt as if sand lay beneath them; blankets seemed to weigh a ton. Teeth chattered; muscles and joints ached. Then came the "sweats," the moment when the fever finally broke, and afflicted folks soaked their clothes and bed sheets. Although Craig shook off his initial fever, the aches and coughing hung on for days, and he felt as weak as a newborn kitten. The disease had struck the McDonnells as well, but their natural resistance enabled them to quickly throw it off. Martin and Stephen tended Craig's livestock in those first days when he could hardly rise from the bed. Agnes came up to care for the family, preparing meals, washing clothes, and caring for the little ones. Although physically weakened by the miscarriage, Mary soon managed to arise and prepare meals. The children began eating miniscule amounts of food, but their little faces remained pinched and wan from the past fever. Mary prepared a chicken soup for them, adding dried garden vegetables from last season and some new peas that escaped the recent frosts.

After three days Craig assumed his regular morning chores, glad he and Romulus had earlier cut great piles of firewood. Painfully he wielded his axe to cut kindling, surprised that it seemed to weigh thrice its normal weight. His burning throat and lungs secreted fluids that induced much coughing and spitting—as if his body was purging itself of the disease. When his appetite finally returned, he began stoking in food, feeling strength surge back into his body.

It would take much longer for his anger and grief to subside. In fact, he doubted if it ever would. As far as he was concerned, God had no right to take his twin sons. Perhaps it was punishment for all the men he had killed, but his stillborn sons were innocent of those crimes. He could never acknowledge their deaths as justified.

Mary seemed to accept it all as part of the grand scheme of life. Many times she commented, "God love their little hearts—their souls are in Heaven. We shall see them again and abide with them for all eternity."

Craig outwardly agreed with her—for her sake—thankful she could rationalize their deaths and get on with living. But her placid acquiescence and supreme confidence in the Almighty's wisdom infuriated him. He wanted to tell her so, but kept all to himself. In truth, his own demons plagued him. Dreadful nightmares tormented his sleep as dead outlaws and pirates, redcoats and slave catchers rose up as ghoulish phantoms, disfigured with gory wounds, blazing with condemnatory stares. Guilt and terror continually assailed him. The torture continued, night after miserable night, until his nerves were frayed. One morning, while playing, Isabel knocked over a broom. The wooden handle clapped loudly onto the hearth, sounding just like a gunshot. Craig leaped from his chair and barely restrained himself from shouting at her. Mary's face reflected his shock and anger. He turned and stormed out of the cabin, feeling guilty, but thankful that Isabel remained unaware.

He hitched up the oxen to the heavy oak harrow, flipped the triangular-shaped implement onto its back, and slung a sack of seed cord and a hoe onto it before crossing the Hardinsburg Road to the Smithhart farm. He had endured enough. This winter—the deadly epidemic, blighted sun, frosts, misery, and death—could all go to hell. This day, despite the fact his breath fogged in the cold air, he would begin planting his corn.

Driving his oxen to the nearest corner, Craig flipped the harrow back over so the rows of sharpened black locust pegs pointed downward into the plowed earth. He stepped the oxen ahead until the traces grew taut. Then, hopping onto the flat platform and slipping the lines over his left shoulder and under his right arm, he clucked to his team. The oxen slowly leaned into their harnesses. The crude all-wood implement broke up the previously worked soil with ease, snagging on an occasional root and jolting him with the impact. After two rounds he felt light-headed and weak, so he pulled the team to a halt and began planting corn, dropping the golden seeds about one foot apart before dropping back to cover them with his hoe. This allowed him a brief respite from the harrowing, and after two more passes he was done in, shaking from weakness, barely able to manage planting and covering.

Shortly past midday he unhooked the oxen and drove them back to the barn where he watered them, and fed them double portions of corn and several forks of hay. At the spring well he drew a bucket of cold water and gulped down several noggins, feeling his body tissues absorb it. Wearily he stumbled back toward the cabin and collapsed into bed, barely conscious when Mary removed his moccasin boots and wrapped the covers around him.

He woke late that afternoon to a howling wind that lashed the trees and buffeted the cabin. Another cold wave plummeted down from the north, pouring masses of frigid air into Kentucky, driving endless rolls of ominous blue-gray clouds southward with frightening speed. It seemed impossible that a blast so cold could strike so late in the season.

"This is unjust!" he exclaimed in outrage. "It is June and yet we must keep a constant fire burning in this house!"

"I know, Craig," Mary murmured. "No one can believe it." She handed him a cup of hot tea.

He swung his legs from the covers and sat upright to sip the black brew to which she had added lemon and honey. "Thank you, Mary. I am truly sorry for this morning. I have not been sleeping well."

"You are troubled, Craig. But you must not blame God for what happened. His ways are not our ways. Perhaps He knew something we did not. It was His decision to take our children and have them live with Him."

"Well, I don't like *His* decision. I hate it."

"That is only natural. But you must rid yourself of the notion that God is punishing you. There is a difference between self-defense, soldiering, and murder. You are not a murderer. He knows that."

"I am sure you are right," he replied without conviction.

"I am, Craig. And you must soon seek counsel about your nightmares. They are destroying you. Please, please speak with Father."

"I will not," he snapped irritably.

Giant rain drops thumped upon the cedar shakes. The clouds opened up for a brief moment and then the rain ceased. Craig downed the cup of tea, pulled on his boots, and shrugged on his coat. It was milking time already, and although much daylight remained, it appeared almost dark as night.

———•———

Next morning Craig discovered that, despite the brief shower, the earth was dry enough to continue harrowing and planting. Romulus joined him, content to drive the oxen and use the old wooden harrow. Craig hitched his big green farm wagon to the tans, loading it with bags of seed corn, hoes, water buckets and feed before transporting the whole lot to the Smithhart farm.

Together they began harrowing rows, smoothing the plowed ground with Romulus leading and Craig following, glad to wear his heavy coat. On this day he felt stronger and managed several rows before calling a halt to plant seed corn. It always amazed him how much more two people could accomplish together. Vergina joined them after dinner and they worked until late afternoon. Over the next week, the weather warmed and this brought out Diogenes and Maggie. Their presence freed Craig and Romulus for almost continual harrowing. In the late afternoon they called a halt and helped plant and cover seed.

Martin came up one morning to inspect their work. He stuck his finger into the soil to gauge its warmth. "I am glad you decided to plant, Craig. This weather could be breaking. If that happens, you may get a fair stand. But if this crop does not make, I would not replant."

"I agree. This is about as late as I dare plant."

"I called on Mary and the children this morning. She seems to be faring well."

"It was terrible for her, being ill and losing the babies."

"She has faith in God, Craig. Armed with faith one can overcome anything—sorrow, fear, *and* guilt."

Craig nodded noncommittally and glanced away, hoping the conversation would not progress further. Mary had obviously spoken to him, and the knowledge made him angry.

"I should know," the old man continued. "Several times in the past I questioned God's judgment—and perhaps even lost faith in Him for a spell. But I soon reckoned that He is all we really have in this world. Everything else, including our loved ones, will pass away; only He is eternal. Faith in Him is what truly helps us survive hard times."

Craig could not meet Martin's eyes. He was glad when he turned to speak with Romulus and examine the oxen and horses. In his characteristic manner Martin took up a hoe and helped them. They finished planting by late afternoon. Usually, Craig experienced a sense of elation after hard work done to the best of his ability. But this evening was not like that. He went through the obligatory motions of dragging harrows back to the barn, knocking mud and roots from the pegs, unhitching the animals, feeding and watering them, and milking the cows. Romulus headed back across the road to work at his own chores. Craig could not remember exactly when he left. He thought cynically that the corn's fate now rested in God's terrible hands. Considering the recent tragedy God had visited upon them, he held little hope for the crop.

That evening Mary prepared a dish of sautéed chicken marinated in peach brandy which she served with roasted potatoes, hominy, new greens, English peas, and green onions. It really was a fine meal, but Craig ate mechanically without enjoying it. Afterwards he took straight to bed—not thanking her, still angry that she had spoken to Martin about his nightmares. Mary sensed the reason for his anger and she left him alone, playing with the children until their bedtime. He was still awake when she slid under the covers beside him.

"Craig?"

He did not answer, fearful of what he might say.

She laid a soft hand on his ribcage "I know why you are angry."

"I asked you not to talk with him."

"I know. But I have been so fearful. You must let go of your guilt and your anger toward God. We have two children who need you very much. *I* need you. The war is over; our stillborn sons are in Heaven. We have all suffered terribly, but we must continue living our lives."

"What do you think I have been trying to do?" he snapped.

"I just want you to be happy again. We must be grateful we have survived. Our garden will make, and these cold snaps must soon end."

Craig experienced a crushing sense of guilt and he pulled her to him. "I'll try," he promised. "I am so lucky I have you. I know you care."

They clung to each other throughout the night, both weeping silently, changed by the tragedy that had befallen them.

New Orleans—June 13, 1816

With his innate cleverness, Pierre Delacroix managed to slip out of New Orleans unobserved. An important court trial regarding monopolistic water rights made this timely escape possible. Delacroix found the case intriguing and spent some time familiarizing himself with the background particulars. A year ago the steamboat *Enterprise* had been seized by city officials, and its captain, Henry Shreve, was arrested and thrown into jail. A punitive lawsuit was brought against the ship's owners by entrepreneur Robert Fulton and his partner Robert Livingston. The two plaintiffs complained that *Enterprise* infringed upon their exclusive rights to navigate steamboats on Louisiana waters, rights previously granted by the Territorial Legislature of Louisiana. The aggrieved pair seemed determined to spend any amount to suppress rival steamboat builders. Accounts of this incident swept throughout the American West, circulating widely in newspapers and creating a popular uproar among those who believed that everyone had the right to navigate America's rivers. Shreve was ultimately released, boldly returning with his steamboat on April, 5th, 1816, well ahead of the impending court date.

The *Enterprise* trial, Judge Dominic A. Hall presiding, was held in the Old Spanish Courthouse at 919 Royal Street. The courtroom filled with New Orleans' most prominent citizens, for all appreciated the potential of steamboat navigation; all realized that the outcome would directly affect them. Co-defendants Daniel French and Henry Shreve intended to break the Fulton-Livingston monopoly. In a brilliant stroke of genius, their defending lawyer, Abner L. Duncan, submitted a federal patent, dated 1809, for *Enterprise's* improved and unique steamboat engine. He argued that this patent protected the owners, French and Shreve, and their Monongahela & Ohio Steamboat Company shareholders from the monopolists' lawsuit. On May 20th, Judge Hall ruled that the old Territorial Legislature had exceeded its authority in granting a steamboat monopoly, and he summarily dismissed the lawsuit. Although the plaintiffs lodged an appeal that might rise all the way to the Supreme Court, Judge Hall's decision would, in the interim, contribute much toward new steamboat commerce and western states' financial growth.

After the trial, *Enterprise* was free to leave. Delacroix sought out Captain Shreve and negotiated for a private cabin. The cost was staggering, but the old merchant did not intend lodging in the common room. Although other steamboats plied the river, *Enterprise* was ready to depart—bound for Shippingport, Kentucky, just below the Falls of the Ohio. Delacroix's destination, the little settlement of Cottonwood Bend, lay about a hundred miles nearer. There, he would visit Lucinde, perhaps for the last time. He had waited too long already. Four years had elapsed since they parted, and the longing was like a physical ache. *Enterprise* would bring that separation to a short end; the vessel had already proven its ability to ascend the Mississippi and Ohio River currents. If past performance meant anything, Delacroix would reach Cottonwood Bend in about three weeks.

On the morning before his departure, he met with his managers and lawyers, providing them with long, carefully-worded written instructions, personal requests, copies of legal papers, bank statements, and other documents. He spent the afternoon with Judge Harkness, Henri de Ste. Gême, and a few of his closest friends. He and Harkness divulged what information they could concerning Jules Signet and Alain Morel, and judging from their reactions, Delacroix felt confident the banker would encounter serious difficulties if he attempted another takeover. Harkness now safeguarded one of several notarized copies of Lucinde's manumission papers, a long letter addressed to Philippe Bouchard, and a document naming the young man as his power-of-attorney, effective upon his return to New Orleans.

At dusk, the merchant assigned four trusted employees to convey his considerable baggage to *Enterprise*. He personally supervised the transfer, satisfied that his three heavy trunks were packed tightly into solid wooden barrels marked '*Whiskey—1811.*' His personal effects fit into another, slightly smaller trunk and a voluminous leather portmanteau. No one noticed the two pistols under his coattails, or the brace of expensive double-barreled shotguns in his portmanteau.

Enterprise was moored at the levee directly in front of his nearest warehouse, tucked in neatly between two flatboats. Even in the dim light, the contrast was striking. The steamboat displaced seventy-five tons, measuring eighty feet in length with a beam of fifteen feet and a draft of just two-and-half feet. Designed by Daniel French, a single high-pressure steam engine powered a massive sternwheel eight feet in diameter. A single black smokestack towered high above the waterline; that and the recessed sternwheel served notice that a new, advanced form of transportation had arrived and would remain. Other features conveyed an air of stark utility, if not beauty—a forward gun for saluting, a rounded bow, deck railings, white-painted cabin, and a blocky pilothouse stacked on top, forward. Delacroix boarded *Enterprise* without hesitation or regret; his course was clearly charted. He locked his cabin door and slept soundly until the blackness of early morning when the stokers began firing the boilers. Apparently it was standard procedure to slow-stoke the fireboxes to avoid stressing and cracking the clay linings and cold iron boilers. The noise woke him and brought him out onto a deck piled high with cords upon cords of firewood. Delacroix locked his door from the outside and pocketed the key before wending his way through the wood stacks to the pilothouse.

Captain Henry Shreve invited him in. "Monsieur Delacroix, you are just in time to observe our departure. I am pleased you have joined us. Would you like some coffee?"

"Indeed," Delacroix smiled.

"I hope your accommodations are satisfactory."

"They are indeed. This is quite a vessel. Congratulations on your recent court decision."

"Fortunately for all enterprising Americans, our western waters are now open for fair competition and investment. We could have easily lost. Judge Hall is a tough customer."

"I agree. The Fulton-Livingston monopoly seemed fairly ironclad, even if it was issued by the Territorial Legislature. Your lawyer employed a brilliant legal defense, invoking patent law."

"That stratagem prevailed. Of course it was the proper approach, for *Enterprise* is unique in so many ways."

"How so?"

"Fulton's boats were all sidewheelers. Our hull design is completely different, and much better suited for shallow waters. The recessed sternwheel is protected and offers a definite advantage on western rivers filled with snags and driftwood. Those obstacles frequently destroy unprotected side-mounted paddlewheels."

"I can appreciate that," Delacroix nodded.

"Our engine is vastly superior in all aspects, designed and constructed by my partner Daniel French."

"What makes it so much better?"

"Fulton's engines have extremely complicated machinery that requires a heavy beam to convert the piston stroke to the sidewheels. Their engines are mounted vertically and the massive, low-pressure cylinder is grossly inefficient."

"And French's engine differs in what way?"

"It is a high-pressure engine with a much smaller, oscillating cylinder, mounted horizontally and directly connected through the piston rod to the sternwheel crank. Our engine is simpler, lower in weight, more efficient, and less costly to manufacture. And engines keep improving with each new design."

"So you feel quite confident the steamboat represents the future?"

"We are already building bigger and faster steamboats in Brownsville, Pennsylvania, some with protected sidewheels. The new designs will astound you."

Delacroix accepted a cup of coffee from a deckhand.

"She's ready, Captain," the deckhand exclaimed. "We have a full head of steam up."

Shreve nodded. "Prepare to cast off all lines."

In the uncertain pearly light Captain Shreve engaged the big wheel and *Enterprise* reversed, backing away from the levee and swinging its stern downriver. The captain pulled on a lever, uncoupling the engine and allowing the paddlewheel to come to a complete halt. They drifted silently backward. For a moment, Delacroix feared the engine had malfunctioned; then Shreve reengaged the machinery by moving the lever into the forward position. The great engine began to thump and *Enterprise* surged forward, its bow cleaving the muddy brown water. This was Delacroix's second ride on a steamboat. The first had been a celebratory excursion on board the *New Orleans* in 1812. That ship was the first-ever steamboat on western waters—at that time he had discounted it as a mere novelty, a passing fad, not at all a practical mode of transportation. So many doubts surrounded the vessel. Her machinery was too complicated, her draft too deep for the Mississippi sandbars, her cost effectiveness diminished by a notoriously short lifespan. The doubters were proven correct when *New Orleans* hit a snag, sinking just two short years after launching.

Despite this failure, new steamboats continued to arrive at the levee, and each vessel incorporated some innovation that showed improvement. Delacroix admitted his world had changed—in fact, it had leapt far beyond him. Yet here he was, embracing the latest wave of progress, glad he could afford the luxury and indulge himself in a grand trip upriver, riding on a new-fangled steamboat.

New Orleans soon fell behind them and disappeared from view. The river sprawled lazily, well over a mile wide, painted chocolate-brown with upstream silt. Delacroix studied the vast plantations crouched behind their natural levees, complete with attendant outbuildings and stables, orange groves, cotton fields, bright green cane shoots, and brick sugar mills. Stilted slave quarters huddled in the shade of live oaks and pecan trees. *Enterprise* carried him past other plantations and small farms, and the vistas flashed like fragments of his bygone life.

Delacroix had arrived in Louisiana in 1763 after the French War—a refugee from the British-captured province of Quebec. Through ingenuity, good luck, and hard work he had acquired farms and, later, several great plantations, then the banks, warehouses, and exchanges, amassing incredible wealth. Now he was turning his back on it all.

The river wound like a tortured snake through a vast southern panorama—towns and settlements along the muddy banks, isolated huts, flatboats, cypress trees and flat cotton fields stretching to the horizon. *Enterprise* never faltered, its pistons hammering and sternwheel churning, leaving a large foaming wake behind them.

The wood supply diminished at an alarming rate, for the engine, an insatiable Baal, required constant stoking. Although substantial reserves still remained, Captain Shreve and crew began scanning the riverbanks for long rows of firewood cut and stacked by resourceful farmers or woodcutters who sold it to the steamboats for two dollars per cord. Usually these suppliers tied a whiskey jug or colored rag to a tree branch to indicate their intent to sell. At present, new sources were unreliable; oftentimes crews must pull ashore and cut their own wood, usually green. If this happened, Delacroix could count on adding days to his travel time. He hoped it would not be the case.

He longed for Lucinde, the grandchildren he had never seen, and his handsome son-in-law, Owen. Like *Enterprise* they represented the future. He wanted nothing more than to consign his great fortune to them, to see it carried forward in their deserving hands.

Salvador da Bahia—June 20, 1816

Doc lingered in Bahia day after miserable day, nursing the unrealistic, desperate hope *Lisette* would soon arrive. Although the city offered plenty of diversions, the passing days began to chafe, then to agonize. Days turned into weeks; weeks into almost two months. He wondered if the schooner had turned back for New Orleans. Had she sailed for another slave port? Perhaps the captain had jettisoned his 'cargo' in the mid-Atlantic and sailed onward to France. Fortunately Judge Harkness had demanded specific orders in his ruling— Philippe must be properly treated and proven alive at the end of one year. It was a slender strand of hope that kept Doc waiting in Bahia, but his hope was fading. He decided to give it one more week; then he would set sail for Martinique. But without Philippe, there was no real reason to go. He had lost again—his good intentions turned sour, like everything else in his rotten life.

Emmett, on the other hand, had found his paradise. One evening he, Louis, and Raoul left *Arabelle* and did not return. Doc learned of his whereabouts two weeks later—and the tale was incredible. Emmett had purchased a small waterfront property, stocked it with liquor, acquired a few slave women, and gone into business. In one month he had picked up rudiments of the Portuguese language and was dealing directly with vendors and suppliers. One night Doc visited the tavern with its mismatched tables and chairs and cast-off furniture. The place was jam-packed with sailors, locals, slaves, and free blacks. Louis and Raoul sat at one corner of the tavern, positioned where they could monitor the patrons' comings and goings, just as they had in New Orleans. Emmett had built a sturdy bar of thick oak planks and ensconced himself in the fort-like structure.

Emmett lit up when he saw him. He emerged from behind the bar, a pathetic but proud little gnome, hobbling on his good leg and one crutch, obviously the ruling king and star celebrity of his establishment.

"What in the hell are you doing, Emmett?" Doc asked.

"I buy this place. I still go with you, kill Signet, then come back here. Big money to make."

"With your brains you will soon be running this city."

"Big part maybe."

"We must leave soon. I fear *Lisette* is not coming."

"She be 'long directly."

"How do you know that?"

"Sailor say she have trouble—stopped in Cuba to fix."

"When did you learn this?" Doc was astounded.

"Last week."

"Damn it, Emmett! You should have told me!"

"I tell when ship gets here."

"Philippe Bouchard is aboard *Lisette*. That is why we are in Bahia, to free him. He will play a major role in destroying Signet."

"I take care of Signet. Count on that!"

"We will handle him legally, that is if we can recover Philippe."

"Your business yours—mine be mine."

Doc left the tavern in a state of bewilderment. There was no reason to doubt Emmett's information, but felt certain Joshua Adams might have some new intelligence to add. Next morning he paid a call to his office.

"No, I have heard no news on *Lisette*," the merchant replied. "I will ask around. Yes, I understand your concern. Perhaps she has stopped to trade elsewhere. The good news is, I have heard of no reports of storms or shipwrecks."

Doc consulted with Nathan West in his cabin and felt even more anxious, for the captain painted a much bleaker picture. "The ship should have arrived weeks ago, but she may have stopped to trade in other ports. Possibly they lied to you about their destination; perhaps she suffered some calamity at sea. There are never guarantees."

Despite these gloomy scenarios, West advised waiting. The original plan, based on current information, was solid. Delacroix had helped devise it, so it must be good. Doc agreed—with trepidation.

His torment ended on the morning *Lisette* limped into the 'Bay of All Saints' –eight weeks after *Arabelle* had anchored. Captain West visited the schooner and learned she had struck a reef off Cuba and was forced to put in at Havana. Repairs had taken more than five weeks. Rough seas had damaged the patchwork and *Lisette* stopped again for repairs, this time in San Juan, Puerto Rico. Further slowed by two trading stops and hampered by cautious sailing, the schooner finally managed to reach her destination.

West returned to *Arabelle* with pertinent intelligence—Philippe and Kayla were on board *Lisette*, both in remarkably good shape, both scheduled for sale at the next auction.

"Did you see them?" Doc asked.

"I did not, but the captain described them exactly as you have—a white man and a young quadroon girl with child."

Doc narrowed his eyes as he counted backward. Had nine months passed since he brought Kayla to Judge Harkness? They had. "By God, I am getting old!" he muttered.

"What?"

"Nothing. Is the child in good health?"

"Apparently, yes. After I left *Lisette* I paid a call on Joshua Adams. He will make a tentative offer this afternoon."

"Good. Let me know when he has lodged them in the barracoons. I will speak with the girl first, then Philippe."

"As you wish."

———————•———————

Adams' slave pens stood well back from the harbor, tucked under sprawling shade trees near where a small rivulet entered the bay. Constructed of palm logs with roofs of bamboo and palm thatch, and underpinned by solid floors of sawn timber, these long sheds occupied the best site in the immediate area. Although the smell of human excrement assaulted the senses, Doc appreciated the sanitation system Adams had devised, for it took advantage of the rivulet's sluggish current.

Kayla sat alone in one corner of the female barracks, cradling a loosely wrapped bundle and cooing softly to it. Doc chose to speak with her first, in the belief that motherhood would soften her temperament. Adams let him in and locked the door. She raised her head and saw him. In that single glance he caught several reactions—an initial flare of recognition, a flicker of hope, an expression of hostility—all replaced by the dull mask of submission affected by most slaves.

"Hello, Kayla," Doc began.

"Hello, Doctor," she replied, her voice a bare whisper.

"I see you have borne your child."

"Yessir."

"May I see it?"

Kayla threw back the linen swaddling. Doc grinned broadly. The baby was the spitting image of the Honorable Judge John Harkness, just a slightly darker version of the original. It bore all the judge's characteristic features—plump body, long toes, enormous ears, bulbous nose and a thick pelt of hair covering its body from knuckles to toes.

"Not bad!" Doc chuckled. "He looks quite the solid little lad. I told you he would turn out just fine, didn't I?" A blessed lie, but it worked like a charm, as he knew it would. All mothers found endearing qualities in their babies, no matter how ugly. Doc was willing to bet that even mother warthogs felt the same way about their young.

Kayla smiled, showing her pearly white, even teeth.

"I predict he will go far in life."

"Not here. Not as a slave."

"Glad you brought that up. I am here to take you back to New Orleans. Judge Harkness wants to care for you and his son."

"Then we be his slaves there."

"No, he wants to free both of you. He plans to provide for you."

"I not be his wench."

"He understands that. You will be a free person. You may not credit this, but he truly regrets his actions and he wants to make things right."

Kayla could not conceal her disbelief, but she remained silent.

"I know it is much to absorb, but the Judge is sincere. We have both made mistakes and want to make amends. That is why I am here—to take you back and help you begin a whole new life. You must put your trust in us and allow events to prove themselves. Can you do that?"

"Yes, Doctor."

———◆———

Philippe recognized Doc immediately. He lunged like a wild animal, his long-bottled rage exploding into a superhuman strength that strained the chains of his iron shackles. The guards rushed forward to subdue him.

"You filthy bastard! I swear to God, I will kill you!" Philippe roared through clenched teeth. He wore such a menacing expression of hate and resolve that Doc recoiled, thankful the young man still wore his slave chains. "So help me, I will get free of this and make you all pay!"

Doc observed him from a safe distance. Philippe had grown leaner. His thick head of hair and dark full beard indicated that he was in the prime of life. He had obviously spent time on deck, for the sun had bronzed him gloriously. Doc had always admired his handsomeness, but it showed even more clearly in its raw, natural state, unadorned by the frills and fineries of civilization. By reputation he knew the young man's intelligence. He allowed the outburst to run its course, ignoring the threats and venomous obscenities, letting him exhaust himself. Finally Philippe subsided and turned to face the back wall.

"Are you quite finished?" Doc inquired, recognizing it was time for reason.

Philippe did not answer.

"I have come to take you back to New Orleans, to rescue you from this hellish place and to restore you, as much as possible, to your rightful position." Again no answer. "Shortly after your hearing, I consulted with Judge Harkness, and we agreed we were terribly wrong. We deeply regret our part in your misery." Doc had rehearsed his admission on the long sea voyage, but no amount of preparation could make the words come out right. He paused, gathering himself for the rest of it.

Philippe turned to glare at him, trembling visibly as he struggled to gain control of his emotions. At least he did not attack. Doc took this as a favorable sign and continued.

"Jules Signet bought my services to use medical science against you. I confess openly that I was in a sorry state when we made our arrangement. He provided money in exchange for my testimony and for the power I held over Judge Harkness. You will not like this, but I played the biggest role in the plot to ruin you. I am thoroughly ashamed of myself."

"Then you admit it?" Philippe croaked hoarsely.

"Oh, yes. I must."

"And that damned judge—passing that despicable ruling!"

"He regretted it from the outset, but you must understand he was grossly manipulated. As his physician, I knew his vulnerability and I used Kayla to entrap him—even prescribed her physical favors as a medical treatment. He is the father of her child. We used her condition as leverage. It was all part of the contract I made with Signet."

"I cannot believe you are telling me this."

"I used Judge Harkness; I used Kayla—and I harmed you, an innocent man." The enormity of it all, telling it face-to-face to the party he had injured, overwhelmed him. Tears slid down his cheeks. "I will never be able to make everything right, but I will spend the rest of my life trying to make it up to you."

This knocked the rough edge off Philippe's expression. "Signet and his lawyer, Morel—they did this because they wanted my wealth?"

"They crafted your hearing to test the legal waters. Signet plans to use scientific classification to seize other estates—including all the holdings of Pierre Delacroix. He even offered me a thousand dollars to put Delacroix down with a strong opiate."

"This grows more unbelievable with each pronouncement."

"Pierre Delacroix needs you in New Orleans. And you will find you have a strong ally in Judge Harkness."

"I will never trust that man. When I return, I will have him hounded from the bench."

"You won't have to. He plans to resign his office as soon as he helps you regain your position. The judge and I confessed our sins to Father Poitier and we set up a secret meeting with Delacroix in the rectory. Together we devised the plan to find you, bring you back, and restore you. Delacroix has financed it; Judge Harkness will reverse his decision and play a major role in your restoration—and I have a few nasty tricks up my sleeve."

"Of that one can be certain."

"All will be employed for your benefit. The salient question is, will you put your trust in the wretch who brought such ruination upon you?"

"I doubt it very much."

"Delacroix has. I told him everything and yet he provided me with the gold coin to purchase you, the ship, captain, and crew to convey you homeward, and this letter—addressed to you. After you have read it, let me know your decision."

Philippe reached for it, his eyes filling with hope. Doc stepped as close as he dared, and handed him the buff-colored letter. Philippe took it and retreated to shed's far corner. On his first night at sea Doc had broken the seal and read the letter penned by Pierre Delacroix in flamboyant, elegant script taught to him by the Catholic nuns in Montreal. If any incriminating contents were written inside, it was best to know beforehand. Doc had read it so often on the long sea journey that he knew the letter by heart. In fact, he could visualize the words as he watched the young man pore over it.

New Orleans, Louisiana
March 21, 1816

My Dearest Philippe,

If you are reading this correspondence, please know that your ordeal has nearly reached the end. You are ever in my thoughts and most fervent prayers, and I continue to light candles for you in the Cathedral of St. Louis. Daily I pray for your safety and good health, and for your speedy return to New Orleans.

It was with broken heart I learned of your recent fate. All indications point to a libelous personal attack—without basis—and a wicked, criminal takeover of your wealth and station. In my wildest imaginations I could never conceive such duplicity, such wickedness. I am thoroughly shaken that a respected federal judge and brilliant physician would abuse their stations and employ their God-given gifts to ruin such a wonderful, innocent young man as yourself. Howev-

er, both rogues have expressed a sincere change of heart, and I am wholly convinced they will strive faithfully to make what amends they can. Their tales are sad—both were manipulated by a sinister force that induced them to commit this heinous wrong. This does not excuse their behavior, but at least you have the full story, plainly.

You must be forewarned that our fair state, Louisiana, is moving in an unsavory direction that will, in time, further entrench slavery. When men like Jules Signet seek to enrich themselves, they will use existing laws to write new laws, especially those statutes concerning race and inheritance. When a man has friends in State Legislature, New Orleans society, and in city government, he becomes enormously, dangerously powerful. And when one considers the influence he wields in the legal profession, banking system, and militia patrol, one realizes the peril of openly challenging him.

Your situation is precarious; that is why I have financed a ship, captain and crew to convey you back to this city. All has been arranged with the utmost secrecy. I beseech you now to place your trust in Doctor Thomas Applegate—as repugnant as that course must seem. You must rise above your injury, consider your current plight, and look wisely to your future. Right now the Doctor holds that future in his crafty and guileful hands. The fellow is a sly old fox, devious beyond belief, yet absurdly shrewd and resourceful. If he could contrive your downfall, he could well engineer your restoration. Bear this in mind as you travel with him. He is forever in your debt—have him help you plan the details of your return.

Meanwhile I will meet with several trusted friends to warn them of the impending danger. Despite my advanced years, I still wield a considerable amount of power—I hope for the good. Judge Harkness is prepared to overturn his ruling, and other legal actions are in progress. I promise to work tirelessly to help you regain your wealth and position.

For that reason you must return with all reasonable haste. Please cooperate with the Doctor and keep him from harm.

Remember this—in His greatest agony, Jesus Christ forgave all mankind from the Cross—His blood was completely innocent; His punishment was undeserved. He commands us to do the same in our lives, to forgive those who trespass against us. Sometimes He tests our loyalty, our professed faith in him. I am certain He has presented you with a rare and precious opportunity, to follow in His footsteps. I pray you will accept this honor and, when you are my age, look back upon the tribulation with gratitude; hopefully you will be able to say—"I forgave." Then I am certain that the Father in Heaven will say to you, "Well done, my good and faithful servant."

Please, take the utmost care of yourself. I long to embrace you and to see you fully restored.

Your humble and obedient servant,
Pierre Delacroix

Philippe bowed his head as tears stung his eyes. He trembled, not from rage but from the old merchant's irresistible power, reaching out to him with a father's steady and proper advice. He slowly turned and looked at Doc.

"There really is no other option, is there?"

"No. It is the best we could manage under the circumstances. We will make up the rest as we go along."

"Then get me out of this place."

"I am an old man, but I am not yet ready to die."

"I won't harm you, you rotten bastard," Philippe grinned wryly. "I trust Delacroix. According to him I need you. But Kayla must go with us."

"We have already purchased her. Delacroix's ship, *Arabelle*, is moored not far from here. We are headed home, but first we must put in at Sainte-Pierre, Martinique."

"Martinique?" Philippe inquired.

"When one gambles, it pays to hold the top cards."

Chapter Fourteen

Breckinridge County—July 3, 1816

Craig worked his long-handled hoe with practiced efficiency, cutting new weeds and grass sprouts, bringing up loose dirt around the waist-high tobacco plants. Heat waves rippled off the field and sweat dropped from his brow, but he did not complain. Despite another brief cold snap, summer finally arrived in the Ohio River Valley. His and Mary's constant care of the tobacco bed paid off. They had spent precious time at both ends of each day, laying cedar boughs and covering it with straw and long bolts of filmy linen cloth, but this kept the bed warm at night, trapping in the sun's heat and, keeping at bay the morning frosts of May and early June. When the plants reached about eight inches high, with leaves the size of a rabbit's ear, they were carefully pulled each morning, bundled into wet sacking, and transported to the field for planting. This required a great deal of stoop work—pulling plants, bending over to stab a ten-inch wooden peg halfway into the ground, taking a single plant and sliding it into the hole, covering it with dirt and then pouring a noggin of water around the stem. The plants wilted over the next few days, but a light rain shower revitalized them and they began to grow.

The warm weather worked wonders on the countryside. Corn sprouted on the high ground and gardens began producing everything from onions, radishes, cabbages, and beets; lettuce, spinach, collards and other greens, to squash, early beans and cucumbers. Potato and yam plants flowered. The sweet corn would take longer to come on, for it was planted afterwards. Fruit trees flowered late and by all appearances apples, pears, plums, sour cherries, and peaches would fare well. Mary's grape arbor, now almost five years old, looked as if it would produce handsomely. Everyone's spirits improved. Craig used the lengthy daylight to keep busy—the only way he knew to combat the ill feelings still plaguing him.

One morning, after their first hay cutting, he drove his horses into Cottonwood Bend to buy supplies at Rosenbotham's store. The riverfront bustled with activity. A flatboat unloaded at the landing as the ferry brought riders over from the Indiana Territory. Although the cold weather was nearly a month behind them, folks still jawed about the strange phenomena. Craig overheard the conversations as he stepped up onto Rosenbotham's long, covered porch.

"Old Gerald Fischer says we ain't done yet with the cold."

"Donn Wimmer done seen a ring around the moon two weeks ago. He counted sixteen stars inside the ring. You know *that* spells trouble!"

"How about you, Paul? Did your corn make?"

"Hell, naw! Damned frost done froze out two crops. Got my terbacky too!"

"What air ye gonna' do?" asked an old timer. He spat a gob of brown tobacco juice off the porch.

"Live off my garden, I reckon. Hunt and trap maybe."

"You boys don't know when you have had it good!" the flatboat captain exclaimed.

"How's that, stranger?"

"I hail from Pittsburgh. Folks north and east of there are completely frozen out—corn and wheat crops ruined, ice on the lakes, a foot of snow in Vermont."

"The hell you say!"

"You can read some of them horror tales in the newspapers I brung Rosenbotham. Frost ruined fruit trees just upstream from Louisville. The forecast in New England says there'll be no fruit harvest at all. Cold weather has ruined the hay crop there. New York, Pennsylvania, and Ohio have suffered as well."

Old Rosenbotham added, "Two days ago a fellow came in on a keelboat from Tennessee. He swore that the June cold spell froze the young cotton plants down there."

"Times are fierce!" the old timer rolled his eyes in terror.

Just then, Judge Bozarth emerged from the store with Violet on his arm. Rosenbotham's son, Isaac, followed dutifully, lugging groceries and supplies. The Judge appeared fully recovered from his bout with the grippe and looked dapper in his powder-blue suit coat, black cravat and top hat. He gave the old timer a look of bemused pity, one usually reserved for lunatics and errant children.

"Pshaw! This is a miraculous era! And it is the opportune time for you farmers to cash in on your investments. Why, you can sell your produce for the best prices ever seen in American history. And I would be delighted to manage your profits, to advise you in a number of sound venture strategies that would make you all as rich as kings!"

"Like yourself, Judge?" one man guffawed.

"I have not done too badly."

"Oh yeah? How come more than twenty people have filed court petitions to force you to pay back the money they loaned you?"

The Judge's countenance registered no change. Instead, he chuckled easily. "I am sure you have been misinformed."

"Well, it's all over the county that you owe money to a bunch of folks."

"Ah, yes! You are referring to those unfortunates who have lost patience with the markets. They will recoup nothing. One must wait for the right moment to capitalize."

"And when is *that*—when the poor lender is dead from starvation?"

Some men drifted off, uncomfortable with the rough taunting. Rosenbotham also turned away to lead the flatboat captain inside. The Judge was a likeable sort and he still retained a reputation of greatness. After all, he had performed numerous heroic deeds throughout the county and beyond, and if truth be known, he had helped most of the men present at one time or another. Others sympathized with Violet. They all knew the Judge had wronged her—far more often than once—and it was grossly disrespectful to abuse the husband in her presence. Craig cast a quick glance at her. She did not possess the Judge's knack for dissembling, and it appeared the accusations struck a sensitive nerve. Perhaps she was as aware of his risky ventures as she was his infidelity.

The Judge cleared his throat and laughed. "It is apparent you have no inkling of what is happening in the world, in America—for that matter in Kentucky. I truly sympathize that you lack the temerity to take a risk or two."

With relief Craig abandoned the confrontation and stepped through the open doorway. Rosenbotham's Store smelled pleasantly of smoked hams, coffee, cigars, leather, lamp smoke, and spices. Buckets, farm implements, gardening tools, lanterns, harnesses and other items hung from the rafters. In one section the old storekeeper stocked his shelves with bolts of cloth, ribbons, pins and needles, thread, shoes, leather goods, undergarments, collars, suspenders, dungarees, hats and shoes. In another he stocked porcelain dishes, crockery, pots and pans, ladles, tableware, candles, and rope. In addition to the food staples he bought from farmers and resold to townspeople, Rosenbotham sold dried coffee beans, loose and pressed tea, spices, and now, more frequently, tropical fruits like oranges, lemons, and limes which were floated downstream on flatboats from Pittsburgh—and now on steamboats from New Orleans. A customer could buy flour, brown and white sugar, salt, apples, cheese, oats, yeast, honey, maple syrup, liquor, jams, and hard candy. There was an icehouse cellar for storing perishables. Behind the front counter Rosenbotham showcased patent medicines, painkillers, soaps, perfumes, and other toiletries.

A dozen jugs of "Widder's Reserve" occupied a place of honor on the center shelf. Each jug was filled with the dark amber-colored whiskey. An unstopped jug sat on the countertop where Rosenbotham poured a sample for the flatboat captain. The two were discussing its merits when Craig walked up.

"This is the best whiskey I have ever tasted," the captain declared, smacking his lips in apparent pleasure. "I could sell barrels of this stuff in New Orleans. Do you have any for sale?"

Rosenbotham glanced guiltily at Craig before answering, "Let's step back into the warehouse to discuss it."

Craig suppressed his amusement. Obviously the old skinflint didn't want him, the wholesaler, overhearing the retail price. But the jugs were clearly marked $1 per quart. Craig spied several glass containers holding Mary's whiskey-infused cigars and flavored chewing tobacco. Glancing over to another section he noticed several spools of hemp twine and a pile of woven hemp sacks, products of Mary's spinning wheel and loom. He realized then how much he and Mary fit into the community's business scheme, how successfully they had captured a niche market with high quality goods.

The Indiana men strode into the store full of news. Some of the locals followed them in, peppering them with questions.

"So Indiana is now a state?"

"Almost. Last time I heard, forty-three delegates were a-writin' the state constitution."

"Were they now?"

"Yep. They've been meetin' in the territorial capital of Corydon. Buildin' couldn't hold 'em all. It's been so damned hot they've done most of their work outside in the shade of a giant elm tree."

Craig wondered how preposterous that scenario would have seemed just a few short weeks ago. This prompted him to ask, "How has the cold weather affected Indiana?"

"Well, that depends on where you go. The farther east and north, the worse it gets. Low-lyin' areas naturally suffered more frost. Some folks have planted corn for the third time."

Another of the men volunteered, "I talked to a feller who come from Ohio. Fruit trees there is frozen. Hay crop's been pitiful—pumpkins, squash and new beans are ruined."

Lillian Rosenbotham, the storekeeper's wife, listened attentively to all conversations—as a result she served as the community wellspring of gossip and local news. She also picked up valuable information from travelers. Now she volunteered, "Just last week a flatboat stopped in. I talked with a young man from Massachusetts who is moving his family lock-stock-and-barrel to the Illinois Territory. He claimed that the devastation in New England defies belief. Birds have died in great numbers in subfreezing temperatures. Farmers are killing or selling their cattle and hogs because they cannot grow enough to feed them."

Craig silently congratulated himself on selling his hogs, for it sounded like there might soon be a glut in the livestock market. He realized that he could never outguess the markets; folks like Rosenbotham who religiously followed business news usually fared no better.

"Steamboat a-comin'!" men shouted in from the porch.

Everyone streamed outside in a singular reflexive action. This was great entertainment for everyone—almost as popular as a spectator sport. Despite their increasing numbers, new steamboats still drew folks to the riverbanks. Craig knew folks who dropped their chores to race two miles, just to catch a glimpse of the new boats—in fact, he had done so on several occasions. The vessel turned from midstream, definitely on course for Rosenbotham's landing. White water curled from her bows and black smoke mushroomed in great volumes from the smokestack.

"Oh, joy! She's a-puttin' in!"

"What boat is she?" someone asked.

"*Enterprise*—built in Brownsville, Pennsylvania."

"Look at her come!"

"Hope I can ride on her one day!"

Craig could hear the engine now, a deep, throbbing beat that seemed to transmit sound through the ground upon which he stood. He noticed the absence of sidewheels and wondered how *Enterprise* was powered. In that instant, the pilot laid on the whistle, a harsh, full-throated blast that startled horses and set young children to crying. The boat maneuvered carefully toward the landing and nosed gently into the mud bank. Everyone watched as the crew tied mooring lines, ran out a sturdy wooden ramp, and began rolling three heavy barrels onto shore. Another crew member lugged a massive ornate traveling trunk. Behind him followed a slight, elderly figure dressed in elegant gray suit and black top hat, carrying a large leather portmanteau. His spade-like beard and pointed moustaches were snowy white. Craig recognized him immediately. He had stayed at the merchant's townhouse during a business venture in 1812, and again during the Battle of New Orleans.

"Monsieur Delacroix!" he cried, waving his arms as he descended the cobblestone landing.

The old man focused on him for a time, unsure of who he was. Walking down the ramp with the jaunty, stride of a much younger man, the merchant drew near and finally broke into a broad grin, showing his long teeth.

"Craig, my boy! Fancy meeting you here!" His handshake was firm and dry. "What are the odds of this encounter?"

"I don't know, but I am glad you have come."

"May I prevail upon you to convey me to Lucinde's house?"

"You may and I will. Might I purchase my supplies first?"

"Indeed. I will stay here with my belongings until you return. Do you have a wagon?"

"I do," Craig replied.

"That is splendid news!" Delacroix sat down on his trunk and glanced around nervously. Craig noticed his unease and hurried filling his order. As he drove his wagon down the steep landing, the steamboat's pistons began to thump. *Enterprise* hauled in her gangplank and backed out into the Ohio, turning sideways to reveal its entire profile. Craig finally noticed the enormous sternwheel. It began to revolve, churning the river into a foaming white surge. A massive column of ink-black smoke roiled from the stack.

Two men helped load the barrels into his farm wagon. "Damn, but they are heavy!" one complained. Craig feared they might break his floorboards. Fortunately the oak planks were thick. He hefted the trunk and slid it in behind the barrels. Delacroix climbed onto the seat and Craig joined him to take up the lines. The big tan horses leaned into the slope, their metal-shod hooves popping on the cobblestones. Just as they pulled onto River Street the black smoke drifted in, shrouding the landing, and almost obscuring the view. Craig turned his nose up at the smell.

"What is that steamboat burning?"

"Coal. We stopped few miles downstream to purchase a huge deckload. Apparently western Kentucky is sitting on a huge coal-field. The coal does smell, but it burns hotter than wood and it lasts longer."

Craig recalled smelling burning coal when he worked in Pittsburgh; it didn't stink like rotten eggs as this did. He reckoned there would be some changes in the Ohio River Valley—not all of them pleasant. But someone might make money digging the mineral out of the ground and piling it on riverbanks to sell to passing steamboats.

The black cloud dissipated. Craig wheeled down River Street past the finer homes and across the timber bridge spanning Cottonwood Creek. They skirted around Cemetery Knob, the town's elevated graveyard. Distant trees shimmered and danced in the heatwaves and perpetual smoky haze no longer attributable to *Enterprise*.

"So what brings you to Cottonwood Bend?" Craig asked.

"I have come to visit my daughter and grandchildren," Delacroix replied. "If you have not noticed, I am not getting any younger."

"You look exactly as you did last year." Craig recalled the merchant helping to organize the defense of New Orleans, opening his blacksmith shop to skilled gunsmiths, busily ferrying troops and arms to Line Jackson.

"Perhaps, but it has been four years since I last saw Lucinde. And I have never seen the grandchildren. At my age I cannot afford to wait."

"I understand."

"Is she well?"

"She is."

"And the family."

"Everyone is fine."

"I give thanks to the Almighty Father for that blessing. Pray, tell me about the cold weather. Folks—especially the New England ship captains—carry frightful stories of hard frosts, frozen crops, ruined orchards, and emaciated livestock."

"It *has* been bad. I learned today that we here in this part of Kentucky are lucky. The last heavy frosts fell in June. We have enjoyed almost a month of fairer weather even though it has been colder and drier than usual."

Delacroix told of frosts in Virginia and the Carolinas, freezing rains and summer snows in New York and Pennsylvania—something Craig had not heard. Craig imagined that the merchant, living in an international port and speaking directly to folks from affected areas, had much better access to distant news.

They exchanged a few more pleasantries, discussing the upcoming Presidential election, the Tariff, and new steamboats on western waters. Soon they reached the long drive to Owen's and Lucinde's plantation. To mark the entrance, Owen had constructed an ornate pair of curving red brick portals. On each wall a stone plaque read: *McDonnell—1812.*

"Ah! They have apparently done well!" Delacroix beamed.

"You might say so," Craig nodded as he turned his team into the drive. "Martin McDonnell purchased this plantation from the slave owner Colonel Franklin Stoner. He then gave it to Owen as a wedding present."

They clipped along the smoothed track that cut between waving wheat and towering hemp—crops that thrived splendidly despite the dismally cold spring. Presently the great white house, with its elegant columns, green shutters, and front porch, hove into view. Surrounded by a white picket fence and shaded by large oaks and maples, it was situated on a gentle rise. Lucinde's lovely flower gardens were in full bloom, adding splashes of color to the lawn. Craig enjoyed the plantation's orderly air, well-appointed vegetable gardens, grape arbors, established orchards, stone silos, barns and neatly arranged outbuildings. The original slave shacks now housed hired farm hands; others served as spinning and weaving sheds, a blacksmith shop, tool shed, mill, and tanning shed.

When they pulled up between the sheds they noticed Owen

standing near the drive, talking with some of his farm hands. He noticed Delacroix and grinned. The workers drifted back to work when Craig pulled up. Delacroix hopped off with the light spring of a much younger man. He embraced Owen warmly.

"I did not know you were coming!" Owen laughed. "Lucinde will be so pleased."

"I departed New Orleans in some haste, "Delacroix explained. "The steamboat *Enterprise* was leaving, and I did not have much time. I have brought you both some extremely valuable gifts." He indicated the barrels. "They weigh a great deal. You and Craig must immediately secure them inside your house. Do you have a strong room?"

"I suppose you could call it that," Owen nodded, his blue eyes flickered with interest.

As soon as they rolled out the first barrel, Craig knew it contained a fortune in gold and silver. Nothing else could weigh that much, and there was no sloshing of internal liquids. It took a great deal of strength to wrestle the barrel just short of the front porch. The commotion brought Lucinde to the door.

"Father!" she cried, bursting outside with abandon.

"Oh, my dearest daughter! You have grown even more beautiful! I feared I would never see you again!"

Father and daughter embraced, weeping with unrestrained joy. Craig always imagined his sister-in-law as quiet and reserved; now she displayed a whole new facet of her personality.

"You look well, Father!"

"Bah! I am an old man and I know it."

"Oh, what a lovely surprise! It must have been a long arduous journey."

"Actually, no. I enjoyed a luxurious twenty-two day cruise aboard the steamboat *Enterprise*, passing through some remarkable countryside. I slept in a private stateroom, ate three good meals a day, drank all the coffee I could drink and was offered a wide assortment of liquors. It really was quite pleasant."

"I do hope you will stay a while."

"As long as you will have me. No doubt you will soon grow tired, caring for an elderly parent."

"Never!"

"Now, where are those grandchildren?"

"Follow me," she beckoned.

Between them Craig and Owen wrangled each barrel off the wagon and up to the porch. It required a great deal of strength to accomplish the task. In an effort to redistribute the weight, Owen fetched some strong wooden buckets into which they unloaded gold bars and coin. They carried these into a back study. The lightened barrels could then be rolled onto the porch without danger of breaking boards. Lucinde laid down heavy rugs on which they positioned the barrels, sliding them easily across polished floors to a back room.

"Thanks, Craig." Owen shook his hand. "We will handle it from here."

"Glad to help. Fortunately I was at Rosenbotham's when Delacroix stepped onto the landing."

"He is here because of trouble."

"I thought he seemed a bit nervous."

"We'll know more this evening. Would you stop in and tell Pa he is here?"

"Of course."

Welcome Hall—July 5, 1816

The arrival of Father Stephen Theodore Badin always created a stir in Breckinridge County. His international background, classical education, and tireless work ethic made him the subject for much interest. Born in Orléans, France, he had fled the French Revolution and arrived in America in 1792. The Catholic Church had assigned him to the wilderness of Kentucky, a cross which he took up willingly. The priest proved unflagging in his efforts to serve the spiritual needs of a parish bigger than some European countries. Despite poor roads and great distances, he always showed up to minister to those in need. Folks claimed he spent most of his life in the saddle, while tales of his physical strength abounded. The priest was constantly organizing congregations and overseeing the actual building of new churches throughout Kentucky. When he came to Breckinridge County, he always stopped in first to inspect St. Rumoldus in Hardinsburg. There he would say Mass, tend to those in need and begin circulating throughout the county. When he moved on to Cottonwood Bend, he invariably stayed at the home of Martin McDonnell. The doors of Welcome Hall were always open to him and the hospitality was legendary.

Martin lodged the priest in one of the big downstairs corner bedrooms, coolest in summer with its high ceilings and floor-to-ceiling windows. Agnes busied herself preparing big breakfasts, keeping cold drinks at hand and making sure the sheets on his bed were clean and crisp. Badin planned to stay an entire week, perhaps more, so the family prepared a massive celebration in his honor. Soon, Pierre Delacroix began showing up at Welcome Hall. He would borrow one of Owen's horses and spend whole afternoons under the shade trees talking with Father Badin and his longtime friend, Martin.

One morning the priest appeared at Craig's barn. Craig had just finished the milking and was surprised to see him. The priest wasted no time getting to the point.

"Young Ridgeway, I heard about Mary's miscarriage. I am so sorry."

"Thank you, Father."

"Would you like me to say a few words with you two?"

"I know it will mean much to Mary," Craig replied. "Let me carry this milk to the springhouse."

When Father Badin entered the cabin Craig noticed the look of joy and peace on Mary's face. If he had known the impact the priest's presence would have, he would have ridden all the way to Bardstown to find him. After they joined hands and prayed, Badin asked Mary to lead them to the place where their stillborn children reposed. Craig carried Ruth, and Mary led Isabel across the pasture to the grove. They had outlined the little grave with stones and fenced it with black locust logs so the cattle would not trod upon it.

"We must be mindful that God's ways are not our ways," the priest began. "He alone holds the complete view of our universe—and *nothing* happens without His express knowledge. There was a reason He chose to bring your children home to live with Him. Perhaps the illness would have left them crippled or mentally impaired. It is possible their deaths occurred so Mary could live. We will never know. What we do know is that God is merciful; God is just. Those children are innocents and they will live with Him in Paradise. Jesus said, 'Suffer the little children that they might come unto me.' So we know without doubt they are with Him."

Craig hoped this was true. He noticed how Mary hung on every word—and realized that he should as well.

"And know this," Badin continued. "He will never burden us with a load so heavy we cannot bear it. At times He will test us. When He does, we should thank Him, for He is refining us as the metalsmith refines purest gold. Always remember, God's refining bowl is the crucible of adversity."

Craig silently admitted he would rather skip the "refining" part of life. It was much too painful.

Father Badin sprinkled some holy water on the gravesite, said a closing prayer and turned to leave. On the way back, the priest sidled up to Craig and spoke softly, "You are a fortunate young man, Ridgeway. Your wife is absolutely beautiful and your children are like young olive trees gracing the table of your life. Look at this pasture with the green grass and the animals that graze upon it. Your crops and fruit trees have survived where others' have not. Your cabin and barn are solid and commodious. Remember to thank God for all of this."

"I will, Father," Craig answered. He suspected then that Martin had spoken to the priest about other things. There would surely be more discussion in the days to come.

Most meals at Welcome Hall took place in the kitchen with its large utilitarian fireplace and cupboards, shelves and cutting tables, and proximity to the back door facing the cookhouse. On extremely rare occasions Agnes McDonnell opened up the formal dining room. This room was usually closed off, reserved for visiting dignitaries and special events. Mary claimed that she had spent far more time polishing the floors, furniture, and silverware than she had dining in it. With its gleaming dark wood floor, pastel blue painted walls, and decorative plaster cornices festooned with leaf designs, Craig decided it was even more elegant than the parlor. The double windows were adorned with damask-patterned drapes made of cotton cloth, and each brass chandelier held twelve of the finest beeswax candles. Tall brass urns flanked the fireplace; a polished mirror hung above the ornamental mantel. Mirrored sconces and paintings adorned the walls at symmetrical intervals. The furniture was fashioned from the richest dark cherry wood—a long polished table that could seat sixteen guests, matching chairs, a massive sideboard with mirror, a china cupboard and serving table.

Father Badin and Pierre Delacroix would occupy the guest seats of honor at each end of the table. Martin invited Judge Wilfred Bozarth and Violet, Hiram Rosenbotham and Lillian, Doc Emmick and his wife, Owen and Lucinde, Craig and Mary. Martin, Agnes, and Stephen rounded out the party. Not counting the children, that made fifteen seats. The young mothers planned to take turns feeding and watching their children in the kitchen.

Preparations had begun the previous day. Martin slaughtered a year-old calf and, after hanging it overnight in the ice house, he began slow-roasting the beef over a hickory wood fire. Craig took several spells at the spit, turning it and making sure the beef was constantly basted in Agnes' marinade, a recipe which she guarded like gold. As a child, Mary had helped her in the kitchen and she knew it contained apple cider vinegar, brown sugar, salt, black and red pepper, chopped onion and garlic, butter, and plum wine. But she admitted that Agnes might add a few more secret ingredients. Craig drizzled it on with a cloth mop, careful not to waste any. The weather had turned sharply cooler so he did not mind working near the big fire.

Martin brought jugs of various wines and a jug of brewed tea down to the ice house for chilling. Stephen fetched a couple dozen potatoes from the root cellar, some of which Agnes would steep in pickled peppers. Mary and Lucinde helped prepare delicious vegetable dishes to grace the table.

Late Saturday afternoon the guests began arriving. The womenfolk brought pies and cakes, and fresh vegetables from their gardens. Miraculously, Doc Emmick had grown a little sweet corn, the first and only ears Craig had seen that year. He anticipated gnawing on the boiled kernels, salted and drizzled with melted butter. Violet Bozarth looked elegant in her dark green dress and matching jewelry, while the Judge strutted about in his coat and tails, glancing periodically at his image in Agnes' parlor mirror. He had filed to run once again in the upcoming elections for the Kentucky State House of Representatives. Craig wondered how the Judge stood the slightest chance of winning, given the fact that everyone knew of his infidelity and shady business dealings.

Stephen took his turn at the spit to allow Craig enough time for milking his cows and to wash and dress up for the occasion. After bathing in the spring below the well, Craig donned his best clothes and hurried back. When he returned, Mary, Agnes and Lucinde had removed their aprons for the evening. Mary took him upstairs, straightened his tie and smoothed out his cream-colored shirt. "There you are!" she spun him around to face the mirror.

"I regret I do not have a suitcoat to wear," he lamented.

"It does not matter, Craig," Mary said, "These are friends and family. Besides, you are the handsomest man here!"

The long table and sideboard was covered with prepared dishes. Father Badin offered up a magnificent blessing and the women of Welcome Hall served food from platters and bowls. Events like this were exceedingly rare and everyone savored the opportunity to enjoy good food and good company. Summer thus far had been bleak with its cold spells, crop failures, influenza, and deaths. Everyone present understood life's uncertainties; no one knew if they would all be together again. Delacroix broke custom and spent half his time in the kitchen amusing the children and teaching them a few French phrases. From time to time they broke into French songs and their happy laughter rang throughout the house.

Agnes was pleased to learn of the new churches and religious orders being established across Kentucky—and she was thrilled to serve as hostess to the priest, a great man who hailed from another country, one who knew bishops, archbishops, and cardinals.

"These hot potatoes are absolutely delightful, Mrs. McDonnell!" Father Badin complimented her. "I can see you have used yellow peppers as the second ingredient, but there is obviously more to the recipe. You must share it with me."

"Why yes, Father!" Agnes blushed.

"And Martin, this beef is delightful. The marinade surpasses anything I have tasted. I am certain Bishop Flaget would be pleased to know its ingredients."

"Then he surely shall," Martin laughed, slicing another cut of the choicest tenderloin.

Conversation was unrestrained and joyful. Violet Bozarth wore an expression of complete satisfaction. This was her life, to hang on the arm of her important husband, despite his many faults, to dine and fraternize with the uppermost citizens of Cottonwood Bend. Craig wondered what she thought of the priest and the esteemed guest from Louisiana, given her Baptist predilection to cast scorn upon other denominations—especially Catholics. He reckoned that wealth and social standing trumped religion for now—at least while she was not ensconced in her usual Sunday pew.

The wind kicked up outside, indicating that another dreaded cold air mass was swooping down upon them. This new phenomenon, occurring in the dead middle of summer, contradicted everything in nature. Craig hoped it would not bring the frosts ushered in by the last cold spell. His crops were thriving and there was no time for another planting.

After dessert, Martin and Owen built a fire in the parlor. The men moved in there for after-dinner liquors and more conversation. Father Badin shared stories of farmers to the east and north who suffered from nature's onslaught.

"It is God's test," he declared. "We do not know why, but we must accept it and work within His parameters, keeping to His commandments, praying for His Divine Mercy."

"Yes, yes," the Judge commiserated. "When I am elected I must look into establishing some form of protection for those who have suffered."

Craig stifled a chuckle. The Judge never failed to take a conversation and turn it upon his latest venture, be it financial or political.

"That is a noble concept," Badin nodded. "If only our politicians would look beyond enriching themselves. Government should exist only to serve its people."

Folks talked long into the night. The children fell asleep in their parents' and grandparents' laps. Fortunately Judge Bozarth remained relatively quiet, asking pertinent questions and actually listening to various opinions without trying to one-up everyone. Craig noticed how he paid close attention to the conversations, perhaps to gauge the political and business climate in Kentucky and beyond. No one could ever accuse him of being stupid.

Delacroix talked of Louisiana—cotton, sugar cane and slavery, changing laws and new dangers. He recounted the tale of young Philippe Bouchard and the plot that had enslaved and condemned him to the plantations of Brazil.

"We have several folks working to make things right. Inevitably I must return to assist them and to see Philippe properly restored and safe from further persecution. "I have sold all my plantations, but have retained my warehouses, exchange and shipping enterprise. After I have advised Philippe, I may sell everything to him and come back to live out my life here."

"I do not wish you to go back, Father!" Lucinde hugged his neck. "You have painted such a dangerous picture."

"We will talk of that later. I am sorry I mentioned it. For now let us enjoy the time God has given us. Isn't that right, Father Badin?"

Chapter Fifteen

Sainte-Pierre, Martinique—July 12, 1816

Arabelle breezed smoothly along in the lee of Martinique, protected from the massive rollers that swept across the Atlantic crashed upon the eastern coast. Here the sea was calm and as clear as gin. White sand beaches rimmed the drier southern shores and, where the Caribbean lapped into scalloped inlets and bays, the water blazed bright turquoise, reflecting sunlight and changing shades with each gentle wave. Farther north, past Diamond Rock, Pointe d'Arlet and Cul-de-Sac Royal, the terrain grew mountainous and beaches ranged in color from dusky gray to darkest black, the result of ash spewed from Montagne Pelée, the great volcano that dominated all other geographic features on the island. Rain fell more abundantly on the steep mountain slopes, watering verdant tropical forests that seemed ready to tumble into the indigo sea.

"We're almost there," Doc observed. "Tomorrow we will visit the priest and have a look at your pedigree."

Philippe stiffened with irritation. "You may as well know, Doctor, I am not concerned that my great grandmother was a slave. If she was, I will wear that knowledge as a badge of honor."

"Go ahead and broadcast *that* when you return to New Orleans and see what good it does you. In case you have forgotten—the court ruling still stands. Signet could have you abducted and shipped back to Brazil in a heartbeat. You had best start praying your great-grandmother was European."

Philippe turned to the rail and watched the mountains slide past in majestic emerald promenade. Graceful palms and flowering trees beckoned from their slopes. Here and there a farmer had cleared a patch of land and, in the open fields, sugarcane grew in great green blocks. Near these fields stood conical stone windmills and sugar refineries. Small fishing villages clustered around most of the bays. The houses appeared primitive, constructed of palm logs, bamboo and palm thatch, nestled among sea grapes, banana plants, and croton hedges.

Captain West broke the relative silence, shouting a command from the foredeck. "Helm to port! Steer clear of those boats!"

The deck canted slightly as *Arabelle* sheered out to sea to avoid the local fishing fleet, presenting Doc with his first full view of Montagne Pelée. The French word *pelée* meant 'peeled' or 'bald,' and Doc considered this name appropriate. The volcano did appear bald, perhaps from previous eruptions that destroyed trees and vegetation near its top. Montagne Pelée loomed ominously behind Sainte-Pierre, rising almost a mile high into the cumulus-filled sky.

"Big ass mountain!" Emmett Barnett observed. "One day it blow this island all to hell!" The little man balanced on his crutch and new wooden leg. The prosthesis differed from the plain peg legs that instantly drew attention. As promised, Willoughby had fashioned a base to hold Emmett's boot in place; then he secured the boot top to the cup with leather thongs that functioned much like garter straps. When Emmett's trouser leg covered the whole, he looked normal in all respects. Of course his gait was awkward, but he could walk. Doc could hear him pacing the deck at night—*step-thump, step-thump*.

"You are getting around pretty well, my friend," Doc remarked. "You'll have the hang of it soon enough."

"I have now."

"What about your new tavern? Did you leave it in someone's care?"

"Locked up. I go New Orleans. Get rest of money, then go back Bahia."

"I implore you once again—do not attempt to seek revenge upon Jules Signet. He is much too powerful. Even if you succeed, which

I doubt, the American justice system will prosecute you for murder. Signet has the law squarely on his side, but we have several legal weapons with which to fight him. And we have strong allies—Judge Harkness, Pierre Delacroix, and other notable figures."

Emmett made no comment. He just puffed on his cigar and swayed with the ship's movement, looking almost elegant in his new clothing, his long, drooping moustaches fluttering in the wind.

"Do you understand me? Let us handle this in the right way."

"Sure!" Emmett grinned cheerily and blew a measured stream of blue smoke downwind before flicking his cigar butt into the sea. Raoul and Louis guffawed at the reply. Doc searched for the faintest trace of sincerity and found none in that glittering black eye.

Philippe watched the exchange with interest. "Why not unleash him, Doctor? Would it not serve everyone involved?"

"I shall ignore that request, young man, and pray that your friend and sponsor never hears of it. Pierre Delacroix believes we can fight fairly, within the strictures of the law. You, above everyone else on this earth, should know that he is an honorable man. He has more scruples than all of us put together."

The young merchant considered the men surrounding him. "That is not saying much."

"He would be vehemently opposed to murdering Signet. I know that."

"You are right, of course."

Late that afternoon, Captain West laid *Arabelle* on its final tack toward the port of Sainte-Pierre. The sun set before they reefed sails and dropped the bow anchor in the calm waters just offshore.

"Sound bottom, Captain," a sailor called.

"Very well," West replied. "Let her come around, drop stern anchor, and post guards."

"Aye, aye, sir."

"Why not go ashore this evening?" Philippe asked.

"I doubt we would accomplish much tonight," Doc replied.

"We will send the first boat ashore tomorrow morning," West stated with finality.

They dined on deck that night, enjoying the soft, refreshing breeze and admiring the city lights. From somewhere on shore, violin music carried across the water, complementing their supper of grilled fish and fresh St. Lucia-grown vegetables seasoned with spices from the Grenadines. West broke out a flagon of his finest claret.

"Finest city in the Windwards," he commented.

"I have heard that," Doc replied. "I believe it is called '*Petit Paris des Antilles*', 'Little Paris of the Caribbean'."

"It is without doubt the commercial, cultural and social center of Martinique. The island's wealth lies in its plantations. Distillers in Sainte-Pierre manufacture some of the world's finest liquors. Rum, sugar, coffee and cocoa have made the planters very rich. The town's upper quarters resemble old France—cobbled lanes of houses with wrought-iron balconies, sculpted botanical gardens and parks, a theatre, and some splendid cafes and restaurants."

"Didn't Napoleon's wife come from Martinique?"

"That was his first wife, Joséphine de Beauharnais. He divorced her to marry Marie Louise of Austria. By all accounts Joséphine was barren; the younger Marie could give him children."

"Terrible thing, divorce," Doc remarked.

"It is, isn't it?" Philippe interjected, his sardonic grin showing clearly in the lantern light. "My wife divorced me because of your vicious lies. That hurt more deeply than everything else."

An awkward silence fell over the table. Doc had not forgotten the role he had played in ruining Philippe, but—perhaps mistakenly—he ranked enslavement, imprisonment, and financial ruin more important than the marriage. This reality struck him like a runaway horse. He fought back an overwhelming surge of guilt, then reasoned—he could only take one step at a time. He had freed the young man and was taking the next step toward restoring his finances and social position.

"I truly am sorry, Philippe. I wronged you, but I am doing all in my power to make amends." Silently he admitted that he might never repair the young man's marriage.

"I loved her."

"Of course you did. Would *you* have abandoned *her* if you found out she carried negro blood?"

"Certainly not," he replied without hesitation.

"Are you quite sure of that?"

"Without a doubt. I loved her completely."

"I believe you. You may try asking yourself this question—although it may be painful—did she love you equally? Did she wait around to find out if the allegations were true?"

"She was horribly misled."

"Yes she was. But she made the conscious choice to leave. At the first sign of trouble she appealed for annulment and fled the country. She did not stand by you in your time of need."

"I have considered that," Philippe admitted.

Captain West and the sailors, clearly embarrassed, talked quietly among themselves, forming a roughly-separate group. The meal was well underway and they would not leave it.

Doc continued, "During the inquest it was clear she and her father were concerned far more with social position than your welfare. It shamed me to see you so abandoned. That is partly why I am here."

Fortunately the conversation shifted to the recent Napoleonic Wars and the vast, far-reaching changes brought about by the Congress of Vienna. Martinique had been recently returned to France as a result of the Congress. Of course plummeting sugar prices, national tariffs, and the future of the slave trade entered into the discussion. All were impacted by the role victorious Great Britain had assumed upon the world's financial stage. Here, Philippe contributed his vast knowledge and experience. Doc watched and listened with increasing respect. The young man had so much to offer. Perhaps the ordeal had not broken him, but had instead, tempered—made him a better person. Sometimes folks must reach rock bottom to know the value of all things.

Sainte-Pierre resembled Paris in many ways, its old world features blending beautifully with the tropical landscape. The port occupied a magnificent setting—overlooking the stunningly blue Caribbean with a backdrop of verdant mountains behind it. Tiered rows of multicolored warehouses and shops fronted the harbor where Doc and Philippe landed. Philippe hailed a carriage and directed the driver to take them to the *Eglise du Mouillage*—the church that might hold the answer to his lineage. The ride took them down cobblestone streets lined with tamarind and chestnut trees, sculpted fountains, magnificent buildings, and a small scale reproduction of the famous theatre in Bordeaux, France.

The city had miraculously rebuilt in the thirty-six years since the "Great Hurricane of 1780," possibly the deadliest storm in recorded history. Then, an entire fleet of French warships had capsized in high winds, killing four thousand soldiers and sailors. English warships in the area suffered as well. In fact, more English soldiers died in that storm than in all battles of the American Revolution. The hurricane produced a twenty-five-foot storm surge that destroyed most houses in Sainte-Pierre; in all, nine thousand people died on Martinique, perhaps twenty-seven thousand throughout the Caribbean. No evidence of the hurricane remained, except that the houses all had a new, fresh-painted look, adding to the vista their pastel colors of peach, jade, rose, aqua, cream, lavender and ochre. Now the home of many banks, churches, consulates and industries, Sainte-Pierre was once again a major city in the Caribbean.

"Well, young man. Are you prepared for what you might find?" Doc inquired.

"I am," Philippe replied. "No court in America will uphold Judge Harkness' decision."

Doc shook his head. Perhaps Delacroix could talk some sense into him. "Just remember that Signet works outside of the law and he somehow manages to blur the distinction between legal and illegal."

They halted outside the lovely church, first built by the Dominicans in 1654. Destroyed by an English naval bombardment in 1667, it had been reconstructed in the neoclassical style in 1675 and had survived wars, volcanic eruptions, British occupation, and hurricanes. Now it nestled among dense foliage on well-manicured grounds, its square bell towers and arched windows reminiscent of the Romanesque churches of medieval days.

Doc paid the driver and sent him on his way. He explained, "We might be here for some time."

Together he and Philippe entered the sanctuary's open-arched doorway, stepping around the place where a native woman mopped the tile floors. Philippe dipped his fingers in the font, crossed himself, and paused to look around. After the tropical sun's brilliance it took some time to adjust to the darkness. Doc noticed the white marble high altar, communion rail, and religious images. A few older folks knelt in prayer.

"You might as well take time to pray," Doc suggested, lowering his voice to a whisper. "You need all the help you can get!"

"Yes," Philippe hissed. "And so do you. I will pray for your sorry soul." He turned into a pew on the right side of the aisle and knelt in silence.

Doc sat across from him on the left hand side; his knees hurt too badly to kneel. In the silence he contemplated their next course of action. Whatever they discovered here in Martinique, favorable or unfavorable, they must return to New Orleans. Judge Harkness had promised to vacate his ruling but that might jeopardize everyone involved. Signet held considerable sway over city and parish lawmakers, the militia patrol, and many prominent businessmen. With his resources he could secretly hire professional killers to deal with his enemies. A series of cold, calculated assassinations could easily be made to look like 'Kaintock violence.' Perhaps Emmett could mobilize a secret army of outlaws, pirates, and other unsavory cohorts to counterbalance such a threat, but the little smuggler was greatly diminished by injury and fire.

Certainly Pierre Delacroix was laying the groundwork for their return. Hopefully he was mobilizing his associates to form an alliance. Perhaps he had engaged lawyers from an Atlantic coastal town or enlisted the aid of sympathetic figures in Louisiana's state legislature. But Signet also had friends in the legislature. Delacroix had mentioned this in his letter to Philippe. An unpleasant thought crept into his mind—the merchant's life was in danger. His death could easily be made to seem a natural occurrence. What if Delacroix was already dead? He pushed the thought from his mind.

"No sense in borrowing trouble," he muttered. So engrossed was he in his thoughts he did not realize he had spoken it aloud. An old couple turned from their prayers and regarded him with annoyance. He touched the brim of his hat in apology. Quickly, he swept it from his head and set it beside him in the pew, closing his eyes and assuming an attitude of prayer.

It was almost midday when the priest arrived. He wore the traditional black robe with white collar. Philippe rose immediately and proceeded to intercept him. They shook hands and conversed quietly. The priest appeared attentive. Doc overheard a few phrases spoken in French, but their voices were too low and rate-of-speech too fast to follow. Finally, Philippe turned to beckon him. Doc rose and made his way down the aisle.

"Let us step into the vestibule," the priest suggested, gesturing to a side room. He ushered them in and closed the door behind them. Doc noted his graying temples and somewhat portly build, guessing him at about forty years of age. He extended his hand.

"Father, I am Doctor Thomas Applegate from New Orleans."

"And I am Father Gérard Gaston, the priest of this parish." His English, although heavily French-accented, was good.

Doc smiled. "Then you are the man we have traveled so far to see."

"According to young Philippe, I am."

"I must know who my great-grandmother was," Philippe interjected with a note of desperation. "More specifically, I must know if she was of African descent—if she was a slave, or not. I need to see her birth and marriage records."

"The woman in question was named Philomène Bouchard. Am I correct?"

"Yes!" Doc and Philippe fairly exploded, taking the priest somewhat aback. It took a few moments for everyone to recover.

"Some time ago a lawyer from New Orleans came to me requesting the same records. I did not help him, for I felt something was gravely amiss. Call it a 'sixth sense', but I sensed true evil in his heart."

"But this is different!" Philippe insisted. "Philomène Bouchard was my great-grandmother."

"Yes, and she was supposedly the man's great aunt—at least that is what he claimed. I asked for some form of verification and he laid a leather purse of coins on the table. At that point I suspected malevolence and proceeded to prevaricate. I stalled long enough, feigning ignorance until he left."

"We already know that," Doc interjected.

"We do?" Philippe asked.

"Correction—I do."

The priest regarded their exchange guardedly, but with intense interest. "I did not tell an outright lie; I told him the exact and literal truth, that all official Sainte-Pierre birth, marriage and death records, along with deeds, bills of sales, and other legal documents, were destroyed by the San Calixto Hurricane of 1780."

"And were they?" Philippe pressed.

"You must understand, the storm surge reached twenty-five feet or more in height. It carried away the biggest part of the town. Whole warehouses and their contents were swept out to sea."

Philippe's countenance fell. "Then there are no records? None at all?"

"He didn't say that," Doc pointed out. "Why would he prevaricate, stall, and feign ignorance, if there were not records?"

Philippe regarded him with the smallest flicker of respect.

"I think you should tell me your story," the priest demanded sternly. "Leave nothing out. If you lie to me, I shall know it."

Philippe began recounting his version of the inquest. As his story progressed, he spouted angrily about the judge's ruling, his imprisonment aboard the *Lisette*, and his arrival in Salvador da Bahia. Doc confessed his prior drunkenness and financial condition, his role in setting up the inquest, his calculated manipulation of Judge Harkness, and 'scientific' courtroom testimony. Father Gaston listened in stunned disbelief, glancing over at Philippe and then back at him. Doc continued, sharing his feelings of guilt and his flirtation with the idea of suicide. He then described in detail his confession to the judge, Father Valentin Poitier, and Philippe's mentor, Pierre Delacroix.

"I cannot believe you have the nerve to sit in the same room with the man you wronged. It defies belief."

"It took some doing," Doc sighed. "Because of me he lost his beautiful wife, his wealth, his position in New Orleans society and God only knows what else. That is why I am here—I had to face Philippe, to apologize and devote my life to restoring him to his rightful place."

"And you, my son," Father Gaston shook his head. "You must be commended for your restraint. Most men would have sought the ultimate revenge."

"Believe me Father, I wanted to kill him. Sometimes I still do."

"And what has stopped you from doing so?"

"This." Philippe fumbled in his coat pocket for Delacroix's letter. He handed it over with shaking hand. Doc watched the priest read it and saw that it affected him. After a few moments Father Gaston returned the letter.

"Have you any other proof of greater value? I am afraid I must have more. How do I know this performance is not an act? We have a fine theater nearby employing some of the most gifted actors in the world. At times they can be extremely convincing. How do I know this is not some stratagem to gain my trust?"

Philippe's head drooped; his misery was complete. He had nothing but words to prove he was Philippe Bouchard, merchant from New Orleans. He realized he must sail to New Orleans to fetch the documents.

At that moment Doc saved the day. Philippe watched, amazed, as the old reprobate produced a court order from the Honorable Judge John Harkness, emblazoned with his seal, letters of introduction from Pierre Delacroix and lastly, Father Valentin Poitier's lengthy chronicle of the whole situation. In this final document the New Orleans priest couched phrases known only to his friend, recounting shared experiences at *Séminaire de Sainte-Sulpice* in Montreal.

"This last letter is incontrovertible proof—but to be honest, I believed your story, for no one on this earth could concoct such a tale. It bears witness to the saying that 'truth is stranger than fiction.' I doubt I will ever hear a confession as—ah— 'remarkable' as yours."

Doc cut in, "That is all well and good, Father. Can you please tell us where we may find the documents?"

"What you seek is not here. It is as I stated—all official records in Sainte-Pierre were destroyed in the hurricane."

"But you said—"Philippe blurted.

"Philomène arrived here with her husband *after* they were married. He was born in Sainte-Pierre; she was not."

"Where *was* she born?" Doc asked.

"In a small town near Bordeaux, in southwestern France."

"France!" Doc and Philippe exclaimed.

"Yes, but she was married in Fort Royal, right here on this island."

"Then she *was* a white woman!" Doc glowed.

"Presumably so. You will find copies of her birth and marriage records safely lodged in her home church."

"Will you write a letter of introduction to the priest in Fort Royal?"

Breckinridge County, Kentucky—August 5, 1816

After a month of near average warmth, crops were growing reasonably well in the Ohio River Valley. Although cool snaps and dry weather had stunted much of Craig's corn, at least it was tasseling and making ears. The tobacco stood shorter than usual with much smaller stalks, but the height was uniform and leaves appeared near average in size. With his much-reduced labor force, Craig began topping plants, beginning work in the early dawn when dew lay heavy upon the plants. 'Topping' involved snapping off the bunch of compact, flowering leaves that formed at the plant's top. Topping kept tobacco plants from wasting precious energy on developing flowers and seeds, inducing them to produce larger leaves. Later in the day, when the sun's warmth heated stalks and made tops less brittle, Craig and Romulus switched from using bare hands to short-bladed knives, taking off the tops with a single cut.

A few days later, the plants developed 'suckers'—shoots that emerged where the big leaves joined the stem. It was imperative that these suckers be removed. If allowed to grow, they would sap strength from the main leaves, resulting in smaller yields, and smaller profits. Throughout its growth, tobacco suffered attacks from numerous insects. Of all the pests in the fields, farmers most feared the green tobacco worm. These fearsome-looking creatures could grow up to four inches long. A plague of worms could destroy a crop in less than a week; this knowledge forced Craig to daily inspect his tobacco plants. If he found worm damage, he must comb the plants and find the worms, pick them off and crush them underfoot. All this was light work, but it required good eyes and many hands. Fortunately Martin's field workers joined in to help clean the fields. Maggie and Diogenes worked in the cool mornings as did Mary and Vergina. The mothers spread blankets under shade trees at the field's edge and allowed the children to play. Leta and Isabel could be somewhat trusted to keep an eye out for their younger siblings, but at least one mother always kept them in eyesight. At other times, Agnes watched the young ones at Welcome Hall. In this manner the families readied their tobacco for harvest.

During this time the nightmares renewed their insidious assault upon Craig's unconscious. He truly believed they had retreated and would in time fade away. Perhaps they would always skulk at the fringes of his consciousness, waiting like wolves to attack. One night they crept in and overwhelmed him with hideous images of bleeding, dead, and rotting corpses, and each successive night the dreams became more real. Mary, ever sensitive to Craig's moods and sincerely convinced he wished to fight the affliction, sent for Father Badin. This time she would not let Craig fall back into the destructive pitfall of guilt and terror.

Fortunately the priest was back in Cottonwood Bend, staying with the McDonnells after almost a month of travel, but preparing for his journey back to Bardstown. Father Badin had dealt with this affliction before, and he intended to end it once and for all. He borrowed one of Martin's mounts and rode up Hardinsburg Road to confront Craig in his home. Mary met him outside the dogtrot and took charge of his horse, tying it to a hitching rail.

"Where is your husband?" Father Badin glowered.

"In the barn," Mary replied. "Please understand, Father. He has suffered greatly."

"It ends today," the priest snapped. The look on his face terrified her. It seemed he intended to fight with all the legions of hell. Without uttering another word, he strode toward the barn.

Mary's covered her mouth, lest she say more, praying silently that she had not brought the proverbial cliff down upon all their heads. She retreated inside to pray further, searching for the right words, asking God for his mercy and intervention, pleading with Him to make everything right again. While she knelt, a horse and buggy clattered past the house. By the time she reached the cabin door, the buggy was halfway to the barn. She recognized Levi Matthews, and another, younger man unknown to her. At first she thought of running them down and asking them to hold back, but she withdrew, choosing to let the chips fall where they would.

Craig was sharpening tobacco knives and hemp hooks when Father Badin's shadow fell across the door.

"Father!" he exclaimed.

The priest wasted no time in offering pleasantries; he had come to do battle. He stepped in close, his face just inches from Craig's. "Your wife tells me you have fallen prey to Satan's ploys, that you have allowed him to ensnare you with his weapons of guilt and shame."

Craig took one look at him and cast his eyes downward. "I do not mean to, Father Badin. It happens mostly when I am asleep."

"That is because you have not let go of your guilt in your waking moments."

"I am trying."

"That is not good enough!" he growled. "You will end this cycle of self-destruction today, do you hear me?"

"I hear you, Father."

"You are to stop this wallowing in self-pity and get on with your life, Craig Ridgeway."

"It is not self-pity," Craig protested.

The priest's open right hand came from almost nowhere, exploding against Craig's temple and jaw, causing him to see stars. It was completely unexpected.

"Do not argue with me, young man! You have been given a great many gifts—a healthy, muscular body, a lovely wife and family, a prosperous farm and business, friends and position in the community. God has kept you alive for a purpose, not to cringe in shame, whimpering from nightmares. It turns my stomach to see you wallow in such a state when I see others dying from disease, living alone in hunger and poverty. People died in that war; others lost their entire fortunes and you lie in the darkness crying because God chose you to live. You will stop this now, do you hear?"

"Yes."

"You *will* stop it!" The priest's left hand wheeled upwards, slapping his jaw, stinging with unbelievable pain, knocking his head sideways. Then the right hand caught him with a thunderous roundhouse clap, and before he could react, Craig found himself being pummeled severely about the head. He stepped back to avoid the flurry of blows and tripped over a big spool of hemp twine. The priest loomed menacingly over him.

"God gave you the gift of life, the other gifts I mentioned, and all those I did not name. He is all-powerful and has already forgiven you for the deaths you inflicted. You will *not* deny His omnipotence and you will not allow Satan to spoil the gifts God intended you to have!"

Craig did not know what to say. He felt safer lying on the ground, but prepared to roll in case Father Badin decided to kick him. Fortunately, the priest's fury abated somewhat.

"Do you acknowledge God's omnipotence, young man?"

"I do, Father."

"Then you accept His absolute power to forgive completely?"

"Yes, Father."

"Do you appreciate the wonderful family and worldly gifts He has given?"

"Very much, Father."

"Then lift yourself up, man!" Father Badin extended his hand. Craig took it apprehensively, allowing the priest to draw him to his feet. "I have commanded you before, young Ridgeway—get on with living. God has other plans for you."

"Thank you, Father."

"Try praying several times during the day, not only at bedtime. And instead of reflecting upon what was wrong in your past life, thank Him for the wonderful things He has given you in *this* life, and ask Him to guide you in the future. Focus your thoughts upon glorifying Him, not upon past sins He wishes you to bury."

"I understand, Father." Craig replied with some conviction. The priest had argued with sound logic based in scripture, although he might have spoken rather than beating on his head.

"When you exercise your thoughts accordingly during the day, you will sleep in peace at night. Are we in agreement?"

"Yes, Father."

"Then good day, young Ridgeway. I must now visit people who are in much greater need."

The priest left the barn, pausing briefly to tip his hat at Levi Matthews and another man with him. They stood respectfully, just outside the door. Craig dusted himself off and steeled himself to look at Levi. The little miller struggled not to laugh; no doubt he would blab this story all over the settlement, to country folks who visited his mill, and especially to members of his church congregation. Given his propensity to embroider in the tellings and multiple retellings, the incident would sound much worse than it actually was.

Levi cast a wary glance over his shoulder to make sure the priest was out of hearing.

"Damn!" he chuckled. "Remind me not to cross *that* one!"

"We were having a conversation," Craig muttered, hoping he had not witnessed the worst of it.

"I saw that conversation," Levi guffawed. "He slapped the literal shit out of you! Remind me not to call for him when I am in need."

"He actually made a good point," Craig recovered his wits enough to defend the priest.

"And you caught the sharp end of it! Now, whenever you want to hear some *real* preaching, our doors are always open—and our preacher won't beat the hell out of you!"

Craig noticed the man with Levi. He hung back, clearly embarrassed by what had transpired. Craig guessed him at about thirty-five years of age, perhaps a few years younger than the miller, judging by his curly brown hair and slender build. "Who did you bring with you this time?"

"Craig, meet Kelwyn Lasher. He was frozen clean out of Vermont and decided to move west to seek his fortune."

"Pleased to meet you," Craig shook his hand. "What is your trade?"

Kelwyn replied, "I am a farmer. But it has become impossible to grow anything in New England. Last autumn early frosts ruined all my crops. I left there in mid-spring and have been moving west and south ever since, searching for lands beyond the reach of summer frosts. This area is about the best I have seen in my travels."

"Well, just so you know, we have suffered our own share of bad weather—frost in June, cold snaps and a patchy light frost in July. Everything is late, and the dry, cold weather has stunted our crops.

We fear early frosts as well."

"You obviously haven't seen the devastation east and north of here."

"He's living in his wagon next to the stable in Cottonwood Bend," Levi volunteered. "I told him you might be interested in having him occupy and farm the Smithhart farm, especially since you lost most of your labor force. Kelwyn has a wife and two growing boys who can work."

Craig fingered his jaw, still smarting from the blows Father Badin had rained upon him. It was an entertaining thought, but his inclination toward close-fistedness gave him pause. He addressed the farmer, "I will need a day to consult with my father-in-law. I am not sure how much I can pay. You may find a better deal with someone else, perhaps farther downriver."

"We can't keep traveling for much longer. Besides, my wife has declared we will settle here. I am willing to work for rent and fair wages. I don't have much money, but I would like to farm on thirds next spring."

"I can hire him this winter when we cut timber," Levi offered. "He claims he is something of a carpenter—I might also employ him on a few odd jobs."

"Well, the place *is* vacant and harvest time is almost upon us. Do you have equipment?"

"I have a team and a good plow. Also a milk cow. "

"How about a harrow?"

"Sold it."

"What else do you have?"

"All the standard farm tools—cradle scythe, corn and hay knives, hoes, rakes, pitchfork, axes, maul, wedges, saws, pruning knives..."

"He's got some good carpentry tools," Levi added. It was plain the little miller saw promise in the man.

"You do realize we could suffer more bad weather?" Craig asked.

"Nothing could be as bad as New England," Kelwyn shook his head. "Farmers have sold and even killed their livestock because they cannot feed them. Orchards are frozen, most crops destroyed."

Craig nodded. "Would you mind walking back toward the cabin? I need to speak with Levi."

"Not at all." He turned and strode back toward the cabin.

Levi advised, "You'd better take him on, before you lose him to someone else. He's a good man. I have seen his family."

"How old are his boys?"

"Thirteen and eleven. His wife is little-bitty mouse of a thing. Peel back all them layers of clothing—I'll hazard you won't find much underneath."

"You are a crude man, but I have told you that many times before."

"She may be little, but let me tell you she reigns supreme in that family. She's got him firmly by the short hairs. Jim Fallin overheard her bitching at him in Rosenbotham's store. Lillian Rosenbotham claims she runs everything on a tight schedule, even while they search for a place to live and work—up at dawn, regular meals, early to bed. Keeps everything in that wagon as neat as a pin."

"Tell him I will talk it over with Mary and then we'll discuss it with Martin."

"Don't dither too long. You might just lose him. My guess is you won't keep him much more than a year, two at the outside. They'll have their own place by then. I say he'll turn you a profit and improve your land. Have I ever steered you wrong?"

Craig admitted he had fared well taking Levi's advice. "You almost have me convinced. Why not take him up to the Smithhart farm and show him around? See if he likes it."

"I already have."

"That's damned presumptive of you."

"Trust me—you won't be sorry. The wife is something of a harpy, and she keeps a tight leash on him, but that might be a good thing."

"Thanks for riding out here. Wish you had come at a different time."

Levi sniggered. "That was the best entertainment I have had all year!" Taking another look at Craig's face, he winced theatrically.

"Gee! You should have Mary lay something cold on that left eye. It's closing shut!"

———————◆●◀———————

Kelwyn Lasher and his family moved into the Smithhart cabin with little fuss. Craig and Mary spent a full day helping them, bringing over a wagonload of firewood, another of kindling, a half load of ear corn for their stock, some fresh-baked goods, a young rooster, six laying hens, and a few other amenities. The family had brought nearly everything else they needed from Vermont, all neatly stowed in the covered wagon that had served as their home during the past months. The heavy wagon cover gleamed snowy white and the wheels appeared oiled and well-cared for. Kelwyn's wife, Prudence, had stowed everything neatly and compactly within, and she made no bones about where she wanted things placed. Craig detected a calculating gleam in her eye as she surveyed the empty cabin, judging where to position their furniture.

"Let us sweep the dust and cobwebs from this place," she ordered. Like a whirlwind she and the boys attacked the corners, eaves, and rafters, sweeping down the walls, hearth and floors. Mary joined in with her broom. Levi had struck the mark when he branded Prudence as the family sovereign. She did not yell or speak in obscenities, but she ruled with a glance, a look of disapproval, and an occasional curt command. It was mid-afternoon when she decreed they could move in their belongings. Craig and Kelwyn began with the heaviest items, working under her stern eye and a barrage of instructions.

"No, put it over there. Have a care with that crate! Let us pick up the pace—it is almost suppertime," she snapped with a businesslike authority that not even Kelwyn dared challenge.

Levi, in his unvarnished manner, had been accurate in his physical description. Prudence was indeed a little thing, dark-haired, dark-eyed, with perhaps a bit of Spanish or Portuguese in her blood.

She appeared several years older than Kelwyn, but her movements were brisk and purposeful, belying a great amount of nervous energy. She wore a heavy coat that blurred any inkling of shape, a broad kerchief tied over her head, round metal spectacles, and heavy, no-nonsense boots. The boys, freshly scrubbed and cleanly dressed, scampered about, silently doing her bidding, carefully handling the breakable items. Fortunately, she took an instant liking to Mary and, on occasion, even broke into a smile.

After they finished unloading, Craig showed Kelwyn the farm—the spring from which he could draw clean water, the best places for a fall garden plot, and where he could cut timber for firewood. Levi and his crew had recently logged, so there was a good supply of downed timber tops for cutting. Finally, they surveyed the barns, sheds, and stone silo.

"I will need the silo when the corn harvest comes in," Craig informed him. "And please do not cut down hickories, walnuts, chestnuts, persimmons, and any wild fruit trees—any tree that bears food. We will share in their bounty. Do you know how to recognize them?"

"I do," Kelwyn replied. "This really is remarkable land."

"Is it so different from Vermont?"

"Oh yes. New England is known for its thin, rocky soil. Most of it has been exhausted by repeated farming. It is becoming harder each year to eke out a living in those hills. There is no new land available and too many immigrants for the land to support. Out here everything is so vast and open—the topsoil is rich and it runs deep."

"You will find rocks here too," Craig pointed out. "And farms do decline with use. My father-in-law Martin McDonnell has followed the European practice of crop rotation and he seems to have found success. What else do you like about Kentucky?"

"There is an abundance of wildlife—ours is about gone."

"Do you have a gun?"

"I do not. Prudence fears them."

"Was it really so bad in New England?"

"It was a frozen wasteland when I left. We suffered terribly in the years before that—the trade embargo and War with Great Britain, repeated bad harvests, frosts, drought, forest fires—it was altogether too much to bear. Many people died of repeated epidemics, usually from fever, coughing, and pneumonia. It was the final straw, at least for Prudence."

"I hate to disillusion you, but we suffered the same epidemics. During that time Mary miscarried of our twin sons."

"I am sorry to hear it."

"What happened then?" Craig asked.

"I finally sold the farm. Do not ask me the price; I am thoroughly ashamed to admit how little money we received."

"Maybe you should have held on."

"I wanted to. I have family there, but Prudence insisted. She had read about Kentucky, the generous terms for sale of public lands, and the cheap and easy credit. In the end she is usually right, so I agreed."

Craig nodded and kept silent. The man had confided an awful lot, but he did not seem bitter or in the least disconcerted. They walked back to the house to find the boys stoking up a fire in the hearth. The mantel gleamed with oil, and two throw rugs gave the place an air of orderliness. Mary and Prudence worked at the table, altering a set of curtains with scissors, needle and thread.

"I am pleased you are back, Kelwyn," Prudence announced. "You must now assemble the beds. I shall call you when supper is ready."

"Is there anything else you need?" Craig asked.

"I think not, Mister Ridgeway," she replied brusquely. Mary took this as her cue and rose to leave.

"Call me 'Craig', please."

"We will soon have everything in order," Prudence assured him.

"I do not doubt it."

"When do we begin work?" Kelwyn asked.

"I will let you know. Get your family settled in first. Have you ever worked in tobacco?"

"No."

"Hemp?"

"We do not grow it in Vermont."

"Then you are in for a real delight."

———◆———

Pierre Delacroix planned to depart for New Orleans on August 8th. He sensed he was needed in New Orleans; the unfinished business with Philippe called him back. Two days earlier, a near-empty keelboat pulled in to Cottonwood Bend and the merchant booked passage on it. Earlier Craig had negotiated the sale of his prime four-year old whiskey; Delacroix had paid him handsomely in gold coin. On Delacroix's orders, the keelboat poled upstream to Mary's Landing where Craig, Romulus, and the new hand, Kelwyn, rolled barrels of whiskey aboard. When they finished loading, the keelboat sat much lower in the water. The crew floated back down to Cottonwood Bend to make ready for the direct voyage to New Orleans.

On the night before Delacroix's departure, the McDonnells held a farewell dinner. It soon turned into an emotional affair. Lucinde wept openly, convinced she would never again see her beloved father.

"Nonsense, my dear," Delacroix comforted. "I may be old, but I still enjoy robust health. As soon as Philippe is restored, I shall conclude my business, sell out to him, and return here to live out my days, puttering away under the shade trees. Surely in that knowledge you can bear my leave. In fact, I am certain you will appreciate the brief respite."

"That is unfair, Father—and you know it!"

"Rest assured, I will miss you and the grandchildren. It has been a splendid visit; it exceeded all my expectations, and I am overjoyed you have found true happiness."

"I do so fear for your safety, Father."

"Then you have little faith in the warrior who fought in and survived three terrible wars. I would loathe to think you regard me a weakling, unable to defend myself."

"It is not that!" Lucinde protested.

"I know, my dearest heart." Delacroix embraced her. "Please promise me this—you will never, never return to New Orleans. No matter what correspondence you may receive, stay away. There are evil forces there, powerful men who would seek to lure you into their grasp. They covet my enterprises and they see you as the key to great wealth. As long as you stay here, you will remain safe. Do you promise?"

"Yes, Father."

"Very well. Let us make merry this night, for I truly rejoice in your good fortune, knowing you have become part of a family that loves you."

Bayou Barataria

In all his years in New Orleans, Doc had never ventured into the bayou country. He knew it by reputation—a dangerous, lawless place teeming with pirates, smugglers, outlaws, and displaced Indian tribes. The word 'bayou', now embedded in the English language, originated from the Choctaw 'bayuk', which meant 'small stream'. There were hundreds of these bayous forming an intricate maze in a vast swamp from which some people never returned.

Arabelle's boat crept over a black, stagnant surface beneath which lurked all manners of dangers—alligators, poisonous cottonmouths, and God alone knew what else. Turtles, frogs, snakes, blue herons, snowy white egrets, and large woodpeckers watched with interest as the boat moved between ill-defined shores and claw-footed cypress trees draped heavily in gray-green Spanish moss. The heat and humidity surpassed anything Doc had experienced. His pores gushed great droplets of sweat and not one breeze stirred to cool him. Instead, the air clung like a hot, damp blanket; breathing it required considerable effort. Although the straw hat shielded his neck from the sun, it provided little protection from the myriad flies, gnats and mosquitoes. In the bow, Philippe and Kayla appeared equally miserable. Kayla kept the baby loosely covered to protect it, wiping him down occasionally with a cloth dipped in water. Emmett and his half-brothers drank dark rum and smoked foul-smelling cigars, unaffected by the stickiness and insects. Two sailors worked the oarlocks, taking it easy in the afternoon heat.

"Look!" Emmett barked, reaching for his shotgun. "Damned big gator." The black reptile lay immobile on a dead log, sunning itself.

"Don't shoot!" Doc ordered. "You will announce our presence!"

"No one care out here."

"Out here? You said we were close—that we would reach New Orleans tonight!"

"I lied."

"We are *not* staying in this swamp tonight."

"It grow dark soon. I send Louis and Raoul into New Orleans to scout—find out what happen while we gone."

Doc cursed under his breath, but appreciated the sensibility of waiting. They should not alert Signet and Morel before meeting with Delacroix and Judge Harkness to set up a hearing. Then, it might be wise to alert some of Delacroix's closest associates and have them present in the courtroom. Doc would add to that guest list Philippe's former father-in-law Gustave d'Alembert. It would be entertaining to watch his reaction. The judge could subpoena him to appear, also some journalists from the *Louisiana Gazette*. When Philippe's lineage became public knowledge, it would be near impossible for Signet to refute. The takeover would be thwarted, legally. If public condemnation ran too strongly, the banker might just pull up stakes and leave New Orleans altogether. But Doc figured Signet would consider resorting to the next recourse—violence. Hopefully Delacroix and Judge Harkness had prepared the groundwork for their safe return and had alerted the authorities about the banker's growing power.

Gradually, the sun dipped behind the treetops and the channel ahead darkened. From time to time a fish rose to snap at an insect, a bullfrog plopped into the water, or a snake cut a wriggling path across the surface. Emmett barked a command and gestured for the sailors to pull to shore. Doc tried unsuccessfully to distinguish land from water as the boat edged through a layer of bright green algae. Up ahead he spied a blue column of wood smoke, then a ramshackle jetty, its posts cock-eyed and planking askew, weathered gray from age and damp. Someone had secured a long pirogue to the post nearest the bank. Behind the jetty, on slightly higher ground, stood a small, moss-covered shack. It also stood askance, looking like it might topple into the bayou. In front of the shack three men worked at skinning an alligator, carefully removing the rough hide which would later be sold for leather. The dead reptile hung from a crude tripod and it required two men to handle the work. One man was slicing meat from the reptile's tail and threading large fillets onto green wood skewers. He jammed these skewers into the ground to roast the meat over the fire.

"Lord have mercy!" Doc muttered. "Pirates!"

Emmett hallooed and the three men started, reaching instinctively for their guns. One of them recognized Emmett and shouted a greeting. "Just in time for supper!" The pirate walked out to the jetty's edge, leaning to one side to compensate for the slant. The other pirates returned to skinning the alligator.

"Damned hungry!" Emmett declared.

"We heard you were dead!"

"Like hell!"

Philippe tossed the rope and the man caught it, expertly drawing them in, then looping and tying the rope around the piling. Philippe lifted Kayla and her baby onto the jetty and lithely joined her. Raoul and Louis stepped forward carefully, and between them the half-brothers helped Emmett onto the jetty. Raoul handed Emmett his crutch and the little tavern owner clunked briskly up the uneven planks. Doc rose shakily and eased forward, allowing *Arabelle's* sailors to assist him out of the rocking boat. He clung tightly to his medical bag, painfully conscious of his coins within, but also those belonging to Pierre Delacroix and, as additional insurance, a second, notarized copy of Philomène Bouchard's birth record. He prayed the pirates would not try to rob or injure him and the members in his party. For now, no one asked questions; no one challenged or threatened them. Apparently, traveling with Emmett made them acceptable. Doc knew that most of these pirates kept their own secrets, close with words like most of their kind. They displayed some furtive interest in Kayla, but she clutched her infant and stayed close to Philippe.

"Where you been, if not dead?" the pirate cook asked Emmett.

"Brazil. Bring Bouchard and Doc back."

"Doc?"

"He save my life." Emmett patted his stump.

The man shrugged and returned to the fire, adjusting the skewers to turn the roasting alligator meat. He produced some coarse salt from one pouch and rubbed it into the sizzling chunks. From another pouch he crumbled red pepper and dried herbs onto the meat. Doc caught the aroma and was suddenly ravenous. He found a roughly suitable seat atop a fallen cypress log and jammed the black leather bag between his legs. Unbuckling the straps, he peered inside to ensure that his pistols rested on top, then turned his attention to the pirates.

They were a rough lot, lean and sun-blackened, unkempt and hardened by rugged conditions in the bayous. These men made their living by illegal smuggling and robbery on the high seas, circumventing American customs and providing tax-free goods for some of New Orleans' wealthiest businessmen. They were almost certainly associated with the notorious Jean Lafitte and his brother Pierre. Cutthroats, thieves, blockade runners, and murderers, these pirates had helped General Jackson defeat the British at the Battle of Chalmette Plantation; some had manned cannons and carronades. In reward for their contribution, Governor Charles Cole Claiborne had granted the pirates full pardons, but most of them continued their criminal activities.

Doc glanced around fearfully, wondering if there were more pirates out there in the growing darkness. Certainly there were. The byzantine labyrinth of bayous served as home and hideout for pirates and smugglers like these men, many who had left the Acadia region of Canada to escape British rule shortly after the French War ended in 1763. Some folks in New Orleans referred to these French refugees as *cajuns,* a shortened version of the word 'Acadians." In just a few years these people had developed their own language, amalgamating words from the various cultures in southern Louisiana. The two men skinning the alligator spoke in a French-Spanish-English-African-Choctaw patois that almost defied understanding.

"You not like the bayou?" Emmett chuckled. He sat on the log next to Doc.

"Can't say I do," Doc grumbled.

"It the perfect hideout. Signet not find us here."

"You may be right."

"Louis and Raoul go into town tonight. Ask questions."

"I agree with that."

"If safe, friends hide us."

"You trust them not to tell Signet?" asked Doc.

"They know I kill."

"You really are one nasty character. I am glad to have you on my side!"

Philippe stood opposite them, listening to the exchange, occasionally slapping at the mosquitos. "When will we have the hearing?"

"That is entirely up to Judge Harkness and Pierre Delacroix. I believe we should make it a public affair, so Signet could never challenge you again. But those gentlemen may have other ideas. We will seek their counsel."

"Meat's ready!" grunted the pirate cook. Everyone helped themselves to a stick. Doc's fillet bubbled and sizzled. He picked off the clinging flecks of soft wood ash and bit in. Flavored with salt and spices, it tasted as good as anything he had eaten. The tail steak was the choicest cut, mild-flavored white meat with a texture similar to veal, lean and high in protein.

"Not bad!" he commented.

Philippe helped himself to another steak; it seemed there was plenty to go around. The pirates passed around a jug of dark rum. Emmett guzzled until his eyeball bulged; then he handed it to Doc who passed it on, choosing to wait for the coffee. The pirate tending the pot boasted that it was the finest variety, grown in Jamaica. At first it seemed strange these pirates would have such luxuries as coffee, spices, liquors, granulated sugar, and even porcelain cups, but then it stood to reason they had access to a lot of things—they simply stole what they wanted.

"No rum, Doctor?" Philippe asked.

"It was the drink that caused me to behave so atrociously. I will need clear wits for what lies ahead."

"Strange, but over these past weeks I have grown to see you do care. I never thought I would feel that way." Slowly, very slowly, he was revising his opinion of the man who had so condemned him.

"Don't get too sentimental. I know I am a monster."

"Well, this experience has changed my life. I see a lot of things differently— especially slavery." He indicated Kayla who had bared a breast to suckle the baby. Her skin glowed like dark honey in the firelight. Doc noticed again how much the chubby, hairy little infant resembled Judge Harkness.

"I do want her freed," Philippe insisted.

"She will be. Judge Harkness and Delacroix will see to that. And the judge will ensure that she and her son are provided for."

"At what price?"

"None to her. He regrets his actions and intends to atone for them."

"I will believe that." Philippe's sarcasm was evident.

"You will see I am right."

The moon rose bright and full, reflecting off white cumulus clouds and transforming the bayou into a highway of quicksilver. Ghostly strands of Spanish moss glowed in the moonlight, adding an eerie beauty to the scene. Emmett stumped down to the jetty and conferred briefly with Raoul and Louis. Doc could not make out all the words, but he caught the authority and intensity in the little man's voice. The two half-brothers boarded the pirogue, cast off the line, and began paddling northeast in the direction of New Orleans. Doc half wished he could go with them, but it would be late when they reached the city and he had no place to stay. No doubt Signet had ordered surveillance on Judge Harkness' house. It would not do to show up there unannounced. Doc also decided he did not relish climbing back into the boat and traveling in near darkness with men who owed him no real allegiance. Better to keep near his protector.

Another commotion occurred down at the end of the jetty—*Arabelle's* sailors were casting off. This concerned him directly. He left the firelight and strode down to where they were.

"Are you sure you gentlemen won't wait until morning?" Doc was far more concerned with his own safety than theirs. Both men were armed with pistols and cutlasses and would help balance out the pirates in the event of a possible conflict.

"We're not staying another moment in this swamp," one of them answered. "If the bugs don't get us, the pirates will."

"You might run into other pirates."

"We'll take that chance."

"Can you find your way back?"

"We'll keep a southerly course. In the end we'll come out into the bay." That was where *Arabelle* was anchored, waiting for the sailors' return. From there Captain West would sail back into the Gulf, then up the Mississippi to New Orleans. Doc watched them go and felt a sense of isolation wash over him. The sailors were his only real link to civilization. He must now rely solely upon Emmett's protection.

The bayou, ghostly silent for most of the afternoon, now resounded with noise, frightfully alive in the darkness. The tree frogs were deafening, their shrill screams underscored by the boom and croak of tens of thousands of bullfrogs. An occasional alligator thrashed about; nothing else could make that much noise or displace that much water. Night birds yammered, owls hooted, and a panther or bobcat yowled in the distance. Doc returned to the fire, grateful for its smoky glow. He drank coffee sweetened with brown sugar and listened to the pirates talking with Emmett. Although they were almost impossible to understand, Doc grasped enough of the conversation to know they were discussing a captured ship laden with Jamaica rum, French cognac, coffee and molasses. Emmett agreed to buy the cargo and arrange for its transport through the bayous to his surviving warehouses. He would then sell to local merchants; some were the wealthiest and most-respected folks in New Orleans. Doc listened to him bargain, fascinated with his command of facts and numbers, impressed by his knowledge of business. The little gnome had a sound head on his shoulders. Apparently he was not as financially diminished as Doc imagined.

Glancing around the clearing, Doc noticed Philippe and Kayla were missing. "Where is the boy?"

"They bed down for night."

"In that shack?"

"It not so bad. You get some sleep. We be in New Orleans tomorrow night."

Doc plucked a burning stick from the fire to use as a torch. He investigated the interior of the little shack. Emmett was right; the interior was much nicer inside—two rooms outfitted with beds and cotton-stuffed mattresses, mosquito netting draped over the windows and a storeroom jammed with various crates and barrels. Philippe and Kayla slept in the same bed; Doc imagined this was for safety rather than for passion's sake. He took the bed next to theirs, patting it down for bugs and the very likely snake. Although the sheets smelled of human sweat and needed washing, the bed was comfortable. Doc tossed the torch outside and groped his way in darkness back to the bed. Using his medical bag as a rough pillow, he fell asleep, too exhausted to worry about pirates and other dangers.

Breckinridge County, Kentucky

August remained dry and cool with a constant breeze blowing in from the northwest. Despite the late start and fluky summer weather; the oat and wheat crops fared surprisingly well. Golden-brown stalks rippled lightly in the wind, strikingly beautiful against the tall, dark green forest of hemp. Martin had earlier predicted they would not be disappointed; these crops were hardier and withstood cold weather much better than others. Daily the old man walked the fields, checking to see when the fields were ready. He squeezed a grain between thumb and forefinger to see if it oozed a milky substance, then he chewed another to test for the same effect.

Craig followed him in his own field and asked, "You have such knowledge. How did you learn all of this?"

"My father taught me. He was an Irish Catholic farmer who became an indentured servant in Maryland. I learned some from the Indians and other farmers. I also learned from books. I still do."

"Is the wheat ready?"

"Not yet, but as soon as the grains pass the 'milk stage' we can begin harvesting. They might need to dry up and harden a bit before they're ready, but it is always best to harvest on the early side."

"Why is that?"

"If you wait too long, the heads will become too dry and more likely to shatter when cutting. Much of the grain will fall onto the ground."

This year, Craig's oats ripened first and workers from four farms converged upon his fields, a veritable army carrying their long-handled cradle scythes, wooden rakes and drinking gourds coated in beeswax. Owen led off on the east end of the oat field, cutting a broad swath with his scythe. Stephen followed with long-practiced strokes. Craig let him get ahead and then followed at a safe distance, swinging his scythe in smooth arcs, clipping the stalks close to the ground, careful to not touch dirt. The wooden tines, or 'fingers', of the cradle caught the falling stalks, enabling him to lay them in neat rows for easy gathering. Other workers positioned themselves strategically in the field, keeping well apart as they joined the harvest. Martin and Owen had previously scoured the countryside for unused scythes and there were plenty available, for many farmers had given up on their fields. They were glad to rent the implements in exchange for foodstuffs. Soon the field was filled with the sounds of harvesters. Blades sang sweetly in the still summer air.

Craig remembered how clumsily he had first handled the cradle scythe. Five years ago Martin showed him how to use it efficiently. Now the oats fell to his blade, slipping evenly off the fingers to dry in rows in the sun. Later in the morning the women began raking and binding the stalks into sheaves. Craig turned to see how his new hand, Kelwyn fared. The slight New Englander was right there with his own sharply-honed and well-oiled implement, keeping up with the best of Martin's workers.

"Where are your sons?" Craig asked.

"Prudence will not allow them to work until they have finished their lessons," he replied with some embarrassment.

"Lessons, you say?" one of Martin's workers laughed derisively as he swung his scythe.

"Every morning, except on the Sabbath, she schools them in reading, writing, mathematics and religion. When they have mastered all lessons to her satisfaction, she will release them for work."

"Sounds more like prison to me," the man sniggered. "Don't she know this is harvest time?"

"She does not alter her schedule for anyone or any reason," Kelwyn replied matter-of-factly. "Do not worry; she has blocked out specific times each day for the boys to join us in the fields. You can count on them to be here. And they will work; I promise you that."

Craig kept silent, wondering what it would be like to live with someone so structured, so uncompromising. He could not imagine that anyone would fail to take full advantage of the narrow window of opportunity nature begrudged. The women working in the fields certainly appreciated the value of hard work during harvest time.

Around mid-morning Prudence arrived, carrying a wooden rake, bustling like a lively little hen, followed dutifully by her sons, Noah and Lemuel. She wore her coat, even in the midday sun, and had tied a woolen scarf around her bonnet, the edging of which extended well beyond her face. One would have to look at her square-on to observe her expression. Dressed in her bulky clothing she resembled the sketch of a little European peasant woman that Craig had once seen in a book. He doubted she would amount to much in the field.

Prudence straightway proved him wrong. She did not wait for instructions—she took one look and ordered the boys to join in with the womenfolk and children, to help gently rake fallen oats into bundles and tie those bundles into sheaves. Obviously experienced in this work, she fussed and clucked to them, cautioning them to handle the oats tenderly to prevent the loss of precious kernels. The boys worked as well as anyone, raking and tying the oats into neat, uniform bundles. Prudence fastidiously stacked the sheaves upright into small stands called 'shocks' or 'stooks.' Craig turned his attention back to cutting the standing oats.

Beside him and slightly behind Kelwyn, Romulus and Vergina swept their cradle scythes with efficiency. They seemed settled in their condition, at least for the present. Earlier in the summer, Romulus had mentioned that he might try for Upper Canada after the harvest. Craig promised to help, whatever decision he made, but both realized that the same fate of capture could befall them. Slave prices were rising higher in post-war America.

———•———

The nights remained unusually cool and dry. Although the sun tried its hardest to warm them, the air felt more like that of early October than mid-August. Martin and Owen had planted fewer acres of wheat and oats, so it did not take long for the combined workforce to harvest the grain on all farms. The upright shocks dried quickly for hauling to the barns and threshing floors. Threshing involved beating the grain heads to separate kernels from supporting straw and husks. First came the removal of long straw, later forked into barn lofts for use throughout the year. Grain was then sifted through a sieve or 'riddle', and tossed into the air from a holding tray or basket so the breeze could blow the lighter chaff and dust away. Cleaned grain was stored in bins or stone silos for farm consumption or for sale to the local miller.

The womenfolk and children proved well-suited for these tasks. Diogenes and Maggie contributed their skill; even Mary managed to help a few hours each day. With uncanny regularity Prudence and her sons arrived each mid-morning to contribute some of the best work on the floor. The little woman worked methodically and efficiently, tolerating no idleness, no wastage; and although her brusque manner and grim visage intimidated some of Martin's workers, she spoke no cross words.

Wheat commanded prices twice the market value of corn, making it an excellent cash crop in 1816. Prices were soaring due to crop failures all across the north and northeastern states, also in Upper and Lower Canada and especially in Europe. Levi Matthews was buying up all he could; shippers and merchants were paying top prices for milled flour. It appeared that France would soon admit American merchants into her lucrative flour trade because she could not supply her Caribbean colonies of Guadaloupe and Martinique.

Unfortunately the corn crop was severely diminished. Even Craig's new field, planted after the last heavy frost and able to withstand the spotty mild frosts of that summer, was stunted by dry weather and repeated cold spells. The ears had formed, but they were poor, measuring about half the size of those grown in previous years. Hopefully there would be enough corn for whiskey distilling.

Levi stopped by one crisp afternoon to comment on it all, catching up with Craig on Martin's farm. Rather than tie his horse and walk into the fields, he pulled under a big oak tree and waited, preferring to sit in his cushioned carriage seat and let the harvesters work their way back to him. The hemp season was in full swing; nearly two dozen men worked in dusty concert, first reaching around the closely-planted stalks, grown nearly twelve feet in height, cutting them off near the ground with curved, razor-sharp reaping hooks, and laying them in long, even rows with butt ends pointing the same direction. Block after block of the tall plants fell to the hooks which were drawn in a smooth slicing motion, rather than chopping. Yellow pollen from the male plants coated everyone. At the near end of the field, the workers halted for a water break, providing the miller his opportunity to approach. He climbed down from his carriage and strode up to Craig.

"Well, how is our friend from New England getting along?" he indicated Kelwyn.

"He's a fine field hand," Craig asserted, pausing to wipe the itchy pollen from his face. "He brings his own tools to the field and he has thrown himself into these new crops with vigor."

"Ah!" Levi exclaimed, addressing the newcomer. "You folks don't grow tobacco or hemp up there, do you?"

"Not that I know of," Kelwyn replied. "At least I didn't."

"I hope you are paying him a man's fair wages, you damned pinchpenny."

"Don't concern yourself," Craig snapped.

"I visited your cornfield today," Levi sniggered, shaking his head in a show of mock pity.

"Which one?"

"The one on Smithhart farm. Pretty puny ears I would say, but then I am no farmer."

"At least I have grown *some* corn. A lot of folks could not."

"That is why I am here. Can you spare a little time from your fields?"

"Not much." Craig added. "I might as well tell you now; I can't sell you any. I may not have enough corn for the livestock, let alone for whiskey-making."

"I saw that. But you do have plenty of hemp. The flatboat men are buying so much grain and milled flour, I am very nearly out of sacking. I don't have to tell you—Rosenbotham and I are making a killing."

"I thought you shipped the flour in barrels."

"Usually I do. But the slack coopers can't keep up with demand. Mary makes those strong feed sacks and I need them now. Tell her I will pay in corn, wheat, oats, or flour."

"I did not hear gold, silver, or copper in that litany."

"That too. I want fifty-pound sacks to bag the corn and wheat. The flour sacks will have to be close-woven."

"Tell her yourself. She's up at the threshing floor with the women and children. But she may not be available for a few days. As soon as we finish cutting and stacking the hemp we must start on the tobacco. The lower leaves are beginning to fire."

"Are you priming this year?"

"I am. I want to harvest all I can before the frost. These nights are getting cooler."

"This is the damnedest weather I have ever seen. One of the flatboat men said this year should be named '*Eighteen-hundred-and-froze-to-death!*'"

"I agree."

"You have a barn full of last year's raw hemp."

"Yes, and I intend to sell it."

"Sell it to me. You will make more than you will selling to the rivermen."

"I might, but it must first be spun and woven."

"Will Mary do it?"

"I know she will—after tobacco season. She has her own spinning wheel, you know."

"I built her that big one for making twine."

"She has another, smaller one; she also has a loom. I am sure we can bring up three more looms from Owen's and Martin's farms. Vergina and Maggie can weave. And I would bet my bottom dollar that Prudence can operate a loom."

Levi made a loud hawking noise in the back of his throat. "Can you imagine living with *that*? I heard she keeps school every morning, allots a set time for field work, and serves meals at the exact same time each day. She has probably scheduled a fixed time for Kelwyn and her to—"

"She is a good worker," Craig interrupted, not wanting to hear the rest of it.

"Well, I reckon I'll drive up and speak to Mary."

"You do that."

Craig returned to the hemp field and joined in the labor, falling quickly into a rhythm—gathering a bunch of standing hemp stalks, slicing through them with his hook, and laying the plants in neat rows—each step connected in a seemingly endless set of motions. Martin moved among the laborers, inspecting their work, offering suggestions and encouragement, and joining in to even up the workers who had fallen behind. As the sun descended, dying in a flaming, blood-orange death, the temperature did likewise. Stars were twinkling faintly through the haze when the field hands placed their hemp hooks in Martin's wagon and said their good evenings.

"Another cold one tonight!" the old man observed.

"You are right," Craig replied.

"I noticed your tobacco is near ready."

"The bottom leaves are already fired yellow. I might prime this year."

"Wise decision. I planned to suggest it to you. That way you can save what you pull. We could have frost any morning. A frost will burn your tobacco and ruin its quality. But if we get freezing temperatures, you can plow the field under, for your tobacco will be ruined."

"This is August—it can't be possible!"

"We have said that again and again. Last week, a man in Rosenbotham's Store called this the 'Year Without a Summer.'"

Craig thought that appellation as fitting as the one Levi had shared. Whatever people chose to call it, the year 1816 would certainly be remembered in the history books.

Chapter Sixteen

Breckinridge County, Kentucky

The tobacco plants stood about four feet high and, although shorter than usual, appeared ready to harvest. No other crop on Craig's farm required such intensive labor. He had worked hard all season, protecting seedlings from freezing and young plants from frost, chopping out the weeds that would choke them, topping flowers and suckering secondary growths. By sheer vigilance he had saved his crop from destruction by the big green tobacco worms. As an experienced grower, he could judge the leaves' maturity by their color, texture and pliancy, or lack thereof. If the leaf was yellow, thick, rough and downy, and if it broke when folded between his fingers, it was ready. In past years he harvested by splitting each stalk lengthwise with a short-bladed knife, stopping about one foot above the ground, cutting it off at the bottom, and then hanging six mature plants over a thin, four-sided stick. He then stood the tobacco into "wigwams" and left it for most of the afternoon to wilt. This resulted in a heavy, moist leaf which fetched a higher price at market. If the plants were harvested before fully mature, the leaf would bring far less. But, if the tobacco stood too long in the field, there was the risk of frost destroying the entire crop.

Frost was now Craig's biggest fear—that is why he planned to 'prime' his tobacco, rather than wait to cut the entire stalk. 'Priming' meant removing individual mature leaves from tobacco plants. Tobacco leaves naturally ripened first at the bottom, then toward the top. In warm weather a farmer could wait and allow the entire plant to ripen, but with frost threatening and upper leaves still green, Craig decided to pull the bottom leaves and work upward.

In mid-August he deployed his workers into the field to crop the dirty leaves at the base of the tobacco stalks. These were the trash or 'sand lugs'—so named because they grew closest to the ground and were splashed with sand and mud when heavy rains hit the soil. These leaves weighed the most, due to their large size and added weight of clinging soil, and were by far the most difficult to work with. The leaves oozed dark tobacco sap that dried into a dark gum to which the soil stuck. Prudence despised having her hands and exposed wrists coated with sticky gum and grainy soil. However, she did not complain and she moved through the field faster than most of the field hands. Craig realized again how fortunate he was to have the whole family working for him.

They tied the leaves into bunches and hung them onto sticks, then transferred the sticks into the barns. Craig, Romulus, and Vergina hung these in the tiers, regulating the bunches to dry evenly on the sticks.

"These sticks are a lot lighter without the stalks," Craig noted.

"They do it this way in ol' Virginie," Romulus said. "It take longer to harvest, but it help when strippin' time come."

"I imagine it does. We're doing it this way because the top leaves are not ready."

Four days later they revisited the field to pluck the next layer of brighter, cleaner leaves. These were ripened to a golden yellow and handled easier without the excessive gum and grime. Fortunately the weather had mellowed and the picked leaves wilted nicely in the midday sunlight.

Craig's luck turned bad the next morning. The dreaded blue-gray clouds rolled in shortly after dawn, dragging a mass of cold air with them. They would harvest no tobacco that day, for the leaves stood no chance of wilting. The wind roared steadily for the entire day. As Craig did the evening milking, he watched his breath fog in the cold damp air. Mary appeared unexpectedly in the barn carrying folded lengths of the light linen cloths they used in springtime to cover the tobacco plant beds.

"Craig, will you please help me cover the grapevines? It might frost tonight."

"I sure will!" he exclaimed, wondering why he had not thought of it.

They worked until just past sunset, spreading cloths over her grapevines. They also forked straw over the potato and pumpkin vines. He was glad they did, for next morning a light frost covered the lower fields. After the milking and wood splitting, Craig steeled himself to venture into the tobacco field. Martin was already there, inspecting the leaves. He combed through them and sadly shook his head.

"Is it ruined?" Craig asked.

"The frost singed it pretty badly, enough to severely depreciate the value."

"Is it all lost?" Craig could see the damage himself.

"You might find some that would pass inspection, but it would consume too much valuable time. You have saved a good portion of it by priming; be thankful for that. Plow it under and look to other endeavors."

Craig felt the rage boil up inside him. He had worked so hard that summer to produce a decent tobacco crop—and more than half was lost. "Well, I'll be damned!" he swore, kicking a shower of dirt into the air.

"Swearing won't help, Craig."

"I apologize, Martin."

"Many farmers have suffered much worse. Think of those who lost their entire fortunes to war. Some folks in Europe will never rebound. Trust me—you will see better years."

"I sure hope so. What galls me is that prices are so high—and we have so little to sell!"

"We fared well, selling our hogs this spring. And your whiskey turned an incredible profit. That is the beauty of that industry—you can manufacture and store the product. Whiskey improves with age and you can sell it when the time is right.

"What about our apples and pears?"

"That depends on how cold it gets. There is always a chance of frost during the apple and pear harvest. But fruit on the tree may survive several frosts with little damage. Whatever happens, we will make out. One thing is certain—our hemp crop fared well last year and again this year. That may be our salvation."

Craig knew then what he must do. It was time to get Mary and the women started on the feed sacks. He shared Levi's offer with Martin.

The old man grinned, his eyes sparkling. "That's the spirit! Levi has provided you with a splendid opportunity. He needs sacking; you need grain to continue your distilling. Wonder if he would allow my women workers to weave sacks? Agnes could show them how."

"I'll ask him. With her and Mary teaching them, I am sure they can meet his standards. We are going to need spinning wheels to make hemp thread and looms to weave it."

"Meet me at the house at dinnertime."

Mary was ready to begin. Last year's hemp was in the barn hanging in huge bundles, each weighing one-hundred fifty pounds or more, just waiting to be sold—or made into fifty-pound grain sacks for a quarrelsome little miller.

"Craig, why don't you walk over to the Lasher's cabin and ask Prudence if she would like to spin thread and make feed sacks?"

"I really do not relish asking her. She might just start ordering *me* about. Have you seen how she treats Kelwyn?"

"She really is a sweetheart, once you get to know her."

"Well, I must ask Vergina and Maggie if they would like to work. I guess a few hundred steps more won't matter."

The two women received the news with joy, for it gave them a chance to earn precious money. There would be work for Diogenes as well; he was best at separating and distributing bundles of the fiber to the hackling tables. He also knew how to comb, or "hackle" the fiber into long straight rows for tow making. This tow would then be spun into strong, durable thread that naturally resisted rot.

On his way to the Lasher cabin Craig ventured into the cornfield to check on the ears. The plants appeared dry and stiffened, almost as if it were late autumn. To inspect an ear he shucked back a husk with very little green left in it. The grains were pathetically small, with almost a shriveled appearance, already hardening. At least the crop would make good fodder.

The youngest boy, Lemuel, opened the door when he knocked. Prudence sat primly at a spinning wheel, quizzing Noah on long division problems. Guiltily, Craig realized he had interrupted her teaching,

"What may we do for you, Mr. Ridgeway?" Prudence asked in her business-like manner.

"Mary and I have contracted with Levi Matthews to manufacture grain sacks for his mill. He is faced with a dire shortage and needs them promptly. Fortunately I have plenty of unsold hemp fiber that will need to be scutched, hackled, spun into thread and then woven into cloth for fifty-pound grain sacks. Mary has the template for making them."

"What about your tobacco? Will we not be working in it today?"

"The frost has destroyed it."

Prudence shook her head, her expression bitter. "That is bad news. I am sorry to hear it."

"Well, the good news is, I need people to work last year's hemp fiber into sacks. You will have to move your wheel over to our place."

"Yes, it would be more practical. What about weaving?"

"We are bringing up looms from Martin McDonnell's place. Owen will lend us two more. It will involve disassembling and moving them to our cabin. But we may set up in the barn, possibly in the dogtrot, and most likely inside the cabin."

"I could have Kelwyn bring my loom," she pointed to a neat four-harness loom in the far corner. "It belonged to my grandmother. She brought it across the ocean from England."

Craig appreciated that it held sentimental value, and was surprised she offered it. "Thank you. Mary will see it comes to no harm."

"I prefer to work with my own loom. That way you can be assured of getting the best quality at the fastest speed."

"I understand," Craig nodded.

"When do we begin?'

"We are setting up today."

"Then I will instruct Kelwyn to disassemble the loom for easy transport."

"He might not need to do that. I can bring my big farm wagon over. We will use the oxen. They are slow and steady."

"Will you hire the boys? They can both spin and weave."

"Yes, by all means bring them. We have other work to do to prepare the hemp fibers for spinning."

Before long, Kelwyn arrived at the door. "Sorry, I missed you, Craig. I came to work and found nobody in the field. Mary told me your tobacco is ruined."

"Frost destroyed what remained outside. We will have to plow it under."

"We saw a lot of that in Vermont with other crops."

"Fortunately the leaves we harvested will be fine."

"Oh! That's good news at least."

"We are spinning and weaving hemp fiber today. Why don't you walk back with me to fetch the wagon and oxen? We'll use it to bring over the loom and spinning wheel."

"Sure," Kelwyn beamed.

"I am sorry, but that is not possible," Prudence contended, shaking her head. "The boys must recite their Bible passages, and I wish you to hear them. You may take care of the loom after that. Then we will all walk over there together."

Kelwyn deflated noticeably, but did not seem dispirited. Craig would later describe his reaction as "resigned."

———————◆———————

Diogenes had worked in hemp and flax for decades. His owner, Colonel Franklin Stoner, had taught him and Maggie the fundamentals of preparing the crop—plowing, hilling, planting, seed harvesting, cutting, shocking, scattering and retting, taking up and "breaking". This knowledge Diogenes had passed on to Martin and his sons. Craig had worked for three years with the crop and was still fascinated with the hemp brake upon which retted stalks passed through "jaws" that crunched the woody stems up and down their lengths. He and his workers would snatch up the broken plants and whip the fibers about so that most of the woody parts, called "hurds," shook free. This semi-cleaned hemp could be bundled, hung in the barns and sold to buyers traveling up and down the river.

But to have fibers suitable for spinning and weaving, it required additional cleaning, a process called "scutching." This meant scraping the fibers with a knife-shaped wooden blade to remove small bits of clinging hurds. When this was accomplished, the fibers would then be "hackled." Hackling involved passing hemp through a stationary table-mounted comb to clean and straighten the fibers, aligning them so they could be spun into continuous thread. This process also separated the long fibers from the shorter tow. These shorter fibers could easily be removed and combed.

Prudence overruled her own pronouncement and insisted on riding over in Craig's wagon to protect her loom and spinning wheel. Fortunately when Craig and Martin decided where these should be positioned, she did not argue.

Kelwyn looked around and exclaimed, "Prudence, you should feel at home! This place resembles a regular New England factory!"

By midday Craig's barn was full of wooden tables and various machines. Martin brought up two wooden tables to lay raw hemp upon for scutching. Craig dragged out his cookhouse trestle table and placed it with the others. These were situated close to the rails upon which hemp bundles hung. Owen delivered two looms and three hackling tables with their sharp, upended pins. Stephen hauled up Agnes' old two-harness loom and two spinning wheels. Some of Martin's hired hands brought their wives and implements for the enterprise.

Shortly after dinner, the first work began. Diogenes and Maggie instructed the field hands how to use the bladeboards to scrape away the hurds.

"You don't want to put much stress on them fibers—jest use the bladeboards soft-like," Maggie said.

Prudence and her boys quickly mastered this process and manned one of the tables. Soon they were scutching, their wooden knives rubbing softly against the planks. Three women from Martin's and Owen's farms worked at another table. Diogenes, Maggie, and two women worked at another.

In the midst of all this industry, Levi Matthews arrived, driving his heavy grain wagon, hauling a spinning wheel and loom. Craig and some of the workers helped him unload it.

The large workforce surprised him. "Here I came to chivvy you along and you've got the whole countryside working!"

"We want some of that gold coin you have amassed," Craig laughed.

"This is better than I hoped! It seems you have the whole process set up."

"We strive to please."

Stephen and Owen drove up with two wagonloads heaped with raw hemp from their farms. They halted just outside the barn where Craig, Romulus and Martin's field hands began unloading, draping big bundles over the bottom tobacco tiers and indoor stall fencing. Mary, Vergina, and Owen's women workers started hackling the first scutched hemp, drawing the fibers through the stationary combs.

Levi said, "I am impressed, truly I am, but I need those grain sacks now. That is why I am here."

"You may be in luck. I have three dozen or so empties inside the distillery. Mary has a big spool of twine for sale as well. As you can imagine it will cost you—in corn."

"You are a hard ass when it comes to a bargain."

"Dealing with you, I must be."

They soon worked out a "hemp for grain" deal that benefitted them both, and Craig led him to the distillery. Levi appeared pleased with his sacks. He held them up to the weak sunlight to examine them.

"These look just as good as the day you fetched them."

"They should. We keep them indoors and off the stone floor."

"And this twine—it is worth its weight in gold."

"I will bear that in mind."

"The flour sacks will require a closer weave."

"Mary knows that. She and her mother are experts and they will make sure the others understand."

"What about that Prudence?" the miller shuddered theatrically.

"She's probably the best worker here. You were right. She's sure got Kelwyn trained."

"He's used to it," Levi chuckled. "As long as she can deliver the grain sacks, I don't care how she treats him!"

———•——

In late August another frost encrusted the meadows, singeing the pumpkin and potato leaves, and ending any further development of corn crops. For all intents and purposes, summer was over. Martin assured them the pumpkins would survive. If there were no hard freezes, Mary's fall garden would produce greens, cabbages, onions, beets, potatoes, and turnips, but everything else would be sorely diminished. As the month melded into September, Craig kept his workers busy. It truly amazed him to have such an industrial endeavor taking place on his farm. Heaps of scutched and hackled hemp piled up behind the spinning wheels; Craig counted eight of those devices whirring at one time. Kelwyn took Prudence's place at the scutching table so she could work at spinning.

Lucinde and Agnes came up most days to help Mary cook meals for the workers, mind the children, and join in the spinning. Agnes showed the spinners how to draw out the fibers for producing finer and more uniform thread. Mary devised a flour sack pattern that incorporated an inner lining. The crude outer layer would also double as a corn or wheat sack, tightly woven and tough enough to withstand loading and unloading along the river.

Eight skilled spinners could not keep up with those who scutched and hackled. Piles of hemp grew faster than fibers could be spun into thread. Prudence rose imperiously from her wheel and installed Kelwyn behind it. The man uttered not one word, but set himself to spinning. Craig was impressed, for Kelwyn clearly knew how to spin, but Prudence clucked and interposed herself, showing him by demonstration and repetition until he spun exactly as she did. At least she exercised the good manners to ask Mary and Vergina to allow her boys to take their places at the wheels.

"Long ago, I taught them how to spin. They will be far more useful at the wheels," she insisted. "The spinners are overwhelmed as it is and we haven't begun weaving yet. It is time to weave." She indicated the big spools of tightly spun hemp thread. No one challenged her.

"Why yes!" Agnes beamed. "I believe you are right. Besides, I prefer to work on the loom!"

Craig fought back a prickle of irritation; as owner it should be his decision to assign the work force. But, like Kelwyn and everyone else, he kept silent—mainly because Prudence was so damned good at everything. Sharp-eyed, quick-handed and methodical, she wasted no time and always produced excellent work. Grudgingly, he admitted she was right about the work force. By shifting her family to the wheels and moving select spinners to the looms, a better balance existed.

Mary had already determined the total yardage needed, and the womenfolk dressed their looms accordingly. This was a time-consuming endeavor, but late that afternoon the barn, cookhouse, distillery, dogtrot and cabin resounded to the rhythmic noises of weaving—the thwacking of heavy battens, pumping of treadles, and the creaking up-and-down movements of the harnesses. Agnes recited her *Our Father*'s and *Hail Mary*'s as she wove cloth, setting her prayers to the rhythm of her work.

Sturdy, yet simple enough to be produced in bulk for sale to Levi Matthews, Hiram Rosenbotham, or any one of the passing flatboat merchants, this rough cloth would naturally repel moisture, insects, and mold. At first Craig had doubted the plant. Hemp was new to him, new to Martin, but it proved itself in many ways to be a wonder crop. Hardy beyond belief, the plants had withstood cold temperatures and the frosts of spring and early summer. It required no weeding—that in itself was a combined miracle and blessing—it just seemed to grow on its own. The crop needed little water and, unlike tobacco, required no worming, suckering or topping. Better yet, hemp renewed the soil with each harvest and retting.

Martin hazarded that hemp might one day become Kentucky's main cash crop, bigger even than tobacco. It seemed that everything was aligning that way. Cotton exports were booming and gave every intention of expanding, especially in the Territory of Mississippi, and the state of Louisiana. Southern planters demanded crude hemp sacking for their European-bound cotton bales. The cloth's natural tendency to resist rot protected the cotton on overseas voyages.

The rough grain sacks and fine flour sacks began to stack up. In less than two weeks' time Craig counted well over two hundred. Levi was beside himself with joy, whistling as Martin helped him load the sacks in his wagon.

"This ought to keep you occupied for a while!" Martin chuckled. The old man was enjoying himself, perhaps even more pleased than Craig with the industry. Like Craig, he stood to make more money than selling raw hemp to the boatmen, while the spinning and weaving enabled him to keep his workers employed. The cold summer and smaller crops had impacted the families who worked for him; hard times would grow more evident as winter came on. This enterprise provided them the opportunity to earn enough money to tide them over until springtime.

September 1816 was a remarkable month in Kentucky for it was the only month without a recorded frost. Other parts of the United States suffered terribly; widespread 'black' frosts froze water in the tissues of plants and killed nearly all crops north of Pennsylvania. In New England, apples withered on their branches and corn cobs froze solid in the fields. Flatboat and keelboat pilots carried tales of prolonged droughts, forest fires, continued frosts, and severe food shortages. These tales continually filtered down from the north and across Pennsylvania to Pittsburgh where the river pilots prepared for their westward journeys.

Fortunately, the Ohio River Valley was spared the worst of this calamity. At month's end, Martin dismissed his field hands for a time to allow them to work their winter gardens, and to harvest the fruit which had fared surprisingly well despite the cold summer. Early on Mary had heeded his advice, covering her grape arbors each night with the same linen cloth she had woven to protect tobacco beds, young garden plants, and vines. Some of the grape leaves singed, but most of the flowers had survived and, if the fruit was small and a bit tart, it rendered well into preserves, raisins, and a passable wine.

This was their first real grape harvest. Martin had planted the arbor for Craig and Mary shortly after they married in 1811, siting it on a slight rise and away from the tall oaks so the vines would receive plenty of sunshine and warmth. Craig remembered him insisting that the Marquis de Lafayette's winemaker, Jean Jacques Dufour, had planted America's 'First Vineyard' in central Kentucky, selected from acreage surveyed by Daniel Boone. According to Dufour, Kentucky possessed the right climate for certain types of grapes.

Of course the past season was a glaring exception. Craig wondered what their harvest would look like in a warmer year. He enjoyed the harvest, snipping the dark purple bunches with his knife, placing them into bushel baskets and carrying them to the wine press. Every now and then he would pop a fresh fruit into his mouth or help himself to a dipper of fresh juice. For days the cookhouse smelled of grape preserves which Mary cooked and stored in crocks, sealing the lids with melted beeswax. One day she pulled a table into the autumn sun and dried some of the grapes on the boards, packing the fruit into crocks and sealing them. In the winter she would use those raisins when making pies, cakes, and bread.

The apple and pear harvest took place in comparatively balmy October weather, even though the sun began banking farther in the south, each day shortening the amount of light the land received. Martin had planted an orchard at Mary's Landing in 1811, instructing Craig to plant several trees of the same variety to ensure better yields. He also advised, as he had over the past four years, to pull the various fruits early, not allowing them to mature so that the trees would put more energy into growing in size and establishing a strong root system.

"It takes six or more years for the tree to mature," he said. "Next year you may let the fruit grow. This year you can help with Owen's and my harvest. We have far more than we can use. And we also have that big orchard on the Arbuckle farm. Take a good share and let Mary work it however she wants."

Martin showed Craig how to watch for the right time to harvest apples. Some of the trees began dropping ripe apples to the ground; that was one indication. By that time most apples had turned the full color they were supposed to be. The old man picked a dark red apple and sliced it open with his knife.

"If the apple seeds are a dark brown color, the apples are ripe." He handed half to Craig. The seeds stood out in dark contrast to the light pulp. "Now taste it. If it is juicy and crisp, the apple is at its best."

Craig bit in, savoring the tart, sweet flavor. No one needed to tell him—these apples were ready. Next morning, while dew lay cold and heavy on the orchard grass, he hitched up his horses and hauled the ladder and bushel baskets down to Martin's orchard. Mary wrapped the children in blankets and brought them along. Agnes would feed them breakfast.

Harvesting apples was pleasant family work, much cleaner than working with gummy tobacco, pollen-laden hemp, or dusty corn stalks. Martin showed them how to twist the apples around and up, removing them without damaging the branches.

"Try to leave the stems on the apples," he advised. "They will keep longer."

Craig and the McDonnell brothers propped their ladders into the branches and climbed up and down, picking apples and placing them gently into sacks or bushel baskets to avoid bruising them. Many of these apples would be stored in a root cellar or ice house and used for several months.

"Don't store them near the potatoes," Martin cautioned. "For some reason, apples spoil faster when they are around potatoes."

Not all apples were destined for such storage. Many were peeled, sliced, cored and juiced. The women cut some apples into thin slices or rings and laid them out on tables to dry in the sun. When the fruit dried to the consistency of leather, it was gathered up and stored in cloth bags, usually hung from hooks in the cookhouse rafters, and later used in cooking. Mary and Lucinde built up a fire and made a large kettleful of apple butter, thick and dark, flavored with brown sugar and spices from Rosenbotham's store—cinnamon, cloves, nutmeg and lemon peel. It took them almost the whole day to make it, and when it was ready, they spooned it into crocks which they sealed with melted beeswax. Martin set up the wooden cider press nearby; into this went the fallen apples and culls, all carefully washed, sliced and cored, the brown spots cut off and thrown into a bucket to feed the fattening hogs.

Craig enjoyed drinking the fresh-squeezed juice about as much as anything. Working the cider press gave him a chance to sneak several dippersful. The leftover pomace was also saved for the hogs. Martin declared that this would make their meat sweeter tasting.

"Nothing like bacon off an apple-fed hog!" he exclaimed.

Of course, some apple cider could be held so it would turn hard—and this would fetch a fair price at Rosenbotham's store, if Martin chose to sell it. Usually he chose to distill the wine into a stout brandy. Agnes always let some turn to vinegar which would go into making her marinades and sauces, adding a nice flavor to cooked greens.

The days remained dry, cool, and hazy with late afternoon "sun dogs" shimmering near the pale yellow orb, still a diminished blob surrounded by an indistinct halo in a smoky sky. It was into this pastoral scene that a farmer on his way home from Cottonwood Bend arrived with a message.

"Craig Ridgeway!" he called.

Everyone stopped working, curious to hear what the farmer had to say. It was always a welcome break to have someone new stop in.

"Yes?" Craig replied.

"You have people in town asking for you. They are waiting at Rosenbotham's store."

"Who are they?"

"Big man from Philadelphia with a tiny wife. Says he's your father."

"What!" Craig could not believe his ears. "Are you sure?"

"Said his name was Gregory Ridgeway. Claims he's some kind of lawyer."

"Thank you for telling me," Craig replied, in a state of near shock. It could not be possible—Philadelphia lay hundreds of miles away, up river, across forests and steep mountains. The roads were tortuous and river fords downright dangerous—but it sure sounded like his folks.

"Go ahead, Craig," Martin advised. "We are almost done for the day. Your wagon is here. Bring them back here and we will feed them supper."

"I can't believe it is them!"

"There is only one way to find out."

Quickly Craig strode over to where Mary and Lucinde stirred the apple butter. "Did you hear?" he asked.

"I did!" Mary exclaimed, smiling. "I am so happy for you. You must go to them, Craig."

As he drove the team into town, Craig reflected upon his childhood in Pennsylvania and on the parents who raised him. Long ago he had neatly tucked them away into a compartment of the past. At age fifteen he had left home without a word—they had not deserved that. They were good providers, and most of all, they loved him. They had raised him to be thrifty, hard-working, and conscientious, supplying him with a wide collection of books, maps, pamphlets, and newspapers, giving him a sound knowledge base. They had sent him to the best schools and saw he was prepared for university. But the wanderlust had struck without warning. One August morning he had packed up and headed westward, settling in Lancaster, Pennsylvania where he became a gunsmith's apprentice. Five years later, again without word, he set out for Pittsburgh and then down the Ohio River to Breckinridge County, Kentucky. Finally, he sent them a series of letters, telling them about his new life—his wife, farm, and family. Now they had traveled—emerging out of his past—to see him. Few people in America paid visits of this magnitude; there was a reason they had come, and Craig feared it was bad.

He recognized them immediately, dressed in their fine clothing and looking somewhat different from the regular folks in the settlement. Newcomers always looked different, at least for a while. They sat on a bench against the front wall of Rosenbotham's store, their travel chests and bags stacked beside them. Craig's father spied him immediately and stood up. His mother remained seated, staring out at the river, seemingly unaware of his presence. Craig pulled his team up to the storefront.

"Hello, Father!" he exclaimed, stepping down from the wagon. "This is a welcome surprise. It is good to see you!" He extended his hand and was pleased to have the greeting returned.

"It is good to finally see you, Craig." Gregory Ridgeway smiled, somewhat preoccupied. He looked remarkably the same—about the same weight as before, but with some graying at the temples. It was to be expected. After all, he was fifty-five years old.

"Mother!" Sarah Ridgeway showed no sign of recognition. Craig experienced a sharp stab of alarm as he noticed the vacant look in her blue eyes. Her light brown hair had turned completely gray.

Gregory's voice steadied him. "I am sorry, Craig. She does not know you. Sometimes she remembers you as a small boy, but five years ago she suffered from a severe fever and it brought on a sharp decline in her mental abilities—an affliction some call 'lunacy'—found more often in the elderly. Doctors attribute her present condition to the initial fever, but also to long-standing grief, anxiety and depression."

Craig did not have to ask the reason for her previous mental distress. His leaving home surely factored into her decline.

"Oh, Mother!" He embraced her, unable to choke back a sob. She did not return the embrace.

"She is tired, Craig. We both could use some rest."

"Mary and I have a fine bed. Her mother is cooking supper for you at Welcome Hall. The house is on the way to my cabin. We were picking apples there and preparing them in different ways for the coming months."

"We would appreciate a good meal. A word of caution—your mother usually fares well in small, quiet gatherings, but sometimes even that overwhelms her. We may have to leave the table early."

"I understand. I will explain this to Mary and she will forewarn her folks."

Together, Craig and his father loaded the luggage into the wagon. As they set off down the road, his mother began talking—babbling in an unceasing torrent of disjointed phrases, incomplete thoughts, and fragmented sentences. She chattered the entire length of River Street and long after they crossed the bridge over Cottonwood Creek. Listening to her, Craig could barely hold back his tears. He could recall her reading stories in an expressive voice and how she almost sang her words with perfect clarity and articulation. Her soprano voice had once soared to the rafters of the church in Philadelphia, so sweet and bell-like that it moved the congregation to tears. But now she gibbered a muddled hodgepodge of sounds that made absolutely no sense. Sometimes she stuck on words that she either repeated, or rhymed nonsensically. It was impossible to decipher, so he let her talk, nodding occasionally or agreeing out loud. About halfway to Welcome Hall, the chattering abruptly ceased.

"That's what I do, Craig," Gregory whispered. "I just let her talk until she runs down. Some days she is clearer, usually in the mornings. When sundown comes, things go downhill."

"Does she sleep at night?"

"Sporadically. Sometimes while I have slept, she has wakened and gone outside. Once, a passerby found her walking in the street. He alerted a neighbor and they brought her home. Since then I have installed locking bolts on all the doors and windows, and have hired a woman to help take care of her, one who has experience caring for the elderly. Needless to say, she has been a godsend. The doctors tell me your mother's condition will grow progressively worse."

"What prompted you to come here?"

"I thought the change might do her good. You need to catch a glimpse of her former self before it vanishes completely. Also, I wanted to see how my son has fared. We would like to meet our grandchildren and your lovely wife."

"You were both wonderful to me. I can't tell you why I left home."

"We are not the only parents to lose our children to the frontier. It is much more common than you might think. We initially tormented ourselves, wondering what we did to make you leave home."

"It is not easy to explain. Maybe I was ashamed to let you know I was finished with schooling. I yearned for adventure, new places. The outdoors beckoned and later, the frontier. I have enjoyed an incredible life and am happy."

"Apparently so. I still read your letters aloud, over and over again. Your mother loves to hear them, although I could probably as well read advertisements from the *Pennsylvania Gazette*. She forgets almost immediately what I read."

Craig stifled another painful sob.

"So you have become a farmer?"

"Yes, sir."

"I would imagine that this summer, or whatever one chooses to call it, has played havoc upon the crops."

"It has, but we have managed to grow some. Our hemp fared

extremely well."

"The farmers in New England have not been so fortunate."

"I have a Vermont family working for me. They told us some terrible tales."

"Do you have enough money to sustain your family?"

"Yes, Father."

"I would advise you to branch out; find ways to invest to minimize the uncertain income of farming."

Craig almost blurted out that he and Mary had established a successful distillery, ran a successful weaving industry, and cut and sold lumber to the local sawyer—but he held back, appreciating that Gregory was trying to make up for the past years, to bridge the gap and be the father Craig had denied. Guiltily he knew he should be the one reaching out, so he replied, "If you have any suggestions, I would sure welcome them."

The late afternoon air grew chill as the sun dipped behind the trees. A sharp breeze sprang up from the river. Gregory reached behind the wagon seat and withdrew a green woolen shawl from Sarah's valise. Tenderly, he wrapped it around her.

She cried shrilly, "Oh! I am cold, fold, bold, old, told, hold, gold, golden, olden, tolden, solden…" and the litany continued.

"Yes, it is a cold afternoon," Gregory agreed. "We will soon sit you by a warm fire and have a nice supper that Craig has arranged for us."

"Who?"

"Craig."

"Who?"

"Your son, Craig."

"What?"

"We are going to stay a while at his home."

"Who?"

His mother gibbered on for at least another mile before she subsided. Through tear-blurred eyes Craig concentrated on his horses and the road ahead, clucking to them to quicken their pace. They trotted past Owen's brick entrance columns and soon turned up the

McDonnell's wide, crushed-gravel driveway. Warm yellow light glowed from the downstairs windows.

"Is this where you live?" Gregory asked.

"No, this is Welcome Hall, Martin McDonnell's house. Mary grew up here."

"Ah, yes. He is the Revolutionary War hero. This is quite a nice house."

Craig pulled up in the back yard and tied the horses to the hitching post. "I will go ahead and let Mary know you are here."

"We will follow."

Everyone had quit the orchard. Stephen was down by the hay barn, washing out the cider press with cold spring water. The womenfolk had finished making apple butter; their fire had burned down to a few red coals. Martin and Owen were nowhere in sight. They were probably tending to the farm animals. Mary met him at the cookhouse door.

"They are here?" she smiled warmly, always intrigued by family drama.

"Yes," Craig replied.

Ever-sensitive to his moods, her expression changed. "What is wrong, Craig?"

He whispered, more from shock than embarrassment. "It is Mother. She is suffering from a cruel form of mental decline. Father says she does not tolerate large crowds and noise. They may have to leave early."

"Say no more, Craig. I will let everyone know. They will understand." She stepped back into the cookhouse.

Craig returned to the wagon to escort his folks inside. They stepped into the covered back stoop and then into the everyday dining room with the large red maple table. Agnes and Lucinde began bringing in covered dishes while Mary met her in-laws.

"So this is the wonderful Mary?" Gregory inquired, smiling. "From his letters, I learned that Craig is completely smitten; now I understand why."

"I am so pleased to finally meet you, dear Father-in-law." Mary kissed his cheek.

"Son, you have done well. Sarah, this is Craig's wife, Mary."

"My little Mother, you are so beautiful." Mary smiled brightly. Craig watched her embrace his mother for the first time. Sarah smiled through her confusion. "Come into the parlor and sit by the fire." Mary led Sarah gently into the front room and sat her in Martin's chair near the hearth, holding her hand and talking softly to her. The crackling warmth imparted an immediate, calming effect. Soon they were conversing, although Craig comprehended none of it. Mary pretended as if she understood every word. Martin and Owen came onto the back stoop with the children. While they removed their shoes, Agnes cautioned them in low tones.

After a time, Isabel poked her head into the room.

"Come, Isabel," Mary beckoned. "These are your other grandparents, all the way from Pennsylvania. They are *your* father's mother and father."

Isabel approached timidly. Sarah perked up and smiled warmly, reaching out her arms. Craig was somewhat apprehensive, but there was no reason. Mary beamed happily, totally unconcerned as the two embraced. Gregory's eyes welled up and Craig felt his own tears begin to flow. Little Ruth, now almost eighteen months old, came in to investigate. After a short time, Owen's children filed into the room. Quietly, Craig led his father out to meet the rest of the family.

Gregory shook hands with Martin. "I understand we are now relations. I appreciate you helping Craig establish himself as a farmer."

"He has fared quite well," Martin assured him. "I could not have picked a better husband for Mary."

Agnes inquired softly from the entranceway. "Would you folks care to join us for a simple supper?"

Craig felt grateful to this wonderful family for so wholly and graciously accepting the situation. Stephen acted a bit awkward, which was understandable; Owen and Lucinde, always quiet and observant, behaved as usual. And the children, even the youngest, conducted themselves like angels, amused at the strange little woman making faces at them from across the table. The transition from arrival to supper was seamless, made smoother by the splendid cooking. The roasted pork loin, baked potatoes, vegetables and new apples fried in butter and sprinkled with cinnamon, tasted delicious after a long day's work. Craig noticed how his folks dug in, realizing how hungry they were from their travels.

After dinner, everyone retired to the parlor for a hot peach brandy. Sarah began yawning and showed signs of sleepiness. Obviously, the day's travels had worn her out. Agnes suggested, "Craig, why don't you let your folks stay here for the night? I'll bet they're tired from their journey. We already have the guest room made up and Martin can build a fire in the end fireplace. We'll feed them a hearty breakfast and you can come down and fetch them in the morning."

"Are you sure, Mother Agnes?"

"Why, yes! We don't want to send them back out into the cold night air."

Craig glanced at Martin. The old man nodded his assurance. Gregory accepted with a relieved glance. Agnes and Mary left with Sarah to help her bed down for the night.

"Thank you so much for your hospitality," Gregory sighed, sipping his brandy. "Usually she does not go to bed so easily. We are exhausted."

Martin replied, "I have had relatives who suffered from the same condition. In fact, I do not know a family who has not experienced it in at least one relative."

Mary appeared from the guest room, whispering quietly. "Craig, your mother needs her nightclothes."

Craig rose to fetch her valise from the wagon. Gregory set his cup onto the brick hearth and rose to follow him. Together they walked out into the darkness where Craig had hitched the horses.

"We will take in just the light valises, Craig. They are all we need."

"You know you are welcome at my home."

"We are so tired; Agnes recognized that. None of us would have enjoyed much of a visit tonight. Take our chests to your house and we will join you tomorrow."

"My place is not nearly as nice as Welcome Hall."

"We came to visit you. We will make do for as long as you will have us."

As his folks prepared for bed, Mary began bundling the girls for the ride back to the cabin. Martin watched all with interest.

"Thank you, Martin," Craig took his hand and shook it. "I appreciate your hospitality more than I can say."

"We are happy to have them here, Craig."

"I never expected to see them again. I am still a bit overwhelmed."

"Just remember this—God has a plan for everything in this world. Nothing happens without His express will. You must accept their presence as His gift to you. He is providing you with a remarkable opportunity to bring closure to that part of your life—or perhaps it is a new beginning."

"I do not deserve it."

"None of us deserve God's grace—it is a gift."

"I wish you could have known Mother in better times."

"We have to take life as it is and work within those boundaries."

After they put the children to bed, Mary began sweeping and dusting, polishing lamps and dishes, making ready for their guests. She brought out the good quilts and sheets, hanging them about the house to air them. There were dozens of particulars that Craig knew to leave in her care. If she needed him, she would call. He must attend to other chores. The cows waited to be milked—all the animals needed feeding. The barn was his retreat; usually he did his best thinking and praying out there, tending to the animals and busying himself at things like sharpening axes, polishing harnesses and turning barrels of whiskey. Craig took his time with the milking, sorting out his thoughts. He realized that Martin was right—he must take things as they are and make the most of them.

He cut up a large supply of kindling and brought it inside. Then he hauled down the corn shuck mattress from the cabin loft, placing it near the girls' beds. He and Mary would sleep on it in coming nights, while giving his folks the fine bed Levi had made. He stoked up the fire and threw in a heavy green log that would still be burning at daybreak.

"I think we are finished, Craig," Mary announced as she put away the last of the dishes. "We should turn in early tonight." She slipped on her nightdress, turned back the covers, and slid beneath them. "Hurry, Craig! The sheets are cold!"

Craig followed her, enjoying how the down mattress enveloped them. Mary snuggled against him, wrapping one arm around his waist and worming her feet in between his legs.

"I know you are hurting, dear. It is terrible thing to see a loved one with a bodily or mental ailment."

"Have you ever had a family member like this?"

"Oh, yes I have—it was my grandfather, Ma's father. After Grandmother died, he lived alone. He became severely depressed; he didn't bathe, he quit doing his chores, and he even forgot to eat. The neighbors first informed us about his straying animals. Local farmers came to tell us that his axe had rusted from disuse and that one of his guns had lain outdoors for several weeks. He began to lose weight because he was not eating. Ma thought her younger sister, who lived nearby, was looking in on him, but she was not. There was nothing to do but take him in. Pa rode over to his house to bring him and his immediate belongings here."

"What happened then?"

"We put him up in the guest room. From the beginning it was hard on everyone. I remember Pa saying that Grandfather never slept. He would wander outside at night; toward the end he fell and broke his arm. Sometimes he would wake us up with his shouting. He would repeat himself, over and over; other times he struggled to find the right words to say. When he could not, he became frustrated and angry."

"That must have been difficult."

"Later, he saw things that weren't there. On the parlor wall he saw a giant French cathedral which he recollected from a pilgrimage to Paris; at another time he spoke with an English general and saluted him as if he were in the room. Later, he became dangerously aggressive. Once he hit Owen across the back with an iron poker. Pa fought with him to wrench it from his grasp. Grandfather retreated to his bedroom and fell into a deep sleep. When he woke, he remembered nothing of the ordeal, and we all sat down together for a meal."

"How old were you then?"

"I was seven years old. One time, Ma told me to take him a cup of water. He dashed the water in my face. I remember crying, it hurt my feelings so."

"So your memories of him are not pleasant."

"Oh, I have wonderful memories of him. Before Grandmother died, they would visit on odd Sundays. Grandfather always dressed up in his best clothes and he would take Owen and me on long walks. I can still see his walking cane and especially his jew's harp. He would sit down on a log and twang it and call out a three or four-handed reel or a jig. He taught Owen and me some of the dances. He was a wonderful man!"

"Mother was wonderful, too. You should have heard her sing. She reminded me of those little wrens that nested in the grape arbor this past summer. You know how they just swell up, cock their heads back, and cut loose with their warbling. She sang like that in church."

"She still is wonderful, Craig. She absolutely loves little children; that is plain to see. She can still feed herself. In the end, Grandfather could not."

"I wish I could understand her better."

"You might find, that over the next several days, you will. Being around her will help. It's like understanding our babies. You do not always need words."

Craig rolled in and kissed her soft, parted lips, tasting her sweetness and feeling her body as she pressed against him. The embrace engendered a wave of passion, so violent and thrilling, it shocked him. Soon they were entangled in each other's arms and legs and he was locked tightly in her grip of velvet softness. Ever since Father Badin had "reasoned" with him, and he had accepted God's forgiveness, the night terrors had noticeably receded. He began sleeping soundly and his interest in Mary naturally awakened. At first he could not hold back, and the storms of lovemaking were brief and violent. But Mary coaxed and cajoled him into drawing out their loving, taking it smooth and slow, so when it did end, they were both spent in body and spirit. Tonight was a slow night, loving and tender.

"I love you so much!" he gasped.

"I love you too, Craig."

"Thank you for helping me take care of Mother. And Father too."

"You do not have to thank me, Craig. It will be nice having them here. You will see. Make the most of it."

Before dropping off to sleep, Craig realized it might be some time before they could indulge in such evening pleasure. But he resolved to make the visit a good one.

Mary's Landing—October 13, 1816

Martin brought Gregory and Sarah to the cabin while Craig was still milking the cows. The day was cold and overhung with gray clouds, and the air smelled of rain. Craig toted in the morning bucket of milk to find Martin, Gregory and Sarah seated at the maple wood table and drinking hot coffee.

"Well, good morning, all! " Craig smiled. "I was just headed down there."

"Your mother woke early," Gregory explained. "She did sleep

through most of the night. I myself feel rested."

"Have you eaten breakfast?"

"We thought we would join you."

"Martin, do you care to stay?"

"I had best get back. Stephen will need help with the stock."

"Thank you again for supper. Please tell Agnes."

He rose and tied his heavy wool scarf around his neck. "We'll do it again soon. Will we work tomorrow?"

"Yes. Levi needs the sacking and I need the money and the corn. When we finish with weaving, I intend to run another batch of whiskey."

"I agree. Strike while prices are high. Make all the money you can and then, when the storms come, you can shorten your sails and ride them out."

Mary buttoned the top button on his coat, kissed him on the cheek, and saw him to the door. Then she began busying herself at the fire, breaking eggs for scrambling and slicing bacon for frying. Bread browned in the Dutch oven. Of course there were plenty of apples for frying.

"Mother, would you like to watch Mary cook?"

"Yes," she replied as plainly as she had ever spoken.

"She might even have something for you to do." Craig brought a chair closer to the hearth where she could sit and watch—and perhaps help with small tasks. He returned to the table where Gregory spoke softly.

"Usually, this is her best time of day. She often experiences several moments of clarity until dinnertime. She takes a nap afterwards and can wake up foul-tempered—especially if startled. There might follow another spell of relative calm, but then, around suppertime, things can go terribly wrong."

"I did not notice that last night."

"She was tired." Gregory hesitated with his words and then spoke. "Do you have an old oilcloth and blankets you can spread on the bed mattress?"

"Yes."

"We sometimes have to wash sheets and blankets in the morning."

"I understand."

The children heard the strange voices and woke together. As
usual they joined Mary at the fireplace. In a short time, Isabel leaned
against her grandmother and they talked and laughed a little. While
Craig took the chamber pots to empty them, he thought how much
old folks could be like children. The outhouse was some distance
from the cabin, down the knoll next to the timbered slope, far below
the spring well which lay behind him. Long ago Martin had advised
where to situate it—and it stood as far away from their cabin as it
did at the McDonnell's house. The old man swore that the long distance was why his family never suffered from bouts of bloody flux
and stomach ailments that afflicted other folks. There was no chance
of anything leaching into their drinking water. Craig had heard of
whole families dying from unknown stomach or intestinal disorders.
Some physicians ascribed deaths to the nearness of the outhouse, or
sometimes the careless dumping of chamber pots too near the water
supply. The McDonnells, although Irish, had some German stock in
their blood and from their ancestors they inherited a penchant for
cleanliness. Later, Mary would wash everything with boiling water
and lye soap, taking time to dump the wash water the full distance
away.

On his way back to the cabin, Craig heard a flock of geese wing-
ing their way southward just above the cloud level. They were honking on both sides, east and west, perhaps hundreds of them, flying
in their usual V-shaped formations. Winter was not far off. Geese
were always a sound indicator of colder weather. Craig still could
not yet see the Ohio through the trees, but leaves were beginning
to fall. Golden beech, red, orange and scarlet sassafras, and purple
sumac leaves still clung to the trees, but early leaves lay underfoot
in the pasture.

The aroma of breakfast greeted him at the dogtrot door. Mary
served it piping hot and the family enjoyed it together. Craig poured
coffee when the cups ran low. The conversation flowed, and it

seemed that his mother followed most of it, even if she did not join in.

Gregory asked, "Is there no church in Cottonwood Bend?"

"Oh yes," Craig replied. "There is a Baptist Church with regular Sunday services. They say Brother Kreisle is a fair preacher. The Methodists and Catholics must content themselves with traveling clergy. Our priest, Father Badin, visits St. Romoldus Church in Hardinsburg every few months. Sometimes he stays at Welcome Hall. He married us on the grounds in August of 1811."

"And there are no other churches?"

"We have traveling evangelists in the summer months. They preach in big brush arbor services."

"I have heard of them—mass conversions, extreme fervor, and strange phenomena. Our preacher says they should be avoided."

"They can be scary," Craig nodded. "But I hear many good things have happened as a result of some of those conversions. And those meetings have spurred folks to demand churches with regular pastors."

After breakfast, Mary suggested, "Craig, why don't you show your father around the farm?"

"I would like that," Gregory nodded.

"Then I suggest you put on your heavy coat. It is cold out there."

Together they stepped out into the dogtrot. Craig led him between two looms to show him into the cookhouse with its fieldstone chimney, open hearth, and glazed brick oven built by Levi Matthews. Gregory inspected it with interest and noticed the grain sacks and foodstuffs on the shelves. As they left, he ran his hand thoughtfully over the loom which stood there.

Craig then described the great barn and cabin raising that took place over a two-day period just before he and Mary were married. "It resembled those big barn raisings in Pennsylvania. I was so appreciative of everyone. Events like that encourage a strong sense of community. Of course, I always return the favor when someone builds a barn or cabin. Everybody helps everybody. We harvest each other's cornfields, and work together in times of trouble."

"Martin told me he is proud of you. He told me about your beginnings. It seems you had a rough start here in Breckinridge County."

"It was a tough time, but looking back, it was a good time."

"I can tell it forged you into a strong man."

"Well, I have had many doubts along the way. The fighting in New Orleans affected me badly. I have been forced to kill—and it has taken some coping to deal with it."

"Many men have been put in that situation. You did what you needed to do."

"We lost twin sons during the flu epidemic. They were stillborn. I was angry with God for a time."

"No man should have to lose a child, but it happens. God's ways are higher than our ways, but most men have questioned Him at one time or other."

"And, Father, I do feel guilty for leaving home without a word."

"We observed the restlessness long before you left. Folks reported they had seen you heading west. I could have chased after you, but I could not have made you return. Your employer, the gunsmith, wrote and told me you were happy and well. I knew that if I tried to force the issue, you would move farther away."

This was a revelation. Craig admired his father for not following him. He was here now only because Craig had invited him in his letters.

"I am so glad you came. It is such a long distance."

"The truth is, I did not know what to expect. I am also glad I came."

Before they visited the barn, they stopped in at the smokehouse, henhouse, spring well, and stone distillery shed. Gregory studied with fascination the cypress wood vats, the copper still, stone-and-clay fire pit, and fireplaces. "Martin told me that you and Mary manufacture an exceptional whiskey, that it brings top dollar."

"We do fairly well. Come and see the barrels." Craig conducted him to the barn's south shed to show him the sturdy oaken racks loaded with aging barrels of whiskey.

"I have tasted Kentucky whiskey. I hope you will let me sample yours."

"We have a jug of our best in the house, set aside for special guests. I think you qualify."

"Why are all these looms and spinning wheels here? I noticed others in the cabin, dogtrot and distillery."

"We have a temporary industry underway."

"What industry?"

"The local miller, Levi Matthews, has contracted with me to provide him with grain sacks made from local hemp. Martin, Owen and I are among the few farmers growing hemp in these parts. In addition to making grain sacks, Mary has devised a close-knit pattern for weaving flour sack linings. Levi pays us in ground corn and hard coin."

"I heard Martin ask if you would work tomorrow."

"Yes, this place will become busy tomorrow morning. Martin, his family and field hands will arrive shortly after daybreak. The Vermont family will come in about mid-morning. My slaves will be here early."

"Slaves?" Gregory raised an eyebrow.

"Yes, Mary and I purchased them, fully intending to set them free. But that has proven difficult, perhaps impossible. They are, for the time being, officially in my care."

"Slavery is truly an abomination."

"I know that. I have seen it at its worst—here in Kentucky, Tennessee and Louisiana."

"What will you do with them?" Gregory asked.

"The old ones will never leave. Their age and condition make it impossible. So I provide them with a home, pay them good wages when they wish to work, give them chickens and hogs, cut firewood, and let them work their gardens. Romulus, and his wife tried to leave, and I helped them across the river, but the attempt failed miserably." He told Gregory about the incident with the slave catchers.

"You know this slavery issue is causing real havoc in American politics. They claim that new states will be admitted on a 'free' or 'slave' holding status. The tariff is another issue altogether. Our brilliant achievement in maintaining freedom may soon be overshadowed by new internal problems."

"Let's hope not."

Craig led him around the barn, pointing out the giant beams and hayloft, tobacco sheds and stalls. Gregory recognized the tan plow horses from the previous day. He studied the oxen, milk cows, and tall blue roan.

"That is the tallest horse I have ever seen. He is beautiful."

"He is a wonderful saddle horse. I love riding him."

"Craig, I came here to see if I could help you. It seems you have made it on your own, which is as much as any man could hope for his son. I am proud of you."

"I wish I was worthy of that. I did you a grave wrong."

"It is all in the past. Let's enjoy today,"

"You are not the first person to tell me that."

The weaving began full force the next morning. A cold wind funneled into the dogtrot, forcing the weavers to move their looms into the barn. After the extended break, everyone enjoyed reconnecting, and work resumed as if there had been no interruption. Craig moved about, coordinating efforts, hauling more hemp from the Arbuckle farm, and helping scutch the raw hemp. Once, Gregory brought Sarah out to the barn, but the commotion was too much for her. She screamed in a high-pitched voice that carried above the clacking and laughter. Everyone quieted down as Gregory conducted her back to the cabin. Mary's loom was set up inside and she did her weaving there. She could look after her mother-in-law, talk quietly with her, and see to her needs. This settled the problem.

Several times over the next two weeks Craig observed his father talking with Martin. Once Gregory accompanied him and Owen down to Welcome Hall. Certainly he was gathering more information, but Craig did not begrudge him that. Better he learn from others. One morning, before work, Craig was pouring a cup of coffee for his mother. As he added two spoonsful of maple sugar, she surprised him with a clear sentence, unmarred by stammering or repetition.

"Once, I had a nice son. But he didn't love me and he moved away. He never came back to see me."

Craig gasped with pain. This was truth in its rawest form, and it laid bare the hurt he had inflicted upon her. "Mother, I *am* your son! I am so sorry I left. I loved you then and I love you now. Please forgive me!" His tears flowed freely.

Sarah hugged him, genuinely confused, not really knowing who he was. Craig retreated to the barn for his morning chores, hoping to regain control before the workers arrived.

The hemp bags piled up. Twice during the week, Levi drove his wagon up for more, pleased to see everyone at work. On his first trip he had barked, "Let's not have any more shutdowns shall we? I was running too damned low on grain sacks. You never know when a flatboat or keelboat will stop in."

"Why can't the coopers help?" Craig asked.

"They are! I have them working night and day. The damned thing is, their barrels cost a lot more than your feed sacks."

"Well, if you keep on complaining, our prices will rise. These folks have to eat! They needed to harvest their fruit and vegetables, and store them for the winter. And I still have corn to cut and hogs to slaughter!"

"Everyone has their troubles," he groused.

The next three weeks passed in a flurry of activity. Craig's raw hemp stock dwindled down to a few remaining hanks. Martin brought up the last of his hemp; Owen's stock was fast declining. It seemed the workers had found the right balance, and finished sacks piled to their highest level. Finally, Levi felt secure enough to announce that he had enough sacking to last for some time. He paid partially in small coin—coppers, dismes, and silver bits—which made it easy to pay out the workers. Martin exchanged gold for some of Craig's small coins, leaving a handling fee that he and Mary worked out. But Craig felt most satisfied with the corn he had amassed. Levi included the grinding fee in his calculations and would store it at his mill. Soon, Craig and Mary could begin another distilling run.

Craig grew comfortable having his folks living with them. As usual, Mary was right. Over time he began to understand his mother, if not in a verbal way. He learned how to communicate, to anticipate her moods, and understand her needs. So it came as a surprise when, on November 16th, his father announced he and Sarah would soon be leaving. Craig felt a pang of remorse.

"I wish you could stay forever. You are always welcome—you know that."

"Of course we do. But you have your life and we have ours. This visit has done us all an extreme amount of good. Who knows? With the new advances in transportation, namely the steamboat, we might visit again someday. But I am still active in my law practice, and from what I have observed, you will never slow down. In fact, you have worn me out with all your working. You never stop."

"Maybe it is the outlet for what you call my 'restlessness.'"

"Perhaps. But I can see—it makes you happy. I only wish I could do something for you. I thought I might find you destitute, or perhaps living at subsistence level. What a surprise to find you are not only a successful farmer, but also a successful businessman. Still, I wish I could give you some money. I brought a thousand dollars to help you get established."

"I would feel guilty accepting it." Over the past few weeks, Craig had thought long and hard on how to make his father feel needed. He decided to appeal to his professional skills. "There *is* one thing I need."

"What is it, son?"

"Legal advice."

"I am at your service."

"Tell me how to ensure that Romulus and his family can reach free territory and remain free. I cannot leave my farm and family to escort them all the way to Canada. They cannot make it on their own. They tried and were apprehended by slave-catchers. It was sheer luck we rescued them."

"You say you have already manumitted them?"

"I have. Romulus has their papers. Fortunately we recovered them from the slavecatchers."

"But you are legally responsible for the family?"

"Yes. I signed a statement to that effect in the Breckinridge County Courthouse. Martin claims they are in a much more precarious position than when they were slaves."

"Let me think on this. Who is your lawyer?"

"Judge Wilfred J. Bozarth in Cottonwood Bend."

"I wish to meet this man."

"Then you are in for a real treat."

"First, I want to meet with Romulus and his wife."

———————————•◄————————————

Early Sunday morning Gregory outlined his plan. Like all good plans it was simple and direct. Although it skirted the bounds of legality, Craig was confident his father possessed the brilliance and clout to execute it. He accepted the plan without reservation. After he finished his morning chores, he led Gregory across the Hardinsburg Road to Romulus' cabin. He rapped once on the weathered wooden door and Romulus invited them in. The slave couple went instantly on guard, aware something was afoot. They knew Gregory was Craig's father, but the frenzied pace of hemp work had precluded any chance for interaction. This was a strange white man in their home and it made them wary.

Craig began, "Romulus, you know I have done all I can to free you. You want to live and work as a free man, and not fear that slavecatchers will snatch and sell you to a southern plantation."

Romulus' face set into a hard mask of bitter remembrance and apprehension. Vergina appeared frightfully hostile.

"My Father has the answer we have looked for."

"What answer?" Romulus asked.

"Father," Craig prompted. "Tell them."

"I propose that Craig turn you over to my custody, as my legal property."

The couple recoiled in defiance; their expressions were equally frightening.

"It sounds terrible, but hear me out. Craig has manumitted you—set you free. The original records are lodged in the Breckinridge County courthouse. But you know from recent experience that your papers are worthless scrap—especially if you fall again into the hands of unscrupulous patrollers."

Romulus stuck out his jaw, resisting the idea of re-enslavement. Vergina shifted uncomfortably, but she listened.

"I propose that Craig draw up a bill of sale for the entire family, and that we take it to Judge Wilfred Bozarth for his official seal. You would be, for a short time, my legal property. Very soon, perhaps this week, I will begin my voyage home to Philadelphia. You may not know this—Pennsylvania was the first state in the Union to pass a law abolishing slavery. This occurred in 1780, while war with Britain raged and Pennsylvania was still a colony in rebellion. Pennsylvania remains one of the strongest 'free' states in the republic. Within our state exist two religious sects—the Quakers and the Mennonites—some of the staunchest abolitionists in the Republic. They constantly help slaves to escape northward, especially those fleeing Maryland and northern Virginia. Some Quakers have even managed to persuade southern slave owners to free their slaves."

"How this help us?" Vergina challenged.

"I am just trying to convey to you the political climate within the state. Pennsylvanians violently oppose slavery. Quakers openly disobey the Fugitive Slave Law and work to frustrate it at every step. No slavecatcher would dare come for you there. As soon as we land in Philadelphia, you and your family will be free—and I know people who help establish freed slaves. I will personally help you settle and find work."

"It hard to believe."

"You own the manumission papers Craig gave you. He has always supported your cause. Has he not proven that time and again?"

The couple began to waver, but it was still too much to assimilate. They had hoped so many times before, only to have those hopes sickeningly dashed; both had experienced brutality that no human being should ever endure. Craig, more than anyone, understood their skepticism—and terror. He had seen them bludgeoned at a local slave auction. Romulus' gaping eye socket and pronounced limp were the most glaring of his many injuries. Craig had seen other scars, much more ghastly, fortunately concealed by clothing. And, not long ago, he had rescued the battered and terrified family from the slavecatchers in that deadly shootout in the hills of southern Breckinridge County. He knew he must press further.

"You will never have a chance like this again, Romulus. This is the answer we have looked for. I believe God had you in mind when he brought my folks here. This time the plan will work."

"I don't know, Craig." Romulus hesitated.

"He is my Father. I trust him completely. You know you can trust me. He will free you."

"We think about it, Craig." Vergina signified that the meeting was over.

"Just don't think too long," Craig advised. "Father is looking for a boat to convey him downriver."

"South!" Romulus gasped.

"It sounds terrible, but it is the quickest and easiest way. After your trip to New Orleans, you will board a sailing ship bound for Philadelphia Harbor. No one can challenge you as long as he legally owns you."

In the end they accepted, as Craig figured they would. He had seen the unmistakable hope in their eyes. They came hand-in-hand that afternoon to tell him. Romulus agreed to play the role of manservant and Vergina would tend to Sarah's needs. Gregory would pay passage and board for the whole family and provide a generous salary for their positions.

Just one obstacle remained—making legal arrangements with Judge Bozarth. The next morning Craig hitched up the wagon and drove the team of big tans into Cottonwood Bend, where he introduced his father to the esteemed Judge, Wilfred J. Bozarth, Attorney-at-Law. On the way, he provided an abridged version of the Judge's character, divulging one piece of knowledge that might prove helpful to their cause.

They found the Judge in a buoyant, almost unrestrained mood. Despite his legendary carousing and shady business dealings, he had won his election to the Kentucky State House of Representatives. This victory advanced him one step closer to the Governorship, the office to which he aspired. He flashed his celebrated, brilliant-toothed grin as he smoked one of Mary's whiskey-soaked cigars and sipped brandy from a glass snifter. His magnificent silver and black mane was neatly trimmed and he looked resplendent in his tailored suitcoat. Violet showed them in to his office and retreated quietly to take up her familiar position just outside the door where she could listen to all particulars.

Craig introduced his father and let him explain the basics of his plan. Judge Bozarth reviewed the details with reservation. He knew that Romulus and his family had been freed, that the original manumission papers resided in the Breckinridge County Courthouse. He explained that the process of re-enslavement would be complex and open to challenge, and in this matter he could not help—he was obliged to follow the law to the letter.

Gregory Ridgeway argued, "Yes, but when Craig signed the manumission papers, he also signed a document taking full responsibility for the freed slaves' welfare to ensure that the county would not be burdened with their upkeep. What we are proposing is this— Craig is unable to continue his support. He wishes to transfer full responsibility to me, his father."

"Then Craig may transfer guardianship to you. That I am willing to do."

"Herein lies the difficulty. On the way home we will be traveling through southern slave states. The officials there may ask me to prove ownership. I need to have legal ownership papers on me."

"I understand, but our statutes are clear. You are certainly not suggesting I circumvent the laws of this fair county."

"I am suggesting this. Romulus and his family are legally free. And when I get them to Philadelphia, they will remain legally free. Their condition will not change. But I am traveling through country where folks are not so understanding. We are asking you to provide 'temporary' documents that declare me their undisputed owner—this to ensure they remain in their current state of freedom."

"This matter should be handled in the Breckinridge County Courthouse."

"It will take precious time I do not have. I am traveling with a sick wife."

"I have heard that. My sympathies."

"Thank you. At the proper time I will destroy the temporary documents and produce the valid manumission papers which will be unquestionably honored in Philadelphia."

"I have just been elected to the Kentucky State House of Representatives! If I am discovered..."

"We will be heading west and south, in the opposite direction of Hardinsburg and Frankfort. Craig's slaves will never again return to this county. And you, Judge—ah, Honorable Representative—you may rest assured you have done a noble service for a deserving family and for my son."

The Judge kept silent, weighing his options. Then, Gregory employed the argument that Craig knew would tip the scales.

"Of course, I am willing to pay handsomely for the execution of these documents. Would a hundred gold dollars suffice?"

Craig thought the Judge's eyeballs would burst from his head. He had heard from local gossips that the Judge was anxious about funding his stay in Frankfort when the Kentucky General Assembly opened for the new legislative session. Sometimes lawmakers met for months, and during this time they would be expected to attend a whirlwind of celebrations, banquets, and expensive venues of entertainment. Judge Bozarth must maintain a certain presence in the capital, especially if he planned to rise higher in state government. Socializing played a critical role during the session, for it was then that legislative deals would be forged and extra money could be made. But socializing would cost him dearly. A hundred dollars would go a long way in bankrolling his stay.

"I see." The Judge cleared his throat, feigning an enlightened expression. "The end result would be the same? The slaves *would* ultimately be free?"

"You have my word and hundred gold dollars on it."

"I will require an extra twenty dollars for the seal and for my wife's signature as witness." The Judge was wheedling, trying to milk all he could from the arrangement. "And I would like to see the money up front. As you may be aware, times are hard."

"That presents no problem." Gregory counted out a dozen shining gold eagles embossed with stars and capped busts, eagles and shields.

The Judge's eyes glittered with greed. "I would not perform this service for anyone. Craig Ridgeway has become one of our most important citizens. He has served our local militia well, and he performed brilliantly at the Battle of New Orleans. You may be proud to call him your son." He called toward the door. "Violet, dear! Would you please help me prepare the necessary papers?" He needn't have called, for Violet had already crossed half the office floor.

———◆———

Two days later, Craig said farewell to his parents and to the negro family that had become such an important part of his life. Mary accompanied him to Rosenbotham's Landing where the giant keelboat waited. She hugged Romulus and little Gabriel first, then turned to Vergina and Leta. She began to cry, tears of happiness mingled with those brought on by impending loss. Five years ago, Vergina had stayed with her while Craig accompanied her brothers on a long voyage downriver to New Orleans. They had forged a bond that had grown stronger over time.

"I shall never forget you, Vergina. We shall see each other again in heaven!"

"Then it not be good-bye, Miss Mary." Vergina's eyes were red-rimmed and overflowing.

Gregory strode over to Mary and hugged her. "You are a wonderful daughter- in-law, Mary. I know my son has found happiness with you."

Craig and Romulus stowed the baggage aboard the keelboat. When they hopped back onto the cobblestone landing, Craig clasped the giant's hand. "Romulus, take good care of my folks. Father will see you established in Philadelphia, and he will write to tell me how you are getting on."

"Thank ye, Craig. It been good livin' with you, but we's got to be free and standin' on our own two feet."

"I understand. I always have."

"Romulus sounds like someone else I know who left his home long ago," Gregory laughed.

Craig embraced him. "Thank you, Father. Thank you for everything. You are simply remarkable! Your visit has been the most wonderful gift."

"Let me know when we have more grandchildren."

"I will." He turned to his little mother. Mary had dressed her in her mauve wool travel coat and taken pains dressing her hair. "Goodbye, little Mother. I love you." He embraced her, sobbing, realizing he would probably never see her again.

"I love you too, Cray."

Craig gasped with shock. 'Cray'—it was a close approximation to his name. The sentence was so clear, he was convinced she knew him; of course it was early morning, the time when she functioned best.

"All aboard!" the keelboat captain called. "Cast off all lines!"

Gregory helped Sarah into the boat cabin. Craig watched the crew take in the gangplank, untie the lines, and pole the long, cigar-shaped keelboat into the main current. Sobbing silently, he watched as it drifted downriver and slowly disappeared behind the bend in the timbered Indiana shoreline.

"Aren't you glad they came to see us, Craig?" Mary asked.

"Yes, I am!" Craig exclaimed. "I am so much richer for it."

"You are indeed," Mary nodded seriously. She waited until they crossed Cottonwood Creek to tell him that Gregory Ridgeway had left him eight hundred and eighty dollars in gold coin.

Chapter Seventeen

New Orleans, Louisiana—November 29, 1816

Jules Signet spent the better part of three months traveling up-river, adding voraciously to his already expansive financial empire. In that time he acquired three well-established plantations that produced cotton, oranges, sugarcane, and brown rice. Each estate came with a large house, numerous barns and outbuildings, a sugar mill, jetty, livestock and other assets, including considerable slave populations. The largest estate listed 104 slaves. Signet purchased this plantation from the state senator who had bought it from Pierre Delacroix. It had cost dearly, and the senator forced him to sweeten the deal by demanding a vice-president's position at the Louisiana Planters Bank in New Orleans. Now, Signet possessed one of Delacroix's finest jewels. He dismissed the current overseers, replacing them with his own men. Next, he procured the adjoining acreage with its vast stand of hardwood timber. He appointed a manager and initiated a massive clearing venture. The giant logs were destined for sawmills in New Orleans. The remainder would be cut into cordwood and piled along the riverbanks to sell to the new steamboats appearing more often on the Mississippi. In time, the cleared land would be transformed into another plantation. Moving north to Baton Rouge, Signet purchased the city's largest shipping firm—docks, warehouses, merchandise and other assets—cash, horses, wagons, and keelboats. He capped off his dealings by acquiring the largest bank in Baton Rouge. In late October, he began the complex process of liquidating its assets, reorganizing the board and restructuring it as a subsidiary of his New Orleans bank. As expected, these dealings required a massive amount of time and attention, yet he still managed his business affairs through a handful of trusted couriers. Detailed correspondences arrived, on average, once a week from New Orleans. Alain Morel kept him up to date on his business and legal activities; he also sent the latest intelligence as it related to him.

In early September, Signet learned that Delacroix had returned home after a lengthy visit to Kentucky. The disappearance had caught him off guard; he was relieved to know the merchant was back in the city. At the time this news arrived, Signet was taking control of the shipping firm. It was late October when Morel informed him that Doc Applegate had also reappeared in New Orleans with Philippe Bouchard. Somehow the old rogue had slipped out of the city, sailed down to Brazil, and rescued the young man before he could be sold to the plantation owners and carted into the interior cane fields. Doc had produced papers proving Philippe's European heritage. Judge Harkness signed the documents and issued a court order directing Alain Morel to assist Philippe in regaining control of his assets. Philippe was already back at Bouchard Exchange, in full control of financial operations.

Signet admitted that the coup was brilliant. It completely surprised him, which meant it had been carefully orchestrated. Doc could not have managed all this on his own. Signet wanted to return to New Orleans and frustrate their scheme, but he could not leave right away—he had just opened negotiations to acquire the Baton Rouge bank. Then he would be entangled in the lengthy process of restructuring. He dashed off orders, instructing Morel to stall the proceedings with delay tactics.

The last courier brought a bundle of letters from his assistant bankers, accountants, and other managers, all inundating him with questions, demanding immediate instructions. Alain Morel urged him to return to New Orleans with all dispatch. Judge Harkness had issued a summons for Signet to appear in court on December 9, 1816. The banker examined it before he laid it aside. This directive did not trouble him as much as the small folded dispatch written ten days ago by one of his hired security men. It read:

New Orleans, Louisiana
November 19, 1816

To Jules M. Signet,

Urge you exercise extreme caution upon return to New Orleans. Reports indicate Emmett Barnett has resurfaced.

Sincerely,
Q.L.

———◄━●━►———

Judge Harkness opened the courthouse for the special, public hearing which had been conspicuously advertised in the *Louisiana Gazette*. The courtroom soon filled with curious citizens, most of them planters, merchants, bankers, and civic leaders. Signet steeled himself to accept the inevitable outcome. He arrived early with Alain Morel and his armed personal bodyguards in tow. The bailiff ordered them to surrender their weapons at the door. Glancing about the courtroom, Signet recognized his longstanding adversaries— Pierre Delacroix, Philippe Bouchard, Henri de Ste. Gême, and some of the older, established planters. He noticed the Catholic priest, Poitier, and the editor of the *Louisiana Gazette* among the gallery spectators. The usual players—clerk, court reporter, and bailiff— took up their places. Signet crossed the floor just as Judge Harkness entered the courtroom.

The bailiff bellowed, "His honor, Judge Harkness! All rise!"

The gallery rose in unison as the judge installed himself on the elevated bench, dressed in his official black robes, prepared to preside over the proceedings. The jury box was vacant, so there would be no trial.

"Be seated," the Judge commanded. Everyone sat down and a hush descended over the room. "I promise you, this hearing will be brief."

"Not good," Morel whispered.

"Any fool can see that," muttered Signet. He was absolutely livid, for Doctor Thomas Applegate had just entered the courtroom. The doctor looked tanned and rested, well-dressed and comfortable in his dark blue suitcoat. No doubt he had coordinated his efforts with that of Delacroix and the judge. Signet knew this was not the battlefield on which to fight. Sometimes in war, one must withdraw tactically to achieve a strategic victory. He resolved to endure this hearing with as much good grace as conditions allowed.

Judge Harkness called Philippe's lawyer to the bench and, after a brief consultation, asked him to address the gallery, to read aloud from a prepared statement. The lawyer, Jameson Howard, a young man newly arrived from Virginia, turned to face the spectators. He was something of a showman, fiery and idealistic.

"Thank you, Your Honor. As you know, a few months back, there arose some question as to the ancestry of my client, Philippe Bouchard. According to at least one interpretation of the Louisiana Digest of 1808, these findings could have disqualified him from inheriting his father's considerable property. Mr. Bouchard would like to thank this court for providing him with the necessary time to investigate and establish his lineage. After a lengthy sea voyage to Martinique, and with the help of French government officials and local priests, he discovered that his ancestry—on *both* sides—traces back to the provinces of southern France. The paternal lineage is thoroughly documented. Mr. Bouchard has recently discovered that his mother's ancestry originates in southwestern France. He wishes to make this knowledge public to the citizens of New Orleans."

"What proof do you have of this finding?"

"These are the official documents."

Howard produced handwritten statements signed by French colonial officials verifying the existence of birth registers and marriage returns. These were affixed with government seals. He also brought out letters from two priests in Martinique. The bailiff conveyed them to the judge.

Judge Harkness studied the documents at length. "How do we know these are not forgeries?"

"Your Honor, I would like to call Father Valentin Poitier."

"Come forward," the Judge ordered. "What can you tell us?"

The priest approached the bench, reviewed the documents, and spoke with confidence. "I solemnly swear that this signature belongs to Father Gérard Gaston, priest in Sainte-Pierre, Martinique. I would recognize it anywhere. We were roommates at seminary and have regularly corresponded over the years." He flourished a piece of paper so the spectators could see. "Father Gaston recently wrote me this letter, detailing Mr. Bouchard's visit to Martinique and the findings regarding his ancestry. He verifies that these documents are authentic in all respects."

The bailiff stepped forward to take it. He handed it up to Judge Harkness. Harkness had already read the letter, but he made a show of accepting and reading it. "Do you have any objections sharing this letter with the court recorder and the journalists from the *Louisiana Gazette*?"

"We do not, Your Honor. In fact, we welcome it."

"Thank you. We will return this letter after the court clerk records it. You may be seated." Judge Harkness then addressed Howard. "What are we, the public, to conclude from all of this?"

The young lawyer stepped forward and answered in a ringing voice, "Philippe Bouchard has provided this court with incontrovertible proof that he descends from white French ancestry. Nothing in his heritage excludes him from inheriting his father's property and wealth. The slave codes of the Louisiana Digest do not apply in his case, and no man may dare lay a claim against him." Howard strode boldly over to Signet, smiling magnanimously. "Mr. Bouchard would like to publically thank Jules Marie Signet for serving

as court-appointed trustee while the question of ancestry was resolved."

"Do you accept his gratitude?" Judge Harkness demanded of
Signet.

"Your Honor—" Morel began.

"Silence!" Harkness thundered. "I did not ask you to speak!"
He glowered again at the ashen-faced banker. "What say you, sir?"

"I accept his gratitude, Your Honor," Signet muttered.

"And you publically acknowledge that Philippe Bouchard is fully entitled to his father's property and that you will provide unre-
stricted access for him, his lawyers and accountants to examine all
legal and bank records related to him, and any transactions made by
you in his behalf?"

"Yes, Your Honor."

"And do you agree the trusteeship you hold is no longer in effect?"

"Yes, Your Honor."

"Is there anyone in this courtroom who doubts Philippe Bouch-
ard's ancestry or his claim to the property left to him by his father?"
Judge Harkness paused and glowered menacingly around the room.
"Let him speak now or forever hold his tongue!"

Doc watched Signet's face and saw intense rage burning beneath
the dignified demeanor. He knew that everyone involved in this
hearing must, from this day forward, guard against retribution. The
banker loathed any challenge, even in minor business affairs. This
time his plans had been completely thwarted. Someone would pay
dearly, perhaps not immediately, but sometime in the future, when
conditions favored.

Judge Harkness ordered Signet to come forward and sign the
legal release forms, also a statement accepting the court's ruling on
Philippe's ancestry. Signet signed the forms, slammed the plumed
quill upon the clerk's table, and strode from the courtroom with Morel and bodyguards hastening to keep pace. Grudgingly, he conceded that Judge Harkness had allowed him to retain his dignity. No one
had leveled charges; no one had hurled recriminations. Instead, the

hearing had taken the form of a celebration, a public announcement handled with a flair of old-world gentility. That bore Delacroix's stamp. The old merchant had fired an unmistakable warning shot, but had conducted himself like a gentleman. Judge Harkness had presided with an iron hand, allowing no diversion from the progression of prepared statements. Signet realized he must resort to other tactics.

The judge rapped his gavel and proclaimed, "These proceedings have concluded!" He sat at his bench, grinning benevolently and enjoying the crowd's reaction. Folks rushed forward to shake Philippe's hand. Many citizens had wondered at his absence, and were intrigued by this affair so shrouded in mystery.

Doc clapped Philippe on the shoulder. "Congratulations, my boy! You have won! I hope I can continue to serve you."

"Thank you, Doctor. You have done quite enough."

Doc wasn't sure if this was a compliment or a dismissal. Probably both.

"My son!" Delacroix wept. "The hearing unfolded even more beautifully than I expected. You are fully restored. Will you now forgive Judge Harkness?"

Philippe cast a murderous glance in the judge's direction. Delacroix observed his hatred. "Philippe, surely your ordeal has taught you something. Forgiving him is the only true way to move on."

Philippe observed Judge Harkness leave the bench and shuffle toward him, rheumy eyes streaming with tears. The judge could not conceal his physical pain; clearly he suffered from bad health. Philippe felt the anger fall away like an irritating scab and his heart soared free. God demanded that His children forgive, just as His son Jesus did from the Cross. Philippe had recently read the story of the Crucifixion from the Gospel of Luke. Delacroix was right—the old man's words would remain forever etched in his memory.

I am certain He has presented you with a rare and precious opportunity, to follow in His footsteps. I pray you will accept this honor and, when you are my age, look back upon

*the tribulation with gratitude; hopefully you will be able to
say—"I forgave."*

The judge stood before him. Philippe could hardly hear him
above the commotion. "I am sorry, son. I wronged you. Please,
please forgive me."

Philippe embraced the judge, while Delacroix looked on, beam-
ing proudly.

Breckinridge County, Kentucky—February 4, 1817

A bale of newspapers, old and recent, arrived by flatboat at
Rosenbotham's store. The year 1816 had passed into history, leaving
a legacy that would long be remembered. As he read the broadside
posted on the store's front wall, Craig could not believe so much
had transpired, that 1816 was such a pivotal year. The American
Republic had celebrated its fortieth birthday, and seemed on the
cusp of embracing a new unity. For the first time Americans viewed
themselves not as members of a loose coalition of states, but part of
a larger 'United States of America.' Nowhere was this better demonstrated than the 1816 presidential election, held from November 1
to December 4, 1816. Americans overwhelmingly sent Democrat-
ic-Republican James Monroe to the Executive Mansion. Monroe had
served as Secretary of State under the outgoing, two-term President,
James Madison. His party basked in wild popularity for prosecuting
and winning the War with Great Britain. The Federalist Party, which
had opposed the war, tottered on the verge of collapse. Discredited
by secessionist rhetoric in New England during the war's bleakest
years, they chose New York senator Rufus King as their candidate,
but did not even bother to make a formal nomination. Monroe won
the Electoral College by the wide margin of 183 to 34.

Kentucky had thrown its twelve electoral votes behind President Monroe. With increased immigration from New England and

eastern states, the state continued to grow, waxing in political and financial influence. A new capitol building was built in Frankfort to take the place of the one that had burned in 1813. Kentucky's great statesman, Henry Clay, was reelected to the U.S. House of Representatives, and he would likely retain the speakership. His extraordinary efforts had helped bring about the Tariff of 1816 and the Second Bank of the United States. He had also proposed a vast scheme of internal improvements to bind the republic together—an elaborate network of roads and canals. This plan was being hailed as "The American System."

Many new developments occurred west of the Appalachians. Congress acknowledged the statehood of Indiana in a joint resolution on December 11, 1816, and it appeared the Territory of Mississippi might be moving toward reorganization. Apparently a plan existed for dividing the territory into the state of Mississippi in the west and the Territory of Alabama in the east. With all the westward migration precipitated by the freezing weather, the Territory of Illinois was experiencing huge growths in population. It would soon apply for statehood.

Craig read stories of the "Year Without a Summer", and he realized how lucky he was, how much devastation Kentucky had escaped. In almost every part of the world, folks continued to experience hunger. Harvests not killed by frost and drought were washed away by flooding rains. Villagers in Vermont survived on hedgehogs and boiled pine needles, while peasants in China sucked on white clay to stave off hunger. Irish peasants begged for alms in the market towns or sold their children in exchange for food. A shortage of bread grains afflicted a European continent devastated by two decades of Napoleonic wars. Craig felt guilty for complaining about his ruined tobacco crop. He and Mary had succeeded at so many other ventures. One thing was certain—there was always plenty of food on their table.

"That Craig sure does love reading the news!" Rosenbotham announced out loud so everyone could hear.

Several folks had come to town to see what new goods the flatboat had brought. The menfolk grinned good-naturedly at Craig. Like him, they were buying garden seeds, select staples, and new harnesses for springtime plowing. Many could not read, but they liked to be informed. They hoped to overhear an enlightened discussion.

"What did you think about our new Governor dying?" the storekeeper inquired.

"I didn't read that," Craig admitted. "What was his name?

"George Madison. He was our sixth governor and, so far, the only one to die in office."

"Heered he was sick afore he decided to run for office," Paul Madden interjected. "He'd done resigned his post as Auditor of Public Accounts due to illness, but his friends pushed him into runnin'."

"That is correct," Rosenbotham nodded.

"I did not vote in the past election," Craig said. "And I am ashamed to confess I thought Shelby was still our Governor,"

"He was, at least until this past September."

"Madison sure didn't serve long."

"Just a few weeks—from September to mid-October. It's a shame to see his career end that way, for he lived such a colorful life. Madison served with distinction in three wars—the Revolutionary War, the Northwest Indian War, and the War of 1812. He was twice wounded and was one of the lucky survivors taken prisoner at River Raisin."

Craig recalled the massacre in the Michigan Territory where Indians burned wounded Kentuckians alive in their cabins. Not many prisoners or wounded soldiers made it home.

"He was second cousin to President James Madison," Jim Fallin volunteered.

"How did he die?" Craig asked.

Rosenbotham continued, "Some ailment—no one really knows. He had been ill for some time. Soon after the election, he traveled to Blue Lick Springs in the hopes he could restore his health. His condition worsened and he was pronounced too weak to return to Frankfort for the inauguration. A justice of the peace from Bourbon

County administered the 'Oath of Office' at the springs. Madison died at age fifty-three in Paris, Kentucky."

"Tell him about the new governor!" Gerald Fischer prompted. "He's in for a rough ride!"

"His name is Gabriel Slaughter—and he has created a mess."

"I remember him!" Craig exclaimed. "He fought at Chalmette. I believe Judge Bozarth knows him."

"Yes, he was there! And yes, the Judge does know him."

Donn Wimmer snorted, "If I had my way, they would throw all those crooks out of office!"

Rosenbotham continued, "After Madison's death, Slaughter replaced the Secretary of State, Charles Stewart Todd, with former Senator John Pope. This smacked of political favoritism—and it was a bad move, for Todd is the son-in-law of Governor Isaac Shelby. To make things worse, Pope, when he was Kentucky's U.S. Senator, voted against war with Britain."

"Everybody is in an uproar!" Richard Waitman threw up his hands. "And if that wasn't bad enough, Slaughter appointed a damned Federalist to fill the vacant Senate seat of William T. Barry."

"There will be more trouble for him down the road," Rosenbotham hazarded. "Kentucky is in for rough time."

"I always try to avoid politics," Craig announced.

"Leave the poltickin' to Judge Bozarth!" crowed an old farmer. The whole store erupted in laughter.

Craig turned his attention back to the newspaper, reading an article about loose credit and land investing. It seemed that investors stood to make a bunch of easy money. While he was engrossed in reading, Levi Matthews burst into the store, interposing himself between Craig and the posted newspaper.

"There you are! Folks said I would find you here!"

"And what of it?"

"Well, here you are reading the newspaper while your Vermont field hand is throwing away all his hard-earned money."

"That doesn't sound like Kelwyn. Where *is* he?"

"Folks saw him going inside Bozarth's law office."

"So?"

"The Judge is always prowling around for investors, and many newcomers have fallen prey to his 'persuasive' charms. Somehow he dupes them into thinking they'll be rich as King George, if only they invest their money into his schemes. We who know him know better!"

"Are you so sure Kelwyn went there to invest?"

"He was carrying a heavy leather bag."

"That doesn't prove anything."

"No? The Judge accosted him last Sunday morning after church. People overheard them talking on the lawn."

"Maybe we should find him." Craig sighed. "But I won't say anything negative in the Judge's presence. I always try to show him a measure of respect."

"Well, if you won't say anything, I will!" Levi announced.

"It's really not my business. You could have gone over there on your own. Why do you need my poor support?"

Together they stepped out onto Rosenbotham's covered, wooden-planked porch. Kelwyn Lasher walked toward them, toting an empty leather bag over his shoulder. He broke into a broad grin. "Where are you two going?" he asked. Craig liked hearing his close-clipped New England accent.

"Well, damn it all to hell!" Levi swore.

"What is wrong with you?" Kelwyn laughed.

"He's just being his usual self!" Craig rolled his eyes.

"Did you give the Judge any money?" Levi prodded.

"Why do you ask?"

"Well, did you?"

"I might have," Kelwyn replied warily.

"I hate to inform you—that man is a crook!"

"He is honorable enough. After all, he is a lawyer, a former judge, local militia leader, official tax assessor and now elected to the Kentucky House."

"He is also in debt to half the county and he has squandered many life savings in his shady, get-rich schemes." Levi paused, so angry he could barely speak. "He's been waiting for a barefoot pilgrim to wander in."

"I don't believe it. The Judge has just returned from the General Assembly. He is a decorated war hero and a deacon at our church."

"He sure as hell is!"

Kelwyn looked to Craig for support. "Judge Bozarth *is* trustworthy, isn't he? He claims you and he are close, that you fought together at the Battle of New Orleans. He said he helped you acquire the deed to your land, and has advised you on several legal matters."

"That is all true," Craig nodded. He would not say more.

"He even told how he led the Regulators that rescued your slaves from the slavecatchers."

"And all *that* is true."

"Then, what is wrong with him? Levi, I believe you have been misinformed. Everything will be fine." Kelwyn recounted what the Judge had told him. "He plans to invest the money in several new state banks. These institutions are starting up free from the usual restrictive regulations, and they will provide ready loans for land investors. He claims the profits will be nothing short of astounding and they could come back to me before spring planting."

"Ask Craig if he has invested any money with the Judge," Levi prodded.

"Well," Kelwyn asked. "Have you?"

Craig hesitated and Kelwyn read the answer in his eyes.

"Why not?"

"I prefer to keep a firm grasp on my money. It is an ineradicable flaw in my character."

"How much did you give him?" Levi asked the New Englander. "You might as well tell us."

"Three hundred dollars."

"Paper or coin?"

"Gold and silver!"

Levi clutched at his forehead and made a cawing, gargling noise as if a fish bone was hung in his throat. He chuckled weakly, "No sense crying about it now!" Then, a sadistic grin broke over his face.

"And what will Prudence have to say about all of this?"

"She doesn't know."

"What!" Levi and Craig exploded in unison. Both realized there would be serious hell to pay.

"Why didn't you just buy a damned farm outright?" Levi asked.

"I wanted to find a way to make more money, faster. The Judge claims I can get a substantial loan from one of the new Louisville banks in which I will own shares."

"So, you gave him good hard coin and let him turn you into a debtor. That's real smart!"

Kelwyn's face reddened and his rate of speech increased. "The Judge insists that being a debtor in this new era is a good thing. The bank will lend cheap paper money to many farmers moving west. Paper is the new currency. Land prices will rise. Grain prices have never been higher."

"I am glad *you* are convinced," Levi snorted. "Let us walk you over there and get your money back!"

"I will do no such thing!"

"Well, you have had your chance. I wish you good luck!"

Kelwyn stomped off into the store, angry over the confrontation. Craig did not wish to see things end on a negative tone, but realized he should let things settle for a while.

"You were a bit hard on him," he said to Levi.

"Just hoping he would see things in the light of God's eternal truth."

"He isn't the first person to make such a mistake."

"Well, at least he won't be leaving you any time soon. You will have a good hired hand for the next several years—the Judge has seen to that."

"I hadn't thought of that."

"Hadn't you?" he chuckled sardonically.

"Don't you have some pressing business at your mill?" Craig asked. "I for one have seen about enough of you for one day."

Levi hunched his shoulders and walked off laughing as if he had been paid the nicest of compliments. Craig returned to the store.

Rosenbotham filled his order and, while he carried the items outside, Kelwyn confronted him.

"Craig, have I made a mistake?" he asked.

"Perhaps and perhaps not. I just read an article about the new state banks and easy credit. It does seem possible that one could catch shares on the rise and sell while the getting is good. One could make money, if he knew when to do all that."

"What would you do?" Kelwyn asked.

"Hold onto the money I have. It is hard enough to come by."

"I can't believe Judge Bozarth would steer me wrong. I can sell my shares of bank stock, borrow money cheap, buy land, perhaps several parcels, sell it when it rises in value, and reap profits from the crops. Sometimes one has to invest."

"You may be right. I sure hope you are."

"The Judge is not a crook, is he?" Kelwyn was trying, unsuccessfully, not to sound anxious.

"Levi was a bit harsh. Don't hold it against him. He can be exasperating."

"You didn't answer my question."

"I don't think the Judge would deliberately cheat anyone. He truly believes he has discovered a good thing, for he invests his own money—and money he does not have—in the same ventures." Craig wasn't completely convinced his assessment was correct, but he knew the Judge was a decent man at heart.

Kelwyn reached his decision. "Then I am relieved. I will stick with the Judge."

New Orleans—March 11, 1817

Two murders rocked the 'Crescent City', putting the whole populace on edge. People began carrying guns and locking doors at night. They traveled in pairs or groups. The torchlight system was reinvigorated. More patrollers were added to the irregular militia force. These reactions stemmed from the shooting of Louisiana State Senator Richaud de Lisle. Unknown assailants had stopped the senator's carriage at twilight on Canal Street. Gunshots rang out and the senator was killed. The murderers slipped unobserved into the haphazard warrens of the American sector. To its credit, the New Orleans militia patrol conducted a spirited investigation, but turned up nothing. No credible witnesses stepped forward.

Jules Signet delivered Senator de Lisle's eulogy, and folks remarked for days upon his distinguished tribute. At the gravesite, he presented the flag of New France to his widow and teenage sons. Louisiana had no official state flag, but De Lisle descended from an ancient French family. The flag, the Royal Standard of Louis XIV, was an outdated, but fitting, gift draped over Lisle's coffin—a white field bearing a blue shield emblazoned with three gold *fleur de lis*, topped by a bejeweled red and gold crown, the whole surrounded by gold adornments. The funeral made all the newspapers and went a long way toward restoring Signet's image. A few days later, a boatman discovered the bloated and partially decomposed body of Jameson Howard, the Virginia lawyer who had so ably championed Philippe Bouchard. The young man floated face down in the muddy river about five miles below the city, an obvious victim of foul play.

Jules Signet shed no tears over either man. In fact, he celebrated Howard's death at the Hotel d'Orleans, splurging on a decanter of fine imported claret. The young upstart had humiliated him, forcing public declarations that would proscribe several future legal actions. Now, he was dead. Senator de Lisle was a fine man, but he had cost Signet a great deal of money, first refusing to sell Delacroix's old plantation, holding out for an obscenely high price and then demanding the vice-presidency at the Louisiana Planters Bank. At least that position was now vacant. Signet would fill it with a more loyal supporter. He chuckled fruitily into his glass when he considered how smoothly both deeds were accomplished. No one could possibly link him to the murders. Morel had hired a third party to engage the killers, and they had proven themselves true professionals. The newspapers attributed the deaths as robberies and mentioned a recently-departed Spanish merchant crew as possible suspects. Signet planned another, similar strike when the next boatload of wild 'Kaintocks' reached the city.

After the private dinner, he visited his regular suite on the third floor. The concierge had already installed the new girl. Fresh from Paris, she was not yet consigned to a local brothel. Signet would enjoy her comforts before anyone else in New Orleans. If she pleased, he might employ her exclusive services, at least until he grew tired of her. He opened the door and gasped. She was a fair-skinned, dark-haired beauty, reclining in the wide four-poster bed, wearing only a filmy chemise, arms over her head so he could see the broad swatches of black hair in her armpits. Her slender thighs parted slightly, providing him with a tantalizing glimpse of her mysterious black forest of dense curls.

He flourished the decanter of claret and announced, "Mademoiselle, we shall celebrate tonight!"

The next morning Signet left the girl, still snoring, entangled in the covers. Exhausted from a night of drinking and pleasure, he decided he would keep the girl for at least a week, perhaps more. Perhaps she reminded him of Lucinde, Delacroix's daughter and only heir. When Lucinde was a young girl, on the brink of womanhood, Signet had offered Delacroix a proposal of marriage. The merchant referred him directly to Lucinde. The haughty heiress had called him an old man and rejected him outright, taking no pains to hide her revulsion. Signet never recovered from that offense. The wound had festered over the years; he continued to obsess over her, lusting for her exquisite beauty and her father's financial empire. He wanted it all.

Signet arrived at the bank, nursing a murderous hangover. A clerk noticed his condition, brought him a porcelain cup of black coffee, and closed the door quietly behind him. In the privacy of his office, Signet plotted his next course of action. It might take months, perhaps even years, but he would have his full revenge, and he would obtain the wealth and power he coveted. Several people still remained on his 'list of expendables'—especially those who had conspired against him. He knew which ones would fall next, but for now he resolved to lay low, digest his recent successes and wait for the right opportunity to strike again.

His only true source of discomfort was Emmett Barnett. The former tavern owner was now a prominent smuggler, circumventing customs officials and allying himself with the bayou pirates. Someone reported that he had lost a leg and now hobbled around on an artificial stump. Sightings of the underworld figure were fleeting and unsubstantiated. Occasionally he did turn up in New Orleans, usually to execute a lucrative business deal. Signet learned that the little man had reorganized a small army of cutthroats, informants, boatmen and 'soldiers' in New Orleans. Most of these were relatives, or men who owed him their allegiance. The customs officials could not catch him, nor could the militia patrol. Signet had clandestinely used the De Lisle murder investigation to scour the streets for the outlaw. Twice he had offered impressive rewards for Emmett Barnett—dead or alive. Some of the takers had ventured into the swamps to search for him and were never heard from again. Signet decided he would raise the reward offer. Eventually, someone would take the bait. He knew from experience that greed would overcome even the strongest fear.

Breckinridge County, Kentucky—March 21, 1817

Although the winter of 1816-1817 had been cold and protracted, and the Ohio River had frozen almost solid, Martin McDonnel claimed he had seen worse. Folks in Breckinridge County were understandably wary, but they could not ignore the encouraging signs suggesting a more normal spring. It was almost as if the veil of smoke or fog had dissipated. On clear days Craig noticed that the sky appeared robin-egg blue; white cumulus clouds had defined edges that did not fade with haze, and the sun shone a brighter yellow. Pasture grass greened and stayed green, rippling in the warm March winds that sprang up from the south. Craig enjoyed listening to those same winds at night, glad for their origins, relieved to know they would not usher in icy air masses. Mary's crocuses and daffodils brightened the front lawn and woodland floors were stippled with various pastels of wildflowers—blue violets, snowdrops, saxifrage, stork's bills, bloodroots and others. White splashes of wild plum and dogwoods, and pink-purple smears of the redbuds daubed greening woods. Long trains of wild geese winged their way northward. Craig shot two of them in the flooded bottomlands and shared them with Martin's family.

Craig's teams of horses and oxen seemed to enjoy working in the fields. Craig sure did. He loved plowing in the bottomlands and inhaling the clean fragrance of freshly-turned soil. He enjoyed watching the robins hunt for earthworms. These orange-breasted beauties would run a few steps, halt, cock their heads to listen, run again and pounce, before gobbling down a pink earthworm. One day he watched Mary working in the new garden, surrounded by three robins, all within an arm's length of her. She talked and cooed to them as she planted English peas, spinach, kale, lettuce, green onions, beets, carrots, broccoli, and cabbage. Craig hankered to taste the new vegetables.

The tomato plants and green pepper seedlings remained safely inside the cabin, growing in small clay pots of soil. As she had last year, Mary pulled a table over to the big south window and let them bask in the sunlight. Martin visited often, offering suggestions on what to plant and where.

"You two are the busiest folks I know!" he laughed. "Just remember, you should always take time off for each other, for family and community. We only have a short time on this earth and you can't spend it all on work!"

Craig realized he was right. Fortunately, farming demanded that the families work together in close proximity. Each family had their everyday chores on separate farms, but something always brought them together. This past winter had proved it. In November, Craig joined the McDonnells when they slaughtered and butchered hogs— cutting up meat, making sausage, rendering fat into lard, smoking hams and sides of bacon. Everyone enjoyed the event—especially the feast after the work was done. Afterwards, the McDonnells returned the favor at Craig's place. That month the families combined their efforts to cut and harvest the meager corn crops. In December and January, they hewed and sawed great blocks of ice from the frozen ponds and river, storing them in underground ice houses and packing them in straw and sawdust. January and February were the months for making maple syrup and sugar. He and Mary distilled two large runs of whiskey, and the barrels now resided in the south shed of his barn. Throughout the winter he cut and sawed firewood, mostly on the Smithhart farm that Kelwyn managed. As Craig expected, Kelwyn's sons were fine hands with axe and saw, and they could rip out a cord almost as fast as the adults. At other times they all split rails to repair the worm fencing lost in flooded bottomland fields. It was amazing to see what everyone could accomplish together.

After Romulus and Vergina moved on, Craig had worried how he would survive, but Kelwyn showed himself as able a plowman as any farmer. Often they would plow with three teams—Craig with his big tans, Kelwyn with his horses, and the boys alternately handling the gentle oxen.

Levi Matthews drove out one Sunday afternoon with his carpentry tools to build Kelwyn a wooden harrow. Craig knew Levi well enough to know it was a peace offering. The miller evidently felt remorse for his harsh comments regarding Kelwyn's investments. Often Levi would say something in jest, laugh at his own wit, then later regret it. Of course that did not stop him from snapping orders while they worked, grousing about how little they knew about carpentry. "Damn it! Have a care with that mallet!" Or, "Keep your damned hands back before I accidentally cut them off!" Craig admitted that the harrow was a beautiful piece of woodcraft, made from heavy twelve-by-twelve white oak beams, joined together by wooden pegs and iron spikes to form a triangle. Levi added a cross beam and sawed it at perfect angles. He then marked the beams with a piece of charcoal and showed Craig and Kelwyn where to drill with their augers. While they did this, Levi cut some thick green chestnut limbs and sawed them into equal lengths, fashioning sharpened stakes from them. He tapered the stakes to fit the holes so tightly that it required a mallet to drive them in.

"You keep those stakes wetted down so they'll swell up and never fall out," he instructed.

Craig admitted it was a finer implement than his own.

"You plan to stay on this summer?" Levi asked Kelwyn. Craig was relieved he asked, for it would help him plan for the upcoming season. He had not felt comfortable asking. Leave it to Levi to broach the subject.

"I suppose I will have to now," Kelwyn shrugged. "The Judge claims that investments take time."

Levi rolled his eyes at Craig. "Uh huh! Well, if this parsimonious niggard doesn't pay you enough, I can find you work elsewhere."

Craig did not feel threatened. Few folks could afford to pay laborers much, if anything. Despite the needling, he admitted he enjoyed the afternoon, spending time with his friends, something he rarely did. Levi was outrageously funny, regaling them with tales about Judge Bozarth's legendary infidelities. He shared how thoroughly shocked he was when the Judge won his election to the Kentucky House of Representatives. "How in the hell he pulled *that* off—I'll never know!" He declared that the Judge would never become governor, but added this qualification, "Mark my words—if they *do* elect that horse's ass, I'm pulling up stakes and moving west!" Levi's wit was cutting as ever, but Craig was relieved to see all was forgiven.

"Ask your employer there about the Judge's mistress, Cecilia Dowell." Levi sniggered. He glanced over his shoulder to make sure

Prudence was not in the vicinity before cupping his hands up to his chest, joggling them up and down to illustrate Cecilia's wobbling bounty. "Craig got himself a real close-up look!"

"Really?" Kelwyn laughed.

"How do you know that?" Craig demanded.

"The Judge told it to Worden Thompkins."

Craig blushed and shook his head in disbelief. The Judge was positively incorrigible. Kelwyn laughed guiltily like a misbehaving boy, glancing back at the cabin, hoping he would not be discovered. Only once was the growing bonhomie darkened. That was when Prudence came out to the barn to ask Kelwyn where he had put an oaken bucket.

"It's right by the well," Kelwyn replied amiably.

"No, it is not!" she snapped.

"I set it right beside the persimmon tree."

"And why is it not in its usual place?"

Craig noticed the controlled ferocity in her gaze and knew that this exchange was not about a bucket. Levi perked up with interest, wincing theatrically as if he expected a thrashing. Prudence shot him a contemptuous stare, wheeled about on her heel and stormed off to the cabin.

"What got under *her* bonnet?" Levi asked in a hoarse whisper.

"She has been this way for some time."

"Do I have to ask why?"

"No," Kelwyn grinned weakly.

"I thought not. Don't worry—I suffered similar circumstances with my first wife, and look at me—I survived. When she turned mean, I found employment that took me away for a few nights."

"I remember all too well," Craig sighed. "He stayed at my place for days at a time. I didn't think he would *ever* go home!"

They spent the remainder of the afternoon together, not really working, putting an edge on a hoe or scythe, rearranging harnesses, mostly talking. As the sun dipped toward the horizon, Craig realized he must get back to care for his animals. Mary would soon be putting on supper. He rode home in Levi's wagon, although the distance was short.

When they pulled onto the road, well beyond earshot, Levi commented. "That Kelwyn is not a bad fellow."

"No, he is not. And he is a great worker."

"I hope to hell you are paying him enough."

"I pay him what I can."

"Do you think Prudence knows the full extent of the—uh—investment?"

"No, I don't think so."

"That's a relief!"

"I know she knows!"

"Man, is he ever in the outhouse! I hope Elizabeth doesn't take an angry turn in her direction."

"She just might—living with you!"

———————◆———————

Next Sunday afternoon Craig rode horses with the McDonnell brothers. He was pleasantly surprised when Martin saddled his chocolate-colored mare and joined them. Craig had seen him ride only a few times, but he was impressed how he handled himself—ramrod straight, but relaxed, in full control, still remarkably robust for a man his age. Perhaps it was because he kept himself fit with hard work. Together they rode over to the Arbuckle farm and inspected it from the riverbank to the base of the high cliffs. Martin's field hands invited them in to see the house and showed them the orchard, deep well, and outbuildings. Martin was pleased to find everything in good shape. After the inspection, they crossed the Hardinsburg Road and visited Craig's farm, the old Smithhart farm, looking over the barns and silos, cleared farmland and standing timber.

"Kelwyn and his family are fine field hands," Martin commented. "I expect you won't keep him for long."

"Perhaps I will." Craig told him what he knew about the investment. "He still hopes the Judge will make him rich."

"A forlorn hope," Martin shook his head.

They stopped in to visit Diogenes and Maggie and then climbed uphill to the extreme southern boundary of Craig's property. Although much of it was comprised of limestone cliffs and other outcroppings, almost three hundred acres of tall timber still awaited Levi's lumber crew. Craig led them to the highest point from which they could turn back and view the picturesque countryside. They could see for miles, up and down the Ohio River. This timbered portion was a gem of unspoiled beauty. Craig could rest assured Levi would not lay it to waste. When Levi finished logging, one would have to look hard to see where he had cut.

They rode over the vast McDonnell farm, taking Craig to places he did not know the old man owned. In the bottomlands they passed a little cabin with its roof fallen in and grease paper hanging in tatters from open windows.

"This is where Mary lived when she first married," Stephen announced.

It had happened a long time ago and Craig gave it no more thought. They threaded their way through Martin's forested bottomlands where they had tapped maple trees a few weeks previously; then they crossed over to Owen's plantation. The house looked dazzlingly white, adorned with fresh coats of paint and trimmings—ornate posts, green shutters, curtained glass windows, porch railings and brightly painted well-house. Owen did not have a suitable river landing, but his farm was massive, much bigger than Martin's home place. He produced more hemp than Martin and Craig combined.

Apparently Owen had told Lucinde to expect them, for she had brewed a pot of hot coffee. She had also baked a fresh batch of beignets, using an old French New Orleans recipe. The dough contained only butter, water, flour and eggs. Instead of yeast, the high moisture content created steam during cooking, and this puffed the pastry. Lucinde heavily sprinkled the beignets with maple sugar, finely ground coffee, and cinnamon, Stephen devoured a half dozen of them.

"My compliments to the chef!" Martin saluted her.

"This is wonderful, Lucinde. Thank you!" Craig said.

Lucinde smiled in return, showing her bright even teeth. Her hair, black as a raven's wing, tumbled down past her shoulders. Her quiet dignity reminded Craig so much of her father.

Afterwards, Craig said good-bye to his in-laws and rode Blue back to his cabin. To make sure the horse did not cool down too quickly, Craig took time to remove the saddle, throw a bigger blanket on him and walk him. He brushed out cockleburs with an iron currycomb and put him in his stall, pouring buckets of fresh water and giving him plenty of oats and hay. While Blue munched on his oats, Craig turned his attention to the other animals pressing in for their share of feed and affection. Somehow, they made him feel part of the great scheme of life.

At the end of March, Craig discovered a massive beehive hidden inside a hollow beech tree and with Diogenes coaching him, he smoked it, pulling out vast combs dripping with golden honey. Craig shared more than half with Diogenes and Maggie. The old couple still managed to get around and were great help in the gardens from which they would share. Diogenes dearly loved his honey. That evening Mary pressed the combs and saved the wax for making fine candles. These candles smelled sweet and burned brighter and cleaner than the tallow variety. Next morning while Mary and the children walked down to Welcome Hall, Craig brought a clay crock of strained honey to Kelwyn and Prudence. He found Kelwyn seated on a hackberry stump in front of the cabin, polishing the surface of his iron plow. When Kelwyn noticed Craig, his countenance brightened and he stood up.

"What have you brought?" he asked.

"A crock of honey to sweeten someone's disposition." He did not notice Prudence standing in the doorway until it was too late.

"I do *not* find that remark amusing, Mister Ridgeway!" she interjected caustically.

"Perhaps I was referring to Kelwyn," he countered. "It *is* fine honey. Mary pressed it from the comb and strained it before sending it over."

"Be sure and thank her for me." She closed the door.

"I didn't mean to make her angry," Craig offered.

"She'll get over it, eventually. It's really not as bad as it seems. I know Levi gets a big laugh out of it."

"That's because he has been there. He told it straight when he said he suffered similar circumstances with his first wife. I knew her well. But know this—everyone has disagreements from time to time. Judge Bozarth has gone through living hell, most of it brought on by his own doing."

"You and Mary seem to get along fine."

"We have had our moments. Bad times usually pass."

"I think everything will work out if Bozarth's investments come through,"

"How much did you leave yourself after you gave him the money?"

"Ten dollars."

Craig said nothing, but he was completely horrified. This admission revealed why Prudence was so angry. She was more than justified. He shuddered to think how he would react if he learned that all his money was squandered. It would take Kelwyn a long time to recoup three hundred dollars. But, the young man had made a conscious decision to risk his money, and refused when Levi offered to try and retrieve it for him. In the end, the Judge had broken no laws when he convinced Kelwyn to invest—unless he used the money for his own personal gain. Craig preferred not to think about it. He had taken a much bigger risk leaving civilized Pennsylvania to come to the wilds of Kentucky. One must live with the consequences of choices, good or bad.

April was always a fickle month in Kentucky. Cold air masses collided with warm air producing frightful thunderstorms, but the rains heralded an end to the cold, dry fog that had gripped the Ohio River Valley over the last terrible months. April brought its usual cold snaps—especially 'redbud' and 'dogwood' winter—sharp reminders of the previous year, but folks could tell that this spring would be different. On Martin's approval, Craig planted red wheat and oats where he had grown corn and tobacco. In early May, he replanted his hemp fields. The fall and winter retting process leached vital minerals back into the ground and renewed the earth so the crop could be grown in the same fields year after year. It seemed that hemp would remain profitable for years to come. Lexington ropewalks demanded tons of hemp for cordage. Ship owners could not stock enough rope for rigging. Neither could another significant consumer of Kentucky hemp—the United States Navy. Factory looms in Lexington, Danville, and Frankfort wove cotton bagging, barely able to keep up with southern planters' demands.

In mid-May, Martin deemed it safe to plant corn. Seed corn was inordinately expensive and, as he had predicted, Levi Matthews made a killing selling it to other farmers. Folks drove their wagons all the way from Hardinsburg and Hartford for a bagful of seed corn. Corn meal and wheat flour brought premium prices from the flatboat men. Fortunately Craig had plenty of seed corn, purchased with hemp sacks. This year he planted patches of five to seven acres in sections of fields where he had never grown corn, mostly on the Jennings place and the Smithhart farm. In all, he planted around thirty-five acres of corn.

At month's end, he shifted to preparing the tobacco plots and transplanting seedlings from the beds. Kelwyn and his boys were great help, as were the womenfolk. Mary helped until mid-morning; Prudence and her boys worked from mid-morning until dinner. Some days, Diogenes and Maggie came over to help. Craig had never liked pulling plants from the beds, so he carried buckets of water and wetted-down sacks full of tobacco plants to the fields where he began pegging holes in straight rows. Kelwyn worked alongside him while his sons kept them supplied with new bags full of plants. After dinner, the boys joined in the pegging. It was constant stoop work that left them all with sore backs and leg muscles.

Craig enjoyed helping Martin and Owen with their planting. This year Martin increased his tobacco plot to ten acres. Kelwyn hired out his team of horses, plowing and harrowing on the Arbuckle farm, at Welcome Hall, and Owen's plantation. The work went smoothly and, on many nights, families and field hands joined together for a meal.

Soon, Mary resumed her weaving industry, but on a much smaller scale, using what women were available. She could always count on Prudence to help. Owen brought up the last bundles from his barns. After that, Levi struggled to find raw hemp, for few people in this part of Kentucky cultivated it. Fortunately, a farmer forty miles upriver heard the little miller was buying and he floated a huge raft laden with hanks of the fiber down to Cottonwood Bend. Levi ordered him to pole it back upriver to Mary's Landing where everyone helped unload it into wagons.

In early June, Mary served yellow crook-necked squash and red-purple beets with fresh butter. Craig loved her cucumbers pickled in apple cider vinegar. He could not wait to taste the first ripe tomatoes and sink his teeth into milky sweet corn. It seemed the earth had finally regained its normalcy.

Craig enjoyed playing with his daughters and hearing their laughter ring throughout the house. They loved to watch him milk cows in the evenings. He lifted Isabel onto one of the big plow horses and walked her around. Ruth was content to have him put her on and hold her there for a short time. Sometimes they played hide-and-seek in the barn loft before bedtime. Every so often, Mary would invite Diogenes and Maggie over and they would enjoy cooking out under the stars. Martin was right—time on this earth was short, and it shouldn't all be spent on work. Craig resolved to make more time for his family and friends.

New Orleans—June 17, 1817

Night closed in, unbearably hot and sticky. Judge Harkness threw off the damp sheets and lay naked, gasping for breath, sweat trickling off him in little rivulets. Lately he had found it more difficult to rise; as a result, he had indefinitely postponed his courtroom trials. His feet and legs were swollen and he felt his lungs filling with fluid; it was impossible to cough it up, but it rattled alarmingly deep inside him. Doc Applegate had examined him the previous day, diagnosing a heart condition. He ground up some medicinal herbs to mix in hot coffee, claiming the concoction would help him eliminate fluids. The herbs helped—some. The judge felt the urge to go again and he reached for his chamber pot, urinating noisily into it. He groaned as the copious outpouring went on and on.

Edna barked angrily from her downstairs room; she was complaining about the noise again. Often times he wakened her with his rasping cough and she would shout for him to quieten down. Something clattered to the floor and, this time, he heard her wail. He struggled to finish his business so he could investigate, but wondered if he should bother. Two nights ago, a frightful pain had squeezed his chest with the grip of a gigantic vice. He had cried out for her, to tell her he might be dying—and he was certain she had muttered, "I hope you do." She did not come to help him and he laid there, somehow surviving the night. Finally, he could put down the pot and reach for his robe. It was as far as he got. Two silent figures entered his room and strode directly toward his bed.

"What do you want?" he demanded.

Something flashed in the darkness and sharp pain stung his throat as a knife was drawn from ear to ear. He tried to shout, but instead coughed up a great fountain of blood. A great weakness washed over him as his vision faded to black. His knees buckled and he struck the floor with a loud thud. Blood pooled around him.

"That was easy," one of the attackers laughed.

"In and out!" agreed the other. "We might take some time to enrich ourselves. There has to be some money in this house."

Solange Tourigny strolled with Doc through the convent gardens. It was still early morning, but the heat and humidity were already oppressive. The sun blazed down upon the lawn; no breeze stirred within the walls. Fortunately, the live oaks provided some relief. They sat on a bench beneath the spreading, interlocking branches, enjoying the shade.

"Well, that is it, I am afraid," Doc finished. "I have faced my devils square on. Now you know why I gambled and drank. I sought to punish myself."

"Your wife—you did all you could to save her. Your last act was a desperate attempt to provide relief. She was already in the throes of death. You cannot blame yourself."

"I know that now," Doc nodded. "I wanted to share it with you. Other than a few colleagues, no one else in this world knows."

"Then I am honored you have confided in me. I shall keep it secret forever."

Doc had already told her about the sea voyage—rescuing Philippe from the slave pens in Brazil, helping him trace his lineage while on Martinique, the return to New Orleans, and the complex legal maneuverings used to outflank Signet. Solange felt that at least some form of justice had been wrought upon the banker, but she was more pleased that Doc had played a major role in Philippe's restoration. Philippe's subsequent rise had proven almost meteoric. The young merchant made the newspapers more often than not; usually there was some new announcement—an acquisition, a new consignment of goods for sale, a new merger, or some civic business worthy of a story. Recently he had outbid Signet in an auction, purchasing the warehouse complex and docks adjacent to his own. A company of French merchants bought his entire grain stock at the highest prices in American history. British factory owners bought up most of his cotton and tobacco. Philippe was back in full swing, thanks to

Delacroix and Judge Harkness.

"You took such great pains to make amends," she said. "I applaud you for that. Most men would have walked away."

"That does not make me worthy of applause. In the first place, most men would not have stooped to such wickedness."

"It is all now behind you. You must move on. You should begin your medical practice anew."

"I have considered that," Doc agreed. "I have saved some money, perhaps enough so I can move up north, take up residence in a small village, and become a country doctor. I read where Kentucky needs doctors. The population there has soared—mostly because of New England immigrants who have fled the cold—and there are not enough doctors to take care of them."

"Yes," Solange nodded thoughtfully. "I can see you as a country doctor."

"He would, of course, need an assistant he could trust. Can you see yourself as a country doctor's wife?" Doc asked the question, almost before he realized it. It startled him.

"I can indeed, Doctor." Solange smiled brightly, taking his arm. "I thought you would never ask,"

Doc stared in disbelief. "You are serious? I thought you might wish to wait, to allow the relationship to develop, to see that I have truly changed."

"I *know* you have changed. At our age we cannot afford to wait."

"My dear, I do not know what to say!"

"You have already said it."

"It won't be an extravagant life."

"Neither is this," she indicated the convent. "But the sisters have shown me what really counts in life. God wishes me to help the sick. That is what you are doing."

"I am no knight in shining armor. I fear the armor has grown somewhat—ah—rusty. I am well past sixty, you know."

"None of us is getting any younger."

"True, but—"

"I am afraid I have already consented. You may not back out

now!"

———◆●◆———

Pierre Delacroix was among the first people in New Orleans to hear about the Harkness murders. This was not surprising. The merchant had cast a wide, well-established net of operatives throughout the city, and up and down the river. As a successful investor, he knew in advance what businesses and properties would come onto the market. No merchant ship or flatboat arrived without his knowledge. Delacroix gleaned other intelligence from the surrounding countryside, America's heartland and coastal cities, and from foreign governments. A chill wriggled up his spine. The murders smacked of Jules Signet. Of course there was no way to prove it; the banker had departed for Baton Rouge some days ago. Signet would naturally remove himself from New Orleans before setting things into motion.

Delacroix's first thought was of Philippe Bouchard. The young man might be in mortal danger. He left his warehouse and strode briskly along the levee, unconcerned for his own safety. The Bouchard Exchange was in an uproar. Philippe and his associates had just heard the news. The young man spied him instantly.

"Monsieur Delacroix!" he called above the clamor. "Come up to my office!"

Delacroix crossed the room and ascended the stairs. Philippe offered to assist, but the old merchant was as quick and sure-footed as any mountain goat. When he closed the door, Philippe asked the critical question, "Is Signet making his move?"

"I fear so."

"The judge's house was rummaged to make it appear like a robbery."

"Yes. And Signet is conspicuously out of town, supposedly on business."

"Can't we make an accusation?"

"Who would act upon it? Judge Harkness is dead. Signet virtually controls the militia, the city and parish lawmakers, state legislators and other prominent citizens. What proof could we bring? "

Philippe thought for an instant. "We could fight him with our own forces—on the same terms."

"And join the Devil in Hell? We must never stoop to his level of barbarity."

"We should at least defend ourselves!"

"By all means, yes."

"Are you carrying a weapon?" Philippe asked.

"I admit I am not. I left my warehouse in great haste."

Philippe opened a desk drawer and handed him a short, loaded pistol crafted from walnut and worked in brass trim. He also gave him a leather shot pouch. "Take this. It shoots beautifully. I have made up several cartridges with powder, wadding and shot. Bite off the ends and ram them in."

"I have weapons, Philippe." Still, Delacroix took the pistol, proof he considered the situation dire.

"You should have someone guard you around the clock. I intend to surround myself with men I can trust."

"Wise choice."

"And now, I will have you escorted back to your warehouse."

"Thank you for your concern, young man. And I appreciate you signing those papers yesterday. I know you will execute my estate honestly."

"Nothing will happen to you."

"Signet will be furious when he discovers what we have done."

"That is a good thing. Take care, monsieur."

The city authorities summoned Doc Applegate late that afternoon. As a physician, Doc was licensed to conduct the official medical examination. He had observed death in many guises, but this one hit him hard—Judge John Harkness was his closest friend. He and Doc had come through the darkest of times, opening their hearts to each other as few men would do. Each knew the other's sins and had struggled together in their long, tortuous climb out of darkness. The sheriff and two militiamen waited in the shaded archway of the carriage entrance. When they saw Doc, they whistled to summon the two slave gravediggers lounging beneath the live oaks. The slaves rose hesitatingly and joined them. The sheriff and his men directed them all inside. Doc followed their example and loosened his cravat, tying it snugly over his mouth and nose, for the stench was unbearable. He ordered the slaves to open the windows. Edna lay face up on the floor, slashed across her breast and stabbed clumsily in four places. It had taken her some time to die. Judge Harkness lay in a congealed puddle of blood, a hairy heap covered with metallic green blowflies. The loathsome creatures had already lain eggs in the open gash and now swarmed greedily in and out of it. Doc ordered the slaves to roll the corpse so he could examine it for other wounds. After determining that the judge had died from the single slash, he informed the sheriff, "Have the slaves transfer the decomposing bodies to the cemetery." That, thankfully, was not Doc's job.

He left the judge's bedroom and descended the same flight of outside stairs on which he had brought the slave girl, Kayla. That spurred a further thought. What would become of her and her child, now her sponsor was dead? Had the judge made provisions? Doc resolved to find her and bring her to Delacroix.

Back at the courthouse Doc recorded the findings of his investigation, filed the proper forms, and made out an invoice for his payment. The official inquest would be held sometime in the future—a new federal judge must be appointed. Doc stepped back into the street and headed for Emmett's safe house tucked away in the American sector. Doc had not seen him since their return from the sea voyage.

The city reeked almost as badly as did the Harkness house. A heavy dome of humidity trapped and intensified the mid-June heat and rotten smells of open gutters. Doc avoided the roughest sections of town. He glanced down each street and alleyway, on guard for possible assailants. His nerves were frayed. Apparently Signet had decided to make his play. Anything could happen. The sun began to sink, but the temperature did not decline. It would be another hot, miserable night. He sighed, weary and dispirited. Then he thought of Solange and his spirits lifted. It was time to leave New Orleans and take her north.

He shifted the black bag from his left hand to his right, awkwardly transferring his cane. At that vulnerable moment, two men appeared beside him. Before he could react, they had grabbed his arms and wrenched the bag from his clutches—the bag with his medical equipment and all his life savings. He would have fought for it, but a pistol jabbed him in the rib cage. He had been foolhardy, carrying his wealth in the American sector without Emmett Barnett's protection. Now, he had lost everything. He had nothing to offer Solange—if he somehow escaped this predicament alive. He raised his cane, prepared to use it.

"Do not make me do it, Doctor." The voice bore a heavy French accent as the cane was snatched away.

An enclosed carriage wheeled out of the shadows and the assailants shoved him roughly inside. The driver sped westward, heading for the city limits. Doc realized that his long run was over. Signet had triumphed. Doc would never experience the new life with Solange; his last chance for happiness and fulfillment had vanished. At least, he could take some comfort, knowing he had turned himself around, and fought the good fight. During that time he had always known the worst could happen. Hopefully God would go easy on Judgment Day. Father Poitier had assured him that God knew each person's heart—that He would forgive, if asked. The knowledge emboldened him.

"Where are we going?" he demanded.

"You'll know soon enough."

Doc studied his abductors and recognized none of them. But he knew enough about human character to know they would kill him at the slightest provocation and dump his body into the gutters along with the other refuse. Fighting was not an option—every one of them aimed a cocked pistol at him. One attacker rested his gun barrel on top of the medical bag, using it as a prop.

Doc recalled that Signet had once offered him a thousand dollars to put Delacroix down with poison. He wondered if he might yet strike a deal, feign acceptance of the offer—and use the opportunity to escape. He immediately discounted this stratagem; the banker knew full well that he had gone down to Bahia to free Philippe and frustrate his plans. With Judge Harkness gone, and with friends controlling the militia and city government, Signet had grown too powerful. Doc's skills were now superfluous. The banker would have his revenge.

Chapter Eighteen

Breckinridge County, Kentucky—June 17, 1817

As the summer solstice approached, the sun brought a clarity and brightness not enjoyed in the Ohio River Valley in well over a year. Giant cumulus clouds sailed like ships in majestic progression from south to north, traversing across a clear blue sky that stretched endlessly overhead. Tree foliage grew full and leafy; grape vines and fruit trees blossomed, and by all appearances would produce bumper crops. The corn, hemp, wheat and oat fields looked especially promising, testament to Martin's insistence on crop rotation. Few other farmers bothered with such "larned foolishness," but even a dullard could see how poorly their crops would turn out in comparison.

Sunshine and warmth worked like a magic elixir, restoring, almost fully, Craig's healing spirit. The long days provided plenty of time for work and allowed precious time for family and friends. Craig's workload eased when two new families arrived from New England, near destitute from the "Year Without a Summer"—clean, thrifty folks searching for a new beginning in western lands. One couple had four children, all of working age, the other had three younger children. Craig installed them in the empty cabins on the Jennings place, breaking new gardens and providing them with vegetable seeds. Mary brought over some laying hens and fresh vegetables, and Craig gave each family a smoked ham. Feeding them proved easy in the summer months. Sometimes, at sunset, Craig shot a deer trying to eat in the gardens. He and Diogenes would skin it and cut it up for immediate consumption. Diogenes also trapped raccoons and possums raiding the gardens. With uncanny skill, he ran trotlines in the river, baiting the hooks with high smelling entrails from his traps. He regularly hauled in a mess of catfish. At first, the families expressed shock when they learned the negroes were slaves, but Diogenes assured them, "Craig done give us our papers. We's here because we want to be."

Like Kelwyn's family, the newcomers proved industrious— and they were great help in the tobacco patch. The plants already stood shoulder high with their fine, broad leaves waxing dark and healthy in the sunlight. On his visit last summer, Pierre Delacroix had brought seeds for a new, sweeter Caribbean strain, and Craig had taken instantly to cultivating it. Six acres now grew in the bottomland pasture where he had grazed cattle for the past four years. Martin had come down in April to approve the site. As usual, his counsel was wise.

"The old Widder just about wore this low ground out, planting tobacco over and over again. But I will tell you a secret. She did not plant anything near my line. If you start out near the rock wall and work back toward your landing, you might produce a fine crop. It is wise you allowed the land to rest. Those four years of grazing will work in your favor, for the respite has given your soil a chance to recover. This spring's flood deposited a thick layer of silt—you can still see it clinging to the tree trunks, so you know much more settled on your fields. Here is something else—the Widder barely scratched the topsoil with that skinny mule and wooden plow. You have teams of oxen and horses and a heavy iron plow. I'll hazard you could plow deep and turn up several inches of rich, river bottom silt deposited over the centuries. Harrow down those ridges, break up the clods, plant your tobacco, and watch it grow!"

Craig had followed his advice and could now see the wisdom in it. This tobacco would make his best crop yet. It amazed him how quickly he and his new field hands could work over the patch. He purchased new hoes at Rosenbotham's store and kept the families busy chopping weeds. When they finished the tobacco patch,

Craig shifted them into the cornfields. Kelwyn, Prudence and sons demonstrated their skill in hoeing and, working with the newcomers, they kept the fields clean. Apparently Judge Bozarth's investment scheme had not materialized, for Kelwyn continued to work, not broaching the subject of buying a farm. Craig figured that the young farmer had accepted the fact his money was gone and was settling in to recoup it. Prudence never abused Kelwyn in public, but she rarely smiled or engaged in small talk. Only when Mary visited the field did she seem to brighten.

Attracted by the promise of good land and cheap money, other New England families arrived in Cottonwood Bend, Hardinsburg, and the scattered little villages in Breckinridge County. All of them hoped for a fresh start in life. Like a spider weaving its web to trap unsuspecting flies, the wily Judge Bozarth formed what he called a "settlement agency" to "assist" the immigrants in their endeavors. He offered commissions to those locals who referred newcomers to him; of course he managed to impose flexible legal terminology to wriggle out of paying for most referrals. For a reasonable fee, the Judge advised the new folks where to settle, showed them what farms they might procure, and conveyed them to places they might find work. For those with a goodly supply of hard coin, he peddled his money-making schemes, convincing them to invest in the new wildcat banks and western lands. Using his credentials to impress, he set himself up as their land agent, lawyer, and investment advisor, quite content to shift business hats on a moment's notice. Folks in Rosenbotham's store marveled at his industry.

One farmer commented, "The Judge might have once been a-skeered he couldn't afford Frankfort—but by dogs, he might just go all the way to Washington D.C.!"

New Orleans

Doc Applegate acknowledged that his life had reached its conclusion. Strangely, he was experiencing more anger than fear, regarding his current plight more as an unwelcome interference than a death sentence. Life with Solange would have been redeeming, worthwhile, sublime. Together they could have done much good. He wondered how Judge Harkness behaved when he met his end. Had he begged for his life? Probably not. The judge was in ill health and approaching death. He had fully honored his commitment to restore Philippe, going so far as to humble himself in the courtroom and ask for the young man's forgiveness. No doubt he had prepared himself. Doc admired him, but did not wish to concede his own hand—at least not yet. He inhaled deeply and cleared his mind. He still had a few cards up his sleeve and he intended to play them.

The carriage turned off the rutted Levee Road onto a smooth plantation driveway of crushed shell lined with white rock and rows of live oaks. As they pulled into the circular drive, Doc noticed the upper veranda of a large French Caribbean-style house. Signet owned several properties along the river; no doubt this was one of them. A half dozen armed horsemen sat their mounts in the shade of sprawling live oak branches. Others lounged on the front porch. Doc's abductors hustled him out of the carriage and onto the wooden porch.

"Inside!" one of them growled.

Doc stepped forward to face his executioner. He stopped in the center of the room and blinked his eyes, hoping they would grow accustomed to the darkness. His abductors lined up behind him. Another half dozen men stood before him, forming a rough semi-circle.

"Hello, Doctor," a voice barked. Doc would have recognized that low growl anywhere. His knees almost buckled from relief.

"Why, Emmett Barnett! You ornery brigand!"

Before he could cross the floor, the swarthy little smuggler walked gamely toward him—*step-thump—step-thump*. He clasped Doc's hand and grinned, his tar black eye disappearing into the deep creases of his sun-blackened face. He had let his curly black ringlets grow longer and, combined with the eye patch, this gave him an even more piratical air.

"You in deep hell trouble!" he laughed.

"Tell me something I don't know. The affliction is chronic, I fear."

"Signet kill Judge and others. He search for you."

"And you also."

Emmett grinned wolfishly. "If he not careful, he find me."

"Where in the hell *are* we?" Doc glanced around at the elegant furnishings—French drapes, marble-topped furniture, paintings, and fine books.

"Ste. Gême's."

"Why did you bring me way out here?"

"Signet hunt you. He also hunt Philippe."

"What?"

"He hire big army of men. Then he go up north—while they kill his enemies. He come back and take over."

Doc reasoned that Emmett commanded his own network of spies and informants. He would know, almost as well as Signet, what was happening in New Orleans. "I must warn Philippe!"

Emmett shook his head, his drooping black moustaches fluttering like tiny ribbons. "Too damn dangerous. Too many men!"

"Still, I must try! After all he has suffered, that boy deserves some help. You might one day find him your best trading partner in New Orleans. Consider this—if they kill him, you will be doing your trade with Signet. Lots of luck there!"

"You packing gun?"

"Yes—when you give back my medical bag."

Emmett nodded to the men behind him. Doc pivoted and snatched the precious satchel out of his abductor's hands, fixing him with an icy glare. The man grinned back, unaffected.

Doc turned back to Emmett. "Will you drive me to the Bouchard Exchange? We might not have much time."

"Come back to bayou with me. I kill Signet—trouble over."

"Delacroix says no."

"He wrong. Only one way to stop."

"Let me meet with Delacroix first."

"I send men with you. Be careful, Doctor."

Baton Rouge—June 17, 1817

Jules Signet dined that evening on roast beef au jus, poached snapper in cream of dill sauce, steamed mushrooms and broiled asparagus tips. After the meal, he enjoyed a fine cigar with champagne and chocolate truffles. His hotel room overlooked the Mississippi River, now almost indigo in the fading light of evening. Two slave boys pulled on cords, operating large, woven-cane ceiling fans to stir the sluggish air. Signet smoked the cigar and read by lamplight the latest intelligences from New Orleans. The Governor would soon appoint Judge Harkness's successor, Emile Blanchard de Carondelet, to the bench. Alain Morel had practiced law with Carondelet, and acting upon Signet's insistence, arranged a congenial introduction. After that, Signet spent valuable time courting Carondelet, feeling him out on various issues. In the end he knew the judge would support his cause. Acquiring Philippe's wealth would present little problem—here Signet could resort to direct action. The levee was a dangerous place, full of foreign sailors and dangerous Kaintocks. Any of these ruffians might lunge from the shadows or shoot from concealment. Fights, robberies and murders had grown increasingly commonplace in New Orleans. Philippe had no heirs; once again Signet's bank would become trustee of his possessions. The new judge would quietly allow Signet to assume control of the estate at a ridiculously low price.

Pierre Delacroix's estate must be handled differently; like an onion, several layers must be peeled back. In this case, a living heir currently existed—in fact, there were grandchildren. First, Delacroix must be removed from the equation. After that, Carondelet would order the clerks to remove all of Lucinde's manumission papers from courthouse files. Delacroix's home and lawyer's office could easily be burgled or set afire. In the end, Carondelet would rule any of Delacroix's surviving manumission papers null and void, declare the daughter a slave with no rights of inheritance, and appoint Signet trustee of the estate with the option to assume control. But that meant bringing the daughter and her children down to New Orleans. The judge would demand her to appear in court in person. Signet could prove that Lucinde Delacroix had at least one-sixteenth negro blood in her veins, that she descended from slave women. By law Signet could possess her, use and dispose of her as he wished. He felt a thrill of excitement course through him. For years he had coveted Delacroix's wealth and position. Now it all lay within his grasp. Owning the daughter and her issue would be the *pièce de résistance*.

Signet quelled the rising sexual urge and studied the dossier again. The mercenary's record was impressive—his little army-for-hire had worked for several rich American landowners, merchants, businessmen, and unnamed legislators, helping them remove various "obstacles" in their paths to success. The Emperor Napoleon had employed him on the European continent in a number of assassination schemes—all had met with success. In November 1815, the mercenary had scouted for Spanish forces in Mexico and helped them surround and apprehend the revolutionary Catholic priest, Jose Morelos. He would be expensive, but he was unquestionably the best.

At that moment, the concierge knocked on the door. "Monsieur Signet, your guest has arrived."

"Thank you. Please have this dinner cleared away."

"Of course, sir."

"You may send him in."

The door creaked open and the mercenary stepped inside. He was the most impressive human figure Signet had ever seen—dark-haired, at least six-feet-six, broad-shouldered, and lean-waisted, with a square-jawed face hard-chiseled by sun and wind. He wore expensive blue dress trousers, white shirt with ruffled collar, and gray linen vest. Bruce Bowman's stride exuded the lithe grace and awareness of a stalking panther. Signet rose and shook his hand, guessing him at about thirty years of age, a bit young to lead such an operation.

"Mr. Bowman, please take a seat." He gestured at the two chairs near the window.

"Thank you." Bowman sat down, never taking his eyes from Signet's.

"Alain Morel informs me you might be available for employment."

Bowman nodded cautiously. "If the price is right and the project feasible, I might just be."

Signet liked his manner of speaking—confident but non-committal, wanting to hear all the facts before agreeing. "Of course you must hold what I tell you in strictest confidence. If you reject the operation, you may not bandy it about."

"If I did that, my reputation would be forever ruined. Discretion is not the least of my virtues."

"Very well. I need you to assemble a force of about a half dozen good men. They must supply their own horses and arms, and be willing to follow you several hundred miles north."

"I am listening."

"Some months ago, the outgoing Governor of Louisiana wrote a letter of introduction and signed a judge's order empowering my designee to locate and bring back to New Orleans a runaway slave woman and her children. They belong to me and I wish them returned unharmed. You will ride to Frankfort, Kentucky and present the document to the new Governor there. He, or someone in his office, will issue you a legal writ authorizing you to seize the slaves. Our Governor, Villeré, has requested that the Kentucky writ require cooperation from local law enforcement officers."

"It sounds straightforward enough."

"Nothing is ever straightforward. Complexities always arise. In this instance the woman has married a white man of some substance. I understand his family is highly regarded in the community. There could be fighting."

"That is what we do best."

"Once you have seized the slaves, you will make all haste to present them to me in New Orleans."

"Understood."

"Let us discuss your fee."

"This will cost you, dearly. I employ thirteen men. They have served me well for five years. It may sound heavy-handed, but we work together as a professional unit—and produce guaranteed results. Each man is a weapons expert, skilled in the art of fighting, tracking and anti-tracking..."

Signet listened in awe as the mercenary expounded on his men's abilities. He knew he need look no farther.

"We pride ourselves on stealth and subterfuge. Wherever we operate, we settle in, get to know the people, then scout the terrain for ambush sites and escape routes. We evaluate all the best options, planning our tactics carefully. We have caught runaway slaves before—as far north as Canada. Often, we make the extraction without killing anyone. That is always the best outcome."

"How much?"

"Three thousand, five hundred dollars."

"What!"

"And I insist upon two thousand dollars in advance."

"That is highway robbery!"

"You admitted yourself—this is a complex mission. I estimate, conservatively, that it will take anywhere from three to five months. In addition to the wages I must pay my men, I will incur charges for hotel bills, food, stable fees, oats for the horses and numerous incidental costs. I may be required to socialize while in Frankfort. All of this requires money."

"Yes, I understand."

"I am considering several lucrative offers at present. Revolutionary leaders in colonial South America have long aspired to break free from Spanish rule. They want guerrilla fighters, but need skilled military planners even more. I may sign a contract with one of them. You would be wise to secure my services before then."

"Can we sign the contract in New Orleans on June twenty-sixth?"

"If you will lay down a retainer of five hundred dollars."

"Done. We'll meet in my office in the Louisiana Planters Bank—early morning. At that time I will provide all remaining particulars."

"And the money, of course." Bowman grinned sardonically.

"Of course."

New Orleans

A carriage emerged from the dusk. Pierre Delacroix's heart raced as he fumbled for his pistol with shaking hands. Decades had passed since he shot a man. Doc Applegate's voice just prevented him from doing so again.

"Pierre! It is me, Doc Applegate!"

Delacroix subsided and leaned against the carriage archway for support. He hung his head and took a few deep inhalations, hoping the dizziness would pass.

"Are you unwell, Pierre?"

"No—please allow me to recover my wits." Delacroix drank in a few more breaths. He had not experienced that kind of fear since the French War in Quebec, decades, almost a lifetime past.

Doc laughed. "These are Emmett Barnett's henchmen. Don't feel ashamed—they scared the literal hell out of *me*." Then he grew serious. "Have you heard about Judge Harkness?"

"I have."

"You and Philippe are next on Signet's list."

"What about yourself?"

"Rest assured, he wants me dead—for personal reasons. I am on my way to warn Philippe. Will you join me?"

"We have already spoken. He understands the situation, completely. By now he has surrounded himself with protection."

"Have you informed the militia patrol?"

"Yes. I fear we may not count on them."

"Well, get yourself inside and lock the doors. Load all your firearms and keep them close."

"Thank you, Doctor. I am much more concerned for Philippe."

"It is *your* wealth for which Signet has lusted."

"Then he will find only an empty shell. Last summer I moved most of my wealth to Kentucky and gave it to my daughter Lucinde. I have rid myself of all remaining assets. They are now safely in the hands of Philippe Bouchard. He will execute the will and see she receives the rest."

"I would love to see Signet's face when he discovers that!"

"It may not be pretty," the old man conceded. "If something happens to me, you must promise that Lucinde remains safely with her family in Kentucky. I have strictly forbidden her to return here. Will you see she stays away?"

"I will try," Doc promised. "I am not sure what I can do."

"You can go to her—tell her what happened and remind her of my words." The merchant seemed shrunken, fragile, and strangely vulnerable.

"Nothing will happen to you, friend." Doc tried to hide his concern. "Won't you come with us?"

"I will lie down now. You have given this old man a terrible fright."

"Very well," Doc tipped his hat. "Good evening, Pierre." He drummed on the roof and shouted, "Drive on!"

The carriage driver cracked his whip and the team of marbled grays clattered along the levee toward the Bouchard Exchange. Doc felt a pang of unease leaving Delacroix alone, but remained focused on the task at hand. If Emmett said Philippe was in danger, one could sure as hell count on it. First, Doc would warn Philippe, then find out where Judge Harkness had housed Kayla.

Night closed over *Vieux Carré*. The spires of St. Louis Cathedral loomed high above *Place d'Armes*, barely visible in a night sky just a few days off the new moon. On their right, the Mississippi sprawled in an empty black expanse. The carriage sped dangerously as they neared the warehouses on the levee's eastern end. Doc caught the distinct popping of firearms. A surge of trepidation rose into his throat. He hadn't counted on riding into a war; he figured he could warn Philippe and still have time to flee New Orleans. Emmett's men exploded into action, drawing pistols or thumbing back their shotgun or rifle hammers, galvanized into a state of awareness. Rather than rein in, the driver cracked his whip and drove the grays harder, charging into the midst of a raging gun battle. He swung the team into a sharp left-hand turn and pulled up hard under a stack of cotton bales. Doc clutched at the door handle for balance, gripping it in white-knuckled fear.

Emmett's men disgorged in hasty accord, two of them clambering roughly over Doc's legs. Doc realized with a sick slide in his guts that these men were absolute maniacs. Apparently, the driver was cut from the same cloth—he looped the reins around the brake handle, snatched up his shotgun and leaped nimbly off the box. Emmett's men fanned out into the warrens of barrels and bales, crates and sheds. In the pitch blackness, Doc wondered how they could distinguish the enemy from Phillipe's men. He had never been in a gun battle before. For some time he sat, frozen with terror and uncertainty, wondering what to do. It seemed far more dangerous outside the carriage. A bullet thwacked into the side paneling, shattering it and stinging him with wood splinters, changing his mind. He scrambled outside and flattened himself against the rough, hemp-covered cotton bales. In the darkness he opened his medical bag and fumbled for a pistol.

"Bang!" A shotgun roared nearby. The report drew several shots from across the square. Bullets ticked and whizzed off the cobblestones or thudded into cotton bales. A man screamed in obvious pain. Doc located his priming flask and struggled to control his nerves. With skilled surgeon's hands he poured a measure of gunpowder into the pan, cocked the hammer and closed the frizzen. He shrank back into a shallow indentation in the cotton bales and let the battle play out. The shooting lasted for some time—a single shot here and there, and then a flurry of reports—big, booming blasts, high-pitched rifle shots, singing bullets, and whining ricochets.

Slowly and erratically, the gun battle moved away, downriver beyond the Bouchard Exchange and Philippe's warehouses. Doc followed the noise cautiously, weaving stealthily between sheds and cargoes, his senses heightened with terror. It grew quiet.

"Over here!" someone hissed.

"Are they gone?" another asked.

Doc wondered if these were Emmett's men, or those hired by Jules Signet. He crept silently among the bales, waiting to hear more.

"Let's chuck this fancy pants into the river!"

"You'd better slice his gullet with that pig sticker. He's still alive."

"Hell, I'll just put a ball through his head. Give me your gun."

"What's wrong with yours?"

"I'm out of shot. Let me shoot him with your pistol!"

"And bring the whole bunch down on us? By now that militia patrol is on its way. They must at least give the impression they played a role in putting down the violence."

Doc froze. These were undoubtedly Signet's men, but how many he could not tell— definitely two, perhaps more.

"Give me a hand, will you?"

Doc caught a blur of movement near him. He could just make out the figures of two men dragging a supine body. Surprisingly, their victim jerked and broke free. In an instant the attackers clubbed him about the head with their gun butts. The unfortunate man slumped back to the ground, unconscious.

"Let me shoot the bastard now!"

"I told you—no!"

"Then I'll stick him!"

"No you won't!" Doc heard himself roar. In his rage, he was not immediately cognizant of his actions; he was shocked that he had stepped forward, and now leveled his cocked pistol at the two men.

"Bang!" An orange flash lit the surrounding bales and a lead ball whizzed past Doc's left ear. One of Signet's men had fired, just missing him.

Doc did not miss. The heavy-caliber pistol thundered and kicked high, but the bullet struck home with a loud, meaty thud. He saw the gunman collapse into an inert mass. There was scarce time to avoid the other attacker who advanced with a long-bladed knife, fast closing the distance between them. Dropping the medical bag, Doc snatched up his cane and swung it with superhuman strength born from abject fear. The cane, fashioned from solid ebony and topped with an ivory head the size of a large duck egg, hissed in a wide arc, smashing with a sickening crunch into the attacker's skull. Doc could tell from the jarring impact that he had killed the man. No human could survive such a blow.

In the silence that followed, he drew out his other pistol and primed it, then reloaded and primed the discharged pistol. He crept cautiously toward the victim and rolled him over. In the darkness he just recognized Philippe Bouchard.

"Oh, my dear God!" Doc gasped in sheer disbelief, wondering what might have happened if he had delayed coming here, even for a few moments. Certainly an unseen hand had intervened, guiding him to this place. He slapped the young man's face. "Philippe! Can you hear me?" No response. Hurriedly he strode over to the team of gray horses. They shied and stomped, still nervous from the gunfire; mercifully, they had not bolted. He led them over and flung his black bag onto the carriage floor. Somehow, Doc managed to half drag, half haul Philippe to the carriage. The young man was slender but tall, weighing about a hundred fifty pounds—more than Doc was used to handling. He struggled to bundle the limp body into the carriage interior. Perhaps residual fear unleashed hidden reserves, for it enabled him to just accomplish the feat. It required even more effort for him to climb up onto the box. He released the brake and sped back toward New Orleans.

———◆———

Doc drove like a berserker, galloping his team recklessly through the streets, wondering where he might find a safe haven. Philippe needed immediate medical attention—God alone knew what internal injuries he had suffered. Doc thought first of taking him to Delacroix's townhouse, but discounted that possibility. Emmett Barnett had claimed that the merchant was on Signet's death list. He might be dead already. Doc then considered the convent as refuge, but he did not wish to involve Solange—at least until they were ready to leave. There was no way of knowing where Emmett was, so he avoided the American sector. His options were dwindling. In the end he decided on the rectory of St. Louis Cathedral. Surely the priest would accept them. Doc cut across Place d'Armes and slowed only when he reached the rectory. He pulled up and wrapped the reins around the brake handle as Emmett's driver had done. Carefully, he climbed down and knocked loudly on the door.

Father Poitier cautiously opened it, holding a candle lamp high. "What is wrong, Doctor?"

"It is Philippe," Doc indicated the closed carriage. "Signet's men attacked him. I fear he is badly hurt."

"Let's bring him inside." No inane questions, no protestations—Doc had rightly figured the priest would prove sympathetic.

Together they lugged Philippe inside and laid him out on the stone floor. A copious spattering of blood trailed into the room. Father Poitier lit another lamp and placed it on the table's edge. Carefully, Doc examined the young man. The knife wielder had inflicted two nasty gashes, one on Philippe's left forearm, another on his right shoulder. Both wounds required stitches. Doc knew he must tend to them immediately, for Philippe had already lost much blood.

"Press the heel of your hand onto the forearm," Doc directed. "No—right there, where it is bleeding. Apply steady pressure until I am ready to work." He retrieved his medical bag, laid out clamps and sutures, surgical needle and cords. Quickly, he fashioned a simple tourniquet which Father Poitier held as Doc heated surgical clamp ends over a candle flame. Then, he located the severed blood vessels, pinching them with the heated clamps. He washed the wounds with wine and closed them with neat stitches, wrapping them with bandages. Gently, he raised Philippe's head to accommodate a pillow which the priest provided. Then he elevated the damaged arm. The young man's breathing seemed regular, but his heartbeat was fast and his skin felt cold and clammy. Doc brought the lamp close and held open each of Philippe's eyes, checking the pupils for signs of concussion. Both appeared normal. Doc would allow him a brief rest before trying to revive him. He spent a few moments wiping blood from Philippe's upper body before carefully sliding a blanket under him.

Father Poitier watched all in quiet amazement. "God has truly gifted you, Doctor."

"Well, it is in His hands now, so you might offer up some prayers. That is *your* specialty. Unfortunately, my poor skills are limited to the earthly realm. Besides, God wouldn't listen to an incorrigible miscreant like me."

"There you are wrong, Doctor."

"While you are at it, pray that Philippe's other injuries are not life threatening. I am concerned his attackers have fractured his skull. Often, a severe head blow can cause bleeding of the brain. This can result in stroke-like damage and, possibly, death."

"How did it happen?"

"They clubbed him with pistol butts."

"Are you sure the attackers were Signet's men?"

"Completely sure. You have heard about Judge Harkness?"

"Yes, God rest his immortal soul." The priest hung his head in sorrow and uttered a prayer.

"Emmett Barnett warned me today that Signet has hired an army to kill Philippe—Delacroix as well."

"You must take this to the law."

"Right now Signet *is* the law," Doc insisted.

"Where is Delacroix now?"

"I last saw him at his townhouse."

"Does he have men to protect him?"

"I saw no one, but surely he has made some sort of arrangement."

"You stay with Philippe. I will bring him here." The priest left quietly and strode toward Delacroix's townhouse.

———◆———

By some unknown miracle, the merchant had escaped Signet's assassins. Perhaps the private army had concentrated their forces to eliminate Philippe, calculating correctly that he would put up stiffer resistance. Perhaps they believed they could take Delacroix at any time. Father Poitier escorted him now through the black streets of *Vieux Carré*, but the spry old man set a hard pace, threatening to leave him. Poitier rationalized that he should bring up the rear in case someone followed them. Certainly Signet had assigned some-one to watch the townhouse. From time to time he halted, listening for footsteps, but he heard nothing. Soon they reached the rectory. The team of unsecured grays still stood motionless in the narrow street behind the building. Delacroix possessed the good graces to wait and allow the priest to let him inside.

Father Poitier opened the rectory door. Doc recoiled and swung a loaded pistol toward them, but lowered it quickly. He growled, "You might have first announced yourself!"

Phillipe now lay in the priest's simple bed. He smiled wanly when he recognized his friend and mentor.

Delacroix crossed the floor, knelt down and touched Philippe's hand. "My boy, I am so glad you are still alive."

"The feeling is mutual, monsieur." Philippe subsided, obviously weak.

Delacroix turned to Doc Applegate. "Will he recover?"

"No guarantees, but he stands a good chance."

"How on earth did you lift him into bed?" Father Poitier asked.

"He woke up and climbed into it himself—with my assistance, of course. He drank some water, which is a good sign. We must get some broth into him."

"This violence must end today!" Delacroix exclaimed, his face a bitter mask.

"I agree," Doc nodded. "Philippe has already taken the initiative and contacted powerful figures like Ste. Gême, de la Ronde and Plauche. They agreed earlier this afternoon to meet with Governor Villeré. Perhaps, if they act together, they can bring Signet to heel."

"Villieré won't believe them. Signet left for Baton Rouge days ago. They will have difficulty proving his involvement. And that damned Morel will muddy the water. To make things worse, Signet has allied himself with the Governor."

"Shh!" Father Poitier gestured for them to stop talking. "Someone is outside." Footsteps sounded on the cobblestones.

"You in there, Doctor?" someone called.

"Who wants to know?"

"Jacques. We're taking Emmett's horses."

"Ah!" Doc crossed the floor and peered cautiously outside. Recognizing most of them, he further opened the door. Emmett's men assumed a rough defensive posture outside the rectory. Doc wondered how they had found him. It was a long walk from the exchange. "I needed to leave in a hurry. Sorry about that."

"You fight pretty damned good!" the gunman, Jacques, exclaimed. Doc recognized him as the one who had earlier appropriated his medical bag. Two of his cohorts supported him between them. He stood on his left leg and seemed to favor the right.

"What's wrong with your leg?"

"Shot."

"Then I should have a look at it."

"Not here." Jacques broke into a broad grin. "I will tell Emmett about you killing the two men. He will like that!"

"What do you mean?" Delacroix asked, shouldering past Doc.

Jacques explained, "I had fired my weapons and was forced to hide among the cotton bales while reloading. I watched the whole fight from just a few feet away!" Apparently, Doc's misadventure elevated him in the gunman's estimation.

Doc glanced guiltily at Father Poitier.

Jacques gestured inside. "If you hadn't killed them, that boy would be dead."

"Truly?" Delacroix marveled.

"They were ready to cut his throat. Doc shot one with his pistol and clubbed the other to death with his cane. Spilled his brains onto the levee!"

"And then he brought Philippe here and tended his wounds," Poitier added.

The merchant turned to embrace Doc. "I abhor violence, but you have saved Philippe's life! You have more than redeemed yourself, Doctor Applegate. We owe you a debt of gratitude."

Doc coughed in startled embarrassment. "I seriously doubt that. Well, there is nothing more for me to do here. I must tend to other wounds. Remember, you should also credit Emmett for saving Philippe's life. And these men who drove me to the levee."

"None too soon!" Jacques exclaimed. "The fight had already begun!"

"Yes, yes." Doc cut him short. "Get off that leg, now. I will fetch my bag and join you."

As he gathered up his instruments, Delacroix grasped his arm. "Will you remember to honor my request? If something happens to me, will you travel to Kentucky to warn my daughter about the danger?"

"As it happens, I am headed north with my intended bride, Solange Tourigny. We intend to start a medical practice there."

Delacroix grinned and winked at Father Poitier. "Then I will provide you with necessary travel funds—and some additional money—a little wedding gift—to establish yourself. I trust you two will do much good, wherever you settle."

"And I would be honored to perform the marriage ceremony," Father Poitier offered. "Of course you must first convert to the true faith."

"I suppose I better had," Doc agreed. He prepared to leave.

Philippe raised himself up and croaked hoarsely. "Good bye, Doctor. And thank you."

"You have nothing to thank me for. Promise to rest, and drink plenty of fluids. We'll soon see the back of this."

———————◆———————

Emmett Barnett watched with interest as Doc extracted lead shot from his gunman's leg. One mushroomed pellet clung with stubborn tenacity, defeating all Doc's efforts to remove it, forcing him to open the wound wider so he could probe at a different angle with the small forceps. Jacques shrieked in agony, struggling wildly against the men holding him. With a short swing of his fist, Emmett clubbed his forehead, knocking out all resistance, allowing Doc to resume work. The pellet came free with a loud sucking noise and clattered onto the table.

"That's the last one," Doc announced. He poured wine over the wounds and bound them with a light dressing.

"You damn fine doctor!" Emmett grinned.

"As long as those wounds do not mortify, he should be fine."

Emmett led him out onto the shaded porch of Ste. Gême's plantation. It was shaping up to be another hot day. Doc washed his hands and instruments before taking a chair and indulging in a single glass of red wine. It had been a long and stressful night; he needed to rest. Emmett joined him. As they sat in what passed as companionable silence, Doc surveyed the plantation grounds and wondered how Emmett had managed to procure it for a base. Perhaps Ste. Gême wanted the smuggler close at hand for his own protection. It was an ideal location, surrounded by drainage ditches, orange groves and near-impenetrable cane fields. To the front lay the Levee Road and the broad Mississippi, both easy to guard; in back, the plantation ran into a cypress swamp. Apparently the place was far enough from New Orleans not to arouse suspicion. Doc counted sixteen men under Emmett's command and figured they could hold off an army. He leaned back in the cane chair, allowing himself to doze, barely conscious of the gunmen who spoke in a heavy Cajun dialect.

After some time, Emmett asked, "When you let me kill Signet?"

"Unfortunately that is not my decision. I know Governor Villeré plans to speak with him. Hopefully this will prevent further violence. Delacroix still insists upon fighting Signet on legal grounds."

"Like going to gunfight with bare hands—can't win!"

"You may be right."

"Old Delacroix be killed soon enough—you see."

"I hope not."

"How the boy?"

"Philippe will live. He plans to return to the Bouchard Exchange and fort up inside with his trusted gunmen. Kayla and her child will stay with him. With Judge Harkness gone, they will live under his protection."

"Good people," Emmett mused.

Doc wondered that this cold-blooded monster could actually feel—let alone express—such sentiment, but upon further reflection he managed to work it out. They had spent a long time together and suffered near-impossible hardships; each had been forced to fight free of their personal, agonizing hell—Doc from his transgressions, Philippe from total ruination, and Kayla from abuse, childbirth and slavery. Emmett had lost his livelihood and suffered the amputation of his leg. The long sea voyage had forged a strange bond that tied them all inextricably together; close circumstances enabled each traveler to know the other and to appreciate their various plights. The journey had been a life-changing experience for them all. It hadn't made Emmett any nicer, but it revealed to Doc that the human spirit could always surprise.

"You want them to live, send for me."

"I will," Doc replied, mostly to appease him.

Breckinridge County, Kentucky

Shimmering heatwaves distorted the tobacco patch as Craig and his workers hoed out new weeds and got an early start picking off tobacco worms. The New England families all came from farming backgrounds and they readily adapted to gently examining leaves and stalks, demonstrating true care for the leaves as they searched for and destroyed the pests. In just a few weeks, they would all be topping blooms.

The summer sun reached its zenith, and the Ohio River Valley air lay in a heavy blue haze. Everyone broke into a sweat long before mid-morning, but after the previous year's cold, Craig resolved never to complain about heat. He knew he was blessed, and he thanked God daily for His many gifts. Regular rains had produced a sizeable hay crop. Kelwyn and the other New England families took to the fields, proving they were skilled hay cutters. As a result of their combined efforts, the first cutting was sun-cured golden brown, raked into windrows, forked into big hayricks or loaded onto wagons and stored in Craig's barn. The hemp plants grew tall and dark green, undulating in rare summer breezes. This summer the tobacco leaves looked most impressive. It appeared that the corn, planted in new fields, would fare well. Both cows calved; hogs farrowed sizeable litters, and fruit trees still promised abundant harvests.

All nature conspired to obliterate the previous year's hardships. There was much reason for hope. Craig's daughters were growing and Mary was, once again, with child. When she told him she was nearly two months along, Craig experienced the familiar initial pang of unease, but he observed her glow of absolute contentment and decided not to spoil her happiness with useless worry. He would put the matter in God's hands and trust completely in Him.

The summer gardens produced some truly spectacular vegetables—and these graced many meals at Welcome Hall. Everyone took advantage of the long summer days. As evening shadows descended upon the front lawn, the children played games of tag or hide-and-seek, running and shrieking with laughter. After supper, the adults moved chairs outside to observe the fun and, at times, assist the youngest children. One night, Lucinde and Owen announced that they, too, would bring a new addition to the family, most likely in early December. Agnes brought out jugs of peach brandy, hard apple cider, and wine, serving everyone their choice. Martin McDonnell, the patriarch, now in his seventy-seventh year, sat back in his chair, stretched his long legs and laughed out loud at the children's antics. He looked relaxed and fulfilled as he sipped on a tumbler of Mary's and Craig's best whiskey, enjoying the gentle breezes wafting in from the river. The family had endured through hard times and could, now more than ever, appreciate the good.

One morning Craig drove Mary and the children into town to shop at Rosenbotham's Store. It had been some time since they had left the farm, and the outing gave Mary the chance to stock up on salt, spices, coffee, tea, fine wheat flour, spools of thread, and bolts of cotton and linsey-woolsey cloth from which she could fashion new clothing.

As he carried out a hemp sack full of supplies, Craig noticed Levi Matthews standing at the corner of the brick storefront. The little miller hissed and waved impatiently for Craig to join him. He was fairly bursting with fresh gossip. When Craig reached him, Levi glanced over his shoulder to make sure no one was listening.

"I guess you have heard the latest on Judge Bozarth?"

"The last time I saw him, he spent half an afternoon rhapsodizing about his grand time in Frankfort," Craig replied. "I learned then to never ask him about the General Assembly. To hear him tell it, he has made a big splash with the legislators and is on easy speaking terms with the Governor."

"That all may be true, but he's in deep trouble here at home with Gill Hagman."

"Who is he?"

"The farmer from up past Hardinsburg who is sweet on Cecilia Dowell."

"I thought the Judge was finished with that foolishness!"

"Nope. Gill caught him at her house and beat the literal hell out of him. Told the Judge he'd kill him if he saw him there again. He blacked both of the Judge's eyes and roughed him up—badly. The old fraud barely made it home. He concocted a tale for Violet. Claimed that his horse spooked, ran him through some trees and threw him. He was laid up for a week or more and he is still hobbling around."

"Poor Judge. He doesn't understand how he hurts people, because it truly is never his intent. He actually sees himself as the victim in the affair."

"Well, he's got worse troubles than Gill Hagman. His investors are threatening to lynch him. Folks in Hardinsburg have hit him with lawsuits. Lenders have filed liens on his property."

"I figured something like this might happen."

"This time, he may actually have to sell his house."

"That is sad. I figured he might find success in Frankfort."

"In all likelihood he has done the same thing up there, perhaps on a larger scale. The more money he has, the more money he spends—or invests in shady schemes. You might think he would at least use new investors' money to pay off his earlier investors, but that is not the case."

"How do you know it is not?"

"He brags after church services; so does Violet. They wined and dined throughout the whole legislative session. She came back from Frankfort with a half dozen new dresses. He purchased two pairs of new boots, some gold cufflinks and an expensive rifle."

"Why did you seek me out to tell me all this?"

"The Judge is desperate. He is renewing his efforts to draw in more investors. No doubt he will soon pay you a visit."

"I have pretty much convinced him that I can't invest."

"Then don't let him swindle your new workers. I am afraid Kelwyn might fall prey to his wiles once again."

"I doubt that very seriously. If the Judge visits the Lashers' cabin, I shudder to think of the consequences. Gill Hagman's thrashing would pale in comparison. He might even end up dead!"

"Come now," Levi laughed. "Kelwyn is as mild and easygoing as anyone I have ever known." Then he caught Craig's meaning and laughed out loud. "You're right! I believe she *would* kill him!"

———•———

Judge Bozarth showed up at Craig's barn early next morning. Mary was cooking breakfast in the cookhouse, something she did in summer to keep the cabin cooler. Craig had just finished milking and was putting the buckets in the springhouse. The smell of frying bacon, eggs and pancakes wafted on the southerly breeze all the way out to the barn, piquing his hunger. The Judge sat regally on his big chestnut mare, dressed in a new dark blue suit coat.

"Good morning, Judge!" Craig greeted him.

"Same to you, young Ridgeway," the Judge boomed in his deep theatrical voice. He dismounted slowly, apparently still sore from his beating. Craig pretended not to notice, but observed his recently-blackened eyes and facial bruises now faded to a sickly greenish-yellow. The Judge watered his horse and watched as Craig used a corn cob-handled file to lay a bright edge on each of the long-handled hoe blades. After breakfast Craig planned to put his workers into the tobacco fields.

"You are an industrious young man, Craig. You have always impressed me with your work ethic." The Judge was a master at buttering up his constituency—or his prospective victims.

"Thanks, Judge. Running a farm takes a great deal of work."

"I honestly cannot name another soul who has accomplished so much from so little."

"Mary and I really don't have that much," Craig replied, including Mary's name and hoping to put him off asking for money.

"Bah! When you arrived here, you were a penniless lad with your buttocks hanging out of the holes in your trousers. It gave me great pleasure to execute the Widow Fuqua's will and to see you

receive your inheritance. It provided your start. You have not forgotten?"

"No," Craig replied. He felt a twinge of remorse. The Judge
was playing the guilt card with uncanny skill, obviously desperate,
bringing up an event from six years ago. Then, Judge Bozarth had
acted as Craig's lawyer and had guided him through the complicated
legal processes of inheritance, paying back taxes, and drawing up a
new deed. But, for that service he had been well recompensed. The
Judge's legal fees took a large portion of the money due Craig.

"And, you will recall I petitioned the Governor of Kentucky that
same year, expediting your reward for killing the outlaws."

"Yes," Craig admitted. Silently he added, *"You were helping
yourself, for you also had a reward coming."* The Judge continued
to build a strong emotional case, one that would be increasingly difficult to refuse. Before Craig could stop him, he resumed his litany
of benevolent deeds.

"Might I add I provided sound military leadership at the Battle
of New Orleans? You desperately needed a strong commander to
follow." Craig did not contend that he and his brothers-in-law had
arrived in New Orleans three weeks ahead of the Judge, and had
served under Pierre Delacroix and later, John Coffee's Tennesseans.
Obviously, the Judge had recounted his own version of the story so
many times that he now believed it.

"Of course, let us not forget the service I performed in rescuing
your abducted slaves. Other officials might have allowed them to
slip away, but I willingly risked life and limb to redeem them."

"Yes, you did." Craig realized that this was mainly why he felt
so beholden to the Judge.

"And I willingly broke the law, drawing up and signing those
false bills of sale for your father."

This argument hardened Craig's resolve, rather than erode it.
A friend would have done it for next to nothing; instead, the Judge
had shaken his father down for a hundred-and-twenty gold dollars.
Craig held his tongue and waited for the great personage to make
his move. Apparently the Judge was having a hard time coming out

with it. He chose a different tack, making an expansive sweep with his arm to indicate Craig's estates.

"So here you are, young Ridgeway. You now own three farms, a profitable distillery, a fine cabin, and several spacious barns. I understand you have partnered with Levi Matthews on a number of lucrative ventures. And you now have workers in your employ. You truly have come a long way in this world, lad."

"I *am* blessed, but expenses are frightful. Last year's cold weather diminished us greatly. And that excise tax on whiskey cuts deeply into any profits."

"There may be good news forthcoming on that front," the Judge volunteered. "I have it on good authority that President Monroe intends to ask Congress to end the whiskey tax."

"I will believe it when I see it."

"Craig! Breakfast!" Mary called from the cabin.

"Won't you join us, Judge?"

"I have breakfasted—thank you, lad."

"Then have some coffee," Craig offered, glad Mary had called. Together they would form a stronger front resisting him. The Judge wouldn't wish to offend the daughter of one of Cottonwood Bend's leading citizens.

"First, I wish to talk with you about a new investment."

"Then you must join us, for I cannot make a financial decision without Mary."

The Judge looked flustered, but resigned. "Very well." Craig noticed his sheepish expression as they walked toward the cabin.

Mary had set the dogtrot table where they could enjoy the light morning breeze drifting through. She poured coffee and forked a stack of bacon, two eggs and three pancakes onto Craig's plate. The Judge watched with interest as Craig buttered the pancakes and poured maple syrup on top.

"Will you have breakfast, Judge?" Mary asked cheerfully.

"I do believe I shall," he beamed.

Craig had already figured he would, for the Judge dearly loved good food. After Levi Matthews, he could eat more than just about anyone. Isabel and Ruth watched in awe, captivated by the elegantly dressed visitor. After a time they lost interest and went inside to play.

"Try the plum preserves, Judge," Craig offered.

"Thank, you, lad."

After breakfast he resumed his assault, beginning with his usual flattery. "Young Ridgeway, you have made good in this world and I am truly proud of you. Cottonwood Bend needs more citizens like you. Mary, you and Craig make a splendid couple."

They nodded and waited expectantly for his next line. Apparently, the Judge expected the praise to soften them but he perceived this was not working. Their direct gaze wrong-footed him and he slurped noisily on his coffee. "You know, a young couple like yourselves should think about investing for the future."

"That is just what we are doing, Judge," Craig replied. "We have everything invested in our farms. We *have* been fortunate, but because we have been thrifty. We must watch every expense."

"Yes, but so many financial opportunities currently abound. Kentucky is truly rising, shedding its frontier image. New banks, steamboat companies, and land ventures have made folks rich—you should consider investing while the times favor. You may never have another chance."

"I appreciate you coming out here, Judge," Craig said. "I just cannot invest money with you."

"Your friend Kelwyn has invested. I plan to ride out and give him another chance to add to his good fortune."

"Please do not do that, Judge."

"And why not?"

Craig struggled to find the least offensive phraseology. "Kelwyn and Prudence are not—uh—pleased with you. He invested almost their entire savings and it has caused much friction in his marriage."

"I did not realize that."

"How much money has he realized from your investments?"

"I cannot divulge a client's financial or legal affairs."

"You don't have to. We both know—he has earned nothing. His family subsists on what wages I can pay them."

"Sometimes it takes years for investments to bear fruit."

"Those investments will never pay off."

"Craig, you do not understand the nature of business." Clearly, the Judge felt insulted.

"I understand *this*—the wildcat banks will fail, and much sooner than you might think. Their paper money will be worthless. Agricultural prices will certainly drop, and outstanding debts will be called. I fear for your investors—and I fear for you, Judge."

Judge Bozarth's countenance darkened. He rose slowly and put on his broad-brimmed hat. "I can see I am not welcome here."

"Judge, you are always welcome," Craig insisted. "Why don't you tell us the real reason you came."

"You would not understand."

"Try me. I count you as my friend. You know I will keep your confidences."

Mary interjected, "Sometimes, true friends must put aside pretenses and speak plainly. Please, sit down." She refilled his coffee cup and this simple act appeared to mollify him.

The Judge sighed wearily and sat down, looking rather deflated. "I know you two must hold me in terrible disregard."

"Not so," Craig argued. "We have been through too much together. You are one of the pillars of our settlement."

The Judge buried his face in his hands. "Not for much longer! I fear I am ruined! I have borrowed heavily to finance my own speculation, and now the lenders are filing liens against my property. My clients' investments may never pay off. For some time I have suspected I have been duped by shady bank agents. I never intended to lose people's money."

"Most folks already know this. But you can't continue your charade for much longer. And you can't keep taking money from families already struggling to exist."

"What am I to do?" Judge Bozarth pleaded. "I readily admit to making poor monetary choices." Craig could not tell if he was acting or sincere.

"Violet is quite astute when it comes to money matters," Mary contended. "She might help you deal with the lenders. Have you spoken with her?"

"Good Lord, no!" the Judge recoiled in genuine alarm. "After my infidelities I could not bear to injure her further. I spend money to keep her happy, to atone for the anguish I have caused. She so enjoys her station." He began to weep and, in his usual manner, it came out loud and full. "What am I to do?"

"You must tell her everything," Craig answered firmly. "I understand she has money of her own."

"That is true, but I cannot ask for it."

"Then you must bear the full consequences of the law. The sheriff will surely come to evict you. And by then, Violet will know anyway. It is best you tell her before it happens."

"Oh! How I desperately need money—right now! Unfortunately there is very little for a lawyer to realize in this one-horse town!"

"How much money?"

"I don't know."

"You must know who your lenders are, Judge."

"Yes, I do."

"Then you must curb your expenses and begin paying off each lender. Even if you are forced out of your home, you must find a way to restore your honor."

"I fear it is not that easy. Liens have been filed."

"How many liens?"

"Two that I am aware of."

"Then you must deal with them—the earliest lienholder first."

"Others will follow," the Judge threw up his hands in despair.

Craig glanced at Mary. He could see the compassion written on her face and he knew what was coming.

She spoke softly and directly. "Judge, we do not have much money. If we let you have some, you must promise to tell Violet all the details of your plight, for she shares in your misfortune. Let her handle the money, and then you must work to pay off your lenders. Violet may love you more, if you confide in her why you spend."

"But I might lose her!"

"That possibility does exist, but I believe she loves you. She may prove your salvation."

"You would loan money to this miserable wretch?" Judge Bozarth asked incredulously. "Perhaps I can invest a small part of it."

"No," Craig shook his head. "You have invested enough. You must apply it exclusively toward your debt."

"I will pay you back!" The Judge declared. He meant this sincerely, but Craig knew he could never repay.

"We can let you have one hundred dollars," Mary offered.

Craig almost choked on his coffee. He had not expected her to give that amount. It took much labor, time and good fortune to earn one hundred dollars. While Craig toiled in his fields, the Judge lived like a king enjoying fine foods, liquors and cigars, buying expensive clothes, guns, horses and rigs, traveling to Frankfort and hobnobbing with the elite. It wasn't fair, but the Judge was in real trouble—and he had helped Craig when he was in trouble.

"God bless you both!" Judge Bozarth boomed.

"It is all we can give," Mary qualified. "And it will hurt us."

"Then, please consider it a loan."

"We want you to have it and do with it as we instructed."

The Judge hung his leonine head and shook it in a theatrical display of sorrow. "I cannot accept."

"You took everything Kelwyn had," Craig pointed out.

"I did not know his situation then. I assumed he had much more."

"Just promise you will not go up there. I warn you—it will not be pleasant."

The Judge considered this as he downed a final cup of coffee. He waited patiently while Mary fetched the hundred dollars in coin. She dropped them into a small cloth bag. Craig heard the clink of heavy coins and felt a pang of remorse with each clink. Then he recalled what Martin once told him—the Judge was a man worth having on one's side. He still retained some influence and might again prove valuable. Mary pressed the little bag into his open hands.

"Why are you doing this?" Judge Bozarth asked, weeping.

"Because you are our friend," Craig answered simply. "We do not wish to see you fail."

"I hope I may one day prove myself worthy of your friendship." The Judge shook Craig's hand and hugged Mary before striding briskly out to the barn where his mare waited. He hauled himself painfully into the saddle and guided the horse back to the cabin. "Thank you, Mary, for the wonderful breakfast!"

"You are welcome, Judge," she replied.

As they watched Judge Bozarth trot the big mare down the lane toward the Hardinsburg Road, Craig wondered which direction he would take. If the Judge turned east toward Hardinsburg, he most likely planned to continue his hopeless fundraising. If west, toward Cottonwood Bend, he might just head home to talk things over with Violet.

"Which way will he turn?" he asked Mary.

"Toward home," she replied with a tone of certainty. "He has much to discuss."

"Did we just throw away a hundred dollars?"

"Probably—I don't know." She shaded her eyes against the rising sun.

"I bet he heads east, toward Cecilia Dowell's house."

"And you are an old cynic!" She elbowed him and play-slapped his arm.

The Judge reached the end of the lane and reined in his mare. Clearly he was tormented. He glanced longingly toward the east. Perhaps he contemplated visiting the families in Craig's employ; maybe he still hoped to prey on new investors recently arrived in Hardinsburg. Almost certainly he thought about Cecilia Dowell. He held his mare in the morning shade, pondering for a long time before finally turning west and heading home. Mary smiled knowingly.

New Orleans—June 26, 1817

Dawn broke over the city in a hot, muggy haze with diffused rays of light slicing through the fog and spilling onto the wooden floor of Louisiana Planters' Bank. Two men sat on either side of a large Louis XIV desk inside the president's office. As previously agreed, Jules Signet paid out fifteen hundred dollars in gold and silver coins. Bruce Bowman counted and swept them into two leather satchels, adding to the five hundred dollar retainer paid him in Baton Rouge. With the required advance in his possession, the mercenary could lower his reserve and adopt a more accommodating manner. After all, Signet now had full rights to dictate specific terms. Bowman carefully examined the official letters, maps, and other documents, probing for possible weaknesses.

"This letter from Governor Claiborne is a masterful piece of work—and the new Governor's request strongly reinforces it. We should have no problem securing the Kentucky writ to seize the woman and her issue."

"How soon can you leave?" Signet inquired.

"In three days," Bowman replied unhesitatingly. "We will begin provisioning this afternoon."

"You do not wish to wait for a steamboat?"

"I do not. Several weeks could pass before a steamboat arrives at the levee. Even if one arrived tomorrow, I doubt we could load fourteen horses on board."

"The builders are manufacturing bigger boats," Signet argued. "The newer ones can carry considerable cargo, including livestock."

"I prefer certainty. I can't control steamboat schedules, trading stops, snags, sandbars, or boiler explosions. But I can dictate our speed overland."

"So, you intend to ride north on the Natchez Trace and return by the same tortuous route?"

"We will decide that when we assess the conditions in—this settlement—Cottonwood Bend." He studied the hand-drawn map of Kentucky, estimating the distance from Frankfort to the little town. "It is located on the Ohio River. We should be able to commandeer a boat for the return. In that case, we could split our force. If we effect a clean getaway, we would need only a half dozen men to return the slaves. The remaining men on horseback could lead the horses back to New Orleans."

"Then I encourage you to consider seizing a steamboat. The return could be accomplished in mere days, rather than weeks."

"We will examine all possibilities." He read the description of the slave woman. "Tell me more about this Lucinde."

"I remember her as a young girl," Signet began. "Her father is Pierre Delacroix, one of the richest men in New Orleans. The man is a legend, a decorated soldier from the French War, and one of the richest men in Louisiana. He married a woman with negro blood in her veins and there were no manumission papers."

"I asked you about Lucinde."

"She is now in her mid-twenties—quite beautiful. Her great-great grandmother was a full-blooded slave on the island of Santo Domingo. Six years ago, she married a young Kentuckian, Owen McDonnell, and moved with him to Cottonwood Bend, about a hundred miles downriver from the Falls of the Ohio. She has borne two children and they must be brought with her."

"How do you know this?"

"Delacroix recently visited her. What grandfather can resist talking about his grandchildren? It is common knowledge among the city's elite."

"What more can you tell me?"

"Lucinde's father-in-law is Martin McDonnell, a Revolutionary War hero, now in his late seventies. He has a wife and teen-aged son living with him. He farms the land immediately upriver from Owen, and a son-in-law owns the farm above him."

"That doesn't sound like much opposition."

"They are popular citizens in the settlement, and good friends with the local militia commander, a Judge Wilfred Bozarth. All are veterans of the Battle of Chalmette Plantation."

"Interesting," Bowman mused. He rose in a smooth, cat-like motion, slid the documents into a leather folder, and shouldered his money satchels. "I will review every document and contact you if questions arise. If not, we will leave on June twenty-ninth. When I reach Kentucky I may have the opportunity to send a cryptic note informing you of our progress, but in all likelihood we will return long before any correspondence could reach you."

"Then I wish you good luck." Signet rose and shook Bowman's hand. The mercenary spun on his heel and exited the office in a deliberate stride. The banker watched him leave, pleased to have finally set the final part of his grand scheme into motion. There were still a few loose ends remaining, but he would eliminate these long before Bowman's return.

He tried to imagine Lucinde's face when he told her she was his slave. Her arrogance had festered for years; finally he could exact revenge. There were hundreds of ways to humiliate her, and he imagined taking advantage of every one. He could lock her up and have her any time he wanted, as often as he wanted. The mere thought of inflicting pain produced an animalistic thrill that overrode all reason. The surge in his groin required instant relief. Hurriedly, he closed his office and walked across the cobblestone street to the hotel where the new girl still slept.

Chapter Nineteen

Mary's Landing—July 2, 1817

"It seems such a shame to break off these lovely flower heads," Prudence shook her head as she examined an early tobacco blossom. "But I understand why we must."

"We want to divert the energy into leaf growth instead of the flowers and seeds," Craig instructed. He beckoned for the New England families to gather round so he could demonstrate how to top tobacco plants. "Fortunately only a few plants have flowered. Before they do, we must break off these tops here, just above the main leaves. Take the stalk between your thumb and first two fingers and simply snap it off. Throw the top onto the ground and be mindful not to break the main leaves as you pass through the rows. Everything we do in this field centers around preserving the leaves and ensuring that they grow large."

When Craig arrived in the Ohio River Valley, he knew nothing about tobacco; now he was teaching others. He walked between two rows and showed them what to do, recalling the day when Martin McDonnell and his sons first stepped into his fields and began snapping the flowering tops from his tobacco. Craig had protested, but Martin explained patiently that this procedure would make the leaves grow larger, and heavier. He continued, "Topping also stimulates root development, makes the plant less top-heavy, and reduces the possibility of it blowing over in a windstorm. Flowers usually attract harmful insects, so when we remove them, the plants become less susceptible to infestation."

Kelwyn and his family were no strangers to tobacco, but they had arrived too late the previous year to break out the flowering tops. They and the other New Englanders watched closely as Craig moved down the row, alternately snapping one stalk on his right and another on his left. "Walk between two rows and break the top out of each plant, right and left," Craig instructed.

On one leaf he noticed some light damage and brought this to the workers' attention. "We also need to search for tobacco worms. We have done this once, but it pays to check every time we are in the field. A big worm can eat an entire leaf in a single afternoon. We are topping a little early, and the worms are still small, but it is better to get ahead than to fall behind."

Just then he spied a small bud of dark green shoots forming at the base of a main leaf where it emerged from the stem. He pinched it off and showed it to them. "This is called a "sucker'. It is a secondary growth that also saps vitality from the main leaves. We will see a lot of them soon after we top."

"Why is that?" Kelwyn asked.

"For some reason, topping stimulates the growth of these shoots. They can grow into quite large 'side stalks' and will rob the main leaves of valuable nourishment. We must get them all."

Kelwyn nodded. "I understand this. We break secondary growths from some vegetable plants and prune our orchards of secondary branches."

"Yes, the same principle applies," Craig nodded, pleased they understood.

Slowly, the families began moving through the field, snapping tops, pinching off suckers, finding and crushing the insidious green tobacco worms. It was tedious work in humid heat; the new workers, used to the long, cold winters and short, cool summers of New England, were not yet totally acclimated to July in Kentucky. Craig made sure they had plenty of water to drink. Earlier that morning he drew several buckets of cold spring water and toted them downhill to the field and set them in the shade. Everyone drank from a communal dipper.

The tobacco plants looked healthy, standing between four and five feet tall, vibrant green leaves gleaming in the sunlight. Even the youngsters understood that these delicate plants needed special care. Craig surveyed their work and decided that this crop was the best he had grown. He dearly hated to pay out the wages, but Mary pointed out that there was much to show for it. Martin counseled him on what was standard farmhand pay.

Late that afternoon, Levi Matthews drove his wagon out to Mary's Landing. Craig heard his horses clattering across the wooden bridge that the carpenter-turned-miller had built five years ago. He had just finished topping his last row and he watched the miller pull into some shade near the riverbank. Levi stepped down and crossed the short distance to the tobacco field. He watched the workers for a few moments.

"Got your white slaves out working on a hot day like this?"

"I am afraid so," Craig nodded, wiping his brow with a handkerchief. "We're almost done with this field."

"Mary is cooking supper. I smelled it as I drove by the cabin. You wouldn't have a crust to spare for your starving friend?"

Craig laughed, "Leave it to you to show up at suppertime. I suppose we could tolerate some of your sick humor. Just promise you won't curse around the children."

The first workers reached the end, and they helped the stragglers finish topping and cleaning their rows.

"Let's go home!" Craig called.

"I'll haul them up the hill," Levi offered.

"You heard him!" Craig said. "All those wanting a ride, hop on to his wagon. He is not usually this generous."

The womenfolk rode while the menfolk walked. Levi's horses dug in on the steep climb up from the bottomland. Craig noticed that they looked a bit stressed.

"Make sure you water those horses when you reach the barn."

"I was thinking the same thing."

After supper, Levi revealed why he had ridden out. He reached into his vest pocket and produced a letter written on expensive buff-colored quarto stationery, folded four ways and sealed with expensive red wax. "This has been waiting in Rosenbotham's store for over a week. Everyone in town has wondered when you would come in to fetch it. The letter is from Philadelphia, Pennsylvania."

Correspondences were rare on the frontier and the arrival of any letter created a great stir of excitement. As Levi passed it to him, Craig immediately recognized his father's bold, cursive handwriting. Mary handed him a knife and he slit the seal, opening the letter with fumbling fingers. He had often thought about his folks—how they had fared, possible troubles they may have encountered. He had tried to estimate the time it would take them to reach New Orleans and then the time required to secure passage on one of the ocean-going vessels. The ensuing sea journey would depend solely upon winds and sea currents; after arrival in Philadelphia it would have taken his father several days to settle in, get his mother back on a schedule, catch up on business, and see Romulus and family established. Most of all, he wondered how his mother was faring. Through tear-filled eyes he read the letter carefully.

Philadelphia, Pennsylvania
April 21, 1817

My Dearest Craig,

I pray this correspondence finds you happy and well. Please convey our warmest regards to your lovely wife and family, to Martin McDonnell and his family. We send our love and our gratitude for the wonderful reunion.

If you are reading this, please rest assured that your mother and I arrived in Philadelphia in good condition on March 2nd of this year. Due to multiple trading stops on the

Ohio and Mississippi Rivers, the keelboat journey took longer than originally expected. Would that we could have engaged passage on a modern steamboat. I learned too late that one of the new vessels passed us in the night, headed non-stop for New Orleans.

We spent the whole of January in that city, resting from our journey and searching for a suitable vessel bound for an Atlantic seaport. Pierre Delacroix assisted in making things easier for us, calling regularly at our hotel and seeing to our needs. In February I secured passage on board the <u>HMS Speedwell</u>, a smart British schooner. The vessel put in at Jamaica before turning north to Philadelphia and Boston. We received another unwelcome surprise when Speedwell anchored in the port of Charleston, adding another week onto our voyage. The important thing is this—we reached home in excellent health.

Your mother's condition is remarkably the same. She maintains her physical fitness, but she experiences the same difficulties in speech, thought processes, and engaging in appropriate human interaction. It may please you to know that on two occasions she has mentioned your children. Although I initially worried about bringing her to Kentucky, I believe the trip was beneficial; it certainly did her no harm. We have settled back into our city life; I have returned to work with a renewed spirit and with visions of your beautiful Kentucky farmland to brighten my memory.

Now, let me update you on your former charges. They played their roles to perfection, convincing everyone of their positions. If truth be known, they enjoyed the charade, buoyed by the knowledge that they would soon be set free. Keelboat crewmen, plantation owners, local officials and British sea captains accepted our ruse so completely, I was never required to show papers. You may now inform the Honorable Judge Bozarth that the "ownership" papers have been destroyed; he is free from all culpability. Romulus, Vergina,

*Leta and Gabriel reside a few streets back from the Dela-
ware River. Quaker merchants immediately hired Romulus
as a laborer; Vergina now tends two Quaker households
and serves as governess for their children. Both Romulus
and Vergina send you and Mary their regards. One Quaker
woman has undertaken the task of teaching both to read and
write. They are regularly attending the newly-formed African Methodist Episcopal Church. Their children will one
day benefit from established, well-financed schools. You may
rest easy on their account—and know that I will look in on
them regularly.*

*I hope one day in this life we shall meet again. One reads
of projected canals that will link upper New York rivers with
the Great Lakes, and canals that will connect the Lakes to a
central Indiana or Illinois river, obviating the need to cross
the Alleghenies or to travel on the high seas and thence upriver from New Orleans to reach Kentucky. Until that time,
I bask in the memory of our recent reunion, feeling secure
in the knowledge we remain a family. A man could not be
happier for his son.*

*Your loving father,
Gregory Ridgeway*

The letter moved Craig deeply. Once again, his father had
reached across the miles to present him with yet another measure of
closure. The letter's deep significance must have shown on his face,
for Levi and Mary maintained their silence until he finally looked
up.

"They are well?" Mary asked. "Did they make it safely home?"

Craig handed her the letter. "Yes, everything is just fine." He
shared with them the contents.

"So you finally freed Romulus and his family?" Levi shook his
head in disbelief. "You always said you would."

"It was Mary who insisted we put up the money to buy them, thinking we could simply free them. Originally, I was dead set against spending any money."

"You would be, you shameful miser. But I admire you for seeking Romulus out and bringing him back from Tennessee. Those slaves will never have it as good as they had it here."

"They weren't free."

"Folks in the county claim they were. You did more for them than most folks would."

"We must also give the Honorable Judge Bozarth his due share of credit. He helped free them from the slavecatchers."

"That old blowhard!"

"You should see him fight. You already know what he did at Tippecanoe and New Orleans."

Levi rolled his eyes and sighed, "Yes, I have heard him tell it over and over again—and the story gets grander every time!"

"Well, I observed him that night we rescued the slaves—how he sent out scouts, positioned our forces, spread us into a semi-circle and ordered 'no quarter' after they fired on us."

"Yeah, yeah, I hope you are convinced."

"How *is* the Judge?" Mary asked.

"You wouldn't believe it. Why, the dirty swindler claims he has turned over a new spiritual leaf! He got up in the pulpit during the last church social and confessed to being a squanderer, a poor investor, a debtor and a weakling."

"I had not heard that," Craig said.

"Well, you country folk don't get out much. Some months back, we suffered through his sordid confessions of adultery and endured a lengthy soliloquy extolling Violet, that puffed-up, high-and-mighty—!"

"Levi!" Mary forestalled him.

"Sorry, but you didn't have to hear it." Levi glanced guiltily at the children. "What a fraud he is!"

"So what happened at this last confession?" Craig asked.

"He wept out loud, begging for forgiveness. He likened himself to the pitiful little tax collector in the Gospel of Luke and promised to pay everyone back, although not fourfold as Zacchaeus did. Then, he hauled up some lender he had brought down from Hardinsburg and paid him the fifty dollars he owed. The man forgave him and tore up his lien—right there, in front of the congregation. Then the Judge invited some other feller up and paid him forty dollars. That man ripped up his lien. Folks fairly ran down the aisle, lining up in the hopes they would get *their* money back, but the Judge announced, 'It is all I have.' One man was so disappointed, he cursed out loud, and Brother Kreisle ordered him to leave the church."

"Well, it sounds like the Judge is on the road to restoring his honor."

"I will believe *that* when I see it. I think Violet found him out and took him in hand. I'll give her this—she has the brains for business where he does not. She announced that she would review his loans and other investments and begged for time to get a payment schedule in order. Apparently the Judge has made a whopping mess of things."

"What happened then?"

"That damned Kreisle got up and ordered us to dig deep into our pockets and help the Judge as he has helped those in the community. Oh, it was an impassioned plea! I almost heard violins playing."

"Hasn't the Judge helped folks?"

"Well, yes. But he didn't deserve the eight dollars they collected. There were poor folks, barely making ends meet, giving him money. Can you imagine that? It is shameful."

Craig shook his head. "You may be right. But wouldn't it be best if he tried to pay everyone back?"

"I suppose so," Levi grumbled.

"Just think, Levi, Mary added. "Jesus forgave little Zacchaeus. Rich men sin, just like the poor. Wouldn't Jesus want us to forgive him, too?"

Levi winced sheepishly and said nothing. He would not argue with Mary.

Craig came to his rescue, "When can I pick up a load of corn?"

"It's waiting for you. I don't deliver."

New Orleans, Vieux Carré —July 3, 1817

In death Pierre Delacroix resembled the image one might see on a papal sarcophagus—a fragile, dignified pope, hands folded neatly upon his chest as if in repose, features sunken inward, eyes and mouth closed in genteel dignity. He looked as if he was taking a nap. The soft morning light illuminated his pale features, giving him an almost-angelic glow. His skin was cool and parchment-thin, the face strangely rose-colored. Philippe touched his hand and crumpled by the bedside, wracked with grief. Across the room, Delacroix's slave girl wailed in a shrill, mournful cry. Before long, Doc arrived with Father Poitier. The priest made the sign of the cross, then dipped and shook his aspergillum, sprinkling the body with holy water as he began reciting a litany of prayers.

For protection, Doc had moved into the Bouchard Exchange with Philippe and Kayla, so he was present when the message came. Philippe had ordered his carriage made ready, taking Doc and two armed gunmen with him, leaving the remainder of his force to guard the exchange and warehouses. As the carriage rolled past the cathedral, Doc realized he must fetch the priest. He convinced Philippe to let him out, knowing they would catch up quickly, for it was but a brief walk to Delacroix's townhouse.

As soon as they entered the room, Doc assumed immediate charge. He would take time to grieve later. "Thank you, my dear," Doc dismissed the wailing girl. "You were right to inform us. You may go outside under the trees, but stay close; the authorities will wish to ask questions—as coroner, I will certainly ask questions."

The girl left hastily and the room fell silent. Doc waited for a respectable moment to say something. In fact, Delacroix's death left him momentarily speechless. For decades the old man had been at the heart of New Orleans' settlement and growth. He had helped to write its history—he *was* history. It was as if an era had passed.

"He looks so peaceful." Philippe sobbed, finally. "Surely he did not suffer."

"That is what I intend to find out," Doc replied, opening his medical bag.

"Will you not allow him to retain the dignity he showed in life?"

"As much as that is possible," Doc agreed. "You will recall that Signet once offered me a large sum to put him down. He wanted me to poison him, declare 'death by natural causes' and then order immediate burial or cremation. He may have hired someone else to do the job."

"Please proceed, Doctor."

Father Poitier bowed his head and recited more prayers in Latin. Doc presumed these involved the Sacrament of Extreme Unction. He traced Delacroix's hairline with his fingertips, then felt under his jaw, tilting back the head to visually observe his neck. He put his nose to Delacroix's mouth and cautiously sniffed, smelling the faint odor of bitter almonds. Then he unbuttoned the shirt and removed it, noticing slight bruising on the wrists, the wine-purple bruising usually found on the elderly's hands and arms, especially on the limb most often used. But these bruises were lateral in shape, located at nearly the same place on each wrist. Someone had held Delacroix down; there had been an obvious struggle. Doc almost uttered his suspicions aloud—but wisely kept silent. No sense in making a diagnosis before he finished. Any declaration of murder would certainly inflame Philippe, goading him into a suicidal mission of revenge. He raised the merchant's skinny arms and noticed that rigor mortis had not yet set in. Carefully he examined both armpits for puncture wounds and found none. He already knew, without doubt, that the attackers had used poison. They had not encountered much resistance—cyanide killed quickly.

Instead of robbery and murder, Delacroix's death was staged, rather clumsily, to resemble a natural passing. The attackers had taken great care to compose the body—closing the eyes and mouth, folding his hands, perhaps even dressing him. It was all too neat.

Signet's choice of doctor would declare "death by natural causes" and, in this summer heat, the body would be quickly interred. Few would question an old man dying in the midst of a summer heat wave. After all, Delacroix had lived four-score years and then some.

"May I kiss him?" Philippe asked, pathetically.

"I would not." Doc had seen a young medical student collapse from cyanide fumes while examining the intestines of a poisoning victim.

"Why not?"

"He may have had an infectious disease. He would not wish you to catch it. I understand he placed great trust in you."

"And in you, Doctor," Father Poitier broke in.

"How do you mean?"

"He left a sizeable bag of money for your travel and relocation expenses."

"Ah, yes. Now I recall." Doc had forgotten about that; somehow he had lost his obsession for money. He donned his hat and picked up his bag and cane before turning to Philippe. "Be vigilant, young man. Take care of Delacroix's burial and get yourself back to the Exchange."

"Why? What are you going to do?"

"You just worry about Monsieur Delacroix's wishes. He has passed on his precious torch of life to you. You must now defend that flame. Do not let Signet extinguish it."

"I won't! But how can we stop him?" Phillipe recognized the compelling tone in Doc's voice and clasped his hand.

"You let me worry about that."

Doc strode from the room, adjusting the loaded pistol stuck into his waistband. Like a gallant knight of old he prepared himself for battle.

———————●◄———————

Signet reserved passage onboard the *Jesse P. Emmick*, one of the new steamboats built in Brownsville, Pennsylvania. The vessel had put in at Baton Rouge two days ago and the whole city turned out to admire it. Dazzling white in a fresh coat of paint, the *Jesse P.* resembled an elaborate "Tower of Babel" with cabin stacked upon cabin—counting the wheelhouse, three decks in all. The vessel performed far beyond Signet's expectations, transporting him downriver at the incredible speed of ten knots. The banker spent most of the trip drinking liquor in the green-curtained saloon. He entered mid-morning to enjoy the congenial setting and to listen to the latest gossip. Although far too early in the day to start in, he indulged himself in a tall whiskey. The passengers were in a celebratory mood, for the upcoming Fourth of July promised a great deal of cannon and rifle fire, parades, street music and drinking. New Orleans was well-known for its noisy festivals and widespread vices. People welcomed any excuse to deviate from normal, day-to-day activity.

Although busy, the mood in New Orleans appeared somewhat somber. Signet surveyed the levee, appreciating the sweeping crescent of the muddy river, long rows of warehouses and jetties, and the many vessels moored beneath the embankment—flatboats, keelboats, rafts, pirogues, and canoes—extending downstream to large ocean-going vessels with their tall sailing masts. Leaning against the polished brass railing of the upper deck, he felt like a king, surveying the activity below, enjoying the fact that the vessel upon which he rode outclassed all the others. Equipped with well-furnished cabins, dining room, and saloon, the *Jesse P.* was propelled by the most modern machinery. This vessel represented real power; after all, it had conquered the mighty Mississippi and Ohio River currents. He resolved to buy shares in a steamboat; perhaps he might one day own an entire fleet. Before disembarking, Signet cast a longing glance at the Bouchard Exchange and adjacent warehouses. Very soon he would own them all.

As he stepped off the gangplank, one of his assistants, a minor clerk, recognized him and ran up, obviously in distress. "Oh, Monsieur Signet! I bring you terrible news! Pierre Delacroix has died!"

"How very sad," Signet murmured and bowed his head, hoping to conceal his delight. "Do you know the cause?"

"He was eighty-two, I think. Need I say more?"

"Get me a carriage."

"Yes sir!" The man hurried off to the public stable located just past Signet's warehouse.

Despite the noonday heat, Signet enjoyed the ride home. There he would luxuriate in a cool bath, read his correspondences, drink more whiskey, and catch up on some needed sleep. He deserved to relax, for he had vanquished a major obstacle—perhaps the most important one. The "Age of Delacroix" had passed; the new age belonged to him. New Orleans seemed more attainable than ever, and a sense of power coursed through his veins. The city would soon be his personal fiefdom in which he would control society, wealth, and law. And in a few short months, Bruce Bowman and his mercenaries would bring Lucinde and her children back from Kentucky, bound in chains before him. Then, he would own everything he desired in this world!

———◆———

Doc's arrival at Ste. Gême's plantation created an understandable stir. Emmett's gunmen were deployed along the riverbank, behind every live oak tree, across the porch, and at every shed and outbuilding, wisely forming a layered defense, one that would rake deadly crossfire against any attackers. These smugglers knew their business. Doc's driver hauled up at the entrance where two gunmen waited with dangerous-looking fowling pieces. He stepped out of the carriage and the guns lowered perceptibly; these gunmen recognized him from previous visits. One of them barked, "What you want?"

"I'm here to see Emmett Barnett."

"He not here."

"Where is he?"

'Who knows? He comes—he goes. Business."

"I need to speak with him. It is urgent. Believe me—he will want to hear what I have to say."

"He come back this afternoon. Ste. Gême here."

Doc perked up. "Is he? May I speak with him?"

"We ask."

Doc waited in the oppressive mid-morning heat while Emmett's gunmen inspected the carriage interior and informed Ste. Gême of his arrival. After some time, a shrill whistle cut through the stillness. The gunmen stepped aside and ordered them onward. As they proceeded up the drive, Doc noticed more smugglers in the dappled shade of the live oaks. Ste. Gême was taking no chances. Doc tried to remember what he knew about the man.

Jean-François Henri de Miquel, Baron de Saintegême, was a genuine nobleman who hailed from the southwestern French province of Languedoc. He had served as high-ranking officer in the French army, and fought in the Revolution of Saint-Domingue under various flags, involving himself deeply in privateering on the Caribbean Sea. After fleeing to New Orleans amongst a tidal wave of refugees, and hoping to escape Napoleon's wrath, Ste. Gême promptly married a wealthy Creole woman who had inherited a plantation from her deceased husband. The estate was situated on Gentilly Ridge, a stretch of relatively high ground along Bayou Gentilly, a few miles from *Vieux Carré*. Merging his own substantial wealth with that of his wife, Ste. Gême built an incredible empire—acquiring plantations, trading with the pirate Jean Lafitte, and even outfitting his own army, the *Dragons à Pied*, during the Battle of Chalmette. The little man, who stood just four feet-eleven inches in height, had become a pillar of society—so people forgave him his eccentricities. During the Battle of Chalmette he had worn a dazzling French uniform bedecked with sashes, tasseled epaulettes, and medals, and, to augment his height, high-heeled boots and an enormously-plumed helmet. Everyone in New Orleans knew that Ste. Gême had come to New Orleans with his companion of color from Saint-Domingue;

their three children had all been born in New Orleans. No one spoke of it.

Ste. Gême emerged onto the porch, dressed in an expensive white suit that matched his moustache and goatee. Doc reckoned him at about fifty, perhaps older. A younger man joined him.

"Doctor! How good of you to come!" Ste. Gême's smile diminished when he noticed Doc's expression. "Is there something wrong?"

"Pierre Delacroix is dead."

Ste. Gême bowed his head and crossed himself. "How did he die?"

"The papers will report natural causes. They will base this on the coroner's report."

"And do you know something else?"

"I do."

"Go on."

"Philippe Bouchard and I examined the body. Delacroix was poisoned orally with a form of cyanide."

"Poisoned!" Ste. Gême sat down heavily in a porch chair and buried his face in his hands.

After some time, Doc continued, "Out of respect for Delacroix, I fought Signet the legal way."

"Yes, you certainly did. Pierre truly was an honorable man. He believed wholly in the laws of God and man—and he succeeded so admirably in restoring Philippe. I truly thought he had won. It is a shame Judge Harkness is no longer with us, God rest his soul."

"He was murdered. So was that young lawyer, Howard, and Senator de Lisle."

"But those deeds were ascribed to a Spanish merchant crew or perhaps to some Kentucky flatboat men. You don't think—!"

"I *know* Signet was responsible," Doc interrupted. "Recently, he tried to murder Philippe. I was in the very midst of that gunfight. The man controls a private army, and he holds sway over half the militia patrol. I believe he is making his final play. We need a real soldier to help fight him."

"Perhaps I should sell out now and leave Louisiana," Ste. Gême mused. "I have already begun planning my return to the family estates in France. The quiet vineyards beckon even more strongly this morning."

"Come now, you have more spleen than that," Doc admonished. "Your conduct at Chalmette Plantation was above reproach."

"It is not for myself that I fear. Do not think that I have quiescently accepted Signet's devious intrigues. I have met on several occasions with the planters and merchants of this city. Most of them are associated with Signet. I have pleaded with Governor Villeré, but he, Signet, and Signet's lawyer, Morel, are good friends. Villeré does not believe Signet is guilty of anything."

"Then we must take matters into our own hands."

"If I do that, I am guilty under the law. If I tried and failed, Signet's men would exact retribution. I have two families, loved ones for whom I care."

Doc nodded sympathetically. Signet had forced just about everyone into a defensive mode while he destroyed his enemies one by one. Phillipe and Kayla were holed up at the Bouchard Exchange; for almost two years, Doc had crept about the city, glancing over his shoulder at every turn; even Emmett Barnett had been driven into the harsh environs of the black-water bayous. Worst of all, good people had died. Signet's shadow army reigned and inflicted terror with complete impunity.

"There *is* something we can do," Doc insisted. "And it would not involve you directly."

"And what is that?" Ste. Gême asked.

"Unleash Emmett Barnett."

Ste. Gême recoiled. "Do you realize what you are suggesting?"

"I do. You may not know this, but Emmett lost his tavern and his leg because of Signet. He has been rearing to have a go at him. I am surprised he hasn't tried something already. It has taken my greatest efforts to hold him in check."

"That speaks highly of you, for Emmett usually does what he wants."

"I think he has the skill and the manpower to get the job done."

"He will never take that townhouse. Signet may have thirty men guarding it. They are some of the hardest men on this earth."

"Emmett Barnett is just as hard. I would not want to pit myself against him or any of his men."

"They may look ferocious, but they are not soldiers; in reality, they are a sad lot of undisciplined rabble. Signet's men would kill them before they got anywhere near. Those ruffians have no idea how to take a walled compound."

"Signet travels to and from other places—various hotels, the bank, his warehouses—even up to Baton Rouge. Perhaps we could take him at the levee."

"Too uncertain. Most of Emmett's men are criminals with a bounty on their heads. They can't show their faces in New Orleans during the daytime. And Emmett is wanted by *both* sides of the law. It will have to be done at night, under cover of darkness. And it should be sooner than later."

"Will you at least help us plan it?"

"What do you think, Jean?" Ste. Gême addressed the younger man. "Forgive me, Doctor, this is my associate, Jean Boze. We have known each other since our time together in Saint-Domingue."

"Pleased to meet you," Doc shook his hand.

The young man had heard the entire conversation, but he pondered a few moments before answering Ste. Gême. "If Signet could do such a thing to Delacroix and Judge Harkness, he could do it to you—*before* you sell out. I believe we should give Monsieur Barnett all the assistance he needs."

Ste. Gême's eyes hardened into cold steel. He clapped his hands and two gunmen ran up to the porch, prepared to do his bidding. "Get my carriage ready. We are going on a reconnoitering mission."

A few of Emmett's men stepped closer. One of them asked, "You want me fetch Emmett?"

"Yes," Doc nodded.

"What I tell him?"

"You tell him Doc Applegate says it is time."

"That all?"
"He'll understand."

———●———

Emmett's tar-black eye glittered with satisfaction as he pored over Ste. Gême's drawings. He chomped on a foul-smelling cigar, listening with great attention to the plantation owner's description of Jules Signet's townhouse. At various times the little smuggler broke into a broad grin and his eye disappeared into the folds of his skin as he imagined the moment when he would confront the banker. Doc shivered when he observed the expression. Although Emmett had afforded protection and treated Doc as one of his own, the man's past was horrifying. If the stories about him were even half true, he eclipsed all definitions of evil.

Some years ago, Doc had read a sickening newspaper account of two brothers—Micajah and Wiley Harpe. The Harpe Brothers were highwaymen, river pirates and murderers. They had operated for years in Kentucky, Tennessee, and the territories of Mississippi and Illinois, committing some of their worst atrocities at the pirate lair called Cave-in-Rock on the Ohio River. Not satisfied with robbery and mere murder, they added torture to their nefarious exploits. In fact, their crimes were more motivated by bloodlust than financial gain. They butchered their victims alive, axed women, children, and babies, murdered entire families, and even stripped captives naked, tying them to blindfolded horses and driving them off the high cliffs above their cave. In all, they boasted of killing thirty-nine people, but authorities ascribed numerous other deaths to them. Doc realized that Emmett was capable of this level of violence.

"What have I done?" he muttered to himself.

Emmett included his brothers Raoul and Louis in the strategic planning session. That morning Ste. Gême and Boze had driven directly to Signet's townhouse, making a complete circuit around the block, negotiating the streets and searching for the best avenues of escape. They had returned shortly after noon. Ste. Gême went straight to his office to draw, in India ink, a plan of the townhouse showing streets, front and back carriage entrances, overhanging live oaks, outbuildings and courtyard. Emmett and his motley entourage arrived in the heat of mid-afternoon charged with anticipation and purpose. Doc noticed the difference in Emmett's manner; he perched on the edge of his seat, leaning forward like an eager gun dog, taut-nerved and ready for hunting.

"Each carriage entrance is guarded by two armed men," Ste. Gême began.

"Hah!" Emmett laughed derisively. "We kill!"

"These men are stationed outside on the street, and they have commanding views in both directions. There are certainly more guards stationed just inside the entrances." He pointed with his silver-handled letter opener. "These are live oak trees—eight of them. Two trees have overhanging branches that can be reached from the street. They can be climbed."

"Hmm!" Emmett raised his black eyebrow and chuckled like a naughty schoolboy, elbowing his brothers. They laughed dutifully.

Ste. Gême glanced up and shook his head, exasperated at the interruption. "The wall is ten feet high. And there are outbuildings here, here, and here."

"We bring ladders?" Emmett suggested.

"Yes. I believe they will serve you well. The assault must be timed perfectly. To enter the courtyard, you must first overwhelm the guards outside. They must be eliminated silently. Then, you can focus on the townhouse. Above all, your objective *is* to kill Signet. When he is gone, all opposition will die. Now, I must know more about the main house and outbuildings."

"I can help you there," Doc volunteered. "I lived with him for a time."

"Proceed."

"There are indeed two entrances to his property. The front lies very close to the street. Consequently, that drive is short, a small, circular cobblestone affair, just big enough for a carriage to pull inside and disgorge guests. The house resembles a tall fortress, with a heavy single front door and barred windows."

"We go in back way," Emmett said.

"That is what I would do," Doc nodded. "Once inside the carriage entrance, you can fan out and take the outbuildings." He indicated one of the squares on Ste. Gême's drawing. "This is the stable. There may be a night watchman posted there. And these are the slave quarters." He glanced at Emmett. "I pray you will not kill them. They will be terrified. One or two men should manage to subdue them and keep them indoors."

Emmett grunted noncommittally.

"Good, what else can you tell us?" Ste. Gême prodded.

Doc closed his eyes and tried to reconstruct the layout in his mind. "You will find good cover by the stone fountain. The back of the house has several large windows, two downstairs doors, an outside stairway leading to the balcony, and multiple balcony doors leading into various upstairs rooms, including Signet's bedroom."

"Multiple points of entry, but many more guards," Ste. Gême mused. "They will certainly see and hear you coming. That will give Signet and his men time to prepare a defense. All they have to do is hold on until the militia patrol arrives."

"I put plenty men front of house," Emmett chuckled. "No one leave that way."

"I was about to suggest that," Ste. Gême agreed. "Make that force strong. A concerted effort could break through." He returned his attention to the sketches.

Doc indicated the northeastern corner of the house. "This is Signet's bedroom. At least it was while I lived there. It is upstairs and a door opens out onto the balcony, an elegant glass-paned affair, easy to force. But there is also an inside door leading to the central hallway." He pointed out various rooms, stairway locations, and possible avenues of escape. Ste. Gême made valuable comments on the plan as the details filled in. Emmett seemed impressed with his suggestions, recognizing their military value.

They continued planning throughout the afternoon, finally stopping to drink a cool beverage on the shaded front porch. By that time, the live oak shadows were stretching across the cane fields, and two boatloads of smugglers arrived by pirogue. Small bunches of men climbed warily up the river bank to cross the road.

"*Mon Dieu!*" Ste. Gême gasped. "What has he brought us now?"

Doc noticed three Choctaw Indians with long wooden bows and leather quivers full of arrows. Four negroes carried armloads of machetes, the kind typically used for cutting cane. Two squat, brown-skinned Indians kept apart from the rest. They came from a different tribe, one with which Doc was unfamiliar, and they looked ill at ease. Doc noticed that they carried two long, slender cane poles, and shouldered stout, woven cane baskets that appeared heavy, judging by how they leaned forward. Other smugglers appeared over the bank; one man rolled a giant barrel ahead of him.

"I had better slaughter a beef to feed this lot," Ste. Gême sighed. He dispatched two men to do the job. Emmett overheard this and added his own orders, then strode out to greet his men, slapping some on the back and laughing.

"What are they bringing?" Doc asked.

"I am afraid to find out," Ste. Gême said, shaking his head. "This could be dangerous—for all of us."

Together they ventured out to inspect the new arrivals. They first discovered that the barrel was full of gunpowder, pirated from a British merchantman. Raoul pried open the lid while Louis distributed gourds and hollow clay pots to the men who promptly lined up to have them filled.

"What are these?" Doc began.

"Bombs!" Emmett chuckled.

Doc noticed the lit cigar stub between his teeth, took it out of his mouth and handed it to him. The little smuggler spit a gob of saliva into his open palm and ground the glowing tip into it.

"No smoke!" Emmett barked to his men.

Moving on, Doc considered the three Choctaws—tall, well-formed men with unstrung persimmon-wood bows almost as tall as they were. Gingerly, he touched one of the arrows. "May I?"

"Be my guest, Doctor." The Choctaw's articulation was far superior to Emmett's.

The arrow measured about three-feet long, fashioned from sturdy river cane, tipped with a razor-sharp point of finely-shaped deer antler and fletched with three turkey feathers, split and trimmed. These feathers were affixed into grooves and secured by some sort of animal hoof glue, the ends bound with thin sinew. All arrows were painted red or black, colors the Choctaw associated with war and death.

"Ah! The *bolas*!" Emmett exclaimed, pushing roughly past him. "Give!"

Timidly, the two strange Indians opened their baskets, and Emmett plunged his hand inside. He hauled out a trio of round stone weights, each wrapped in tight leather webbing that formed a secure pouch. The ends of these pouches were woven into braided leather cords. While the two heavier weights were attached to short cords about three feet long, the lighter weight had a longer cord.

"What is this?" Doc asked.

"You watch!" Emmett exclaimed. He was almost manic with delight.

Doc heard laughing behind him. Emmett's men clapped and cheered loudly, as if they were at a cockfight. Doc wheeled to behold the reason for this commotion—two of Emmett's men were chasing a yearling steer down the lane.

"Get ready, Brother!" Louis shouted from his position near the powder keg.

The steer had run a couple hundred yards, but still had plenty of wind. It darted this way and that, tearing up chunks of Ste. Gême's lawn. At one point it almost broke free, but inexorably the men drove it back toward the little smuggler. Emmett grasped the center knot and shook free the stone balls. He had obviously done this before. Lifting his hand high overhead, he began twirling the balls. As he worked up speed, they whistled in the disrupted air. The whole process looked and sounded dangerous. Doc stepped back to avoid being brained, praying that the webbing held up. At that moment, the steer jogged past them and Emmett released the weapon. The *bola* hissed away in a deadly, spinning path of destruction. The stone balls wrapped around the steer's hind legs and brought it down with a crash. Doc was stunned at how easily Emmett accomplished the feat. The steer bellowed in agony and tried to rise. Doc noticed the right hind leg, bent at an impossible angle, shattered by one of the weights.

A big negro stepped forward to swing his machete downward in a powerful two-handed blow. The blade bit clean through the steer's neck bone. Blood sprayed as the steer rolled over, stiffened, and voided its bowels in a bright green gush. Emmett held up both hands like a champion gladiator, strutting around as much as his wooden leg allowed. The smugglers cheered in a blood roar, their faces flushed from watching the grisly spectacle. Certainly they had guessed they would soon engage in a dangerous confrontation. The highly-charged atmosphere was palpable.

"Let us move these people behind the house," Ste. Gême suggested. "The ground is more suitable there and we will not be seen from the road."

"Good idea," Doc agreed.

While the men prepared the steer for cooking, Ste. Gême ordered his kitchen slaves to lay on a meal for his guests. A fire was built in the stone pit near the orange grove. Some men stayed in the side yard to finish scooping gunpowder into clay pots, tying on the lids with dampened leather strings and inserting fuses into holes bored into them. The leather would tighten down as it dried.

"I thought this was to be a silent attack," Doc commented.

"It be until our cover blown," Emmett said.

"How soon do you plan to attack?" Ste. Gême asked.

"Tomorrow night—late!

"Not with bombs! You'll wake the whole town!"

"They be wake anyway. It Fourth of July!" Emmett guffawed.

Ste. Gême's jaw dropped in realization. He turned to stare at Doc who wore a similar, stunned expression. Both realized that Emmett

Barnett had figured this out long ago. Gunfire and cannon booms would reverberate all night in a city drunken with patriotism and liquor. Doc tried to suppress a nervous chuckle, but the dam burst and he laughed out loud, releasing the tension that had built up inside. Ste. Gême and Boze laughed too, but Doc could not tell if they were laughing at him, or at Emmett's declaration.

The little smuggler dispatched armed guards along the road and plantation lane as Ste. Gême ordered torches lit on the back lawn. Two slaves dragged out a giant, hemp-wrapped cotton bale from Ste. Gême's brick warehouse and stood it up on its end. One of them snatched a blackened stick from the fire and drew a rough human figure on the hemp cloth. At forty paces the Choctaws gave a splendid demonstration with their bows. Doc watched as arrow after arrow whizzed across the distance, each projectile striking the target in the upper torso or neck. Emmett's men cheered with each hit. After the Choctaws finished their display of skill, the smugglers practiced with their long throwing knives. A few of them hurled wooden-handled tomahawks.

Finally, Emmett whistled for the two squat Indians in charge of the bolas. Doc observed their dress, bowl-shaped haircuts, and overall demeanor, wondering what made them so different from the others. Emmett uttered some unintelligible language and the men unslung long, hollow tubes from their shoulders. These tubes stood much taller than the Indians.

"Who *are* these gentlemen?" Doc asked Emmett.

"They from Brazil. Escape Portuguese slavers—hide in my bayou. Fight for me tomorrow night—I take when I go Bahia."

"You really *are* going back?" Doc remembered how quickly the little smuggler had adapted to his new life.

"I be rich man after tomorrow night—live like king in Bahia."

"I believe you, friend," Doc nodded soberly. He then recognized the cane poles as blowguns, weapons sometimes used by the Cherokees.

The Indians reached into their cane baskets and withdrew a pair of flat leather quivers. They opened these to reveal several dozen round hardwood darts, ten inches long, fletched, and dangerously sharp looking. Around the backside of each dart they had twirled a small tuft of cotton fiber to create a pressure seal which would enable the blower to propel the dart at great speed. Each Indian thumbed a dart into one end of the tube which flared out into a mouthpiece. The tube exteriors were wrapped in thin strips of plant material and sealed with a resin coat to make them airtight. Doc watched with interest as one Indian put his lips to the mouthpiece, aimed the long tube, and blew a sharp puff of air. At twenty-five paces the dart shot across the lawn and struck the charcoaled target in the neck. The crowd roared its pleasure. Both Indians fired darts in rapid succession, much faster than a man could reload his gun.

"Those darts not poison," Emmett offered. "Tomorrow night they use poison. It work fast!"

Doc considered one of a half-dozen spears the Indians had brought and wondered how effective these primitive weapons would prove against modern firearms. It seemed impossible that this rough assortment of humanity could prevail against well-trained gunmen. But then Doc noticed the firepower these smugglers carried—rifles, muskets, shotguns, and pistols; naval cutlasses and officers' swords, seized perhaps from some merchant ship or fighting vessel. While these men were not professional soldiers, they knew something about weapons and fighting. It would be interesting to see how events would turn out.

The pirates spent most of the night feasting and drinking. Ste. Gême ordered a big barrel of dark rum rolled out and he served the men with his own hand. One of Emmett's men brought a banjo and struck up a tune. A Brazilian Indian produced a wooden instrument with multiple horizontal tubes that made flute-like noises and he joined in. Some pirates clacked spoons or drummed on upturned bowls while others sang, danced, leaped and gyrated.

After midnight, the merriment died down. Emmett called a quick assembly and ordered everyone to get a good night's sleep. They understood that a major attack was eminent, but knew nothing of the objective, let alone specific details. Emmett promised to brief them entirely the following afternoon, emphasizing that this would be a coordinated attack, wholly dependent upon stealth and lightning speed. He assured them that a successful outcome would earn each a substantial reward. The smuggler switched in the midst of his sentences from English to French, to Choctaw, and various Indian and African dialects. Doc could scarcely follow him, but the men seemed to assimilate all of it.

Most men wrapped in a single blanket and slept on the porch to avoid the ants and other ground insects, while others found places in various barns and sheds on the plantation. Emmett posted fresh guards along the road before he turned in. Ste. Gême provided the smuggler with a fine guest room; a slave directed Doc into the corner bedroom next to Emmett's. Thoughtfully, someone had provided a jug of fresh water, scented-soap, clean washcloths, and towels. The corner windows, covered in filmy mosquito netting, admitted a barely noticeable breeze.

Doc washed and climbed into bed, tired and sick with grief and apprehension. He thought about Delacroix, the cheerful, sprightly merchant who had at all times conducted himself with such exemplary dignity. He reflected on how Delacroix had cared for Philippe and his daughter Lucinde, how he had guided his beloved New Orleans from territorial times, through wars and tumultuous growth. Finally, Doc tried to imagine the city without Delacroix. The old man had made an indelible impression and had changed Doc's life for the better.

But Doc understood that life was all about change—nothing ever stayed the same. Soon, he and Solange must leave the city; then they could begin their new life together. Sometime, much later in the night, he offered Delacroix a silent apology for what would soon transpire. Whether or not Emmett's attack succeeded, much blood was sure to spill.

Welcome Hall, July 4, 1817

"How did you feel when you first learned that the colonies chose to declare independence from Great Britain?" Craig asked. Night had almost fallen—it was nearly dark under the trees where the family gathered after a big Independence Day supper. Agnes served refreshments from a large pewter tray and poured after-dinner drinks. The family leaned forward to hear Martin's response.

The patriarch sipped on his whiskey and pondered for a time. "It gave me a dreadful, hollow sensation, for it meant we were lawbreakers, traitors against king and country. Although we despised 'taxation without representation' and the fact we could trade only with the mother country at prices set by her, most of us did not want war. However many of our prominent businessmen saw it as a way to become richer."

"Didn't you fight for the crown in the French War?"

"I did. For six years I served alongside some of Britain's finest soldiers and even taught a few of them how to fight American-style—those who wished to learn. We campaigned in Upper and Lower Canada, and not only against French forts. Indian tribes harassed us at every turn. They were on home ground and used their knowledge against us."

"You were a scout," Owen stated. "What did that entail?"

"Well, mostly I moved ahead of the main forces, searching the forest for signs of enemy movements. The Iroquois worked with us on most campaigns. If we discovered signs of large troop concentrations, I hurried back to report to the commanders. Good scouting saved a lot of British lives."

"What do you mean by fighting American-style?" Stephen asked. "How does that differ from British fighting?" The youngest McDonnell brother was now eighteen and the tallest member in the family.

"You should know," Martin replied. "You fought at New Orleans. The British marched right up to your guns in perfect rank and file, completely exposed to your guns. Some people call it 'Continental warfare'—open, set-piece battles, massing troops in great blocks with wings on either side. You fought from cover, like the Indians did. The Indians opposing us in the French War were mobile, using hit-and-run tactics. At first, the British refused to adopt the strategy and it cost them dearly."

"Where did you fight?" Craig asked.

"Pennsylvania at first, then New York and up into Canada."

"What is Canada like?" Lucinde asked.

With a mild degree of surprise everyone turned to look at her, for she rarely interjected herself into a conversation.

"It is beautiful country," Martin replied. "Especially the Niagara Falls and the river gorge below. Some of those cliffs must be three hundred feet high, and the river is dark green, etched with white rapids. All the water from the upper Great Lakes thunders over the falls and compresses into the gorge before the river discharges into Lake Ontario."

"Niagara—is that where you saved Father's life?"

"Yes, at a place very near there."

"He often mentioned your act of mercy. He lit candles daily in the cathedral, and we said prayers for you at every Mass we attended, but he never discussed the particulars. Could you tell me about the battle?"

"It is difficult to relive; it was so brutal."

"I ask, because yesterday I thought a lot about him. All day I felt a strange sense of unease. I believe he came here, realizing it would be the last time we would see each other."

Her appeal affected Martin deeply. He sipped again on his whiskey and Craig noticed him struggling to dredge up details of the long-ago event. Craig felt a special empathy for him, knowing firsthand the effort and pain it took to revisit such terrible times. As dusk closed round them, insects chirped and sang rhythmic melodies and counter-melodies in concert with the tree frogs and other night noises.

Martin gathered himself a few moments longer. "I suppose you deserve to know what happened. You must realize that Britain's colonial settlements, especially those west of the Appalachians, were endangered. The French did not like foreign settlers in their lands; they saw it rightly as British encroachment. Most Indian tribes favored the French who lived and traded among them, even intermarrying with them. When the British erected a fort in disputed territory, a fight ensued. The conflict spread into a world war that spilled across continents and oceans. I was just fourteen when war broke out in 1754. I was tall and looked older, and growing up with the Indians gave me certain skills that made me desirable from a commander's standpoint."

"Fourteen!" Agnes shook her head.

"I saw things that would curdle a grown man's blood. People talk about Indians as savages, but the white men were just as brutal. Both sides offered generous bounties for enemy scalps taken in the war. The fighting was extremely bloody. After five full years in the field, the commanders regarded me as a veteran scout—even though I was just nineteen. I signed on for a generous bounty and scouted for Brigadier General John Prideaux. Our objective was Fort Niagara."

"Why was that fort so important?" Stephen asked.

"It was the main supply point for all French forts in the Ohio Country. In 1759, British Major General Jeffrey Amherst drew up plans to capture the stronghold and he chose Prideaux to lead the expedition. Fort Niagara occupied a strategic site, a rocky point above the Niagara River where it flows into Lake Ontario. You should see that fort—nothing could get past it—high walls and revetments, moats and oak palisades, entrenchments, cannons and carronades, and a commanding field of fire. The French built a remarkable stone chateau there, complete with two stories and a vast attic. Just before our attack, they improved the fort, adding buildings for barracks and supplies. But we learned that the French commander, Pouchot, had sent the bulk of his soldiers south to reinforce forts in the Ohio Country; we hoped to move fast and capitalize on that weakness. But high water on the Mohawk River delayed us and we were forced to wait for some of the local soldiers."

"What was Prideaux like?" Owen asked.

"He was a quiet fellow. I didn't speak much with him. When we reached the ruins of Fort Oswego, he seconded me to Sir William Johnson, the Indian agent who led the Iroquois forces. I scouted with them. We marched across New York that summer, then embarked in a fleet of bateaux and rowed west along the south shore of Lake Ontario. We slipped unnoticed past French naval forces and landed at the mouth of Little Swamp River, about three miles from Fort Niagara. We had achieved surprise and immediately laid siege to the fort. Fortunately I escaped the trench digging and heavy work. I was watching the road about two miles south when we heard that one of our cannons had exploded, struck Prideaux in the head, killing him instantly. My commander, Sir William took command—I recall this was on July nineteenth. He was a provincial officer, not in the regular army, so some officers questioned his right to command. But Sir William held a royal colonel's commission as commander of the Iroquois, and he stood his ground."

"That helped you, didn't it, Pa?" Stephen asked.

"Not really. A scout's work is dangerous no matter who his commander is. Each day during the siege, we ranged far, searching for the enemy. Then the British experienced a stroke of luck—about a hundred Seneca Indians negotiated a truce with the Iroquois and filed out of Fort Niagara. We learned from them that a French relief force was on its way. Sir William ordered me to take twenty Iroquois to scout the approaching force."

"That must have been exciting!"

"I was terrified. The French Army's Indian allies also knew how to advance stealthily. Usually, one side will spot the enemy first and lay a clever ambush. Often, I fought against French scouts—and each time, I was lucky to survive. In 1757, I was hit by musket fire and laid up for a month. I still have the ball lodged in my lower rib."

"What happened then?" Lucinde prodded.

"We high-tailed it back to Sir William and informed him the force was approaching."

"How many were there?" Craig asked.

"We guessed about fifteen hundred men. Although the French

knew Indian ways, they advanced without taking normal precautions—so I proposed an elaborate trap, a surprise attack near the ravine at La Belle-Famille." Martin hesitated guiltily, his eyes glistening with tears, clearly visible in the gathering darkness.

"Please, go on," prompted Lucinde.

"Your father was in that relief force. My plan could have killed him."

"Fortunately it did not. You saved him."

"Many other soldiers died, hundreds of them—and I played a major role in their deaths." He paused for an instant, and it seemed he might stop talking.

Craig said, "Your situation is somewhat similar to mine. I killed a lot of soldiers at New Orleans, but I saved one—a man named Eric Ashley. A Tennessean was about to shoot him point blank. I have often wondered what happened to him."

This seemed to spur Martin onward. "I suggested we build an abatis—an obstacle of trees cut and laid in a row with sharpened tops pointing outwards toward the enemy. Sir William approved the plan and ordered Lieutenant Colonel Eyre Massey to execute it. We blocked the portage road near the ravine and manned it with about one hundred colonial troops and a few regulars. We constructed the abatis to make it look vulnerable, easy to storm. We guessed correctly that the French would play from strength—because they outnumbered us three to one. We could only muster four hundred and fifty regulars. The six hundred Iroquois were unreliable at best."

"What happened next?" Owen asked.

"Massey ordered us to lie down in the forest on either side of the road with guns loaded and bayonets fixed—and the French marched right into our trap. As soon as they emerged, they deployed into a line. Massey waited until they were in close range, and commanded us to rise and fire. The French attack collapsed and they retreated in panicked disarray. It turned into a massacre. We chased some of them for over five miles. The Iroquois, ever-ready to take advantage, fell upon the survivors and began scalping and disemboweling them. I came upon three Indians about to tomahawk a French officer. He was already badly wounded. There was no sense in what they planned to do."

"Wasn't it dangerous to interfere?"

"It was indeed, but the madness of battle had left me—in fact, I was sickened to my very soul, knowing I had planned the ambush. Over three hundred Frenchmen died. Perhaps I thought an act of humanity would serve as some sort of atonement. I intervened, reasoned quite strongly with the Iroquois, and threatened to fight them, but in the end I gave them most of my enlistment bonus and saved the officer's life." Martin turned to Lucinde. "It was your father— Pierre Delacroix."

"What did you do with him then?" she asked softly.

"I carried him back to our encampment and kept him there throughout the remainder of the siege. Pouchot continued his defense of Fort Niagara for two more days. Somehow, despite the heat and rough conditions, your father survived. I shared my rations with him and treated his wounds the best I could. After the surrender, we marched into the fort where a British surgeon cared for your father. I made sure they safely transferred Pierre to a stockade before setting out on another expedition. You know the rest of his story."

"I thank you for saving him," Lucinde whispered.

"You have thanked me on many occasions."

"But now I know the whole story." She rose from her blanket and kissed his cheek in gratitude.

"It really was a pathetic gesture on my part, considering how many men died."

Craig glanced around at the McDonnell clan. The entire family had listened Martin's recounting with a strange attentiveness; clearly this was the first time they had heard the chronicle described in such detail. For Lucinde it was a revelation, an undiscovered thread newly woven into the tapestry of her heritage. Craig considered Martin's war experience, how closely it mirrored his own. He appreciated firsthand the courage it took to resurrect such terrible memories.

Agnes rose from her wooden chair and said, "Well, I don't know about you folks, but after that, I think we all deserve another round of refreshments!" Mary helped her pour.

"To our country!" Martin toasted them. "It is forty-one years old today!"

"To our country!" everyone echoed.

Chapter Twenty

New Orleans—July 4, 1817

Doc's stomach churned as the carriage turned off North Rampart onto St. Peter and into the heart of *Vieux Carré*. Although Ste. Gême had argued forcefully that he should remain behind and leave the fighting to Emmett's men, Doc knew he must see this attack to its conclusion, no matter what the outcome. If it failed, he must warn Philippe and spirit Solange safely out of town. He had let loose one of the most hideous monsters upon the world; he could not turn his back now. Ste. Gême's pleas for him to stay behind had fallen upon a hardened resolve, but as they neared their destination, Doc felt himself wavering.

Although it was late, gunfire crackled and cannons boomed near the river, evidence that the citizens were still celebrating. Emmett had commandeered a number of wagons and two covered carriages to convey his motley army into New Orleans. As planned, they came in from the west, skirting the western fringe of *Vieux Carré*, hanging just inside the American sector before crossing Canal Street to take North Rampart, which ran along the city's back side. People still reveled in the streets; many showed signs of drunkenness and seemed generally unconcerned at their passage. The wagons began peeling off individually on preassigned routes that would converge near Signet's townhouse. From the afternoon briefing Doc understood that Emmett's drivers would halt at various locations; the attackers would get out and approach the townhouse on foot from different streets. After the attack, the survivors would return to their carriages and disappear into the night.

The air lay hot and humid, making it difficult to breathe. The crowded carriage rolled to a halt, just one street west of the town-house. Six men stepped out, joined by four more who were riding on top.

"You come with me, Doctor," the gunman Jacques ordered. "Emmett ordered me to watch out for you." He still limped from his gunshot wound.

Doc stepped down cautiously and whispered. "Are you sure you can run on that leg?"

"I can outrun you with your gimp! Are those pistols loaded?"

"They are."

"This is the first time I have seen you without your black bag."

"I left it with Ste. Gême. If something happens to me, he will give it to Solange Tourigny, the nurse to whom I am engaged. Why do you mention it?"

"We might need it."

"Of that I am sure. If I live, I will patch up those I can when we return to Ste. Gême's."

Silently, they approached the townhouse. No one spoke. Full moon was just six days past, and when it emerged from behind the clouds, it flooded the cobblestone street with disconcerting bright-ness, gleaming off the palm fronds and illuminating the Spanish moss into strands of ghostly white. Doc glimpsed several shadowy figures already crouched along the stone walls, most of them bunched in the dark shade of a live oak tree. Beyond these men, Doc spied the arched carriage entrance—much closer than he had reckoned—just thirty feet away. He flattened himself against the wall and wondered briefly where Emmett was.

Unexpectedly, two of Signet's guards emerged from the arch-way. Both men smoked cigars, ends glowing red in the darkness. They appeared casual in attitude; then, one of them noticed the clus-ter of men under the tree, backlit by the moonlight. He swung his gun around and Doc heard the twang of three bowstrings, the whiz-zing of arrows, and the 'thunking' noises of arrow strikes. Both men jerked violently backwards and slammed onto the street, neither making a sound. The Choctaw Indians had successfully pulled off their phase of the attack. In that instant, the knot of pirates under the trees sprang into action. Some darted silently toward the entrance; others boosted the two Brazilians into the live oak branches, while others raised crude ladders and placed them gently against the courtyard walls.

"Let's go!" Jacques whispered, slapping him on his shoulder.

Doc drew both pistols and followed, his powder horn and leather shot pouch bouncing awkwardly against his right hip. Other men approached from the east, their footsteps scuffling on the cobblestones, although they tried hard to move quietly. When they reached the entrance, Doc noticed Signet's guards lying face-up in the street, fletched arrow shafts protruding from their necks, their vocal chords severed as the Choctaws had intended.

Inside the courtyard, Doc observed Emmett's men fanning out to neutralize the slave quarters and check out the stables, blacksmith's forge, and other outbuildings. Someone in the courtyard yelped in pain and outrage. To his right, Doc spotted a guard staggering in a wild circle, his hands clutching at something in the back of his neck. Another guard ran toward the house, but he too began to stagger in a crabbing, sidewise motion. Three of Emmett's men ran him down and threw their long knives. Every knife struck, although in odd places. The man stumbled and fell face forward onto the ground where the pirates finished him off. The first guard escaped the knifing, but had lost complete control of his functions. He lay on the ground, legs twitching and drumming convulsively. Doc edged over to investigate, paying no attention to Emmett's men dropping agilely from the walls. Two long wooden darts were embedded deeply in the guard's neck. He had been hit from behind—the Brazilians had done their work.

"Alarm! Alarm!" shouted someone from the upper balcony. A muzzle blast lit the entire courtyard and one of Emmett's men went down. A Choctaw Indian materialized beside Doc, drew his long bow and released an arrow. Doc watched the missile flit away in the moonlight; then he lost track of it in the dark live oak shadows. But an instant later he heard the strike and saw the gunman pitch forward over the wrought iron railing to smash headfirst onto the flagstones below.

After that, all hell broke loose—the time for stealth was past. Emmett's men opened up with a deadly hail of gunfire, but Doc was not quite sure what they were shooting at. Fighting erupted behind him at one of the long stone buildings. Perhaps this was where most of Signet's men were quartered. A bomb exploded from that direction. Gunfire blazed from the townhouse—perhaps as many as eight to ten guns rained lead shot into the courtyard. More of Emmett's men fell. Doc sought cover behind the closest live oak tree, glancing nervously over his shoulder to see where the Brazilians were, praying they would not mistake him for one of Signet's men. He did not wish to die from a poison dart—or for that matter, gunfire. Out on the front street more gunfire crackled; this noise was abruptly overwhelmed by a deafening explosion. One of Emmett's men had set off a homemade bomb.

A bold knot of pirates reached the balcony stairs. One of them lit the fuse on a huge bomb, once an old whiskey keg, and rolled it up to the heavy back door, the fuse crackling and sparkling brightly under the balcony overhang. Other pirates hurled small, fist-sized bombs onto the balcony, smoke trails arcing upward in the moonlight. The men scarcely had time to scatter before the big bomb exploded in a thunderous boom, smashing in the door and shattering glass windows. The small bombs burst and another of Signet's guards plummeted into the courtyard with a sickening impact.

Through clouds of gun smoke, Doc spied Emmett Barnett, "step-thumping" up the balcony stairs with a half dozen of his men. He rushed forward, climbing as fast as his bad knee would allow, to join them. Others followed closely behind. They inched their way up the stairs and along the balcony.

"Bang!" A musket blast shattered the glass door in front of Doc; the impact of a lead ball clubbed one of Emmett's men over the railing. The man had stood less than a foot away. In an incredible blur of reaction, Emmett spun on his wooden leg, lit the fuse to a small bomb, and tossed it through the shattered glass door into the room. All of this happened in a blur of motion. Doc winced and drew back, covering his ears and ducking as the bomb exploded, blasting shards of glass outward in a silvery spray. The shrieks inside the bedroom were piteous. Emmett sniggered like he had played some naughty trick, then dispatched two men to enter the room and finish off the survivors. The remaining three—Emmett, Raoul and Doc—crept cautiously toward Signet's bedroom. They reached the last door, a delicate, glass-paned affair.

"Bomb?" Raoul whispered.

"No bomb!" Emmett growled. "Want Signet alive!"

The fighting fizzled out in the courtyard below. Emmett's men swarmed the lower level of the townhouse, looting and laughing, shooting stray survivors. Out on the front street, a fusillade of con-certed gunfire indicated that some of Signet's men attempted escape in that direction. More bombs exploded. Doc wondered if the banker was involved in that luckless attempt. Emmett would be sorely dis-appointed if he had, for no one could have survived such an ambush.

The little smuggler seemed unconcerned. He tapped Raoul on the shoulder and gestured at a wrought iron chair. The half-broth-er understood and chuckled silently. He leaned his musket against the wall, lifted the chair and swung it with all his might though the French double doors, shattering the glass panes, smashing the brass latch, and tearing both doors from their hinges. A blaze of gunfire erupted from the room, confirming that at least three men were holed up in there.

"Bomb?" Raoul asked again.

"No bomb!"

Doc wondered what Emmett would do next. More of Emmett's men climbed the stairs to the balcony, bunching up behind them.

"Eh?" Emmett asked quizzically. Raoul nodded in agreement as he picked up his musket. Emmett stepped forward, removed his big hat and swept it over the open doorway. More shots rang out, very nearly tearing it from his grasp. He had obviously employed this ruse before.

"Now!" Emmett barked.

Raoul and Emmett barged in through the door and Doc followed right behind them. From across the room a gun fired and Raoul reeled backward, falling with a hard thud. Emmett fired his pistol and in the flash of that muzzle blast Doc glimpsed a massive bed with perhaps a dozen guns laid out on it. He also spied three startled faces—those of Jules Signet, the lawyer, Alain Morel, and another man, obviously a gunman. It was that man who Emmett had shot. He sat in an awkward, twisted position against an armoire, hands clamped onto his midsection, blood spewing from his mouth. Morel snatched up a musket. Reflexively, Doc pointed his pistol and shot him in the abdomen, doubling him over. He drew his other pistol and fired into the darkness where he last saw Signet, praying for his sake he had killed him.

In the darkness he heard a strange whistling noise. It grew louder and louder in volume, the noise filling the confines of the room. One of Emmett's men appeared in the doorway with a blazing torch. The flames lit the room with an eerie, flickering glow, intensifying the already-surreal scene. Doc saw Emmett twirling his short bola, and the savage gleam in his single eye revealed fully his unholy nature. Doc imagined this might be a glimpse into hell itself. In desperation, Signet reached for one of the guns, obviously uncertain as to which had been discharged.

"I wouldn't!" Doc roared, pointing an unloaded pistol at him.

The bluff worked. Signet fled for the hallway door, taking his chances with those fighting men he might have remaining outside. Emmett cast the bola in a deadly throw. The weapon spun across the room, just missing the bedposts, catching Signet about his legs. In a whirling blur, the stone weights wrapped the cords tightly, thwacking soundly against shins and knees. The banker crashed to the floor, wailing in agony.

"For the love of God, have mercy!" he wailed.

"Haw! Haw!" Emmett laughed, advancing triumphantly across the room—*step-thump, step-thump*. "This night I get payment for leg."

"I can pay you—lots of money," Signet gasped.

"I take all you have."

"It is not hidden in this house. Only I know where it is."

"You tell," the pirate chortled. "We have whole night." He reminded Doc of a cat, toying with a wounded mouse—in total control of the situation.

Signet glared madly at Doc. "You can stop this. As a physician you swore an oath to save lives and ease suffering."

"That is what I am doing," Doc replied. "I should have released Emmett long ago. You have killed too many good people already. And for what—financial gain? Power?"

"You were nothing when I dragged you from the gutter—nothing but a sorry drunk wallowing in your own piss and vomit!"

Doc recognized the truth of this and sat on the bed, carefully reloading his pistols. He still entertained thoughts of mercy-killing, but Emmett anticipated this and shook his head. "Take Doc's guns. We give back to him soon." One of his men took charge of the pistols. More of Emmett's men filed into the room. "See to Raoul," Emmett ordered.

Obligingly, Doc crossed the floor to where Raoul lay on his back—shot through the chest, his breath rasping loudly, bright blood frothing at his mouth. Doc recognized this instantly as a lung shot; the man was drowning in his own blood. He rose shakily and stepped out onto the balcony, sickened at what was yet to come. Some of Emmett's men carried items from the house and across the courtyard. Others guarded the streets in case the militia patrol showed up. In that event there would be another bloody shootout.

"No!" screamed Morel. "Have pity!"

Doc glanced back into the room. The men had lit a couple of lamps. Stripping Morel naked, they laid him out on the floor in front of Signet. Doc saw the bullet wound where he had shot him—low and to the left—a gut shot, the most painful of all wounds. He wished he had killed him, but he had been forced to shoot fast—and he was no gunman. The man lay crumpled in agony.

"Watch what we do your friend," Emmett guffawed, kicking Signet in the shin. "You next."

The little pirate drew a small knife, scooped up a handful of Morel's genitalia and sliced off the whole lot. Morel thrashed and squealed like a butchered pig. Emmett fell upon his victim, cutting off ears, nose, fingers and toes, slicing off strips of flesh, flaying him alive. Blood covered the little monster. The screams grew weaker and weaker before dying out altogether. Doc returned his gaze onto the courtyard, trembling and faint, knowing he had instigated this hell. After some time, it was over—at least for Morel. Emmett's gruff voice grated in the stillness that followed.

"Now my friend—you talk. Where gold and silver?"

Signet attempted a show of strength. "You will torture me anyway. Why should I tell you anything?"

"You tell!"

Doc turned to behold the wooden parquetry covered in blood, hunks of internal organs, and pieces of flesh; Morel's head had been severed and jammed onto one of the bedposts. The mouth was agape and stuffed with the man's genitals. Without warning, Emmett struck Signet on the hand with a cast-iron fire poker. The two-handed blow landed with a sickening thud, very obviously breaking bones. Emmett went deliberately for the hand, knowing he could inflict excruciating pain without killing his victim. Signet screamed in a high-pitched wail. His fingers were bent back at impossible angles and the hand dangled limply from the wrist.

"Where the gold?"

"Right here—in this room—wall safe behind the armoire!" Signet gasped.

"See?" Emmett laughed delightedly. "You talk."

One of his men crossed the floor and laboriously moved the heavy furniture. The safe was unlocked. The gunmen withdrew numerous leather satchels, each heavy with gold and silver coin.

"Where else?" Emmett prodded.

Signet hesitated and Emmett whacked him hard on the knee, shattering the joint, another blow calculated to inflict maximum pain, but not to kill. Doc wished he could end Signet's suffering, but the smuggler would not permit it; besides, his gunmen were already onto him. They would block any attempt on his part to alleviate Signet's pain. This was pirate justice—a highly dangerous situation in which he could not interfere. Quickly he left the room, strode the balcony's length, and descended the stairs, oblivious of possible danger. Another scream pierced the night. When he reached the fountain, he dipped his handkerchief in the water, laying it on the back of his neck as he struggled to keep his gorge from rising. He glanced back at the 'townhouse-turned-torture chamber'. One of the finest residences in New Orleans was now a hell of unspeakable horrors. He heard more thuds and screams and occasional outbursts of laughter, so he stepped through the carriageway and onto the street where some of Emmett's men stood guard. The street remained empty of passersby or the curious. Presently, the outlaws began hauling out gold and silver coin, precious jewelry and personal effects, expensive weapons and silverware.

"What is happening?" one of the street guards asked.

"Emmett cut off the man's private parts," the bearer announced. "Then he cut off both legs and both hands—all while he still lived."

"Merciful God!" Doc breathed. "What have I done?"

"What else happened?" the guard prodded.

Doc learned that Signet had suffered the same grisly fate as Morel had—both heads were jammed on the bedposts and— He turned sadly away and began walking back toward the carriage.

"Doctor!" Jacques accosted him. They had lost contact during the assault. Jacques appeared relieved to have found him.

"Yes?"

"Emmett says I must take you back to Ste. Gême's plantation."

"Very well."

"Are you sick, Doctor?"

"We should all be sick this day."

Two of Emmett's men caught up with them. They panted heavily as they lugged blood-spattered satchels of money and hemp sacks stuffed with silver plate and cutlery. Apparently the little pirate had made the haul of a lifetime, taking revenge upon his would-be killer and more than recouping his financial losses. Judging from the weight of those satchels, he had seized an enormous plunder—and this load did not represent the total amount. Much had already been spirited away. Doc wondered if some of the pirates might try to filch a small portion of the loot, then he thought again. After tonight, no one would dare attempt to rob the little monster.

They soon reached the carriage. Jacques ordered the driver to head directly to Ste. Gême's, even though the entire complement of gunmen had not yet made it back. Doc imagined that several men would not return. He also knew that Emmett's priority was to safeguard his plunder. Those who missed the carriages must find their own way back. When they turned onto North Rampart, the driver cracked his whip and quickened the pace, urging the team into a brisk trot toward the relative safety of the American sector. They crossed over Canal Street and soon hit *Rue de la Levee*, the road toward Ste. Gême's plantation.

Ste. Gême met Doc on the front porch. The planter blanched when he observed Doc's face in the torchlight. "The deed is done?" he inquired bleakly.

"May God forgive me, yes," Doc muttered.

"Signet is dead?"

"He is. So is Alain Morel and perhaps twenty other men."

"I warned you not to go. I knew it would be horrific."

"You were right," Doc croaked.

"Come inside and I will pour you a drink. I will order the slaves to draw a hot bath, and they will clean and press your clothing."

"I fear I shall never be clean again."

Although he yearned for a strong drink, Doc settled for hot tea with lemon. While this was prepared, a slave woman removed his boots and brought him a porcelain basin of cold water mixed with mineral salts. Tenderly she bathed Doc's feet while another, younger woman brought a cold compress to lay across his eyes. Ste. Gême ordered the woman to massage Doc's temples, neck and shoulders. During this time, Jacques and the other pirates deposited their loot with the planter and quietly left the plantation.

After a time, Ste. Gême spoke softly, in case Doc had fallen asleep. "Can I get you anything else, Doctor?"

"No, thank you. This is just fine. Has Emmett arrived?"

"Not yet. You may speak freely; his men have gone."

"Then we must thank Almighty God."

"I am sorry you did not heed me. By all accounts Emmett Barnett is a dangerous customer."

"That is an understatement," Doc replied without removing the compress. "I knew he was evil, but never in my wildest imaginings could I have foreseen such macabre behavior. Henri, we have joined hands with the Devil's minion on earth. I have read about gruesome slayers throughout history, but this man takes all prizes. The ancient Assyrians and the Huns have nothing on him."

"What must we do with the man?"

"He has confided in me. He plans to set up a tavern in Bahia da Salvador in Brazil. We must hope he does so—and very soon. I will do all I can to aid him in his endeavor."

"You may count on my support. Perhaps I can make discreet inquiries about a ship. In the meantime, we must consider a New Orleans without Signet. It will be a brighter, safer place. We no longer live in mortal danger."

"That is some comfort."

"Philippe Bouchard may take his place among the ranks of our finest citizens."

"Yes, you are correct." Doc lowered his voice. "Henri, you must not let Emmett know I told you about him going to Brazil. He will not wish the law to follow him. If he thought you knew, he might—"

"Say no more, my friend. Your secret—Emmett's secret—is safe with me. Like you, I was complicit in this evening's assault. In fact,

I planned it. Emmett knows this, so he may eventually ask for my help in securing transportation. And he shall have it. When Emmett goes away, so goes our secret. We must then pray daily for him to stay away."

Later, while Doc soaked in a tub of hot water, another group of Emmett's men arrived. They straggled in throughout the night, in bunches of four or five men, silent figures laden with all sorts of plunder. Each group deposited their loot with Ste. Gême, and instead of staying on, they disappeared over the river bank to return to the bayou. Apparently all this was done on Emmett's command. The pirate trusted Ste. Gême as Doc had trusted him with his medical bag. The planter locked the plunder safely away in Emmett's bedroom.

———————•———————

The little monster did not show up until late the following afternoon, attended by his surviving brother, Louis, Jacques, and a half dozen other of his most trusted pirates. No longer the blood-covered ghoul, he appeared clean in immaculate clothing—dark blue shirt, black cravat, cream-colored trousers, leather vest, and new black eyepatch and hat. His boots were brightly burnished. Ste. Gême received him on the front porch, paying him all the respect due a foreign dignitary, pouring him a tall cognac and ordering the slaves to bring other refreshments. Doc forced himself to play the role of admirer, compartmentalizing the disdain and terror he felt.

"I put end to all your troubles," Emmett chuckled, sipping on the cognac.

"You sure as hell did!" Doc exclaimed.

"He not bother Philippe or anyone else."

"Right again."

"I go Bahia."

Doc glanced at Ste. Gême and shrugged. Apparently, the pirate trusted the planter with the secret of his destination. "When?" he asked.

"Soon."

"Let me know. I will see you off. We have suffered much together."

The little pirate barked an order. Jacques stepped forward, reached into a leather pouch and handed Doc his pistols. "You one damn good doctor—good fighter too!" Emmett exclaimed

"I'm not so sure about that," Doc demurred.

"What happen you now?"

"Well, first I am getting married."

"You too damned old!" Emmett laughed out loud, slapping his good leg.

"I know—I know," Doc held up his hands. "But she is a nurse and together we plan to take our skills north, perhaps to Kentucky, maybe Ohio."

"Good to hear."

As dusk fell, Emmett inspected his plunder. Even he was amazed. "Too much to carry in boats," he announced. "I come back for more tomorrow." Carefully he counted out a large stack of coins. Louis handed him a strong leather bag and the pirate swept the coins into it. He gave it to Doc.

"For you, my friend."

"What for? Doc asked, shocked. "I do not understand." He guessed there must be a thousand gold dollars in that bag.

"Take—wedding present. Enjoy new life, like me. We all have new start."

"You and I know about new beginnings," Doc agreed, recalling their sea voyage to Brazil. "Life is all about change, you know. It is how we meet those changes that count."

"You damn right, Doctor."

The Natchez Trace—July 15, 1817

They came upon the boy shortly after dawn. One of Bruce Bowman's outriders heard him whimpering in the underbrush and pulled in to investigate. The boy had been shot through his abdomen and he now lay writhing in mortal agony, black blood coating the green cane stalks. His crying was pathetic to see and it affected even the hardened soldiers.

"Water!" the boy croaked through cracked white lips, his face ashen from death's pallor. Bowman guessed him at about thirteen years of age, taking mental note of his fine clothing and well-made shoes. He snapped his fingers for the outrider to bring him a leather pouch of fresh water. The boy guzzled it greedily, then doubled up in pain.

"Can you tell us what happened?" Bowman asked.

It was a familiar tale on the Natchez Trace. The boy, his father and two brothers had teamed up with a neighbor and his sons, building a large flatboat, assembling a cargo, and floating it downriver from the state of Ohio. Loaded with barrels of salt pork, wheat flour, cornmeal, salt, leather, wool and tobacco, they had gone to New Orleans to make their fortune, traveling down the Great Miami River to the Ohio, and thence to the mighty Mississippi—all without incident. By all accounts they had fared well, selling their goods at high prices. They had walked back on the Trace. A band of robbers learned of their wealth, tracked them from the town of Natchez, fell upon them, and—as far as the boy knew—killed his entire family, and the other family as well. The boy had been shot, but managed to escape into the brush.

"I am sorry for you, lad," Bowman sighed. Truly he was. "Do you know where the men were headed?"

"Toward Nashville. They have already robbed and killed other travelers. I heard them say so. They plan to rob again."

Bowman considered this. "Can you describe the men?"

"Yes. Two were fat, freckled, and red-headed. One was tall, skinny, and black-haired. There were four or five others, maybe more. One rode a brown horse and led a big gray mule."

'It gives us a leg up," Bowman thanked him. "Let's have a look at that wound."

"Oh, it hurts something awful!"

"I'll bet it does," Bowman sympathized. Gently, he peeled back the boy's linen shirt. The blood had congealed and the cloth stuck to his body. At first glance Bowman could tell that the wound was mortal. The gut was punctured and the stench from the leaking contents was sickening. Infection was spreading throughout the young man's body.

"Am I to die, sir?"

"We all are, lad."

"Can you give me something for the pain?"

"I think we might have something." He nodded significantly at his outrider who instantly understood the unspoken command. Bowman swung back into his saddle and rode off. He had scarcely gone fifty yards before the gunshot popped on the warm morning air. It was a sad case—but the boy was certainly better off. The outrider soon caught up with them.

"Shall we pursue?" he asked.

"We shall," Bowman nodded. "We are, at present, the only source of justice in this area. They deserve punishment—and when we vanquish them, we will reap the rewards."

"The boy looked quite well-to-do." The outrider had searched the body and found six Spanish mill dollars, made of pure silver. He handed these over.

"He was—and that means his family was. According to him, the outlaws have robbed others, so I suspect they are carrying a great deal of money. Ride ahead and let me know what you discover."

The outrider spurred his horse into a lope and headed up the trail. Bowman did not worry about him. He was the best tracker in his outfit. He could tell how many horses they were pursuing, whether they were carrying heavy loads, what the riders ate for breakfast, and how far they were ahead—he could glean all sorts of information from signs along the trail.

Around mid-afternoon the outrider returned, bringing plenty of news. He had stopped in at a crude tavern just inside the southern boundary of Tennessee. The keeper had seen the outlaws pass, but insisted they had not stopped. Farther along the road, a local farmer saw a rough-looking band of riders, perhaps twelve or thirteen men—far more than the boy had counted—riding good mounts and leading pack horses, oxen, and mules, all laden with goods.

"Are these the men we seek, Jeff?" Bowman asked.

"The boy had it about right. Two fat, red-haired men lead the party—ne'er-do-wells by the name of McPherson, from south of Nashville. There is a tall, skinny black-haired man and a big gray mule in the bunch. As the farmer guessed, there are a dozen or more men in all."

"Did you see them?"

"I saw their sign. They are definitely headed up the Trace toward Nashville."

"Can we get ahead of them?"

"I believe so. I scouted a game trail that turns south and then east for several miles. It appears to run parallel to the main road."

"Yes, but for how far?"

"I am not certain, but it will keep them from seeing us."

"How far are they ahead?"

"We could catch them by sunset, but that might rush things. I pulled in close enough to hear them talking. They are taking their time, planning another ambush."

"On this occasion *they* will be the prey." With a sharp whistle, Bowman called in his soldiers. They drew in close, with no wastage of time, ready to follow his instructions. "Men, the outlaws are just a few miles ahead. They have robbed and killed several travelers. I plan to cast ahead and lay a trap from which they will not escape. You have done this kind of work before, so you know what that means. We kill quickly and efficiently—no one lives to report us. I promise you will receive the usual share of spoils. And, you may rest assured, we do a good deed for humanity. Are you with me?"

No one dissented; these men functioned as a single unit, ready to engage on a moment's notice, their weapons loaded and primed, horses well-fed and rested. Bowman would use this ambush as a practice drill, taking notes on individual conduct and overall outcome, providing feedback where needed. "Let us ride."

The Natchez Trace—July 16, 1817

The outlaws knew their business; Bowman immediately saw this was evident. Perhaps one or more of them had fought in the military, for they wisely sent ahead scouts, three men on fast horses to reconnoiter in case lawmen or—worse—other outlaws lay in wait. They also looked out for likely victims, farmers returning from New Orleans with bags full of money.

The outlaws had camped the previous night, making it possible for Bowman to cast ahead of them. Following the well-worn game trail, which was much smoother than the main road with its stumps and wagon ruts, they gained plenty of time to stake out the killing ground, making sure the false camp lay in a depression next to the road with plenty of solid cover from which to shoot. Jeff, the outrider, selected the site when he discovered that the road formed a gut, with steep banks and narrowed ends, making escape near impossible.

Some miles back, Bowman baited the initial trap with four of his best men, making sure they dressed in their finest attire. Their horses carried leather satchels bulging with small rocks gathered from a nearby creek bank. The men had played this game before. They would keep their guns ready to discourage an attack, and boast openly of a successful trip to New Orleans. From the brushy bluff twenty feet above the road, Bowman and three other mercenaries provided additional protection, each taking aim at the outlaw scouts, ready to shoot them dead if they tried to attack. From their hideout they could overhear the entire conversation.

The outlaws rode up from behind and one of them shouted, "Hello, friends!"

Bowman's men wheeled their horses in feigned surprise, aiming their weapons. "What do you want?" Jeff asked.

"We don't want nuthin'! This here is a dangerous road. Would you mind us joining you for extra protection?"

"We would."

"There is safety in numbers."

"Then find someone else."

"Ya'll ain't very friendly."

"If you were carrying as much money as we are, you wouldn't be friendly either."

"Had a good trip to New Orleans, did you?

"We can't complain. Do you know of a good tavern nearby?"

"You won't find one before nightfall."

"Then we will have to make camp," Jeff sighed. "I am getting damned tired of this road."

"Don't stray too far off it," the outlaw advised. "You never know what kind of riff-raff is out there. You'll be safer if you camp near the road."

"Thanks for the advice, friend," Jeff replied.

To avoid suspicion, the outlaw scouts continued onward. Bowman knew they would soon turn off the road and backtrack through the brush, returning to report their findings. Bowman suppressed a chuckle. Making open camp on the Natchez Trace was the worst of all possible suggestions. He waited until the outlaws had gone before rising to brush the grass off his clothing.

"You think they'll try?" Jeff called up to him.

"I am certain of it. We will make ready."

At dusk, Bowman ordered his men to build a blazing camp-fire in the shallow depression. The mercenaries staked four horses where they could be seen from the road, while camp gear was positioned in likely places. Four bedrolls, stuffed with leaves and arranged to resemble sleeping figures, added a final touch of reality. The remaining horses were concealed some distance beyond the depression, but close enough to mount, if needed.

The mercenaries deployed in a semi-circle along the rim that ringed the open depression, crouching like predators among trees. Each man carried two rifles and two pistols. No one smoked or talked. Presently, the sun sank behind forested hills and the road grew dark. The fire flickered in the hollow, lighting tree branches overhead and making the camp clearly visible. Finally, the moon rose, illuminating the hollow with ghostly silver light. An owl hooted mournfully in the distance, and the jar flies began their repetitive chirping.

A twig snapped out on the road. Bowman curled his hand gently around the cross-hatched wrist of his long rifle. Peering hard into the darkness, he counted five men. Then, he heard footsteps crackling in the brush behind them. Outlaws were encircling the hollow, adopting his ambush plan. As they approached, they ran the risk of stepping on his men. Bowman knew his mercenaries would lie perfectly still, ready to use their knives, if it came to that. Silently, he admitted that these outlaws were very good, but even so, his men still held the advantage.

Someone whispered very near him. "They are asleep—let's go in!"

Bowman drew his long knife. In one accord the outlaws screamed like panthers—horrific, blood-curdling screeches intended to terrorize their prey. The entire band poured into the hollow, guns blazing, startling the tethered horses. One outlaw, slower than the others, ran to within two feet of where Bowman lay. Bowman sprang up and swung his knife in a powerful arc, plunging the blade deep into the man's throat.

The mercenaries opened up in a single volley, dropping outlaws all over the hollow. In one smooth motion, Bowman sheathed the knife and aimed his rifle at a tall man dodging sideways toward the horses. Gently he touched the trigger and watched with gratification as the man collapsed. Methodically, he reached for his other rifle and searched for a target. He heard shooting out on the road. As planned, the two mercenaries posted on both ends of the narrow gut shot their respective targets. Like hinged gates, they were closing off both avenues of escape. Silently, he ran toward the shooting. An outlaw appeared from behind a giant silver beech and fired at him from twenty paces, missing completely. How that man had escaped the massive volley, Bowman could not guess. He aimed and fired, hitting the outlaw squarely in the center of his chest, blasting him into the brush.

Hoof beats thundered out on the road. An outlaw had apparently reached his horse and was trying to break free of the trap, fleeing the "gatemen" on the western road. Guns fired from that direction, but the outlaw came on. Incredibly, another outlaw appeared behind him, also on horseback. Bowman ran into the road, drew his pistol and fired, spilling the nearest outlaw from his saddle. His second pistol misfired. He had nothing else to shoot, and the other horse bore down hard upon him. Instinctively, he reversed the grip on his empty rifle, grabbing it two-handed by the barrel, swinging hard and smashing the horse on its nose, breaking the wooden butt. The animal screamed, swerved violently, and stumbled, unbalancing the rider. Bowman sprang forward and yanked the outlaw from his saddle. He drew his knife and slashed the man's throat. The battle was over.

It took most of the night to round up the outlaws' horses, collect their guns, count the dead, and pick the bodies clean of money and stolen jewelry. Financially, the engagement was a rousing success, for the outlaws were carrying well over two thousand dollars in coin. That did not count the jewelry, some of which was valuable. In addition, there were horses and livestock, guns and personal belongings that would fetch a fair price in Nashville, less than one week's journey away.

But Bowman was not satisfied with the ambush. Much had gone wrong. One of his men was seriously wounded, shot in the lower right rib. The outlaws had outflanked them and come in from behind. That was his fault, really—he should have anticipated that. Additionally, there were far too many missed shots in the engagement. Granted, the light was bad, and the outlaws attacked from several directions, but there were too many survivors of the initial volley. In the end they killed sixteen outlaws—more than Jeff counted the day before. Bowman suspected they had not killed all the outlaws. A distinct possibility existed that one or more had escaped. As soon as daylight broke, he ordered his men to search the forest and ride back along the road in bands of two and three, to hunt for survivors. They found no outlaws, but did catch up with a big gray mule carrying saddlebags filled with Spanish mill dollars, shiny silver coins that jingled musically whenever the animal trotted. Bowman was pleased to see those saddlebags, for the silver more than doubled their gains.

Ten miles northeast of the hollow, the mercenary called for a halt. The men breakfasted late on coffee, bacon, and bread. After the meal, Bowman held a conference. He asked questions, not making judgments, not blaming anyone; he was logically probing for answers. Jeff was the best tracker he had ever known; it was highly unlikely he had miscounted. Perhaps other outlaws had joined the band after his report. The four "gatemen" swore that no riders had gotten past them on the road. The two guarding the western end had fired at the mounted outlaws, but were hindered by brush and overhanging limbs. Those would-be escapees turned, but would have run into the "gatemen" on the eastern end, had Bowman not stopped them. In the end, the mercenary admitted he had acted too hastily; perhaps he was guilty of underestimating his enemy—one of the biggest mistakes a soldier could make. He also realized that his men were exhausted. They would rest up in Nashville and enjoy the amenities of that city before pressing on to Frankfort.

Cottonwood Bend—July 21, 1817

The Honorable Judge Wilfred J. Bozarth, Kentucky State Representative, Attorney-at-Law, and noted war hero, surveyed the ragged militia company under his command. Once a year the company met on the open pastures of Charles Cox's farm to conduct military drills. Everyone enjoyed the event, but no one more than Judge Bozarth. While the regulars dressed in common homespun or buckskins, moccasins, farm boots, or shoes and leggings, the Judge wore a pair of polished black boots and an impressive blue uniform complete with gleaming officer's saber, gold buttons and epaulets, and a long red plume stuck into his stiff officer's hat.

From the time statehood was declared in 1792, Kentucky maintained some form of its original militia system, and every able-bodied male from eighteen to forty-five was obligated to serve. This system had been proclaimed in the *Militia Act of 1792*, but that law was almost immediately repealed when it proved "inadequate to answer the purpose intended." This act was first of many legislative attempts to govern militias, and most counties continued militias in one form or another. The annual muster provided valuable practice in case of another war, and it helped train men for law enforcement. All of the Cottonwood Bend Regulators served in the militia.

Each county was laid off into "bounds" large enough to produce a company of men, and each household was required to own a gun and keep a generous supply of powder and lead. Breckinridge County adhered to this practice. Kelwyn Lasher had lived in the county long enough to be summoned, but the New Englander had never fired a gun. Craig loaned him one of his old reliable rifles, and spent an evening teaching him to load and shoot. Kelwyn learned quickly enough, but his unfamiliarity with weapons showed that the militia system served a useful purpose.

At first, Prudence ordered him to ignore the summons—any variation in her schedule caused her great distress—but Craig informed her of the penalty for not showing up. If a member failed to answer roll call without legitimate excuse, he would be fined two dollars. Grudgingly, she acquiesced, but when Mary visited and explained what happened during the day, she ceased her grumbling.

In truth, most folks looked forward to the annual muster. Already heightened by recent Independence Day celebrations, patriotism soared to new heights as the militia marched under fluttering flags and stepped to the beat of fife and drums. Womenfolk showed up at the event in equal numbers, waving handkerchiefs and homemade flags, cheering loudly for their men. Even Prudence seemed to enjoy herself. After a morning of hard marching, arms inspection, and shooting in mass volleys, the men disbanded for dinner. The women had cooked all morning under sprawling shade trees at the pasture's edge.

After the dinner and a brief rest, Judge Bozarth assembled his men in ranks to read aloud from the long-defunct *Militia Act of 1792*, his stentorian voice carrying to the far corners of the field.

"Be it enacted that the Militia Companies within the several Counties in the State shall on the twenty-first day of July meet at some convenient place in the bound of their respective Company, and by ballot choose a Captain, Lieutenant and Ensign, balloting for the Captain first, and so on in order until the whole are elected!"

He paused theatrically and added, "I would be deeply honored if you kind folks could see fit to elect your humble servant for yet another year!"

The voting took place by acclamation and the Judge was summarily reelected. Craig suppressed a chuckle as he watched him strut about the field like a peacock, sucking in his gut and proudly displaying his magnificent uniform. Craig knew what others present did not—Violet had come to Mary two weeks ago, asking for her help in sewing a corset to tame the Judge's waistline which was showing increasing signs of rebellion. Despite that comic bit of knowledge, Craig readily admitted that the Judge knew all the intricacies of the drill; he also knew the law, and no one in the county could match his deep, booming voice. He was a true commander and his wit was, at times, razor-sharp.

At one point during the drill he asked the men, "Is everything in order?"

A young man, known for his fondness for the drink, replied, "I would like some whiskey, sir."

The Judge replied in his gruff manner, "Yes—and people in Hell want ice water!" Waves of suppressed laughter rippled through the ranks and someone snorted uncontrollably. "For that comment we shall march up and down the length of this field twice more!" the Judge's voice thundered. "Left face! On the double! March!"

They drilled for the remainder of the afternoon. Then, the real entertainment began—horse shows held on the parade grounds, horseraces, wrestling, footraces, tomahawk and knife-throwing, and individual rifle fire at various distances. Craig won the shooting contest for the fifth year in a row, but Owen, Calvin Ward and Judge Bozarth gave him stiff competition. There were others in the militia who proved themselves excellent marksmen.

That evening, the women served supper. Charles Cox had donated the beef and pork which slow-roasted most of the day over a low fire while the womenfolk prepared a wide assortment of dishes. As expected, several men began drinking and some terrible fights ensued, but Craig loaded Mary and the children into the wagon before things got too far out of hand. He recalled last year when Bill Lyle's son had an eye gouged out in a drunken brawl. Others suffered lost teeth, knife cuts, bite wounds, and broken bones.

"Well, another muster has come and gone," Craig observed.

"And you won the shooting contest again," Mary replied. "You have certainly earned the Judge's respect. That was clear. Several times he deferred to you."

Craig said nothing. He enjoyed driving home in evening's cool shadows. As they crossed the timber bridge over Cottonwood Creek, he spied numerous fish rising in the glass-smooth water, snatching insects that landed on the surface. A big blue-gray heron winged its way over the willows, heading east. Bullfrogs croaked from reedy banks where the creek flowed into the Ohio.

"Are you tired from all the marching?" Mary asked.

"Not really, but I would like a cool bath."

"It was awfully hot today. The Judge ran his men hard this afternoon."

"He sure did."

"Has anyone mentioned how is he faring—financially?"

"I heard someone say that Violet has paid off all their creditors. There are no more liens against them. That is something, for the Judge owed a lot of money."

"She confided the same thing to me. It has taken almost all she had."

"Will Kelwyn and Prudence be repaid?"

"They didn't loan money to him; Kelwyn fully considered the risks and speculated—as the Judge has done. Violet has no intention of refunding anyone's investments."

"Good for her." For the first time Craig admitted that Violet was made of strong stuff. The Judge had cheated on her and wasted their money, yet she chose to stand by him, endure humiliation, and hold him up in the community, while managing something of a social comeback using the last of her personal wealth. Perhaps the saying was accurate—it took tribulation to bring out one's strengths.

"She confessed they are in dire financial straits," Mary added. "There is so very little of her money left. The Judge works hard at his law practice, as he always does, but there are few prospects for him in Cottonwood Bend. When he attends court in Hardinsburg, he can realize a little money, but Violet worries he will fall prey again to a shady financier. And of course, she is terrified he will succumb to the charms of Cecilia Dowell."

"I wish that woman would go ahead and marry Gill Hagman!" Craig exclaimed, wondering if the man was up to the task, unconvinced that marriage would contain her sexuality.

"Perhaps she will. The point is, Violet still fears the Judge's weaknesses."

"She also respects his strengths. I have revised my opinion of her."

"I thought you might."

"There was a time when I would have rejoiced to see her taken down a peg."

"Many people would. Sometimes it takes something terrible in life to bring out the best in people."

"You see and understand so much that I do not. I love you." Craig leaned over to kiss her. The horses plodded surefootedly along the road—around Cemetery Knob and into the darkening country-side, and later, past Owen's driveway and the brick home of Martin McDonnell. Stars appeared overhead, gradually forming the sprawl-ing summer constellations that filled and spangled the sky. Mary pointed out some of these to the children, cooing with wonder at na-ture's artwork. As he did several times each day, Craig thanked God for blessing him with a loving wife and family, productive farmland, nice cabin and secure place in the community. The quiet, everyday routine had worked miracles upon his soul. In that moment he felt he was the luckiest man in the whole world, and he resolved to make the most of what God gave him.

St. Louis Cathedral, New Orleans—August 2, 1817

Hundreds turned out to attend the wedding of Doctor Thom-as Applegate and the widow Solange Tourigny. Many of New Or-leans' wealthiest citizens showed up, including Governor Jacques Villeré. Philippe Bouchard arrived with Henri Ste. Gême and his protégé Boze. Yves Guillot and family, including the young mother and child, occupied one of the front rows; a delegation of sisters attended from the Ursuline Convent. Old, young, rich, and poor came to share in the ceremony. Doc had treated most of them over the past twenty-five years—patched them up, cured their illnesses, eased their suffering, delivered their babies, and much more. Like the supporting cast from some vast dramatic production—his life—

they appeared for his final New Orleans performance. The wedding was, in every way, a deeply reaffirming experience. It surprised him that he had touched so many folks—that he had actually made a real difference in their lives. As the wedding procession left the cathedral, many came up to bestow their blessings and their thanks.

"I have told you often that people hold you in high esteem," Solange whispered as she held onto his arm. "You have steadfastly refused to believe that."

"It is you they admire, my dear." Doc replied, still unsure if this was a dream. Solange was an absolute vision in her cream-colored floor-length dress, lilac ribbons and matching bonnet. His heart soared when she smiled back at him.

"Will you promise to keep this old rogue in check?" Father Poitier laughed.

"I will, Father," Solange replied.

The celebration took place in the grand ballroom of the Hotel d'Orleans. Earlier, Philippe and Ste. Gême had agreed between them to foot the bill; consequently the food was exquisite and drinks flowed generously. Doc and Solange took the first dance across the floor and then gave it over to their guests. Experiencing a brief pang of remorse, Doc wished that Pierre Delacroix and Judge Harkness were there to share in his joy. For some strange reason he also thought of Emmett Barnett who, for obvious reasons, could not attend.

Father Poitier joined them at the head table. "I am so glad you chose to join the Holy Church, my son. In many cases, converts make the best Catholics."

"I am glad also," Doc agreed. He winked at Solange. She, Delacroix, Philippe, Ste. Gême, Father Poitier, and others were exemplary models of Christianity—they, more than anyone, had convinced him to join the Catholic faith, not by their words, but in how they conducted their lives. His recent experiences had taught him a great deal about life, and even more about himself. He had decided, once and for all, to place his trust in the highest power, the Almighty God.

For years Doc had read the works of French *philosophes* and

Enlightenment scientists. These scholars believed that everything in the Universe could be defined by Reason—by precise, mathematical, scientific truths. But one dissenting *philosophe*, Pierre Bayle, argued that this could only mean one thing—Reason is limited by those truths. Bayle had argued that Faith could not be proven; therefore, it transcended the boundaries of mere Reason. Doc liked to consider himself "enlightened" and he accepted this philosophy. But he had also read the Bible and had firmly decided where to put his faith.

The celebration lasted long into the night. Doc had reserved a corner room at the hotel; he and Solange would reside there until a steamboat arrived to provide passage north. He could easily afford both. In addition to his own money, Emmett Barnett's wedding present of one thousand dollars made him a wealthy man. But Pierre Delacroix had trebled that wealth with a princely gift of two thousand dollars. Doc would use a portion of that money to honor his request. Although the danger no longer existed, Doc would seek the daughter, Lucinde, and relate Delacroix's warning for her to stay away from New Orleans. He knew he must also bring her the news of her father's death—a task he dreaded.

"I am a sentimental old fool!" he rebuked himself. "This is my wedding night!" He turned his focus onto his lovely bride and their guests, joining in the conversations and adding all the wit and charm he could muster. It came naturally and he soon had everyone laughing and gathering round to hear his tales. Folks remarked how happy the couple looked together, marveling at how the years seemed to have rolled back for them both. All agreed that good fortune could not have visited a more deserving pair.

Chapter Twenty-One

Breckinridge County, Kentucky—August 22, 1817

This year Craig split and cut his tobacco with short, T-shaped knives, pleased with how fast the New England farmers learned to use them. Gently, they split and laid the plants in piles of six so these could wilt in the hot sunlight. The workers' children carried armloads of four-foot wooden lathes, one-inch square, dropping one near each pile. The wilted plants were later slid onto these lathes and crossed at angles to stand like wigwams, the butts pointing southward toward the Hardinsburg Road. Everyone understood that this work was all about preserving the leaf. The womenfolk directed their children to pick up leaves broken off in the handling, and these were strung onto hemp string and hung in the barn to cure.

From early August onward, various fields—oats, hemp, and tobacco—toppled before the army of workers, all harvested in their proper order and, fortunately, in excellent weather. Martin McDonnell commented on how smoothly everything transpired, how well the hands coordinated their efforts. Most of them had worked together for several years, hired shortly after the first New Madrid earthquakes when Martin had purchased two additional farms.

To Craig, harvest time seemed more like a social event than labor. First, the workers swept their long, two-handed cradle scythes through the oat fields that rippled in sluggish breezes like waves on a golden sea. These fields rustled with the crisp strokes and gentle laying of stalks in even rows. All the New Englanders knew how to harvest oats. Womenfolk raked and bound the stalks into sheaves, loading them into wagons and hauling them to the threshing floors.

Following Martin's advice, Craig had increased his hemp acre-age. The old man predicted that Kentucky's corn harvest might break records and corn prices would begin to fall. On the other hand, hemp looked to enjoy a healthy future market; even Hiram Rosen-botham offered to buy at respectable prices. This year the crop grew exceptionally well, densely-planted fields towering like dark green forests beside other, shorter crops. In April or May, these "fiber fields" were sown heavily—between forty-four and fifty pounds per acre—the closeness forcing the plants to grow upward to a height of ten to twelve feet. Ideal stalks would be thin-shelled with large hol-lows containing tough fibers valued by rope and sack makers. Hemp harvesting began when the plants began shedding pollen. Each af-ternoon, the workers emerged from the fields covered in a sticky coat of sweat and yellow pollen that itched and irritated. Craig took evening plunges in the river to wash it off. The water was warm this time year, but cool enough to refresh. Three days after each cutting, workers flipped the hemp stalks for even sun curing. When the plants had thoroughly dried, they were stacked in great shocks on crude platforms of fence rails lain in ten-foot squares. These plat-forms kept the shocks from touching wet ground. Craig showed his workers how to crisscross short bunches and lay them in the centers and then angle the taller bundles, butts downward, tops upward to form giant cones some twelve feet high. Finally, the cones were cov-ered with an outer, rain-proof thatch of sheaves, tightly-bundled and well-tied, to resist the strong winds of early winter. The fields soon abounded with these colossal shocks which would remain upright until late November when they would be torn down. At that time, workers would spread the stalks onto the ground. Cold rains, frosts, and melting snows would leach out the gum binding interior fibers to woody stems. Hemp retted in cold weather produced a fine, bright fiber that fetched top dollar.

Of all the crops grown in Kentucky, tobacco improved the most. Free from the frosts and cold of 1816, it flourished handsomely— big golden-green leaves that promised a good income. From the beginning Craig knew his crop would turn out well, and he was glad for the additional tobacco barn Levi had built a few years back. In previous years, he had committed his field hands to help Martin and Owen; now they returned the favor. This year, Craig's tobacco went in first. Then, the combined work force moved into Martin's fields. With so many hands at work, they could run multiple tiers in the barns. Tobacco was handed from flatbed wagons and passed upward to the top man who hung the stick and "regulated" the stalks, spacing them for even airflow. While he did this, the man below him repeated the process—and so on, down to the bottom man. With four separate runs going up, the wagons were unloaded quickly. It felt rewarding to hang the last tobacco in the barn.

The workers finished housing Owen's tobacco on September 1st. To celebrate, Owen killed a hog for the field hands and their families who came to enjoy dinner on the plantation lawn. These were happy times. Lucinde's belly began to show; Doc Emmick announced that she would deliver in early December, just three months distant. Craig could not believe how fast time was passing and he voiced this out loud.

Martin laughed, "Wait until you reach my age! You won't believe how short the years become. You will see the world changing right before your eyes—new developments will amaze, perhaps unsettle you. I read there are water-powered textile mills in New England that employ hundreds of workers. We have already seen how the steamboats are changing. The newer ones are bigger, faster and far more elegant. This is just the beginning!" Craig listened to him, recognizing the wisdom of his years.

Once, during a family dinner, Agnes asked, "Martin, you have lived a long time. What has surprised you the most about life?"

He answered without hesitation, "How short it is. Just yesterday I was in Maryland, playing with Indian children my own age, learning from them the ways of the woods. Now I am seventy-seven years old. The Lord gives most of us three-score-and-ten years. Anything after that is a bonus." That answer instilled in Craig the desire to live life to its fullest.

A couple of weeks remained before the corn harvest. The weather turned cooler, making for good sleeping nights. Craig and Mary spent much of that time together, working and playing. They distilled another batch of whiskey in this off time while corn turned brown and ears hardened. In the evenings they strolled through their orchards and surveyed the plums, apples and pears. It was plain to see that the fruit harvest would be abundant. The grape arbors sagged with heavy purple clusters. Soon they would be making jam, preserves, and wine.

In the down time, Craig took Kelwyn deer hunting. They went out one early morning and took up a position near the man's fall garden. The New Englander had never shot an animal before, but he had killed chickens and hogs. He dropped a fat doe at about eighty yards out. The families would dine that night on roast venison. Craig showed him how to dress the deer and wash it down with cold spring water. They hung it just inside the ice house and built a fire behind the stone silo while the womenfolk prepared a host of side dishes. Mary shared the secret of her marinade with Prudence. The venison soon roasted on the spit. Kelwyn's sons turned and basted it. Early that afternoon, Craig saddled his horse and rode into town to invite Levi Matthews to the dinner. The quarrelsome miller seemed surprised, but pleased, that Craig asked. He showed up with his family long before suppertime, quite content to fill everyone in on the latest town gossip. With such a large audience present, he embroidered his tales and soon had everyone in stitches. He was not above sharing memories of his and Craig's early experiences, and he could not resist telling his eyewitness account of Father Badin beating Craig. Obviously this tale had been honed from multiple tellings and retellings. Several times he prodded Kelwyn for confirmation. The New Englander nodded and added a few of his own details.

"What are your middle names?" Craig asked them. "Judas and Brutus?"

It was an enjoyable evening—a small preview of the upcoming corn shuckings when families gathered from all over the settlement and beyond. The season marched on in a quiet, glorious procession of autumn colors and changing scenery. Each morning the sun rose at a lower angle, days grew shorter, and nights turned crisp. Autumn usually induced in Craig a mild melancholy, but this year was different. He had too much to be thankful for and too much work to do.

New Orleans—September 19, 1817

After several weeks of running cargo and passengers from New Orleans to Natchez and back, *Jesse P. Emmick* moored at the levee with momentous news—the steamboat would soon journey north to Pittsburgh, with stops in various towns and cities along the way. Philippe Bouchard informed Doc Applegate of the eminent departure scheduled for September 26th. Consequently, Doc was the first traveler to reserve passage. He and Solange, although still enjoying wedded bliss, looked forward to leaving; they were ready to practice medicine in a cooler, northern climate. Doc believed the new location would bring finality to his past life. No one would know him; it would herald a whole new beginning. He still recalled that horrible night at Signet's townhouse and wanted to put as much distance between him and New Orleans as possible.

The city had undergone a quiet, but miraculous change. Still a wicked place full of vice and corruption, it felt cleaner and safer with Signet gone. Philippe Bouchard had worked together with other merchants to parcel the banker's vast holdings and put them up for auction. A new city council was formed. In the afternoons, Doc could walk hand-in-hand with Solange on the streets and not worry about the banker's minions stalking him. Despite this, he still carried his pistols. New Orleans hadn't changed that much. The ubiquitous "Kaintocks" and foreign ship crews, pickpockets, thieves and pirates still lurked along the levee, and in back streets and alleyways.

As promised, Philippe manumitted his slaves and began putting his plantations up for sale, choosing to purchase warehouses along the levee and expand the Bouchard Exchange. The estates of

D'Alembert, his former father-in-law, came under his control. The man who should have championed him in his misfortune had sold out and left New Orleans for good. Philippe soon resold these estates at an enormous profit. He moved Kayla into his townhouse and employed her full time as a housekeeper. Some folks gossiped that the relationship went much farther, but if so, this was an arrangement common in New Orleans. As long as Philippe did not flaunt her openly, he would suffer no societal repercussions. Doc was glad to know that Kayla and her child would be cared for. Philippe would not take advantage; if something did exist between them, Doc would not be one to criticize. Like Philippe and Judge Harkness, he had changed his thinking on numerous issues.

It was almost a perfect closure to his years in New Orleans—except for one nagging detail. Doc often wondered about Emmett Barnett. The man had seemingly dropped off the planet. Perhaps he was already in Bahia da Salvador. Doc figured it was best he had disappeared; perhaps that in itself was closure.

Then, Henri Ste. Gême's letter arrived at the hotel. As soon as Doc opened it, he experienced a shiver of apprehension—Emmett was requesting a meeting at the plantation, obviously wishing to share some critical news. Memories of the butchery in Signet's townhouse flooded back in giant, gruesome waves. In his mind, Doc could see the little monster splattered from head to toe in blood, sawing with his knife, swinging a heavy iron poker and breaking bones, laughing triumphantly with that unholy gleam in his eye. Doc considered ignoring the invitation, but Ste. Gême reiterated in closing that Emmett bore news of great significance.

Reluctantly, Doc hired a carriage and ordered the driver to convey him westward, toward the plantation. On the way he racked his brain, wondering what the little man could possibly have to tell him. From the time they parted ways, Doc had felt a sense of unease, believing there was something left undone or perhaps unspoken. Soon, he was rolling along on the *Rue de la Levee*, following the muddy river with the aroma of sugar refineries in his nostrils. It was that time of year when the refineries burned all day and all night.

The smuggler waited outdoors on the long front porch, seated with his friend Ste. Gême. Doc got out and walked across the shaded lawn to where they were. "Hello, Doctor!" Emmett called, grinning widely, his good eye closed tightly with genuine happiness. He and Ste. Gême rose to shake his hand.

"So, you are still in New Orleans?" Doc greeted Emmett, surprised he could still feel some affection for the man.

"Sit down, Doctor and have some coffee," Ste. Gême offered.

"Don't mind if I do." Doc took one of the cane-backed chairs. A uniformed slave poured black coffee into a porcelain cup. Doc added a liberal dash of cream, then stirred and sipped on it as he considered Emmett. The man looked remarkably fit, as hard as nails, almost the image of a dashing, miniature buccaneer. "I thought you left town long ago."

"Soon."

"Me as well. Solange and I have reserved passage on the steamboat *Jesse P. Emmick.* We are heading north to Kentucky."

"You need go damned quick."

"What do you mean?" Doc asked. He noticed the smuggler was no longer grinning.

"Should have told long ago. Did not think important."

"What is important?"

"That night at Signet's—you remember?"

"I remember." Doc nodded grimly, trying to suppress the memory.

"I torture him. I ask who he kill. He tell many names."

"Yes. Did he admit to killing Delacroix and Judge Harkness?"

"Delacroix, Harkness, Senator, young lawyer—many more."

"Unfortunately none of those murders will ever be proven. Your testimony would never stand up in court. First of all, you could never show up to testify, for the officials would arrest you on sight. And, because of your nefarious past, no court would accept your sworn deposition."

"I not go court—I tell you. There more to tell."

"And what is that?"

"Signet send small army to Kentucky."

A chill snaked up Doc's spine, numbing his lips. "Why would he do that?

"Get Delacroix's daughter—bring her back as Signet's slave."

"What!" Doc thundered. "He told you *that?*"

Emmett actually showed some semblance of remorse. "He say much that night. I force him talk. He tell everything."

"Why didn't you share this earlier?"

"I not think important then—forgot. But it bother me. When I remember—I send for you."

"Well, I thank you for that. How many men did Signet dispatch?"

"Fourteen."

"Did he really say all that—in his condition?"

"He tell me truth—no worry. He send good fighting men. Pay three thousand, five hundred."

Doc knew Emmett would not fabricate such a story. The smuggler always spoke directly, or refused to speak at all. Additionally, these particulars were too specific—they must be true. In order to avoid pain and dismemberment, Signet had spilled everything, most likely in broken sentences during lulls in the torture, the information becoming more incoherent as blood loss weakened him. Emmett could not possibly have remembered it all. He had been far too occupied with inflicting pain, and later stealing, transporting, counting, and storing the plunder, then guarding it while arranging for the long journey to Brazil. Apparently, this detail had escaped his recollection for some time and had resurfaced only recently. Doc would not chastise him, but he must know more.

"What else can you tell me?"

"They go see Governor of Kentucky."

"What for?"

"Give him order to take girl."

"Who wrote the order?"

"Villeré."

"Perhaps Philippe and I can petition him to rescind the writ. When did the men leave?"

"Last of June."

"Good Lord!" Doc gasped. "They must be there by now!"

"Sorry not remember sooner."

"Well, better late than never—I hope."

"You try stop men?"

"Yes. A steamboat leaves New Orleans one week from today. It will take approximately three weeks to reach Cottonwood Bend where Lucinde lives."

"You be careful. These men real soldiers. Fight in France and Mexico."

Doc realized this was a paid army of mercenaries, highly skilled professionals who sold their guns to the highest bidders. It mattered not whether they worked on the side of law enforcement or its frustration—they would fight for anyone as long as the price was right. If Signet had paid that dearly for their services, they must be good.

"Emmett, you take care of yourself in Brazil. Try to stay out of trouble."

"I bring plenty men with me. Buy warehouses. Set up damned fine tavern—smuggle goods, trade slaves."

Doc nodded thoughtfully. It was exactly the same underworld activity in which Emmett had engaged in New Orleans. The new tavern would serve as a front for the more lucrative businesses of smuggling and slave trading. With Signet's money, Emmett could start anew in a country where he had no criminal record.

"It appears you have things well-planned. I wish you a prosperous life, my friend."

"And you Doctor."

Doc, Emmett and Ste. Gême enjoyed another serving of coffee and pastries, listening to the chorus of cicadas and other insect noises rising and falling in the mid-morning heat. Emmett's news instilled in Doc a sense of extreme urgency; he wanted to depart that very day. Signet's men could have already seized Lucinde. But *Jesse P. Emmick* operated on a set schedule and would not leave for seven days. It was exasperating, but the steamboat was the fastest mode of transportation he could hope to engage. In the meantime, he would secure Philippe's aid in meeting with Governor Villeré. The young man might succeed in getting a new writ signed and could perhaps alert his business associates upriver to look out for the mercenaries.

As soon as the mercenaries learned of Signet's death, they would in all likelihood release their captives. After all, there would be no one in New Orleans to pay for them. But Doc must prevent the seizure from happening. Men like this could play rough, taking the worst kind of advantage of a defenseless woman. And, without Signet's payment, they might decide to hold her and the children hostage, forcing the Kentucky family to pay ransom. By all accounts the husband was wealthy.

It seemed wrong that Signet, who had wrought such havoc and inflicted so much pain, could still reach from beyond the grave to cause even more trouble. Doc realized that his past association with the banker continued to hurt others. Delacroix had charged him with his family's safety and Doc knew he must honor that trust.

Breckinridge County, Kentucky—September 21, 1817

"Wasn't that the most wonderful Mass?" Agnes declared. Attending Mass meant a great deal to her, and Martin always obliged when Father Badin came to Hardinsburg. They had arrived early Sunday morning, so she could recite the complete Rosary with the other womenfolk of Breckinridge County. The little church at St. Romuald, formerly St. Rumoldus, now boasted a sturdy roof constructed of yellow poplar beams, white oak boards and cedar shingles cut during the dark of the moon in the belief they would lie flatter. Materials and labor were donated by the Wheatley and Mattingly families, prosperous farmers who knew how to build. To add beauty and symmetry to the place, the Beavins had planted dark cedars and flowering trees around the church grounds and graveyard. Father Badin conducted a glorious Mass on the beautiful autumn day, reading from the Bible about bountiful harvests, fruitful wombs, and God's wish for all his children to prosper. He performed baptisms and marriages, heard confessions and granted absolutions.

The dinner was something to behold, enjoyed out on the lawn under a clear, blue sky with long fire pits, trestle tables and wagons covered with food. Farmers had donated beef, pork, lamb, turkey, goose, chicken, rabbit, and venison—roasted, baked, fried or stewed. The wafting aromas tantalized hungry folks waiting for the blessing. Fortunately, there was plenty of food to go around. Agnes had brought a pot of her hot potatoes. Lucinde brought a half dozen pies, while Mary had prepared a savory venison stew. Folks could choose from all kinds of vegetables cooked separately, mixed in combination with other vegetables, or prepared in deep dishes. Secret marinades and sauces added new flavors to the palate. There were loaves of freshly-baked breads, some still warm from the ovens. Desserts filled a dozen wagons—cakes, pies, cobblers, pastries, sweetbreads and much, much more. There was cold water to drink, fresh and hard ciders, wines, brandies, beer and whiskey. Craig had brought a half barrel of his best whiskey, partially as a promotional move. After a few sips, several farmers and businessmen approached him to ask if he had any to sell.

As expected, there were musicians present. Father Badin did not forbid it, as long as things did not get out of hand. At one point, Mary nudged Craig and pointed discreetly. Stephen danced with a young lady from Hardinsburg, a short auburn-haired sprite with a lovely smile and lissome figure.

"Who is *she*?" Craig whispered.

"That's the Cummings girl—Alicia," Mary replied. "Her father is a storekeeper in Hardinsburg, but her aunt Beatrice lives in Cottonwood Bend."

"Interesting," Craig mused.

"I think she plans to visit Beatrice during corn shucking time."

"Sounds like we might have another wedding on our hands."

"I think it is likely," Mary agreed. "I know my baby brother well, and he seems very obviously smitten."

They drove home in two wagons. Martin handled the first wagon with Agnes, Owen, Lucinde and their children; Craig drove his big tans with Mary, Stephen, Isabel and Ruth riding in the rear wagon. After his runs to fetch Judge Bozarth, Craig knew this road well. Fortunately, it was still daylight as they descended into Hite's Run and crossed the wooden bridge. When they topped the next ridge, they beheld a beautiful sunset of golds and apricots, oranges and reds lighting the hills that descended down to Mary's Landing and Welcome Hall. The Ohio River lay to their north, glistening like a giant, copper-colored snake, twisting and looping in vast bends bordered by hills covered with tall trees whose leaves had begun to change colors. The air grew cool and it felt invigorating to breathe it in. Craig could smell sassafras leaves, cornfields, fragrant weeds, and horses. Finally, they reached the Smithhart farm. Kelwyn was chopping wood for the fireplace and he waved at them.

"How come he didn't go to church, Daddy?" Isabel asked.

"Because he goes to a different church in Cottonwood Bend," Craig replied.

They passed the Jennings place and noticed some of the New Englanders outside working in the fall gardens, perhaps gathering something to bring to the supper table. Diogenes and Maggie sat on their porch in the waning sunlight, enjoying the last rays. Finally Craig turned onto the lane leading to the cabin and barn.

"See you tomorrow, Craig!" Stephen hopped off and ran to catch his father's wagon.

"Good-bye, baby brother!" Mary called after him.

Mary built up the fire while Craig unhitched the horses, then watered and fed them measures of new hay and double handfuls of oats. The cows had already come up for milking. Blue and the oxen crowded in, waiting for their feed. Craig went about his chores, happy for the blessed regularity of life, thanking God for yet another wonderful day.

New Orleans—September 26, 1817

"Now, do you have the Governor's letter safely stashed away?" Phillipe asked.

"Yes, I do," Doc replied. He and Solange stood together on *Jesse P. Emmick's* upper deck, happy to be leaving for new horizons.

"And the official copy of Lucinde's manumission papers?

"That, a copy of Delacroix's will, and Signet's death record—and, as a last resort, your written financial offer."

"If they refuse to call off the abduction, you will refer them to me and let them know I will pay out their contract?"

"Of course. But remember, they left New Orleans months ago. We must consider the possibility they have already seized her."

"Let us pray they have not."

"What measures have you taken in case I miss them and they bring her here?" Doc asked.

"I have dispatched notices north to city officials and business associates in Baton Rouge and Natchez. Our militia patrol and *collectionneur* have been alerted. As soon as the mercenaries show themselves, they will be informed of Signet's death. I have ordered this information conveyed to every northbound keelboat and steamboat captain leaving New Orleans—and that includes the captain of the *Jessie P. Emmick.*"

"It sounds like you have done your part—now, I must do mine."

"Please take care of yourself, Doctor Applegate. They are dangerous men."

"Of that I am sure."

"I wish you the best of everything in life—and I am so happy for you and Madame Solange." Solange smiled at him warmly. Philippe continued, "Funny, but there was a time I could not have said it, let alone feel it. I was so filled with hate and bitterness. But that seems like another person, long, long ago."

"I know just what you mean," Doc agreed. "The Great Physician has truly healed us. Now we must trust and serve Him."

Philippe smiled and tipped his hat, then slid down the brass ladder to hop nimbly ashore. The steam whistle blasted, crew members hauled in the gangplanks and *Jesse P. Emmick* backed smoothly away from the Levee. Doc waved at the young man, happy to know he was fully restored and at peace.

"You really have gone to the ends of this earth to make amends, Thomas," Solange said, putting her arm in his. "Few men could have done what you have. Philippe is truly happy and much better off than before. "

"You are a dear," Doc smiled, patting her affectionately. "Let us now hope we can spare that girl and her family any hardship. Signet wanted her children too, for they are next in line to inherit the Delacroix estate. He sent professional soldiers—of the roughest ilk. Men like them have been known to abuse their female captives."

"Oh, no!"

"And do you imagine Lucinde's husband will stand idly by and let them take her and his children? He will fight them to the death; his father will fight, as will the whole family. Remember, these mercenaries have served foreign governments and killed their own countrymen for money. Unless I can arrive in time to alert the family, a lot of good people will die."

"Thomas! I never knew, until now, what a burden you have carried."

"Brought on by myself."

"You are not to blame. Signet planned on doing this all along."

"I know dear. But I promised Delacroix I would keep his daughter safe. I am responsible."

"Doctor, I have never loved you more than at this moment," Solange said, leaning her head against his shoulder. Doc embraced her tenderly. It was a great feeling to be loved.

"Let's take a chair under the awning and enjoy the scenery."

A uniformed servant brought them tea and cakes as the stately sidewheeler churned resolutely upriver. Doc and Solange sat in silence, taking in the sweeping panorama of cotton, rice, and sugarcane plantations. Some planters' homes were truly magnificent, white gems in the midst of sprawling live oaks and rows of orange trees. Doc recognized Ste. Gême's plantation and the wooden jetty where Emmett's motley band of pirates had tied up and come over the bank—the night before they accomplished the impossible and exterminated the evil specter that had threatened them all. Soon the plantation slid past, disappearing completely from view, as did his life in New Orleans. Doc looked upriver and felt the relative cool of the morning breeze on his face. A strange sense of excitement stirred through him. This truly was a new beginning!

Breckinridge County—October 6, 1817

"Mercy, that Cummings girl moved fast!" Levi Matthews sniggered. "She cleaned Stephen's plow on day one! Shame on her, taking advantage of such a young lad."

"He is nineteen years old, going on twenty!" Craig pointed out.

"Going on twelve. That one is a Mama's boy if ever I saw one."

"He fought like a man in New Orleans."

"Yeah? That was war; this is marriage, a horse of an entirely different color. Women have been known to bring ruin upon the greatest of kings!"

"I think he knows what he is getting himself into."

Levi changed the subject. "Are you going to let me have Kelwyn for another few days? After all, I *am* paying him more than you are, you old pinchpenny."

"That is entirely up to him. I am still cutting and shocking corn, and the tobacco will soon come into case."

"You farmers are always complaining about something."

"When will you finish work?"

"By week's end, if I can have your man."

"Is he really that good?"

"He is as good as me. He should go full time into carpentry. If it was still my main profession, I would have stolen him from you long before now."

"Aren't you needed at your mill this time of year? The harvests are in full swing."

"Your father-in-law made an offer I could not refuse."

Craig knew this was true. After the second corn shucking, Stephen announced he was marrying Alicia Cummings. The girl was in total agreement; in fact Tom Wheatley had spied the young couple slipping over the riverbank, blanket in hand. Word got back to Martin, but he kept silent and let events run their course. In the end he was pleased with the match. Agnes was happy too, but her joy was mixed with a twinge of sadness. Her last child was leaving the nest—she was losing her baby boy. Stephen looked forward to his new life at the Arbuckle farm, sharing it with the girl he loved.

The farmhouse was a big, two-story structure, built mostly of dressed stone block with glass window panes and end chimneys. Barns, silos, and sheds, also built of stone, stood in good condition. A deep well produced clear, sweet drinking water, and the orchard was larger than Martin's and Craig's combined. The farm itself consisted of rich bottomland, rolling pasture and woods. Stephen's move meant displacing the family Martin had installed there. The man was a good field hand and his wife and children made dependable workers, so Martin chose to build them a house. Three other workers and their families lived in houses near the river, so the fourth house would go there. Martin engaged Levi Matthews for the job.

Levi was perhaps Cottonwood Bend's best carpenter, but he now invested his time and effort fully into his grain and saw mills. It took a great sum of money to entice him to leave these enterprises and work on constructing a house. But Martin could well afford the price—after all, it was an indirect wedding present for his youngest son. Craig realized that, after this venture, Kelwyn might just decide to strike out on his own—as a carpenter. Levi could be planning to hire him to lead construction crews. Craig decided not to worry—he would cross that bridge when he came to it. He dearly wanted to stop in and work with his friends, but the weather was clear and sunny, the nights cool and crisp with bright moonlight to work by. Craig, Martin, and Owen kept the field hands late each night. During that time, Kelwyn's family worked without him; Prudence brought the boys into the fields on a regular schedule, and she cut and bound corn alongside them, as fast and as efficient as any man. Craig was proud to have her there. He realized he must look hard to find someone as skilled, dependable, and hard working as this New England family.

Cottonwood Bend—October 7, 1817

Thirteen men, mounted on fine horses and armed with expensive weapons, clattered across the big wooden bridge and rode into Cottonwood Bend. It was a warm, overcast night. A light drizzle blurred the house lights, turning them into fuzzy halos. Rosenbotham's store had closed for the night. There was some activity down on the riverfront, but the townspeople had just about all turned in. Bruce Bowman drew his oilskin cloak around his shoulders and tipped his broad-brimmed hat sideways, hoping to shed the water. He would be happy to dry out by a crackling fire. It had been a long ride from Elizabethtown.

One of the flatboat men led a tired-looking nag up the landing, obviously heading somewhere, perhaps a stable.

"Hello!" Bowman hailed him.

"Hello, yourself!" the man answered gruffly.

"Can you point us in the direction of a good boarding house?"

"You might try Maple Manor. It's run by old man Axton and his wife."

"Where would we find it?"

The man pointed. "Turn down there, on Maple Street. Go back until you come to the next cross street. The house sits on the corner on the right-hand side."

"Do they have a stable?"

"Nope. But if you follow me, I'll show you where one is."

Although his men were tired and sore, Bowman made sure they

first saw to their mounts. It took some time to unsaddle and dry their horses, stable, feed and water them. The night watchman showed them where to hang the saddles and wet blankets. When all was in order, Bowman led his men, lugging their bags and bedrolls, down River Street, then up Maple Street to Maple Manor. Fortunately it was a short walk. Golden maple leaves covered the streets like a soft carpet. The houses on either side were large clapboard affairs; one on the right looked especially nice. A wooden signboard hung on chains from an elaborately decorated post. Bowman stepped in close and just made out the wording: *Judge Wilfred J. Bozarth: Attorney-at-Law.*

"That is convenient," he laughed.

"What is?" Jeff, his outrider, asked.

"The man whose help we seek lives here."

They came to the big, rambling boarding house surrounded by tall, spreading maple trees. Bowman stepped up onto the porch and knocked on the front door. The bearded innkeeper, an elderly, fragile-looking man, cautiously opened it and held up a lamp. He looked startled by so many men standing outside.

"Yes?"

"We are looking for a place to sleep."

"How many are you?"

"Thirteen. We have a commission from Governor Slaughter."

"You'll have to sleep four or five to a room, I'm afraid. Two of our five rooms are occupied."

"We wish to stay a couple of weeks, perhaps more." He hauled out his doeskin pouch and jingled it. "We want all your rooms. I can pay you in gold—in advance."

The man's eyes bugged out. "I guarantee we will have vacancies after tomorrow morning."

"That is suitable. Can you cook us some supper?"

"We have served supper."

"I will pay extra."

"It will take some time, but yes. I will have to send for my cook."

"Very well."

"Come in—come in!" the innkeeper opened the door wider.

Bowman strode into the front parlor, almost filling it with his great height and presence. He allowed the innkeeper to lead him into a small side room to conduct business. The man ducked behind a wooden counter, set down the lamp and fetched a black ledger book. He performed some mental calculations, scrawling numbers with a turkey feather which he dipped at intervals into an inkwell, mumbling as he figured. He wrote down a sum.

"How's that?"

"Does it include full board?"

"Breakfast and supper. You will show up on time or miss out."

"Agreed." Bowman dropped six gold coins into the innkeeper's hands.

The man gaped in astonishment. It was doubtful he had seen so much money at one time. He shouted down the hall. "Jenny?"

"What is it?" an elderly female voice answered, rather tiredly.

"Get your coat on and run down to Lila Dobbs' place. Tell her to bring a couple of girls with her. We've got thirteen hungry guests who need supper."

Bowman heard her sigh.

The innkeeper shouted, "Hurry, now! They have paid us in gold!"

* * *

Bowman woke after a restful night's sleep, glad to have finally reached his destination. Three of his men still slept in their bedrolls on the hardwood floor. The innkeeper was up early, hustling his girls around, ordering them to set the table, fetch washing water and deliver it to the rooms, and carry out the guests' chamber pots. Lila Dobbs and her kitchen crew fried thick slabs of smoked ham, bacon, sausage links, eggs, potatoes, onions, and pancakes. They cooked oatmeal in an enormous pot and baked fresh bread in the Dutch oven. The aromas wafted through the house. One girl brought in fresh butter from Rosenbotham's icehouse. Bowman knew this because the walls were thin and he could hear conversations in the other rooms. He filed this knowledge away for future use. He had caught Lila Dobbs' eye and, judging from the way she flirted and fussed after him, he knew they would soon be together. She would find a way; women always did. He was accustomed to this. By virtue of his leadership he would have a room to himself—but they would have to keep quiet.

As he washed and shaved, Bowman considered the current state of the mission. It was taking much longer than he had calculated. Frankfort lay some eight hundred miles distant from New Orleans. The Natchez Trace had proven no easy road, made harder by the oppressive heat and humidity of July. He had lost one man in the shootout with the outlaws. The mercenary had died of wound mortification long before they reached Nashville and they had buried him on the trail. By then, the horses were nearly shot, and his men ready for a rest. Bowman had called for a one week halt to give the horses ample opportunity to recover. Splendid animals, they responded to shade, ample water, and extra feed. During this time, Bowman sold the outlaws' horses, oxen, and guns, realizing a handsome sum. He kept the stolen jewelry, convinced he could do better selling it in New Orleans.

On August 4th they had set off for Frankfort, keeping their horses at a slow, steady pace to avoid overheating. It was August 15th when they descended the high hills ringing Kentucky's capital. From the rim they enjoyed a bird's eye view of Frankfort, situated in a deep valley and bisected by the Kentucky River which made an S-turn as it flowed through the city's center. The new two-story brick capitol building with its tall, stately cupola was clearly visible among the trees. Instead of splashing across the river at 'Frank's Ford', Bowman and his men clattered across the new timber-and-chain stationary bridge at St. Clair Street and found a wide choice of stables and hotels that catered to lawmakers and businessmen who visited the city.

It took two weeks to arrange a meeting with Governor Slaughter's closest aides. Part of this stemmed from the fact he was weakened by political infighting. Formerly Lieutenant Governor, Slaughter had assumed the governorship upon the death of his predecessor. Many legislators questioned the legality of Slaughter's status; earlier in the year, some had accused him of political favoritism and argued for a special election to replace him. This scheme had failed, but most of his enemies refused to call him "Governor", preferring the title, "Acting Governor". Bowman had never seen or heard anything like it. Worse, no one seemed in a hurry to please an out-of-state traveler, even when he dropped Governor Villeré's name. It took all his charm and intellect, and a crafty bit of detective work, to position himself in the right social event to speak to one of the aides. Governor Slaughter proved amenable and, after a brief review period, requested that the aide draw up a writ, ordering the Cottonwood Bend militia leader to assist with returning the slave, Lucinde Delacroix. This process took another two weeks. It might have taken longer, but gold had effectively greased obstinate political skids. The writ was drafted, amended, and finally sent to the Governor for signing. An official seal was affixed and the writ delivered on September 12.

Bowman was free to leave, but he had earlier dispatched two riders to Louisville to investigate steamboat schedules, hopefully to reserve passage on one of them. At this time of year, the Ohio River was low and vessels would be moored above or below the falls, waiting for high water to cross over them. The men returned on the 18th. Unfortunately, they had not seen one steamboat above or below the falls. Bowman decided to move his entire force to Louisville where they waited for another week. It seemed that no set steamboat schedules existed; arrivals and departures were "hit or miss." Bowman interrogated teamsters on the portage road and dockworkers at Shippingport, totally unprepared for the anger these men felt toward the steamboats. Apparently, several principals—merchants, civic leaders, bankers and legislators—were calling for a big canal to bypass the falls. The most vocal advocates of this proposal were the steamboat builders, but a canal would mean the loss of many hauling and transfer jobs. As a result, no one seemed eager to share information about possible steamboat arrivals. In the end, a few silver coins produced the answers Bowman already knew—steamboats, although becoming more commonplace, were still quite sporadic. After waiting a few more days in Louisville, Bowman made the executive decision to ride south and west. He would post a lookout at the Cottonwood Bend riverfront to watch for an approaching steamboat. These vessels were easily flagged down, for captains were always seeking paying passengers or merchants with cargo.

Someone knocked softly on the door—one of the maids.

"Yes?" he answered.

"Judge Wilfred Bozarth is waiting in the parlor, sir."

"Thank you. I will join him shortly."

He adjusted his cravat, slid on his jacket and stepped into the hallway. As soon as he entered the parlor, the Judge came forward to greet him in a gushing display of hospitality, pumping his hand vigorously, his face lit in a broad, gap-toothed grin. Bowman was instantly amused at his stylish clothing, deep voice and effusive manner. The man was definitely a poser. In England they would call him a fop. The Judge seemed equally impressed at Bowman's clothing, very obviously sizing up his wealth.

"Welcome, sojourner, to our humble little settlement of Cottonwood Bend! With whom have I the honor of speaking?"

"Bruce Bowman, from New Orleans, Louisiana—by way of Frankfort."

The Judge perked up noticeably at his mention of the capital city. "I am Judge Wilfred J. Bozarth, Attorney-at-Law, Kentucky State Representative, and Commander of the Cottonwood Bend Militia." He obviously recited this litany of titles in an effort to impress.

Bowman bowed slightly. "You must know you are quite the luminary. Everyone in Frankfort holds you in high regard. The Governor himself has assured me of your sterling reputation." This was not altogether true. Two of the Governor's assistants did indeed know Judge Bozarth, and one of them had snarled, "Next time you see that damned Bozarth, you tell the sorry son-of-a-bitch I want my money back!"

The Judge blushed at the compliment, whisking at an imaginary piece of lint on the felt hat he held in his hands. "Yes, yes—we know each other well. We were fellow warriors—fought side-by-side at the Battle of New Orleans."

"Apparently you conducted yourself with distinction."

"And what was your business with the Governor?" the Judge asked, genuinely interested.

"Government business," Bowman answered cryptically. "I will disclose that when we are alone. Will you breakfast with me?"

"Perhaps some coffee."

"Very well—after you."

Together they entered the dining room. The young women waited on them, forking meats and eggs onto Bowman's plate, ladling oats and pouring coffee. The Judge fiddled nervously with his spoon.

"Are you sure you won't have some breakfast?" Bowman offered. "I am paying, for it is you I came to see."

"Oh, I couldn't accept!" the Judge protested, hands extended, but eyes resting hungrily on the steaming slabs of smoked ham.

"I insist."

"In that case..." The Judge signaled briskly for the servers, gesturing for them to pile his plate high. He began talking, slathering on his best charm as the servers ladled gravy on his ham steak and buttered the toasted bread.

Bowman watched in amazement. Judge Bozarth was a true specialist when it came to putting away food. He knew how to handle silverware and use his napkin; he had obviously acquired social skills proper for public engagements, but he could stoke away food with astonishing speed. Bowman allowed the Judge time to enjoy breakfast before sharing the carefully rehearsed version of his commission.

"The Governor of Louisiana has charged me to search for a valuable runaway slave in the Kentucky counties of Hardin, Nelson, Ohio and Breckinridge."

"Yes?" Just now, the Judge was concentrating more on pouring a generous puddle of maple syrup onto his pancakes.

"I represent a wealthy plantation owner from New Orleans. Some months ago this planter received reliable correspondences that his escaped slave had settled in one of the aforementioned counties and is living under the protection of an abolitionist. The planter then obtained a letter from the Governor of Louisiana asking your Governor to provide aid in the search. I recently presented that letter to Governor Slaughter in Frankfort."

"Wouldn't the slave have crossed long ago into Indiana or Ohio?" the Judge asked. "Those are 'free states' that have outlawed slavery."

"We are close on the trail. We intend to seize this slave in Kentucky, and prevent him from crossing the river."

The Judge looked a bit skeptical. No doubt he was calculating time and distances, wondering how someone from Louisiana could learn about a slave in Kentucky and then hope to catch him before he crossed the river. Bowman played his next card to keep him off balance.

"Your Governor, Gabriel Slaughter, has empowered me to search for this slave in your county. If successful, I will return the property to the rightful owner. Naturally, the planter has offered a handsome reward."

The Judge's eyes glittered with greed and he laid down his fork, now all ears. "A reward, you say?"

Bowman nodded. "This planter is rich beyond belief. I am prepared to share a portion of the reward with the official who assists me in tracking down the slave. We have eliminated all the other counties. Breckinridge is last on our list, so the odds are, he is here."

"I am not sure how much I can help," the Judge demurred. "There are very few slaves in this county."

"Can you, in your capacity, obtain a list of county slave owners?"

"It would involve a ride to Hardinsburg, but I believe so."

"Then, could you conduct me on a tour of the various farms?"

"How would that help you?"

"Oftentimes, slaves will hide runaways right under their mas-

ters' noses. If this is not the case, slave owners know who the abolitionists are and will, most usually, inform on them."

"True," the Judge nodded.

"I need a guide who is familiar with the countryside. Please understand that I can recompense you handsomely."

The Judge was truly impressed, but knowledge of the law tempered his greed. "This would require a warrant."

"You are a Judge."

"I am a former Judge—the title is now an honorific. What you
ask is beyond my authority. We will have to petition the judge in
Hardinsburg."

"Governor Slaughter has granted me written authority to search
for the slave. His writ requests local officials to provide assistance.
The Governor has assured me that I can count on you."

"May I see the writ?"

"You may indeed, but for reasons of privacy I must conceal a
small portion of the document. Please understand, we will not be
using strong-arm tactics—no ransacking of farmhouses and barns—
just paying informal visits. When I locate the slave, I will take
charge at a later date. That phase will not involve you." Bowman
casually opened his travel purse and spilled a small pile of gold
American eagles and half eagles onto the tablecloth. He noticed how
the Judge's eyes bulged. "I am happy to pay up front. Would fifty
dollars suffice?"

"The sum of eighty crossed my mind. This will mean rearranging my busy calendar, and I may have to refund some clients' money." The Judge had no set schedule, and he would never, ever refund
money paid him, but he played his card with admirable skill.

"That is acceptable," Bowman conceded. "Oh, I almost forgot—
the Governor instructed me to thank you for supporting his cause.
He knows you stood by him in the House and he will not forget it.
He said it took real courage for you to vote in the minority—and he
knows who his true friends are." The Governor had told him no such
thing; Bowman had learned of the vote through conversations, old
newspapers and legislative records.

If Judge Bozarth had any reservations about Bowman, this declaration swept them aside. This man spoke the literal truth. In January, when political enemies hoped to remove Governor Slaughter from office, the Kentucky State House of Representatives bowed to widespread discontent, passing a bill by the vote of 56-30, calling for a new gubernatorial election. During the heated deliberations, the Judge had kept his cards close, sorely tempted to vote with the majority. In the end, he voted for his fellow soldier and made damned sure the Governor knew it. Slaughter was grateful, but his assessment of Judge Bozarth's political courage was misplaced. The Judge, in the course of his considerable legislatorial wining and dining, had learned in advance, and on the best authority, that the measure would never pass the Senate. It had failed, as he knew it would, 18-14.

He chuckled self-deprecatingly. "Yes, yes. It was the right thing to do. I did nothing more than adhere to my convictions."

"Then it appears I have found my man."

Chapter Twenty-Two

Welcome Hall—October 10, 1817

The weather turned crisp and dry. Craig was cutting corn on Martin McDonnell's farm when Judge Bozarth paid his official visit. The Judge led the way on his chestnut mare; six well-armed men followed behind him in a staggered, slightly extended formation, looking as if they could wheel off in various directions on a moment's notice. The field hands stopped their labor and stood up to have a better look at these newcomers. Everyone present knew that thirteen strange men had ridden in from Frankfort and were staying at Maple Manor Boarding House. News like that traveled fast. Of course, the Judge boasted about town that Governor Slaughter had personally sent these men to him, Wilfred J, Bozarth, and he deemed their mission an important one, in fact, it was top-secret. Even the Judge did not know the exact details, but he was hired as an official guide to conduct the men throughout Breckinridge County to inspect the farms of those landowners who owned slaves.

Had the Judge not been leading, Craig would have felt more apprehension than he did. Something about these men seemed wrong. They looked dangerously aware, almost like soldiers—all of them tough, in their late twenties or early thirties—each man carried a bristling assortment of weapons, although none of these were drawn. Beside him, Martin stirred uneasily

"Hello, young Ridgeway!" the Judge boomed, making a big show of his arrival.

"Hello, Judge," Craig replied.

"What can we do for you?" Martin asked.

"Actually, I need to borrow Craig for a short time."

"What about?" Craig felt a rising snake of alarm.

"I am here on official business, commissioned by the Governor of Kentucky, to inspect the slaves of all slaveholders in Breckinridge County."

""What for? I have done nothing wrong. The three slave women died of the grippe last year. I reported this to you. Now I have only Diogenes and his wife Maggie." He wondered if this had anything to do with Romulus and his family, but discounted that notion for Judge Bozarth had played a major role in freeing them. Craig did not mention them and neither did the Judge.

The Judge turned in his saddle to speak to the apparent leader of the newcomers, a giant of a man with a muscular frame. The man sat his horse with relaxed ease, almost boredom, but he still looked dangerous.

"Bruce Bowman, this is Craig Ridgeway, number eleven on your list. He is undoubtedly one of Cottonwood Bend's finest citizens."

"Pleased to meet you, Craig," Bowman greeted him formally.

"Likewise," Craig replied without much feeling.

"And that stately gentleman is his father-in-law, Martin McDonnell." The Judge was laying it on thick.

"The hero of the American Revolution?" Bowman's gaze shifted. "I am honored, sir."

Martin nodded stiffly, clearly unimpressed.

"And that young man over there is his son, Owen."

Owen continued cutting and shocking corn, so absorbed in his work that he did not hear. Craig noticed a slight change in Bowman's carriage. Had he not been looking directly at the man, it might have escaped him. Bowman sat up straighter and pulled his horse slightly left to get a better look. He studied Owen far much longer than he did anyone else.

"This young man is Stephen, the youngest brother. He is about to take the plunge and marry his sweetheart from Hardinsburg. It is a true love match."

Stephen grinned in sickly embarrassment. Bowman smiled fleetingly and stared once again at Owen. His men glanced casually, but constantly, over their shoulders, ever-watchful of their surroundings.

"Well, Craig, will you show us your slaves?" the Judge asked.

"I suppose so. I hate to leave my crew."

"We won't keep you long. In fact, I'll give you a ride up there. Hop up behind me and hold onto the saddle. Don't worry; I promise this mare will not turn a hair at an extra rider."

The Judge extended his hand and helped Craig swing up onto the mare's rump, then eased into a gentle canter. When they reached his property, Craig hopped off to open the gate. He let the Judge and his men through, closed it and swung up again. They clattered across the little wooden bridge before climbing the steep lane to Craig's high pasture. From this vantage point they could see his cabin and barn, and the river behind them. Bowman whistled shrilly and held up his hand for them to stop. The Judge gently reined in the mare. She responded beautifully.

"What is this place?" Bowman asked.

"Flatboat men once called it 'Widder's Landing', but that was long ago," the Judge replied. "It is called 'Mary's Landing' now, after Craig's wife."

"Landing?" Bowman asked. He pointed down to the break in the dark cedar trees that framed the rock landing. "Is that it?"

"Yes," replied Judge Bozarth. "Why, in its day, the landing accommodated all sorts of flatboats and keelboats. Young Ridgeway inherited this land from an old hag, Gertrude Fuqua. To evade taxes, she used to ship her whiskey and tobacco from here. It is a solid rock landing with a gradual slope that drops off sharply about ten yards out. You can load and unload all year round—even in a downpour."

"How deep is it?" Bowman asked, his interest more than passing.

"Craig?" Judge Bozarth prompted. "Can you help him with an answer?"

Everything about these strangers unsettled him. There was far more involved here than inspecting slaves. To humor the Judge he answered, "I'm not sure. It varies with the river level."

"Is it deep enough for a steamboat?" Bowman asked.

"That would depend on the boat, how much water it draws."

"Has a steamboat ever pulled in here?"

"No." This was not true, but Craig would not volunteer any further information about his land—not to these men.

Bowman nodded at the Judge and they rode on past the cabin. Mary was outside, taking in clothes from the line. She paused to look at the riders, then recognized Craig, waved and smiled. Craig waved back, uncomfortable with how the men gawked at her. They rode on and he studied their guns. Bowman carried two fine rifles in oiled leather scabbards and wore two pistols tucked in his belt. In addition, he carried a big, wide-bladed knife and a small tomahawk with a well-worn handle, indicating that it had been often wielded— or thrown. The other men were more or less equally armed. Craig regretted that he did not carry a gun. He realized with a sickening rush, just how vulnerable he and Mary were out here in the country-side, so far from town.

They crossed the Hardinsburg Road and pulled up in front of Diogenes' cabin. Craig slid off the big mare, glad not to have his legs stretched further from straddling those broad hindquarters.

"Diogenes!" Craig called. "Can you come out?"

The old, white-haired tanner opened the door. His face registered alarm when he saw the men.

"There is nothing wrong, Diogenes. The Judge needs to see you and Maggie. He is doing some sort of population count."

Old Maggie came to the door and stood at her husband's shoulder. She looked a pathetic sight, for she had recently lost all her teeth. Craig had paid Doc Emmick to draw the last of her abscessed snags, just to give her relief from pain and fever. Consequently, her face had collapsed, folding in upon itself.

"This is it!" the Judge boomed. "Just the two slaves, possibly in their late seventies. Craig takes excellent care of them. Would you care to see ownership papers or look around the place? You wouldn't mind, would you Craig?"

"There is not much to see. I have two families from New England who live in the other cabins, but they are working in the fields I had to leave."

"No, I have seen enough," Bowman replied with that same uninterested look. He resembled an adult forced by circumstance to supervise someone else's children, wishing he were somewhere else.

Craig felt relieved to know he would not be forced to pay out money, which was what usually happened when Judge Bozarth arrived on official business. "I hope you are satisfied, Judge."

"Yes, young Ridgeway—as I knew I would be. Thank you for your time. I regret I cannot convey you back down to Martin's cornfield; we are off for Hardinsburg. There are a few slaveholders who live in the vicinity." He clucked to his mare and led the newcomers back onto the Hardinsburg Road. They turned east and loped away.

Craig watched them go, perplexed and still feeling uneasy. Some inner instinct warned him that the Judge was in water way over his head. He did not belong with those men. They were searching for something—and it was not old slaves. Additionally, he hated to see him ride in the direction of Cecilia Dowell's home—the Judge was not strong enough to resist her temptations.

"We not in trouble, Craig?" Diogenes asked.

"No," Craig assured him. "Maggie, Mary dug a row of potatoes this morning. I think she is making a pot of mashed potatoes to bring over. How is your mouth?"

"Still sore, but gettin' better."

"She cry when Doctor Emmick pull her teeth," Diogenes volunteered.

"I imagine so," Craig sympathized. The only painkiller available was Craig's whiskey. Afterwards, Mary had mashed up a poultice of black cherry bark to pack the bleeding gums. That had provided some relief. "Well, I reckon I should get back down to Martin's farm. It will be dark soon."

"Dark of the moon tonight!"

"You are right about that!"

Instead of immediately returning to Martin's cornfield, Craig took the deer trail over to the Smithhart farm, following the riders on a parallel course. Weeds grew thickly on either side—goldenrod, ironweed, cocklebur, foxtail and cane. He emerged from the woods and ran along the cornfield's edge behind cabin and outbuildings before ducking back into more timber. Finally he reached a limestone outcropping from which he could view the Hardinsburg Road. For some reason, he feared that Mary and his children could be in danger. He wanted to make sure the men did not double back and pay a surprise visit to his cabin. Of course, the Judge would not allow anything bad to happen, but he was just one man. Craig watched until he spied the bright red coat of the chestnut mare as she emerged into a patch of sunlight in an open place in the road. Carefully, he counted six more riders—clearly the men were headed for Hardinsburg, climbing the tall rise before descending into Hite's Run.

He breathed a sigh of relief and headed back for the cornfield. On the way, he stopped in to visit Mary. Happy to see him, she gave him a warm embrace. He crossed over to the hearth where Isabelle and Ruth played with corn husk dolls, and hugged both of them.

Mary asked, "What were you doing with Judge Bozarth and those men?"

"Apparently, the Judge is escorting them around the county, inspecting slaves. He wanted to see Diogenes and Maggie."

"Why on earth? Has there been a new law passed?"

"He claims the Governor has commissioned him to inspect."

"We aren't in violation of any laws?"

"No. They aren't concerned about two old slaves."

"What are you saying, Craig?"

"Something is wrong with those men. They are up to no good. Their leader seemed awfully interested in our landing."

"Are they part of that group staying in town?" She handed him a cup of coffee and cream.

"I assume so."

"Lila Dobbs is quite smitten by their leader. She described him in detail—perhaps too much detail. That was him with you and the

Judge, wasn't it?"

"Maybe he was." Craig noticed her blushing.

"His name is Bruce Bowman. He *is* quite handsome—I can see why Lila likes him."

"Lila Dobbs is a—"

"Craig!" she cautioned, glancing at the children.

"Well it's true!" he exclaimed. Lila Dobbs was known for the hot nature of her blood, and folks rumored she often took up with selected male guests at the boarding house.

"My dear husband, I do believe you are jealous!" she laughed.

"Not of him. I want you to bolt the door when I am in the fields."

"Why?"

"I don't like these men. They are heavily armed and here on a mission—not related to legal slaveholders. The average family could not hope to defend themselves against such men."

"Have you spoken to Pa?"

"I didn't have time. But I can tell, he doesn't like them either."

Craig loaded the shotgun, rifles, and pistols, and he made sure Mary could reach them. He left the cabin with his favorite .40 caliber rifle, possibles bag, and powder horn. When he reached the field, the sun was sinking below the mass of limestone hills to the west of Cottonwood Bend. There would be no moon that night, so Martin decided to finish early. He noticed Craig laying his rifle in the wagon.

"So, they bothered you too?" he asked.

"Those men are not here to inspect slaves."

"Wonder what the Judge has gotten himself into this time."

"There is no telling. He is puffed up with self-importance—once again. They weren't interested in Diogenes at all."

"What about Romulus?"

"The Judge never mentioned him and neither did I. After they left, I followed them past the Smithhart farm. They are headed for Hardinsburg."

Martin raised his eyebrows as he considered this. Craig knew he was worried about the Judge. "So why the rifle?"

"Did you see the weapons those men carried? Not one of us had a gun. We were absolutely powerless. I got a sick feeling when we rode past our cabin, for Mary was outside. What if those men had chosen to come in from the Hardinsburg Road? She was there alone, with the children. Before I left, I loaded our guns and told Mary to bolt the doors."

Martin nodded. "I see your point. Agnes is alone at Welcome Hall. Lucinde and the children are alone on their plantation. But, if Bozarth is certain they hold a governor's commission, they should represent no danger."

"I have seen no such commission."

"The Judge obviously has. I am reasonably confident he can handle them. Hopefully they will move on in a few days. Folks like that usually do."

"Until that time, I plan to be vigilant. Did you see how the big one stared at Owen? He got himself a long hard look—and then looked again."

Martin looked at him quizzically. "I didn't notice."

"When the Judge made introductions, he hardly glanced at us."

"He spoke to me, and I thought his praise a bit heavy. He also smiled at Stephen."

"Maybe I am wrong," Craig admitted. But he didn't think so.

October 16, 1817

Levi Matthews drove his buggy out to the cabin late Thursday afternoon. Craig was milking cows and feeding the stock when he rolled up. From behind the western hills, the sun's last rays fanned upward into an indigo sky; there was little daylight left. The little miller tied his horses near the water trough as Craig finished milking.

Craig set the two covered milk buckets near the door and forked some more hay from the loft. "What brings you all the way out here,

Levi? Could it be that it is almost suppertime?"

"Glad you have invited."

"First, I must put this milk in the springhouse."

"I'll follow."

"Here." Craig handed him the Lancaster rifle. "Carry this for me."

"No thanks! I'll carry a bucket."

"Suit yourself, just don't spill any." He handed Levi the bucket of butterfat milk. "Did you come here to buy corn?"

"Not sure how much I will buy this autumn. Prices have dropped—the boatmen are paying less. We're getting reports that the European harvest has recovered—no war, no frosts this year—and they do a much better job farming than we do."

"That is what Martin claims. He tries to follow their practices."

"Well, your farms do look better than most."

"Why did you drive out here?"

"I reckon you have heard about the new visitors in Cottonwood Bend—the thirteen men?"

"Half of them visited me last week."

"Said they were checking on slaves?"

"That's what the Judge said."

"Well, you can be sure *that* is a load of bullshit—for that is what the Judge usually serves up."

"He is certain the governor has commissioned those men."

"Of course, he is! The leader pays him in gold eagles, so the Judge is eager to please, fawning all over him."

"You mean, Bruce Bowman?"

"So, you know his name?"

"The Judge introduced us."

"Well, here is some news—Bowman has the Dobbs girl slobbering all over him every night. She slips in a side door and they make so much noise they keep the whole boarding house awake."

Craig glanced toward the cabin, hoping Mary would not hear. Then he reckoned Lila had already shared her experiences with her. He set the buckets in the springhouse and covered them with wooden lids. Together they walked toward the cabin with the smell of supper on the breeze.

Levi continued. "Of course Lila told her fellow workers all about it."

"All very interesting, I am sure."

"There's more! Yesterday morning one of the maids went in to clean a room and Bowman's man jumped her. He had stayed behind to lie in wait."

"Oh, dear God! I figured those men were dangerous. Did he rape her?"

"Not exactly."

"Either he did or he didn't."

"Old Axton's wife sent for the Judge. That ingratiating bastard did nothing but muddy up the water. He questioned the other maids and they all claimed the girl had flirted and invited the man's favors. In the end, Bowman paid her enough money to keep quiet."

"Apparently not quiet enough—*you* seem to know all about it."

"Well, you know Cottonwood Bend. No secrets in our town!"

"What *are* those men doing here?"

"No one knows—except perhaps the Judge. Donn Wimmer says they are riding all over the county in groups of twos or threes, checking out the roads, asking folks where each one leads to."

"Strange. I thought they were inspecting slaves."

"Some are; some aren't. They've got one man watching the riverfront; that's all he does. He stays there all day—claims he hopes to hail a steamboat."

"Let's hope one arrives soon." Craig shuddered.

"I don't think our womenfolk are safe—especially those on farms far from town, living in isolated cabins."

"Funny you should say that. I voiced the same concerns to Martin."

They sat on a bench in the dogtrot and kicked their boots off before going inside. The door was barred. Craig knocked and Mary asked, "Is that you, Craig?"

"Yes."

"I heard another voice."

"It is just Levi. Surprise! He showed up for supper."

The heavy oaken bar slid back and the door opened slowly. Mary cradled a stubby double-barreled shotgun in the crook of her right arm.

Levi recoiled when he spied it. "Those men had best keep away from this place. You folks are dangerous."

"Levi! Won't you come in for supper?" she exclaimed.

———————◆•◆———————

Craig headed in near-darkness down the steep lane. As it usually did on cold mornings, a heavy fog rose from the warmer river, thick white clouds billowing perhaps a hundred feet high. His breath fogged in the crisp air. Today, he would help cut and shock Owen's cornfield. In the evening his brother-in-law planned for another corn shucking. Craig intended to return home that afternoon, feed and milk, and then drive Mary and the children down to the festivities.

He had begun carrying a reliable .50 caliber rifle and possibles bag with a dozen paper cartridges made up with powder and ball. Martin might think he was acting overanxiously, but said nothing about it. Each day, Craig stood his weapon against the wagon and worked as usual; its proximity made him feel somewhat more comfortable. His only source of unease stemmed from leaving his family alone. During the daytime, when he worked in Owen's fields, he was farthest away from them. Turning west, Craig prepared to cut across his and Martin's pastures where the frost sparkled like diamond crystals on beige autumn grass. As he crossed the bottomland, a heavy splash broke the silence—the sudden "ker-plunk" was followed by a man's voice.

"Damn! That water is cold! Don't chuck that rock in again. Lower it easy, so it won't splash."

Craig felt the hair stand up on his arms. Cautiously, he crept along the tree line, moving silently as possible toward the riverbank. At the landing's edge he ducked into a thick clump of dark green cedars. This provided excellent cover, enabling him to observe the strange activity without being seen. Through the fog he could make out two ghostly figures manning a big canoe. It was the ferry boat Rosenbotham used to haul passengers traveling on foot. He gripped his rifle more tightly.

"Over there," a voice directed.

Craig watched as one man lowered a heavy rock into the water, waiting until it touched bottom before hauling it up. "Ten feet. Hell, this landing is plenty deep enough. I am ready to head back to the boarding house. Those girls sure can cook!"

"We aren't leaving until we use the poles. You heard what he said. We can't risk getting the bottom torn out."

The men probed the landing floor, working their long cane poles side to side, searching for a boulder or hidden outcrop. Craig could hear rattling vibrations as they scratched their poles along the rock bottom. The men were extremely thorough, paddling the boat in a systematic pattern, gradually working farther out from the shore. It looked like they were mapping the landing.

One of them announced, "Here is where it drops off."

The other said, "That landing runs smooth, all the way out to here."

"Good. That's what the captain wants to know. We're done."

The men tossed their poles into the river and began paddling. Craig followed quietly, making sure they headed downriver toward Cottonwood Bend. He hopped the rock fence and held to the lower end of Martin's pasture, not his usual path, staying with the men, hearing their voices occasionally. They were making good time, for their conversation grew ever fainter. The river curved sharply northward, forcing Craig to break off toward Owen's plantation. He followed a well-worn cow path across hilly pastureland. The sun's first rays enabled him to see how much of Martin's land actually abutted the river which snaked sharply back to the west to touch Owen's plantation. By water, the distance to Owen's fields was less than walking by land. Craig had never realized this. But he knew it was a much longer journey by boat to Cottonwood Bend, because the river twisted northward again, and then northeast, making a gigantic loop around some low hills, then bending west and south before hooking west again to sweep past the settlement.

By the time he arrived at Owen's cornfield, some of the workers were already cutting. Martin spied him walking in from the back way.

"Decide to go for a stroll today, Craig?" he asked.

"You won't believe what I saw this morning." He told Martin about the strangers surveying his landing with sounding rocks and cane poles, and he related Bruce Bowman's earlier interest in it. "You don't think he wants my land, do you?"

Martin frowned. "I wouldn't think so."

"He seemed awfully interested in knowing how deep the landing is. Perhaps he has convinced Judge Bozarth to invalidate the Widder's will,"

"No, your deed was formally recorded in the clerk's office. No one can take your land from you."

"Then why were those men poking around at my landing? Levi says some of them have ridden all the way to Hartford and Yellow Banks, studying roads and trails. One man does nothing all day but watch the river."

"It does sound strange."

"They need to leave Cottonwood Bend—and sooner the better. I hope I never see them again."

"Well, you had best brace yourself. The Judge has invited himself—and the men—to Owen's corn shucking tonight."

"No! Why didn't Owen refuse?"

"They are supplying a whole beef. Apparently, this Bowman can afford it. You will never guess who he bought it from."

"Who?"

"Gill Hagman, Cecilia Dowell's husband."

"She finally married him?" Craig gasped.

"She did."

"Let's hope this puts an end to the Judge's tomcatting."

"It might—for a spell."

"Those men shouldn't be here tonight, not with women and children about. I don't want their guns around my family."

"The Judge has taken care of that. They must leave all guns and knives at the boarding house. Bowman has contracted for Axton's cooks to prepare other foods for the shucking. Why not let them come? It will save us a beef and with thirteen extra field hands at work, we will get the corn in faster."

Craig shrugged in displeasure and walked over to lean his gun against the wagon. He noticed, with some surprise, that Martin's double-barreled shotgun and leather shot pouch lay on the inside floorboards.

———◆———

Four of Bowman's men arrived shortly, driving a fat black steer ahead of them. This was not one of the rangy, grass-fed cattle one usually saw in western Kentucky—Gill Hagman had fattened it on corn to sell at a premium price, perhaps to boatmen who contracted with one of the finer hotels upriver. The men rode past Owen's white plantation house, pausing to look at it in obvious admiration. At that time, the field hands were cutting a broad swath of corn just below the house. Everyone paused in their labors to admire the steer, a magnificent animal—low slung, well rounded, and glossy black..

"Where can we butcher this steer?" one of the men asked.

"Come on; I will show you," Owen offered, leading them past the tobacco barn and slightly downhill. "This is the place."

Several times Craig had helped kill hogs and beef cattle there. The heavy timber post-and-crossbeam structure was perfect for hanging and dressing slaughtered animals. The stone cooking pit lay uphill, closer to the house.

"You will find a stack of firewood by the pit. Hope you fellows can cook."

"Oh, don't worry about that. But if we run into trouble, may we call on your missus?"

"You may not. If you need anything, come down into the fields and find me."

"Sure thing," the man replied in an over-friendly tone.

Gradually, everyone returned to work. Craig muttered to himself as he swung the corn knife, angry that these men had come to upset the balance of their little settlement. Suddenly, a sharp report cracked the stillness—a pistol shot. Craig jumped at the sound, nerves tingling. He felt every bone in his body shaking.

"I thought they could not bring their guns!" he called to Martin.

"That rule holds for tonight, Craig. They needed something to kill the steer with."

The workers advanced swiftly through the field, cutting sizeable blocks of cornstalks and binding them into great shocks—every person anticipating the evening corn shucking, which would take place in the fields they had earlier cut. At the noonday halt, Owen invited Martin, Stephen and Craig for dinner. Craig brought his rifle with him, but Martin left his shotgun in the wagon. They walked past the men who turned the now-dressed beef over a slow fire, keeping it well away from the flames. They knew how to cook, for they had split the beef and splayed it with green oak sticks. Craig noticed with a shudder that they all carried guns.

At the house they kicked off their boots and washed their hands. It was cool under the shade trees still in leaf. Lucinde had built up a small fire in the kitchen. She looked fresh and radiant, although she had spent much of her morning in the cookhouse preparing food for the corn shucking. Owen had obviously told her to expect them, for she had set out three extra stoneware platters, each with a roasted half chicken, baked potatoes, beans and cornbread. She had already seated the children. Martin said the blessing and everyone dug in. There was cold buttermilk, hot coffee, apple cider, and well water to drink.

"How is Mary this week?" Lucinde asked. "I have missed her."

"She is well," Craig replied. "She looks forward to getting out tonight. We are both tired of forting up and carrying guns."

"My goodness! What is the matter?"

"Craig has it in his head that the town's newcomers are dangerous," Martin replied. "I agree there is something peculiar about them, but they carry a governor's commission. The Judge claims he is in charge of them."

"In my opinion, the Judge is riding a runaway horse," Craig said. "He may think he is in charge, but there are too many men carrying too many guns for my liking."

"They do behave strangely," Lucinde volunteered. "Two of them walked around the entire house, looking at the doors and windows."

Owen's blue eyes flashed with concern. "They didn't ask to come inside, did they?"

"No. Perhaps they were just admiring the house."

"I want you to lock the doors when we return to the fields."

"Are we in danger?" Lucinde asked.

Owen's expression softened. "Probably not, but it might be wise if you locked them."

"But I must go outside to the cookhouse," Lucinde insisted. "There are several more dishes I must prepare."

"Just be aware and lock the doors when you come back inside."

They finished their meal, somewhat subdued. Owen brought a rifle with him when he returned to the fields. He carried it casually on the far side, but it did not go unnoticed. One man basted the beef with a marinade from Rosenbotham's store. The other men squatted near the fire. Owen stopped when he drew level with them.

"I want you men to stay down here. Do not go anywhere near the house."

"We were just admiring it. You have beautiful place."

"Just stay down here." It was a flat, direct command, spoken quietly but with authority. Craig was surprised at the tone. Usually Owen was quiet-spoken, spare with his words.

"Oh, yes sir," the man answered. "You're the owner. Sorry if you are upset."

Craig could not conceal his disgust, for although the man tried to appear obedient, his apology was blatantly insincere. After they returned to the field, Craig noticed Owen glancing up periodically toward the men—he was definitely keeping watch on them. Around mid-afternoon, Owen left his work and strode up to the men. Martin casually drifted over to the wagon, making a conspicuous show of getting a drink, but Craig saw that he positioned himself to keep a watchful eye on his son—and, if necessary, reach his guns. Owen returned as three of the men rode off on horseback.

"What was that all about?" Martin asked.

"I told them it was time to take their guns back to town."

"What did they say?"

"They agreed. The cook handed his gun to one of them."

"Feel better now, Craig?" Martin asked.

"I suppose so. I just wish they weren't coming."

"Well, we will make the most of it. Don't let their presence spoil it for you."

<hr />

Big Tom Wheatley's slave, Old Eleazar, had perished last year from the grippe, but his protégé, Young Ben, could play almost as well. With unrestrained abandon the teenaged slave tickled the banjo strings as he strode about the wagon, kicking his heels, rolling his eyes and howling from time to time, usually at the climax of a number. Young Ben possessed a powerful baritone voice, and folks called upon him more than once to sing. He performed lively ditties and crooned mournful ballads so compelling that he silenced the talking audience. This was a new and pleasant addition to the corn shucking. Craig figured his voice was the best he had ever heard. Otherwise, things remained remarkably unchanged—Ed Mattingly and Bill Tindle still played their fiddles, while James Earl Flood and Dan Skaggs plucked sparkling accompaniments on their fiddles. Tim McCoy twanged his jew's harp; Lester Hinton puffed on various water-filled jugs to produce alternate bass tones. The Coomes brothers clattered sets of spoons to create counter-rhythms.

Last year's corn crop was so poor that Owen had cancelled his shucking; this autumn, folks turned out in much bigger numbers. As usual, families poured in from all over the county and the food was as varied and plentiful as ever. The thirteen newcomers created a stark difference in this year's shucking. Craig admitted grudgingly that they had brought some delicious food, for the girls at Maple Manor Boarding House were renowned for their cooking. And Hagman's grain-fed beef—a rarity in this part of Kentucky—was absolutely among the best Craig had tasted, tender and juicy, full of flavor. So far, the newcomers seemed to behave themselves. They showed up without firearms and worked in the fields like regular field hands. With their help, Martin figured Owen would finish shucking soon after midnight.

After supper, almost everyone returned to shuck corn and toss ears into the wagons—full ears with golden kernels. Agnes and some of the older womenfolk stayed inside the house to watch the children and keep an eye on things. Craig, Stephen, Owen, and Kelwyn drove wagons by the light of a waxing half-moon and helped each other unload into the corncribs. When they returned to the river bottoms, they found more wagons filled and waiting for them. At that point, the musicians struck up another round of tunes and everyone stopped to clap hands and sing. Several couples danced while others whooped and cheered, joining in on three and four-handed reels, square sets, and jigs.

That was when one of the strangers shouted, "Found me a red ear!"

Another stranger declared. "Me too!"

Usually, when this rarity occurred, the host inspected it for color and a young man kissed his sweetheart, or a husband kissed his wife; on occasions someone might kiss an unmarried woman in good-natured fun. These two strangers had imbibed too much of Craig's whiskey, or perhaps Martin's brandy, and they were feeling silly and cocksure of themselves. Both men swaggered up to where Mary and Lucinde worked.

"Hello, darlin'! How about a kiss?" one of the men reached for Lucinde.

Lucinde recoiled and snapped, "Find someone else, please!"

The man pulled her roughly to him and forced his mouth upon hers. Mary yanked at his arm, and the other man reached for her. Craig hauled back on the reins and sprang off his wagon. Owen bolted across the field, head down and running hard. "Hands off!" he roared.

Both strangers turned, ready to fight. Owen charged in and slammed his man onto the ground. The other stranger swung, but Craig ducked and side-stepped, unleashing a powerful kick to the man's shin and spinning a backward blow to his head. It wasn't solid, but it staggered the man. Owen and his man rolled on the ground, punching and growling like two wild animals. Craig's opponent stepped in and shot out a fist that grazed his temple, then landed a solid punch to the gut. Craig doubled over and saw the uppercut coming, dodged sideways and kicked again, connecting with the same shin. Then he punched straight in, connecting hard, knocking the man onto his haunches. In one simultaneous reflex, both strangers reached into their boots and whipped out long-bladed knives that flashed silver in the moonlight.

"That is enough!" Martin's voice boomed like a cannon. He stepped out of a corn shock shadow with his double-barreled shotgun trained on Owen's opponent. Both hammers were thumbed back. Craig could tell by Martin's stance he was ready to pull the triggers.

In a single instant, Bruce Bowman appeared from nowhere, striking two powerful blows that felled both men. He scooped up their knives and hauled them to their feet.

"My apologies, Mister McDonnell. They know better. I suspect they had too much to drink."

"You should take all your men back into town—immediately."

"I will do that, sir. Again, my apologies." He whistled once for his men and the response was instantaneous.

The music ceased and everyone turned, curious to see what

had happened, most unaware of how serious the situation was. A hundred folks watched as the strangers abandoned their places and quietly left the cornfield. Martin, Owen, and Craig followed them past the house, making sure they headed down the plantation drive. Martin waited just below, wondering if they had left weapons at the road, fearful they might return. Belatedly, the Judge swaggered up to weigh in with his opinion, arriving from another part of the field where he had been regaling guests with tales of Tippecanoe, New Orleans, and Frankfort.

"What happened, Martin? Why did you insult the Governor's men?"

"Are you so sure they are the Governor's men?"

"I myself have seen the writ."

"How do you know it is not a forgery?"

"Martin, credit me with the ability to recognize government documents. After all, I am a lawyer; I *have* worked and lived in Frankfort—and I know the Governor's signature well. The document is legitimate."

"The document may be, but they are not. They are dangerous men; I know their kind. They will not come onto our land again. Do I make myself clear?"

"Perfectly clear. You will pleased to know this—Bowman assured me this afternoon that his mission is nearly complete. He and his men will soon leave Cottonwood Bend, so I can confide in you now—I am also uneasy about them."

"Almost everyone in the settlement feels that way."

The Judge hesitated, weighing what he should share. On one hand, Bowman carried a Governor's writ and paid generously in gold coin; even more, he had promised to write a letter of commendation to Governor Slaughter. But the Judge knew that Martin McDonnell and his family could be trusted.

"Bowman is not here to inspect slaves. He is searching for a particular runway slave."

"Has he found this slave?"

"If so, he has not informed me."

"Have you seen in this writ the slave's name, or at least his description?"

"Bowman concealed that from me. He could have saved himself a great deal of time and expense by telling me up front. Instead, he has ordered me to escort him and his men all over the countryside."

"No doubt you have profited well from it."

"I admit that is true."

"Does their behavior not seem strange? Why would they engage in useless searches if they know the slave's name and whereabouts?"

"There you have me, sir. I have oft asked myself the same question, but have been content to accept their payments, and conduct the search in the manner Bowman prescribed. It seemed harmless enough."

"Just make sure you tell him to keep his men off our land."

"Consider the deed done."

Martin stayed to keep watch while Owen, Craig and Judge Bozarth returned to the field. Folks saw them return and they stopped to whoop and cheer.

"That was good fightin', son!"

"I thought Owen was wrestlin' a bear, there wuz so much growlin'!"

"You knocked him flat, Craig. Wished he'd a-fought fair and square, for I wanted you to finish the fight!"

Owen and Craig went straight to Mary and Lucinde. Both wives embraced them warmly.

"Are you injured?" Craig asked Mary.

"I am fine! You were magnificent! Did he hurt you?

"No, but your father stepped in at the right time."

Lucinde appeared unharmed. Owen led her off behind a corn shock to talk with her. The musicians struck up another reel and everyone returned to work and play.

Cottonwood Bend Riverfront—October 20, 1817

From the steamboat's deck, the town of Cottonwood Bend

looked as promising as any place on the western Ohio River. Nestled between Spigot Run and Cottonwood Creek, it possessed an orderliness not found in most western settlements. Most of those places were haphazard in construction with residences built mostly of crude logs. Here, a row of fine, two-story brick or clapboard, glass-paned houses lined a high bank, and several businesses bespoke of an obviously vibrant economy. The townspeople had constructed a heavy timber bridge over a big creek to the east, indicating that some sort of civic order existed. A red-brick cobblestone landing led up to the town's centerpiece—Rosenbotham's Store. Golden maple and red gum leaves rippled in the early morning breeze, made more colorful by morning sunlight reflecting off the river's surface. High limestone hills were daubed in oranges, yellows, reds, and purples.

"Oh, Thomas! Is this truly the place?" Solange asked.

"That's what the captain said." Doc could not quell the happiness inside him. After a fine breakfast, he and Solange had gone onto the top deck to enjoy the crisp autumn air. She looked beautiful in the sunlight, and happiness emanated from her as well.

"It is beautiful!" she cried.

"Are you sure you wish to settle here?"

"If we do not like it, we can travel farther east and north. I am just happy to be with you!"

"It *has* been an adventure, hasn't it?"

The accommodations on board *Jesse P. Emmick* had proven luxurious beyond belief. Doc had paid fifty-five dollars for the journey; that included room and board. For three weeks, he and Solange had enjoyed the changing countryside, fraternized with the passengers, and—practiced medicine.

Wherever they put into shore, it seemed that folks needed their medical expertise. When the steamboat stopped in Baton Rouge to pick up cargo, one of the new businessmen came down with a serious fever. Doc and Solange treated him for three days, keeping him cool, feeding him liquids, and administering doses of willow bark powder. The man's health improved and he paid generously in Spanish mill dollars. A little boy, the son of a traveling young couple, suffered from a toothache and Doc had drawn the tooth, making the operation seem more like an escapade. He entertained the lad with a few magic tricks and told a story about a brave young bear who needed his tooth pulled. Late one afternoon, the *Jesse P.* tied up at the notorious Natchez wharf. There they took on two flatboat merchants, both shot from ambush two days previously, when river pirates tried to seize their cargoes. Doc and Solange treated their wounds. One man was shot in the lower arm, and it showed beginning signs of mortification. The physician ashore recommended amputation. The wounded merchant cursed that physician and sought a second opinion. After a cursory examination, Doc took two loaded pistols and ascended the steep bluff in search of a slaughterhouse or tannery. At the tannery he found a hanging hide removed from a recently-slaughtered cow; from this he collected a tin of white, writhing maggots. He returned to the *Jesse P.* shortly before dusk, just as the hell-hole below Natchez came to life. This was the lawless part of town known as 'Natchez-Under-the-Bluff.' The wildest sort of men and women began their work—and play—amid music, shouts, laughter, and drunken revelry. Shots rang out, a woman screamed, and a stray lead ball struck the port smokestack with a resounding clang. Doc hurried up the ramp and took cover inside the merchant's cabin. Solange was treating his patient who, by this time, was near delirious. She peeled back a poultice of grated raw potato and slippery elm to reveal a feverish arm swollen twice its normal size from infection. Red streaks ran from the bullet wound which had scabbed over and turned black. Solange handed Doc the muslin bandage and he took a whiff of the infection.

"We are going to try something a bit unorthodox," Doc announced. "A few years back, I read in two medical papers that Revolutionary War doctors treated infection, namely gangrene, with maggots. I plan to introduce them into this wound and allow them to eat away any dead flesh. They will leave the healthy flesh alone, open up the wound, and reduce swelling. Then I can probe for lead fragments, which I suspect have caused much of the infection."

"You won't put those goddamned maggots in my arm!" the merchant swore.

"Then I recommend you go ashore and allow the doctor to amputate."

The merchant shut up and turned his head while Doc used a pair of tweezers to introduce the maggots into the wound. He covered the arm with a loose bandage and let nature take its course. On the following day, Doc extracted three lead splinters, two bone chips, a sodden mess of wadding, and a patch of the man's shirt. Infection bubbled out of the wound with the consistency of thick custard, loathsome and foul-smelling. Solange assisted Doc during the surgical procedure and, after washing the wound in hot wine, applied a mustard poultice to draw out the remaining infection.

Within the first day, the man showed signs of recovery. Later, he showed his gratitude, paying Doc a sum so generous that it more than covered the full cost of his passage. From that time on, everyone vied for his and Solange's company—especially at evening meals. This included the lad whose tooth Doc had pulled. The mite was six, perhaps seven years of age and an uncontrollable terror, running up and down the deck, throwing items overboard, screaming, throwing tantrums, and constantly interrupting adult conversations, gleefully making so much noise that he rendered talking impossible. The young parents apparently accepted this behavior, for they steadfastly refused to discipline, spending most of their time appeasing him and attempting to redirect his unruliness. Doc could see they were exasperated and always relieved to have other adults entertain him for a time. One afternoon, the lad snatched an elderly woman's porcelain cup from the deck table and, without looking, hurled it backwards over his shoulder. It just missed another passenger and shattered on the deck below.

"That one needs a sound thrashing!" Doc muttered.

"Thomas!" Solange scolded. "He is only a little boy."

"Yes, but he knows better. If they don't rein him in now, they'll have trouble down the road."

"He thinks the world of you!"

"Look at that—the parents are trying to reason with him. He

controls *them*—watch how he will hold them hostage for most of the afternoon. They can talk until they are blue in the face. One good swat to the behind would send a much clearer message."

Later that afternoon the lad disappeared. His parents searched frantically, knocking on cabin doors, pleading with the captain to conduct a search. Passengers turned out to help, most fearing the lad had fallen overboard. The possibility certainly existed, but Doc had a hunch where he might be. Painfully, he descended the rear ladder to search the livestock deck. The lad was down there, poking his fingers into a large wooden-doweled chicken coop. He had upset the six hens which now cackled in terror, but the big black rooster, with iridescent tail feathers and a pair of sharp, curved spurs, appeared riled. It swelled up and strutted about in an aggressive manner.

"What are you doing?" Doc asked the lad gruffly. "You stop that right now!" The lad grinned devilishly, acting as if he hadn't heard, and continued wiggling his fingers at the rooster. "Go ahead then, and let that mean rooster peck your eyeballs out."

With astonishing speed, the enraged fowl darted across the cage and jabbed the lad's finger with its beak, catching hold of it and shaking its head. Doc could not help but feel a bit of satisfaction at the lad's blood-curdling scream of pain and outrage.

"You didn't listen, did you, you monstrous little turd!" he chuckled. "You are lucky it wasn't worse. Try that in a barnyard and see what happens. That rooster would flog you with its wings and cut you up with its spurs! Come on; your folks are beside themselves." He shepherded the shrieking lad up the ladder and onto the top deck.

"Oh, Fitzroy!" The mother spied him and came running. She held him close and wept with relief. "What happened? Where were you?" The father joined them, still shaking, pale from fear his son had drowned.

"I found him down on the main deck," Doc replied. "Despite my warnings, he insisted on tormenting a caged rooster. Natural consequences occurred before I could intervene."

In a short time everyone on deck knew that Doc had found the boy. They gathered round to watch Solange assist as he washed the small wound and wrapped it in a light linen bandage. It really was a fuss over nothing. The lad had made a conscious decision to commit a wrong and had suffered the consequences. Silently, Doc admitted he had made much worse choices in his own life. Adults made conscious, bad missteps all the time. But he felt it would be wrong not to chide the lad a little further.

"Next time your elders—and especially your folks—tell you not to do something, you had better damned well listen. You have worried everyone on board. And you have worn us out with your constant demands and misbehavior. It is time you straightened up and stopped acting like a spoiled infant. Now run along." The parents were not pleased with those words, but Doc figured he possessed enough years and authority to speak freely. Most passengers silently applauded him; more than one whispered that a little natural justice might just teach the lad some self-control. The family disembarked where the Ohio entered the muddy Mississippi. They were headed north to settle near the growing settlement of St. Louis. From that point they must hire a keel boat; Doc had not heard of steamboats traveling upriver beyond the Ohio.

The rest of the journey passed without incident and *Jesse P. Emmick* powered its way up the glassy smooth Ohio River, sometimes slowing to avoid sandbars and stopping occasionally to load cordwood, before finally bringing them to their destination. The captain eased into the landing, disengaging the paddlewheels and ordering ropes tossed ashore. Deckhands secured the vessel and ran out the brass-railed gangplank. Two lounging river hands stepped forward and offered to carry Doc's and Solange's baggage. A crowd gathered, curious to see the new double-decked steamboat, one of the largest seen on western rivers. Just as Doc reached the top, six armed men shouldered through the throng, jostling folks as they hastily made their way down to the steamboat, obviously hoping to book passage before it departed.

Doc decided to head toward the brick-fronted store. If anyone knew where to find lodging and locate the sheriff, it would be the storeowner. The man was wearing a homespun apron and sorting new red potatoes into wooden bins. He stood up and greeted Doc warmly.

"What can I do for you, stranger?"

"My name is Thomas Applegate."

"*Doctor* Thomas Applegate," Solange added. Not usually one for bragging, she had learned early on that the title commanded some respect and made their journey easier.

"Hiram Rosenbotham at your service."

"Can you tell me who your law enforcement official is, and where I might find him?"

"That would be Judge Wilfred J. Bozarth."

"Is he the sheriff?"

"No, the sheriff is in Hardinsburg. Bozarth is our local militia commander. As such he possesses some jurisdiction when it comes to lawbreaking. Is anything wrong?"

"I cannot say for sure," Doc replied. "If you would kindly point us in his direction, I would be forever in your debt. After we hand him an official correspondence, we would like to find a good board-ing house." Doc noticed others in the store listening intently, wholly engrossed in the conversation, and he figured that strangers made for big news in this settlement.

"Well, you are almost there. The Judge lives right around the corner on Maple Street. You can't miss his place—he has a sign-board hanging out front. Maple Manor Boarding House is just past his house. I think they are full up, but you can sure ask."

"Thank you, sir." Doc nodded. He and Solange exited the store. The river hands conducted them up Maple Street to Judge Bozarth's magnificent two-story home where a heavyset, middle-aged woman answered the door.

"Yes?" she inquired, displaying a somewhat reserved and haugh-ty air. Doc was not impressed.

"I am Doctor Thomas Applegate and this is my wife, Solange. We have come from New Orleans to see your husband, Judge Bozarth.

"I am his wife, Violet Bozarth. What is your business with him?"

"I bear a message from the Governor of Louisiana. It must be hand-delivered to the local law enforcement officer. I understand that is Judge Bozarth."

"You should find him next door at the boarding house." She pointed south at the next building, a rambling two-story structure covered in white planking.

"Thank you, madam."

"If he is not there, you may bring the letter to me. I will make sure he gets it." Doc could see she was dying to know its contents.

"I certainly shall." Doc tipped his hat, took Solange's hand in the crook of his arm and led the way to Maple Manor Boarding House.

He found the parlor a scene of turmoil and consternation, men packing their gear and checking weapons. He tipped the river hands and turned to observe the spectacle. A giant man was issuing commands with authority and urgency. "Get down to that boat and make sure Jeff and his men hold it there. No one else may board. If he has things in hand, you know what to do. Tell him to meet me as planned. Saddle my horse and tie the gray mule to it."

Two men emerged from a back bedroom lugging their guns and bedrolls. They crossed the parlor without words and quit the boarding house.

"Leaving so soon?" inquired an older, well-dressed man. This man possessed a big, booming bass voice, impressive girth, and splendid mane of salt-and-pepper hair. "Am I to conclude your business is finished here?"

"You may so conclude."

"Ah, there remains the matter of final payment."

The giant, younger man withdrew a small bag of coins from his coat pocket and paid out five gold American eagles. "Thank you, Judge. Now I must be off to the stables to see to our horses. I am anxious to return to New Orleans."

"You may be disappointed, my friend," the Judge countered. "I understand that your steamboat is headed upriver to Louisville and, when high water favors, beyond to Cincinnati and Pittsburgh."

"I think we can suffer a few days riding that boat to Louisville.

We may then offer sufficient inducement for passage to New Orleans."

"You never found your runaway?"

"He has gotten clean away. We gave it our best try."

Doc watched as four more men emerged from the hallway to join their leader. In that instant, the puzzle pieces merged to form a clear image. With a shock Doc realized that these men were part of the mercenary force sent by Jules Signet. Thank God they had not yet seized their quarry.

"Are you Judge Wilfred Bozarth?" Doc interrupted.

"I am indeed," the Judge replied imperiously.

"We need to talk in private."

"Not now, man!"

"It is important."

"And so is my present business. I must conduct these men safely to their boat. They have been with us for some time."

"I bear an important correspondence from—"

"I said, not now!" Judge Bozarth thundered. "My law office is next door. See my wife—she will make an appointment."

The giant man spoke again. "We need no further assistance from you, Judge. Trust me—you have more than done your part. I will remember your help for years to come."

Doc noticed how he suppressed his mirth as he shouldered a pair of heavy saddlebags. Clearly he held the Judge in disregard. He and his men abruptly left the boarding house and strode briskly down Maple Street. One might describe them as running. They were halfway to the river before anyone thought to speak.

"You will listen to me now, you insufferable windbag!" Doc snapped.

The Judge wheeled angrily. "I beg your pardon!"

"Read this letter. It is from Jacques Villeré, Governor of Louisiana. In it he asks the Governor of Kentucky to disregard the writ those men carried."

The Judge broke the seal and opened the letter. "I see no reason why this should have precedence over our Governor's decision."

"Do you know why those men came here?" Doc asked.

"They were searching for a valuable runaway slave."

"She is not a runaway slave."

"*She?*" the Judge looked perplexed.

"Lucinde Delacroix, now McDonnell." Doc handed Judge Bozarth Lucinde's manumission papers and the death records of Delacroix and Jules Signet as additional proof. In a few concise sentences, he shared the story, "They are a professional mercenary force hired to deliver her to a man who had conspired to seize her inheritance and enslave her and her children. That man is dead, but these men do not know it."

The Judge's jaw dropped as full realization struck him; his eyes bulged from their sockets and his hands began to tremble. "Oh, merciful God! I have helped them all along! I did not know their real business! They concealed Lucinde's identity from me—I swear it!"

Doc took charge of the papers. "You should not be surprised why they did. She is, after all, Delacroix's daughter and the daughter-in-law of your most prominent citizen."

"We must tell Bowman about this letter—the changed situation!"

"You can try," Doc agreed. "But those mercenaries may decide to hold Lucinde hostage to cover their losses. I understand that Martin McDonnell is a wealthy man. So is his son, Owen."

The Judge's complexion darkened; clearly he was outraged. "They have played me as their fool and, by all that is sacred in Heaven, they will pay!"

"Yes, and 'a stitch in time may save nine.' You had best call out your militia and ride over to save Lucinde from catastrophe. Her family will undoubtedly fight to protect her, and they could be killed. Remember, these men are professional soldiers."

"So am I," the Judge growled. Moving unbelievably fast for such a big man, he raced outside toward his home where he would get his guns, saddle his horse, and ride out to muster the Cottonwood Bend Regulators.

Chapter Twenty-Three

Welcome Hall

"Where is Owen?" Craig asked. They were sharpening corn knives in the noonday sun that flooded through the open south doors of Martin McDonnell's barn. It felt good to sit on a stone block in warm sunlight after a big dinner, and to smell the cured tobacco hanging behind them. The weather had turned too dry for stripping; that was why Martin chose that afternoon to cut corn. Before dinner, the workers had complained that their knives were dull, so Craig and the McDonnells used long files to lay a bright edge on each knife.

"Could be Lucinde cooked him an extra special meal," Martin mused. "He's been late before."

"I can't remember when."

"He'll be along, directly."

After they had sharpened the knives, Martin led them into the field nearest Owen's plantation. Craig noticed how he kept casting concerned glances to the northwest, looking for his son's familiar, lanky silhouette. Soon, he motioned for Stephen to join him. "Would you see what is keeping your brother?"

"Sure, Pa!" Stephen replied. He broke into a light run that carried him swiftly across the bottomland to Owen's boundary which was marked by a ditch and small fencerow. Presently, he disappeared from view. Martin and Craig found the field hands still snoozing after their noonday meal, many enjoying the bright rays of autumn sunshine. Everyone took a sharpened knife and began chopping at the brittle cornstalks, gathering and shocking them, using the new hemp twine Mary had fashioned.

A short time later, Craig heard a voice crying in the thin autumn air. He straightened up and peered northwest to focus on the figure hurrying toward them—it was Stephen. Craig shouted to get Martin's attention, for the old man was becoming somewhat hard-of-hearing. Martin straightened up and shaded his eyes against the sun as Craig did. Stephen was a long way off, still too far to understand, but Craig could tell he was distressed and running toward them at top speed.

"Something is wrong, Martin!" Craig flung down his corn knife and sprinted hard toward his brother in law, not bothering to regulate his stride in the corn stubble. Somehow, he managed not to trip and fall, and he reached the fencerow just as Stephen vaulted clumsily over it to collapse onto the field. When Craig reached him, the lad was winded, lying flat on his back, breathing air in great, ragged gulps, and choking with sobs. He had run over a mile, mostly at top speed, to reach the pasture.

"What is it, Stephen?" Craig demanded.

"It's O-Owen!" the young man gasped, his eyes rolling in his head.

"What is wrong with him?"

"Bleeding from the head—couldn't wake him!"

"Breathe deeply," Craig counseled. "Tell me what you saw."

Gradually, Stephen's gasps subsided and he relayed his discovery. "Owen is lying in the front yard with his head covered in blood. I think he is dead." He began to weep.

"Did you tell Lucinde?"

"She and the children are gone! I called and called for them. Oh, Lord! My brother is dead!"

Craig deduced instantly what had happened. The strangers Judge Bozarth had so willingly escorted around the county had attacked Owen and seized Lucinde and the children. He knew it was so, without knowing why. "Come on! Get on your feet! We have to find them. We must fetch Judge Bozarth!"

Martin ran up. "What is wrong?"

"Owen is bleeding from the head!" Craig answered. "Lucinde and the children are gone."

"Is this true?" Martin laid a hand on Stephen's shoulder.

"I called and called for them, Father!"

"Perhaps they are in hiding," Martin replied.

"Owen is dead!"

"Are you sure?" His face revealed his horror.

"I could not wake him."

"Perhaps he still lives. We must go to him."

"I will fetch the guns." Craig volunteered. His .50 caliber rifle and Martin's double-barreled shotgun lay in back of the flatbed wagon. He dashed across the field to where the confused workers stood. Few, if any, owned a weapon. "Go home and bolt your doors!" he told them. "If you have guns, load them and keep them ready." He snatched up the guns and leathers and sprinted back to the fencerow.

Martin took his shotgun and doeskin shot pouch with paper-wrapped charges. "Stephen, you run up to Welcome Hall and saddle the horses. Get my rifle and yours—and bring some spare rifles—pistols too."

"Yes, Father!"

"Don't push yourself so hard that you collapse. You must bring the horses and guns. We may need them."

"I'll see you at Owen's house, Father."

"Good."

With his long legs, Martin stepped easily over the fencerow that Craig had to jump. Together they trotted across Owen's fields. After a few hundred yards, the old man began to lag. Craig was amazed he had run so far.

"You run ahead, Craig. I'll be there shortly."

"Yes, Martin."

"And watch yourself. There may be gunmen there, waiting in ambush."

Craig crouched low and rushed over the low rise, darting at angles through the orchard before reaching the double grape arbor. He ducked behind a thick locust post that served as an end support, thumbed back the hammer of his rifle, and scanned the house and yard. Owen lay flat on his stomach a few steps from the side door. Craig thought he saw his right foot twitch. After he regained his normal breathing, he ran to the cooking pit and took cover behind the stone blocks. The place lay silent and appeared completely abandoned. It seemed strange that such a beautiful home could look so bleak. He glanced over his shoulder. Martin had covered about two-thirds of the distance, so he decided to throw caution to the wind. He left his cover and ran to where Owen lay. The young man's black curls were matted with dark blood.

"Owen!" he called. "It's Craig." Craig saw he was still breathing. "You are safe now." He glanced again at the house, ready to shoot at any stranger. Owen groaned and turned painfully onto his side. His blue eyes appeared oddly unfocused. Martin ran up, breathing heavily.

"Hold on, son. We have horses coming. We will take you to your mother. She will know what to do."

"Lucinde!" Owen croaked hoarsely. He thrashed weakly as he tried to rise.

"Just lie still. You have lost some blood."

Craig darted inside the house and found a folded sheet in the linen closet. He brought it outside and tore it into long strips. Martin bound Owen's head with those strips.

"Has he been shot?" Craig asked.

"Tomahawked, judging from the gash. They meant to incapacitate, not kill, but they have come close."

"Let's not wait for the horses. I will hook up his wagon. He might do better with us holding him upright between us."

"Good idea."

By the time Craig hitched the wagon and drove it into the yard, Stephen arrived with the horses and guns. "You did well, Stephen," Martin commended him.

"He's alive!" Stephen exclaimed in wonder.

"By God's good graces. Let's get him over to your mother."

Stephen broke down completely, crying from relief, pressing the palms of his hands against his eyes. When he recovered his composure, he asked, "What about Lucinde and the children?"

"Let us take one step at a time."

They tied the horses behind the wagon and laid their guns on the floorboards. Martin and Craig helped Owen into the back and sat on either side, supporting him upright while Stephen drove.

Obviously, the young man had informed Agnes to expect trouble, but despite his terrible fear, he did not tell her Owen might be dead. She had already boiled water and laid out various herbs to mash into poultices. Concern showed on her pale, grim features as she watched them help Owen inside. With assistance, Owen walked upright, although jerkily, and Craig felt relieved to see both his feet working. Owen seemed to see where he was walking. Perhaps his vision had returned.

Agnes sat him in a wooden chair and went to work on the scalp wound. "Have some black tea, Owen," she cooed. "It will help clear your head." She skillfully blotted the laceration and packed it with a mushy green root poultice. "That should stop the bleeding," she announced. "It's best you sit upright and stay real still. Keep on drinking your tea."

"What happened, son?" Martin asked.

"Four men came. They stepped down from their mounts and left their rifles in their scabbards. I remember ordering them to move on. One man drew his sword and brought it down on my head. Everything went black."

"What about Lucinde and the children?"

"I don't know!" His eyes registered panic. "Did they take them?"

"We suspect so."

"But why?"

"Who knows? Remember, Pierre Delacroix warned Lucinde to never return to New Orleans. I suspect someone down there wants her."

"We must find them!"

"We will!" Martin assured him. "I truly don't think they would kill her or the children. They could have killed you where you lay."

"I'll go with you!"

"You are in no condition to ride. Stay here. We will ride into Cottonwood Bend and fetch the Judge. He will have to call out the Regulators."

Craig said, "I want to warn Mary, and fetch my horse and other weapons. May I take one of your horses?"

"Go," Martin nodded. "We may not be here when you get back, but you can catch up with us."

"Thanks, Martin." Craig dashed outside and untied a solid-chested bay gelding. They cut across the bottomland pasture, taking the most direct route. Long before Craig came to Breckinridge County, Martin had constructed a low stone fence to separate his land from the Widder Fuqua's. With Craig as his son-in-law, the fence served no real purpose, and when, during a freeze, some of the top stones fell, Martin had not bothered to replace them. Craig charged directly at the gap and urged the horse into a jump. They sailed cleanly over the wall with a good foot to spare and raced across the forty-acre pasture. Instead of taking Levi's wooden bridge, Craig jumped the narrow ditch and whipped the gelding into a hard gallop up the steep lane toward his cabin. He burst out over the rise and drove fast toward the cabin.

Hopping off just short of the dogtrot, he shouted for Mary to unbolt the door. "Mary! I need my guns!"

Mary slid back the oaken bolt and opened the door. "What is it, Craig?" she asked, eyes filled with fear. She knew him well enough to know the situation was dire. He strode directly to the mantle and began taking down his guns—his favorite, the .40 caliber rifle, the other .50 caliber, and the short double-barreled Spanish-made shotgun given to him by Pierre Delacroix six years ago. All guns were loaded, but he would later check the priming on each one. Long ago he had fashioned leather straps to serve as slings. He shrugged each one onto his shoulders.

"What has happened?" she insisted.

"Bruce Bowman's men have taken Lucinde and the children."

"Oh no!" Mary exclaimed. She handed him his possibles bag

filled with loaded paper cartridges made up to fit each weapon. "What will you do?"

"I am saddling Blue. Your father, Stephen, and I are riding in to Cottonwood Bend to alert the Judge. He will call out the Regulators."

"Do you think Lucinde is in Cottonwood Bend?"

"If not there, they are taking her out on one of three main roads. It makes good sense—ever since they came here, they have ridden the roads and trails, asking folks where they lead. We may have to split our forces."

"How is Owen taking this?"

"He has been seriously injured by the mercenaries. Your mother is caring for him."

Mary's eyes widened with shock. "I must help her."

Craig shook his head. "You must stay put. We don't know where the men are. They might even come here, so keep your shotgun and pistols close at hand. Bolt the door and don't open it unless you hear my voice—or that of someone you know."

"I understand."

Craig liked that about her. She trusted his judgment and would carry through his instructions. He made to leave.

Mary stepped into his path and hugged him with all her strength. "Be careful, Craig! I am more afraid for you now than when you went off to war." The children were quiet, obviously frightened by their conversation. Craig stooped to hug them.

"You girls look after your mother," he instructed.

"We will, Father," they replied.

"I love you, girls!" he told them. He rose, kissed Mary and embraced her, "I love you so much!"

"Just come back to me," she whispered.

"I plan to," he replied. He waited until he heard Mary bolt the door before he led Stephen's horse to the barn.

Martin McDonnell checked the loads on his .36 and .50 caliber rifles. He advised Stephen to do the same with his weapons. They worked quickly, inspecting their possibles bags and shot pouches, packing an extra blanket and filling their drinking water tins.

Agnes watched from the parlor with trepidation. With their help she had propped Owen in a reclining position on the parlor couch, and elevated his head with pillows from the guest bedroom. She kept vigil on him while her husband and youngest son made ready for battle. It brought back memories of Martin heading off to fight in the American Revolution, first in the brutal fighting at Guilford Courthouse in North Carolina and later in Kentucky at the disastrous Battle of Blue Licks. The agony and fear she faced then was almost too much to bear. She could hardly trust herself to speak.

"You men be careful, now. You hear?"

"We will, Ma!" Stephen tried to assure her. She could tell he was frightened.

"Don't let anything happen to your Daddy. We have been together too long."

"You just keep a close eye on Owen," Martin counseled. "Don't let him sleep too much. When we reach Cottonwood Bend, I will find Doc Emmick and send him here. Don't let him do anything drastic. It is best Owen heals on his own, but the Doc may have some words of medical wisdom."

"Is Craig going with you?"

"He will catch up."

Agnes could not hold back her tears. "Why did those men come to our quiet settlement? Why would they take Lucinde and my precious grandbabies? We weren't bothering them!"

Martin crossed over and enfolded her in his corded, sun-blackened arms. He let her weep for a few moments before answering, "It's not about us."

"What then?"

"Money, power and greed. We are meaningless figures in their calculations."

Agnes sniffed and straightened up, squaring her shoulders in defiance. "Well, you just go and fetch Lucinde and those grandbabies back!"

Cottonwood Bend

Doc Applegate paid a full week's rent for one of Axton's recently vacated rooms, and he made sure Solange was safely ensconced in it. She began hanging clothing in the large armoire, arranging shoes in the cavernous bottom, and folding her undergarments to place them into dresser drawers. She noticed Doc rummaging through his black leather medical bag, examining its contents, and checking the priming of his two pistols.

"What are you doing, dear?" She could not conceal her alarm.

"I intend to see my promise to its conclusion," he answered simply.

"But, Thomas—you have already done your duty."

"I cannot rest until I know that girl is safe. I promised Pierre Delacroix I would protect her."

"You have done more than could be reasonably expected."

"I am not sure this Judge Bozarth character is up to the task."

"He must be, or he would not be the local militia commander."

"I am sure you are right, but if there is a gunfight, and I believe there will be one, they will need a doctor to patch them up. We may be bringing wounded men back here, and in that event I will need you. Remember, you alone are responsible for guarding our belongings."

"You must guard yourself—against danger. Thomas, you have said it more than once—Signet's men are professional soldiers. You are not a soldier. You have no business engaging them."

"I have every business engaging them."

"I do not wish to be left alone again in this world—not after finding such happiness."

"You must realize how important this is."

"I know you would not be yourself if you left others to finish the job. I love you all the more for your decision. Please, please be careful!"

"On that score you may rest easy."

———————◆———————

"Wilfred, I fear for your life!" Violet Bozarth wept aloud.

The Judge stuck his polished rosewood dueling pistols into his wide leather belt, sucked in his gut and sleeked back his impressive mane with a dab of expensive French pomade he had purchased in Louisville. He lifted his ornate rifle from the cabinet and struck a pose, admiring his imperial figure in the full-length mirror.

Violet fussed over him, brushing his suitcoat with her hands, her fear clearly evident. "You old bull, you are not as young as you once were."

"I am just a hair past fifty! Still a young man—full of vim and vigor. You should know, Madam!" He chortled recklessly, displaying the magnificent gap-toothed grin that won her heart years ago— and flustered the hearts of various female companions in years since.

"You are too old to be chasing outlaws—I know that! Remember, you are a state representative with a bright future in politics. Please, please, do not act rashly and throw all that away."

"Violet, I have unwittingly betrayed one of my closest friends. Those mercenaries wish to abduct Lucinde McDonnell and her children, and haul them down to New Orleans in chains. As the commander of the Cottonwood Bend Regulators, I am duty-bound to prevent that from happening."

"Don't use that high-and-mighty tone with me, Wilfred!" Violet retorted. "I am your wife. I know all your sins—and your weaknesses. You welcome this conflict as another chance to prove you are still a brave young warrior able to fight with the younger men, but you must realize your time for fighting is over. Let others handle this problem. What is this McDonnell girl to you?"

"I shall not dignify that question with an answer. It is the whole McDonnell family for whom I fight. It is for duty dear, honor, friendship, and human decency—the real reasons for which we should live—and the values for which most men never get to fight."

"People say the mercenaries are dangerous men. You may not fully comprehend what you are up against."

"I too, am a dangerous man, and they most assuredly do not comprehend the peril *they* face." The Judge was on a roll; there was no stopping him now. He expanded on the importance of law and its execution, the right of every man to enjoy freedom from persecution, and of government's duty to protect its citizens. It was a longish speech. A passerby might imagine him addressing a large crowd from the steps of the Kentucky Capitol. He cocked one shoulder, swelled up his chest and boomed, "I shall teach them not to mess with the likes of Judge Wilfred Bozarth, Attorney-at-Law, Representative of the great State of Kentucky, and Commander of the Cottonwood Bend Party of Regulators!" He finished his grandiose soliloquy with arms spread wide, rifle clutched in his right hand, jaw extended in a bellicose manner—deeply satisfied with his reflection in the mirror. At that moment, someone rapped on the front door and the distraction spoiled his rhapsodizing.

"Yes!" he roared.

"Judge, I have brought four men." Judge Bozarth recognized the voice and nodded. Five was about what he initially expected. However, this was a matter that impacted an important Cottonwood Bend family—more militiamen would surely follow.

"Enter," Judge Bozarth beckoned. Calvin Ward opened the door, removed his hat in Violet's presence, and nodded in respect to both of them.

"Shall I saddle your mare, Judge?"

"She is saddled and ready." The Judge slid the leather possibles bag over his right shoulder and adjusted it so he could open the flap and reach his paper-wrapped cartridges. "Fare thee well, my lovely wife!" He crossed the floor and blew her a magnanimous kiss from the doorway. "I shall return before you know I am gone!" Violet could not stifle her cry and, before he closed the door, she ran for the cupboard where she kept her jug of "Widder's Reserve." She knew it would be a long night and this would be her only source of comfort.

Out on the lawn the Judge asked in a low voice. "Do you know why I have summoned you—why I am calling out the Regulators?"

"Seth Toler said we might be ridin' over to Owen McDonnell's place—that Owen's wife and children might be in danger."

"Yes, that is correct. I have just learned that the men who stayed in Maple Manor Boarding House plan to seize Lucinde and spirit her down to New Orleans. We must take drastic measures to prevent them from doing so."

"I imagine Owen will have something to say about them taking her. So will old man McDonnell."

"Yes, but there are thirteen of them and only four on Owen's side—if you count young Stephen and Craig Ridgeway. Owen and Craig are battle-tested and both good shots. Stephen is unproven and Martin, bless him as a decorated hero of the Revolution, must be nearing eighty. Not much of a force, even when you add our half-dozen men. We shall need more. I have it on good authority that Bowman's men are professional soldiers—mercenaries. They are not the common outlaws with whom we usually deal. Therefore, we must exercise utmost caution. That means shooting first and asking questions later. If they are as good as I fear, several of our Regulators may perish."

Calvin knew his man well. The Judge was telling it straight now, with no exaggeration or embellishment. He waited for him to fetch his mare from the stable and lead it around to the front lawn. Other Regulators soon joined them, leading their mounts, ready to receive instructions. The Judge had not yet formulated a detailed plan. His first instinct was to ride over and alert the McDonnells. If he arrived early enough, he could position his men in an ambush, utilizing the additional McDonnell firepower. He was about to speak when a voice interrupted him.

"You *do* realize they intend to smuggle Lucinde aboard the *Jesse P. Emmick*?"

The Judge spun on his boot heel. The well-dressed man who called himself a doctor had walked over from the boarding house and now leaned against the big maple tree near the street. He had obviously heard everything.

"When I need commentary from strangers and amateurs, I shall ask for it," the Judge retorted, still smarting from the man's earlier rebuff.

"You are correct, Judge. I *am* a stranger and an amateur—but you must hear me out. As soon as we docked, a half dozen armed men boarded the steamboat upon which I traveled. You and I heard Bowman order his men to make sure that—and I quote—'Jeff and his men hold it there.'"

"Yes?"

"My guess is that half of Bowman's men are aboard the steamboat. The other half plans to snatch Lucinde McDonnell and bring her here to Cottonwood Bend. The steamboat is the fastest and most reliable mode of transportation in America. They could have her in New Orleans in two weeks, maybe less."

Calvin interjected himself into the conversation. "The men have also been riding out on our main roads and trails, asking where they lead. They might be planning to take her back overland."

"They have already commandeered the boat. Put yourself in their position. Which mode of transportation would you choose?"

"There is something in what you are saying, Doctor," Bozarth admitted. "Calvin, we still need someone to ride out to the McDonnells and warn them. Send Will Meriwether. And damn it to hell, we need more men!" His voice thundered up and down the street, reverberating against the houses. "I want every available man to meet me at Rosenbotham's store. Get Rosenbotham! Find Brother Kreisle and that damned Levi Matthews! Fetch any citizen with a gun! I care not about their military experience. We *must* keep those gunmen from boarding with Lucinde!"

His men scattered to raise a citizen army. Judge Bozarth knew that most folks in Cottonwood Bend could shoot. He began walking toward the river, leading his big chestnut mare. Doc fell in beside him.

"Could you use a couple more guns?"

"Not those antiquated horse pistols. I am willing to bet you couldn't hit a barn at thirty paces."

"In New Orleans I shot and killed two men—one at ten paces and one at three. With my cane I clubbed another man to death. All three were linked to this business. I have traveled twelve hundred miles to ensure Lucinde's safety and I intend to see this through. I *am* on your side, you know."

"Well-spoken, Doctor. You may join us, but do not expect to be anywhere near the fighting. I predict these men will shoot from great distances to keep us at bay. They are professionals in every sense of the word. Even if we can amass fifty settlers, we are outgunned and out-soldiered."

"Then you had better come up with a plan."

"I'm working on it. Sometimes a gun battle will unfold in diametric contrast to what is planned; there are always human variables that require flexibility."

"I have seen that in action."

"What is in the black bag?"

"Why, my medical instruments of course—bandages, medicines, and the like. From what you have told me, your men are going to need them."

———◆———

Craig caught up with Martin and Stephen at Cemetery Knob a few hundred yards before the timber bridge that crossed Cottonwood Creek. Stephen rode a buckskin horse, looking awkward and tense in the saddle, his right hand gripping the rifle so tightly that his knuckles showed white. Martin rode his chocolate-colored mare with the awareness of an experienced soldier, rifle laid across his saddle in ready position. Craig edged in on Martin's right. Blue had handled superbly and allowed him to lead the McDonnell's bay horse back to Welcome Hall. Craig had then pushed him into an easy lope which he could maintain for almost a half day. The horse was not extended after the six mile ride.

"Is Mary safe?" Martin asked as he pulled up alongside.

"The cabin door is locked and she is well-armed."

"Which is more than I can say for Agnes. Poor Owen is unable in his condition to defend her."

Craig thought about that. He realized how much folks had been forced to alter their daily lives to guard against possible danger. Now, everything was coming to a terrible, explosive conclusion—and turning out worse than anyone could have imagined. They must fight, against terrible odds, to free Lucinde and her children—and drive out those men who had infected Cottonwood Bend with their virulent poison. He felt no doubts about the upcoming conflict—there would be no trouble sleeping at night, no matter what violence he committed. At the bridge, one of the Cottonwood Bend Regulators, Will Meriwether, met them. The fair-haired bachelor was riding from town on Judge Bozarth's orders.

"Mister McDonnell, the Judge sent me to warn you that your daughter-in-law is in danger. Those men—"

"Too late," Martin cut him off. "They already have her."

"The Judge is trying to raise the whole town, not just the Regulators, against them. There is a big steamboat tied up at the waterfront, the *Jesse P. Emmick*. We believe the men are holding it there until they get Lucinde on board."

Craig felt a faint flicker of hope. If the steamboat was still moored at Cottonwood Bend, there was a good chance Lucinde's captors were somewhere near, and more likely than not, headed there. The Judge obviously planned to recapture the steamboat, station his forces aboard it and along the riverfront, denying the abductors access to the river.

"How do you know she is not already aboard?" Martin asked.

"She can't be. It hasn't pulled out yet. The Judge heard Bowman order his men to hold it there. Why else would they do that?"

"A diversion?" Martin hazarded.

"What I want to know is how we missed them." Craig mused. "It is about five miles from town to Owen's plantation and another mile to yours. If they are on their way into town, you would think we, or someone else, would have seen them. The river squeezes in and funnels them in toward the bridge."

They crossed the timber structure that Levi Matthews had built after the massive earthquakes of 1811-1812. Hewn from squared yellow poplar logs four feet thick, the main beams were supported by giant log pillars angling upwards from both banks rising above the planks and joined with thick hickory pegs in the middle. The bases of those pillars were anchored in heavy stone. In 1816 Levi added chains to provide additional support. The bridge afforded the only passage across Cottonwood Creek. The abductors must bring Lucinde across it—unless they had a boat waiting upstream.

Craig noticed the big steamboat at the foot of the town landing. It resembled an ornate wedding cake adorned with delicate scroll-work that looked similar to icing. Two giant smokestacks towered high above the water, just forward of the cabins. Without speaking, Martin turned off River Street to tie his horse at the hitching post alongside the warehouse. Craig and Stephen followed his example, realizing that he intended to keep the horses out of harm's way.

Judge Bozarth assembled more than thirty men inside Rosenbotham's Store. Most had attended the recent militia muster, so they understood the rudiments of following commands. This dubious force included the cooper and blacksmith, several local farmers, Rosenbotham, Reverend Kreisle, and Levi Matthews, who was not armed.

"Martin!" Judge Bozarth turned to greet his respected friend. His countenance sank when he saw the old man's face. "I wish to offer my concern and to extend my hand in eternal friendship. I want you to know I am as surprised as anyone."

"No one else in the county was surprised. But then they were not blinded by the brightness of gold and silver. This time you have gone too far! You have hurt your friends, those of us who have tolerated your behavior and cared for you when you went astray."

"Oh, Martin! You have cut me to the quick! As God is my witness, I did not wish for any of this to happen."

"What do you intend to do about it?" Martin demanded. Craig had never seen his father-in-law so angry. He was glad he was not the focus of that icy glare.

"Well, I shall go on board the *Jesse P.* and bargain with the men for your daughter-in-law's return. I will announce that their guarantor is dead, and convince them that there is no justifiable reason for bringing Lucinde to New Orleans."

"They may still decide to hold her as a hostage, and force me and Owen to pay—that is, if Owen lives."

"What happened to him?"

"He suffered a cut to the head while defending his wife and children from the abductors. We need the doctor."

Rosenbotham interjected, "Doc Emmick rode out to deliver a baby early this morning. Said he was headed to the southern reaches of the county and might not be back until nightfall."

"So it is as I feared—the abductors do have them." Judge Bozarth mused.

"They do," Martin confirmed.

"I hoped we might prevent that." The Judge scratched his chin and, after some silent deliberation, began issuing a string of militarily sound orders. First, he dispatched four men to watch the bridge over Cottonwood Creek. Two men were posted at the tobacco inspection station to watch the river in case the abductors brought Lucinde and the children by boat. In addition, they would search the warehouse to make sure the hostage takers were not hiding among the hogsheads of tobacco. Rosenbotham's oldest son, Isaac, climbed up into the store attic where he could peer down from obscurity at the steamboat's upper deck. Other men were stationed downstream, below the *Jesse P.* to guard the western approaches. Finally, the

Judge commanded the whole town to turn out and search homes, shops, stables, outbuildings, sheds, wells and icehouses, to make sure the abductors did not have their captives hidden away. Apparently he wished to eliminate the possibility that Lucinde was already in town, fearing that her abductors would, at the last instant, rush from hiding and board the steamboat, using her and the children as human shields.

"You!" he thundered, pointing at a chubby little merchant no one had seen before. He scowled menacingly and the man tried to duck behind the potato bins, fearful of his anger.

"Me?"

"Yes! You were on that steamer. How many passengers were aboard?"

"Well, the Doctor and his wife were on it. That man over there was."

"You?" the Judge asked.

"Yes."

"How many passengers are on board?" he demanded.

"None now. They chucked us all off."

"How many gunmen were there?"

"Six."

"How many crew members?"

"Eight, plus the captain. There are a few others—cooks, cabin hands and such. All scared to death."

"You have told me all I need to know," the Judge replied. Craig watched as he reached a decision. The Judge began laying out his classic ambush tactics. "I want men spread out all along the riverbank, and for God's sake, keep concealed. You will be fighting professional soldiers and they are armed to the teeth. Make sure of your targets before you shoot. You don't want to hit the captain or crew members. The upper deck planking is paper thin, so make sure you don't kill someone unconnected with this crime!"

"How can we tell who is who?" one citizen asked.

"If they have a gun and they are shooting at you, I guarantee you'll damned well figure it out!" the Judge thundered.

"Oh, that was rich!" Doc commented, laughing.

"When do we open fire?" someone asked.

"When I throw down the white flag of truce."

"That ain't honorable!" another man shouted.

"You are correct! It is because those men are not honorable human beings. They are predators who have swooped in and snatched one of your own, right from your very midst. Next time it could be you! Somewhere out there is a scared young woman—carrying a child, no less—and two scared young ones. If we fail to act, we may never see them again. Owen McDonnell may not survive his injuries. And you *dare* speak to me about honor? We must eliminate the gunmen holding that steamboat. When I give the signal, you will rush the boat and board it. This is our best chance to save Lucinde."

Everyone fell silent as they considered their role in the upcoming battle. Craig did not envy the *Jesse P.*'s captain or crewmembers, for the steamboat was about to become a dangerous place. Trigger happy citizens, untrained in warfare, could not avoid shooting unarmed civilians. Once the firing began, everyone on board the boat would be a likely target.

"Well, it is almost time," the Judge announced.

"I am going with you," Doc offered. "I have spoken with Signet on numerous occasions and was present at his death. I have carried these papers all the way from New Orleans." He turned to Martin McDonnell. "There are many good people in that city. One of them has offered to pay the abductors if they will release her. I bear his letter and seal."

"Delacroix?"

"No, it is Delacroix's young protégé, Philippe Bouchard. Pierre Delacroix is dead—murdered by the man who ordered Lucinde's seizure."

Martin hung his head and made the sign of the cross upon his chest. He and Delacroix had shared much together—from war to grandchildren. Already shaken by the injury of his son and the abduction of his family, news of Delacroix's murder struck an especially hard blow.

"These men must be stopped."

"No better time than the present!" the Judge boomed. He swept his arm at the crowd inside the store. "Move!"

Everyone filed out, crouching low so they could not be seen from the river. They began picking their way toward choice spots—a row of cottonwood trees lining the bank, the limestone outcropping above the steamboat, and a pile of cull bricks heaped near the stables. Some folks ducked inside the combined cooper's and blacksmiths' shop. The long building fronted River Street, but the back wall faced the Ohio. There was a lengthwise gap running between the wall and low roof that allowed forge smoke to escape, and most men planned to stand on something and shoot through it. Craig climbed up into Rosenbotham's warehouse attic and found a small vent through which he could ease his rifle barrel. He surveyed the scene below and counted the guns trained on the steamboat—thirty or more of various makes and calibers.

The Judge stepped boldly out onto Rosenbotham's porch. "Hand me that white flag." The storekeeper had fashioned a crude flag from an old, torn bedsheet and tacked it to a wooden broom handle. The Judge took it from him, shaking out the cloth so it would show. Solemnly he announced, "Let's go!"

Together he and Doc left the store and crossed River Street. The landing fell precipitously away and the *Jesse P. Emmick* loomed below them.

"You in the boat!" Judge Bozarth boomed. "I must speak with Bruce Bowman!" His voice carried clearly on the still autumn air.

"He ain't here, Judge!" a gunman shouted up. Craig could just make him out, standing inside the wheelhouse, holding a pistol on captain and crew. The other gunmen recognized the Judge readily; after all, they had spent the past few weeks riding with him.

"Well, he should be present, for he needs to hear this! May I come aboard?"

"Stay where you are! I can hear you just fine. Say your piece!"

The Judge identified him as Jeff, Bruce Bowman's right hand man, and he announced, "The man who hired your boss is dead." A long silence followed. Two gunmen, one on either side of the *Jesse P.'s* top deck, edged forward, clearly interested in this development. Another gunman, with rifle held ready, stepped out of a doorway on the main deck. The Judge shouted again, "Did you hear me? Your financier is dead."

"That's word-for-word what the steamboat captain told us!" one of the gunmen insisted, his voice unintentionally carrying up to the street. "Do you believe it now?"

"Who's that with you?" Jeff demanded.

"My name is Doctor Thomas Applegate, recently arrived from New Orleans!" Doc replied. "I have Jules Signet's death record, and a letter from Governor Villeré of Louisiana, asking you to stand down. The McDonnell girl is not a slave. I have her manumission papers."

Judge Bozarth continued, "It would be foolish for you to proceed on this course! There will be no money waiting when you reach New Orleans. As militia commander of this district, I am offering you the chance to leave now, free from prosecution. Where is Lucinde McDonnell?"

The gunman, Jeff, stepped outside and leaned out over the brass railing. "You don't think I would make a decision without hearing from Captain Bowman?" Craig laid his rifle sights on the gunman's chest, snugged his cheek against the curly maple stock, and waited. He could feel tension building around and within him.

The Judge pressed on with his negotiations. "I am asking you to appeal to your own common sense and turn the girl over to me."

"She ain't here."

"Where is Bowman?"

"Out ridin' the countryside, I reckon."

"I know where he is. He has gone to snatch Lucinde McDonnell. Do not bother to deny it. I already know—she has been taken from her home."

"Well ain't that just a damned dirty, cryin' shame!" Jeff laughed, aiming his rifle at the Judge. "Now, git!"

The Judge threw down his flag and dragged Doc behind a big,

golden-leafed maple tree. Craig squeezed the trigger and dropped the gunman with a clean shot. After that opening bang, a literal firestorm broke loose. Guns boomed all along the riverbank, peppering the steamboat with deadly crossfire. White wood splinters flew in all directions while whole sections of lacy scrollwork were shot to pieces. Blue smoke fairly obscured the landing. As Craig slid his .50 caliber rifle barrel through the vent, he spied muzzle flashes blooming from various upper cabin doors, and he noticed disconcertedly, several Cottonwood Bend folks falling from well-aimed hits. From his vantage point he spied a gunman taking refuge on *Jesse P.'s* upriver side. Craig lined up his sights and fired. The ball raked the man's spine, knocking him into full view where several citizens finished him off, rifle balls clubbing him into the river. With a well-placed shot, Isaac Rosenbotham brought down another gunmen.

A massive hail of gunfire raked the riverbank. Before Judge Bozarth could signal his men to rush, *Jesse P.'s* paddlewheels began turning, and the big steamboat backed ponderously away from the landing. Black smoke belched from twin stacks and the engine rumbled audibly. The Judge's plan had gone completely awry.

"She's a-gettin' away!" a Cottonwood Bend citizen shouted. Carelessly, he stepped from behind a tree and was shot dead by a gunman on the *Jesse P.* The steamboat chugged backward, well into the deep channel, while Cottonwood Bend citizens traded random shots with the remaining gunmen on board. Craig aimed his third rifle at the steamboat's hull, hoping to hit her at the waterline. The boat was about two hundred yards away and steaming backwards, downstream. As a result, he was a fraction low and his shot hit short, striking water with a powerful splash. He climbed down from the warehouse attic, angry at his miss. Perhaps the ball ricocheted and hit somewhere, but not near the waterline where *Jesse P.* would take on water. Perhaps other shots had struck low enough to create minor havoc. He dodged outside and peered cautiously around the store's front corner. The *Jesse P.* backed downriver another three hundred yards and there held a stationary position, just visible through the trees.

Although the Judge left the cover of his maple tree and others stood unconcernedly in River Street, Craig remained in his protected position in the shaded eastern side of Rosenbotham's Store. He was taking no chances as he leaned his rifles against the orange brick wall and carefully reloaded each one. Martin also occupied a position at the store's corner. He had obviously fired a shot, for he was reloading his rifle.

"How did you fare, Craig?" he asked.

"I killed one and wounded another. Where is Stephen?"

"He volunteered to help guard the bridge at Cottonwood Creek. Bozarth believes they will bring Lucinde in from that direction. I pray she is not on board that boat."

"The Judge doesn't think she is."

"That old fool doesn't know where she is. I shudder to think about all those random shots tearing through that steamboat. Folks were just shooting blindly at it."

"Wonder why they are holding position out there?" He followed Martin into the street, noticing how he kept within the line of cottonwoods edging the waterfront. There they learned that three Cottonwood Bend citizens were killed, five wounded. The New Orleans physician tended to them in the street.

"I told you Lucinde is not aboard the vessel!" the Judge roared triumphantly. "They are waiting for Bowman to bring her in!"

"Good shootin', Craig." Isaac Rosenbotham congratulated him.

"Yes," Bozarth nodded. "Young Ridgeway, I figured it was you up there in the warehouse. You fired the first shot of the battle."

Craig nodded at Isaac. "You did well yourself,"

"Well, we enjoyed clear shooting from up there."

"I suspect we accounted for most of the godless ones," Bozarth hazarded.

"Perhaps three or four," Martin said. "But the boat has gotten clean away. Diplomacy might have served us better."

"Those men cared nothing for diplomacy! They would not even let me on board."

"Still, you might have waited for Bowman to return and tried to reason with him, rather than shoot that boat full of holes." His face froze and he stared beyond the Judge, pointing downstream. "Look, they are up to something!"

Craig saw the big steamboat surging full ahead—upstream—with waves of white water curling under its sleek bow. As he watched, he kept expecting it to execute a turn and head south for New Orleans, but this maneuver did not occur. Smoke billowed from the tall stacks as *Jesse P.* picked up speed. When it drew level with Cottonwood Bend, Martin ducked wisely behind the store, and Craig followed his example. The Judge tugged Doc Applegate behind the big maple in the barest nick of time. Rifle balls tore great shards from its silver trunk. The air sang with whooshing sounds and two rifle balls struck random citizens, producing a chorus of yelps. More bullets thwacked against the bricks of Rosenbotham's store, but by then, everyone had taken cover. The *Jesse P.* passed the giant limestone bluff above the city and steamed out of sight.

"We shall pursue!" the Judge commanded.

"To what end?" Doc asked. "You said yourself they must bring Lucinde here to Cottonwood Bend."

"They may be heading upstream to some other pickup point, perhaps even Louisville. Bowman did mention that city!"

A wave of horror washed over Craig; it was so powerful he was forced to steady himself. Suddenly, sickeningly, he knew where they were heading.

"The landing!" he gasped.

"What!" Martin roared.

"They are headed for Mary's Landing! That is why those men were throwing in rock-weighted ropes and probing with cane poles! They were measuring its depth! It is the closest landing to Cottonwood Bend!"

"You may be right!" Martin exclaimed, startled with the realization.

"I'd bet my last dollar they snatched Lucinde and headed east, clinging to the river bottoms until they made their way to my farm.

They are hidden in those trees near the landing."

"We must inform the Judge!"

Judge Bozarth listened intently as Craig outlined his suspicions. He recoiled when Craig told him about the men mapping his landing. "I do recall Bowman's interest in your landing! By the heavens, I fear you have struck gold! Mary's Landing *is* the nearest serviceable mooring, albeit a remote one. I shall select and lead a force of our best Regulators to your landing. But I must leave a large number of men in Cottonwood Bend, in case the boat returns. That means I must divide our forces."

"You divide them—I am riding ahead!" Craig spun about and sprinted for his horse.

Martin stepped into his path and grabbed his arm. "Craig, you can't charge in there by yourself. Those men are too good. I suspect they are the better half since Bowman is with them. They will shoot you dead."

"They are at my landing, and Mary and the children are alone," he replied.

Martin nodded and turned him loose. "Just be careful. I will try to hurry the Judge along."

——————◆◀—————

Craig reined in when he approached the bridge. Judge Bozarth's men were positioned on the settlement side. Stephen was one of them.

"What is wrong, Craig?" he asked. "We heard shooting in the town."

"You won't like it—the steamboat got away."

"The Judge ordered us not to leave this post. We saw it pass—steaming upriver."

"They are headed to Mary's Landing. We suspect Bowman's men are holding Lucinde there."

Stephen's eyes registered shock. "Should I follow?"

Craig shook his head. "Stay here like the Judge ordered. He should be along shortly. He'll instruct you what to do. I suspect Martin will be riding with him."

"Take care, Craig."

"I will."

He had to nudge Blue forward to cross the bridge. The roan skittered dangerously close to the edge, his hooves clattering loudly on the heavy puncheons. Craig glanced down at the still green waters of Cottonwood Creek covered in bright, multi-colored leaves. Just a hundred yards to his left, the creek debouched into the mighty Ohio River. Indiana's forested hills blazed with autumn colors under a cloudless, achingly blue sky. It was a crisp afternoon, brilliant in every respect, an absurdly incongruous backdrop for such grim human drama. From his vantage point he could see traces of black smoke still hanging on the air. However, the *Jesse P. Emmick* had disappeared from view as it began its northwest turn through the hills.

When he reached the other side, Craig urged Blue into a brisk gallop—not full out, but faster than the lope to which he was accustomed. He fully intended to arrive ahead of the steamboat—and his expectations were well-justified. During the past six years he had ridden atop many of Levi Matthew's timber rafts, guiding them from his landing to Spigot Run where the sawmill was located. He knew from hard-earned experience how long the journey was. If one examined this section of the river on a map, they would describe it as "mushroom-shaped." Martin estimated the large northerly loop at about fourteen miles—a much longer journey than traveling overland. Craig knew that the distance across the "stem" to Mary's Landing, as a crow flies, was just over six miles. Blue seemed to sense his urgency and it took a great deal of strength to restrain him. They galloped around Cemetery Knob and along the tree-covered stretch of road leading to Owen's plantation entrance. Craig slowed to a lope as he neared the house, sliding his rifle forward, ready to use it. The hair stood up on his arms until he was past. Laying the reins onto Blue's neck, he steered him left, past the cooking pit and butchering site and then alongside the barn, keeping in its shadow. He listened for sounds of horses—watching Blue's ears, aware that he might detect them first. They cut across the buff-colored cornfield, recent scene of Owen's corn-shucking party. When they reached the riverbank with its dense canebrakes and tall timber, he slowed to a walk, and after a time, dismounted. Blue was blowing heavily from the run.

"Good horse," he praised. "You are the best!"

Cautiously, he led Blue along the tree line, searching ahead for any movement. When they reached Martin McDonnell's boundary fence, he led the big roan down to the river and allowed him to drink. It was cool under the shade, and the air smelled like old leaves. The countryside was perfectly still, except for the warble of small birds and the occasional cry of a distant blue jay. Craig glanced downstream where he expected to see the *Jesse P.* emerge. The steamboat was nowhere in sight and no telltale smoke heralded its approach. He had beaten it! Upstream, the river bowed sharply, and the far bank concealed his rock landing. Mary's Landing occupied a unique setting, easily recognizable from the river, with limestone pillars on each side flanked by clumps of tall, dark cedars. He reckoned it lay about a mile-and-a-half distant. They climbed back up the steep bank and emerged onto Martin's pasture to follow an old cow path.

In a short time, he reached the boundary fence to his land. This time, he would not jump the gap in the stone wall, nor would he go through the gate. Both sites lay higher up, away from the trees, and each location would expose him to the gunmen's view—if they were down there. Along the riverbank, Martin had not built with stone, choosing instead to construct a fence of split rails. Craig lifted rails from a section and stacked them aside. He led Blue along the river timber and onto his bottomland pasture. They came out in a little half-moon indentation of flat ground surrounded on three sides by trees. The roan lowered his head to nibble at some green fall grass, and in that instant Craig decided to tether him. With his tomahawk he cut a wooden stake and tapped it in deep, tying the reins to it. He hated to leave his trusty mount behind, but would not take him in where he could be shot.

Glancing downriver, he searched for smoke and spied none. He listened for sounds of the steamboat's engine and heard nothing but birds singing. Then he peered upriver, looking for signs of the gunmen. Doubts began to assail him. What if the *Jesse P.* had stopped somewhere else? It would be no great feat for the steamboat captain to pull close to shore and send out a boat for the gunmen and their captives. He closed his mind against those possibilities. He now understood the Judge's burden of leadership—in battle one must make a sensible plan based on evidence at hand, and then try to execute it. It might be the wrong decision, but once initiated, one must cast aside all misgivings and follow through, yet remain flexible to deal with changing conditions. At this moment, the Judge was wisely covering other contingencies and would soon arrive on the scene. Craig knew he must press ahead alone. Carefully he checked and re-primed his weapons. All his senses were heightened as he set out on perhaps the most dangerous undertaking of his life.

The shadows lengthened as he ran softly along the bottomland, staying close to the tall trees. The sun had long ago begun its descent, angling through the branches with that spectacular brightness so characteristic of a Kentucky autumn. Big yellow grasshoppers leaped and flitted among the goldenrods and ironweeds. He smelled overripe pawpaws, old leaves, the cidery tang of fallen crabapples, and the scent of curing tobacco wafting down from his barn atop the hill. He leaped the little creek and ducked into a thick clump of cedars. His landing lay just ahead, about eighty paces away. Abruptly, he crouched down in the tall grass, frozen by a heart-rending noise—the cry of a small child.

Chapter Twenty-Four

The Ohio River

Hoof beats thundered on the Hardinsburg Road as fifteen of Cottonwood Bend's finest galloped toward Mary's Landing. Judge Bozarth led the way on his chestnut mare, comfortable in his saddle and hungry for action. His expensive weaponry seemed like natural extensions of his body. Martin McDonnell followed on his big chocolate-colored mare—his and the Judge's mounts pulled effortlessly away from the others. Calvin Ward followed several lengths behind, trailed by Seth Toler, Gavin Richardson, Carroll Muffett, Jimmy Newton, and Derek Miller. Jan Petersen and young Casey Heath came next, then Stephen McDonnell, who had, under the Judge's orders, allowed Doc Applegate to ride double. Because the others rode poorer mounts, they were strung out behind the main force, but they goaded them onward, not wanting to miss the fight.

At Owen's plantation, the Judge reined in and waited for his Regulators to catch up. When everyone drew round, he had to shout his orders over the blowing horses.

"Men! We shall divide and attack in a two-pronged pincer movement. I will lead a small force through the bottomlands; the rest of you will take the Hardinsburg Road and come in on Craig Ridgeway's lane. Ride past his cabin and barn, then follow the lane down to the river. When you reach the crest, you will see the landing. The abductors will most likely spot you and start shooting. As you are already aware—they are proficient marksmen. Swing out wide when you cross that field. Keep to the trees and approach with caution.

And make damned sure of your targets. Craig is already on site and we soon will be. Don't hit one of us—and for God's sake, do not hit Lucinde McDonnell and the children. The abductors may use them as protection. If you are not sure of your target, do not shoot. I chose you because you are my best fighters and you excelled at this year's muster; you will not be like the townspeople blazing indiscriminately away at a two hundred-foot steamboat. Bear this in mind—if the boat comes in, its upper deck planking is paper-thin."

The Judge chose Calvin Ward, Martin McDonnell, and Jan Petersen to ride with him across the bottomlands, ordering the rest to take the Hardinsburg Road. He made one exception. "Stephen, I want you to convey Doc Applegate to Welcome Hall and have him look in on your brother. He is a trained physician—and from what I saw in Cottonwood Bend, a damned good one."

"What are my other orders?" Stephen asked.

"Keep him and your mother safe."

"With all respect, sir—"

"You will *not* disobey a direct order!" the Judge roared.

"I am sorry, Judge." Stephen stood his ground. "They have taken my sister-in-law, nephew, and niece. I will follow as soon as I can."

The Judge glanced at Martin who nodded his approval. "Very well," he relented. "But keep out of sight as you approach. Make sure you know who you are shooting."

"I will. Thank you, Judge."

The main force of Regulators galloped away. Judge Bozarth turned his mount and led his small band up Owen's lane to take the shortest route across the bottomlands. He led them cautiously past the house to halt behind Owen's tobacco barn. There he laid out his intentions.

"Martin, I chose you because I know you are intimately familiar with the terrain. I want you to guide us in so we will not be seen."

"I can do that."

"Craig is there by now, monitoring the situation. We will ride up and provide support. If all goes as planned, our men will pour over that hill and draw their fire. We will have the gunmen flanked and take them by surprise. We will also gain an advantageous position from which to hit the steamboat—before it reaches the landing. If we can prevent it from pulling ashore, we will frustrate Bowman's scheme. Then, I may be able to negotiate."

"Why not negotiate first?"

"I will try, if conditions allow, but in my experience, the best course is to shoot them all dead—problem forever solved."

Martin shook his head, but did not verbally disagree. "Are you ready?"

"We are."

"Then let's go." The old war hero led them across the cornfield toward the river, well aware how long the afternoon shadows had grown. When they reached the bank, they heard the distant blast of a steamboat whistle—perhaps a mile behind them. Everyone turned at the sound.

"Let us make haste!" the Judge roared.

"Ah, a little scratch like that!" Doc Applegate marveled. "I can't see what all the fuss is about." He tied off the last suture on Owen's scalp. "With that mop of black curls, no one will ever know that someone split your head open. Why, it must be constructed of solid iron!"

Owen repressed a wry grin at the reference to his curly black hair. Agnes was still considerably shaken.

"I must say, Mrs. McDonnell, you have done a splendid job mending him. You should consider taking up nursing!"

"Oh, I am much too old!"

"No, I am serious—your poultice really did the trick. Feeding him broth was a wise decision, but he did not lose as much blood as you feared. A scalp wound always bleeds heavily. It will scare the hell out of you every time, especially if you are not accustomed to it.

But in his case there were no major arteries involved. Quite frankly, I was more concerned about concussion, but his pupils appear normal and he has no weakness on either side of his body."

"Thank God!" Agnes wept.

"Yes, this young man will be fine. Keep him still for a few days and he will be as right as rain."

"I will," she promised.

"Very well. Now, I must go to where folks truly need me."

"And where is that?"

"Mary's Landing," Doc replied.

Agnes shot a worried glance at Stephen as she addressed Doc Applegate. "Why would you be needed there?"

Stephen announced, "That's where the gunmen are holding Lucinde and the children. They are waiting for the steamboat. Pa and Judge Bozarth are headed there now."

Owen struggled to sit up. "I must go too!"

"No!" Doc and Agnes cried in unison.

"Lucinde is my wife! Those are my children. I will not leave their safety in others' hands."

Doc said, "I absolutely forbid it. You could aggravate your condition."

"If my wife and children die, I might as well die too."

"I'll help you saddle your horse," Stephen volunteered, clearly moved.

"Saddle one for me too," Doc sighed. "I came all the way from New Orleans to make sure your family remains safe. Who in the hell am I to tell you no?"

Owen rose shakily. "Is there a good rifle in the house?"

———————◆———————

Craig inched forward through the tall grass with his shotgun and .50 caliber rifles on his back secured snuggly by leather straps.

Wriggling as silently as possible on knees and elbows, he tried not to disturb the grass while keeping the smaller .40 caliber rifle forward, ready for instant use. He had fashioned it the fall of 1810 when he was a gunsmith's apprentice in Lancaster, Pennsylvania—and it was as fine a weapon now as it had ever been. The other rifles were good, reliable guns, and he was comfortable with them, but the Lancaster was his favorite, especially over long distances. In contrast, the stubby, double-barreled shotgun was good for deadly, close-quarter fighting, but it kicked like a mule and threw a wide pattern of shot. He would not use it with Lucinde and the children in the vicinity.

A rotting beech trunk, washed up by some previous flood, blocked his path. It provided ideal cover, mostly concealed by weeds and tall golden grass. Cool shadows lengthened as the sun mellowed and sank lower in the west. Overhead, the sky remained bright blue, and a near-full moon showed clearly, even though it was still daytime. Crickets began chirping, signifying that the afternoon was drawing to a close. Craig wondered where Judge Bozarth and the Regulators were, hoping they would arrive soon. The *Jesse P. Emmick* must be getting close. He knew for certain it was headed for the landing, thankful he had made the right decision. Although he could not see his adversaries, he knew they were there. The child wailed again; Craig recognized her as Owen's youngest.

In the distance he heard the faint shriek of the steamboat's whistle. His heart leaped into his throat. There was not much time left. He lay silent, listening for several moments, before he finally heard the pulsing beat of the approaching engine. The whistle blew again, this time much closer, perhaps a half-mile distant. Just then, he spied movement among the cedars flanking the landing. The gunmen had obviously spread out and sought cover to hide their horses and guard all approaches. Bruce Bowman emerged from the trees, heading away from him. He sat astride a dun-colored horse, leading a giant gray mule with monstrous ears loaded with two sets of bulging saddlebags. Other gunmen appeared from the landing's eastern side. The whistle blew again—this time very close. The engine thump grew louder and hissing steam escaped from pressure valves. *Jesse*

P. Emmick was visible through the trees, smokestacks towering high above a white superstructure and paddlewheels churning the river surface. One could easily hear the sloshing of the buckets.

Shakily, Craig considered his options. If he killed Bruce Bowman outright, the others might abandon the entire scheme. Then again, they might not. There were at least seven men against him, all professional soldiers. They might come at him in a well-rehearsed attack, striking from various angles. The time for decision was upon him. Bowman presented a tempting target, but he would soon disappear, for he was nearing the landing. It seemed wrong, cowardly, to shoot a man in the back, but Craig recalled Judge Bozarth's assessment of the gunmen:

"...those men are not honorable human beings. They are predators who have swooped in and snatched one of your own, right from your very midst. Next time it could be you! Somewhere out there is a scared young woman—carrying a child, no less—and two scared young ones. If we fail to act, we may never see them again."

The heavy pounding of *Jesse P.*'s engine underscored its awesome power. The vessel steamed past where Craig lay and he imagined it lining up to approach the landing. The child wailed again, frightened of the looming monstrosity bearing down upon them. Craig noticed how the mule's ears laid flat. Despite his strength, Bowman was having trouble holding onto it. Thumbing back the hammer of his rifle, Craig aimed and squeezed the trigger. In that instant, the steamboat whistle roared—a double-throated, high-pitched blast. The volume was tremendous and seemed to shake the earth upon which he lay. Bowman's horse skittered sideways just as the flash pan ignited. The rifle fired. Through the smoke Craig saw the big mercenary spill from the saddle, but he knew with dismay that his ball had not struck center. The mule bolted and fled. Two gunmen dashed out from the landing, hoping to catch the stampeding animal. On foot, they stood little chance. They succeeded only in turning it and driving it straight toward Craig's hideout. Someone shouted, "Catch that damned mule! Shoot it if you must!"

The animal tore wildly through the pasture, kicking and bucking in sheer terror, quickly outdistancing its pursuers. Both gunmen knelt and fired as the mule galloped past Craig's hideout. Two shots rang out, accompanied by two meaty slaps. The stricken mule screamed and whirled about. Another well-placed shot bowled it over the riverbank. It cartwheeled messily into a cane-covered fissure before lodging against a shaggy-barked sycamore. Craig shrugged off his weapons, aimed his .50 caliber rifle, and shot the closest gunman before he could reload. There was no doubt about that shot; the man fell dead. Before Craig could fire his third rifle, the other gunman melted into the trees. Several mercenaries crashed toward him through the brush. In true military fashion, they planned to flank him. With sickening dread, he knew there were others approaching he could not hear. He feared to raise his head, for the silent ones would have already taken up positions, ready to shoot.

"Hold on, Craig!" Judge Bozarth's familiar voice boomed like a cannon, rolling across the field behind him. "We are coming!" Craig laid low and worked feverishly to reload his expended rifles. The sound of horses' hooves rumbled behind him. His heart leaped with joy and relief—the Regulators had arrived! They galloped from behind the bend of trees, pulled in toward the bank, and charged toward the sounds of gunfire. Several rifles blazed in unison, all fired from hidden positions. Craig glanced back and saw three Regulators spill from their saddles—one of them was the Honorable Judge Wilfred J. Bozarth. His mare somersaulted in midair and crashed to the ground, reduced in one instant from gallant charger to a heap of inert horseflesh. The Judge was thrown clear into the tall grass. He did not get up. All Craig could see was two fleeing horses and the red belly of the once-magnificent chestnut mare. As he finished loading the rifles, a twig snapped below him on the riverbank. One gunman was very close, just beneath the rim, out of sight. Goosebumps prickled across Craig's arms and neck, and he suppressed a shiver. Abandoning his earlier caution, he reached for his double-barreled shotgun. Lucinde and the children were down at the landing, some sixty yards away. In this instance, he would be shooting in the direction of the river, not toward them.

Two rifle shots cracked behind him. He heard a distinctive slog and the sound of a rolling body below the bank. Another gunman cursed and retreated, crunching through the dry leaves back toward the boat. Craig popped up and spotted another mercenary crouched and aiming at something downriver. He pulled both triggers of his shotgun, dropped the man in a hurricane of lead shot, and ducked behind the log to take up one of his rifles.

"Men are coming down the hill!" Bruce Bowman shouted from on board the *Jesse P.* "Leave it! We are pulling out!"

Craig glanced uphill toward his lane. Although trees partially blocked his view, he glimpsed riders emerging onto the little bottomland field, spreading out and heading at a dead run toward the trees. Gunshots crackled near the landing. Another shot roared behind him.

"Got the bastard!" It was Judge Bozarth. Somehow, he had managed to survive his ordeal and crawl through the grass until he gained cover along the riverbank. He now wriggled up to the beech log where Craig lay, his fine suit coat smeared with dirt and grass stains. Obviously he had taken a hard fall, but seemed little worse for wear.

"What can you tell me, Craig?" He kept his voice low as he reloaded his rifle.

"I shot Bowman, but I didn't kill him. I did shoot two more. One is lying in the grass about halfway to the landing."

"Are you sure he is dead?"

"Oh, yes."

"Are Lucinde and the children there?"

"I heard the young one crying."

"It is as I expected."

The steamboat whistle roared again. Smoke billowed upwards in thick clouds. Clearly, the vessel was about to depart.

"Come on!" Bowman called. "We are pulling out! We have the girl and her children aboard!"

Another rifle shot boomed below the bank.

"Who *is* that?" Craig asked.

"Your venerable father-in-law," he replied. "He hung back and dismounted like the Indian fighter he once was—a wise move on his part."

Craig thought the same thing. It had been foolish for the Judge and his men to charge headlong into such an army. "Are you reloaded?"

"I am."

"Should we move forward?"

"Slowly. Let our Regulators take them. We'll edge along this timber to support them. Martin has the riverbank covered. He killed a mercenary just below this log. I killed another on the run—shot him square in the back. They were all headed back to the boat." Craig felt a little more justified, shooting Bowman as he did.

Jesse P. Emmick backed away from the landing and, when its wheels disengaged, slid sideways until the bow pointed downstream. At that moment the pilot reengaged the engine and *Jesse P.* surged forward. Fruitlessly, Craig searched its decks for a target. In that moment he realized they had lost. It mattered not how much punishment they had inflicted upon the mercenary force; they had failed to rescue Lucinde and her children. Bowman had stashed his captives safely aboard a fast steamboat headed for New Orleans. Nothing on earth could catch him.

"Damn that man!" Judge Bozarth swore, obviously reaching the same conclusion. He rose onto one knee, aimed his expensive rifle, and fired. His ball shattered wheelhouse glass and struck a mercenary who showed his face. The man crashed backward and disappeared from sight. Craig silently commended the Judge for his marksmanship.

The Regulators swarmed over the landing, fanning out through the brush on both sides, searching for dead mercenaries and possible survivors.

"Here's a dead one!" a Regulator shouted.

"And one over here!" called Derek Miller.

"Found a dead'un up in the pasture!" Carroll Muffett announced.

"And another!" someone cried.

Martin's baritone voice carried up to them. "They are all gone. I watched them leave." Craig and Judge Bozarth rose from their hiding place as Martin wended his way through the trees and emerged onto the pasture about forty paces behind them. He approached quickly, taking long, angry strides.

"Well, Judge. You seem to keep closing the barn door after the horse has flown. You have failed us again."

"I have not failed. We shall ride back to Cottonwood Bend this very instant."

"Much good that will do anyone."

The Judge turned away, clearly chastised, not wanting to argue with his friend. He knew full well he had failed, but steadfastly refused to admit it was because of ineptitude. His original plan was sound, relying upon stealth, letting the main force of Regulators first draw the mercenaries' fire. He had planned to sneak in and take Bowman's men in the flank, killing most of them and driving a wedge between them and the river. Three variables changed that plan—the *Jesse P. Emmick* steamed much faster than anticipated; his main force had arrived late, and Craig Ridgeway opened up before he could deploy his marksmen for an ambush. The Judge had felt compelled to support Craig by throwing his men headlong into the fracas, charging in on the gallop, hanging close to the trees. But this decision killed two of his best men—Calvin Ward and Jan Petersen. And it cost him his beautiful chestnut mare. Only Martin McDonnell had kept his head and hung back, dismounting and sneaking up the riverbank, gliding silently among the trees until he found cover from which he could take a calculated shot. He had probably saved his son-in-law with that well-aimed ball.

Judge Bozarth's voice boomed like a cannon across the now-silent field. "Gather round, men!" He waited until they formed a tight circle. "We are returning at once to Cottonwood Bend. Two of you gather up our dead and wrap them in blankets. You must treat them with utmost respect. Bring their rifles and other belongings." Then, he learned that the mercenaries had killed Seth Toler as the Regulators charged down Craig's lane and across open bottomland. He paused for a brief moment of silence and removed his hat. Everyone bowed their heads. Then the Judge continued, "Collect the mercenaries' horses, weapons and personal belongings, and see you deposit them at Rosenbotham's store. There will be no looting! I shall see all items disposed of in the proper manner." Craig understood exactly what that meant. The old reprobate would sell them all and keep the money.

"What about the dead mercenaries and dead horses?" someone asked.

"We shall return later to dispose of them. Hasten now! We must reach town before the boat passes!"

Craig wondered what he planned to do, for *Jesse P. Emmick* was long gone, its paddlewheel buckets throwing surges of white water behind them. The sun dipped behind the limestone hills to the west, throwing shadows over the fields. There was enough remaining light to allow the Regulators to catch the runaway horses and locate their fallen compatriots—and for the Judge to remove his saddle, bridle, and other belongings from the chestnut mare.

"Oh, Lord, what a dastardly deed! I knew the instant she was killed—for I literally felt the life go out of her. She was as dead as a stone before she hit the ground." He wept unashamedly over his beautiful mount. Jimmy Newton brought over Jan Petersen's horse, still saddled and unscathed. The Judge would ride it into town.

As the men dispersed, Stephen and Owen crossed the field, relieved to find Martin unscathed. Their father was equally thankful to see them. He glanced concernedly at Owen. "Son, you don't look so good. You should be at home, taking it easy."

"Not while Lucinde is in their hands," Owen replied.

Martin nodded his understanding. "Don't worry. We will get her back. I am prepared to pay what they ask."

"I have plenty of money."

"I know. Let's get my horse and we'll cut across the pasture, look in on your mother, and join the others when they come down the road."

Craig walked with them to where Martin had tied his chocolate-colored mare. The old man turned and said, "Perhaps I have spoken too harshly to the Judge."

"How so?" Craig asked.

"He could not have prevented this. Both his plans were militarily sound; both required extreme bravery on his part. It took real courage to approach that steamboat when it was moored in town. And again, here at your landing, when his cover was blown, he heard shooting and rode forward to support you. A bit foolhardy, but gallant."

"I was glad when he arrived. He said you did a great job fighting down on the riverbank."

"The truth is, I am far too old for this business. How did the shooting begin?"

"The steamboat was here and they were preparing to board. I had Bowman dead in my sights. I thought I could bring him down and end it all in one shot."

"What happened?"

"Just as I fired, the steamboat whistle roared and scared his horse. The horse skittered sideways and I just winged Bowman. I realize now, it is my fault the mercenaries succeeded."

"Perhaps not. The *Jesse P.* arrived sooner than anyone imagined. It is faster than any boat on the river. You were forced to take that shot."

Craig visualized Bowman spilling from the saddle and concluded that his ball had struck the mercenary's upper left shoulder. He opened his mouth to tell more and immediately shut it, for in that instant he recalled the gray mule breaking away and galloping toward him—a big mule with two sets of heavy saddlebags aboard. They had just passed the spot where it fell. He forced himself not to look over at it.

"Don't blame yourself," Martin said. "Do you want a ride to where you staked your horse?"

"He is not far. I will catch up shortly. Blue has plenty of speed."

While Martin and his sons angled across the pastures toward Welcome Hall, Craig raced on foot across the bottomland to untie Blue. The roan nickered in recognition. "Good horse," Craig praised, patting his neck. He pulled up the stake, took the reins and swung aboard, galloping back to where the mule had fallen. Daylight had faded into darkness. The Regulators had departed for Cottonwood Bend, but he paused for a few moments, searching the field, making sure it was deserted. He listened further for any movement along the riverbank, and heard nothing. The crickets and other night insects sang a reassuring chorus as he dismounted. It was uncomfortably dark under the trees, but he spied the sycamore's white bark and the mule's light gray carcass. He tied Blue's reins to a maple sapling and scrambled down the bank. Tall cane concealed a sandy fissure and he tumbled headlong into it, landing on top of the dead mule. His face hit a smear of congealed blood. With thumping heart, he felt for the saddlebags. He traced the leather straps and fumbled in darkness for a buckle. Somehow, he managed to uncinch the first set and wrench it free. The bags felt impossibly heavy. He found the second set, strapped farther back, and unbuckled it. Again he paused, listening for footsteps or voices, and heard nothing.

The loose sandy soil gave way under his feet, making for a difficult climb. In the end, he realized he could only lug one set of saddlebags at a time. After depositing both sets on flat ground, he risked unbuckling a flap and sliding his hand inside. He felt the smooth surface of metal coins and heard them clink as he stirred his hand. Quickly, he closed and buckled the flap.

It took some effort to hoist and place the first set across Blue's withers. Blue shied at first; perhaps he smelled the dead mule's blood. Certainly he was not accustomed to such weight. Craig draped the second set over the saddle and led him in a light trot up to the cabin, resolving to never again extend him like this.

"Mary!" he called. "Open up! It is Craig!" He halted under the dogtrot, lifted the saddlebags from Blue's back and set them down, patting the horse again. Mary opened the door, set down her shotgun and squeezed him tightly, burying her face in his neck.

"Oh Craig! So many men have ridden by our cabin—it sounded like an army!"

"They were our Regulators."

"I heard terrible bursts of gunfire down by the river. I dared not open the door! We were so frightened!"

"I think all the mercenaries are gone, but they have spirited Lucinde and the children away on a steamboat, the *Jesse P. Emmick*. It is one of the biggest steamboats on the river, and I think the fastest. They are taking her to New Orleans."

"The Judge could not stop them?"

"He tried. The mercenaries killed three of our Regulators in town and three more down below."

"And they got clean away?"

"Not exactly. There were thirteen of them when the fighting began. I believe we killed eight, possibly more—and wounded others. But they got who they came for."

"What will you do?"

"The Judge ordered us all to meet him in town."

"I do not understand. How can he hope to stop the steamboat?"

"He can't." Craig appreciated the Judge's efforts, but realized that he—all of them—were pitted against an unstoppable adversary. "We may have to ride south to New Orleans. Or we could wait for another boat. It is the fastest way to travel."

"But steamboats come so rarely. And the river is so low this time of year. Nothing is coming over the falls at Louisville. It could be days, weeks, or even months."

"I realize that, but I must ride into town to see what can be done. In the meantime would you please count what is in these saddlebags and stash it all under the floor in our secret hideaway?" Mary's eyes opened wide as he dragged in the two sets of saddlebags. "I need to ride into town now."

"The cows desperately need milking."

"You may do that when you have hidden the money."

"Is it safe to go outside?"

"I believe so. But keep the shotgun with you. I'll be back as soon as I can."

"Be careful, Craig."

The children gathered round and they all embraced in a family hug before he left. Once again, he was setting out on a dangerous enterprise—a worthy one, but one that might prevent him from returning home to live out his life with the family he loved. He thought about the six local men who died that day—he knew most of them—and he realized it could have been him, Martin, Stephen, or Owen. Lucinde and her children were family and they desperately needed his help. He welcomed his obligation to them. That was what family was all about. It seemed such a shame evil men could disrupt good folks' lives. He now understood Judge Bozarth's lifelong commitment to making others safe, and realized what it meant for citizens to work together to ensure that safety.

The Ohio River

The engine pounded mightily as *Jesse P. Emmick* built up speed. Bruce Bowman fought to ignore his shoulder wound. The rifle ball had torn through muscle and nicked his shoulder blade, but the injury was negligible. Two neat holes indicated that the ball had passed clean through. He drank whiskey from a tin cup and peered ahead into the night. The Ohio River lay like a bed of quicksilver, marking the route west and south. By any standards, events had played out miserably. The steamboat's arrival was a fortunate occurrence, but it had brought that doctor from New Orleans, and it was he who sounded the alarm. That could not have been foreseen. In truth, he had grossly underestimated Judge Wilfred J. Bozarth, viewing him as a malleably pompous, over-greedy fool, and it cost him the lives of eight men. Only five of his thirteen mercenaries remained, and three of them were wounded—including himself. Five could still accomplish this mission—the problem was, the men were approaching a state of mutiny. All of them argued with him, something completely out of character. He decided to hear them out, let them vent. He listened to two of them now. One mercenary held his guns on the crewmen below, ensuring they kept the furnaces stoked with wood. One more guarded Lucinde and her children.

"I'm tellin' you, cap'n sir, the Judge said our money man in New Orleans is dead. Said there would be no payment when we get there."

"How do you know that is true?"

"There was a New Orleans doctor with him who claimed he carried the official death record. He also said the girl ain't a slave at all—had her freedom papers with him."

"Yeah," the other one growled. "He also bore a letter from the Governor of Louisiana, tellin' us to stand down."

"Did either of you see the papers, letter, or death record?"

"I didn't let 'em on board."

"Perhaps you should have."

"Now we have no money. That mule got clean away with all of our plunder."

"I have plenty of gold and silver on my person. We have gunpowder and lead to force our passage to New Orleans. And, as long as we have the hostages, no one can touch us."

"I think we should put 'em all ashore at the first opportunity."

"You do?" Bowman asked. "Well, you should realize that the woman and her children are worth their full weight in gold, perhaps more. Old man McDonnell and his son are filthy rich—you saw them! I guarantee they will pay a fortune for her return. I will demand twice what Signet offered for her. And consider this—there are far fewer men to split it among."

This argument struck home. They knew that Bowman always paid—he had never let them down. They lapsed into a sullen silence. With some relief, Bowman recognized their acceptance. They would remain loyal, as they had earlier that day, against impossible odds. On his orders, they had held the steamboat at Cottonwood Bend, executing the ruse that gave him time to seize Lucinde and her children. They fended off a massive attack and, despite fearful losses, forced the captain to steam upriver to Mary's Landing.

"Go below and spell the others," he ordered. "Send them up here so I may speak with them." As soon as he said it, he realized how thinly spread they were. In addition to preserving the morale of his depleted force, he must hold his two pistols on *Jesse P.*'s captain, just to keep him at the wheel. It was shaping up to be a long two weeks. To make things worse, the captain was rebelling.

"I'm telling you, it is unsafe to travel at night," he grumbled. "We'll run up on a sandbar—or worse, a snag. If we rip our bottom out, we're done for."

"You just keep heading downriver, or I'll blow your brains out."

"Then who would steer? You don't know this river like I do."

"There is plenty of light."

"It is four days off full moon. "It's not safe steaming under a full moon, especially when the water is this low."

"Is it that low?" Bowman asked.

"Lower than I can remember. It is dangerous even in the day-time—boats run upon snags all the time. We should put in to shore, at least until sunup. "

"Enough talk—you will maintain this speed until we pass Cottonwood Bend. Then I will consider what we should do."

———◆———

Craig arrived in Cottonwood Bend shortly after *Jesse P. Emmick* had steamed full-speed past the town. It seemed impossible that it could have already gone by; then, he remembered—the boat was traveling downriver, its steam power aided by the current, however sluggish. The whole town was heavily armed and in an uproar. Martin and Stephen were down at the water's edge; they and two Regulators struggled to restrain a distraught Owen who was screaming and crying like a madman.

"What happened?" Craig asked an onlooker.

The reply was chilling. "When Owen McDonnell saw that steamboat comin', he tried to take Rosenbotham's ferry boat. He didn't stand a dog's chance, for the *Jesse P.* was goin' like hell afire, flames shootin' out of both smokestacks and engine a-poundin'. If those men had spotted him, they would have shot him dead. McDonnell ran down to stop him. It took four men to wrestle Owen out of that boat."

"Oh my God!" Craig croaked. His brother-in-law was usually so quiet, given more to thoughts than words. He choked back a sob as he tied his horse at the side of Rosenbotham's warehouse. Folks quietened down as Judge Bozarth made the ponderous descent to offer his official words of comfort. Craig followed tentatively, not knowing what to expect.

"Son, I want you to know that I will employ all my powers—as militia commander and Kentucky State Representative, to get your wife and children back. We shall apprehend the abductors, even if it means traveling to New Orleans with a letter from Governor Slaughter. I shall ride to Frankfort—"

"Judge, shut your pretentious mouth!" Owen barked. "They are gone! You helped those men learn everything about us. You made the job easy for them." He broke down, sobbing as if his heart would break. Martin laid a hand upon his shoulder, his face contorted in agony. Stephen wept unashamedly. The crowd watched the scene of despondency in silence, every one of them sympathizing.

"Son, I did not realize their intent."

"You escorted them around the county so they could plan their best avenue of escape. We will never catch them!"

"That may not be necessarily true, young man." Everyone turned to look at the newcomer, Doctor Thomas Applegate, who pointed upriver with an elegant ebony-wood cane. "If my eyesight does not fail me, I *do* believe that is another steamboat."

A hundred pairs of eyes followed the direction of his cane. Everyone uttered a gasp of incredulity. A tower of shimmering yellow lights emerged from around the eastern bend, moving downriver with a steady speed—still a mile distant, but coming fast. In the moonlight the townsfolk could just make out the stark lines of the upper deck and pilothouse of a steamboat. No one had ever seen two steamboats traveling in such proximity, and certainly not at night—even during high water. It was so improbable, it had to be a miracle.

"To the ferry boat!" Judge Bozarth boomed.

Craig beat him to it, hopping in and taking his position at the oars. The Judge, due to his considerable weight and size, experienced more difficulty climbing in, and he rocked the boat dangerously. Several of his Regulators stepped forward to assist him. When he was seated, they ran into the river, shoving the boat outward with a powerful thrust. Craig began to row. His friend Levi Matthews had built this boat. The oars were secured in circular oarlocks and there was a solid wooden support against which he could brace his feet. This enabled him to use his entire body—arms, shoulders, back, legs, and feet—in a concerted effort.

"Oh, dear Lord!" the Judge prayed aloud, his hands raised in a gesture of supplication. "Give young Ridgeway the strength of ten Samsons! Let the captain of this fair vessel see us, and lay it upon his heart to stop and render aid!"

Craig grunted with effort as he dipped the blades into the water and pulled with all his might, over and over again—broad strokes that bit deep. The ferry boat surged ahead with each stroke. Sweat popped out on his body and little rivulets ran down his face. He worked the oars in a flat, circular motion and felt the fibers of his muscles burning from the intense effort.

"Row, my good fellow! Row as if your very life depends upon it!"

Craig kept up the brutal pace, watching the Kentucky shoreline shrink with increasing distance. He dared not look around, but he reckoned they had crossed more than half the river. By studying the Judge's face, he could partially gauge their success.

"Row, young Ridgeway! Row! The captain intends on passing close to the Indiana shore! If we miss this opportunity, Lucinde and the children truly are gone!"

Craig glanced sideways and saw the steamboat, a sidewheeler, gleaming white in the moonlight, bearing downriver with impossible speed, twin smokestacks belching black smoke. The yellow lights glowed brighter, and the boat seemed to grow taller as it neared them. Craig redoubled his efforts and he pulled harder, his breathing exploding in harsh grunts.

"Oh, no! We have missed them!" the Judge cried.

"Fire your pistol!" Craig gasped.

The Judge pulled a rosewood dueling pistol from his belt and fired it in the air. It flashed brilliantly in the growing darkness. Craig could hear the pounding of the great pistons and the hissing of steam as the leviathan approached, its paddlewheel buckets churning. He continued pulling, even though he felt his lungs would burst. The Judge fired his second pistol and shrugged frantically out of his coat. He tried to stand, but thought better of it when the boat began rocking. From a sitting position, he waved the coat and shouted, his bellowing roar carrying clearly over the pounding. Craig reckoned that only the Judge could roar louder than a steamboat engine. The captain laid on his whistle to signify he had seen them. The pounding ceased as paddlewheels disengaged and a great gush of steam escaped from the valves. Craig realized that the boat was stopping— they had intercepted it! He stopped rowing, his heart pounding like the steamboat's engine as he inhaled and exhaled great gasps of air. He imagined fate was repaying him for driving Blue so hard. They continued drifting toward the sleek steamer and soon bumped alongside, just ahead of the enclosed paddlewheels, riding up and down on the giant waves of the steamboat's wake. Crew members used hooked poles to hold them steady. Craig sprang onto the low deck just a foot-and-a-half above the river. The Judge's disembarkation proved much more difficult, but after a considerable struggle, the crew members managed to haul him on board. They secured Rosenbotham's ferryboat to a side rail and watched with interest as the Judge slipped on his suitcoat, slicked back his mane, adjusted his cuffs and replaced his broad-brimmed hat.

"I must speak with your captain on a point of extreme urgency!" Judge Bozarth demanded.

"First thing he'll want to know is—can you pay?"

"How dare you ask such a question!" the Judge blustered. "Take me to him at once."

"We oughta toss you into the river!" a crewman growled and stepped forward.

Craig watched the Judge adopt the mien of a berserker, his great white teeth flashing in the moonlight, eyes bulging glassily. He drew and cocked his pistols, both recently discharged, and pointed them directly at the crewmen. They backed down immediately. "I am Judge Wilfred J. Bozarth, Attorney-at-Law, Kentucky State Representative, and Commander of the Cottonwood Bend Militia. I have no time to bandy words with the likes of you."

Just then, a silver-haired gentleman called down from the upper deck. "What can I do for you, sir?"

"Are you the captain of this vessel?"

"I am Captain Lafe Fortescue. "Welcome aboard the *J.D. Estes*."

———————●———————

Almost all of Cottonwood Bend turned out to view the majestic steamer as it pulled in to shore. For the McDonnells, its arrival was a miracle from God. The steamboat made a splendid sight, luminescent in the moonlight with lanterns glowing at regular intervals beneath the awnings, and yellow light spilling from various cabins. It looked gigantic, perhaps taller than *Jesse P. Emmick*. No one had ever seen a steamboat close up at night, and no one recognized the *J.D. Estes*—they figured it had been recently launched.

As soon as the crew members ran out the gangplank, Judge Bozarth commanded his Regulators to board. A half dozen answered his call.

"Now, see here!" Fortescue roared. "This was not part of our bargain."

"Regrettably, our bargain has changed!" the Judge retorted. "I am commandeering this vessel for the purpose of apprehending a gang of savage abductors and murderers. In addition to seizing one of our fairest young mothers—for reasons unknown to us—they have killed a half dozen of our finest citizens. We shall depart as soon as possible."

"You have no legal right to impose your problems upon me and my crew!" the captain protested. "I will report you to the law."

"I *am* the law!"

"The shipbuilders and investors will hold me responsible for delays or any damage to their cargo."

"You are not to fear. As a Kentucky State Representative, I shall see you are generously recompensed." Craig knew this was in all likelihood an empty assurance, but he admired how cleverly the Judge pulled it off.

Several more Regulators, perhaps fifteen in number, boarded with rifles and leather satchels. Guiltily, Craig remembered his horse and spare weapons. He asked Judge Bozarth, "May I take Blue to the stable? He is tied up at Rosenbotham's warehouse and I want him cared for. I also wish to fetch my other weapons."

"Hurry along, young Ridgeway. You have a little time before we depart. I am waiting on a few more of my men." Craig dashed up the cobblestone slope, still lightheaded from his herculean feat of rowing. He untied Blue and led him onto River Street, crossing well behind the crowd of onlookers. Fortunately, the stable lay nearby, and the owner took Blue into his care. When Craig returned to the *J.D. Estes*, Martin and Stephen were helping Owen aboard. The young man looked wobbly on his feet, and fresh blood seeped through his bandages. Doc Applegate directed them into the main saloon.

"What in hell's name happened to him?" a deckhand asked.

"Saber-cut on his own lawn by the predators who stole his wife and children!" Judge Bozarth roared. "They left him for dead!"

"Damn! They must be awful."

"They are the worst sort of humanity."

The Judge and two Regulators took up positions near the pilothouse. Craig climbed up to join them. Fortescue had seemingly resigned himself to his fate, but he did he not like it. He protested volubly, "This river is dangerously low, and fraught with all sorts of hazards—sandbars, snags, hidden rocks—all of which could tear the bottom out of this lovely vessel."

"That did not seem to bother you before."

"I was just looking for a place to anchor."

"Sure you were," the Judge raised a disbelieving eyebrow.

"This boat is brand new—just off the stocks in Cincinnati."

"Cincinnati, you say?" The Judge looked even more skeptical.

"Yes."

"Then how did you get this vessel across the falls in this low water?"

"The builders constructed the hull and installed boilers and engine in Cincinnati and, in anticipation of low water, sent her over the falls during the June rise. We completed the superstructure in Shippingport and spent September below the falls, mostly on the Indiana side, amassing cargo to transport to New Orleans. You interrupted us on our maiden voyage to New Orleans."

"My apologies."

"We simply cannot risk sinking this boat. It would be wise to wait until morning so we can more clearly spot the dangers."

"But if *Jesse P. Emmick* chooses to steam all night, Lucinde's abductors will build an insurmountable lead. As things stand, we will never catch such a fast boat. And each hour we delay, we leave that poor woman in the hands of those foul monsters."

"*Jesse P. Emmick*, you say?" Fortescue muttered something to himself, perhaps a curse word, and he cast his eyes westward, downriver.

"That is the steamboat upon which they hold her." In a prescient flash, the Judge, who prided himself on understanding human nature—if one did not count Bruce Bowman—recognized his adversary's weakness. Up and down the western rivers, steamboat captains prided themselves on the speed and maneuverability of their vessels, and they bragged incessantly about their piloting skills. It was a humiliating blow to one's reputation to lose a race to a rival. "Of course, it is apparent that *Jesse P.* is the product of superior craftsmanship—it is certainly a bigger vessel, and I am willing to bet the engines are more powerful."

"Like hell they are!"

The Judge chuckled easily, "When it steamed by here, *Jesse P.* was going like an angel from hell, smokestacks blazing, water curling from the bow. No one here has seen a faster ship."

"The *J.D. Estes* can outrun it."

"Poor man, you suffer from delusions of grandeur."

"I know for a fact we are faster. Our engines are exactly the same size and of the same construction."

"That makes you equal at best. Your boat is noticeably smaller."

"Precisely—*Jesse P.* is a hundred and fifty-two feet in length and two hundred twenty tons. We are a hundred and forty-one feet long and a hundred seventy tons."

"So?"

"*Jesse P.*'s engines must push much more tonnage through the water—fifty tons to be exact. We are a smaller, narrower boat, outfitted with the same high-pressure engines. Our length-to-beam ratio is greater; that also helps make us faster. What is more, our paddle-box enclosures are better angled to reduce water resistance, and the curved guards will shed logs and debris that might damage the buckets. I am telling you, we *can* catch that boat."

"But you just enumerated a dozen dangers why we should not travel at night," the Judge pointed out.

"We enjoy another advantage over *Jesse P.* that makes the risk worth taking—our draft is shallower. Both boats are side-wheelers and share similar features, but *Jesse P.* draws six feet of water; we draw just three. Our shipbuilders boast we can steam across dew-covered grass. They constructed the *J.D. Estes* to ride *on* the water, not in it."

"We shall see. Perhaps events will prove you correct."

The last Regulators arrived, two marksmen Judge Bozarth had summoned from the countryside. They handed their horses' reins to folks they knew and ran down the cobblestone landing. As soon as they crossed the gangplank, Captain Fortescue laid on his boat whistle. The great engine began to pound and the paddlewheels reversed. Slowly *J.D. Estes* backed out into deeper water. In a few moments, they were steaming downriver, readying their weapons, and themselves, for confrontation. Fortescue intended to prove his new steamboat and piloting skills superior. The Regulators itched for another fight; this was more excitement than they had encountered in years. Martin McDonnell, Owen, Stephen and Craig were wholly committed to rescuing Lucinde and children; everything else was secondary. Judge Bozarth—while fully intending to restore the captured family to their home—had a score to settle.

"Now, we shall see who the fool really is," he muttered darkly, checking the load on his rifle and reloading his rosewood pistols.

Chapter Twenty-Five

The Ohio River—J.D. Estes

Shortly after darkness closed in, the temperature plummeted with alarming swiftness. Craig decided it was much colder out on the river. He shivered miserably in his homespun shirt as he scanned the surface for snags and sandbars. Captain Fortescue ordered his negro cook to brew several pots of fresh coffee. The hot drink warmed and revitalized the men. Twenty-two Regulators, mostly from Cottonwood Bend and the surrounding countryside, had answered the call to arms. The scales of justice seemed to tilt somewhat in the Judge's favor, at least numerically. Mile after mile, the steamboat pounded onward; still, they raised no lights or other trace of *Jesse P. Emmick.* As the moon rose higher, its light brightened, rendering both shorelines visible. Martin McDonnell joined the Judge's small party near the pilothouse. Later, he came forward to stand by Craig at the rail. Wisely he had stopped in at Welcome Hall to don a coat.

"See anything?"

"Not yet. The river is as still as a millpond. I am not sure that is a good thing. How is Owen?"

"The New Orleans doctor, Applegate, is with him. He stopped the bleeding and re-bandaged Owen's head. I am not yet sure about him."

"They say he traveled all the way from New Orleans to warn the Judge about Bowman."

"I am sure there is more to his story, but I am grateful to him."

"How do you like this steamboat?"

"I never thought I would ride on one," Martin grinned wryly. "Especially not under these circumstances." On another occasion Craig knew he would have loved it. Martin pointed to the men down on the main deck. Some were rolling heavy hogsheads of pressed tobacco and positioning them along the bow and outer rails. Others wrestled with compressed bales of hemp sacking and barrels of whiskey. Still others built fortifications from firewood already stacked upon the deck. "What are those men doing?"

Craig replied, "The Judge has ordered them to set up a barricade—for two reasons. First, *Jesse P.'s* planking is almost paper-thin. Our men need solid protection from which to shoot."

"What is his second reason?"

"He wants us concealed until the very last instant. That way we will not alarm the gunmen. The Judge plans for us to board *Jesse P.* and take them all in one massive ambush."

"It sounds feasible—if everyone keeps their head and remembers that Lucinde and my grandchildren are on board."

From the pilothouse, Captain Fortescue roared his displeasure. "You can't shift the cargo like that! A slight list could do irreparable damage to the boilers."

"Then order your crew to compensate," the Judge snapped.

"I do not wish to have this cargo damaged in a gunfight."

"Better they hit it than your dainty little boat. Think about it—if my men are shooting from behind cargo, they will draw fire away from the superstructure. It may impact your trade goods somewhat, but you will be selling it all in New Orleans. None of your investors need know you engaged in a gunfight."

"Please, do not call this boat 'dainty.' *J.D. Estes* is one of the toughest steamboats on the Ohio."

"Hah!" laughed the Judge. "Try taking this gewgaw out onto the Gulf of Mexico. The first playful wave would smash it into thousands of pieces. Why, folks ashore would be picking up stove wood for the next five years!"

"At another time I would ask you to withdraw that statement," Fortescue hissed. "It is plain you know nothing about steamboats."

"I know enough—even a blind man could see *Jesse P.* has left you in its wake!"

"Not for long."

A crewman climbed up to replace Craig at the pilothouse rail. Gratefully, Craig relinquished this position and moved sternward. Martin followed. They took cover behind the giant port smokestack and enjoyed the heat emanating from it. High above them, ahead of the smokestacks, stars twinkled in limitless darkness.

"You reckon we are far behind them?" Craig asked.

"It is hard to say," Martin replied. "The other boat looked very fast."

"But Captain Fortescue claims he has the same-sized engines driving a much smaller boat. His 'faster speed' arguments make good sense."

"The Judge sure is goading him. To say the *Jesse P. Emmick* is a better boat is much like casting indirect disparagement on a mother's child. Fortescue feels he must prove his boat's worth and defend his reputation. That puts us all in danger."

"At least he claims we have a much shallower draft. He believes *Jesse P.* should run aground before we do."

"I hope he is correct."

Craig took a moment to observe the clean lines of *J.D. Estes* and to appreciate its proportional beauty. It was a handsome craft, glistening white, ornamented with brass railings, elaborate scrollwork, rectangular paddle-boxes arched in the centers to accommodate the circular wheels, and curtained passenger cabins spaced along the upper deck. From his elevated position, he could see bow and stern, port and starboard, and he noted how the main deck flared gracefully outward to provide practical breadth amidships. Twin side-by-side smokestacks rose high above the top deck, and great volumes of black smoke erupted from the chimneys. The steamboat seemed almost alive as it propelled them downstream at frightening speed. Craig watched water churn behind the great paddlewheels, fascinated by the long waves rolling toward both shores.

The Judge appeared beside them. "Craig, will you help the crew take down those lanterns? We don't need them for navigation, nor do we wish to announce our presence any sooner than we should."

"Yes, Judge," Craig agreed.

There were dozens of glass and tin contraptions hung from the awning supports and rails. While Craig and *Jesse P.'s* crew members swarmed up and down ladders to snuff them out and take them in, Judge Bozarth ordered all cabin lights doused. Then he commanded, "Pass the word. I want all Regulators in the saloon—immediately."

In a short time, armed men filed in, leaving doors and windows open to admit the bright moonlight. Craig could just make out Judge Bozarth's figure in the near darkness, but the deep bass voice rang to every corner of the room, charged with urgency. This was the crucial meeting before the battle—everyone would hear the same instructions at the same time, so they would act with one accord. The Judge still employed his usual eloquence, but spoke straight and to the point.

"Men, I want to thank you for answering my summons. It is never easy to leave home and family to fight for someone else, but I know you understand that one day you could suffer a similar calamity, and you might need the help of your fellow citizens. You realize we face an armed force of extremely dangerous men—skilled mercenaries, the lot of them. This afternoon they killed six of our finest citizens and abducted Owen McDonnell's wife and children. We shall bring these monsters to justice. But bear this in mind— there are innocent hostages aboard. I ask you to make certain of your targets and to take no unnecessary actions that would endanger their lives. Our primary objective is to return mother and children safely to their home. "

"Are we a-gettin' close, Judge?" a Regulator asked.

"We could overtake the *Jesse P. Emmick* at any moment. The vessel may be just around the next bend. I wish for all men to hear my instructions and take them to heart. Lives depend upon your actions."

Craig listened carefully as Judge Bozarth outlined his deadly plan, awe-struck at its boldness and relative simplicity. Martin nodded thoughtfully and his expression showed that it might just work. On the surface it seemed brilliant—as long as conditions turned out the way the Judge envisioned. The Cottonwood Bend Regulators would have to execute his plan without flaw.

The Judge continued, "It is damp down here on the river. After you take up your positions, I want you to re-prime your flash pans. Cover them and your muzzles snugly with a dry cloth. Check your loads. We will need every gun for this plan to succeed. Any questions?"

No one asked, for the instructions were crystal clear.

The Ohio River—Jesse P. Emmick

They began as ghostly wisps in the wee morning hours, but these phenomena soon mushroomed into writhing, misshapen wraiths, expanding rapidly in height and breadth. Both shorelines disappeared as a heavy fog rose from the river's warmer surface. Shortly before dawn, the air turned as thick as pea soup, and men could not see from pilothouse to jack staff. Fog beaded heavily on the few remaining glass panes, water dripped copiously from brass railings, and continual condensation rendered the deck slippery underfoot. Bruce Bowman did not protest when the captain shut down *Jesse P.*'s mighty engine and disengaged the paddlewheels. They crept slowly forward, groping blindly in the darkness.

"That's it," the captain said. "Shoot me if you must, but not another mile until this fog lifts."

"Why don't you shut up?" Bowman groused. "Anyone can see that further travel is impossible. Just keep up a good head of steam for the instant we can proceed."

The night passed miserably. His wound had stiffened, making the smallest movement painful. Lack of sleep added to his irritation; twice he caught himself drifting off in an oppressive shroud of pain and fatigue far more encompassing than the fog outside. His men worked out a practicable schedule of shifts—one guard for the captain, one to watch the captives, and two to guard the crew. One gunman remained free to enjoy a brief respite; after that, they would rotate positions. They drew straws for first break. Bowman drew second straw. He hoped that sleep would clear the cobwebs of fatigue and allow him to think more sensibly.

When his break finally came, he shuffled tiredly along the top deck and into the main saloon; there he smashed a locked cabinet, helped himself to a jug of whiskey, drank a few medicinal slugs, and collapsed onto one of the long couches set against the paneling. The heavy hand of fatigue crashed upon him, plunging him into a deep sleep. For that reason he did not feel or hear the soft crunch as *Jesse P. Emmick* coasted gently to rest upon a midstream sandbar. Although dragging two anchors and drifting slowly, the boat's momentum shoved it deeper into the bar and the deck canted slightly to starboard. The mighty steamboat was stuck fast.

The captain ordered his crew to take immediate action. One ducked below and forward to inspect the hull. Another tossed more anchors astern, working the bottom, hoping to find solid purchase so they could haul *Jesse P.* backward off the sand. Yet another two crewmen moved along the main deck, probing the sandbar with long poles. Damage assessment came back in a flurry of reports.

"We're grounded solid, portside!" one deckhand claimed.

"Dry as a mouse's ear below!"

"Can't find suitable anchorage astern—bottom's just mud and sand!"

"Then tomorrow morning we shall send a boat ashore and tie to a big tree," the captain decided. "We'll use the windlass to pull her off."

"Aye-aye, Cap'n."

"We may try reversing the paddlewheels. Please check to see they are clear."

Sometime later, the report came back, "Port wheel's dug deep into the bar. I wouldn't risk it tonight."

"Very well," he sighed.

"What'll we do now, Cap'n?"

"We'll wait until daybreak—when we can see."

The Ohio River—J.D Estes

Dawn came late to the river, delayed by the milky curtains that clung heavily to the bottomlands. Although the mist brightened somewhat, the men on board *J.D. Estes* could do nothing but peer hopelessly downstream and wait for the sun's rays to burn off the fog. On Judge Bozarth's orders, the negro cook fried up giant platters of bacon, eggs, apples, and cornbread—and he prepared pots of steaming hot coffee. The Regulators lined up for more. When Captain Fortescue complained, the Judge advised, "Write up an invoice and I shall deliver it to Frankfort."

Martin raised a skeptical eyebrow and sipped on his hot coffee. Craig repressed a smile and shook his head. He glanced around the saloon. Almost all the men had managed to snatch some sleep and this seemed to renew their vitality. Judge Bozarth had requisitioned a private cabin and slept on a comfortable bed, rising early to order hot water for a bath and shave. This was readily obtained from the ship's steam pipes. While he bathed, crew members sponged and pressed his suit coat and trousers, so he appeared at breakfast clean and completely refreshed. Owen and Stephen still slept in the saloon, but both woke to the aroma of steaming black coffee.

"How are you faring, young man?" the Judge inquired as he helped himself to a plate of bacon and eggs.

"I'm better, Judge." Owen replied. He sat up, unaided. "I apologize for my harsh words last night. I should be thanking you for what you are doing."

"No apology necessary, my good fellow. I am pleased to see you on the mend. None of us wanted this. I shall try my hardest to get your loved ones back."

Doc Applegate examined his patient, checking his eyes first, one pupil and then the other. He inspected the wound, still a dreadful looking slash, crisscrossed with black sutures and clotted with blood. Satisfied, he joined the line for hot coffee. The Regulators talked quietly among themselves, enjoying the breakfast. They appeared relaxed, but ready for battle. The Judge cleaned his plate before addressing them once more.

"Men, I ask you to review your instructions from last night. You should recheck your loads, especially your pans. Re-prime if you must, for it was an extremely damp night." He paused meaningfully before continuing. "Remember, stealth is our key to victory. You will remain completely hidden until you hear my command. Take cover behind the deck fortifications and do not, under any circumstances, let them see you. When we approach, think of these rules— no talking, no coughing, no smoking, no movement of any kind. For those non-combatants here, I suggest you go below. This is about to become a dangerous place. The side planking on this deck will not stop a rifle ball—if you stay here, you are apt to be killed. You may climb into the hold or perhaps take refuge on the main deck behind the cargo. Now I must speak to Captain Fortescue and his crew. They may be able to help us achieve total victory."

Craig doubted how unarmed crew members could help, but when the Judge asked him and Martin to follow, he figured he might just learn. As they made their way forward, Craig heard the distant chirping of a bird on shore. High overhead, a patch of blue sky was visible above the white layer of mist. A pale, rose-gold ray of sunlight angled in from the east. The fog was breaking up.

Fortescue's mood did not improve when they entered the pilothouse. He looked even more ill-tempered when the Judge announced cheerily, "Well, well! It appears the fog is finally lifting. We may soon resume our blessed mission of mercy."

"Yes, and my boat and cargo will be shot all to hell!"

"Perhaps not!" the Judge contended. "A couple of likely options exist where you and your crew could prevent that."

"I'm listening," Fortescue grumbled.

The Judge laid out the possible scenarios. Craig and Martin listened and then stared at each other in disbelief. Fortescue's surly expression changed slowly to one of conspiratorial interest. As captain he felt entitled to play a role in the attack. He liked what he heard, and he liked even more having some control in the matter. Of course he lodged objections, but the Judge was on his home turf, explaining how each phase of the attack would transpire, and how the captain and crew could help.

Fortescue's arguments grew successively weaker and finally he lapsed into silence. Then he asked the all-important question. "Do you really believe it will work?"

"No other outcome possible!" the Judge assured him, full of his old braggadocio. "And, if you execute your part as I instructed, we will rescue the girl and you shall be famous up and down the river. I'll even stand up on the Kentucky House Floor and recommend you for a commendation!"

With startling swiftness, the sun hit them with the full brilliance that could only come from a transparent, mid-autumn sky. The fog seemed to dissipate all at once, rising into the warming air. In a few moments the great sweep of the Ohio River stretched before them.

"Haul in all lines!" Fortescue commanded. "Build up a good head of steam so we can finish this business!"

———◆———

Craig felt relieved to see the Judge's old demeanor returning. The Judge had clearly set aside self-reproach, shaking off his two previous defeats, concentrating wholly on the upcoming battle. He spoke with renewed authority, sounding and looking stronger, more sure of himself. Somehow, the opportunistic rogue sensed that events were turning his way and would continue to do so. By the greatest stroke of luck, or possibly Divine intervention, he had commandeered a fast steamboat and acquired overwhelming numerical superiority. The same heavy fog that impeded *J.D. Estes* had surely forced the *Jesse P.* to suspend its voyage. Any further travel would increase that steamboat's chances of running aground. That is precisely what the Judge hoped would happen. Craig felt himself caught up in the Judge's growing optimism, admitting he would much rather have a self-confident leader than one who was guilt-ridden and vacillating.

Shortly before noon, *J. D. Estes* rounded a sweeping bend several miles below Yellow Banks. There, three quarters of a mile distant and a hundred yards off the south bank, lay *Jesse P. Emmick*, grounded firmly upon a sandbar, deck canted slightly downward on the starboard side. Craig ducked below the pilothouse windows.

"Hah! Just as I expected!" The Judge's voice boomed the entire length of the steamboat, clearly audible above the mighty engine. "Everyone to your stations! Take care they do not see you! Be ready to board upon my command!"

"Half speed!" Fortescue ordered.

"No more talking!" cautioned the Judge.

The Regulators scrambled hastily to their positions behind hogsheads, barrels, and cordwood. Most crouched inside the main cabin, protected by the temporary fortifications, yet concealed by cabin walls—ready at an instant to charge through open doors. Doc watched these maneuvers, regarding Judge Bozarth with an increasing measure of respect. He laid out his medical instruments and made ready for the wounded. Owen joined the Regulators inside; Stephen took his place beside Martin near a row of tobacco hogsheads. Following Judge Bozarth's orders, Craig moved sternward where deckhands had stacked a long row of cordwood.

The Judge whispered, "I want you on my right flank, Craig. Remember this—nothing stands between us and Lucinde. Shoot *anyone* with a gun—that includes crew members. When this fight begins, it will be hard to distinguish who is who."

Craig wondered if he could do this. He felt sure he would recognize the gunmen, but the Judge had a valid point—*Jesse P.'s* crew might believe they were repelling river pirates. Closing his eyes tightly, he whispered a silent prayer that the mission would turn out well for all concerned, but especially for Lucinde and her children.

The pounding of the great pistons slowed markedly and *J.D. Es-*

tes reduced speed. Craig glanced forward and spied his fellow Regulators hunkered down and crouched close behind the barricades. He could hear the sloshing paddles and gurgle of displaced water—then the engine disengaged. They were almost level with *Jesse P. Emmick.* Through chinks in the cordwood he could see the other steamer, its white planks and upper works splintered and riddled with holes. *Jesse P.'s* captain emerged from the pilothouse, walking hesitantly and looking ill-at ease. He appeared under obvious duress.

"Ha!" Captain Fortescue roared with laughter. "Got yourself caught on a sandbar, did you? That was one hell of a fog last night!"

"I am not in a mood to bandy words with you, Fortescue! Throw us a line and haul us off this bar!"

"You are grounded solid—we might not be able to pull you free!" Fortescue surveyed the upper works damage. "What in the hell happened to you? Looks like somebody shot your ass full of holes!"

"I prefer not to discuss it."

"Well, you're not very friendly. Maybe I will just continue on my way."

"No! You can't leave us stranded."

"I have already lost valuable time. The river is dropping. I'd rather be on the Mississippi." Craig admired the argumentative Fortescue. By acting reluctant, he was increasing their chances of success. Often, the trick in selling was not to appear too eager.

"We can pay!"

"It will cost you money—payment in advance and no guarantees."

The Judge chuckled softly in appreciation. "Not a bad job of acting, that!"

Jesse P.'s captain called out, "We have several passengers on board who wish to transfer to your boat." A chill ran up Craig's spine. He knew without doubt who they were; the original passengers were thrown off in Cottonwood Bend.

"Not interested! We are full up as it is; you can see for yourself how crowded our decks are!" He gestured down at the cargo.

"They can pay—name your price!"

"How many?"

"Eight! Five men, a woman and her two young children."

"I'll have no crying brats on this vessel!"

Another voice rang out—Bruce Bowman's. "I'll pay you one hundred gold dollars per person—that is eight hundred dollars total! But it includes the woman and her children."

"One hundred each?" Fortescue sounded doubtful.

"That is the price."

"Show me the money," he demanded.

Bowman held up a leather satchel and jingled it before withdrawing a handful of gold coins. While this haggling went on, the Regulators remained perfectly still. Craig reckoned *J.D. Estes* lay about ten yards off *Jesse P*'s starboard beam. He wondered how Fortescue would maneuver the steamboat close enough for them to board. The captain answered that question by reversing and cutting in closer behind the stranded boat, then allowing it to drift forward with the current. Footsteps moved on both decks as Fortescue's deckhands made ready to tie up alongside.

The Judge nodded, pleased so far with the way events were unfolding. He whispered, "Our crew's movement sends them a message of normalcy—and it draws their attention. They are not looking for us."

Heavy hemp ropes landed with a thump on *Jesse P. Emmick*'s main deck and the deckhands began hauling them in. Bruce Bowman's men appeared from various doors. The two steamboats bumped together.

"Now!" Bozarth hissed.

Craig picked his target through the cordwood. The mercenary who had pulled a knife on him during Owen's corn shucking party now stood on the main deck, heavily armed and prepared to seize command of *J.D. Estes*. Craig popped up, aimed his .40 caliber Lancaster, and pulled the trigger. The ball struck the gunman squarely in his chest, breaking the breastbone and tearing out through his back, its passage marked by a fine spray of blood. In the same instant, the

Judge fired his expensive rifle and brought down another gunman. A hailstorm of gunfire swept the larger steamboat and one more abductor fell. Craig laid down his Lancaster and unslung one of the big .50 caliber rifles as *J.D. Estes'* crewmen dove for cover.

"Boarding party away!" Judge Bozarth roared.

Like a band of high seas pirates, the Cottonwood Bend Regulators stormed *Jesse P. Emmick*, leaping onto the main deck, swarming over cargo, kicking in doors, and sweeping their rifles from side to side, ready to shoot dead any adversary. The *Jesse P.*'s crewmen had the good sense to lie flat on the decks, showing their hands.

The Judge boomed, "Remember! We are here to save Lucinde McDonnell and her children! Keep your eyes wide open!" He and Craig climbed the stern ladder to the upper deck as Regulators charged from bow to stern, kicking in doors and searching cabins.

"Bang!" A Regulator reeled back and somersaulted over the rail to crash onto *J.D. Estes'* main deck. The shot came from a stateroom just two doors away. Craig and Judge Bozarth inched their way forward as five Regulators charged headlong into the cabin, met by a massive flurry of gunfire. Three of them fell dead; the remaining two crawled away, severely wounded.

"Have a care!" the Judge roared. "They are all in there—the woman too!"

Two more Regulators attempted an assault; both were instantly killed. This time Craig and Judge Bozarth charged in. One mercenary worked frantically to reload his weapon. Without hesitation, Craig fired his rifle and shot him dead. As he unslung his last weapon, he spied Bruce Bowman crouched in the corner, clutching Lucinde in a vice-like grip, using her body as a shield. The giant could not hope to completely conceal himself behind her, but he pressed a pistol into her thick black hair, screwing the muzzle painfully against her skull. Lucinde looked completely traumatized, her complexion deathly pale. She struggled unsuccessfully to hold back her sobs. The children were screaming, trying somehow to seek comfort from their captive mother. It was a pathetic, terrible scene.

"Back out of this cabin!" Bowman snarled. "Back out now, or

I'll shoot her in the head."

"You can't be serious!" the Judge roared. "It's over, man! All your cohorts are dead." More Regulators filed silently into the stateroom, their expressions grim and foreboding. One of them was Martin McDonnell.

Bowman barked menacingly, "Drop those guns! If you don't, I'll shoot her just to spite you."

Martin put down his rifle. Several others followed his example and backed cautiously out of the room.

"You too, Ridgeway."

Slowly, Craig knelt to lay his rifle on the floor. Without warning, the Judge attacked with the speed of a striking rattlesnake. In a bedazzling blur of motion he whipped up one of his long-barreled, rosewood dueling pistols and fired, blowing off a large chunk of Bowman's skull, splattering bright red blood and custard-like brain matter over the freshly-painted cabin walls, Lucinde and children. The mercenary leader toppled sideways, his gun unfired. Had Craig blinked, he would have missed it. It was an incredible feat, one that folks would recount for years to come. The Judge, after suffering two harsh setbacks, had persevered and triumphed, ending all with a final, heroic action.

"Make a fool out of me, will you!" he snarled, taking the mercenary's pistol and carefully lowering the hammer.

Some Regulators filed quietly back into the stateroom. Others searched the hold and every other possible hiding place before declaring the ship safe. Martin embraced his daughter-in-law and scooped up the children in his long arms. Stephen led his brother into the cabin, half supporting him. Owen looked as if he would collapse, but when he saw his family safe and sound, relief washed across his face. The reunion was something to behold.

"Oh, Owen!" Lucinde gasped. "You are alive!" She softly touched his bandaged forehead. "Your poor head!"

"It's just a scratch. Thank God you are all safe and sound!" Owen's voice broke with emotion. "Did they hurt you?"

"No. I fought them at first, but one of them snatched the children and I was forced to cooperate. Fortunately they did not harm us."

"We have a Doctor on board. He is busy at this moment, but he can make sure our expected child is unharmed."

"I am fine," Lucinde insisted. "Let us find a quiet place where we can all rest together."

"Father!" Both children cried, reaching out for Owen. Martin continued to hold them, stepping in close so they could all embrace. After a few moments, the family left. Stephen and Martin helped them cross over to *J.D. Estes* to find an empty cabin. The Regulators looked on, happy for the family and pleased with the final outcome, but they had paid an appalling price for their success—six dead and four seriously wounded. The Judge ordered his forces to transfer the dead Regulators and all weapons, including those of the mercenaries, to *J.D. Estes*.

"What about the other bodies?" a Regulator asked.

"We'll let *Jesse P.*'s captain dispose of them. They were on this boat to begin with."

Oddly, Craig saw good sense in his rationale, although *Jesse P.*'s captain might not agree.

The Judge continued, "Search the mercenaries' bodies for coins and personal effects. I'll handle things in this cabin. Craig, I want you to stay here with me. Guard this door while I search Bowman and take charge of his belongings. Anything I find might be useful in an official inquest."

As the remaining men filed out, the Judge worked quickly over the two bodies, employing all the finesse of a professional pickpocket—or perhaps a battlefield scavenger—appropriating a heavy gold ring, odd coins, gold cufflinks, and the grand prize—Bowman's leather purse filled with gold and silver coins, He brandished the leader's fine pistol. "I shall keep this weapon and mount it above my parlor fireplace as a trophy—for today's action represents my finest triumph! Whatever else happens in my life, good or bad, I can lay claim to this day." He pocketed the smaller treasures and loose coins, and clutched the purse tightly. "Let us go home!"

Before turning back toward Cottonwood Bend, Captain Fortescue consulted with *Jesse P. Emmick*'s captain about towing the stranded steamboat off the bar. He could afford to behave magnanimously. Helping a fellow captain would only enhance his already considerable reputation.

"Of course I will not charge you for the service! I apologize for my seeming callousness. It was the best story I could manufacture under the circumstances. Besides, I may need your help one day."

"Then I am in your debt," the captain shook his hand.

Fortescue reversed his engines and ordered lines tossed to *Jesse P. Emmick*'s stern. Crew members worked to secure ropes for towing. In this lull, Judge Bozarth went to his cabin to stow away the mercenaries' guns, coins, and personal effects. *J.D. Estes* eased backward until the ropes grew taut. Both vessels reversed their paddlewheels and churned up vast amounts of water and muddy sand, but *Jesse P.* would not budge.

"Let me work my engines alone!" Fortescue called. "Your paddlewheels are bailing water out from under you!"

This stratagem produced an instant, positive effect. Craig noticed how the water displaced by *J.D. Estes* seemed to wash over the bar, lifting and rocking *Jesse P. Emmick*. Finally, the bigger steamboat pulled free with a loud squelching noise. Men cheered loudly on both vessels.

The *J.D. Estes* steamed majestically into Cottonwood Bend Landing to a rousing reception, one that would be remembered for decades. When they closed to within a half mile, Fortescue announced their arrival, blowing repeated blasts on the whistle and taking the approach slowly to give everyone time to gather along the riverfront. The entire population turned out to greet them. Folks cheered and waved. Some fired their rifles into the crisp afternoon air, creating heavy clouds of blue gun smoke. The town looked wonderfully golden in the slanting rays of autumn sunlight, nestled snugly between the river and steep limestone hills.

Judge Bozarth stood at the pilothouse rail surveying the scene, waving his hand, nodding to his constituents, and occasionally bowing. He reminded Craig of a victorious Roman emperor returning from the battlefield—the old ham was obviously enjoying every moment of it. The magnificent steamer glided into shore with the grace of a swan. Crew members worked to secure bowlines and run out the gangplank. Fortescue cut loose with a long whistle blast and Judge Bozarth held up his hands to indicate he wished to speak. In the silence that followed, Craig recognized many townsfolk— Rosenbotham, Brother Kreisle, Paul Madden, Donn Wimmer, Jim Fallin, Doc Emmick, Gerald Fischer, Violet Bozarth and others.

"My fellow citizens and dear friends!" Judge Bozarth boomed. "Please listen to what I have to say!" He leaned over and whispered to Craig. "Are they ready?"

"Yes, Judge. They are right behind the pilothouse."

The Judge turned his full focus back onto the crowd. "It delights me to inform you that our mission to rescue Lucinde McDonnell and her children was a complete success!"

The crowd roared and clapped until Fortescue cut loose with a couple of short blasts on the whistle.

Again, the Judge stilled them with a sweep of his hands. "Our esteemed Captain Fortescue of the *J.D. Estes* graciously volunteered his magnificent vessel and incomparable expertise to overhaul the mighty *Jesse P. Emmick*—and he provided valuable assistance in helping me and your Regulators apprehend the abductors! We have slain them all!"

"Huzzah!" the audience shouted.

"Three cheers for the Judge!" shouted an old timer.

"We knew you could do it!"

"Ain't no better law officer this side of the Alleghenies!"

"God bless you, Judge!"

In the din that followed, the Judge wheeled and forestalled Fortescue from laying on the whistle. "Don't you *dare* override them again! It gives me great joy to hear them cheer! Besides, I want them to remember this moment come election time."

Craig and some of the Regulators grinned knowingly.

"Yes!" Judge Bozarth thundered, his voice carrying easily up to River Street. "We pursued those evildoers through the darkest of nights on a perilously low river in the densest of fogs—and we fought a terrible battle, one that cost us dearly. Still, we prevailed! I want you to know that there are no braver men on earth than the Cottonwood Bend Regulators!"

The crowd roared again, but the exhilaration was somewhat diminished in the knowledge that some of their friends and family had fallen in action. The Judge knew he must deliver a fitting eulogy while at the same time allowing the crowd to enjoy the fruits of his splendid success.

"Yes, our brave men fully understood the circumstances—they knew that one day it could be any one of you! They put themselves squarely in Owen McDonnell's shoes—your shoes! And oh, how they fought! They served notice to the world that the citizens of Cottonwood Bend will always fight to protect their own!" He turned to Craig and uttered a stage whisper, "Now!" Craig eased behind the wheelhouse as the Judge resumed his speech. "Our men were willing to lay down their very lives..." He turned theatrically and held his arm high. "For this!"

Almost as if scripted, Owen and Lucinde emerged from behind the pilothouse lit dramatically by the afternoon sun. The crowd gasped in wonderment. Lucinde cradled the youngest child who was still crying, badly frightened by the steamboat whistle. Martin McDonnell followed, carrying his grandson. Never one for show, he appeared uncomfortable, but the Judge had convinced him that this appearance was necessary; it would provide visible proof of the mission's success and, more importantly, let folks know that the Regulators did not die in vain. Of course Martin expected the Judge to use the incident to make political hay, but he also figured that maybe, just maybe, the scoundrel had earned the right.

The crowds roared and wept, clapped and laughed. "Let them celebrate!" the Judge called to Fortescue. "No more whistle. Some will soon receive bad news. They deserve to rejoice." He waited for the crowd to calm down before he continued, "Our deepest thanks go out to those Regulators who have fallen, and to those who served—Craig Ridgeway, Martin McDonnell, and others—also to Doctor Thomas Applegate who traveled all the way from New Orleans to warn us of the danger. Doc Applegate treated our wounded and they will survive." He presented Doc to the crowd, then called out, "Where is Doc Emmick?"

"Here!" the doctor waved his hand.

"Looks like you might have some competition in the near future."

"Competition hell! We *need* another doctor. With all these newcomers moving in, I can't take care of the folks we have. Welcome to you, sir!"

Doc Applegate tipped his hat to his new colleague. Below them, the Regulators began filing off the foredeck, across the gangplank and onto the cobblestone bank. They formed two rows with rifles held at "make ready" position—an honor guard to flank and escort their fallen companions. Suddenly, Craig remembered Mary and his children alone in their cabin. The yearning to be with them hit with all the force of a flash flood.

"Martin, may I ride ahead to check on Mary?"

"Yes, if you will first stop to look in on Agnes. Let her know we are all safe and sound."

"Consider it done."

Craig asked for and received Judge Bozarth's permission to leave. He bade farewell to Captain Fortescue, thankful to leave before the Regulators brought off their dead. He ran up the cobblestone landing and headed directly for the stables. Blue nickered a warm greeting. Craig saddled him and paid the stable master. He led the tall roan into the waning sunlight, mounted, and picked his way through the crowded street, glancing down inadvertently at *J.D. Estes*. The first body was brought ashore to a high, piercing wail that rose above the crowd's rumble. Craig felt his eyes burn with tears, knowing that some folks had lost sons; wives were now widowed; children were fatherless. He realized that his little family could have been among those suffering, and he ached with greater desire to reunite with them.

As soon as they crossed the bridge, Craig nudged Blue into his easy, long-reaching lope. He thanked God out loud for bringing him home, for giving him the family he loved so dearly, for his farmland, friends and acquaintances, good health and youth—knowing full well he had survived a danger as deadly as war. As promised, he stopped in at Welcome Hall. Agnes was building a fire in the cookhouse; she emerged when she heard Craig ride up. In the gathering darkness he could see the apprehension on her worn face, and for the first time he noticed more gray in her hair than red. But she was still a beautiful woman.

"Are they—" she broke off, hardly trusting herself to speak. "Did they bring back Lucinde and the children?"

"They did!" Craig beamed at her. "It cost us some good men, but our family is safe and sound."

"Owen?"

"He's fine. Doc Applegate took good care of him."

"Praise God!" she wept.

"They will be home shortly. I will fetch Mary."

"Yes! Let's all have supper together. We have so much to be thankful for."

"We'll see you tonight, then." Craig wheeled Blue around and cantered down the gravel drive and onto the Hardinsburg Road. Blue recognized the sweeping turn and long climb as the last part of the journey. He knew the barn was near—and anticipated that a good feed of oats would follow. It took a great deal of restraint to keep him in check.

Craig recognized Levi Matthew's buggy tied at the hitching rail just past the dogtrot. He pulled up under the roof and shouted. "Mary! I am home!"

The door opened and Mary stepped outside, looking more beautiful than ever in her cornflower-blue dress. "Oh Craig! You are home! Is everyone unharmed?"

"They are," he assured her, dismounting. "Owen will survive and we have brought back Lucinde and the children."

"Pa and Stephen?"

"They are fine!"

Levi Matthew's gravelly voice came from inside. "Well, kiss her, you idiot! She's been worried sick!"

Craig enfolded Mary in his arms and kissed her with wild abandon, unconcerned with who saw them. The kiss went on for a long time. When they finally drew apart, he noticed Levi and his big wife, Elizabeth sitting inside at the maple wood table. Beyond that, he could see Isabel and Ruth playing with the Matthews children, all of them laughing and having a grand time, so engrossed in fun that Craig resolved to hug them later.

Mary spoke softly, "Levi and Elizabeth came out last night to stay with us. They spent the night and all of today here. Levi drove his buggy down this morning to look in on Ma!"

"I just saw her. She has invited us all for supper. Levi, you and Elizabeth should come too."

"I'll never turn down a meal cooked by Agnes McDonnell."

"Or anyone else!" Craig qualified. "Thank you for looking in on my family."

"It was the least I could do. I wouldn't know what to do with a gun. Figured we could be of better service here."

While Mary prepared a dish to take down to Welcome Hall, Craig led Blue to the barn, unsaddled him, brushed his coat, and fed him a double handful of oats, an ear of corn, and a good-sized chunk of hay. He drew buckets of well water and filled the watering trough. At that moment he realized he was just in time for milking and feeding. As they always did, the giant oxen and plow horses crowded in for their share of feed and attention. While Craig milked the cows, listening to them crunch on shelled corn, a pigeon cooed in the rafters. The sounds of his farm were like the voices of old friends, comforting and unchanging, instilling within him a sense of calm and permanency.

———————•———————

After the children were asleep, Craig and Mary held each other in the darkness, talking quietly and listening to the owls outside and the coals hissing in the fireplace. Craig felt at peace, despite the terrifying experiences. He recounted his many blessings, naming them out loud for Mary to hear. She would give birth in January; this time, he did not experience his usual sense of dread. Perhaps he finally realized that life was a gift from God and he must live it to the utmost. They talked for a long time about Owen and Lucinde, Martin and Agnes, and young Stephen who would marry in just eight days.

Later, Craig recounted the entire story, describing Judge Bozarth's bravery—his daring negotiations at the riverfront, his valiant charge in the bottomland pasture, and his storming of the *Jesse P. Emmick*. He also described how the Judge stripped the mercenaries of their valuables.

"Oh, Craig!" Mary gasped. "Speaking of valuables—you will not believe what you brought in those four saddlebags!"

"I truly forgot," Craig confessed. "So much has happened. When you go through what I did, you realize how unimportant money really is."

"Well, we have a major decision to make. I counted over fifty-one hundred dollars in those bags, most of it in Spanish mill dollars."

"Did you hide it under our floorboards?"

"Yes. I had just nailed down the last puncheons when Levi and Elizabeth arrived. One bag was filled with gold and silver jewelry, including some beautiful brooches, one encrusted in diamonds, rubies, and emeralds. Most pieces are small personal items like rings, bracelets, cufflinks, and chains."

"I am certain no one knows about this—for all the mercenaries are dead." He told her how the gray mule died and tumbled over the bank into a deep fissure. "The pasture was deserted when I brought the saddlebags here."

"I have struggled with this. Should we turn it over to the officials? It is not ours to keep."

"Why is it not?" Craig asked. "It was ill-gotten no matter how you cut it."

"I have thought the same thing," Mary confessed. "But there is so much of it, and we already have huge stash of coins under the floorboards."

Craig thought on this a while. A few years ago they had stumbled upon the Widder Fuqua's treasure, certainly stolen. A gang of river pirates had operated out of her little hovel in the bottomlands, robbing and killing settlers on the Ohio. After an extremely large haul, the Widder had poisoned the pirates and appropriated their loot, hiding it under the hearthstones of her hovel. Craig and Mary had accidentally stumbled upon it. With no one living to whom they could return the money, they had kept it, using a portion to redeem Romulus from a Nashville slaveholder—and another portion to purchase land and new farm implements. Most of the Widder's money, several thousand dollars' worth of gold and silver coins of various nationalities, still resided under the same floorboards as did the coin-filled saddlebags. Craig tried to speak and could not. Using the Widder's money had not plagued him in the slightest.

Mary continued, "We could put it to good use and build a strong financial future for our growing family."

"I am thinking similar thoughts."

"We should turn in the jewelry, for I will not wear it in any circumstance. Perhaps we could turn over some of the money."

"Who to?"

"Who else?" Mary replied. "Our esteemed militia commander."

"You know what he will do with it."

"We could present it to him in Violet's presence. She deserves it more than him. After all, she singlehandedly pulled him out of debt and has since kept him on a tight leash. If they choose to keep the money—as we have—she can at least control how the Judge spends it."

"How much should we turn over? A thousand dollars?"

"The sum of five hundred crossed my mind."

Craig hugged her close, conscious of the growing life within her. "I love you more than I could ever hope to say!" he exclaimed, so overcome with emotion that he wept silent tears of joy. They lay in each other's embrace, talking about their lives and sharing their hopes for the future.

Epilogue—July 11, 1818

A harsh summer sun sank behind the wooded limestone hills, and almost immediately the lengthening shadows tempered the heat, aided by soft, northwesterly breezes stirring beneath the sprawling oaks and maples on Welcome Hall's front lawn. Cicadas and jar flies strummed a rhythmic cadence in growing darkness as Martin McDonnell lit the torches. Wood smoke from the cooking pit drifted away from the gathering. It was high summer, the best time for a grand meal cooked outdoors, shared by family and friends. This year, Craig furnished a young steer from Gill Hagman's finest grain-fed stock. After his recent financial gains, he figured it was his turn to spend. He and Mary also supplied a keg of their finest aged whiskey.

It was a grand gathering. Both physicians and their wives attended. The doctors had become good friends, drawn closer by shared medical experiences. Doc Applegate and his wife, Solange, had purchased a nice house on River Street and were well received in the community. Hiram and Lillian Rosenbotham came, bringing a variety of delicacies from their store; Levi Matthews and his family arrived early in the afternoon. Elizabeth, known countywide for her fine cooking, helped prepare and serve side dishes. Father Badin was visiting on his circuit ride, staying in the guest room at Welcome Hall. As usual, his presence added immensely to the event. Judge Wilfred J. Bozarth and Violet rolled up in style, driving their elegant carriage pulled by a pair of matched bays with the Judge's new chestnut mare in tow. Dressed in expensive clothing, the couple carried themselves with all their past pride. Mary noticed that Violet was wearing the finest brooch from the mercenaries' saddlebags and she discreetly pointed this out to Craig. He could only chuckle—he certainly could not condemn, for he and Mary had chosen to keep the lion's share of the findings.

Over the past eight months, the Judge had experienced a true renaissance of financial fortune. It began when he scavenged the mercenaries' money and property; then he realized a fine profit from the sale of their weapons and other belongings. Next came the five hundred dollar windfall from the outlaws' saddlebags which Craig and Mary delivered to him—in Violet's presence. In early November, two of the Judge's elderly clients passed away, each childless and without other heirs. Incredibly, both had named Judge Wilfred J. Bozarth as their sole beneficiary. The Judge found himself the owner of a small farm and a comfortable townhouse in Cottonwood Bend which he promptly sold to Kelwyn Lasher, the town's new carpenter sponsored by Levi Matthews. From his deceased clients, the Bozarths also inherited a hefty amount of gold and silver coin. Quite rightly, Violet took immediate charge of this fortune.

In December 1817, Violet embarked upon her most brilliant triumph. She and the Judge had traveled to Frankfort for Kentucky's Twenty-Sixth General Assembly. The Judge thoroughly enjoyed working on and voting, for or against, various bills, and playing an important role in establishing new banks, towns, roads and turnpikes, tolls, taxes, and lotteries. The Assembly passed resolutions, one "relative to the extinguishment of Indian titles to certain lands in the Commonwealth bordered by the Tennessee, Ohio, and Mississippi Rivers." Another resolution dealt with the Kentucky-Tennessee boundary, and an important one provided funding for the removal of navigational obstructions on the Ohio River. There was even a bill passed to prevent "wanton destruction of fish." Violet had let him have his fun, but after the Assembly adjourned, she sat him down in their hotel room to tap his considerable legal knowledge concerning contracts. Meshing that knowledge with her own financial insight, she formulated a scheme to coerce those speculators who had taken his money to buy out the Judge's numerous holdings in wildcat banks and other risky ventures.

First, she paid off his Frankfort debts with accrued interest. Then she ordered him to travel to Louisville and Lexington to hunt down the bankers and financiers with whom he had invested. Not trusting Wilfred to follow through alone, she accompanied him on those trips and succeeded in strong-arming most of the financiers into purchasing his considerable investments. In this optimistic climate, some were willing, but others were not. She hammered together almost impossible deals, while threatening the more reluctant bankers with expensive lawsuits, and she managed to recoup more than the Judge's original outlay. Like Martin and Craig, Violet anticipated an inevitable crash—knowing that people would, in the end, demand hard coin instead of printed paper. Craig genuinely admired her and reckoned that if the Judge allowed her to control their purse strings, they would surely prosper.

The American Republic also continued on a path of remarkable, almost unrestrained growth. The state of Mississippi was admitted in December, 1817—the twentieth state in the union. Alabama was now an official territory, destined soon for statehood. It appeared that Illinois would join before year's end. On April 4, 1818, Congress adopted a new American flag—thirteen red and white stripes to represent the original states, and one star for each of the current twenty states, with additional stars to be added whenever a new state joined the Union. Republicans wished to encourage further westward migration and so extended their generous credit practices. The Second Bank of the United States opened eighteen branch offices across the country, and these operated with little or no oversight from Philadelphia headquarters. These banks injected so much paper money into circulation that they could never hope to demand specie—hard coin—as payment. But in this heady environment, rapid expansion, speculation, and "wildcat banking" ruled the day. Kentucky rode this tidal wave of business and political expansion. The Bank of the United States established branches in Louisville and Lexington, and these banks augmented an already wild availability of credit.

Kentucky continued to maintain its ascendancy on the national stage. State newspapers predicted that Henry Clay would win re-election and retain the Speakership in the U.S. House where Kentucky's representatives held considerable clout. During his time in Europe, the statesman had toured a number of English farms, and was captivated by a breed of white-faced, burgundy-red beef cattle from Herefordshire. He had recently stocked his Ashland Estate with these hardy animals called "Seventeens," named for the year he imported them. Hemp continued to remain Kentucky's wonder crop as demand for cotton bagging continued to soar. Tobacco and whiskey continued to bring fair prices.

Finally, it appeared that America would become more secure on the world stage—especially as ties with Great Britain improved. Father Badin brought news of the Rush–Bagot Agreement, signed by the United States and Great Britain and ratified in the U.S. Senate on April 16, 1818. The former combatants had agreed to remove large warships from the Great Lakes and Lake Champlain and to exercise joint control over the Oregon Territory. This agreement would create the world's longest unfortified border. Perhaps peace would win out after all. It truly seemed like they were living in an "Era of Good Feelings."

After supper, Craig joined the menfolk to examine Judge Bozarth's new mare—a magnificent creature, sixteen hands high and almost as broad as his previous mare, with glossy red coat and bold white markings.

"Yes, yes—I am blessed to have found such a splendid, docile mount," the Judge waxed eloquently. "She has a soft, cat-footed gait and responds beautifully to my every command. Riding her is like sitting in a parlor rocking chair, yet she is capable of tremendous speed. I have seen proof positive that she has garnered several racing purses. The owner personally demonstrated her ability to jump a four rail fence—but let me assure you I will not be attempting that feat!"

"Where on earth did you find her?" Martin asked.

"While engaged in our numerous financial dealings, Violet and I stopped in to visit Patrick McDonnell's farm just outside of Bardstown. His stables are well-known in Frankfort, patronized by many of our state legislators. Your son had trained the mare himself and valued her as his finest horse. I admit he charged a dear price for her, but I could not be happier, for she is almost a younger reincarnation of my past beloved mare."

Martin looked pleased, knowing that his oldest son had sold a fine horse to the Judge. With deepest admiration, Craig observed his father-in-law. He hoped that when he reached Martin's age, he could look back on a long life filled with accomplishments, blessed with a loving wife, children, and grandchildren. Perhaps he was well on his way.

As the womenfolk began serving desserts and after-dinner drinks, Craig glanced around at his family and friends. Last autumn's ordeal seemed long ago, put firmly behind them. Stephen's wife, Alicia, was with child; she would deliver in August. Beside him, Mary cooed and smiled at their latest addition, a son they named Gregory, after Craig's father. Owen and Lucinde fussed over their new son, now more than six months old. Craig understood enough of their past ordeal to know that the expanding evil of slavery had reached out its tentacles to ensnare them, and it was only by God's good grace they had escaped. He realized suddenly, that in his own small way, he had struck a few blows against that cruel institution.

After dessert, Father Badin rose to address the gathering. He waited until the only sounds were those of the nighttime insects. When everyone was listening, he spoke of God's many gifts—good health, fertile soil, warm sunshine and cool rain; tall trees and grass-filled pastures; freshwater springs, the mighty Ohio River, and all of nature's handiwork the Almighty provided to support life, the greatest gift of all. The priest offered a blessing upon all present, thanking God for each individual and charging each person by name to live life as best they could—enjoining them to always care for each other. Craig knew that God had planted him right here, in the Ohio River Valley of western Kentucky, to do just that.